PENGUIN BOOKS

BURNING YOUR BOATS

Angela Carter was born in 1940. When she published her first novel, *Shadow Dance*, in 1966, she was immediately recognized as one of Britain's most original writers. Eight other novels followed: *The Magic Toyshop* (1967, John Llewellyn Rhys Prize), *Several Perceptions* (1968, Somerset Maugham Award), *Heroes and Villains* (1969), *Love* (1971), *The Infernal Desire Machines of Doctor Hoffman* (1972), *The Passion of New Eve* (1977), *Nights at the Circus* (1984, James Tait Black Memorial Prize), and *Wise Children* (1991). Angela Carter also published three collections of short stories—*The Bloody Chamber* (1979, Cheltenham Festival of Literature Award), *Fireworks: Nine Profane Pieces* (1984), and *Saints and Strangers* (1985, published in the UK as *Black Venus*)—a book of essays called *The Sadeian Woman*, two collections of journalism, (*Nothing Sacred* and *Expletives Deleted*), and a volume of radio plays. She translated the fairy stories of Charles Perrault and edited collections of fairy and folk tales as well as *Wayward Girls & Wicked Women: An Anthology of Subversive Stories* (1986). She also wrote the screenplay for the 1984 film *The Company of Wolves*, based on her short story. A fourth collection of stories was published in the United Kingdom in 1993 as *American Ghosts and Old World Wonders*. Her journalism and essays are available in *Shaking a Leg*.

From 1976 through 1978 Angela Carter was Arts Council of Great Britain Fellow in Creative Writing at Sheffield University, and from 1980 through 1981 she was visiting professor in the Writing Program at Brown University. She traveled and taught widely in the U.S. and Australia but lived in London. Angela Carter died in February, 1992.

Praise for Angela Carter and *Burning Your Boats*

"What a pyrotechnic display this is, like nothing else between book covers. Gothic, bizarre, perverse, wondrous, and the language—lush, rich. . . . It's like Edgar Allan Poe teams up with Flannery O'Connor to ghostwrite for Scheherazade."   —*Mirabella*

"Carter created an original, distinctive world . . . [her] short stories are the most concentrated expression of her talent [with] hothouse prose, sumptuous, morbid, self-caressing, deliberately claustrophobic."
    —*San Francisco Chronicle*

"If you were writing her literary *naissance* in the manner of Angela Carter, you'd have to provide a troupe of ghostly godpersons gathered round her typewriter. Oscar Wilde would be there, whispering 'Nothing succeeds like excess' and bestowing the gift of the inversion of truisms; Sylvia Townsend Warner, with her clutch of ruthless fairies; Edgar Allan Poe, the subject of one of her more spectacular stories, although Carter wears her Rue Morgue with a difference. And Bram Stoker, and Perrault, and Sheridan LeFanu, and George MacDonald, and Mary Shelley, and perhaps even Carson McCullers and a whole gaggle of disreputable tale-telling old grannies."
    —Margaret Atwood, *Toronto Globe & Mail*

"Carter's rambunctiousness escaped from literary cubbyholes was a testament to the twisty playfulness of her sensibility, the obscene amorousness of her imagination. . . . Ripe and rank, Carter's loamy style was artificial, but that doesn't mean it was unnatural—her sentences violently pull us from the everyday, conjuring up repressed worlds of desire and fear that, by necessity, bear the bruises of purple prose."
    —*The Boston Globe*

"In Carter's formulation, you have the basics of a plot, you have the subconscious . . . and you have a rich literary palette—but the *meaning* of the work is completely flexible, contingent, multifarious . . . it's hard not to encounter Angela Carter's spectacular fictional legerdemain without the certainty that it will last, that it will be read, that it will be admired."
    —Rick Moody, *VLS*

"A book of wonders . . . and a welcome occasion for reassessing the work of one of the most unusual writers of recent emergence."
    —*Kirkus Reviews* (starred review)

"Tales, legends, variations on mythic themes, sparked by writing of great vitality, color and inventiveness, and a deeply macabre imagination. . . . A generous treat."   —*Publishers Weekly*

Burning Your Boats

The Collected Short Stories

Angela Carter

With an Introduction by Salman Rushdie

PENGUIN BOOKS

PENGUIN BOOKS
Published by the Penguin Group
Penguin Group (USA) Inc., 375 Hudson Street, New York, New York 10014, U.S.A.
Penguin Group (Canada), 90 Eglinton Avenue East, Suite 700, Toronto,
Ontario, Canada M4P 2Y3 (a division of Pearson Penguin Canada Inc.)
Penguin Books Ltd, 80 Strand, London WC2R 0RL, England
Penguin Ireland, 25 St Stephen's Green, Dublin 2, Ireland (a division of Penguin Books Ltd)
Penguin Group (Australia), 250 Camberwell Road, Camberwell, Victoria 3124,
Australia (a division of Pearson Australia Group Pty Ltd)
Penguin Books India Pvt Ltd, 11 Community Centre, Panchsheel Park,
New Delhi – 110 017, India
Penguin Group (NZ), 67 Apollo Drive, Rosedale, North Shore 0632,
New Zealand (a division of Pearson New Zealand Ltd)
Penguin Books (South Africa) (Pty) Ltd, 24 Sturdee Avenue, Rosebank,
Johannesburg 2196, South Africa

Penguin Books Ltd, Registered Offices: 80 Strand, London WC2R 0RL, England

First published in Great Britain by Chatto & Windus Limited 1995
First published in the United States of America by
Henry Holt and Company, Inc. 1996
Published in Penguin Books 1997

25   24   23

Copyright © The Estate of Angela Carter, 1995
Introduction copyright © Salman Rushdie, 1995
All rights reserved

Black Venus was first published in the United States of America under the
title *Saints and Strangers* and is used by permission of Viking Penguin,
a division of Penguin Books USA Inc. Copyright © Angela Carter 1985, 1986.

Salman Rushdie's introduction is reprinted by permission of The Wylie Agency, Inc.

THE LIBRARY OF CONGRESS HAS CATALOGUED THE HENRY HOLT EDITION AS FOLLOWS:
Carter, Angela, 1940–1992.
Burning your boats: the collected short stories/Angela Carter;
with an introduction by Salman Rushdie.
p.   cm.
"A John Macrae book."
Includes bibliographical references.
ISBN 0-8050-4462-0 (hc.)
ISBN 978-0-14-025528-7 (pbk.)
I. Title.
PR6053.A73B87   1996   95-26312   823'.914—dc20

Printed in the United States of America
Set in Sabon

CONTENTS

CONTENTS

INTRODUCTION

The last time I visited Angela Carter, a few weeks before she died, she had insisted on dressing for tea, in spite of being in considerable pain. She sat bright-eyed and erect, head cocked like a parrot's, lips satirically pursed, and got down to the serious teatime business of giving and receiving the latest dirt: sharp, foulmouthed, passionate.

That is what she was like: spikily outspoken – once, after I'd come to the end of a relationship of which she had not approved, she telephoned me to say, 'Well. You're going to be seeing a *lot* more of me from now on' – and at the same time courteous enough to overcome mortal suffering for the gentility of a formal afternoon tea.

Death genuinely pissed Angela off, but she had one consolation. She had taken out an 'immense' life insurance policy shortly before the cancer struck. The prospect of the insurers being obliged, after receiving so few payments, to hand out a fortune to 'her boys' (her husband, Mark, and her son, Alexander) delighted her greatly, and inspired a great gloating black-comedy aria at which it was impossible not to laugh.

She planned her funeral carefully. My instructions were to read Marvell's poem *On a Drop of Dew*. This was a surprise. The Angela Carter I knew had always been the most scatologically irreligious, merrily godless of women; yet she wanted Marvell's meditation on the immortal soul – 'that Drop, that Ray / Of the clear Fountain of Eternal Day' – spoken over her dead body. Was this a last, surrealist joke, of the 'thank God, I die an atheist' variety, or an obeisance to the metaphysician Marvell's high symbolic language from a writer whose own favoured language was also pitched high, and replete with symbols? It should be noted that no divinity makes an appearance in Marvell's poem, except for 'th'Almighty Sun'. Perhaps Angela, always a giver of light, was asking us, at the end, to imagine her dissolving into the 'glories' of that greater light: the artist becoming a part, simply, of art.

She was too individual, too fierce a writer to dissolve easily, however: by turns formal and outrageous, exotic and demotic, exquisite and coarse, precious and raunchy, fabulist and socialist, purple and black. Her novels are like nobody else's, from the transsexual coloratura of *The Passion of New Eve* to the music-hall knees-up of *Wise Children*; but the best of her, I think, is in her stories. Sometimes, at novel length, the

distinctive Carter voice, those smoky, opium-eater's cadences interrupted by harsh or comic discords, that moonstone-and-rhinestone mix
of opulence and flim-flam, can be exhausting. In her stories, she can
dazzle and swoop, and quit while she's ahead.

Carter arrived almost fully formed; her early story, 'A Very, Very
Great Lady and Her Son at Home', is already replete with Carterian
motifs. Here is the love of the gothic, of lush language and high culture;
but also of low stinks – falling rose-petals that sound like pigeon's farts,
and a father who smells of horse dung, and bowels that are 'great
levellers'. Here is the self as performance: perfumed, decadent,
languorous, erotic, perverse; very like the winged woman, Fevvers,
heroine of her penultimate novel *Nights at the Circus*.

Another early story, 'A Victorian Fable', announces her addiction to all
the arcana of language. This extraordinary text, half-*Jabberwocky*, half-
Pale Fire, exhumes the past by exhuming its dead words:

> In every snickert and ginnel, bone-grubbers,
> rufflers, shivering-jemmies, anglers, clapperdogeons,
> peterers, sneeze-lurkers and Whip Jacks with
> their morts, out of the picaroon, fox and flim
> and ogle.

Be advised, these early stories say: this writer is no meat-and-potatoes
hack; she is a rocket, a Catherine Wheel. She will call her first collection
Fireworks.

Several of the *Fireworks* stories deal with Japan, a country whose tea-
ceremony formality and dark eroticism bruised and challenged Carter's
imagination. In 'A Souvenir of Japan' she arranges polished images of
that country before us. 'The Story of Momotaro, who was born from a
peach.' 'Mirrors make a room uncosy.' Her narrator presents her
Japanese lover to us as a sex object, complete with bee-stung lips. 'I
should like to have had him embalmed . . . so that I could watch him all
the time and he would not have been able to get away from me.' The
lover is, at least, beautiful; the narrator's view of her big-boned self, as
seen in a mirror, is distinctly uncosy. 'In the department store there was a
rack of dresses labelled: "For Young and Cute Girls Only". When I
looked at them, I felt as gross as Glumdalclitch.' In 'Flesh and the Mirror'
the exquisite, erotic atmosphere thickens, approaching pastiche – for
Japanese literature has specialised rather in these heated sexual perversities
– except when it is cut through sharply by Carter's constant self-
awareness. ('Hadn't I gone eight thousand miles to find a climate with

enough anguish and hysteria in it to satisfy me?' her narrator asks; as, in 'The Smile of Winter', another unnamed narrator admonishes us: 'Do not think I do not realize what I am doing,' and then analyses her story with a perspicacity that rescues – brings to life – what might otherwise have been a static piece of mood-music. Carter's cold-water douches of intelligence often come to the rescue of her fancy, when it runs too wild.)

In the non-Japanese stories Carter enters, for the first time, the fable-world which she will make her own. A brother and sister are lost in a sensual, malevolent forest, whose trees have breasts, and bite, and where the apple-tree of knowledge teaches not good and evil, but incestuous sexuality. Incest – a recurring Carter subject – crops up again in 'The Executioner's Beautiful Daughter', a tale set in the kind of bleak upland village which is perhaps the quintessential Carter location – one of those villages where, as she says in the *Bloody Chamber* story 'The Werewolf', 'they have cold weather, they have cold hearts'. Wolves howl around these Carter-country villages and there are many metamorphoses.

Carter's other country is the fairground, the world of the gimcrack showman, the hypnotist, the trickster, the puppeteer. 'The Loves of Lady Purple' takes her closed circus-world to yet another mountainous, Middle-European village where suicides are treated like vampires (wreaths of garlic, stakes through the heart) while real warlocks 'practised rites of immemorial beastliness in the forests'. As in all Carter's fairground stories, 'the grotesque is the order of the day'. Lady Purple, the dominatrix marionette, is a moralist's warning – beginning as a whore, she turns into a puppet because she is 'pulled only by the strings of Lust'. She is a female, sexy and lethal rewrite of Pinocchio, and, along with the metamorphic cat-woman in 'Master', one of the many dark (and fair) ladies with 'unappeasable appetites' to whom Angela Carter is so partial. In her second collection, *The Bloody Chamber*, these riot ladies inherit her fictional earth.

The Bloody Chamber is Carter's masterwork: the book in which her high, perfervid mode is perfectly married to her stories' needs. (For the best of the low, demotic Carter, read *Wise Children*; but in spite of all the oo-er-guv, brush-up-your-Shakespeare comedy of that last novel, *The Bloody Chamber* is the likeliest of her works to endure.)

The novella-length title story, or overture, begins as classic *grand guignol*: an innocent bride, a much-married millionaire husband, a lonely castle stood upon a melting shore, a secret room containing horrors. The helpless girl and the civilised, decadent, murderous man: Carter's first variation on the theme of Beauty and the Beast. There is a feminist twist:

instead of the weak father to save whom, in the fairy tale, Beauty agrees
to go to the Beast, we are given, here, an indomitable mother rushing to
her daughter's rescue.

It is Carter's genius, in this collection, to make the fable of Beauty and
the Beast a metaphor for all the myriad yearnings and dangers of sexual
relations. Now it is the Beauty who is the stronger, now the Beast. In
'The Courtship of Mr Lyon' it is for the Beauty to save the Beast's life,
while in 'The Tiger's Bride', Beauty will be erotically transformed into
an exquisite animal herself: '. . . each stroke of his tongue ripped off skin
after skin, all the skins of a life in the world, and left behind a nascent
patina of hairs. My earrings turned back to water . . . I shrugged the
drops off my beautiful fur.' As though her whole body were being
deflowered and so metamorphosing into a new instrument of desire,
allowing her admission to a new ('animal' in the sense of *spiritual* as well as
tigerish) world. In 'The Erl-King', however, Beauty and the Beast will
not be reconciled. Here there is neither healing, nor submission, but
revenge.

The collection expands to take in many other fabulous old tales; blood
and love, always proximate, underlie and unify them all. In 'The Lady of
the House of Love' love and blood unite in the person of a vampire:
Beauty grown monstrous, Beastly. In 'The Snow Child' we are in the
fairy-tale territory of white snow, red blood, black bird, and a girl, white,
red and black, born of a Count's wishes; but Carter's modern imagination knows that for every Count there is a Countess, who will not tolerate
her fantasy-rival. The battle of the sexes is fought between women, too.

The arrival of Red Riding Hood completes and perfects Carter's
brilliant, reinventing synthesis of *Kinder- und Hausmärchen*. Now we are
offered the radical, shocking suggestion that Grandmother might
actually be the Wolf ('The Werewolf'); or equally radical, equally
shocking, the thought that the girl (Red Riding Hood, Beauty) might
easily be as amoral, as savage as the Wolf/Beast; that she might conquer
the Wolf by the power of her own predatory sexuality, her erotic
wolfishness. This is the theme of 'The Company of Wolves', and to
watch *The Company of Wolves*, the film Angela Carter made with Neil
Jordan, weaving together several of her wolf-narratives, is to long for the
full-scale wolf-novel she never wrote.

'Wolf-Alice' offers final metamorphoses. Now there is no Beauty,
only two Beasts: a cannibal Duke, and a girl reared by wolves, who
thinks of herself as a wolf, and who, arriving at womanhood, is drawn
towards self-knowledge by the mystery of her own bloody chamber;
that is, her menstrual flow. By blood, and by what she sees in mirrors,
that make a house uncosy.

> At length the grandeur of the mountains becomes
> monotonous . . . He turned and stared at the mountain
> for a long time. He had lived in it for fourteen years
> but he had never seen it before as it might look
> to someone who had not known it as almost a part
> of the self . . . As he said goodbye to it, he saw it turn into
> so much scenery, into the wonderful backcloth for
> an old country tale, tale of a child suckled by
>
> wolves, perhaps, or of wolves nursed by a woman.

Carter's farewell to her mountain-country, at the end of her last wolf-story, 'Peter and the Wolf' in *Black Venus*, signals that, like her hero, she has 'tramped onwards, into a different story'.

There is one other out-and-out fantasy in this third collection, a meditation on *A Midsummer Night's Dream* that prefigures (and is better than) a passage in *Wise Children*. In this story Carter's linguistic exoticism is in full flight – here are 'breezes, juicy as mangoes, that mythopoeically caress the Coast of Coromandel far away on the porphyry and lapis lazuli Indian Shore'. But, as usual, her sarcastic common-sense yanks the story back to earth before it disappears in an exquisite puff of smoke. This dream-wood – 'nowhere near Athens . . . (it) is really located somewhere in the English midlands, possibly near Bletchley' – is damp and waterlogged and the fairies all have colds. Also, it has, since the date of the story, been chopped down to make room for a motorway. Carter's elegant fugue on Shakespearean themes is lifted towards brilliance by her exposition of the difference between the *Dream*'s wood and the 'dark necromantic forest' of the Grimms. The forest, she finely reminds us, is a scary place; to be lost in it is to fall prey to monsters and witches. But in a wood, 'you purposely mislay your way'; there are no wolves, and the wood 'is kind to lovers'. Here is the difference between the English and European fairy tale precisely and unforgettably defined.

Mostly, however, *Black Venus* and its successor, *American Ghosts and Old World Wonders*, eschew fantasy worlds; Carter's revisionist imagination has turned towards the real, her interest towards portraiture rather than narrative. The best pieces in these later books are portraits – of Baudelaire's black mistress Jeanne Duval, of Edgar Allan Poe, and, in two stories, of Lizzie Borden long before she 'took an axe', and the same Lizzie on the day of her crimes, a day described with slow, languorous precision and attention to detail – the consequences of overdressing in a heat-wave, and of eating twice-cooked fish, both play a part. Beneath the hyper-realism, however, there is an echo of *The Bloody Chamber*, for Lizzie's is a bloody deed, and she is, in addition, menstruating. Her own life-blood flows, while the angel of death waits on a nearby tree. (Once again, as with the wolf-stories, one hankers for more; for the Lizzie Borden novel that we cannot have.)

Baudelaire, Poe, *Dream*-Shakespeare, Hollywood, panto, fairy tale: Carter wears her influences openly, for she is their deconstructionist, their saboteur. She takes what we know and, having broken it, puts it together in her own spiky, courteous way; her words are new and not-new, like our own. In her hands Cinderella, given back her original name of Ashputtle, is the fire-scarred heroine of a tale of horrid mutilations wrought by mother-love; John Ford's *'Tis Pity She's a Whore* becomes a movie directed by a very different Ford; and the hidden meanings – perhaps one should say the hidden natures – of pantomime characters are revealed.

She opens an old story for us, like an egg, and finds the new story, the now-story we want to hear, within.

No such thing as a perfect writer. Carter's high-wire act takes place over a swamp of preciousness, over quicksands of the arch and twee; and there's no denying that she sometimes falls off, no getting away from odd outbreaks of fol-de-rol, and some of her puddings, her most ardent admirers will concede, are excessively egged. Too much use of words like 'eldritch', too many men who are rich 'as Croesus', too much porphyry and lapis lazuli to please a certain sort of purist. But the miracle is how often she pulls it off; how often she pirouettes without falling, or juggles without dropping a ball.

Accused by lazy pens of political correctness, she was the most individual, independent and idiosyncratic of writers; dismissed by many in her lifetime as a marginal, cultish figure, an exotic hothouse flower, she has become the contemporary writer most studied at British universities – a victory over the mainstream she would have enjoyed.

She hadn't finished. Like Italo Calvino, like Bruce Chatwin, like Raymond Carver, she died at the height of her powers. For writers, these are the cruellest deaths: in mid-sentence, so to speak. The stories in this volume are the measure of our loss. But they are also our treasure, to savour and to hoard.

Raymond Carver is said to have told his wife before he died (also of lung cancer), 'We're out there now. We're out there in Literature'. Carver was the most modest of men, but this is the remark of a man who knew, and who had often been told, how much his work was worth. Angela received less confirmation, in her lifetime, of the value of her unique oeuvre; but she, too, is out there now, out there in Literature, a Ray of the clear Fountain of Eternal Day.

Salman Rushdie, May 1995

EARLY WORK

The Man Who Loved a Double Bass
A Very, Very Great Lady and Her Son at Home
A Victorian Fable (with Glossary)

The Man Who Loved
a Double Bass

All artists, they say, are a little mad. This madness is, to a certain extent, a self-created myth designed to keep the generality away from the phenomenally close-knit creative community. Yet, in the world of the artists, the consciously eccentric are always respectful and admiring of those who have the courage to be genuinely a little mad.

That was how Johnny Jameson, the bass player, came to be treated – with respect and admiration; for there could be no doubt that Jameson was as mad as a hatter.

And the musicians looked after him. He was never without work, or a bed, or a packet of cigarettes, or a beer if he wanted one. There was always someone taking care of the things he could never get around to doing himself. It must also be admitted that he was a very fine bass player.

In this, in fact, lay the seed of his trouble. For his bass, his great, gleaming, voluptuous bass, was mother, father, wife, child and mistress to him and he loved it with a deep and steadfast passion.

Jameson was a small, quiet man with rapidly receding hair and a huge pair of heavy spectacles hiding mild, short-sighted eyes. He hardly went anywhere without his bass, which he carried effortlessly, slung on his back, as Red Indian women carry their babies. But it was a big baby for one so frail-looking as he to carry.

They called the bass Lola. Lola was the most beautiful bass in the whole world. Her shape was that of a full-breasted, full-hipped woman, recalling certain primitive effigies of the Mother Goddess so gloriously, essentially feminine was she, stripped of irrelevancies of head and limbs.

Jameson spent hours polishing her red wood, already a warm, chestnut colour, to an ever deeper, ever richer glow. On tour, he sat placidly in the bus while the other musicians drank, argued and gambled around him, and he would take Lola from her black case, and unwrap the rags that padded her, with a trembling emotion. Then he would take out a special, soft silk handkerchief and set to work on his polishing, smiling gently at nothing and blinking his short-sighted eyes like a happy cat.

The bass was always treated like a lady. The band started to buy her coffee and tea in cafés for a joke. Later it ceased to be a joke and became a habit. The extra drink was always ordered and placed before her and they ignored it when they went away and it was still on the table, cold and untouched.

Jameson always took Lola into cafés but never into public bars because, after all, she was a lady. Whoever drank with Jameson did so in the saloon and bought Lola a pineapple juice, although sometimes she could be prevailed upon to take a glass of sherry at festive occasions like Christmas or a birthday or when someone's wife had a child.

But Jameson was jealous if she got too much attention and would look daggers at a man who took too many liberties with her, like slapping her case or making facetious remarks.

Jameson had only ever been known to strike a man once when he had broken the nose of a drunken, insensitive pianist who made a coarse jest about Lola in Jameson's presence. So nobody ever joked about Lola when Jameson was there.

But innocent young musicians were hideously embarrassed if ever it fell out that they had to share a room with Jameson while on tour. So Jameson and Lola usually had a room to themselves. Away from Jameson, the trumpeter, Geoff Clarke, would say that Jameson was truly wedded to his art and perhaps they ought to book the bridal suite for the pair at some hotel, sometime.

But Clarke gave Jameson a good job in his trad group that was called the West End Syncopators. Ignoring the august echoes of the name, they dressed themselves up in grey toppers and tail coats when performing and their souped-up version of 'West End Blues' (plus new vocal) had penetrated to the lower reaches of the top twenty.

They all looked grotesque in grey toppers and none more grotesque than Jameson; but the band still made money.

Making money, however, meant day after day spent in a converted Green Line bus travelling up and down the country from one one-night-stand to the next. It meant dates at corn exchanges, town halls, grimy back rooms in pubs. It meant constant bone-weariness and constant cash and credit and the band all loved it. They all shared a crazy jubilation.

'The trad boom ain't going to last for ever, so let's enjoy it!' said Len Nelson, the clarinettist.

He was an incorrigible fornicator, whose idea of profiting from the trad boom was to lure star-struck young girls from the provincial clubs and concerts up into his hotel bedroom and there copulate with them. He loved success. And, to a lesser extent, they all exulted.

Except, of course, Jameson, who did not even notice that trad was booming. He played just whatever he was told to play. He never really cared what it was as long as the quality of the sound he produced did not offend Lola.

One night in November, they were engaged to play at a small town in the Fenland wastes of East Anglia. Darkness came with the afternoon, dragging mist with it to fill the dykes and shroud the pollard willows. The band bus followed a straight road with never a turn or dip and when they reached the pub where the jazz club at which they were to perform was held, and climbed from the bus, the darkness fell around their shoulders like a rain-soaked blanket.

'Are they expecting us?' asked Dave Jennings, the drummer, anxiously. Not a light shone in the pub.

A frayed poster pinned to the closed main door announced their coming. But the chronic Fenland rain had so softened the paper that the slogan: 'Friday night is rave night – with the raving, rioting, hit parade happy West End Syncopators' was almost indecipherable.

'Well, it's not opening time, yet,' comforted Len Nelson.

'More's the pity,' grunted Jennings.

'Of course they're expecting us,' said Geoff firmly. 'The club booked us up months ago, before the record even. That's why we accepted a date in this God-forsaken hole, isn't it, Simeon?'

The manager was a peripatetic Jew named Simeon Price, a failed tenor sax man who travelled with them out of nostalgia for his swinging days. Simeon was staring at the pub with bright, frightened eyes.

'I don't like it here,' he said and shivered. 'There's something in the air.'

'Bloody lot of wet in the air,' grumbled Nelson. 'Bet the dollies round here all got webbed feet.'

'Don't come the mysterious East,' Geoff urged Simeon.

Simeon shook his head agitatedly and shivered in spite of the great, turned-up collar of his enormous cashmere coat. He always dressed like a stage Jew. His race was his gimmick and he always affected a strong Yiddish accent although his family had been respected members of the Manchester bourgeoisie for nearly 150 years.

But then the landlord appeared and then the two sixth form grammar school boys who ran the club and there was beer and chat and warmth and laughter. Jameson was very worried in case the damp should hurt Lola, warp her, rot her strings. He allowed one of the grammar school boys, they called him the Boy David at once, to buy her a rum and orange, for her health's sake. Nelson and Jennings had to take the wondering Boy David off into the Gents and explain about Lola, quietly.

But Simeon's slender, delicately pointed nose was almost aquiver

with sensibility, smelling something wrong, trouble in the wet air. The
East Anglian air was bad for his weak lungs. The Boy David was talking
about his club.

'Bit old world, the membership, really, though we get people in for the
club from quite a way away – art students, even, and a few sharp
youngsters, and leather jackets who come from miles on their motorbikes. But the local teds, well, they still even have sideboards and velvet
collars to their jackets!'

There was a chorus of incredulous mirth and the boy at once became
embarrassed and bought more drinks to cover his confusion. The band
were to stay the night at the pub, which hid a number of bedrooms
behind its unimposing façade. Simeon crept away from the bar to feel the
sheets on his bed. They were damp. His throat immediately set up a
sympathetic tickling.

Jameson, humping Lola, also crept away, to the back room where
music and dancing were permitted. He unwrapped his instrument and sat
huddled over it in the cold, caressing with his silken rag. The room
around him waited for the club to open, the shabby lines of quiet chairs
waited, the little platform for the musicians waited.

But there was a potent unease in the night. The musicians sensed it and
their laughter became defiant as they tried to frighten the uneasiness away
with their merriment. And they failed. Their young hosts caught the
silent, depressed infection until they were all just sitting around, drinking
for want of something else to do. But Jameson was happy; he was the
only one happy, sitting away from them all, with Lola between his knees.

As the band assembled on the cramped platform, the first customers
arrived and stood around with their first half pints of bitter. Music began;
the customers waited passively for the first extrovert couple who would
start to dance.

They were an easily recognisable type, these early ones. The boys wore
pale, loose sweaters with paisley silk scarves tucked casually into the vee
necks and the girls were tricked out in pseudo beat style, black or heavy
mesh stockings, loose dresses heavily fringed. They were the children of
local doctors, clergymen, teachers, retired soldiers, probably students in
their last school year. They wore duffel coats and drove battered old cars
and had a tendency to collect those little china ashtrays with veteran cars
on them.

Just before the first break, a black-legged girl in a short little pleated
skirt and a youth in cavalry twill trousers ventured, giggling, on to the
floor to dance; they did so in a peculiarly self-conscious way that made the
musicians wink and grin at one another. Gradually the room began to fill.
Art students from a nearby town, sniggering at the bourgeois who aped

them; a party of crop-haired modernists, who had also travelled some distance. The modernists had sharp, pointed noses and Italian suits. Their girls dressed with studied formality, faces stylised, pale cheeks and lips, vividly painted eyes, hair immaculate, stiff with lacquer.

The modernists chaffed Simeon, who lingered by the pay desk because the boys in charge were so young that he worried for them. The modernists joked about the grey top hats and the striped trousers and were patronising about 'West End Blues' and, in fact, the whole trad set-up altogether; they were here, they implied, just because there happened to be nothing else doing that night. Simeon smiled with professional warmth and wondered whether he dare slip away to spray his throat.

But his eyes slitted with suspicion when he saw a group of youths were parking motorcycles outside the pub; he could see them through the open door. They took off their crash helmets and left them under their cycles, where they gleamed whitely, like mushrooms or new laid eggs. Then the boys approached, plastic jackets creaking. Simeon personally tore off their jackets for them and watched them anxiously as they fought for brown ales at the bar.

'Now, those chaps are really far less potential trouble than those modernist friends of yours,' admonished the Boy David. Simeon sighed.

'You wouldn't have, by any chance, such a thing as an aspirin – and perhaps, might it be possible, could I get a glass of hot milk?'

Inside the club room, a thick smoke haze dimmed the already low lighting and the room was in semi-darkness. Arms and legs flailed, beer slopped. The music was so loud it seemed almost a tangible, brazen wall. The West End Syncopators were half-way through another successful date.

But the leatherjackets kept apart from the main, happy crowd. They had taken over one particular corner for themselves and were not dancing but standing up to their beer, laughing and grinning.

The boys in the band played and sweated and gulped restorative bitter between choruses. They undid their silk waistcoats and their black ties and mopped the red indentations made on their foreheads by their top hats. It was just like any other date.

Just like any other date until one of the leatherjackets spilled his beer all over the olive green buttocks of a thin girl in a sheath dress who jived backwards into him. She turned, angry. He apologised with profuse irony and that made her more angry still. The girl complained to her sharp, short-jacketed escort and the leatherjackets stood all round and leered.

'And aren't you going to say sorry to this young lady, then, mate?' the girl's dancing partner shouted above the music.

The leatherjackets closed ranks like a snapped clasp-knife. Their indistinguishable, pallid, slack-jawed faces all grinned at once.

'And what if I ain't particularly sorry? Wasted all my beer, I have.'

A group of Italian youths deserted their girls to gather behind the olive-sheathed girl's defender. And that was how it started. The quarrel boiled up into a fine ragout of cries, shouts, blows and the dim interior whirled with thrusting limbs and crashing bottles as the eager youths met in fight. A bottle smashed the single, red-painted electric bulb and there was a horror of darkness. In the chaos, a pair of leatherjackets launched an attack on the musicians who were moaning and terrified and striking little matches to see something of the battle.

'That such a thing should happen when we're in the top twenty!' gasped Simeon.

The Young Conservatives came scurrying past shepherding frightened Susans, Brendas, and Jennifers. But the art students clustered safely at the door to giggle. The tight-skirted teddy girls dropped their impassivity; like valkyries they rode the battle, cheering the fighters on. Their exalted faces flickered in and out of the light that trickled through from the public bar.

Now the musicians cast aside their top hats, their instruments and their neutrality. Simeon saw Len Nelson – as jerky and uncertain in the intermittent light as a man in an early film – leap from the dais and seize an Italian youth by his narrow and immaculate lapels and shake, shake, shake him until the boy's mouth gaped open, howling.

'Nothing like it ever happened before!' the Boy David kept exclaiming in an apologetic frenzy. There were crashes and splinterings and the landlord appeared, trembling. Simeon took him into the private bar to soothe him with his own Scotch.

'Quite like the old days, before we got famous,' panted Nelson, defending the microphone.

But it was all over very quickly, when someone shouted something about the police and the room emptied like a bath when the plug is pulled out. The musicians' heavy breathing and little exclamations of triumph and sighs were the only sounds in the room.

'Would I be such a fool as to call the police?' demanded Simeon rhetorically. So they all laughed and went for a drink.

'Here,' said someone later, 'has anyone seen Jameson?'

'Not since the lights went out.'

'Well, what does it matter? I'm going to bed,' said Simeon. 'I've a dreadful cold coming, I feel it. Not that going to bed will do me much good; wringing wet, the sheets are . . .'

Then they all of them forgot about Jameson until very much later, when all but Geoff and Nelson had finally followed Simeon up the stairs to bed. Geoff and Nelson, decently happy, decided to go and have a look at the damage in the club room. They took a light bulb from the bar and plugged it into the socket where the red light had once been. And into focus leapt all the shattered glass and broken chairs and brown beer puddles soaking into the floor.

Sobered at once, Geoff climbed on to the stage and poked anxiously among the instruments remaining. Miraculously, the drum and its accessories had survived and – he sighed – there seemed not a casualty on the dais. Then he found a terrible thing. Where Jameson had sat with Lola, there remained nothing on the floor but a heap of chestnut-coloured firewood.

'Oh, Christ,' he said. Nelson looked up, startled at the tone of the other's voice. 'Jameson, how are we going to tell Jameson, Len? His bass . . . '

They stood together and gazed at Lola's pathetic fragmented corpse. Both were touched with a cold finger of awe and dread and a superstitious sorrow; the lady who did not go into public bars was suddenly no more than a few graceless splinters.

'Do you know if he knows?' whispered Nelson. It did not seem right to talk in a loud voice.

'I haven't seen him since the trouble began.'

'Even if he does know, well, he ought to have a bit of company, at a time like this, a few friends around him . . . '

'Maybe he's up in his room.'

They found out from the landlord that Jameson had been lodged in an attic room high at the top of the old rabbit-warren of a place. Fenland mist had crept into the pub and it blurred their vision as Geoff and Nelson climbed flight after flight of stairs. It was very late, now, and cold, with a bone-chilling, wet, cold. Then, without warning, every light went out. Stricken, Nelson clutched at Geoff.

'Len, it's all right, don't take on. It must be a fuse, or something, perhaps the wiring – rotten old wiring they have in houses as old as this.'

But he himself was badly scared. They both felt an alien, almost tangible something in the darkness, felt it in the damp kiss of the mist-soaked air on their cheeks.

'A light, Geoff, now.'

Geoff clicked his cigarette lighter. The tiny flame only intensified the darkness around them. They reached the topmost landing.

'Here we are.'

The door swung open. Geoff held his lighter high. They saw first a chair, overturned on the floor. Then they saw the open, empty case of a double bass on the cheap taffeta bedspread. The case was shaped for all the world like a coffin. But Lola would not lie in it, although it was her own.

And in the still circle of light, swung a pair of feet, gently, backwards and forwards, forwards and backwards . . . Geoff raised his lighter above his head until they could see all of Jameson, hanging from a disused gas bracket, his gentle face black and twisted. Bedded deep in his neck was a brilliant silken rag, the rag he had used for so long to polish his bass. Something glinted on the floor beneath him – his glasses, dropped, broken.

A sodden wind came in through the open window and swallowed the lighter flame at once. Then there was engulfing darkness and in the darkness no noise but the slow creak, creak, creak. And the two men grabbed at each other's hands like frightened children.

In a room beneath them, the same little wind trickled through an ill-fitting window frame and tickled Simeon Price's throat so that he coughed and stirred a little, uneasily, in his sleep.

A Very, Very Great Lady and Her Son at Home

'When I was adolescent, my mother taught me a charm, gave me a talisman, handed me the key of the world. For I lived in terror, I, so young, so shy of so many people – i.e. those who spoke with soft voices and sounded the h in "which"; cinema usherettes who, in those days wore wide satin pyjamas which mocked my unawakened sex with unashamed lasciviousness; suave men who put cold hands on my defenceless, barely formed breasts on the tops of lonely November buses. So many, many people.

'My mother said: "Child, if such folks awe you, then picture them on the lavatory, straining, constipated. They will at once seem small, pathetic, manageable." And she whispered to me a great, universal truth: "THE BOWELS ARE GREAT LEVELLERS."

'She was a rough woman, my mother. She picked her teeth ceaselessly with a fork and she would take off her felt slippers, in the evenings, and probe out the caked, flaked skin and dirt from between her toes with a sensual, inquisitive finger. But she was possessed of great wisdom – the brutal, yet withal vital, wisdom of a peasant.'

The woman's voice, high and clear as the sound of a glass rapped with a spoon to summon a waiter, ceased in meditation for a moment. Only two endlessly long miraculously slender legs emerged from the pool of coagulated shadow in the corner where she sat.

Petals dropped from a red rose in a silver bowl on to the low, round, blood-coloured mahogany table with a soft, faint, exhausted sound, as of a pigeon's fart. The woman recrossed her legs; rasping planes of silk flashed out as they caught the light, like the blades of scissors, slicing all that came between them. She resumed her narrative.

'I had been a shy child. A lonely child, lost in the middle of a large family – twenty-three children, of whom eighteen reached maturity! – cooped up in a meagre dwelling, the loft above my father's stable. Ah!' she cried, 'how often I lay awake at night comforted by the gentle whickering of great, grey Dapple, with the ruffs over his hooves, like a pierrot!'

Again she paused for a moment's recollection; then resumed her narrative.

'By tragic paradox, so crowded was our home, so continual the to-ing and fro-ing, that my isolation was total. I was alone, so alone; so tentative, unable to grasp the fact of myself as an entity, a personality.

'I was introverted to the point of extinction, and in that great, surging mêlée of humanity – my family – only behaviour extroverted to the point of sheer exhibition drew attention to oneself.

'I remember how one of my brothers – or perhaps it was a sister: one forgets, one forgets – plunged his little bare feet in the suppertime soup one night, to bring to my parents' attention how great his need was for new boots. Or shoes. Or sandals. Or socks . . .'

The voice died away and then welled out again in passionate regret: 'The significant detail – one forgets it! One forgets it!' But soon she resumed her narrative.

'Poor little fellow, he – or was it she – was scalded almost to the knee. The suppertime soup, the cabbage leaves bobbing in it – I remember, though, the suppertime soup. And the faces round the table, so many, many faces. And such meagre soup that many a time, my small stomach sonorous as a pair of maracas, I would creep down in the silence of the night to scoop up a little of Dapple's steaming mash on my fingers, for myself.

'Indeed, though one would scarcely credit it, for many years my mother, in error, called me by the name of an elder sister who had died in infancy. My father, on the other hand, a grey, precise man who smelled of horse dung and kept a list of all our names (together with brief descriptive notes) sewn to the inside of his black greasy hat, scrupulously referred to me by my baptismal name whenever he chanced to see me, removing his hat and running a gnarled finger down the columns until he came to the thumbnail sketch which tallied with the wide-eyed, pigtailed child before him. Those were the only occasions on which I recall him taking off his hat.

'Jason, cigarettes.'

The boy, cross-legged at her feet, leapt into darkness; came the sound of an unsnapped case, a clicked lighter. The red tip of the cigarette glowed in the shadows like a warning traffic-light – STOP – and the petals on another full-blown rose trembled but did not fall.

'Forced into myself, I became bookish, walking five miles to the free library in my cracked clogs. I read, I read, I read. Anything, everything . . . My father, dipping the quill in the penny bottle of ink, laboriously added "steel-rimmed spectacles" to the note beside my name in his directory. Charity spectacles. I was so ashamed.

'But I was a helpless addict; so precious were those books to me that I carried them around next to my heart, beneath the ragged liberty vest from the parish poor-box but above the layer of newspaper that, for warmth, my mother sewed around us, renewing it each autumn.

'My mind grew in the darkness like a flower. But my isolation increased. I could not communicate my love, my wonder, my veritable lust for things of the spirit, the intellect, with my parents – nor, indeed, with my teachers, for them I hated. They bound my face in iron: first my eyes, then my teeth.

' "Teeth in brace," my father amended by the guttering light of the farthing candle. Or was it a penny candle? Or a halfpenny rush dip? One forgets – one forgets.'

Again the brief cry; then she resumed her narrative.

'Life went on. The years passed. The bright peonies of the menstrual flow blossomed. My breasts grew like young doves. I had a fever and they cropped my hair. To my wonder and delight it grew again in little soft curls.

'I stared at my reflection in Dapple's trough. I took off my spectacles and pulled the brace from my mouth. I dimly saw this white face and this golden topknot and I was afraid, for the child I had been was dead; dead and replaced by a beautiful woman whom I did not know.

'Jason, the candles.'

He – the boy; slight, fair, delicate – struck matches, and the branched candlesticks sprang to life.

Her face was a painted mask of beauty. Eyes bluer than their blue-stained lids, precise discs of scarlet on her white cheeks, lambent hair piled above the winking lights of her tiara. And the diamonds burned with no more dangerous fire than did her white breasts, exposed to the nipples by the black chiffon robe that fell away from her thighs.

She was as beautiful as Venus rising from the waves in the celebrated picture by Botticelli, only more so. She was as beautiful as the celebrated bust of Nefertiti in the Louvre, only more so. She was as beautiful as the statue of the young David by the celebrated Michelangelo that gazes on the thronged traffic of Milan with such serenity, only more so.

Slowly she ground out her cigarette in the wounded onyx of an ashtray on the arm of her chair. She resumed her narrative.

'At fifteen, I went walking in the park. I glowed with beauty on the boating pond, in a canoe, at half a crown an hour. I disputed about Plato, whose books I read deeply, with a small brown man in a loin cloth, and all the time I gazed on my reflection in the rippling water.

'When I concentrated on my reflection, I *was* that lovely being. *Je suis un autre.* Dizzied, drunk on the miracle of arriving at a personality with the suddenness of epiphany, I turned from the pool to make some brilliant point to my companion – and my new self fell away like a cloak. I wept, stammered: ten years old again.

'I ran, stumbling, back to the familiar warmth of the stable, to weep saltily into Dapple's warm mane. And there my mother, coming from the streets with her hands full of potato peelings that she gleaned from the ashcans of our neighbours (when no one was looking; she had a fierce pride), to enrich Dapple's mash . . . my mother, returning, saw me.

' "Susan," she said, "hush your moitherings." And then she paused, bewildered, laid her burden on a nearby tea chest and came close to me, so close that I could count the grey hairs growing from her nostrils. Her rheumy eyes filled, overflowed.

' "But you be not my Susan!" she cried. "My Susan didn't live to be as old as you!" And she buried her head in her apron and her shoulders heaved with sobbing. But, selfishly, I dried my own tears on Dapple's tail, for my mother had at last recognised my true identity and I perceived a glimmer of hope.

'Jason, my knee.'

He knelt at once and began to massage her knee. The bones clicked under his long fingers. A candle flame flickered, casting a momentary shadow over the lower part of her face resembling a small black moustache and imperial.

' "Mother," I said, "I am so shy." It was the first remark I remember addressing to her in my whole life. "Mother," I repeated; the word tasted wholesome as bread and milk in my mouth.

'She gazed at me thoughtfully, rolling a corner of her apron into a probe and cleaning wax from her ear with it. Then she gave me the formula, irradiating my life.

' "If you picture them all on the lavatory, constipated, straining, then all the toffee-nosed bastards will seem defenceless and pathetic," she said.

' "THE BOWELS ARE GREAT LEVELLERS."

'It was a revelation. I rushed out into the world, never to return, repeating those words, living by them.

'Jason, the world was my OYSTER!'

Her voice rang like a sudden, brass-throated trumpet. The full-blown rose at last allowed itself to collapse, almost with the quality of muffled applause. The woman's beauty was so intense that it seemed to have the quality of a deformity, so far was it from the human norm. The bones in her knees jostled one another with a faint mumbling.

As if recollecting vague, soft, fragrant, long-ago things, she murmured (more to herself than to the boy): 'Ah, Jason, the childish thighs and baby buttocks of great men. You can stop massaging.'

He drew away. She lit another cigarette at the candle flame. Blinking, he drew a hand through his hair. The candle light shone along the brace in his teeth, made blinding pools in the steel-rimmed spectacles over his eyes. He backed, bumping against the mahogany table where the petals pooled redly.

'Jason,' she asked sharply, 'why are you staring at me? Jason?'

He coughed. He fidgeted, the toes of his bare feet curling and uncurling in the thick carpet.

'Jason?' more urgently.

'And do you look pathetic on the lavatory, mother?'

The cigarette fell from nerveless fingers; she opened and closed her mouth but not a sound came out. She crashed forward on to the carpet and lay there, a tree felled, motionless.

The boy went to the door and vanished, laughing, into the night.

A Victorian Fable

(with Glossary)

The Village, take a fright.
In the rookeries.

Here the sloops of war and the dollymops flash it to spie a dowry of parny; there the bonneters cooled their longs and shorts in the hazard drums.

In every snickert and ginnel, bone-grubbers, rufflers, shivering-jemmies, anglers, clapperdogeons, peterers, sneeze-lurkers and Whip Jacks with their morts, out of the picaroon, fox and flimp and ogle.

A Hopping Giles gets a bloody Jemmy on the cross of a cut-throat; the snotters crib belchers, bird's eye wipes, blue billies and Randal's men.

In a boozing ken in the Holy Land, a dunk-horned cutter – a cock-eyed clack box in flashy benjamin and blood red fancy – shed a tear by the I desire.

But when he got the water of life down the common sewer, he bullyragged so antiscripturally that the barney hipped and nabbed the rust.

'This shove in the mouth makes me shoot the cat! Me dumpling depot is fair all-overish!'

He certainly had his hump up. He absquatulated. The bung cried: 'Square the omee for the cream of the valley!' But the splodger had mizzled with his half-a-grunter.

At his ruggy carser, his poll – a killing, ginger-hackled skull-thatcher – kept on the nose for her jomer.

She had faked the rubber for her mendozy and got him up an out and out glorious sinner. There was an alderman in chains, a Ben Flake, a neddy of Sharp's Alley blood worms, with Irish apricots, Joe Savace and storrac.

'Pray God,' she said, 'that he be neither beargeared, bleary, blued, primed, lumpy, top-heavy, moony, scammered, on the ran-tan, ploughed, muddled, obfuscated, swipy, kisky, sewed up nor all mops and brooms! Or that he hasn't lapped the gutter, can't see a hole in a ladder or been to Bungay Fair and lose both his legs!'

But what a flare-up in the soush! He dropped into her on the spot. He'd got a capital twist for a batty fang and he showed her it was dragging time; she was sick as a horse. He was a catchy fancy-bloke.

'You mouldy old bed-fagot, you rotten old gooseberry pudden, you ugly old Gill, you flea-ridden old moll!' he blasted. 'I'll give you jessie, you Mullingar heifer!'

A barnacled cove (a spoffy blackberry swagger with a Newgate fringe) from the top floor back sang out: 'Knife it, you head beetler! Stow faking!' But got a stunning fag on the twopenny that sent him half-way to Albertopolis.

She had bought the rabbit with that slubberdegullion. He peppered her and clumped her and leathered her till she went flop down on the Rory O'More and then he stepped it for the frog and toad, to go to Joe Blake the Bartlemy.

He hopped the twig on her.

'He ought to go to the vertical care-grinder!' she chived. 'He ought to be marinated! I'll never poll up with a liver-faced, chatty, beef-headed, cupboard-headed, culver-headed, fiddle-faced, glumpish, squabby dab tros like him again!

'I'm fairly in half-mourning – it won't fadge, it just won't fadge. He gives me the Jerry go Nimbles. I'll stun him – I'll streak. I'll pick up my sticks and cut.'

So she bolted and took a speel on the drum to the top of Rome.

On Shitten Saturday, the worms pinned that scaly shaver of hers in a Tom and Jerry for starring the glaze; he went over the stile at Spike Park and got topped.

Glossary

Village, the	London
take a fright	night (rhyming slang)
rookeries	a slow neighbourhood inhabited by dirty Irish and thieves
sloop of war, a	whore (rhyming slang)
dollymop, a	a tawdrily dressed maid-servant, a street-walker
flash it, to	show it, to display one's wares

dowry of parny, a	a lot of rain
bonneter, a	one who induces another to gamble
cool, to	to look, to look over (back slang)
longs and shorts	cards made for cheating
hazard drum, a	gambling dens, where the honest escape penniless, if at all
snickert, a	low alley way
ginnel, a	still lower alley way
bone-grubber, a	a person who hunts dust-holes, gutters, and all likely spots for refuse bones, which he sells at the ragshops, or to the bone-merchants
ruffler, a	beggar pretending to be an old, maimed soldier
shivering -jemmy, a	a begger who exposes himself, half-naked, on a cold day to obtain alms. This occupation is unpleasant but exceedingly lucrative
angler, an	a thief who goes about with a rod, having a hook at the end, which he inserts into open windows at night on the chance of a catch
clapperdogeon, a	a beggar who uses children, either of his own or borrowed, in order to stir the sympathy of the charitable
shed a tear, to	to take a dram or glass of neat spirits; jocular phrase used, with a sort of grim earnestness, by old topers. The origin may have been that ardent spirits, taken neat by younger persons, usually bring water to their eyes
I desire	fire (rhyming slang)
water of life	gin (from aqua vitae?)
common sewer	the throat
bullyrag, to	to abuse or scold violently; to swindle out of money by intimidation and sheer abuse
antiscriptural	adj – applied to oaths when they are composed of foul language

barney	the company
hip, to	to be offended
nab the rust, to	to take offence
shove in the mouth, a	glass of spirits
shoot the cat, to	vomit
dumpling depot	belly
all-overish	adj. – sick, unwell, out of order
have one's hump up, to	to be in a fearful rage
absquatulate, to	depart from an establishment without paying one's score
bung	landlord
square, to	to settle a bill
omee	man-in-charge; governor; landlord (when used by a landlord about himself)
cream of the valley	gin
splodger	lout
mizzle, to	to depart with great speed; to vanish
half-a-grunter	sixpence
ruggy	adj. – frowsty, unclean
carser	house, home
poll	young lady with whom a gentleman is having an irregular relationship
killing	adjective of high commendation; outstanding; unique
ginger-hackled	adj. – having auburn or flaxen hair
skull-thatcher	a straw-bonnet maker
on the nose, to be	on the look-out
jomer	sweetheart
fake the rubber, to	stand treat in an extravagant manner

mendozy	dear, darling; a term of endearment probably from the valiant fighter, Mendoza
out and out	adj. – first-rate; splendid
glorious sinner	dinner (rhyming slang)
alderman in chains, an	a turkey hung with sausages
Ben Flake, a	a steak (rhyming slang)
neddy, a	a large quantity of commodity, as in 'a neddy of fruit', 'a neddy of fish'
Sharp's Alley blood worms	black puddings. Sharp's Alley was very recently a noted slaughtering place near Smithfield
Irish apricots	potatoes
Joe Savage	cabbage (rhyming slang)
storrac	carrots (back slang)

beargeared
bleary
blued
primed
lumpy
top-heavy
moony
scammered
on the ran-tan
ploughed   adjectives and phrases denoting various stages
muddled   of drunkenness
obfuscated
swipy
kisky
sewed up
all mops and brooms
lap the gutter, to
not be able to see a
hole in the ladder, to

go to a Bungay Fair and lose both legs, to	to have reached the ultimate degree of intoxication. In the Ancient Egyptian language, the determinative character of the hieroglyphic verb 'to be drunk' has the significant form of the leg of a man being amputated
flare-up, a	row
soush	house (back slang)
drop into somebody, to	give them an unprovoked beating
twist	appetite, e.g. 'Will's got a capital twist for a Ben Flake' or, in the case of the hero of our anecdote, a capital twist for . . .
batty fang, a	a sound beating, a drubbing
dragging time	the evening of a country fair day, when the young fellows begin pulling the wenches about
sick as a horse	popular simile denoting extreme ennui
catchy	inclined to take undue advantage
fancy-bloke	gentleman friend
bed-fagot	bed companion
gooseberry pudden	woman (rhyming slang)
Gill Moll }	terms of disapprobation applied to females
blast, to	to curse
give jessie, to	to commit assault and battery upon someone
Mullingar heifer	said of a lady whose ankles are 'beefy', or thick. A term of Irish origin. It is said that a traveller passing through Mullingar was so struck with this pecularity in the local women that he determined to accost the first he met next. 'May I ask,' said he, 'if you wear hay in your shoes?' 'Faith, an what if I do?' said the girl. 'Because,' says the traveller, 'that accounts for the calves of your legs coming down to feed on it.'

barnacled	adj. – applied to a wearer of spectacles (corruption of Latin *binnoculi*?). Derived by some from the barnacle (*Lepas Anatifera*), a kind of conical shell adhering to ships' bottoms. Hence a marine term for goggles, and for which they are used by sailors in a case of ophthalmic derangement
cove	or covey; a man or boy of any age
spoffy	adj. – officious, intrusive
blackberry swagger	a person who hawks tapes, bootlaces, etc.
Newgate fringe, a	the collar of beard worn under the chin; so called from its indicating the position of the rope when Jack Ketch operates
sing out, to	exclaim in a loud voice
knife it, to	to stop, to bring to a halt
stow faking, to	to cease evil activity
stunning	adj. – astounding
fag	blow
twopenny	head
Albertopolis	a facetious appelation given by Villagers to the Kensington Gore district
buy the rabbit, to	make a bad bargain; obtain a deal of trouble and inconvenience by some action
slubberdegullion	worthless wretch
pepper, to clump, to leather, to	degrees of beating
flop down, to go	to collapse totally
Rory O'More	floor (rhyming slang)
step it, to	abscond
frog and toad	main road (rhyming slang)

Joe Blake the Bartlemy, to go to	to visit a low woman in a house of ill-repute
hop the twig, to	to run away; to leave someone in the lurch
vertical care-grinder	treadmill
chive, to	to shout
marinated, to be	transported; from the salt pickling herrings undergo in Cornwall
poll up, to	to live with a member of the opposite sex in a state of unmarried impropriety
liver-faced	adj. – mean, cowardly
chatty	adj. – infested with lice
beef-headed	adj. – stupid
cupboard-headed	an expression designating one whose head is both wooden and hollow
culver-headed	adj. – weak and stupid
fiddle-faced	adj. – applied to those with wizened countenances
glumpish	adj. – of a stubborn, sulky temper (our hero certainly fits the bill here!)
squabby	adj. – fat, short and thick
dab tros	bad sort (back slang)
in half-mourning, to be	to have sustained a black eye, or 'mouse', in the course of a tussle
fadge, it won't	expression meaning 'it just won't do', or 'it just won't work'
Jerry go Nimbles	diarrhoea
stun, to	to astonish
streak, to	to abscond
pick up one's sticks and cut, to	to collect one's possessions and leave an establishment without notice; to do a 'moonlight flit'

bolt, to	to run away, escape
a speel on the drum, to take	to take a trip to the country
top of Rome	home (rhyming slang)
Shitten Saturday	corruption of 'Shut-in Saturday'; the day between Good Friday and Easter Sunday
worm	policeman
pin, to	to arrest, to apprehend
scaly	adj. – unpleasant, disgusting
shaver	young person
Tom and Jerry, a	a drinking shop
star the glaze, to	to break the window or show-glass of a jeweller or other tradesman, and take any valuable articles and run away. Sometimes the glass is cut with a diamond, and a strip of leather fastened to the piece of glass cut out to keep it from falling in and making a noise. Another plan is to cut the sash
go over the stile, to	to go for trial (rhyming slang)
Spike Park	the Queen's Bench prison
topped, to be	to be executed. Which the brute richly deserved

FIREWORKS:
NINE PROFANE PIECES

A Souvenir of Japan

When I went outside to see if he was coming home, some children dressed ready for bed in cotton nightgowns were playing with sparklers in the vacant lot on the corner. When the sparks fell down in beards of stars, the smiling children cooed softly. Their pleasure was very pure because it was so restrained. An old woman said: 'And so they pestered their father until he bought them fireworks.' In this language, fireworks are called *hannabi*, which means 'flower fire'. All through summer, every evening, you can see all kinds of fireworks, from the humblest to the most elaborate, and once we rode the train out of Shinjuku for an hour to watch one of the public displays which are held over rivers so that the dark water multiplies the reflections.

By the time we arrived at our destination, night had already fallen. We were in the suburbs. Many families were on their way to enjoy the fireworks. Their mothers had scrubbed and dressed up the smallest children to celebrate the treat. The little girls were especially immaculate in pink and white cotton kimonos tied with fluffy sashes like swatches of candy floss. Their hair had been most beautifully brushed, arranged in sleek, twin bunches and decorated with twists of gold and silver thread. These children were all on their best behaviour because they were staying up late and held their parents' hands with a charming propriety. We followed the family parties until we came to some fields by the river and saw, high in the air, fireworks already opening out like variegated parasols. They were visible from far away and as we took the path that led through the fields towards their source they seemed to occupy more and more of the sky.

Along the path were stalls where shirtless cooks with sweatbands round their heads roasted corncobs and cuttlefish over charcoal. We bought cuttlefish on skewers and ate them as we walked along. They had been basted with soy sauce and were very good. There were also stalls selling goldfish in plastic bags and others for big balloons with rabbit ears. It was like a fairground – but such a well-ordered fair! Even the patrolling policemen carried coloured paper lanterns instead of torches. Everything was altogether quietly festive. Ice-cream sellers wandered among the crowd, ringing handbells. Their boxes of wares smoked with cold and they called out in plaintive voices, 'Icy, icy, icy cream!' When young lovers dispersed discreetly down the tracks in the sedge, the shadowy, indefatigable salesmen pursued them with bells, lamps and mournful cries.

By now, a great many people were walking towards the fireworks but their steps fell so softly and they chatted in such gentle voices there was no more noise than a warm, continual, murmurous humming, the cosy sound of shared happiness, and the night filled with a muted, bourgeois yet authentic magic. Above our heads, the fireworks hung dissolving earrings on the night. Soon we lay down in a stubbled field to watch the fireworks. But, as I expected, he very quickly grew restive.

'Are you happy?' he asked. 'Are you sure you're happy?' I was watching the fireworks and did not reply at first although I knew how bored he was and, if he was himself enjoying anything, it was only the idea of my pleasure – or, rather, the idea that he enjoyed my pleasure, since this would be a proof of love. I became guilty and suggested we return to the heart of the city. We fought a silent battle of self-abnegation and I won it, for I had the stronger character. Yet the last thing in the world that I wanted was to leave the scintillating river and the gentle crowd. But I knew his real desire was to return and so return we did, although I do not know if it was worth my small victory of selflessness to bear his remorse at cutting short my pleasure, even if to engineer this remorse had, at some subterranean level, been the whole object of the outing.

Nevertheless, as the slow train nosed back into the thickets of neon, his natural liveliness returned. He could not lose his old habit of walking through the streets with a sense of expectation, as if a fateful encounter might be just around the corner, for, the longer one stayed out, the longer something remarkable might happen and, even if nothing ever did, the chance of it appeased the sweet ache of his boredom for a little while. Besides, his duty by me was done. He had taken me out for the evening and now he wanted to be rid of me. Or so I saw it. The word for wife, okusan, means the person who occupies the inner room and rarely, if ever, comes out of it. Since I often appeared to be his wife, I was frequently subjected to this treatment, though I fought against it bitterly.

But I usually found myself waiting for him to come home knowing, with a certain resentment, that he would not; and that he would not even telephone me to tell me he would be late, either, for he was far too guilty to do so. I had nothing better to do than to watch the neighbourhood children light their sparklers and giggle; the old woman stood beside me and I knew she disapproved of me. The entire street politely disapproved of me. Perhaps they thought I was contributing to the delinquency of a juvenile for he was obviously younger than I. The old woman's back was bowed almost to a circle from carrying, when he was a baby, the father who now supervised the domestic fireworks in his evening undress of loose, white drawers, naked to the waist. Her face had the seamed reserve of the old in this country. It was a neighbourhood poignantly rich in old ladies.

At the corner shop, they put an old lady outside on an upturned beer crate each morning, to air. I think she must have been the household grandmother. She was so old she had lapsed almost entirely into a somnolent plant life. She was of neither more nor less significance to herself or to the world than the pot of morning glories which blossomed beside her and perhaps she had less significance than the flowers, which would fade before lunch was ready. They kept her very clean. They covered her pale cotton kimono with a spotless pinafore trimmed with coarse lace and she never dirtied it because she did not move. Now and then, a child came out to comb her hair. Her consciousness was quite beclouded by time and, when I passed by, her rheumy eyes settled upon me always with the same, vague, disinterested wonder, like that of an Eskimo watching a train. When she whispered, *Irrasyaimase*, the shop-keeper's word of welcome, in the ghostliest of whispers, like the rustle of a paper bag, I saw her teeth were rimmed with gold.

The children lit sparklers under a mouse-coloured sky and, due to the pollution in the atmosphere, the moon was mauve. The cicadas throbbed and shrieked in the backyards. When I think of this city, I shall always remember the cicadas who whirr relentlessly all through the summer nights, rising to a piercing crescendo in the subfusc dawn. I have heard cicadas even in the busiest streets, though they thrive best in the back alleys, where they ceaselessly emit that scarcely tolerable susurration which is like a shrill intensification of extreme heat.

A year before, on such a throbbing, voluptuous, platitudinous, subtropical night, we had been walking down one of these shady streets together, in and out of the shadows of the willow trees, looking for somewhere to make love. Morning glories climbed the lattices which screened the low, wooden houses, but the darkness hid the tender colours of these flowers, which the Japanese prize because they fade so quickly. He soon found a hotel, for the city is hospitable to lovers. We were shown into a room like a paper box. It contained nothing but a mattress spread on the floor. We lay down immediately and began to kiss one another. Then a maid soundlessly opened the sliding door and, stepping out of her slippers, crept in on stockinged feet, breathing apologies. She carried a tray which contained two cups of tea and a plate of candies. She put the tray down on the matted floor beside us and backed, bowing and apologising, from the room whilst our uninterrupted kiss continued. He started to unfasten my shirt and then she came back again. This time, she carried an armful of towels. I was stripped stark naked when she returned for a third time to bring the receipt for his money. She was clearly a most respectable woman and, if she was embarrassed, she did not show it by a single word or gesture.

I learned his name was Taro. In a toy store, I saw one of those books for children with pictures which are cunningly made of paper cut-outs so that, when you turn the page, the picture springs up in the three stylised dimensions of a back-drop in Kabuki. It was the story of Momotaro, who was born from a peach. Before my eyes, the paper peach split open and there was the baby, where the stone should have been. He, too, had the inhuman sweetness of a child born from something other than a mother, a passive, cruel sweetness I did not immediately understand, for it was that of the repressed masochism which, in my country, is usually confined to women.

Sometimes he seemed to possess a curiously unearthly quality when he perched upon the mattress with his knees drawn up beneath his chin in the attitude of a pixy on a door-knocker. At these times, his face seemed somehow both too flat and too large for his elegant body which had such curious, androgynous grace with its svelte, elongated spine, wide shoulders and unusually well-developed pectorals, almost like the breasts of a girl approaching puberty. There was a subtle lack of alignment between face and body and he seemed almost goblin, as if he might have borrowed another person's head, as Japanese goblins do, in order to perform some devious trick. These impressions of a weird visitor were fleeting yet haunting. Sometimes, it was possible for me to believe he had practised an enchantment upon me, as foxes in this country may, for, here, a fox can masquerade as human and at the best of times the high cheekbones gave to his face the aspect of a mask.

His hair was so heavy his neck drooped under its weight and was of a black so deep it turned purple in sunlight. His mouth also was purplish and his blunt, bee-stung lips those of Gauguin's Tahitians. The touch of his skin was as smooth as water as it flows through the fingers. His eyelids were retractable, like those of a cat, and sometimes disappeared completely. I should have liked to have had him embalmed and been able to keep him beside me in a glass coffin, so that I could watch him all the time and he would not have been able to get away from me.

As they say, Japan is a man's country. When I first came to Tokyo, cloth carps fluttered from poles in the gardens of the families fortunate enough to have borne boy children, for it was the time of the annual festival, Boys' Day. At least they do not disguise the situation. At least one knows where one is. Our polarity was publicly acknowledged and socially sanctioned. As an example of the use of the word *dewa*, which occasionally means, as far as I can gather, 'in', I found in a textbook a sentence which, when translated, read: 'In a society where men dominate, they value women only as the object of men's passions.' If the only conjunction possible to us was that of the death-defying double-somersault of love, it is, perhaps, a better thing to be valued only as an object of passion than never to be valued at all. I had never been so absolutely the mysterious other. I had become a kind of phoenix, a fabulous beast; I was an outlandish jewel. He found me, I think, inexpressibly exotic. But I often felt like a female impersonator.

In the department store there was a rack of dresses labelled: 'For Young and Cute Girls Only'. When I looked at them, I felt as gross as Glumdalclitch. I wore men's sandals because they were the only kind that fitted me and, even so, I had to take the largest size. My pink cheeks, blue eyes and blatant yellow hair made of me, in the visual orchestration of this city in which all heads were dark, eyes brown and skin monotone, an instrument which played upon an alien scale. In a sober harmony of subtle plucked instruments and wistful flutes, I blared. I proclaimed myself like a perpetual fanfare. He was so delicately put together that I thought his skeleton must have the airy elegance of a bird's and I was sometimes afraid that I might smash him. He told me that when he was in bed with me, he felt like a small boat upon a wide, stormy sea.

We pitched our tent in the most unlikely surroundings. We were living in a room furnished only by passion amongst homes of the most astounding respectability. The sounds around us were the swish of brooms upon *tatami* matting and the clatter of demotic Japanese. On all the windowledges, prim flowers bloomed in pots. Every morning, the washing came out on the balconies at seven. Early one morning, I saw a man washing the leaves of his tree. Quilts and mattresses went out to air at eight. The sunlight lay thick enough on these unpaved alleys to lay the dust and somebody always seemed to be practising Chopin in one or another of the flimsy houses, so lightly glued together from plywood it seemed they were sustained only by willpower. Once I was at home, however, it was as if I occupied the inner room and he did not expect me to go out of it, although it was I who paid the rent.

Yet, when he was away from me, he spent much of the time savouring the most annihilating remorse. But this remorse or regret was the stuff of life to him and out he would go again the next night, or, if I had been particularly angry, he would wait until the night after that. And, even if he fully intended to come back early and had promised me he would do so, circumstances always somehow denied him and once more he would contrive to miss the last train. He and his friends spent their nights in a desultory progression from coffee shop to bar to *pachinko* parlour to coffee shop, again, with the radiant aimlessness of the pure existential hero. They were connoisseurs of boredom. They savoured the various bouquets of the subtly differentiated boredoms which rose from the long, wasted hours at the dead end of night. When it was time for the first train in the morning, he would go back to the mysteriously deserted, Piranesi perspectives of the station, discoloured by dawn, exquisitely tortured by the notion – which probably contained within it a damped-down spark of hope – that, this time, he might have done something irreparable.

I speak as if he had no secrets from me. Well, then, you must realise that I was suffering from love and I knew him as intimately as I knew my own image in a mirror. In other words, I knew him only in relation to myself. Yet, on those terms, I knew him perfectly. At times, I thought I was inventing him as I went along, however, so you will have to take my word for it that we existed. But I do not want to paint our circumstantial portraits so that we both emerge with enough well-rounded, spuriously detailed actuality that you are forced to believe in us. I do not want to practise such sleight of hand. You must be content only with glimpses of our outlines, as if you had caught sight of our reflections in the looking-glass of somebody else's house as you passed by the window. His name was not Taro. I only called him Taro so that I could use the conceit of the peach boy, because it seemed appropriate.

Speaking of mirrors, the Japanese have a great respect for them and, in old-fashioned inns, one often finds them hooded with fabric covers when not in use. He said: 'Mirrors make a room uncosy.' I am sure there is more to it than that although they love to be cosy. One must love cosiness if one is to live so close together. But, as if in celebration of the thing they feared, they seemed to have made the entire city into a cold hall of mirrors which continually proliferated whole galleries of constantly changing appearances, all marvellous but none tangible. If they did not lock up the real looking-glasses, it would be hard to tell what was real and what was not. Even buildings one had taken for substantial had a trick of disappearance overnight. One morning, we woke to find the house next door reduced to nothing but a heap of sticks and a pile of newspaper neatly tied with string, left out for the garbage collector.

I would not say that he seemed to me to possess the same kind of insubstantiality although his departure usually seemed imminent, until I realised he was as erratic but as inevitable as the weather. If you plan to come and live in Japan, you must be sure you are stoical enough to endure the weather. No, it was not insubstantiality; it was a rhetoric valid only on its own terms. When I listened to his protestations, I was prepared to believe he believed in them, although I knew perfectly well they meant nothing. And that isn't fair. When he made them, he believed in them implicitly. Then, he was utterly consumed by conviction. But his dedication was primarily to the idea of himself in love. This idea seemed to him magnificent, even sublime. He was prepared to die for it, as one of Baudelaire's dandies might have been prepared to kill himself in order to preserve himself in the condition of a work of art, for he wanted to make this experience a masterpiece of experience which absolutely transcended the everyday. And this would annihilate the effects of the cruel drug, boredom, to which he was addicted although, perhaps, the element of boredom which is implicit in an affair so isolated from the real world was its principal appeal for him. But I had no means of knowing how far his conviction would take him. And I used to turn over in my mind from time to time the question: how far does a pretence of feeling, maintained with absolute conviction, become authentic?

This country has elevated hypocrisy to the level of the highest style. To look at a samurai, you would not know him for a murderer, or a geisha for a whore. The magnificence of such objects hardly pertains to the human. They live only in a world of icons and there they participate in rituals which transmute life itself to a series of grand gestures, as moving as they are absurd. It was as if they all thought, if we believe in something hard enough, it will come true and, lo and behold! they had done and it did. Our street was in essence a slum but, in appearance, it was a little enclave of harmonious quiet and, *mirabile dictu*, it was the appearance which was the reality, because they all behaved so well, kept everything so clean and lived with such rigorous civility. What terrible discipline it takes to live harmoniously. They had crushed all their vigour in order to live harmoniously and now they had the wistful beauty of flowers pressed dry in an enormous book.

But repression does not necessarily give birth only to severe beauties. In its programmed interstices, monstrous passions bloom. They torture trees to make them look more like the formal notion of a tree. They paint amazing pictures on their skins with awl and gouge, sponging away the blood as they go; a tatooed man is a walking masterpiece of remembered pain. They boast the most passionate puppets in the world who mimic love suicides in a stylised fashion, for here there is no such comfortable formula as 'happy ever after'. And, when I remembered the finale of the puppet tragedies, how the wooden lovers cut their throats together, I felt the beginnings of unease, as if the hieratic imagery of the country might overwhelm me, for his boredom had reached such a degree that he was insulated against everything except the irritation of anguish. If he valued me as an object of passion, he had reduced the word to its roots, which derives from the Latin, *patior*, I suffer. He valued me as an instrument which would cause him pain.

So we lived under a disorientated moon which was as angry a purple as if the sky had bruised its eye, and, if we made certain genuine intersections, these only took place in darkness. His contagious conviction that our love was unique and desperate infected me with an anxious sickness; soon we would learn to treat one another with the circumspect tenderness of comrades who are amputees, for we were surrounded by the most moving images of evanescence, fireworks, morning glories, the old, children. But the most moving of these images were the intangible reflections of ourselves we saw in one another's eyes, reflections of nothing but appearances, in a city dedicated to seeming, and, try as we might to possess the essence of each other's otherness, we would inevitably fail.

The Executioner's
Beautiful Daughter

Here, we are high in the uplands.

A baleful almost-music, that of the tuneless cadences of an untutored orchestra repercussing in an ecstatic agony of echoes against the sounding boards of the mountains, lured us into the village square where we discover them twanging, plucking and abusing with horsehair bows a wide variety of crude stringed instruments. Our feet crunch upon dryly whispering shifting sawdust freshly scattered over impacted surfaces of years of sawdust clotted, here and there, with blood shed so long ago it has, with age, acquired the colour and texture of rust . . . sad, ominous stains, a threat, a menace, memorials of pain.

There is no brightness in the air. Today the sun will not irradiate the heroes of the dark spectacle to which accident and disharmony combined to invite us. Here, where the air is choked all day with diffuse moisture tremulously, endlessly the point of becoming rain, light falls as if filtered through muslin so at all hours a crepuscular gloaming prevails; the sky looks as though it is about to weep and so, gloomily illuminated through unshed tears, the *tableau vivant* before us is suffused with the sepia tints of an old photograph and nothing within it moves. The intent immobility of the spectators, wholly absorbed as they are in the performance of their hieratic ritual, is scarcely that of living things and this *tableau vivant* might be better termed a *nature morte* for the mirthless carnival is a celebration of a death. Their eyes, the whites of which are yellowish, are all fixed, as if attached by taut, invisible strings upon a wooden block lacquered black with the spilt dews of a millennia of victims.

And now the rustic bandsmen suspend their unmelodious music. This death must be concluded in the most dramatic silence. The wild mountain-dwellers are gathered together to watch a public execution; that is the only entertainment the country offers.

Time, suspended like the rain, begins again in silence, slowly.

A heavy stillness ordering all his movements, the executioner himself adopts beside the block an offensively heroic pose, as if to do the thing with dignity were the only motive of the doing. He brings one booted foot to rest on the grim and sacrificial altar which is, to him, the canvas on which he exercises his art and proudly in his hand he bears his instrument, his axe.

The executioner stands more than six and a half feet high and he is broad to suit; the warped stumps of villagers gaze up at him with awe and fear. He is dressed always in mourning and always wears a curious mask. This mask is made of supple, close-fitting leather dyed an absolute black and it conceals his hair and the upper part of his face entirely except for two narrow slits through which issue the twin regards of eyes as inexpressive as though they were part of the mask. This mask reveals only his blunt-lipped, dark-red mouth and the greyish flesh which surrounds it. Laid out in such an unnerving fashion, these portions of his meat in no way fulfil the expectations we derive from our common knowledge of faces. They have a quality of obscene rawness as if, in some fashion, the lower face had been flayed. He, the butcher, might be displaying himself, as if he were his own meat.

Through the years, the close-fitting substance of the mask has become so entirely assimilated to the actual structure of his face that the face itself now seems to possess a parti-coloured appearance, as if by nature dual; and this face no longer pertains to that which is human as if, when he first put on the mask, he blotted out his own, original face and so defaced himself for ever. Because the hood of office renders the executioner an object. He has become an object who punishes. He is an object of fear. He is the image of retribution.

Nobody remembers why the mask was first devised nor who devised it. Perhaps some tender-heart of antiquity adopted the concealing headgear in order to spare the one upon the block the sight of too human a face in the last moments of his agony; or else the origins of the article lie in a magical relation with the blackness of negation – if, that is, negation is black in colour. Yet the executioner dare not take off the mask in case, in a random looking-glass or, accidentally mirrored in a pool of standing water, he surprised his own authentic face. For then he would die of fright.

The victim kneels. He is thin, pale and graceful. He is twenty years old. The silent throng in the courtyard shudders in common anticipation; all their gnarled features twist in the same grin. No sound, almost no sound disturbs the moist air, only the ghost of a sound, a distant sobbing that might be the ululation of the wind amongst the scrubby pines. The victim kneels and lays his neck upon the block. Ponderously the executioner lifts his gleaming steel.

The axe falls. The flesh severs. The head rolls.

The cleft flesh spouts its fountains. The spectators shudder, groan and gasp. And now the string band starts to bow and saw again whilst a choir of stunted virgins, in the screeching wail that passes for singing in these regions, intones a barbaric requiem entitled: AWFUL WARNING OF THE SPECTACLE OF A DECAPITATION.

The executioner has beheaded his own son for committing the crime of incest upon the body of his sister, the executioner's beautiful daughter, on whose cheeks the only roses in these highlands grow.

Gretchen no longer sleeps soundly. After the day his decapitated head rolled in the bloody sawdust, her brother rode a bicycle interminably through her dreams even though the poor child crept out secretly, alone, to gather up the poignant, moist, bearded strawberry, his surviving relic, and take it home to bury beside her hen-coop before the dogs ate it. But no matter how hard she scrubbed her little white apron against the scouring stones in the river, she could not wash away the stains that haunted the weft and warp of the fabric like pinkish phantoms of very precious fruit. Every morning, when she goes out to collect ripe eggs for her father's breakfast, she waters with felt but ineffectual tears the disturbed earth where her brother's brains lie rotting, while the indifferent hens peck and cluck about her feet.

This country is situated at such a high altitude water never boils, no matter how deceptively it foams within the pan, so their boiled eggs are always raw. The executioner insists his breakfast omelette be prepared only from those eggs precisely on the point of blossoming into chicks and, prompt at eight, consumes with relish a yellow, feathered omelette subtly spiked with claw. Gretchen, his tender-hearted daughter, often jumps and starts to hear the thwarted cluck from a still gelid, scarcely calcified beak about to be choked with sizzling butter, but her father, whose word is law because he never doffs his leather mask, will eat no egg that does not contain within it a nascent bird. That is his taste. In this country, only the executioner may indulge his perversities.

High among the mountains, how wet and cold it is! Chill winds blow soft drifts of rain across these almost perpendicular peaks; the wolf-haunted forest of fir and pine that cloak the lower slopes are groves fit only for the satanic cavortings of a universal Sabbath and a haunting mist pervades the bleak, meagre village rooted so far above quotidian skies a newcomer might not, at first, be able to breathe but only wheeze and choke in this thinnest of air. Newcomers, however, are less frequent apparitions than meteorites and thunderbolts; the villages breathe no welcome.

Even the walls of the rudely constructed houses exude suspicion. They are made from slabs of stone and do not have any windows to see out with. An inadequate orifice in the flat roof puffs out a few scant breaths of domestic smoke and penetration inside is effected only with the utmost difficulty through low, narrow doors, crevices in the granite, so each house presents to the eye as featureless a face as those of the Oriental demons whose anonymity was marred by no such commonplace a blemish as an eye, a nose or a mouth. Inside these ugly, unaccommodating hutches, man and domestic beast – goat, ox, pig, dog – stake equal squatting rights to the smoky and disordered hearths, although the dogs often grow rabid and rush frothing through the rutted streets like streams in spate.

The inhabitants are a thick-set, sullen brood whose chronic malevolence stems from a variety of both environmental and constitutional causes. All share a general and unprepossessing cast of countenance. Their faces have the limp, flat, boneless aspect of the Eskimo and their eyes are opaque fissures since no eyelid hoods them, only the slack skin of the Mongolian fold. Their reptilian regards possess an intensity which is in no way intimate and their smiles are so peculiarly vicious it is all for the best they smile rarely. Their teeth rot young.

The men in particular are monstrously hirsute about both head and body. Their hair, a monotonous and uniform purplish black, grizzles, in age, to the tint of defunct ashes. The womenfolk are built for durability rather than delight. Since all go always barefoot, the soles of their feet develop an intensifying consistency of horn from earliest childhood and the women, who perform all the tasks demanded by their primitive agriculture, sprout forearms the size and contour of vegetable marrows while their hands become pronouncedly scoop-shaped, until they resemble, in maturity, fat five-pronged forks.

All, without exception, are filthy and verminous. His shaggy head and rough garments are clogged with lice and quiver with fleas while his pubic areas throb and pulse with the blind convulsions of the crab. Impetigo, scabies and the itch are too prevalent among them to be remarked upon and their feet start early to decompose between the toes. They suffer from chronic afflictions of the anus due to their barbarous diet – thin porridge; sour beer; meat scarcely seared by the cool fires of the highlands; acidulated cheese of goat swallowed to the flatulent accompaniment of barley bread. Such comestibles cannot but contribute effectively to those disorders that have established the general air of malign unease which is their most immediately distinctive characteristic.

In this museum of diseases, the pastel beauty of Gretchen, the executioner's daughter, is all the more remarkable. Her flaxen plaits bob above her breasts as she goes to pluck, from their nests, the budding eggs.

Their days are shrouded troughs of glum manual toil and their nights wet, freezing, black, palpitating clefts gravid with the grossest cravings, nights dedicated solely to the imaginings of unspeakable desires tortuously conceived in mortified sensibilities habitually gnawed to suppuration by the black rats of superstition whilst the needle teeth of frost corrode their bodies.

They would, if they could, act out entire Wagnerian cycles of operatic evil and gleefully transform villages into stages upon which the authentic monstrosities of Grand Guignol might be acted out in every unspeakable detail. No hideous parody of the delights of the flesh would be alien to them . . . *did they but know how such things were, in fact, performed.*

They have an inexhaustible capacity for sin but are inexorably baulked by ignorance. They do not know what they desire. So their lusts exist in an undefined limbo, for ever *in potentia.*

They yearn passionately after the most deplorable depravity but possess not the concrete notion of so much as a simple fetish, their tormented flesh betrayed eternally by the poverty of their imaginations and the limitations of their vocabulary, for how may one transmit such things in a language composed only of brute grunts and squawks representing, for example, the state of the family pig in labour? And, since their vices are, in the literal sense of the word, unspeakable, their secret, furious desires remain ultimately mysterious even to themselves and are contained only in the realm of pure sensation, or feeling undefined as thought or action and hence unrestrained by definition. So their desires are infinite, although, in real terms, except in the form of a prickle of perturbation, these desires could hardly be said to exist.

Their lives are dominated by a folklore as picturesque as it is murderous. Rigid, hereditary castes of wizards, warlocks, shamans and practitioners of the occult proliferate amongst these benighted mountain-dwellers and the apex of esoteric power lies, it would seem, in the person of the king himself. But this appearance is deceptive. This nominal ruler is in reality the poorest beggar in all his ragged kingdom. Heir of the barbarous, he is stripped of everything but the idea of an omnipotence which is sufficiently expressed by immobility.

All day long, ever since his accession, he hangs by the right ankle from an iron ring set in the roof of a stone hut. A stout ribbon binds him to the ceiling and he is inadequately supported in a precarious but absolute position sanctioned by ritual and memory upon his left wrist, which is strapped in a similar fashion with ribbon to an iron ring cemented into the floor. He stays as still as if he had been dipped in a petrifying well and never speaks one single word because he has forgotten how.

They all believe implicitly they are damned. A folk-tale circulates among them, as follows: that the tribe was originally banished from a happier and more prosperous region to their present dreary habitation, a place fit only for continuous self-mortification, after they rendered themselves abhorrent to their former neighbours by the wholesale and enthusiastic practice of incest, son with father, father with daughter, etc. – every baroque variation possible upon the determinate quadrille of the nuclear family. In this country, incest is a capital crime; the punishment for incest is decapitation.

Daily their minds are terrified and enlightened by the continuous performances of apocalyptic dirges for fornicating siblings and only the executioner himself, because there is nobody to cut off his head, dare, in the immutable privacy of his leathern hood, upon his blood-bespattered block make love to his beautiful daughter.

Gretchen, the only flower of the mountains, tucks up her white apron and waltzing gingham skirts so they will not crease or soil but, even in the last extremity of the act, her father does not remove his mask for who would recognise him without it? The price he pays for his position is always to be locked in the solitary confinement of his power.

He perpetrates his inalienable right in the reeking courtyard upon the block where he struck off the head of his only son. That night, Gretchen discovered a snake in her sewing machine and, though she did not know what a bicycle was, upon a bicycle her brother wheeled and circled through her troubled dreams until the cock crowed and out she went for eggs.

The Loves of Lady Purple

Inside the pink-striped booth of the Asiatic Professor only the marvellous existed and there was no such thing as daylight.

The puppet master is always dusted with a little darkness. In direct relation to his skill he propagates the most bewildering enigmas for, the more lifelike his marionettes, the more godlike his manipulations and the more radical the symbiosis between inarticulate doll and articulating fingers. The puppeteer speculates in a no-man's-limbo between the real and that which, although we know very well it is not, nevertheless seems to be real. He is the intermediary between us, his audience, the living, and they, the dolls, the undead, who cannot live at all and yet who mimic the living in every detail since, though they cannot speak or weep, still they project those signals of signification we instantly recognise as language.

The master of marionettes vitalises inert stuff with the dynamics of his self. The sticks dance, make love, pretend to speak and, finally, personate death; yet, so many Lazaruses out of their graves they spring again in time for the next performance and no worms drip from their noses nor dust clogs their eyes. All complete, they once again offer their brief imitations of men and women with an exquisite precision which is all the more disturbing because we know it to be false; and so this art, if viewed theologically, may, perhaps, be blasphemous.

Although he was only a poor travelling showman, the Asiatic Professor had become a consummate virtuoso of puppetry. He transported his collapsible theatre, the cast of his single drama and a variety of properties in a horse-drawn cart and, after he played his play in many beautiful cities which no longer exist, such as Shanghai, Constantinople and St Petersburg, he and his small entourage arrived at last in a country in Middle Europe where the mountains sprout jags as sharp and unnatural as those a child outlines with his crayon, a dark, superstitious Transylvania where they wreathed suicides with garlic, pierced them through the heart with stakes and buried them at crossroads while warlocks continually practised rites of immemorial beastliness in the forests.

He had only the two assistants, a deaf boy in his teens, his nephew, to whom he taught his craft, and a foundling dumb girl no more than seven or eight they had picked up on their travels. When the Professor spoke, nobody could understand him for he knew only his native tongue, which was an incomprehensible rattle of staccato ks and ts, so he did not speak at all in the ordinary course of things and, if they had taken separate paths to silence, all, in the end, signed a perfect pact with it. But, when the Professor and his nephew sat in the sun outside their booth in the mornings before performances, they held interminable dialogues in sign language punctuated by soft, wordless grunts and whistles so that the choreographed quiet of their discourse was like the mating dance of tropic birds. And this means of communication, so delicately distanced from humanity, was peculiarly apt for the Professor, who had rather the air of a visitant from another world where the mode of being was conducted in nuances rather than affirmatives. This was due partly to his extreme age, for he was very old although he carried his years lightly even if, these days, in this climate, he always felt a little chilly and so wrapped himself always in a moulting, woollen shawl; yet, more so, it was caused by his benign indifference to everything except the simulacra of the living he himself created.

Besides, however far the entourage travelled, not one of its members had ever comprehended to any degree the foreign. They were all natives of the fairground and, after all, all fairs are the same. Perhaps every single fair is no more than a dissociated fragment of one single, great, original fair which was inexplicably scattered long ago in a diaspora of the amazing. Whatever its location, a fair maintains its invariable, self-consistent atmosphere. Hieratic as knights in chess, the painted horses on the roundabouts describe perpetual circles as immutable as those of the planets and as immune to the drab world of here and now whose inmates come to gape at such extraordinariness, such freedom from actuality. The huckster's raucous invitations are made in a language beyond language, or, perhaps, in that ur-language of grunt and bark which lies behind all language. Everywhere, the same old women hawk glutinous candies which seem devised only to make flies drunk on sugar and, though the outward form of such excessive sweets may vary from place to place, their nature, never. A universal cast of two-headed dogs, dwarfs, alligator men, bearded ladies and giants in leopard-skin loin cloths reveal their singularities in the sideshows and, wherever they come from, they share the sullen glamour of deformity, an internationality which acknowledges no geographic boundaries. Here, the grotesque is the order of the day.

The Asiatic Professor picked up the crumbs that fell from this heaping table yet never seemed in the least at home there for his affinities did not lie with its harsh sounds and primary colouring although it was the only home he knew. He had the wistful charm of a Japanese flower which only blossoms when dropped in water for he, too, revealed his passions through a medium other than himself and this was his heroine, the puppet, Lady Purple.

She was the Queen of Night. There were glass rubies in her head for eyes and her ferocious teeth, carved out of mother o' pearl, were always on show for she had a permanent smile. Her face was as white as chalk because it was covered with the skin of supplest white leather which also clothed her torso, jointed limbs and complication of extremities. Her beautiful hands seemed more like weapons because her nails were so long, five inches of pointed tin enamelled scarlet, and she wore a wig of black hair arranged in a chignon more heavily elaborate than any human neck could have endured. This monumental *chevelure* was stuck through with many brilliant pins tipped with pieces of broken mirror so that, every time she moved, she cast a multitude of scintillating reflections which danced about the theatre like mice of light. Her clothes were all of deep, dark, slumbrous colours – profound pinks, crimson and the vibrating purple with which she was synonymous, a purple the colour of blood in a love suicide.

She must have been the masterpiece of a long-dead, anonymous artisan and yet she was nothing but a curious structure until the Professor touched her strings, for it was he who filled her with necromantic vigour. He transmitted to her an abundance of the life he himself seemed to possess so tenuously and, when she moved, she did not seem so much a cunningly simulated woman as a monstrous goddess, at once preposterous and magnificent, who transcended the notion she was dependent on his hands and appeared wholly real and yet entirely other. Her actions were not so much an imitation as a distillation and intensification of those of a born woman and so she could become the quintessence of eroticism, for no woman born would have dared to be so blatantly seductive.

The Professor allowed no one else to touch her. He himself looked after her costumes and jewellery. When the show was over, he placed his marionette in a specially constructed box and carried her back to the lodging house where he and his children shared a room, for she was too precious to be left in the flimsy theatre, and, besides, he could not sleep unless she lay beside him.

The catchpenny title of the vehicle for this remarkable actress was: *The Notorious Amours of Lady Purple, the Shameless Oriental Venus.* Everything in the play was entirely exotic. The incantatory ritual of the drama instantly annihilated the rational and imposed upon the audience a magic alternative in which nothing was in the least familiar. The series of tableaux which illustrated her story were in themselves so filled with meaning that when the Professor chanted her narrative in his impenetrable native tongue, the compulsive strangeness of the spectacle was enhanced rather than diminished. As he crouched above the stage directing his heroine's movements, he recited a verbal recitative in a voice which clanged, rasped and swooped up and down in a weird duet with the stringed instrument from which the dumb girl struck peculiar intervals. But it was impossible to mistake him when the Professor spoke in the character of Lady Purple herself for then his voice modulated to a thick, lascivious murmur like fur soaked in honey which sent unwilling shudders of pleasure down the spines of the watchers. In the iconography of the melodrama, Lady Purple stood for passion, and all her movements were calculations in an angular geometry of sexuality.

The Professor somehow always contrived to have a few handbills printed off in the language of the country where they played. These always gave the title of his play and then they used to read as follows:

> Come and see all that remains of Lady Purple, the famous prostitute and wonder of the East!

A unique sensation. See how the unappeasable appetites of Lady Purple turned her at last into the very puppet you see before you, pulled only by the strings of *lust*. Come and see the very doll, the only surviving relic of the shameless Oriental Venus herself.

The bewildering entertainment possessed almost a religious intensity for, since there can be no spontaneity in a puppet drama, it always tends towards the rapt intensity of ritual, and, at its conclusion, as the audience stumbled from the darkened booth, it had almost suspended disbelief and was more than half convinced, as the Professor assured them so eloquently, that the bizarre figure who had dominated the stage was indeed the petrification of a universal whore and had once been a woman in whom too much life had negated life itself, whose kisses had withered like acids and whose embrace blasted like lightning. But the Professor and his assistants immediately dismantled the scenery and put away the dolls who were, after all, only mundane wood and, next day, the play was played again.

This is the story of Lady Purple as performed by the Professor's puppets to the delirious *obbligato* of the dumb girl's samisen and the audible click of the limbs of the actors.

The Notorious Amours of Lady Purple

the Shameless Oriental Venus

When she was only a few days old, her mother wrapped her in a tattered blanket and abandoned her on the door-step of a prosperous merchant and his barren wife. These respectable bourgeois were to become the siren's first dupes. They lavished upon her all the attentions which love and money could devise and yet they reared a flower which, although perfumed, was carnivorous. At the age of twelve, she seduced her foster father. Utterly besotted with her, he trusted to her the key of the safe where he kept all his money and she immediately robbed it of every farthing.

Packing his treasure in a laundry basket together with the clothes and jewellery he had already given her, she then stabbed her first lover and his wife, her foster mother, in their bellies with a knife used in the kitchen to slice fish. Then she set fire to their house to cover the traces of her guilt. She annihilated her own childhood in the blaze that destroyed her first home and, springing like a corrupt phoenix from the pyre of her crime, she rose again in the pleasure quarters, where she at once hired herself out to the madame of the most imposing brothel.

In the pleasure quarters, life passed entirely in artificial day for the bustling noon of those crowded alleys came at the time of drowsing midnight for those who lived outside that inverted, sinister, abominable world which functioned only to gratify the whims of the senses. Every rococo desire the mind of man might, in its perverse ingenuity, devise found ample gratification here, amongst the halls of mirrors, the flagellation parlours, the cabarets of nature-defying copulations and the ambiguous soirées held by men-women and female men. Flesh was the speciality of every house and it came piping hot, served up with all the garnishes imaginable. The Professor's puppets dryly and perfunctorily performed these tactical manoeuvres like toy soldiers in a mock battle of carnality.

Along the streets, the women for sale, the mannequins of desire, were displayed in wicker cages so that potential customers could saunter past inspecting them at leisure. These exalted prostitutes sat motionless as idols. Upon their real features had been painted symbolic abstractions of the various aspects of allure and the fantastic elaboration of their dress hinted it covered a different kind of skin. The cork heels of their shoes were so high they could not walk but only totter and the sashes round their waists were of brocade so stiff the movements of the arms were cramped and scant so they presented attitudes of physical unease which, though powerfully moving, derived partly, at least, from the deaf assistant's lack of manual dexterity, for his apprenticeship had not as yet reached even the journeyman stage. Therefore the gestures of these *hetaerae* were as stylised as if they had been clockwork. Yet, however fortuitously, all worked out so well it seemed each one was as absolutely circumscribed as a figure in rhetoric, reduced by the rigorous discipline of her vocation to the nameless essence of the idea of woman, a metaphysical abstraction of the female which could, on payment of a specific fee, be instantly translated into an oblivion either sweet or terrible, depending on the nature of her talents.

Lady Purple's talents verged on the unspeakable. Booted, in leather, she became a mistress of the whip before her fifteenth birthday. Subsequently, she graduated in the mysteries of the torture chamber, where she thoroughly researched all manner of ingenious mechanical devices. She utilised a baroque apparatus of funnel, humiliation, syringe, thumbscrew, contempt and spiritual anguish; to her lovers, such severe usage was both bread and wine and a kiss from her cruel mouth was the sacrament of suffering.

Soon she became successful enough to be able to maintain her own establishment. When she was at the height of her fame, her slightest fancy might cost a young man his patrimony and, as soon as she squeezed him dry of fortune, hope and dreams, for she was quite remorseless, she abandoned him; or else she might, perhaps, lock him up in her closet and force him to watch her while she took for nothing to her usually incredibly expensive bed a beggar encountered by chance on the street. She was no malleable, since frigid, substance upon which desires might be executed; she was not a true prostitute for she was the object on which men prostituted themselves. She, the sole perpetrator of desire, proliferated malign fantasies all around her and used her lovers as the canvas on which she executed boudoir masterpieces of destruction. Skins melted in the electricity she generated.

Soon, either to be rid of them or, simply, for pleasure, she took to murdering her lovers. From the leg of a politician she poisoned she cut out the thighbone and took it to a craftsman who made it into a flute for her. She persuaded succeeding lovers to play tunes for her on this instrument and, with the supplest and most serpentine grace, she danced for them to its unearthly music. At this point, the dumb girl put down her samisen and took up a bamboo pipe from which issued weird cadences and, though it was by no means the climax of the play, this dance was the apex of the Professor's performance for, as she stamped, wheeled and turned to the sound of her malign chamber music, Lady Purple became entirely the image of irresistible evil.

She visited men like a plague, both bane and terrible enlightenment, and she was as contagious as the plague. The final condition of all her lovers was this: they went clothed in rags held together with the discharge of their sores, and their eyes held an awful vacancy, as if their minds had been blown out like candles. A parade of ghastly spectres, they trundled across the stage, their passage implemented by medieval horrors for, here, an arm left its socket and whisked up out of sight into the flies and, there, a nose hung in the air after a gaunt shape that went tottering noseless forward.

So foreclosed Lady Purple's pyrotechnical career, which ended as if it had been indeed a firework display, in ashes, desolation and silence. She became more ghastly than those she had infected. Circe at last became a swine herself and, seared to the bone by her own flame, walked the pavements like a desiccated shadow. Disaster obliterated her. Cast out with stones and oaths by those who had once adulated her, she was reduced to scavenging on the seashore, where she plucked hair from the heads of the drowned to sell to wigmakers who catered to the needs of more fortunate since less diabolic courtesans.

Now her finery, her paste jewels and her enormous superimposition of black hair hung up in the green room and she wore a drab rag of coarse hemp for the final scene of her desperate decline, when, outrageous nymphomaniac, she practised extraordinary necrophilies on the bloated corpses the sea tossed contemptuously at her feet for her dry rapacity had become entirely mechanical and still she repeated her former actions though she herself was utterly other. She abrogated her humanity. She became nothing but wood and hair. She became a marionette herself, herself her own replica, the dead yet moving image of the shameless Oriental Venus.

The Professor was at last beginning to feel the effects of age and travel. Sometimes he complained in noisy silence to his nephew of pains, aches, stiffening muscles, tautening sinews, and shortness of breath. He began to limp a little and left to the boy all the rough work of mantling and dismantling. Yet the balletic mime of Lady Purple grew all the more remarkable with the passage of the years, as though his energy, channelled for so long into a single purpose, refined itself more and more in time and was finally reduced to a single, purified, concentrated essence which was transmitted entirely to the doll; and the Professor's mind attained a condition not unlike that of the swordsman trained in Zen, whose sword is his soul, so that neither sword nor swordsman has meaning without the presence of the other. Such swordsmen, armed, move towards their victims like automata, in a state of perfect emptiness, no longer aware of any distinction between self or weapon. Master and marionette had arrived at this condition.

Age could not touch Lady Purple for, since she had never aspired to mortality, she effortlessly transcended it and, though a man who was less aware of the expertise it needed to make her so much as raise her left hand might, now and then, have grieved to see how she defied ageing, the Professor had no fancies of that kind. Her miraculous inhumanity rendered their friendship entirely free from the anthropomorphic, even on the night of the Feast of All Hallows when, the mountain-dwellers murmured, the dead held masked balls in the graveyards while the devil played the fiddle for them.

The rough audience received their copeck's worth of sensation and filed out into a fairground which still roared like a playful tiger with life. The foundling girl put away her samisen and swept out the booth while the nephew set the stage afresh for the next day's matinée. Then the Professor noticed Lady Purple had ripped a seam in the drab shroud she wore in the final act. Chattering to himself with displeasure, he undressed her as she swung idly, this way and that way, from her anchored strings and then he sat down on a wooden property stool on the stage and plied his needle like a good housewife. The task was more difficult than it seemed at first for the fabric was also torn and required an embroidery of darning so he told his assistants to go home together to the lodging house and let him finish his task alone.

A small oil-lamp hanging from a nail at the side of the stage cast an insufficient but tranquil light. The white puppet glimmered fitfully through the mists which crept into the theatre from the night outside through all the chinks and gaps in the tarpaulin and now began to fold their chiffon drapes around her as if to decorously conceal her or else to render her more translucently enticing. The mist softened her painted smile a little and her head dangled on one side. In the last act, she wore a loose, black wig, the locks of which hung down as far as her softly upholstered flanks, and the ends of her hair flickered with her random movements, creating upon the white blackboard of her back one of those fluctuating optical effects which make us question the veracity of our vision. As he often did when he was alone with her, the Professor chatted to her in his native language, rattling away an intimacy of nothings, of the weather, of his rheumatism, of the unpalatability and expense of the region's coarse, black bread, while the small winds took her as their partner in a scarcely perceptible *valse triste* and the mist grew minute by minute thicker, more pallid and more viscous.

The old man finished his mending. He rose and, with a click or two of his old bones, he went to put the forlorn garment neatly on its green-room hanger beside the glowing, winy purple gown splashed with rosy peonies, sashed with carmine, that she wore for her appalling dance. He was about to lay her, naked, in her coffin-shaped case and carry her back to their chilly bedroom when he paused. He was seized with the childish desire to see her again in all her finery once more that night. He took her dress off its hanger and carried it to where she drifted, at nobody's volition but that of the wind. As he put her clothes on her, he murmured to her as if she were a little girl for the vulnerable flaccidity of her arms and legs made a six-foot baby of her.

'There, there, my pretty; this arm here, that's right! Oops a daisy, easy does it . . .'

Then he tenderly took off her penitential wig and clucked his tongue to see how defencelessly bald she was beneath it. His arms cracked under the weight of her immense chignon and he had to stretch up on tiptoe to set it in place because, since she was as large as life, she was rather taller than he. But then the ritual of apparelling was over and she was complete again.

Now she was dressed and decorated, it seemed her dry wood had all at once put out an entire springtime of blossoms for the old man alone to enjoy. She could have acted as the model for the most beautiful of women, the image of that woman whom only a man's memory and imagination can devise, for the lamp light fell too mildly to sustain her air of arrogance and so gently it made her long nails look as harmless as ten fallen petals. The Professor had a curious habit; he always used to kiss his doll good night.

A child kisses its toy before she pretends it sleeps although, even though she is only a child, she knows its eyes are not constructed to close so it will always be a sleeping beauty no kiss will waken. One in the grip of savage loneliness might kiss the face he sees before him in the mirror for want of any other face to kiss. These are kisses of the same kind; they are the most poignant of caresses, for they are too humble and too despairing to wish or seek for any response.

Yet, in spite of the Professor's sad humility, his chapped and withered mouth opened on hot, wet, palpitating flesh.

The sleeping wood had wakened. Her pearl teeth crashed against his with the sound of cymbals and her warm, fragrant breath blew around him like an Italian gale. Across her suddenly moving face flashed a whole kaleidoscope of expression, as though she were running instantaneously through the entire repertory of human feeling, practising, in an endless moment of time, all the scales of emotion as if they were music. Crushing vines, her arms, curled about the Professor's delicate apparatus of bone and skin with the insistent pressure of an actuality by far more authentically living than that of his own, time-desiccated flesh. Her kiss emanated from the dark country where desire is objectified and lives. She gained entry into the world by a mysterious loophole in its metaphysics and, during her kiss, she sucked his breath from his lungs so that her own bosom heaved with it.

So, unaided, she began her next performance with an apparent improvisation which was, in reality, only a variation upon a theme. She sank her teeth into his throat and drained him. He did not have the time to make a sound. When he was empty, he slipped straight out of her embrace down to her feet with a dry rustle, as of a cast armful of dead leaves, and there he sprawled on the floorboards, as empty, useless and bereft of meaning as his own tumbled shawl.

She tugged impatiently at the strings which moored her and out they came in bunches from her head, her arms and her legs. She stripped them off her fingertips and stretched out her long, white hands, flexing and unflexing them again and again. For the first time for years, or, perhaps, for ever, she closed her blood-stained teeth thankfully, for her cheeks still ached from the smile her maker had carved into the stuff of her former face. She stamped her elegant feet to make the new blood flow more freely there.

Unfurling and unravelling itself, her hair leaped out of its confinements of combs, cords and lacquer to root itself back into her scalp like cut grass bounding out of the stack and back again into the ground. First, she shivered with pleasure to feel the cold, for she realised she was experiencing a physical sensation; then either she remembered or else she believed she remembered that the sensation of cold was not a pleasurable one so she knelt and, drawing off the old man's shawl, wrapped it carefully about herself. Her every motion was instinct with a wonderful, reptilian liquidity. The mist outside now seemed to rush like a tide into the booth and broke against her in white breakers so that she looked like a baroque figurehead, lone survivor of a shipwreck, thrown up on a shore by the tide.

But whether she was renewed or newly born, returning to life or becoming alive, awakening from a dream or coalescing into the form of fantasy generated in her wooden skull by the mere repetition so many times of the same invariable actions, the brain beneath the reviving hair contained only the scantiest notion of the possibilities now open to it. All that had seeped into the wood was the notion that she might perform the forms of life not so much by the skill of another as by her own desire that she did so, and she did not possess enough equipment to comprehend the complex circularity of the logic which inspired her for she had only been a marionette. But, even if she could not perceive it, she could not escape the tautological paradox in which she was trapped; had the marionette all the time parodied the living or was she, now living, to parody her own performance as a marionette? Although she was now manifestly a woman, young and beautiful, the leprous whiteness of her face gave her the appearance of a corpse animated solely by demonic will.

Deliberately, she knocked the lamp down from its hook on the wall. A puddle of oil spread at once on the boards of the stage. A little flame leaped across the fuel and immediately began to eat the curtains. She went down the aisle between the benches to the little ticket booth. Already, the stage was an inferno and the corpse of the Professor tossed this way and that on an uneasy bed of fire. But she did not look behind her after she slipped out into the fairground although soon the theatre was burning like a paper lantern ignited by its own candle.

Now it was so late that the sideshows, gingerbread stalls and liquor booths were locked and shuttered and only the moon, half obscured by drifting cloud, gave out a meagre, dirty light, which sullied and deformed the flimsy pasteboard façades, so the place, deserted, with curds of vomit, the refuse of revelry, underfoot, looked utterly desolate.

She walked rapidly past the silent roundabouts, accompanied only by the fluctuating mists, towards the town, making her way like a homing pigeon, out of logical necessity, to the single brothel it contained.

The Smile of Winter

Because there are no seagulls here, the only sound is the resonance of the sea. This coastal region is quite flat, so that an excess of sky bears down with an intolerable weight, pressing the essence out of everything beneath it for it imposes such a burden on us that we have all been forced inward on ourselves in an introspective sombreness intensified by the perpetual abrasive clamour of the sea. When the sun goes down, it is very cold and then I easily start crying because the winter moon pierces my heart. The winter moon is surrounded by an extraordinary darkness, the logical antithesis of the supernal clarity of the day; in this darkness, the dogs in every household howl together at the sight of a star, as if the stars were unnatural things. But, from morning until evening, a hallucinatory light floods the shore and a cool, glittering sun transfigures everything so brilliantly that the beach looks like a desert and the ocean like a mirage.

But the beach is never deserted. Far from it. At times, there is even a silent crowd of people – women who come in groups to turn the fish they have laid out to dry on bamboo racks; Sunday trippers; solitary anglers, even. Sometimes trucks drive up and down the beach to and fro from the next headland and after school is over children come to improvise games of baseball with sticks and a dead crab delivered to them by the tide. The children wear peaked, yellow caps; their heads are perfectly round. Their faces are perfectly bland, the colour as well as the shape of brown eggs. They giggle when they see me because I am white and pink while they themselves are such a serviceable, unanimous beige. Besides all these visitors, the motorcyclists who come at night have left deep grooves behind them in the sand as if to say: 'I have been here.'

When the shadows of the evening lie so thickly on the beach it looks as though nobody has dusted it for years, the motorcyclists come out. That is their favourite time. They have marked out a course among the dunes with red wooden pegs and ride round it at amazing speeds. They come when they please. Sometimes they come in the early morning but, most often, by owl-light. They announce their presence with a fanfare of opened throttles. They grow their hair long and it flies out behind them like black flags, motorcyclists as beautiful as the outriders of death in the film *Orphée*. I wish they were not so beautiful; if they were not so beautiful and so inaccessible to me, then I should feel less lonely, although, after all, I came here in order to be lonely.

The beach is full of the garbage of the ocean. The waves leave torn, translucent furls of polythene wrapping too tough for even this sea's iron stomach; chipped jugs that once held rice wine; single sea-boots freighted with sand; broken beer bottles and, once, a brown dog stiff and dead washed up as far as the pine trees which, subtly wrapped by the weather, squat on their hunkers at the end of my garden, where the dry soil transforms itself to sand.

Already the pines are budding this year's cones. Each blunt, shaggy bough is tipped with a small, lightly furred growth just like the prick of a little puppy while the dry, brown cones of last year still cling to the rough stems though now these are so insecure a touch will bring them bounding down. But, all in all, the pines have a certain intransigence. They dig their roots into dry soil full of seashells and strain backwards in the wind that blows directly from Alaska. They are absolutely exposed to the weather and yet as indifferent as the weather. The indifference of this Decembral littoral suits my forlorn mood for I am a sad woman by nature, no doubt about that; how unhappy I should be in a happy world! This country has the most rigorous romanticism in the world and they think a woman who lives by herself should accentuate her melancholy with surroundings of sentimental dilapidation. I have read about all the abandoned lovers in their old books eating their hearts out like Mariana in so many moated granges; their gardens are overgrown with goosegrass and mugwort, their mud walls are falling to pieces and their carp pools scaled over with water-lily pads. Everything combines with the forlorn mood of the châtelaine to procure a moving image of poignant desolation. In this country you do not need to think, but only to look, and soon you think you understand everything.

The old houses in the village are each one dedicated to seclusion and court an individual sequestered sadness behind the weather-stained, unpainted wooden shutters they usually keep closed. It is a gloomy, aridly aesthetic architecture based on the principle of perpetual regression. The houses are heavily shingled and the roofs are the shapes and colours of waves frozen on a grey day. In the mornings, they dismantle the outer screens to let fresh air blow through and, as you walk past, you can see that all the inner walls are also sliding screens, though this time of stiff paper, and you can glimpse endlessly receding perspectives of interiors in brownish tones, as if everything had been heavily varnished some time ago; and, though these perspectives can be altered at will, the fresh rooms they make when they shift the screens about always look exactly the same as the old rooms. And all the matted interiors are the same, anyway.

Through the gaping palings of certain fences, I sometimes see a garden so harmoniously in tune with the time of year it looks forsaken. But sometimes all these fragile habitations of unpainted wood; and the still lives; or *natures mortes*, of rusting water pumps and withered chrysanthemums in backyards; and the discarded fishing boats pulled up on the sand and left to rot away – sometimes the whole village looks forsaken. This is, after all, the season of abandonment, of the suspension of vitality, a long cessation of vigour in which we must cultivate our stoicism. Everything has put on the desolate smile of winter. Outside my shabby front door, I have a canal, like Mariana in a moated grange; beyond the skulking pines at the back, there is only the ocean. The winter moon pierces my heart. I weep.

But when I went out on the beach this morning with the skin on my face starched with dried tears so I could feel my cheeks crackle in the wind, I found the sea had washed me up a nice present – two pieces of driftwood. One was a forked chunk like a pair of wooden trousers and the other was a larger, greyish, frayed root the shape of the paw of a ragged lion. I collect driftwood and set it up among the pine trees in picturesque attitudes on the edge of the beach and then I strike a picturesque attitude myself beside them as I watch the constantly agitated waves, for here we all strike picturesque attitudes and that is why we are so beautiful. Sometimes I imagine that one night the riders will stop at the end of my garden and I will hear the heels of their boots crunch on the friable carpet of last year's shed cones and then there will be a hesitant rattle of knuckles on the seaward-facing door and they will wait in ceremonious silence until I come, for their bodies are only images.

My pockets always contain a rasping sediment of sand because I fill them with shells when I go on to the beach. The vast majority of these shells are round, sculptural forms the colour of a brown egg, with warm, creamy insides. They have a classical simplicity. The scarcely perceptible indentations of their surfaces flow together to produce a texture as subtly matt as that of a petal which is as satisfying to touch as Japanese skin. But there are also pure white shells heavily ridged on the outside but within of a marmoreal smoothness and these come in hinged pairs.

There is still a third kind of shell, though I find these less often. They are curlicued, shaped like turbans and dappled with pink, of a substance so thin the ocean easily grinds away the outer husk to lay bare their spiralline cores. They are often decorated with baroque, infinitesimal swags of calcified parasites. They are the smallest of all the shells but by far the most intricate. When I picked up one of those shells, I found it contained the bright pink, dried, detached limb of a tiny sea creature like a dehydrated memory. Sometimes a litter of dropped fish lies among the shells. Each fish reflects the sky with the absolute purity of a Taoist mirror.

The fish have fallen off the racks on which they have been put out to dry. These bamboo racks spread with fish stand on trestles all along the beach as if a feast was laid for the entire prefecture but nobody had come to eat it. Close to the village, there are whole paddocks filled with bamboo racks. In one of these paddocks, a tethered goat crops grass. The fish are as shiny as fish of tin and the size of my little finger. Once dried, they are packed in plastic bags and sold to flavour soup.

The women lay them out. They come every day to turn them and, when the fish are ready, they pile up the racks and carry them to the packing sheds. There are great numbers of these raucously silent, and well-muscled, intimidating women.

The cruel wind burns port-wine whorls on their dour, inexpressive faces. All wear dark or drab-coloured trousers pinched in at the ankle and either short rubber boots or split-toed socks on their feet. A layer of jacket sweaters and a loose, padded, cotton jacket gives them a squat, top-heavy look, as if they would not fall over, only rock malevolently to and fro if you pushed them. Over their jackets, they wear short, immaculate aprons trimmed with coarse lace and they tie white babushkas round their heads or sometimes wind a kind of wimple over the ears and round the throat. They are truculent and aggressive. They stare at me with open curiosity tinged with hostility. When they laugh, they display treasuries of gold teeth and their hands are as hard as those of eighteenth-century prize-fighters, who also used to pickle their fists in brine. They make me feel that either I or they are deficient in femininity and I suppose it must be I since most of them hump about an organic lump of baby on their backs, inside their coats. It seems that only women people the village because most of the men are out on the sea. Early in the morning, I go out to watch the winking and blinking of the fishing boats on the water, which, just before dawn, has turned a deep violet.

The moist and misty mornings after a storm obscure the horizon for then the ocean has turned into the sky and the wind and waves have realigned the contours of the dunes. The wet sand is as dark and more yieldingly solid than fudge and walking across a panful is a promenade in the Kingdom of Sweets. The waves leave behind them glinting striations of salt and forcibly mould the foreshore into the curvilinear abstractions of cliffs, bays, inlets, curvilinear tumuli like the sculpture of Arp. But the storms themselves are a raucous music and turn my house into an Aeolian xylophone. All night long, the wind bangs and rattles away at every wooden surface; the house is a sounding box and even on the quietest nights the paper windows let through the wind that rattles softly in the pines.

Sometimes the lights of the midnight riders scrawl brilliant hiero-glyphs across the panes, especially on moonless nights, when I am alone in a landscape of extraordinary darkness, and I am a little frightened when I see their headlamps and hear their rasping engines for then they seem the spawn of the negated light and to have driven straight out of the sea, which is just as mysterious as the night, even, and also its perfect image, for the sea is an inversion of the known and occupies half, or more, of the world, just as night does; whilst different peoples also live in the countries of the night.

They all wear leather jackets bristling with buckles, and high-heeled boots. They cannot buy such gaudy apparel in the village because the village shops only sell useful things such as paraffin, quilts and things to eat. And all the colours in the village are subfusc and equivocal, those of wood tinted bleakly by the weather and of lifeless wintry vegetation. When I sometimes see an orange tree hung with gold balls like a magic trick, it does nothing but stress by contrast the prevailing static sobriety of everything, which combines to smile in chorus the desolate smile of winter. On rainy nights when there is a winter moon bright enough to pierce the heart, I often wake to find my face still wet with tears so that I know I have been crying.

When the sun is low in the west, the beams become individually visible and fall with a peculiar, lateral intensity across the beach, flushing out long shadows from the grains of sand and these beams seem to penetrate to the very hearts of the incoming waves which look, then, as if they were lit from within. Before they topple forward, they bulge outward in the swollen shapes and artfully flawed incandescence of Art Nouveau glass, as if the translucent bodies of the images they contain within them were trying to erupt, for the bodies of the creatures of the sea are images, I am convinced of that. At this time of day, the sea turns amazing colours – the brilliant, chemical green of the sea in nineteenth-century tinted postcards; or a blue far too cerulean for early evening; or sometimes it shines with such metallic brilliance I can hardly bear to look at it. Smiling my habitual winter smile, I stand at the end of my garden attended by a pack of green bears while I watch the constantly agitated white lace cuffs on the colourful sleeves of the Pacific.

Different peoples inhabit the countries of the ocean and some of their emanations undulate past me when I walk along the beach to the village on one of those rare, bleak, sullen days, special wraiths of sand blowing to various inscrutable meeting places on blind currents of the Alaskan wind. They twine around my ankles in serpentine caresses and they have eyes of sand but some of the other creatures have eyes of solid water and when the women move among trays of fish I think they, too, are sea creatures, spiny, ocean-bottom-growing flora and if a tidal wave consumed the village – as it could do tomorrow, for there are no hills or sea walls to protect us – there, under the surface, life would go on just as before, the sea goat still nibbling, the shops still doing a roaring trade in octopus and pickled turnips' greens, the women going about their silent business because everything is as silent as if it were under the water, anyway, and the very air is as heavy as water and warps the light so that one sees as if one's eyes were made of water.

Do not think I do not realise what I am doing. I am making a composition using the following elements: the winter beach; the winter moon; the ocean; the women; the pine trees; the riders; the driftwood; the shells; the shapes of darkness and the shapes of water; and the refuse. These are all inimical to my loneliness because of their indifference to it. Out of these pieces of inimical indifference, I intend to represent the desolate smile of winter which, as you must have gathered, is the smile I wear.

Penetrating to the Heart
of the Forest

The whole region was like an abandoned flower bowl, filled to overflowing with green, living things; and, protected on all sides by the ferocious barricades of the mountains, those lovely reaches of forest lay so far inland the inhabitants believed the name, Ocean, that of a man in another country, and would have taken an oar, had they ever seen one, to be a winnowing fan. They built neither roads nor towns; in every respect like Candide, especially that of past ill-fortune, all they did now was to cultivate their gardens.

They were the descendants of slaves who, many years before, ran away from plantations in distant plains, in pain and hardship crossed the arid neck of the continent, and endured an infinity of desert and tundra, before they clambered the rugged foothills to scale at last the heights themselves and so arrive in a region that offered them in plentiful fulfilment all their dreams of a promised land. Now, the groves that skirted those forests of pine in the central valley formed for them all of the world they wished to know and nothing in their self-contained quietude concerned them but the satisfaction of simple pleasures. Not a single exploring spirit had ever been curious enough to search to its source the great river that watered their plots, or to penetrate to the heart of the forest itself. They had grown far too contented in their lost fastness to care for anything but the joys of idleness.

They had brought with them as a relic of their former life only the French their former owners had branded on their tongues, though certain residual, birdlike flutings of forgotten African dialects put unexpected cadences in their speech and, with the years, they had fashioned an arboreal argot of their own to which a French grammar would have proved a very fallible guide. And they had also packed up in their ragged bandanas a little, dark, voodoo folklore. But such bloodstained ghosts could not survive in sunshine and fresh air and emigrated from the village in a body, to live only the ambiguous life of horned rumours in the woods, becoming at last no more than shapes with indefinable outlines who lurked, perhaps, in the green deeps, until, at last, one of the shadows modulated imperceptibly into the actual shape of a tree.

Almost as if to justify to themselves their lack of a desire to explore, they finally seeded by word of mouth a mythic and malign tree within the forest, a tree the image of the Upas Tree of Java whose very shadow was murderous, a tree that exuded a virulent sweat of poison from its moist bark and whose fruits could have nourished with death an entire tribe. And the presence of this tree categorically forbade exploration – even though all knew, in their hearts, that such a tree did not exist. But, even so, they guessed it was safest to be a stay-at-home.

Since the woodlanders could not live without music, they made fiddles and guitars for themselves with great skill and ingenuity. They loved to eat well so they stirred themselves enough to plant vegetables, tend goats and chickens and blend these elements together in a rustic but voluptuous cookery. They dried, candied and preserved in honey some of the wonderful fruits they grew and exchanged this produce with the occasional traveller who came over the single, hazardous mountain pass, carrying bales of cotton fabrics and bundles of ribbons. With these, the women made long skirts and blouses for themselves and trousers for their menfolk, so all were dressed in red and yellow flowered cloth, purple and green checkered cloth, or cloth striped like a rainbow, and they plaited themselves hats from straw. They needed nothing more than a few flowers before they felt their graceful toilets were complete and a profusion of flowers grew all around them, so many flowers that the straw-thatched villages looked like inhabited gardens, for the soil was of amazing richness and the flora proliferated in such luxuriance that when Dubois, the botanist, came over the pass on his donkey, he looked down on that paradisial landscape and exclaimed: 'Dear God! It is as if Adam had opened Eden to the public!'

Dubois was seeking a destination whose whereabouts he did not know, though he was quite sure it existed. He had visited most of the out-of-the-way parts of the world to peer through the thick lenses of his round spectacles at every kind of plant. He gave his name to an orchid in Dahomey, to a lily in Indo-China and to a dark-eyed Portuguese girl in a Brazilian town of such awesome respectability that even its taxis wore antimacassars. But, because he loved the frail wife whose grave eyes already warned him she would live briefly, he rooted there, a plant himself in alien soil, and, out of gratitude, she gave him two children at one birth before she died.

He found his only consolation in a return to the flowering wilderness he had deserted for her sake. He was approaching middle age, a raw-boned, bespectacled man who habitually stooped out of a bashful awareness of his immense height, hirsute and gentle as a herbivorous lion. The vicissitudes of a life in which his reticence had cheated him of the fruits of his scholarship, together with the forlorn conclusion of his marriage, had left him with a yearning for solitude and a desire to rear his children in a place where ambition, self-seeking and guile were strangers, so that they would grow up with the strength and innocence of young trees.

But such a place was hard to find.

His wanderings took him to regions ever more remote from civilisation but he was never seized with a conviction of home-coming until that morning, as the sun irradiated the mists and his donkey picked its way down a rough path so overgrown with dew-drenched grass and mosses it had become no more than the subtlest intimation of a direction.

It took him circuitously down to a village sunk in a thicket of honeysuckle that filled with languorous sweetness the rarefied air of the uplands. On the dawning light hung, trembling, the notes of a pastoral aubade somebody was picking out on a guitar. As Dubois passed the house, a plump, dark-skinned woman with a crimson handkerchief round her head threw open a pair of shutters and leaned out to pick a spray of morning glory. As she tucked it behind her ear, she saw the stranger and smiled like another sunrise, greeting him with a few melodious phrases of his native language she had somehow mixed with burned cream and sunshine. She offered him a little breakfast which she was certain he must need since he had travelled so far and, while she spoke, the yellow-painted door burst open and a chattering tide of children swept out to surround the donkey, turning up to Dubois faces like sunflowers.

Six weeks after his arrival among the Creoles, Dubois left again for the house of his parents-in-law. There, he packed his library, notebooks and records of researches; his most precious collections of specimens and his equipment; as much clothing as he felt would last him the rest of his life; and a crate containing objects of sentimental value. This case and his children were the only concessions he made to the past. And, once he had installed all those safely in a wooden farmhouse the villagers had interrupted their inactivity long enough to make ready for him, he closed the doors of his heart to everything but the margins of the forest, which were to him a remarkable book it would take all the years that remained to him to learn to read.

The birds and beasts showed no fear of him. Painted magpies perched reflectively on his shoulders as he pored over the drawings he made among the trees, while fox cubs rolled in play around his feet and even learned to nose in his capacious pockets for cookies. As his children grew older, he seemed to them more an emanation of their surroundings than an actual father, and from him they unknowingly imbibed a certain radiant inhumanity which sprang from a benign indifference towards by far the greater part of mankind – towards all those who were not beautiful, gentle and, by nature, kind.

'Here, we have all become *homo silvester*, men of the woods,' he would say. 'And that is by far superior to the precocious and destructive species, *homo sapiens* – knowing man. Knowing man, indeed; what more than nature does man need to know?'

Other carefree children were their playfellows and their toys were birds, butterflies and flowers. Their father spared them enough of his time to teach them to read, to write and to draw. Then he gave them the run of his library and left them alone, to grow as they pleased. So they thrived on a diet of simple food, warm weather, perpetual holidays and haphazard learning. They were fearless since there was nothing to be afraid of, and they always spoke the truth because there was no need to lie. No hand or voice was ever raised in anger against them and so they did not know what anger was; when they came across the word in books, they thought it must mean the mild fretfulness they felt when it rained two days together, which did not happen often. They quite forgot the dull town where they had been born. The green world took them for its own and they were fitting children of their foster mother, for they were strong, lithe and supple, browned by the sun to the very colour of the villagers whose liquid *patois* they spoke. They resembled one another so closely each could have used the other as a mirror and almost seemed to be different aspects of the same person for all their gestures, turns of phrase and manner of speech were exactly similar. Had they known how, they would have been proud, because their intimacy was so perfect it could have bred that sense of loneliness which is the source of pride and, as they read more and more of their father's books, their companionship deepened since they had nobody but one another with whom to discuss the discoveries they made in common. From morning to evening, they were never apart, and at night they slept together in a plain, narrow bed on a floor of beaten earth while the window held the friendly nightlight of a soft, southern moon above them in a narrow frame. But often they slept under the moon itself, for they came and went as they pleased and spent most of their time out of doors, exploring the forests until they had gone further and seen more than ever their father had.

At last, these explorations took them into the untrodden, virginal reaches of the deep interior. Here, they walked hand in hand beneath the vaulted architraves of pines in a hushed interior like that of a sentient cathedral. The topmost branches twined so thickly that only a subdued viridian dazzle of light could filter through and the children felt against their ears a palpable fur of intense silence. Those who felt less kinship with the place might have been uneasy, as if abandoned among serene, voiceless, giant forms that cared nothing for man. But, if the children sometimes lost their way, they never lost themselves for they took the sun by day and the stars by the otherwise trackless night for their compass and could discern clues in the labyrinth that those who trusted the forest less would not have recognised, for they knew the forest too well to know of any harm it might do them.

Long ago, in their room at home, they began work on a map of the forest. This was by no means the map an authentic cartographer would have made. They marked hills with webs of feathers of the birds they found there, clearings with an integument of pressed flowers and especially magnificent trees with delicate, brightly coloured drawings on whose watercolour boughs they stuck garlands of real leaves so that the map became a tapestry made out of the substance of the forest itself. At first, in the centre of the map, they put their own thatched cottage and Madeline drew in the garden the shaggy figure of their father, whose leonine mane was as white, now, as the puff ball of a dandelion, bending with a green watering can over his pots of plants, tranquil, beloved and oblivious. But as they grew older, they grew discontented with their work for they found out their home did not lie at the heart of the forest but only somewhere in its green suburbs. They were seized with the desire to pierce more and yet more deeply into the unfrequented places and now their expeditions lasted for a week or longer. Though he was always glad to see them return, their father had often forgotten they had been away. At last, nothing but the discovery of the central node of the unvisited valley, the navel of the forest, would satisfy them. It grew to be almost an obsession with them. They spoke of the adventure only to one another and did not share it with the other companions who, as they grew older, grew less and less necessary to their absolute intimacy, since, lately, for reasons beyond their comprehension, this intimacy had been subtly invaded by tensions which exacerbated their nerves yet exerted on them both an intoxicating glamour.

Besides, when they spoke of the heart of the forest to their other friends, a veil of darkness came over the woodlanders' eyes and, half-laughing, half-whispering, they could hint at the wicked tree that grew there as though, even if they did not believe in it, it was a metaphor for something unfamiliar they preferred to ignore, as one might say: 'Let sleeping dogs lie. Aren't we happy as we are?' When they saw this laughing apathy, this incuriosity blended with a tinge of fear, Emile and Madeline could not help but feel a faint contempt, for their world, though beautiful, seemed to them, in a sense, incomplete – as though it lacked the knowledge of some mystery they might find, might they not? in the forest, on their own.

In their father's books they found references to the Antiar or Antshar of the Indo-Malay archipelago, the *antiaris toxicaria* whose milky juice contains a most potent poison, like the quintessence of belladonna. But their reason told them that not even the most intrepid migratory bird could have brought the sticky seeds on its feet to cast them down here in these land-locked valleys far from Java. They did not believe the wicked tree could exist in this hemisphere; and yet they were curious. But they were not afraid.

One August morning, when both were thirteen years old, they put bread and cheese in their knapsacks and started out on a journey so early the homesteads were sleeping and even the morning glories were still in bud. The settlements were just as their father had seen them first, prelapsarian villages where any Fall was inconceivable; his children, bred in those quiet places, saw them with eyes pure of nostalgia for lost innocence and thought of them only with that faint, warm claustrophobia which the word, 'home', signifies. At noon, they ate lunch with a family whose cottage lay at the edges of the uninhabited places and when they bade their hosts goodbye, they knew, with a certain anticipatory relish, they would not see anyone else but one another for a long time.

At first, they followed the wide river which led them directly into the ramparts of the great pines and, though days and nights soon merged together in a sonorous quiet where trees grew so close together that birds had no room to sing or fly, they kept a careful tally of the passing time for they knew that, five days away from home, along the leisurely course of the water, the pines thinned out.

The bramble-covered riverbanks, studded, at this season, with flat, pink discs of blossom, grew so narrow that the water tumbled fast enough to ring out various carillons while grey squirrels swung from branch to low branch of trees which, released from the strait confines of the forest, now grew in shapes of a feminine slightness and grace. Rabbits twitched moist, velvet noses and laid their ears along their backs but did not run away when they saw the barefoot children go by and Emile pointed out to Madeline how a wise toad, squatting meditatively among the kingcups, must have a jewel in his head because bright beams darted out through his eyes, as though a cold fire burned inside his head. They had read of this phenomenon in old books but never seen it before.

They had never seen anything in this place before. It was so beautiful they were a little awe-struck.

Then Madeline stretched out her hand to pick a water-lily unbudding on the surface of the river but she jumped back with a cry and gazed down at her finger with a mixture of pain, affront and astonishment. Her bright blood dripped down on to the grass.

'Emile!' she said. 'It bit me!'

They had never encountered the slightest hostility in the forest before. Their eyes met in wonder and surmise while the birds chanted recitatives to the accompaniment of the river. 'This is a strange place,' said Emile hesitantly. 'Perhaps we should not pick any flowers in this part of the forest. Perhaps we have found some kind of carnivorous water-lily.'

He washed the tiny wound, bound it with his handkerchief and kissed her cheek, to comfort her, but she would not be comforted and irritably flung a pebble in the direction of the flower. When the pebble struck the lily, the flower unfurled its close circle of petals with an audible snap and, bewildered, they glimpsed inside them a set of white, perfect fangs. Then the waxen petals closed swiftly over the teeth again, concealing them entirely, and the water-lily again looked perfectly white and innocent.

'See! It *is* a carnivorous water-lily!' said Emile. 'Father *will* be excited when we tell him.'

But Madeline, her eyes still fixed on the predator as if it fascinated her, slowly shook her head. She had grown very serious.

'No,' she said. 'We must not talk of the things we find in the heart of the forest. They are all secrets. If they were not secrets, we would have heard of them before.'

Her words fell with a strange weight, as heavy as her own gravity, as if she might have received some mysterious communication from the perfidious mouth that wounded her. At once, listening to her, Emile thought of the legendary tree; and then he realised that, for the first time in his life, he did not understand her, for, of course, they had heard of the tree. Looking at her in a new puzzlement, he sensed the ultimate difference of a femininity he had never before known any need or desire to acknowledge and this difference might give her the key to some order of knowledge to which he might not yet aspire, himself, for all at once she seemed far older than he. She raised her eyes and fixed on him a long, solemn regard which chained him in a conspiracy of secrecy, so that, henceforth, they would share only with one another the treacherous marvels round them. At last, he nodded.

'Very well, then,' he said. 'We won't tell father.'

Though they knew he never listened when they spoke to him, never before had they consciously concealed anything from him.

Night was approaching. They walked a little further, until they found pillows of moss laid ready for their heads beneath the branches of a flowering tree. They drank clear water, ate the last of the food they had brought with them and then slept in one another's arms as if they were the perfect children of the place, although they slept less peacefully than usual for both were visited by unaccustomed nightmares of knives and snakes and suppurating roses. But though each stirred and murmured, the dreams were so strangely inconsequential, nothing but fleeting sequences of detached, malign images, that the children forgot them as they slept and woke only with an irritable residue of nightmare, the dregs of unremembered dreaming, knowing only they had slept badly.

In the morning, they stripped and bathed in the river. Emile saw that time was subtly altering the contours of both their bodies and he found he could no longer ignore his sister's nakedness, as he had done since babyhood, while, from the way she suddenly averted her own eyes after, in her usual playful fashion, she splashed him with water, she, too, experienced the same extraordinary confusion. So they fell silent and hastily dressed themselves. And yet the confusion was pleasurable and made their blood sting. He examined her finger and found the marks of the lily's teeth were gone; the wound had healed over completely. Yet he still shuddered with an unfamiliar thrill of dread when he remembered the fanged flower.

'We have no food left,' he said. 'We should turn back at noon.'

'Oh, no!' said Madeline with a mysterious purposefulness that might have been rooted, had he known it, only in a newborn wish to make him do as she wanted, against his own wishes. 'No! I'm sure we shall find something to eat. After all, this is the season for wild strawberries.'

He, too, knew the lore of the forest. At no time of the year could they not find food – berries, roots, salads, mushrooms, and so on. So he saw she knew he had only used a pale excuse to cover his increasing agitation at finding himself alone with her so far from home. And now he had used up his excuse, there was nothing for it but to go on. She walked with a certain irresolute triumph, as though she were aware she had won an initial victory which, though insignificant in itself, might herald more major battles in the future, although they did not even know the formula for a quarrel, yet.

And already this new awareness of one another's shapes and outlines had made them less twinned, less indistinguishable from one another. So they fell once more to their erudite botanising, in order to pretend that all was as it had always been, before the forest showed its teeth; and now the meandering path of the river led them into such magical places that they found more than enough to talk about for, by the time the shadows vanished at noon, they had come into a landscape that seemed to have undergone an alchemical change, a vegetable transmutation, for it contained nothing that was not marvellous.

Ferns uncurled as they watched, revealing fronded fringes containing innumerable, tiny, shining eyes glittering like brilliants where the ranks of seeds should have been. A vine was covered with slumbrous, purple flowers that, as they passed, sang out in a rich contralto with all the voluptuous wildness of flamenco – and then fell silent. There were trees that bore, instead of foliage, brown, speckled plumage of birds. And when they had grown very hungry, they found a better food than even Madeline had guessed they might, for they came to a clump of low trees with trunks scaled like trout, growing at the water's edge. These trees put out shell-shaped fruit and, when they broke these open and ate them, they tasted oysters. After they consumed their fishy luncheon, they walked on a little and discovered a tree knobbed with white, red-tipped whorls that looked so much like breasts they put their mouths to the nipples and sucked a sweet, refreshing milk.

'See?' said Madeline, and this time her triumph was unconcealed. 'I told you we should find something to nourish us!'

When the shadows of the evening fell like a thick dust of powdered gold on the enchanted forest and they were beginning to feel weary, they came to a small valley which contained a pool that seemed to have no outlet or inlet and so must be fed by an invisible spring. The valley was filled with the most delightful, citronesque fragrance as sharply refreshing as a celestial eau-de-cologne and they saw the source of the perfume at once.

'Well!' exclaimed Emile. 'This certainly isn't the fabled Upas Tree! It must be some kind of incense tree, such as the incense trees of Upper India where, after all, one finds a similar climate, or so I've read.'

The tree was a little larger than a common apple tree but far more graceful in shape. The springing boughs hung out a festival of brilliant streamers, long, aromatic sprays of green, starlike flowers tipped with the red anthers of the stamens, cascading over clusters of leaves so deep a green and of such a glossy texture the dusk turned to discs of black glass those that the sunset did not turn to fire. These leaves hid secret bunches of fruit, mysterious spheres of visible gold streaked with green, as if all the unripe suns in the world were sleeping on the tree until a multiple, universal dawning should wake them all in splendour. As they stood hand in hand gazing at the beautiful tree, a small wind parted the leaves so they would see the fruit more clearly and, in the rind, set squarely in the middle of each faintly flushed cheek, was a curious formation – a round set of serrated indentations exactly resembling the marks of a bite made by the teeth of a hungry man. As if the sight stimulated her own appetite, Madeline laughed and said: 'Goodness, Emile, the forest has even given us dessert!'

She sprang towards the exquisite, odoriferous tree which, at that moment, suffused in a failing yet hallucinatory light the tone and intensity of liquefied amber, seemed to her brother a perfect equivalent of his sister's amazing beauty, a beauty he had never seen before that filled him, now, with ecstasy. The dark pool reflected her darkly, like an antique mirror. She raised her hand to part the leaves in search of a ripe fruit but the greenish skin seemed to warm and glow under her fingers so the first one she touched came as easily off the stem as if it had been brought to perfection by her touch. It seemed to be some kind of apple or pear. It was so juicy the juice ran down her chin and she extended a long, crimson, newly sensual tongue to lick her lips, laughing.

'It tastes so good!' she said. 'Here! Eat!'

She came back to him, splashing through the margins of the pool, holding the fruit out towards him on her palm. She was like a beautiful statue which had just come to life. Her enormous eyes were lit like nocturnal flowers that had been waiting only for this especial night to open and, in their vertiginous depths, reveal to her brother in expressible entirety the hitherto unguessed at, unknowable, inexpressible vistas of love.

He took the apple; ate; and, after that, they kissed.

Flesh and the Mirror

It was midnight – I chose my times and set my scenes with the precision of the born artiste. Hadn't I gone eight thousand miles to find a climate with enough anguish and hysteria in it to satisfy me? I had arrived back in Yokohama that evening from a visit to England and nobody met me, although I expected him. So I took the train to Tokyo, half an hour's journey. First, I was angry; but the poignancy of my own situation overcame me and then I was sad. To return to the one you love and find him absent! My heart used to jump like Pavlov's dogs at the prospect of such a treat; I positively salivated at the suggestion of unpleasure, I was sure that *that* was real life. I'm told I always look lonely when I'm alone; that is because, when I was an intolerable adolescent, I learned to sit with my coat-collar turned up in a lonely way, so that people would talk to me. And I can't drop the habit even now, though, now, it's only a habit, and, I realise, a predatory habit.

It was midnight and I was crying bitterly as I walked under the artificial cherry blossom with which they decorate the lamp standards from April to September. They do that so the pleasure quarters will have the look of a continuous carnival, no matter what ripples of agitation disturb the never-ceasing, endlessly circulating, quiet, gentle, melancholy crowds who throng the wet web of alleys under a false ceiling of umbrellas. All looked as desolate as Mardi Gras. I was searching among a multitude of unknown faces for the face of the one I loved while the warm, thick, heavy rain of summer greased the dark surfaces of the streets until, after a while, they began to gleam like sleek fur of seals just risen from the bottom of the sea.

The crowds lapped around me like waves full of eyes until I felt that I was walking through an ocean whose speechless and gesticulating inhabitants, like those with whom medieval philosophers peopled the countries of the deep, were methodical inversions or mirror images of the dwellers on dry land. And I moved through these expressionist perspectives in my black dress as though I was the creator of all and of myself, too, in a black dress, in love, crying, walking through the city in the third person singular, my own heroine, as though the world stretched out from my eye like spokes from a sensitised hub that galvanised all to life when I looked at it.

I think I know, now, what I was trying to do. I was trying to subdue the city by turning it into a projection of my own growing pains. What solipsistic arrogance! The city, the largest city in the world, the city designed to suit not one of my European expectations, this city presents the foreigner with a mode of life that seems to him to have the enigmatic transparency, the indecipherable clarity, of dream. And it is a dream he could, himself, never have dreamed. The stranger, the foreigner, thinks he is control; but he has been precipitated into somebody else's dream.

You never know what will happen in Tokyo. Anything can happen.

I had been attracted to the city first because I suspected it contained enormous histrionic resources. I was always rummaging in the dressing-up box of the heart for suitable appearances to adopt in the city. That was the way I maintained my defences for, at that time, I always used to suffer a great deal if I let myself get too close to reality since the definitive world of the everyday with its hard edges and harsh light did not have enough resonance to echo the demands I made upon experience. It was as if I never experienced experience *as* experience. Living never lived up to the expectations I had of it – the Bovary syndrome. I was always imagining other things that could have been happening, instead, and so I always felt cheated, always dissatisfied.

Always dissatisfied, even if, like a perfect heroine, I wandered, weeping, on a forlorn quest for a lost lover through the aromatic labyrinth of alleys. And wasn't I in Asia? Asia! But, even though I lived there, it always seemed far away from me. It was as if there were glass between me and the world. But I could see myself perfectly well on the other side of the glass. There I was, walking up and down, eating meals, having conversations, in love, indifferent, and so on. But all the time I was pulling the strings of my own puppet; it was this puppet who was moving about on the other side of the glass. And I eyed the most marvellous adventures with the bored eye of the agent with the cigar watching another audition. I tapped out the ash and asked of events: 'What else can you do?'

So I attempted to rebuild the city according to the blueprint in my imagination as a backdrop to the plays in my puppet theatre, but it sternly refused to be so rebuilt; I was only imagining it had been so rebuilt. On the night I came back to it, however hard I looked for the one I loved, she could not find him anywhere and the city delivered her into the hands of a perfect stranger who fell into step beside her and asked why she was crying. She went with him to an unambiguous hotel with a mirror on the ceiling and lascivious black lace draped round a palpably illicit bed. His eyes were shaped like sequins. All night long, a thin, pale, sickle moon with a single star pendant at its nether tip floated upon the rain that pitter-pattered against the windows and there was a clockwork whirring of cicadas. From time to time, the windbell dangling from the eaves let out an exquisitely mournful tinkle.

None of the lyrical eroticism of this sweet, sad, moon night of summer rain had been within my expectations; I had half expected he would strangle me. My sensibility wilted under the burden of response. My sensibility foundered under the assault on my senses.

My imagination had been pre-empted.

The room was a box of oiled paper full of the echoes of the rain. After the light was out, as we lay together, I could still see the single shape of our embrace in the mirror above me, a marvellously unexpected conjunction cast at random by the enigmatic kaleidoscope of the city. Our pelts were stippled with the fretted shadows of the lace curtains as if our skins were a mysterious uniform provided by the management in order to render all those who made love in that hotel anonymous. The mirror annihilated time, place and person; at the consecration of this house, the mirror had been dedicated to the reflection of chance embraces. Therefore it treated flesh in an exemplary fashion, with charity and indifference.

The mirror distilled the essence of all the encounters of strangers whose perceptions of one another existed only in the medium of the chance embrace, the accidental. During the durationless time we spent making love, we were not ourselves, whoever that might have been, but in some sense the ghosts of ourselves. But the selves we were not, the selves of our own habitual perceptions of ourselves, had a far more insubstantial substance than the reflections we were. The magic mirror presented me with a hitherto unconsidered notion of myself as I. Without any intention of mine, I had been defined by the action reflected in the mirror. I beset me. I was the subject of the sentence written on the mirror. I was not watching it. There was nothing whatsoever beyond the surface of the glass. Nothing kept me from the fact, the act; I had been precipitated into knowledge of the real conditions of living.

Mirrors are ambiguous things. The bureaucracy of the mirror issues me with a passport to the world; it shows me my appearance. But what use is a passport to an armchair traveller? Women and mirrors are in complicity with one another to evade the action I/she performs that she/I cannot watch, the action with which I break out of the mirror, with which I assume my appearance. But *this* mirror refused to conspire with me; it was like the first mirror I'd ever seen. It reflected the embrace beneath it without the least guile. All it showed was inevitable. But I myself could never have dreamed it.

I saw the flesh and the mirror but I could not come to terms with the sight. My immediate response to it was, to feel I'd acted out of character. The fancy-dress disguise I'd put on to suit the city had betrayed me to a room and a bed and a modification of myself that had no business at all in my life, not in the life I had watched myself performing.

Therefore I evaded the mirror. I scrambled out of its arms and sat on the edge of the bed and lit a fresh cigarette from the butt of the old one. The rain beat down. My demonstration of perturbation was perfect in every detail, just like the movies. I applauded it. I was gratified the mirror had not seduced me into behaving in a way I would have felt inappropriate – that is, shrugging and sleeping, as though my infidelity was not of the least importance. I now shook with the disturbing presentiment that he with his sequin eyes who'd been kind to me was an ironic substitute for the other one, the one I loved, as if the arbitrary carnival of the streets had gratuitously offered me this young man to find out if I *could* act out of character and then projected our intersection upon the mirror, as an objective lesson in the nature of things.

Therefore I dressed rapidly and ran away as soon as it was light outside, that mysterious, colourless light of dawn when the hooded crows flap out of the temple groves to perch on the telegraph poles, cawing a baleful dawn chorus to the echoing boulevards empty, now, of all the pleasure-seekers. The rain had stopped. It was an overcast morning so hot that I broke out into a sweat at the slightest movement. The bewildering electrographics of the city at night were all switched off. All the perspectives were pale, gritty grey, the air was full of dust. I never knew such a banal morning.

The morning before the night before, the morning before this oppressive morning, I woke up in the cabin of a boat. All the previous day, as we rounded the coast in bright weather, I dreamed of the reunion before me, a lovers' meeting refreshed by the three months I'd been gone, returning home due to a death in the family. I will come back as soon as I can – I'll write. Will you meet me at the pier? Of course, of course he will. But he was not at the pier; where was he?

So I went at once to the city and began my desolate tour of the pleasure quarters, looking for him in all the bars he used. He was nowhere to be found. I did not know his address, of course; he moved from rented room to rented room with the agility of the feckless and we had corresponded through accommodation addresses, coffee shops, poste restante, etc. Besides, there had been a displacement of mail reminiscent of the excesses of the nineteenth-century novel, such as it is difficult to believe and could only have been caused by a desperate emotional necessity to cause as much confusion as possible. Both of us prided ourselves on our passionate sensibilities, of course. That was *one* thing we had in common! So, although I thought I was the most romantic spectacle imaginable as I wandered weeping down the alleys, I was in reality at risk – I had fallen through one of the holes life leaves in it; these peculiar holes are the entrances to the counters at which you pay the price of the way you live.

Random chance operates in relation to these existential lacunae; one tumbles down them when, for the time being, due to hunger, despair, sleeplessness, hallucination or those accidental-on-purpose misreadings of train timetables and airline schedules that produce margins of empty time, one is lost. One is at the mercy of events. That is why I like to be a foreigner; I only travel for the insecurity. But I did not know that, then.

I found my self-imposed fate, my beloved, quite early that morning but we quarrelled immediately. We quarrelled the day away assiduously and, when I tried to pull the strings of my self and so take control of the situation, I was astonished to find the situation I wanted was disaster, shipwreck. I saw his face as though it were in ruins, although it was the sight in the world I knew best and, the first time I saw it, had not seemed to me a face I did not know. It had seemed, in some way, to correspond to my idea of my own face. It had seemed a face long known and well remembered, a face that had always been imminent in my consciousness as an idea that now found its first visual expression.

So I suppose I do not know how he really looked and, in fact, I suppose I shall never know, now, for he was plainly an object created in the mode of fantasy. His image was already present somewhere in my head and I was seeking to discover it in actuality, looking at every face I met in case it was the right face – that is, the face which corresponded to my notion of the unseen face of the one I should love, a face created parthenogenetically by the rage to love which consumed me. So his self, and, by his self, I mean the thing he was to himself, was quite unknown to me. I created him solely in relation to myself, like a work of romantic art, an object corresponding to the ghost inside me. When I'd first loved him, I wanted to take him apart, as a child dismembers a clockwork toy, to comprehend the inscrutable mechanics of its interior. I wanted to see him far more naked than he was with his clothes off. It was easy enough to strip him bare and then I picked up my scalpel and set to work. But, since I was so absolutely in charge of the dissection, I only discovered what I was able to recognise already, from past experience, inside him. If ever I found anything new to me, I steadfastly ignored it. I was so absorbed in this work it never occurred to me to wonder if it hurt him.

In order to create the loved object in this way and to issue it with its certificate of authentication, as beloved, I had also to labour at the idea of myself in love. I watched myself closely for all the signs and, precisely upon cue, here they were! Longing, desire, self-abnegation, etc. I was racked by all the symptoms. Even so, in spite of this fugue of feeling, I had felt nothing but pleasure when the young man who picked me up inserted his sex inside me in the blue-movie bedroom. I only grew guilty later, when I realised I had not felt in the least guilty at the time. And was I in character when I felt guilty or in character when I did not? I was perplexed. I no longer understood the logic of my own performance. My script had been scrambled behind my back. The cameraman was drunk. The director had had a *crise de nerfs* and been taken away to a sanatorium. And my co-star had picked himself up off the operating table and painfully cobbled himself together again according to his own design! All this had taken place while I was looking at the mirror.

Imagine my affront.

We quarrelled until night fell and, still quarrelling, found our way to another hotel but this hotel, and this night, was in every respect a parody of the previous night. (That's more like it! Squalor and humiliation! Ah!) Here, there were no lace drapes nor windbells nor moonlight nor any moist whisper of lugubriously seductive rain; this place was bleak, mean and cheerless and the sheets on the mattress they threw down on the floor for us were blotched with dirt although, at first, we did not notice that because it was necessary to pretend the urgent passion we always used to feel in one another's presence even if we felt it no longer, as if to act out the feeling with sufficient intensity would re-create it by sleight of hand, although our skins (which knew us better than we knew ourselves) told us the period of reciprocation was over. It was a mean room and the windows overlooked a parking lot with a freeway beyond it, so that the paper walls shuddered with the reverberations of the infernal clamour of the traffic. There was a sluggish electric fan with dead flies caught in the spokes and a single strip of neon overhead lit us and everything up with a scarcely tolerable, quite remorseless light. A slatternly woman in a filthy apron brought us glasses of thin, cold, brown tea made from barley and then she shut the door on us. I would not let him kiss me between the thighs because I was afraid he would taste the traces of last night's adventure, a little touch of paranoia in *that* delusion.

I don't know how much guilt had to do with the choice of this décor. But I felt it was perfectly appropriate.

The air was thicker than tea that's stewed on the hob all day and cockroaches were running over the ceiling, I remember. I cried all the first part of the night, I cried until I was exhausted but he turned on his side and slept – he saw through that ruse, though I did not since I did not know that I was lying. But I could not sleep because of the rattling of the walls and the noise of traffic. We had turned off the glaring lamp; when I saw a shaft of light fall across his face, I thought: 'Surely it's too early for the dawn.' But it was another person silently sliding open the unlocked door; in this disreputable hotel, anything can happen. I screamed and the intruder vanished. Wakened by a scream, my lover thought I'd gone mad and instantly trapped me in a stranglehold, in case I murdered him.

We were both old enough to have known better, too.

When I turned on the lamp to see what time it was, I noticed, to my surprise, that his features were blurring, like the underwriting on a palimpsest. It wasn't long before we parted. Only a few days. You can't keep *that* pace up for long.

Then the city vanished; it ceased, almost immediately, to be a magic and appalling place. I woke up one morning and found it had become home. Though I still turn up my coat-collar in a lonely way and am always looking at myself in mirrors, they're only habits and give no clue at all to my character, whatever that is.

The most difficult performance in the world is acting naturally, isn't it? Everything else is artful.

Master

After he discovered that his vocation was to kill animals, the pursuit of it took him far away from temperate weather until, in time, the insatiable suns of Africa eroded the pupils of his eyes, bleached his hair and tanned his skin until he no longer looked the thing he had been but its systematic negative; he became the white hunter, victim of an exile which is the imitation of death, a willed bereavement. He would emit a ravished gasp when he saw the final spasm of his prey. He did not kill for money but for love.

He had first exercised a propensity for savagery in the acrid lavatories of a minor English public school where he used to press the heads of the new boys into the ceramic bowl and then pull the flush upon them to drown their gurgling protests. After puberty, he turned his indefinable but exacerbated rage upon the pale, flinching bodies of young women whose flesh he lacerated with teeth, fingernails and sometimes his leather belt in the beds of cheap hotels near London's great rail termini (King's Cross, Victoria, Euston . . .). But these pastel-coloured excesses, all the cool, rainy country of his birth could offer him, never satisfied him; his ferocity would attain the colouring of the fauves only when he took it to the torrid zones and there refined it until it could be distinguished from that of the beasts he slaughtered only by the element of self-consciousness it retained, for, if little of him now pertained to the human, the eyes of his self still watched him so that he was able to applaud his own depredations.

Although he decimated herds of giraffe and gazelle as they grazed in the savannahs until they learned to snuff their annihilation upon the wind as he approached, and dispatched heraldically plated hippopotami as they lolled up to their armpits in ooze, his rifle's particular argument lay with the silken indifference of the great cats, and, finally, he developed a speciality in the extermination of the printed beasts, leopards and lynxes, who carry ideograms of death in the clotted language pressed in brown ink upon their pelts by the fingertips of mute gods who do not acknowledge any divinity in humanity.

When he had sufficiently ravaged the cats of Africa, a country older by far than we are yet to whose innocence he had always felt superior, he decided to explore the nether regions of the New World, intending to kill the painted beast, the jaguar, and so arrived in the middle of a metaphor for desolation, the place where time runs back on itself, the moist, abandoned cleft of the world whose fructifying river is herself a savage woman, the Amazon. A green, irrevocable silence closed upon him in that serene kingdom of giant vegetables. Dismayed, he clung to the bottle as if it were a teat.

He travelled by jeep through an invariable terrain of architectonic vegetation where no wind lifted the fronds of palms as ponderous as if they had been sculpted out of viridian gravity at the beginning of time and then abandoned, whose trunks were so heavy they did not seem to rise into the air but, instead, drew the oppressive sky down upon the forest like a coverlid of burnished metal. These tree trunks bore an outcrop of plants, orchids, poisonous, iridescent blossoms and creepers the thickness of an arm with flowering mouths that stuck out viscous tongues to trap the flies that nourished them. Bright birds of unknown shapes infrequently darted past him and sometimes monkeys, chattering like the third form, leaped from branch to branch that did not move beneath them. But no motion nor sound did more than ripple the surface of the profound, inhuman introspection of the place so that, here, to kill became the only means that remained to him to confirm he himself was still alive, for he was not prone to introspection and had never found any consolation in nature. Slaughter was his only proclivity and his unique skill.

He came upon the Indians who lived among the lugubrious trees. They represented such a diversity of ethnic types they were like a living museum of man organised on a principle of regression for, the further inland he went, the more primitive they became, as if to demonstrate that evolution could be inverted. Some of the brown men had no other habitation than the sky and, like the flowers, ate insects; they would paint their bodies with the juice of leaves and berries and ornament their heads with diadems of feathers or the claws of eagles. Placid and decorative, the men and women would come softly twittering round his jeep, a mild curiosity illuminating the inward-turning, amber suns of their eyes, and he did not recognise that they were men although they distilled demented alcohol in stills of their own devising and he drank it, in order to people the inside of his head with familiar frenzy among so much that was strange.

His half-breed guide would often take one of the brown girls who guilelessly offered him her bare, pointed breasts and her veiled, limpid smile and, then and there, infect her with the clap to which he was a chronic martyr in the bushes at the rim of the clearing. Afterwards, licking his chops with remembered appetite, he would say to the hunter: 'Brown meat, brown meat.' In drunkenness one night, troubled by the prickings of a carnality that often visited him at the end of his day's work, the hunter bartered, for the spare tyre of his jeep, a pubescent girl as virgin as the forest that had borne her.

She wore a vestigial slip of red cotton twisted between her thighs and her long, sinuous back was upholstered in cut velvet, for it was whorled and ridged with the tribal markings incised on her when her menses began – raised designs like the contour map of an unknown place. The women of her tribe dipped their hairs in liquid mud and then wound their locks into long curls around sticks and let them dry in the sun until each one possessed a hairdo of rigid ringlets the consistency of baked, unglazed pottery, so she looked as if her head was surrounded by one of those spiked haloes allotted to famous sinners in Sunday-school picture books. Her eyes held the gentleness and the despair of those about to be dispossessed; she had the immovable smile of a cat, which is forced by physiology to smile whether it wants to or not.

The beliefs of her tribe had taught her to regard herself as a sentient abstraction, an intermediary between the ghosts and the fauna, so she looked at her purchaser's fever-shaking, skeletal person with scarcely curiosity, for he was to her no more yet no less surprising than any other gaunt manifestation of the forest. If she did not perceive him as a man, either, that was because her cosmogony admitted no essential difference between herself and the beasts and the spirits, it was so sophisticated. Her tribe never killed; they only ate roots. He taught her to eat the meat he roasted over his camp fire and, at first, she did not like it much but dutifully consumed it as though he were ordering her to partake of a sacrament for, when she saw how casually he killed the jaguar, she soon realised he was death itself. Then she began to look at him with wonder for she recognised immediately how death had glorified itself to become the principle of his life. But when he looked at her, he saw only a piece of curious flesh he had not paid much for.

He thrust his virility into her surprise and, once her wound had healed, used her to share his sleeping bag and carry his pelts. He told her her name would be Friday, which was the day he bought her; he taught her to say 'master' and then let her know that was to be his name. Her eyelids fluttered for, though she could move her lips and tongue and so reproduce the sounds he made, she did not understand them. And, daily, he slaughtered the jaguar. He sent away the guide for, now he had bought the girl, he did not need him; so the ambiguous couple went on together, while the girl's father made sandals from the rubber tyre to shoe his family's feet and they walked a little way into the twentieth century in them, but not far.

Among her tribe circulated the following picturesque folk-tale. The

jaguar invited the anteater to a juggling contest in which they would use
their eyes to play with, so they drew their eyes out of the sockets. When
they had finished, the anteater threw his eyes up into the air and back they
fell – plop! in place in his head; but when the jaguar imitated him, his eyes
caught in the topmost branches of a tree and he could not reach them. So
he became blind. Then the anteater asked the macaw to make new eyes
out of water for the jaguar and, with these eyes, the jaguar found that it
could see in the dark. So all turned out well for the jaguar; and she, too,
the girl who did not know her own name, could see in the dark. As they
moved always more deeply into the forest, away from the little
settlements, nightly he extorted his pleasure from her flesh and she would
gaze over her shoulder at shapes of phantoms in the thickly susurrating
undergrowth, phantoms – it seemed to her – of beasts he had slaughtered
that day, for she had been born into the clan of the jaguar and, when his
leather belt cut her shoulder, the magic water of which her eyes were
made would piteously leak.

He could not reconcile himself to the rain forest, which oppressed and
devastated him. He began to shake with malaria. He killed continually,
stripped the pelts and left the corpses behind him for the vultures and the
flies.

Then they came to a place where there were no more roads.

His heart leaped with ecstatic fear and longing when he saw how
nothing but beasts inhabited the interior. He wanted to destroy them all,
so that he would feel less lonely, and, in order to penetrate this absence
with his annihilating presence, he left the jeep behind at a forgotten
township where a green track ended and an ancient whisky priest sat all
day in the ruins of a forsaken church brewing fire-water from wild
bananas and keening the stations of the cross. Master loaded his brown
mistress with his guns and the sleeping bag and the gourds filled with
liquid fever. They left a wake of corpses behind them for the plants and
the vultures to eat.

At night, after she lit the fire, he would first abuse her with the butt of
his rifle about the shoulders and, after that, with his sex; then drink from a
gourd and sleep. When she had wiped the tears from her face with the
back of her hand, she was herself again, and, after they had been together
a few weeks she seized the opportunity of solitude to examine his guns,
the instruments of his passion and, perhaps, learn a little of Master's
magic.

She squinted her eye to peer down the long barrel; she caressed the
metal trigger, and, pointing the barrel carefully away from her as she had
seen Master do, she softly squeezed it in imitation of his gestures to see if
she, too, could provoke the same shattering exhalation. But, to her

disappointment, she provoked nothing. She clicked her tongue against her teeth in irritation. Exploring further, however, she discovered the secret of the safety catch.

Ghosts came out of the jungle and sat at her feet, cocking their heads on one side to watch her. She greeted them with a friendly wave of her hand. The fire began to fail but she could see clearly through the sights of the rifle since her eyes were made of water and, raising it to her shoulder as she had seen Master do, she took aim at the disc of moon stuck to the sky beyond the ceiling of boughs above her, for she wanted to shoot the moon down since it was a bird in her scheme of things and, since he had taught her to eat meat, now she thought she must be death's apprentice.

He woke from sleep in a paroxysm of fear and saw her, dimly illuminated by the dying fire, naked but for the rag that covered her sex, with the rifle in her hand; it seemed to him her clay-covered head was about to turn into a nest of birds of prey. She laughed delightedly at the corpse of the sleeping bird her bullet had knocked down from the tree and the moonlight glimmered on her curiously pointed teeth. She believed the bird she shot down had been the moon and now, in the night sky, she saw only the ghost of the moon. Though they were lost, hopelessly lost, in the trackless forest, she knew quite well where she was; she was always at home in the ghost town.

Next day, he oversaw the beginnings of her career as a markswoman and watched her tumble down from the boughs of the forest representatives of all the furred and feathered beings it contained. She always gave the same delighted laugh to see them fall for she had never thought it would be so easy to populate her fireside with fresh ghosts. But she could not bring herself to kill the jaguar, since the jaguar was the emblem of her clan; with forceful gestures of her head and hands, she refused. But, after she learned to shoot, soon she became a better hunter than he although there was no method to her killing and they went banging away together indiscriminately through the dim, green undergrowth.

The descent of the banana spirit in the gourd marked the passage of time and they left a gross trail of carnage behind them. The spectacle of her massacres moved him and he mounted her in a frenzy, forcing apart her genital lips so roughly the crimson skin on the inside bruised and festered while the bites on her throat and shoulders oozed diseased pearls of pus that brought the blowflies buzzing about her in a cloud. Her screams were a universal language; even the monkeys understood she suffered when Master took his pleasure, yet he did not. As she grew more like him, so she began to resent him.

While he slept, she flexed her fingers in the darkness that concealed nothing from her and, without surprise, she discovered her fingernails were growing long, curved, hard and sharp. Now she could tear his back when he inflicted himself upon her and leave red runnels in his skin; yelping with delight, he only used her the more severely and, twisting her head with its pottery appendages this way and that in pained perplexity, she gouged the empty air with her claws.

They came to a spring of water and she plunged into it in order to wash herself but she sprang out again immediately because the touch of water aroused such an unpleasant sensation on her pelt. When she impatiently tossed her head to shake away the waterdrops, her clay ringlets melted altogether and trickled down her shoulders. She could no longer tolerate cooked meat but must tear it raw between her fingers off the bone before Master saw. She could no longer twist her scarlet tongue around the two syllables of his name, 'mas-tuh'; when she tried to speak, only a diffuse and rumbling purr shivered the muscles of her throat and she dug neat holes in the earth to bury her excrement, she had become so fastidious since she grew whiskers.

Madness and fever consumed him. When he killed the jaguar, he abandoned them in the forest with the stippled pelts still on them. To possess the clawed she was in itself a kind of slaughter, and, tracking behind her, his eyes dazed with strangeness and liquor, he would watch the way the intermittent dentellation of the sun through the leaves mottled the ridged tribal markings down her back until it seemed the blotched areas of pigmentation were subtly mimicking the beasts who mimicked the patterns of the sun through the leaves and, if she had not walked upright on two legs, he would have shot her. As it was, he thrust her down into the undergrowth, amongst the orchids, and drove his other weapon into her soft, moist hole whilst he tore her throat with his teeth and she wept, until, one day, she found she was not able to cry any more.

The day the liquor ended, he was alone with fever. He reeled, screaming and shaking, in the clearing where she had abandoned his sleeping bag; she crouched among the lianas and crooned in a voice like soft thunder. Though it was daylight, the ghosts of innumerable jaguar crowded round to see what she would do. Their invisible nostrils twitched with the prescience of blood. The shoulder to which she raised the rifle now had the texture of plush.

His prey had shot the hunter, but now she could no longer hold the gun. Her brown and amber dappled sides rippled like water as she trotted across the clearing to worry the clothing of the corpse with her teeth. But soon she grew bored and bounded away.

Then only the flies crawling on his body were alive and he was far from home.

Reflections

I was walking in a wood one late spring day of skimming cloud and shower-tarnished sunshine, the sky a lucid if intermittent blue – cool, bright, tremulous weather. A coloratura blackbird perched on a bough curded with a greenish may-blossom let fall a flawed chain of audible pearl; I was alone in the spring-enchanted wood. I slashed the taller grasses with my stick and now and then surprised some woodland creature, rat or rabbit, that fled away from me through long grass where little daisies and spindly branches of buttercups were secreted among gleaming stems still moist at the roots from last night's rain that had washed and refreshed the entire wood, had dowered it with the poignant transparency, the unique, inconsolable quality of rainy countries, as if all was glimpsed through tears.

The crisp air was perfumed with wet grass and fresh earth. The year was swinging on the numinous hinges of the solstice but I was ingenuous and sensed no imminence in the magic silence of the rustling wood.

Then I heard a young girl singing. Her voice performed a trajectory of sound far more ornate than that of the blackbird, who ceased at once to sing when he heard it for he could not compete with the richly crimson sinuosity of a voice that pierced the senses of the listener like an arrow in a dream. She sang; and her words thrilled through me, for they seemed filled with a meaning that had no relation to meaning as I understood it.

'Under the leaves,' she sang, 'and the leaves of life – ' Then, in mid-flight, the song ceased and left me dazzled. My attention abstracted from my surroundings, all at once my foot turned on an object hidden in the grass and I tumbled to the ground. Though I fell on the soft, wet grass, I was shaken and winded. I forgot that luring music. Cursing my obstacle, I searched among the pale, earth-stained rootlets to find it and my fingers closed on, of all things, a shell. A shell so far from the sea! When I tried to grasp it in order to pick it up and examine it the better, I found the act unexpectedly difficult and my determination to lift it quickened although, at the same time, I felt a shiver of fear for it was so very, very heavy and its contours so chill that a shock like cold electricity darted up my arm from the shell, into my heart. I was seized with the most intense disquiet; I was mystified by the shell.

I thought it must be a shell from a tropic ocean, since it was far larger and more elaborately whorled than the shells I'd found on the shores of the Atlantic. There was some indefinable strangeness in its shape I could not immediately define. It glimmered through the grass like a cone of trapped moonlight although it was so very cold and so heavy it seemed to me it might contain all the distilled heaviness of gravity itself within it. I grew very much afraid of the shell; I think I sobbed. Yet I was so determined to wrench it from the ground that I clenched my muscles and gritted my teeth and tugged and heaved. Up it came, at last, and I rolled over backwards when it freed itself. But now I held the prize in my hands, and I was, for the moment, satisfied.

When I looked at the shell more closely, I saw the nature of the teasing difference that had struck me when I first set eyes on it. The whorls of the shell went the wrong way. The spirals were reversed. It looked like the mirror image of a shell, and so it should not have been able to exist outside a mirror; in this world, it could not exist outside a mirror. But, all the same, I held it.

The shell was the size of my cupped hands and cold and heavy as death.

In spite of its fabulous weight, I decided to carry it through the wood for I thought I would take it to the little museum in the nearby town where they would inspect it and test it and tell me what it might be and how it would have arrived where I found it. But as I staggered along with it in my arms, it exerted such a pull downwards on me that, several times, I nearly fell to my knees, as if the shell were determined to drag me, not down to the earth but into the earth itself. And then, to complete my confusion, I heard that witching voice again.

'Under the leaves – '

But, this time, when a gasp stopped the song, the voice changed at once to the imperative.

'Sic 'im!' she urged. 'Sic 'im!'

Before I had a chance to do more than glance in the direction of the voice, a bullet whirred over my head and buried itself in the trunk of an elm tree, releasing from their nests in the upward branches a whirring hurricane of crows. An enormous black dog bounded towards me from the undergrowth so suddenly I saw no more than his yawning scarlet maw and lolling tongue before I went down on my face beneath him. The fright nearly bereft me of my senses. The dog slavered wetly over me and, the next thing I knew, a hand seized my shoulder and roughly turned me over.

She had called the dog away and now it sat on its haunches, panting, watching me with a quick, red eye. It was black as coal, some kind of lurcher, with balls the size of grapefruit. Both the dog and the girl glanced at me without charity. She wore blue jeans and boots, a wide, vindictively buckled leather belt and a green sweater. Her tangled brown hair hung about her shoulders in a calculated disorder that was not wild. Her dark eyebrows were perfectly straight and gave her stern face a gravity as awful as that of the shell I held in my hand. Her blue eyes, the kind the Irish say have been put in with a sooty finger, held no comfort nor concern for me for they were the eyes that justice would have if she were not blind. She carried a sporting rifle slung across her shoulder and I knew at once this rifle had fired the shot. She might have been the gamekeeper's daughter but, no, she was too proud; she was a savage and severe wood-ranger.

Why I do not know, but every impulse told me to conceal my shell and I hugged it close to me, as if my life depended on keeping it, although it was so heavy and began to throb with a wild palpitation so that it seemed the shell had disordered my own heart, or else had become my own disordered heart. But my brusque captress poked at my hands with the barrel of her rifle so roughly my bruised fingers let the shell fall. She bent forward so that her necromantic hair brushed my face and picked up the shell with amazing ease.

She examined it for a moment and then, without a word or sign to me, tossed it to her lurcher, who seized it in his mouth ready to carry it for her. The dog began to wag his tail. The rhythmic swishing of his tail upon the grass was now the only sound in the clearing. Even the trees had ceased to murmur, as though a holy terror hushed them.

She gestured me to my feet and, when I was upright, she thrust the mouth of the gun in the small of my back and marched me through the wood at gunpoint, striding along behind me while the dog padded beside her with the shell in his mouth. All this took place in unadulterated silence, but for the raucous panting of the dog. The cabbage white butterflies flickered upon the still air as if nothing whatsoever were out of the ordinary, while delicious-looking apricot and violet-coloured clouds continued to chase one another across the sun according to the indifferent logic of the upper heavens, for the clouds were moved by a fierce wind that blew so high above the wood everything around me was as tranquil as water trapped in a lock, and mocked the inward perturbation that shook me.

Soon we reached an overgrown path that took us to a gate set in a garden wall where there was an old-fashioned bell-pull and, dangling above it, a bell stained with moss and rust. The girl with the rifle rang this bell before she opened the gate as if to warn whoever was at home that visitors were arriving. The gate led into a graceful and dilapidated walled garden full of the herbaceous splendours of early summer, hollyhocks, wallflowers, roses. There was a mossed sundial and a little stone statue of a nude youth stretching his arms up out of a cuirass of ivy. But, though the bees hummed among the flower bells, the grass was as long as it had been in the wood and just as full of buttercups and daisies. Dandelions expired in airy seed heads in the flowerbeds; ragged robin and ground elder conspired to oust the perennials from the borders and a bright sadness of neglect touched everything as though with dust, just as it did the ancient brick house, almost covered with creepers, that slept within the garden, an ancient, tumbledown place with a look of oracular blindness in windows that were stopped up with vines and flowers. The roof was lichened quite over, so that it seemed upholstered in sleek, green fur. Yet there was no peace in the dishevelled loveliness of the place; the very plants that grew there seemed tensed in a curious expectancy, as though the garden were a waiting room. There was a short, crumbling flight of steps that led to a weathered front door, ajar like the door of a witch's house.

Before the door, I involuntarily halted; a dreadful vertigo seized me, as if I stood on the edge of an abyss. My heart had been thumping far too hard and far too fast since I had picked up the shell and now it seemed about to burst from too much strain. Faintness and terror of death swept over me; but the girl prodded me cruelly in the buttocks with her rifle so I was forcibly marched into a country-house hall with dark stained floorboards, a Persian carpet and a Jacobean oak chest with an antique bowl on it, all complete yet all as if untouched for years, for decades. A maze of dust danced in the beam of sunshine that disturbed the choked indoors air when we broke into it. Every corner was softened by cobwebs while the industrious spiders had wound filaments of geometric lace this way and that between the crumbling furniture. A sweet, rank smell of damp and decay filled the house; it was cold, inside, and dark. The door swung to behind us but did not close and we went up a staircase of worm-eaten oak, I first, she after and then the dog, whose claws clattered on the bare wood.

At first I thought the spiders had cast their nets on both sides of the stair but then I saw the workmanship that wound down the inner side of the staircase was not that of the spiders for, though it was the same colour, this web had a determinate pattern that resembled nothing so much as open-work knitting, the kind of featherlike, floating stuff from which they make courtesans' bedjackets. This knitting was part of an interminable muffler that, as I watched it, crept, with vegetable slowness, little by little downstairs towards the hall. Yard upon yard of the muffler was coiled up in airy folds on the landing and there I could hear the clack, clack, clack of a pair of knitting needles ticking away monotonously near at hand. The muffler came out of a door that, like the front door, stood a little open; it edged through the gap like a tenuous serpent.

My captress motioned me aside with the muzzle of her rifle and knocked firmly on the door.

Inside the room, someone coughed dryly, then invited us: 'Come in.' It was a soft, rustling, unemphatic, almost uninflected, faded, faintly perfumed voice, like very old lace handkerchiefs put away long ago in a drawer with potpourri and forgotten.

My captress thrust me through the door before her; when I was close to her, my nostrils quivered at the vicious odour of her skin. It was a large room, part drawing room, part bedroom, for the being who lived in it was crippled. She, he, it – whoever, whatever my host or hostess may have been – lay in an old-fashioned wicker Bath chair beside a cracked marble fireplace bossed with swags and cupids. Her white hands finished in fingers indecently long, white and translucent as candles on a cathedral altar; those tapering fingers were the source of the bewildering muffler, for they held two bone needles and never ceased to move.

The volatile stitchery they produced occupied all the carpetless area of the floor and, in places, was piled up as high as the crippled knees of its maker. There were yards and yards of it in the room, perhaps even miles and miles of it, and I stepped through and across it very carefully, nudging it out of the way with my toes, to arrive where the girl directed me with her gun, in the position of a suppliant before the Bath chair. The crippled being who lay in it had the most regal cast of chin and mouth imaginable and the proud, sad air of the king of a rainy country. One of her profiles was that of a beautiful woman, the other that of a beautiful man. It is a defect in our language there is no term of reference for these indeterminate and undefinable beings; but, although she acknowledged no gender, I will call her 'she' because she had put on a female garment, a loose negligee of spider-coloured lace, unless she, like the spiders, spun and wove her own thread and so had become clothed, for her shadowy hair was also the colour of the stuff she knitted and so evanescent in texture it seemed to move of its own accord on the air around her. Her eyelids and the cavernous sockets of her eyes were thickly stuck with silver sequins that glittered in the strange, subaqueous, drowned, drowning light that suffused the room, a light filtered through windows caked with grime and half covered by creeper, clairvoyant light reflected, with an enhanced strangeness, by the immense mirror in a chipped gilt frame hanging on the wall opposite the fireplace; it seemed the mirror, like the moon, was itself endowed with the light it gave back to us.

With a touching fidelity, the mirror duplicated the room and all it contained, the fireplace, the walls covered with a stained white paper

stippled with fronds of greenery, every piece of neglected ormolu
furniture. How pleased I was to see my experiences had not changed
me! though my old tweed suit was stained with grass, my stick gone –
left behind where I had dropped it in the wood. And so much dirt on
my face. But I looked as if I were reflected in a forest pool rather than by
silvered glass for the surface of the mirror looked like the surface of
motionless water, or of mercury, as though it were a solid mass of
liquid kept in place by some inversion of gravity that reminded me of
the ghastly weight of the shell that now dropped at the androgyne's feet
from the dog's mouth. She never stopped knitting for one moment as
she nudged it with a beautiful toe painted with a rime of silver; woe
gave her a purely female face.

'Only one little stitch! And I only dropped one little stitch!' she
mourned. And she bowed her head over her work in an ecstasy of
regret.

'At least it wasn't out long,' said the girl. Her voice had a clanging
resonance; mercy was a minor key that would never modify its martial
music. 'He found it!'

She gestured towards me with her gun. The androgyne directed upon
me a pair of vague, too large, stagnant eyes that did not shine.

'Do you know where this shell comes from?' she asked me with a
grave courtesy.

I shook my head.

'It comes from the Sea of Fertility. Do you know where *that* is?'

'On the surface of the moon,' I answered. My voice sounded coarse
and rough to me.

'Ah,' she said, 'the moon, the source of polarised light. Yes and no to
your reply. It is an equivalence. The Sea of Fertility is a reversed system,
since everything there is as dead as this shell.'

'He found it in the wood,' said the girl.

'Put it back where it belongs, Anna,' said the androgyne, who
possessed a frail yet absolute air of authority. 'Before any harm is done.'

The girl bent and picked up the shell. She scrutinised the mirror and
took aim at some spot within it that seemed to her a logical target for the
shell. I saw her raise her arm to throw the shell into the mirror and I saw
her mirrored arm raise the shell to throw it outside the mirror. Then she
threw the duplicated shell. There was no sound in the room but the click
of the knitting needles when she threw the shell into the mirror while
her reflection threw the shell out of the mirror. The shell, when it met
its own reflection, disappeared immediately.

The androgyne sighed with satisfaction.

'The name of my niece is Anna,' she said to me, 'because she can go both ways. As, indeed, I can myself, though I am not a simple palindrome.'

She gave me an enigmatic smile and moved her shoulders so that the lace negligee she wore fell back from her soft, pale breasts that were, each one, tipped by nipples of deep, dark pink, with the whorled crenellations of raspberries, and then she shifted her loins a little to display, savage and barbaric in their rude, red-purple repose, the phallic insignia of maleness.

'She can,' said Anna, 'go both ways, although she cannot move at all. So her power is an exact equivalent of her impotence, since both are absolute.'

But her aunt looked down at her soft weapon and said gently: 'Not, my darling, *absolutely* absolute. Potency, impotence *in potentia*, hence relative. Only the intermediary, since indeterminate.'

With that, she caressed her naked breasts with a stunted gesture of her forearms; she could not move her arms freely because she did not stop knitting. They looked at one another and laughed. Their laughter drove icicles of fear into my brain and I did not know which way to turn.

'You see, we must do away with you,' said the androgyne. 'You know too much.'

Panic broke over me like a wave. I plunged across the room towards the door, careless of Anna's gun in my attempted flight. But my feet were snared by the knitting and once again I plunged downwards but this time my fall half stunned me. I lay dazed while their renewed laughter darted cruelly about the room.

'Oh,' said Anna, 'but we shan't kill you. We shall send you through the mirror. We shall send you where the shell went, since that is where you belong, now.'

'But the shell vanished,' I said.

'No,' replied the androgyne. 'It did not vanish in reality. That shell had no business in this world. I dropped a stitch, this morning; only one little stitch . . . and that confounded shell slipped through the hole the dropped stitch made, because those shells are all so very, very heavy, you see. When it met its reflection, it returned to its proper place. It cannot come back, now; and neither will you, after we have sent you through the mirror.'

Her voice was so very gentle, yet she offered me a perpetual estrangement. I let out a cry. Anna turned to her aunt and placed her hand on her genitalia, so that the cock sprang up. It was of redoubtable size.

'Oh, Auntie, don't scare him!' she said.

Then they tittered, the weird harpies, so that I was quite beside myself with fear and bewilderment.

'It is a system of equivalences,' said the androgyne. 'She carries the gun, you see; and I, too.'

She displayed her towering erection with the air of a demonstrator in a laboratory.

'In my intermediary and cohesive logic, the equivalences reside beyond symbolism. The gun and the phallus are similar in their connection with life – that is, one gives it; and the other takes it away, so that both, in essence, are similar in that the negation freshly states the affirmed proposition.'

I was more bewildered than ever.

'But do all the men in the mirror world have guns between their thighs?'

Anna exclaimed with irritation at my simplicity.

'That's no more likely than that I could impregnate you with this – ' she said, pointing her gun at me, 'here or in any other world.'

'Embrace yourself in the mirror,' said the androgyne, knitting, knitting, knitting away. 'You must go, now. Now!'

Anna maintained her menace; there was nothing for it but to do as they bid. I went to the mirror and examined myself in its depths. A faint ripple ran over its surface; but when I touched it with my fingers, the surface was just as smooth and hard as it should have been. I saw that my reflection was cut off at the thighs by the gilt frame and Anna said: 'Climb on a stool! Who'd want you truncated, here or there?'

She grinned in an appalling fashion and slipped back the safety catch on her rifle. So I pulled a little, cane-seated, gilt-backed chair to the mirror and clambered up. I gazed at myself in the mirror; there I was, complete from head to toe, and there they were, behind me, the androgyne weaving her ethereal coils and the armed young girl, who, now that she could kill me with one little flick of her finger, looked as beautiful as a Roman soldier plundering a North African city, with her unkind eyes and her perfume of murder.

'Kiss yourself,' commanded the androgyne in a swooning voice. 'Kiss yourself in the mirror, the symbolic matrix of this and that, hither and thither, outside and inside.'

Then I saw, even if I could no longer be astonished, that though she knitted in both the room and the mirror, there was, within the room, no ball of wool at all; her yarn emanated from inside the mirror and the ball of wool existed only in the medium of reflection. But I did not have time to wonder at this marvel for the rank stench of Anna's excitement filled the room and her hand trembled. Out of rage and desperation, I advanced my own lips to meet the familiar yet unknown lips that advanced towards mine in the silent world of the glass.

I thought these lips would be cold and lifeless; that I would touch them but they could not touch me. Yet, when the twinned lips met, they cleaved, for these mirrored lips of mine were warm and throbbed. This mouth was wet and contained a tongue, and teeth. It was too much for me. The profound sensuality of this unexpected caress crisped the roots of my sex and my eyes involuntarily closed whilst my arms clasped my own tweed shoulders. The pleasure of the embrace was intense; I swooned beneath it.

When my eyes opened, I had become my own reflection. I had passed through the mirror and now I stood on a little, cane-seated, gilt-backed chair with my mouth pressed to an impervious surface of glass I had misted with my own breath and moistened with my own saliva.

Anna cried: 'Hurrah!' She dropped her rifle and clapped her hands while her aunt, continuing, all the time, to knit, gave me a peculiarly sultry smile.

'So,' she said. 'Welcome. This room is the half-way house between here and there, between this and that, because, you understand, I am so ambiguous. Stay in the field of force of the mirror for a while, until you are used to everything.'

The first thing that struck me was, the light was black. My eyes took a little time to grow accustomed to this absolute darkness for, though the delicate apparatus of cornea and aqueous humour and crystalline lens and vitreous body and optic nerve and retina had all been reversed when I gave birth to my mirror self through the mediation of the looking-glass, yet my sensibility remained as it had been. So at first, through the glass, I saw darkly and all was confusion but for their faces, which were irradiated by familiarity. But, when the inside of my head could process the information my topsy-turvy senses retrieved for me, then my other or anti-eyes apprehended a world of phosphorescent colour etched as with needles of variegated fire on a dimensionless opacity. The world was the same; yet absolutely altered. How can I describe it . . . almost as if this room was the colour negative of the other room. Unless – for how could I ever be certain which was the primary world and which the secondary – the other room, the other house, the other wood that I saw, transposed yet still peeping through the window in the other mirror – all that had been the colour negative of the room in which I now stood, where the exhalations of my breath were the same as the inhalations of my mirror anti-twin who turned away from me as I turned away from him, into the distorted, or else really real, world of this room beyond the mirror, reflected all of this room's ambiguities and was no longer the room I had left. That endless muffler or web wound round the room, still, but now it wound round contrariwise and Anna's aunt was knitting from left to right, instead of from right to left, with hands that, I realised, had they wished, could have pulled a right-hand glove over the left hand and vice versa, since she was truly ambidexterous.

But when I looked at Anna, I saw she was exactly the same as she had been on the other side of the mirror and knew her face for one of those rare faces that possess an absolute symmetry, each feature the exact equivalent of the other, so one of her profiles could serve as the template for both. Her skull was like a proposition in geometry. Irreducible as stone, finite as a syllogism, she was always indistinguishable from herself whichever way she went.

But the imperturbably knitting androgyne had turned its face contrariwise. One half of its face was always masculine and the other, no matter what, was feminine; yet these had been changed about, so that all the balances of the planes of the face and the lines of the brow were the opposite of what they had been before, although one half of the face was still feminine and the other masculine. Nevertheless, the quality of the difference made it seem that this altered yet similar face was the combination of the reflection of the female side of the face and the masculine side of the face that *did not appear* in the face I had seen beyond the mirror; the effect was as of the reflection of a reflection, like an example of perpetual regression, the perfect, self-sufficient nirvana of the hermaphrodite. She was Tiresias, capable of prophetic projection, whichever side of the mirror she chose to offer herself to my sight upon; and she went on knitting and knitting and knitting, with an infernal suburban complacency.

When I turned from the mirror, Anna was holding out her right or left hand towards me but, although I felt sure I was walking towards her and lifted up my legs and set them down again with the utmost determination, Anna receded further and further away from me. Niece and aunt emitted a titter and I guessed that, in order to come to Anna, I must go away from her. Therefore I stepped sturdily backwards and, in less than a second, her hard, thin, sunburned hand grasped mine.

The touch of her hand filled me with a wild loneliness.

With her other hand, she opened the door. I was terribly afraid of that door, for the room that contained the mirror was all that I knew, and therefore my only safety, in this unknown world that Anna, who now smiled inscrutably at me, negotiated as skilfully as if she herself, the solstice in person, went on curious hinges between this place and that place unlike her aunt, who, since she was crippled, could not move unless her condition of permanent stasis meant she was moving too fast for me to see, with a speed the inertia of the eye registered as immobility.

But, when the door creaked open on everyday, iron hinges that had never been oiled in this world or any other world, I saw only the staircase up which Anna had led me, down which she would now lead me, and the muffler that still curled down to the hall. The air was dank, just as it had been. Only, all the alignments of the stairwell had been subtly altered and the light was composed of a reversed spectrum.

The webs of the spiders presented structures of white fire so minutely altered from those I had passed on my way upstairs that only memory made me apprehend how their geometrical engineering had all been executed backwards. So we passed under the spectral arch they had prepared for us and out into the open air that did not refresh my bewildered brain, for it was as solid as water, dense and compact, of an impermeable substance that transmitted neither sound nor odour. To move through this liquid silence demanded the utmost exertion of physical energy and intellectual concentration, for gravity, beyond the mirror, was not a property of the ground but of the atmosphere. Then Anna, who understood the physical laws of this world, exerted a negative pressure upon me by some willed absence of impulse and to my amazement I now moved as if propelled sharply from behind along the path to the gate, past flowers that distilled inexpressible colours from the black sky above us, colours whose names only exist in an inverted language you could never understand if I were to speak it. But the colours were virtually independent of the forms of the plants. Haloes of incandescence, they had arbitrarily settled about spread umbrellas of petals as thin yet as hard as the shoulder blade of a rabbit, for the flesh of the flowers was calcified and lifeless; no plant was sentient in this coral garden. All had suffered a dead sea-change.

And the black sky possessed no dimension of distance, nor gave none; it did not arch above us but looked as if it were pasted behind the flat outlines of the half ruinous house that now lay behind us, a shipwreck bearing a marvellous freight, the female man or virile woman clicking away at her needles in a visible silence. A visible silence, yes; for the dense fluidity of the atmosphere did not transmit sound to me as sound, but, instead, as irregular kinetic abstractions etched upon its interior, so that, once in the new wood, a sinister, mineral realm of undiminishable darkness, to listen to the blackbird was to watch a moving point inside a block of deliquescent glass. I saw these sounds because my eyes took in a different light than the light that shone on my breast when my heart beat on the other side of it, although the wood through whose now lateral gravity Anna negotiated me was the same wood in which I had been walking when I first heard her sing. And I cannot tell you, since there is no language in this world to do so, how strange the antithetical wood and sweet June day were, for both had become the systematic negation of its others.

Anna, in some reversed fashion, must still have been menacing me with her gun, since it was her impulse that moved me; on we went, just as we had come – but Anna, now, went before me, with the muzzle of her gun pressed in the belly of nothingness, and the dog, her familiar, this time in the van. And this dog was white as snow and its balls were gone; on this side of the mirror, all dogs were bitches and vice versa.

I saw wild garlic and ground elder and the buttercups and daisies in the fossilised undergrowth now rendered in vivacious yet unnamable colours, as immobile arabesques without depth. But the sweetness of the wild roses rang in my ears like a peal of windbells for the vibrations of the perfumes echoed on my eardrums like the pulse of my own blood since, though they had become a kind of sound, they could not carry in the same way that sound did. I could not, for the life of me, make up my mind which world was which for I understood this world was coexistent in time and space with the other wood – was, as it were, the polarisation of that other wood, although it was in no way similar to the reflection the other wood, or this wood, might have made in a mirror.

The more my eyes grew accustomed to the dark, the less in common did the petrified flora seem to have with anything I knew. I perceived all had been starkly invaded with, yes, shells, enormous shells, giant and uninhabited shells, so we might have been walking in the ruins of a marine city; the cool, pale colouring of those huge shells now glowed with a ghostly otherness and they were piled and heaped upon one another to parody the landscape of the woodland, unless the trees parodied them; all were whorled the wrong way round, all had that deathly weight, the supernatural resonance of the shell which seduced me and Anna told me in a soundless language I understood immediately that the transfigured wood, fertile now, only of metamorphoses, was – for how could it be anything else – the Sea of Fertility. The odour of her violence deafened me.

Then, once again, she began to sing; I saw the mute, dark, fire burning like Valhalla in *Götterdämmerung*. She sang a funeral pyre, the swan's song, death itself, and, with a brusque motion of her gun, she forced me forward on my knees while the dog stood over me as she tore open my clothes. The serenade smouldered all around us and I was so much at the mercy of the weight of the air, which pressed down on me like a coffin lid, and of the viscosity of the atmosphere, that I could do nothing to defend myself, even if I had known how, and soon she had me, poor, forked thing, stretched out upon a bank of shells with my trousers round my knees. She smiled but I could not tell what the smile meant; on this side of the mirror, a smile was no clue whatsoever to intention or to feeling and I did not think she meant to do me a good deed as she unbuckled her uncouth leather belt and stepped out of her jeans.

Parting the air with the knives of her arms, she precipitated herself upon me like a quoit on a peg. I screamed; the notes of my scream rose upon the air like ping-pong balls on a jet of water at a funfair. She raped me; perhaps her gun, in this system, gave her the power to do so.

I shouted and swore but the shell grotto in which she ravished me did not reverberate and I only emitted gobs of light. Her rape, her violation of me, caused me atrocious physical and mental pain. My being leaked away from me under the visitation of her aggressive flesh. My self grew less in agony under the piston thrust of her slender loins, as if she were a hammer and were forging me into some other substance than flesh and spirit. I knew the dreadful pleasure of abandonment; she had lit my funeral pyre and now would kill me. I felt such outrage I beat in the air behind my head with my helpless fists as she pumped away indefatigably at my sex, and to my surprise, I saw her face cloud and bruises appear on it, although my hands were nowhere near her. She was a brave girl; she only fucked the harder, for she was intransigent and now resembled the Seljuk Turks sacking Constantinople. I knew there was no hope for me if I did not act immediately.

Her gun lay propped against the shells beside us. I reached the other way and seized it. I shot at the black sky while she straddled me. The bullet pierced a neat, round, empty hole in the flat vault of the heavens but no light, no sound, leaked through; I had made a hole without quality but Anna let out a ripping shriek that sent a jagged scar across the surface of the wood. She tumbled backwards and twitched a little. The dog growled at me, a terrible sight, and leaped at my throat but I quickly shot her, also, in this negative way and, now free, there remained only the problem of the return to the mirror, the return to the right-hand side of the world. But I kept tight hold of the gun, by grasping it loosely, because of the guardian of the mirror.

To return to the house, I struck out from the shell grotto where Anna lay, in the opposite direction from the one we had come from. I must have fallen into a mirror elision of reflected time, or else I stumbled upon a physical law I could not have guessed at, for the wood dissolved, as if the blood that leaked from Anna's wound was a solvent for its petrified substance, and now I found myself back at the crumbling gate before her juices were dry on my cock. I paused to do up my flies before I made my way to the door; I used my arms like scissors to snip through the thickness of the atmosphere, for it grew, moment by moment, less liquid and more impalpable. I did not ring the bell, so great was my outrage, so vivid my sense of having been the plaything of these mythic and monstrous beings.

The knitting curled down the stairs, just as I expected, and, in another moment, I saw, on a staccato stave, the sound of the needles.

She, he, it, Tiresias, though she knitted on remorselessly, was keening over a whole dropped row of stitches, trying to repair the damage as best she could. Her keening filled the room with a Walpurgisnacht of crazy shapes and, when she saw I was alone, she flung back her head and howled. In that decompression chamber between here and there, I heard a voice as clear as crystal describe a wordless song of accusation.

'Oh, my Anna, what have you done with my Anna – ?'

'I shot her,' I cried. 'With her own weapon.'

'A rape! She's raped!' screamed the androgyne as I dragged the gilt chair to the mirror and clambered up on it. In the silvered depths before me, I saw the new face of a murderer I had put on behind the mirror.

The androgyne, still knitting, kicked with her bare heels upon the floor to drive her Bath chair over the wreathing muffler towards me, in order to attack me. The Bath chair cannoned into the chair on which I stood and she rose up in it as far as she could and began to beat me with her tender fists. But, because she did not stop knitting, she offered no resistance when I brought my ham-hand crashing down on her working face. I broke her nose; bright blood sprang out. I turned to the mirror as she screamed and dropped her knitting.

She dropped her knitting as I crashed through the glass
    through the glass, glass splintered round me driving
        unmercifully into my face
        through the glass, glass splintered
            through the glass –
                half through
Then the glass gathered itself together like a skilful whore and expelled me. The glass rejected me; it sealed itself again into nothing but mysterious, reflective opacity. It became a mirror and it was impregnable.

Balked, I stumbled back. In Tiresias' bed-sitting room, there was the most profound silence, and nothing moved; the flow of time might have stopped. Tiresias held her empty hands to her face that was now irretrievably changed; each one snapped clean in two, her knitting needles lay on the floor. Then she sobbed and flung out her arms in a wild, helpless gesture. Blood and tears splashed down on her robe, but in a baleful, hopeless way she began to laugh, although time must have started again and now moved with such destructive speed that, before my eyes, that ageless being withered – a quick frost touched her. Wrinkles sprang out on her pale forehead while her hair fell from her head in great armfuls and her negligee turned brown and crumbled away, to reveal all the flesh that sagged from the bone as I watched it. She was the ruins of time. She grasped her throat and choked. Perhaps she was dying. The muffler was blowing away like dead leaves in a wind that sprang up from nowhere and raced through the room, although the windows stayed shut tight. But Tiresias spoke to me; she spoke to me once again.

'The umbilical cord is cut,' she said. 'The thread is broken. Did you not realise who I was? That I was the synthesis in person? For I could go any way the world goes and so I was knitting the thesis and the antithesis together, this world and that world. Over the leaves and under the leaves. Cohesion gone. Ah!'

Down she tumbled, the bald old crone, upon a pile of wisps of unravelled grey wool as the ormolu furniture split apart and the paper unfurled from the wall. But I was arrogant; I was undefeated. Had I not killed her? Proud as a man, I once again advanced to meet my image in the mirror. Full of self-confidence, I held out my hands to embrace my self, my antiself, my self not-self, my assassin, my death, the world's death.

Elegy for a Freelance

I remember you as clearly as if you'd died yesterday, though I don't remember you often – usually I'm far too busy. But I told the commissar about you, once. I asked him if I'd done the right thing; would he have done the same? But he said, if I wanted absolution, that he was the last person to ask for it, and, besides, everything is changed now, and we are not the same.

I remember that I was living high up in an attic, in a house in a square. Most of the windows in the other houses round the square were boarded up and planks were nailed across the doors but they were not uninhabited. Although all these houses were waiting to be pulled down, they contained a handful of small, scarcely licit households whose members crept in and out through secret entries, lived by candlelight, slept upon the filthy mattresses the dossers who lived there before them had used and ate stews made from vegetables picked out of the greengrocers' garbage cans and butchers' bones begged for dogs that did not exist.

But our landlord – it was legal to own private property, to rent it out, in those days – refused to sell his house to the speculators who wanted to pull the entire terrace down. He'd spent the Blitz in his house; it was his foxhole. He pulled the carious walls up snug around his ears and felt himself enveloped in a safety that, although it was fictive, he believed in completely. He rented his rooms out at old-fashioned rents because he did not know that times had changed; how could he? He never left home. He was confined to a chair and almost blind. His room was his world, his house the unknown universe he knew of but never ventured into. Everything else was unknowable. He did not even know that the boys who lived in the basement filled milk bottles with petrol in their back room and made explosions.

A girl lived with them in the basement. She was fifteen. Her face was pale, mild and plump and always seemed a little surprised that she found herself stumbling under the weight of a pregnancy that had stunned her. She hardly ever spoke and moved with the heaviness of somebody moving under water. You kept a rifle in our room and loved to sit and scan the square and the street below us from the open window.

A young man and a girl came to do yoga in the square every morning.

They adopted the tree position. A child on the swings swung more and more idly; he twisted round to watch them. They always had the same audience, the child in the playground and the apprentice sniper. They unfurled their right legs from the hip and reefed them in at the knee in order to place the soles of their bare right feet against the inner sides of their upper left thighs. They joined their hands together as if in prayer and then raised their joined hands above their heads. In order to keep their balance, they fixed their eyes on the worn grass in front of them with the utmost concentration. They maintained this position for an entire minute – I watched the hand on my watch move – and then they returned their right feet to the ground as they lowered their hands and arms and now raised their left legs in order to repeat the exercise. When it was over, they decorously stood on their heads. They were rapt with devotion.

X watched them through the sights of his rifle while they went through the entire repertory of movements. I was scared out of my wits when he slipped back the safety catch and did not dare to say anything. I knew the couple below by sight. They squatted in a house on the other side of the square. They were harmless as the pigeons who lived on the roof. When they had finished, they went away again. X replaced the safety catch and laughed. I was very frightened of him in his feral moods but he told me an authentic assassin ought to be as indifferent as the weather and, when he scanned the square, all he was doing was practising indifference.

I went into his world when I fell in love with him and felt only a sense of privilege in its isolation. We had purposely exiled ourselves from the course of everyday events and were proud to live in parentheses. I went out for a little air at night, sometimes, when the streets were flooded with the ghastly yellow light that bleaches the blood that runs out of road accidents so that it doesn't look real. I used to walk through the streets for miles and I would clap my hands with childlike pleasure, I would enthusiastically applaud the detonating termini.

It hardly seemed possible the city could survive the summer. The sky opened like the clockwork Easter eggs the Tsars gave one another. The night would part, like two halves of a dark shell, and spill explosions. Because I lived in a house full of amateur terrorists, I felt I myself lit the fuses and caused these displays of pyrotechnics. Then I would feel almost omnipotent, just as X did, when he sat with his rifle above the square at the window of my room.

I was living high up in an attic. I hung over the summer in my attic as though it were the gondola of a balloon. London lay below me with her legs wide open; she was a whore sufficiently accommodating to find room for us in her embraces, even though she cost so much to love.

She is so old she ought to be superannuated, you said, the old cow. She paints so thickly over the stratified residue of yesterday and the day before yesterday and the day before the day before's cosmetics you can hardly make out the wens and blemishes under all the layers of paint, graffiti and old posters – voluptuous, oppressive, corrupt, self-regarding London marinating in the syrup of her own decay like *baba au rhum*, while the property speculators burrow away at her guts with the vile diligence of gonococci.

A feverish, hysterical glamour played over this wasting city like summer lights. While I watched it, the city changed shape. Towers of steel and glass thrust their way through the soft, soiled velvet rind of the rotting fruit. Nobody lived in these towers; how could anybody live there – like the architecture of the Third Reich, they looked as if they were intended to be most beautiful in ruins. Amongst this architecture of desolation, haunting the rat-infested rubble, mendicants and proselytisers rang bells and rattled tambourines as they offered to the passer-by a bewildering variety of salvations. Those in saffron robes who had shaved their heads invoked the gods of the Indian subcontinent though our neighbours told us we ought to trust in Jesus. But *our* salvation would be gelignite; the basement of the house in which I lived had become a little arsenal. Any wise child can get a hand grenade together; it was the time of the Children's Crusade.

It was a strange, suspended time. The city had never looked more beautiful but I did not know, then, that it seemed to me beautiful only because it was doomed and I was the innocent slave of bourgeois aesthetics, that always sees an elegiac charm in decay. I remember velvet nights spiked with menace and the beautiful showers of sparks when an amateur incendiarist ignited a police station. My house was always full of the shimmering sound of the trees in the square moving in the wind, so that it seemed the sea was rushing through the corridors, the rooms.

I was living on the fourth floor although I had such vertigo that the sight of an abyss, however insignificant, excited in me, almost intolerably, the desire to plunge. I was quite helpless before the attraction of gravity. I was overwhelmed. I became powerless. Therefore to live on the fourth floor meant-that every day began with a small triumph of will over instinct. I wanted to jump; but I must not jump. Pallor, shallow breathing, a prickle of cold sweat – I exhibited all the symptoms of panic, as I did when I met X. *That* was like finding myself on the edge of an abyss but the vertigo that I felt then came from a sense of recognition. This abyss was that of my own emptiness; I plunged instantly, for my innocence was so perfect that I saw in this submission the height of sophistication.

It was as lovely a summer as those that precede wars. The West Indian lady who ran the neighbourhood launderette always wore a small felt hat with a veil, as if she were determined to keep up the appearances even in the most extreme circumstances. She pushed the dirt around the floor with a sodden mop and, when her tasks were finished, she would sit on a chair and read her well-thumbed Bible aloud to herself in that ineffable, querulous lilt, like the voice of a reproachful bird. Sometimes she would exclaim over the things she found in the book; when I looked over her shoulder, once, while she was crying: HOSANNA I saw she was reading the Apocalypse.

The squatters consecrated the house next door. All night long, while we fixed up our explosive devices in the basement, they chanted: BABY JESUS, BABY JESUS, BABY JESUS.

I would not have believed Lenin was right when he said there was no place for orgy in the revolution, even if I had read Lenin. What we were about in bed seemed to be activity that could in itself overturn the world. X's lycanthropic eyes glowed in the dark like fuses. I found most pleasure of all in the delicious dread that seized me when he clung too close. I wanted to be the Madonna of the Barricades; I would have shot anybody you told me to but only if they did not get hurt. I felt I needed to understand nothing beyond my own sensations. I felt, as primitives do, that ceremonials such as the ones we made could revivify dead earth. Your kisses along my arms were like tracer bullets. I am lost. I flow. Your flesh defines me. I become your creation. I am your fleshly reflection.

('Libido and false consciousness characterised sexual relations during the last crisis of Capital,' says the commissar.)

A man constructs his own fate out of his sense of the world. You engaged in conspiracies because you believed the humblest objects were engaged in a conspiracy against you. Your conviction was contagious; it impressed me. 'Even the strawberries smell of blood, this summer,' you remarked with anticipatory relish. I found you more and more often at the window, practising indifference.

You described the state of permanent revolution to me. It sounded like a series of beautiful explosions. Volcano after volcano would erupt under their own internal stresses in an endless reduplication of ecstasy. When the bed creaked beneath us, it sounded like the *Liebestod* from *Tristan and Isolde* performed with vehemence by a military band. The grand design of glorious convulsions you depicted was so beautiful I wept; but we would begin, you said, in small ways, we would begin with a single shooting. You made assassination sound as enticing as pornography. A, B and C were suspicious of me since you abandoned the basement for my bed. Now we were all gripped in the same obsession, they treated me more politely. *Folie à deux, à trois, à quatre*. We were living on the crater of a

volcano and felt the earth move beneath us. What stirring times! What
seismographic times!

('The bourgeoisie turned politics into an aspect of romanticism,' says
the commissar. 'If it was only an art form, how could it threaten them?')
The city unravelled like knitting as the transport workers' strikes
imposed vast distances between its various sections but we never went
beyond walking distance of our house so the strikes did not affect us.

Our house was tall and narrow. Worn steps led down to the area. Our
landlord lived in the front room on the ground floor. He crouched in
front of his television set making what sense he could out of the random
flickering that was all his eyes registered, poor old thing, with his stick
and his cats. He had a sink and a gas ring and a little cupboard where he
kept his cats' fish. He boiled up their dinners twice a week and stored their
food in a plastic washing-up bowl when it was cooked. The house stank
of stale fish; we had to burn incense all the time to cancel out the smell. He
spread his table with clean newspapers and set out the fish for his cats in
separate saucers. They all jumped up to eat. There was a soup plate full of
water which although it was refreshed each day, always managed to
drown a fly or two by lunchtime, and a saucer of milk that had turned into
junket by the six o'clock news. His three-legged chairs were balanced on
piles of old newspapers and upholstered with cast-off garments. Cats of
all colours sat upon the sideboard amongst the empty brown ale bottles,
the open cans of condensed milk, the stopped clock, the yellowing
circulars, the football coupons, the curded milk bottles, the plaster
Alsatian dog with one ear chipped. There he sat, a king of his kingdom,
thumping upon the floor when the conspirators in the basement went
bang! by accident.

Once a week, in turn, we visited him to pay our rents for we were
determined to be scrupulous and, if you must have a landlord at all, it's
best if he's purblind. It was like paying tribute to a holy statue. Age had
drawn his yellow, freckled skin so tight across his skull his head shone
like polished bone and his eyes had faded to the innocent blue of baby
ribbon – wandering, rheumy eyes, gummed at the corners. His bony
fingers clutched the handle of his stick with a certain balked ferocity.

He was afraid of us, I suppose, and so he pretended to be fierce. In the
pub, they said he kept roll upon roll of banknotes stored in Old Holborn
tins tucked away here and there amongst the clutter. He ingested his rents
like a sponge but he suspected nothing although the cats did and threshed
their tails when we went into his room. Sometimes they spat. The ginger
one once scratched you.

A middle-aged transvestite lived on the first floor but he was too
immersed in his aberration to pay us much attention. He ventured out for

little walks around the square in the dusk that tenderly veiled his
eccentricity, tottering on his five-inch heels, spiking the ground before
him in the manner of a climber with the point of his long, furled
umbrella. He wore a black gaberdine two-piece with a pencil skirt for
these expeditions and slung a fox-fur round his neck. The mask hung
over his left shoulder and kept a good lookout behind with its little beady
eyes. Above him, a slack-witted unmarried mother pigged it with her
brood. She did the old man's shopping for him, when she remembered,
but he only wanted the fish, twice a week, a can or two of beans and the
occasional bottle of brown ale.

A perpetual twilight dominated that house, with its characteristic
odours of stale cooking, phantom bacon, lavatories and the cats who
pissed in the hall. The bulbs on the stairways were always blown. It was
an old, dark house; it was a cave. We saw visions on the walls. It was a
slum. It was a citadel. That was the time of the freelance assassins; our cell
was self-sufficient and took no orders nor cognisance of any other cell in
the cancerous growth of the deathwardly inclining city. You had the
plausibility of a Nechaev; a plot a murder became your sole pre-
occupation.

You arbitrarily selected a member of the cabinet. We consulted the
I Ching, we threw the coins. The oracle seemed to be propitious,
although, as always, its tone was guarded. We drew lots. Inexorably, the
marked card found you. In the full consciousness of a young man about to
become an assassin, you made love to me like the storming of the Bastille.
But then I found you'd somewhere encountered an obstacle to indifference for now you were crying, though, when I asked why you were
crying, you hit me.

Our neighbours were chanting so loudly they might have been
chanting in the same room and I had no curtains at the window so the
glaring, yellow light balefully illuminated your unhappy face, but I was
too much under your spell to guess why you were crying. Hadn't
everything been decided? Tomorrow we would go and murder the
politician. I would ring the doorbell and then you would fire the gun. I
could not understand why you were crying, you had so successfully
impressed me with the model simplicity of the plan, so that I was sure we
were in the right. I went to sleep again, sulking because I had been hit.
The monotonous, droning chant – BABY JESUS, BABY JESUS, BABY JESUS –
lulled me to sleep.

What an awakening! – there was so much blood on your shirt. You
spilled the banknotes over me. They were in tight little blue rolls that
bounced off my body, unfurling as they fell to the floor. Such a lot of
money! I blinked in the violet dawn, astounded at the extravagance of

your hysteria. You sobbed and babbled and hurled the furniture to the ground, smashed cups, overturned the wastepaper basket. I made you tea and slyly stoked up the mug with sleeping pills. I choked it down you and got you into the bed I had vacated for I could never lie in the same bed with you, now. I stayed with you until I was certain you were sleeping and locked the door behind you.

A, B and C had finished the night's work and were frying eggs and bread on their gas ring. A's girl lay on the mattress under her belly which was the size and shape of a dirigible, round enough, big enough to rise up into the air and carry her away with it from this vale of tears, over the rainbow, to a happy land far, far away. I told them what you had said to me, that you killed him for practice. We had intended to be such philosophic assassins! But what were your existential credentials when you murdered the landlord? Was it the dress rehearsal for an assassination or the audition of an assassin?

The old man lay on the floor in his rank pyjamas. His debilitated, senescent tool dangled out of his yellowed fly. The cats milled about him, mewing ravenously. There was blood on their whiskers and on their inquisitive paws. X had smashed in the old man's skull and he'd tumbled off the bed in his death agony. In spite of his age and weakness, he had put up a struggle; we could see the signs of it all over the room. The bedclothes were disordered and his little night-table had been knocked over. The chamber-pot it contained had fallen out on its side, spilling its contents on the floor. Then X must have gone through every cupboard and drawer in the room to find the fabled tobacco tins of money. We looked at the evidence in silence though all the time the neighbours went on wailing very loudly. We could hear them downstairs, even here, on the ground floor. The cats pressed against us, yowling, and I thought I had better feed the cats because I did not want them to practise necrophagy upon the landlord. I opened the food cupboard and took out their fish. I spread the table and laid out their meal as if nothing had happened. They all jumped up and tucked in, purring as they swallowed their dinners.

We had not let A's girl into the room because of her condition. Now, from behind the lace curtain, we saw her, with her shawl flung carelessly round her shoulders, pursuing her burden as it stumbled away down the street. A said: 'She's broken – she's gone for the police.' I rushed out of the house and ran after her. I soon caught up with her; she was too fat to run fast. She wept. She said how much she always disliked X; that he had cold eyes. Then she fainted. A came and helped me carry her back to the basement. Shortly after that, she went into labour. The neighbours continued to chant: BABY JESUS, BABY JESUS, BABY JESUS. While I held A's girl's frightened, hot, sticky hand and A heated water, B and C took some rope, went to my attic and tied X up. They said he was too surprised to struggle when they woke him. He must have felt it was the revolt of the toys.

Then a police car drew up outside and we shrank into ourselves, we were so scared. Poor Susie moaned and tore at the mattress on which she lay. But the police had come for our neighbours. The transvestite had complained about the noise and we watched from the area steps as the police took an axe to the boards that were nailed over the front door and entered it. A little while later, they came out again, half leading, half carrying the dazed and shaking occupants, who were all as white as sheets, tranced, emaciated, their eyes staring as still they mumbled their orisons, too limp and listless to protest.

I sterilised my scissors in the gas jet and A held his wailing son in his arms after I cut the cord. But, however pleased A was to be a father, he insisted on a fair trial for X. Perhaps, even then, B and C didn't quite trust me; I'd been a rich girl. But X confessed everything to us all quite freely.

We tried him in the attic. We left Susie downstairs nursing her baby. We untied X's legs and let him sit down on a chair but we did not untie his arms. He confessed as follows; he seemed agonisingly torn between humiliation and self-justification.

'I wasn't sure, I wasn't sure of myself. I kept thinking, what if I blow it? If I blow the whole thing, hadn't been able to pull the trigger, and just stood there in the doorway staring vacantly at him. What if I can't kill when I want to kill and am in the right to kill? What if I were paralysed? What if I'd spent so long looking at people through the sights of the rifle and holding back from shooting that I could never shoot? Fear I'd be weak shook me.

'What good did the landlord do to anyone? Sitting in his room, sucking in his rents. Nobody loves him. He's significant to nobody. He's hardly alive at all, he can't talk, hardly, he's almost blind, squatting like a toad on all that money.

'I was in a frenzy, I prayed. Yes, I did. The fear I'd fail threw me into a frenzy. I prayed and the answer came. I left her sleeping and took the gun and went to his room. He didn't wake up when I went in but the cats all woke and stretched themselves and jumped off the chairs and the sideboard and the bed and came towards me, mewing; it was a tide of fur with eyes and mouths in it. He woke up when he heard the cats and began to mew, too. "Who's there, pussies, what's the matter, pussies?" I had nothing against him when I went into the room – nothing. It was only an exercise in self-control.

'But I began to hate him when I saw how helpless he was. When I saw how easy it would be to kill him, nothing to it, then I began to hate him. I raised the rifle and looked at him through the sights. The sights changed the way I saw him. Through the sights of the rifle, now I saw he was not human, not even an old wreck of humanity. He was only an object to be extinguished. He asked some menacing person he could not see if that person had come for his money. When I realised that person was I, I thought that I might just as well take his money, while I was there, since he offered it to me. But I said nothing and my hands were shaking. He told me not to kill him. That was how he reminded me I *could* kill him, if I wanted to. Up till then, I had not wanted to but when he called me his murderer, I became so. He sealed his own fate. It was his own fault, what happened.

'Next door they were chanting away like mad things. He rolled about on his filthy bed clutching his head with his hands as if his hands would protect it. His pyjamas burst open and the old flesh spilled on the sheets. I felt nauseated to see his old flesh. My fingers tightened on the trigger. The cats screamed and pressed against my legs. The ginger one scratched me. They reared up on their hind legs and snarled, I could have sworn they were attacking me. How disgusting the old bed-bug was, now he was at my mercy! But just as I was about to shoot, I thought: what a noise the gun will make. It will be much louder than the chanting, even. The noise will wake Sister Boy. Sister Boy will wake and throw his negligee around his shoulders and come and see what is the matter. The woman upstairs will wake, or her kids will wake. They'll all come down, even the four-year-old, wiping the sleep out of his eyes. I thought of a holocaust – mow them all down. But I was too self-restrained.

'I lowered the gun. He was fumbling in his little night-table, where he keeps his pisspot. The night-table rocked, he was fumbling so. Out jumped the pisspot and crashed on the ground. All the cats puffed out their fur, stuck up their backs and hissed and shrank away from me, because the crash of the pisspot startled them, but he was rummaging for his savings in the night-table and found one little tin. He shook the banknotes all over the floor, they were rolled up in the tin like curling papers, they fell in the spilled piss and the cats pounced on them and began to pat them this way and that way with their paws. He scooped up some banknotes in his fists and shoved them towards me. He said: "Take it, it's all I've got." But I knew he had lots of other old tobacco tins full of money, doesn't everybody say so? When he tried to buy me off so cheaply, I lost all mercy and bludgeoned him about the head with the butt of the rifle until he stopped moving.'

He looked at us as though he was certain we understood everything perfectly. I closed my eyes; I had the sensation of falling. Yet, when I opened my eyes, the abyss remained; I stood only upon its brink. Now my eyes were open, perception, lucidity became my new profession. At the conclusion of his story, X began to cry like a child, as though he were to be pitied, and then I felt most afraid of him, in case I began to pity him. While we watched him snivelling, we grew older. He cried like a baby and we became his parents. We must decide what would be best for him. Now I was his mother, they his father and we saw our common responsibility as his cause in the random nature of his effect.

'It must be worst for you,' A said to me, because I'd been the lover of this person; but the same terror gripped us all, for our complicity with him was over once he had acted only for himself and by himself and now we could stand apart from him and, in judging him, judge ourselves.

I will try and describe you better. I am glad you died before the barricades went up. We served our time and took our punishment upon them but I would not have liked to have you beside me with a machine-gun because you were your own hero, always your own hero, and would not have taken orders easily. But you might have made an exceptional kamikaze pilot, had you not been so scared of dying. You made us believe you were our leader; so, while you were ordering us about, how could we become a confederacy? We were in the deepest complicity with you; we admired your paranoia. While we admired it, we believed it formed an explanation of events in itself. But I was always a little afraid of you because you clung to me far too tightly and made me come with the barbarous dexterity of a huntsman eviscerating a stag.

After we heard X's confession, we gave him some water to drink and tied up his legs again before we gagged him, in case he tried to cry to Sister Boy or the unmarried mother below for help. Then we went down to the basement to discuss what we should do with him. A's girl was suckling her baby. She seemed obscurely but entirely content with her own miracle. She was angry we had locked her into the basement and said she would never leave A because he was the father of her child but I thought she said that due to the emotion generated in the generation of the baby and we should still be wary of her. A cooked her some brown rice and vegetables and added a couple of eggs, because she needed nourishment. After a great deal of discussion, B took some food to X also, but X dashed the dish to the floor. He was petulant, now, B told us; he thought we were behaving irrationally.

He had quite recovered his old self-confidence, it seemed, but we no longer retained confidence in him. We reached our decision in unison, although C – what memories of old movies! – at first wanted to lock X alone in my attic with a revolver and let him take his own way out. But our consensus convinced C that X would not have done so, had we given him the chance.

B took a coil of stout rope from the cupboard under the sink. We waited until dark; we listened desultorily to the radio and heard the army had been called in to break the car-workers' strike but we were all stricken with such dreadful gravity at the unexpected turn of events in our cell that the news did not move us. Our private situation seemed to us far more significant.

X was in a foul state since we had not untied him all day so now he rolled in his own excrement and stank. He was in a filthy temper and cursed us but, when he saw the rope, first he laughed to try to bluff his way out of the noose; and then he blubbered – there is no other word for his collapse in tears and pleadings. He seemed astonished we were capable of acting without him. A held the revolver. It wasn't far to Hampstead Heath.

We forced X along with his arms bound and the muzzle of the revolver in his back. We did not meet any others on the streets; those whom we did pass by edged away from us, they must have thought we were all drunk, and the Heath itself was empty apart from a distant bonfire that marked, probably, the camp of some homeless family. By now the moon was up; we soon found a suitable tree.

When X realised there was no hope for him, he relapsed into silence but, when I slipped the noose around his neck, he asked me if I loved him. I was surprised at that – it seemed to me so far from the point; but I replied, yes, I *had* loved him and I tested the running knot. B and C pulled the rope. Up, he went, like a flag. There was a russet-coloured moon of ominous size too low above the whispering bushes; he danced exuberantly for five minutes beneath it after the click when his neck broke. His bowels opened. What a mess!

When it hung limp, we cut his body down and threw it in the undergrowth. A vomited and B wept a little, but C and I covered it with leaves, like the robins in *Babes in the Wood*. I retained such a ferocious calm that C said to me, you are turning into a tiger lady when I always thought you were such a pussycat. I think that justice had been done, although we ourselves had been the perpetrators of both crime and punishment and we did not dig a hole to bury X because we wanted to leave a loophole in which the everyday circumstances of justice might catch up with us. We were beginning to behave with a certain dignity. Our illogic began to approach a kind of harsh virtue, although we looked at one another with veiled, estranged eyes; who were we, what were we becoming?

Was it possible we could have done what we had done; how could it have been possible we had planned what we had intended?

A's girl and the child slept quite peacefully in the basement where we made ourselves tea that did not taste any different from the tea we had drunk before we hanged him.

Now B revealed an intransigent morality. He wanted us to go to the police, make a clean breast of all and take our punishment, since we had done nothing of which we ourselves were ashamed. But A had his baby son to think of and wanted to take Susie and his child to a Welsh mountain where he had friends on a commune, there to recuperate from these excesses in the clean air. Apropos of nothing, he declared he'd never be able to look at meat again and would walk on the other side of the road when he passed a butcher's shop. He sat on the mattress by the sleeping girl and looked, every moment more and more like an ordinary husband and father. But C and I did not know what to do, now, nor what to think. We felt nothing but a lapse of feeling, a dulled heaviness, a despair.

The pure, cool light of early September touched the contents of the room with fastidious fingers; we looked at the day with mild surprise, that it should be as bright as any other day, brighter, in fact, than most. Then I felt a drop like a heavy raindrop fall on the back of my hand but it was not a raindrop, for the sun was shining, nor a drip from a leaking cistern, because the landlord's room was directly over our heads. This was a red drop. Horror! It was blood; and looking up, I saw the stain on the ceiling where the old man's blood was leaking through. Soon he would begin to smell.

We began to argue. Should we dig a hole in the backyard and bury the old man in it, pack our few things and leave the house under false names for secret destinations, as A wanted to do; or should we throw ourselves upon the law, as B thought was right? Instinct and will, again; I was poised on the windowledge of a fourth floor of a building I had never suspected existed and I did not know which was will and which was instinct that told me to jump, to run. While we were discussing these things, we heard a low rumble in the distance. We thought it was thunder but, when A turned on the radio to find out what time it was, only martial music was playing and the newsflash informed us the coup had taken place; the army was in power, as if this was not home but a banana republic. They were encountering some resistance in the north but were rapidly crushing it. All the time we had been plotting, the generals had been plotting and we had known nothing. Nothing!

The thunder grew louder; it was gun and mortar fire. The sky soon filled with helicopters. The Civil War began. History began.

THE BLOODY CHAMBER AND OTHER STORIES

The Bloody Chamber

The Courtship of Mr Lyon

The Tiger's Bride

Puss-in-Boots

The Erl-King

The Snow Child

The Lady of the House of Love

The Werewolf

The Company of Wolves

Wolf-Alice

The Bloody Chamber

I remember how, that night, I lay awake in the wagon-lit in a tender, delicious ecstasy of excitement, my burning cheek pressed against the impeccable linen of the pillow and the pounding of my heart mimicking that of the great pistons ceaselessly thrusting the train that bore me through the night, away from Paris, away from girlhood, away from the white, enclosed quietude of my mother's apartment, into the unguessable country of marriage.

And I remember I tenderly imagined how, at this very moment, my mother would be moving slowly about the narrow bedroom I had left behind for ever, folding up and putting away all my little relics, the tumbled garments I would not need any more, the scores for which there had been no room in my trunks, the concert programmes I'd abandoned; she would linger over this torn ribbon and that faded photograph with all the half-joyous, half-sorrowful emotions of a woman on her daughter's wedding day. And, in the midst of my bridal triumph, I felt a pang of loss as if, when he put the gold band on my finger, I had, in some way, ceased to be her child in becoming his wife.

Are you sure, she'd said when they delivered the gigantic box that held the wedding dress he'd bought me, wrapped up in tissue paper and red ribbon like a Christmas gift of crystallised fruit. Are you sure you love him? There was a dress for her, too; black silk, with the dull, prismatic sheen of oil on water, finer than anything she'd worn since the adventurous girlhood in Indo-China, daughter of a rich tea planter. My eagle-featured indomitable mother; what other student at the Conservatoire could boast that her mother had outfaced a junkful of Chinese pirates; nursed a village through a visitation of the plague, shot a man-eating tiger with her own hand and all before she was as old as I?

'Are you sure you love him?'

'I'm sure I want to marry him,' I said.

And would say no more. She sighed, as if it was with reluctance that she might at last banish the spectre of poverty from its habitual place at our meagre table. For my mother herself had gladly, scandalously, defiantly beggared herself for love; and, one fine day, her gallant soldier never returned from the wars, leaving his wife and child a legacy of tears that never quite dried, a cigar box full of medals and the antique service revolver that my mother, grown magnificently eccentric in hardship, kept always in her reticule, in case – how I teased her – she was surprised by footpads on her way home from the grocer's shop.

Now and then a starburst of lights spattered the drawn blinds as if the railway company had lit up all the stations through which we passed in celebration of the bride. My satin nightdress had just been shaken from its wrappings; it had slipped over my young girl's pointed breasts and shoulders, supple as a garment of heavy water, and now teasingly caressed me, egregious, insinuating, nudging between my thighs as I shifted restlessly in my narrow berth. His kiss, his kiss with tongue and teeth in it and a rasp of beard had hinted to me, though with the same exquisite tact as this nightdress he'd given me, of the wedding night, which would be voluptuously deferred until we lay in his great ancestral bed in the sea-girt, pinnacled domain that lay, still, beyond the grasp of my imagination . . . that magic place, the fairy castle whose walls were made of foam, that legendary habitation in which he had been born. To which, one day, I might bear an heir. Our destination, my destiny.

Above the syncopated roar of the train, I could hear his even, steady breathing. Only the communicating door kept me from my husband and it stood open. If I rose up on my elbow, I could see the dark, leonine shape of his head and my nostrils caught a whiff of the opulent male scent of leather and spices that always accompanied him and sometimes during his courtship, had been the only hint he gave me that he had come into my mother's sitting-room, for, though he was a big man, he moved as softly as if all his shoes had soles of velvet, as if his footfall turned the carpet into snow.

He had loved to surprise me in my abstracted solitude at the piano. He would tell them not to announce him, then soundlessly open the door and softly creep up behind me with his bouquet of hot-house flowers or his box of marrons glacés, lay his offering upon the keys and clasp his hands over my eyes as I was lost in a Debussy prelude. But the perfume of spiced leather always betrayed him; after my first shock, I was forced always to mimic surprise, so that he would not be disappointed.

He was older than I. He was much older than I; there were streaks of pure silver in his dark mane. But his strange, heavy, almost waxen face was not lined by experience. Rather, experience seemed to have washed it perfectly smooth, like a stone on a beach whose fissures had been eroded by successive tides. And sometimes that face, in stillness when he listened to me playing, with the heavy eyelids folded over eyes that always disturbed me by their absolute absence of light, seemed to me like a mask, as if his real face, the face that truly reflected all the life he had led in the world before he met me, before, even, I was born, as though that face lay underneath this mask. Or else, elsewhere. As though he had laid by the face in which he had lived for so long in order to offer my youth a face unsigned by the years.

And, elsewhere, I might see him plain. Elsewhere. But, where?

In, perhaps, that castle to which the train now took us, that marvellous castle in which he had been born.

Even when he asked me to marry him, and I said: 'Yes', still he did not lose that heavy, fleshy composure of his. I know it must seem a curious analogy, a man with a flower, but sometimes he seemed to me like a lily. Yes. A lily. Possessed of that strange, ominous calm of a sentient vegetable, like one of those cobra-headed, funereal lilies whose white sheaths are curled out of a flesh as thick and tensely yielding to the touch as vellum. When I said that I would marry him, not one muscle in his face stirred, but he let out a long, extinguished sigh. I thought: Oh! how he must want me! and it was as though the imponderable weight of his desire was a force I might not withstand, not by virtue of its violence but because of its very gravity.

He had the ring ready in a leather box lined with crimson velvet, a fire opal the size of a pigeon's egg set in a complicated circle of dark antique gold. My old nurse, who still lived with my mother and me, squinted at the ring askance: opals are bad luck, she said. But this opal had been his own mother's ring, and his grandmother's, and her mother's before that, given to an ancestor by Catherine de Medici . . . every bride that came to the castle wore it, time out of mind. And did he give it to his other wives and have it back from them? asked the old woman rudely; yet she was a snob. She hid her incredulous joy at my marital coup – her little Marquise – behind a façade of fault-finding. But, here, she touched me. I shrugged and turned my back pettishly on her. I did not want to be reminded how he had loved other women before me, but the knowledge often teased me in the threadbare self-confidence of the small hours.

I was seventeen and knew nothing of the world; my Marquis had been married before, more than once, and I remained a little bemused that, after those others, he should now have chosen me. Indeed was he not still in mourning for his last wife? Tsk, tsk, went my old nurse. And even my mother had been reluctant to see her girl whisked off by a man so recently bereaved. A Romanian countess, a lady of high fashion. Dead just three short months before I met him, a boating accident, at his home, in Brittany. They never found her body but I rummaged through the back copies of the society magazines my old nanny kept in a trunk under her bed and tracked down her photograph. The sharp muzzle of a pretty, witty, naughty monkey; such potent and bizarre charm, of a dark, bright, wild yet worldly thing whose natural habitat must have been some luxurious interior decorator's jungle filled with potted palms and tame, squawking parakeets.

Before that? *Her* face is common property; everyone painted her but the Redon engraving I liked best, *The Evening Star Walking on the Rim of Night.* To see her skeletal, enigmatic grace, you would never think she had been a barmaid in a café in Montmartre until Puvis de Chavannes saw her and had her expose her flat breasts and elongated thighs to his brush. And yet it was the absinthe doomed her, or so they said.

The first of all his ladies? That sumptuous diva; I had heard her sing Isolde, precociously musical child that I was, taken to the opera for a birthday treat. My first opera; I had heard her sing Isolde. With what white-hot passion had she burned from the stage! So that you could tell she would die young. We sat high up, halfway to heaven in the gods, yet she half-blinded me. And my father, still alive (oh, so long ago), took hold of my sticky little hand, to comfort me, in the last act, yet all I heard was the glory of her voice.

Married three times within my own brief lifetime to three different graces, now, as if to demonstrate the eclecticism of his taste, he had invited me to join this gallery of beautiful women, I, the poor widow's child with my mouse-coloured hair that still bore the kinks of the plaits from which it had so recently been freed, my bony hips, my nervous, pianist's fingers.

He was rich as Croesus. The night before our wedding – a simple affair, at the Mairie, because his countess was so recently gone – he took my mother and me, curious coincidence, to see *Tristan*. And, do you know, my heart swelled and ached so during the *Liebestod* that I thought I must truly love him. Yes. I did. On his arm, all eyes were upon me. The whispering crowd in the foyer parted like the Red Sea to let us through. My skin crisped at his touch.

How my circumstances had changed since the first time I heard those voluptuous chords that carry such a charge of deathly passion in them! Now, we sat in a loge, in red velvet armchairs, and a braided bewigged flunkey brought us a silver bucket of iced champagne in the interval. The froth spilled over the rim of my glass and drenched my hands, I thought: My cup runneth over. And I had on a Poiret dress. He had prevailed upon my reluctant mother to let him buy my trousseau; what would I have gone to him in, otherwise? Twice-darned underwear, faded gingham, serge skirts, hand-me-downs. So, for the opera, I wore a sinuous shift of white muslin tied with a silk string under the breasts. And everyone stared at me. And at his wedding gift.

His wedding gift, clasped round my throat. A choker of rubies, two inches wide, like an extraordinarily precious slit throat.

After the Terror, in the early days of the Directory, the aristos who'd escaped the guillotine had an ironic fad of tying a red ribbon round their necks at just the point where the blade would have sliced it through, a red ribbon like the memory of a wound. And his grandmother, taken with the notion, had her ribbon made up in rubies; such a gesture of luxurious defiance! That night at the opera comes back to me even now . . . the white dress; the frail child within it; and the flashing crimson jewels round her throat, bright as arterial blood.

I saw him watching me in the gilded mirrors with the assessing eye of a connoisseur inspecting horseflesh, or even of a housewife in the market, inspecting cuts on the slab. I'd never seen, or else had never acknowledged, that regard of his before, the sheer carnal avarice of it; and it was strangely magnified by the monocle lodged in his left eye. When I saw him look at me with lust, I dropped my eyes but, in glancing away from him, I caught sight of myself in the mirror. And I saw myself, suddenly, as he saw me, my pale face, the way the muscles in my neck stuck out like thin wire. I saw how much that cruel necklace became me. And, for the first time in my innocent and confined life, I sensed in myself a potentiality for corruption that took my breath away.

The next day, we were married.

The train slowed, shuddered to a halt. Lights; clank of metal; a voice declaring the name of an unknown, never-to-be-visited station; silence of the night; the rhythm of his breathing, that I should sleep with, now, for the rest of my life. And I could not sleep. I stealthily sat up, raised the blind a little and huddled against the cold window that misted over with the warmth of my breathing, gazing out at the dark platform towards those rectangles of domestic lamp light that promised warmth, company, a supper of sausages hissing in a pan on the stove for the station master, his children tucked up in bed asleep in the brick house with the painted shutters . . . all the paraphernalia of the everyday world from which I, with my stunning marriage, had exiled myself.

Into marriage, into exile; I sensed it, I knew it – that, henceforth, I would always be lonely. Yet that was part of the already familiar weight of the fire opal that glimmered like a gypsy's magic ball, so that I could not take my eyes off it when I played the piano. This ring, the bloody bandage of rubies, the wardrobe of clothes from Poiret and Worth, his scent of Russian leather – all had conspired to seduce me so utterly that I could not say I felt one single twinge of regret for the world of tartines and maman that now receded from me as if drawn away on a string, like a child's toy, as the train began to throb again as if in delighted anticipation of the distance it would take me.

The first grey streamers of the dawn now flew in the sky and an eldritch half-light seeped into the railway carriage. I heard no change in his breathing but my heightened excited senses told me he was awake and gazing at me. A huge man, an enormous man, and his eyes, dark and motionless as those eyes the ancient Egyptians painted upon their sarcophagi, fixed upon me. I felt a certain tension in the pit of my stomach, to be so watched in such silence. A match struck. He was igniting a Romeo y Julieta fat as a baby's arm.

'Soon,' he said in his resonant voice that was like the tolling of a bell and I felt, all at once, a sharp premonition of dread that lasted only as long as the match flared and I could see his white, broad face as if it were hovering, disembodied, above the sheets, illuminated from below like a grotesque carnival head. Then the flame died, the cigar glowed and filled the compartment with a remembered fragrance that made me think of my father, how he would hug me in a warm fug of Havana, when I was a little girl, before he kissed me and left me and died.

As soon as my husband handed me down from the high step of the train, I smelled the amniotic salinity of the ocean. It was November; the trees, stunted by the Atlantic gales, were bare and the lonely halt was deserted but for his leather-gaitered chauffeur waiting meekly beside the sleek black motor car. It was cold; I drew my furs about me, a wrap of white and black, broad stripes of ermine and sable, with a collar from which my head rose like the calyx of a wildflower. (I swear to you, I had never been vain until I met him.) The bell clanged; the straining train leapt its leash and left us at that lonely wayside halt where only he and I had descended. Oh, the wonder of it; how all that might of iron and steam had paused only to suit his convenience. The richest man in France.

'Madame.'

The chauffeur eyed me; was he comparing me, invidiously, to the countess, the artist's model, the opera singer? I hid behind my furs as if they were a system of soft shields. My husband liked me to wear my opal over my kid glove, a showy, theatrical trick – but the moment the ironic chauffeur glimpsed its simmering flash he smiled, as though it was proof positive I was his master's wife. And we drove towards the widening dawn, that now streaked half the sky with a wintry bouquet of pink of roses, orange of tiger-lilies, as if my husband had ordered me a sky from the florist. The day broke around me like a cool dream.

Sea; sand; a sky that melts into the sea – a landscape of misty pastels with a look about it of being continuously on the point of melting. A landscape with all the deliquescent harmonies of Debussy, of the études I played for him, the reverie I'd been playing that afternoon in the salon of the princess where I'd first met him, among the tea-cups and the little cakes, I, the orphan, hired out of charity to give them their digestive of music.

And, ah! his castle. The faery solitude of the place; with its turrets of misty blue, its courtyard, its spiked gate, his castle that lay on the very bosom of the sea with seabirds mewing about its attics, the casements opening on to the green and purple, evanescent departures of the ocean, cut off by the tide from land for half a day . . . that castle, at home neither on the land nor on the water, a mysterious, amphibious place, contravening the materiality of both earth and the waves, with the melancholy of a mermaiden who perches on her rock and waits, endlessly, for a lover who had drowned far away, long ago. That lovely, sad, sea-siren of a place!

The tide was low; at this hour, so early in the morning, the causeway rose up out of the sea. As the car turned on to the wet cobbles between the slow margins of water, he reached out for my hand that had his sultry, witching ring on it, pressed my fingers, kissed my palm with extraordinary tenderness. His face was as still as ever I'd seen it, still as a pond iced thickly over, yet his lips, that always looked so strangely red and naked between the black fringes of his beard, now curved a little. He smiled; he welcomed his bride home.

No room, no corridor that did not rustle with the sound of the sea and all the ceilings, the walls on which his ancestors in the stern regalia of rank lined up with their dark eyes and white faces, were stippled with refracted light from the waves which were always in motion; that luminous murmurous castle of which I was the châtelaine, I, the little music student whose mother had sold all her jewellery, even her wedding ring, to pay the fees at the Conservatoire.

First of all, there was the small ordeal of my initial interview with the housekeeper, who kept this extraordinary machine, this anchored, castellated ocean liner, in smooth running order no matter who stood on the bridge; how tenuous, I thought, might be my authority here! She had a bland, pale, impassive, dislikeable face beneath the impeccably starched white linen headdress of the region. Her greeting, correct but lifeless, chilled me; daydreaming, I dared presume too much on my status . . . briefly wondered how I might install my old nurse, so much loved, however cosily incompetent, in her place. Ill-considered schemings! He told me this one had been his foster mother; was bound to his family in the utmost feudal complicity, 'as much a part of the house as I am, my dear.' Now her thin lips offered me a proud little smile. She would be my ally as long as I was his. And with that, I must be content.

But, here it would be easy to be content. In the turret suite he had given me for my very own, I could gaze out over the tumultuous Atlantic and imagine myself the Queen of the Sea. There was a Bechstein for me in the music room and, on the wall, another wedding present – an early Flemish primitive of Saint Cecilia at her celestial organ. In the prim charm of this saint, with her plump, sallow cheeks and crinkled brown hair, I saw myself as I could have wished to be. I warmed to a loving sensitivity I had not hitherto suspected in him. Then he led me up a delicate spiral staircase to my bedroom; before she discreetly vanished, the housekeeper set him chuckling with some, I dare say, lewd blessing for newlyweds in her native Breton. That I did not understand. That he, smiling, refused to interpret.

And there lay the grand, hereditary matrimonial bed, itself the size, almost, of my little room at home, with the gargoyles carved on its surfaces of ebony, vermilion lacquer, gold leaf; and its white gauze curtains, billowing in the sea breeze. Our bed. And surrounded by so many mirrors! Mirrors on the walls, in stately frames of contorted gold, that reflected more white lilies than I'd ever seen in my life before. He'd filled the room with them, to greet the bride, the young bride. The young bride, who had become that multitude of girls I saw in the mirrors, identical in their chic navy blue tailor-mades, for travelling, madame, or walking. A maid had dealt with the furs. Henceforth, a maid would deal with everything.

'See,' he said, gesturing towards those elegant girls. 'I have acquired a whole harem for myself!'

I found that I was trembling. My breath came quickly. I could not meet his eye and turned my head away, out of pride, out of shyness, and watched a dozen husbands approach me in a dozen mirrors and slowly, methodically, teasingly, unfasten the buttons of my jacket and slip it from my shoulders. Enough! No; more! Off comes the skirt; and next the blouse of apricot linen that cost more than the dress I had for first communion. The play of the waves outside in the cold sun glittered on his monocle; his movements seemed to me deliberately coarse, vulgar. The blood rushed to my face again, and stayed there.

And yet, you see, I guessed it might be so – that we should have a formal disrobing of the bride, a ritual from the brothel. Sheltered as my life had been, how could I have failed, even in the world of prim bohemia in which I lived, to have heard hints of *his* world?

He stripped me, gourmand that he was, as if he were stripping the leaves off an artichoke – but do not imagine much finesse about it; this artichoke was no particular treat for the diner nor was he yet in any greedy haste. He approached his familiar treat with a weary appetite. And when nothing but my scarlet, palpitating core remained, I saw, in the mirror, the living image of an etching by Rops from the collection he had shown me when our engagement permitted us to be alone together

. . . the child with her sticklike limbs, naked but for her button boots, her gloves, shielding her face with her hand as though her face were the last repository of her modesty; and the old, monocled lecher who examined her, limb by limb. He in his London tailoring; she, bare as a lamb chop. Most pornographic of all confrontations. And so my purchaser unwrapped his bargain. And, as at the opera, when I had first seen my flesh in his eyes, I was aghast to feel myself stirring.

At once he closed my legs like a book and I saw again the rare movement of his lips that meant he smiled.

Not yet. Later. Anticipation is the greater part of pleasure, my little love.

And I began to shudder, like a racehorse before a race, yet also with a kind of fear, for I felt both a strange, impersonal arousal at the thought of love and at the same time a repugnance I could not stifle for his white, heavy flesh that had too much in common with the armfuls of arum lilies that filled my bedroom in great glass jars, those undertakers' lilies with the heavy pollen that powders your fingers as if you had dipped them in turmeric. The lilies I always associate with him; that are white. And stain you.

This scene from a voluptuary's life was now abruptly terminated. It turns out he has business to attend to; his estates, his companies – even on your honeymoon? Even then, said the red lips that kissed me before he left me alone with my bewildered senses – a wet, silken brush from his beard; a hint of the pointed tip of the tongue. Disgruntled, I wrapped a negligee of antique lace around me to sip the little breakfast of hot chocolate the maid brought me; after that, since it was a second nature to me, there was nowhere to go but the music room and soon I settled down at my piano.

Yet only a series of subtle discords flowed from beneath my fingers: out of tune . . . only a little out of tune; but I'd been blessed with perfect pitch and could not bear to play any more. Sea breezes are bad for pianos; we shall need a resident piano-tuner on the premises if I'm to continue with my studies! I flung down the lid in a little fury of disappointment; what should I do now, how shall I pass the long, sea-lit hours until my husband beds me?

I shivered to think of *that*.

His library seemed the source of his habitual odour of Russian leather. Row upon row of calf-bound volumes, brown and olive, with gilt lettering on their spines, the octavo in brilliant scarlet morocco. A deep-buttoned leather sofa to recline on. A lectern, carved like a spread eagle that held open upon it an edition of Huysmans's *Là-bas*, from some over-exquisite private press; it had been bound like a missal, in brass, with gems of coloured glass. The rugs on the floor, deep pulsing blues of heaven and red of the heart's dearest blood, came from Isfahan and Bokhara; the dark panelling gleamed; there was the lulling music of the sea and a fire of apple logs. The flames flickered along the spines inside the glass-fronted case that held books still crisp and new. Eliphas Levy; the name meant nothing to me. I squinted at a title or two: *The Initiation, The Key of Mysteries, The Secret of Pandora's Box*, and yawned. Nothing, here, to detain a seventeen-year-old girl waiting for her first embrace. I should have liked, best of all, a novel in yellow paper; I wanted to curl up on the rug before the blazing fire, lose myself in a cheap novel, munch sticky liqueur chocolates. If I rang for them, a maid would bring me the chocolates.

Nevertheless, I opened the doors of the bookcase idly to browse. And I think I knew, I knew by some tingle of the fingertips, even before I opened that slim volume with no title at all on the spine, what I should find inside. When he showed me the Rops, newly bought, dearly prized, had he not hinted that he was a connoisseur of such things? Yet I had not bargained for this, the girl with tears hanging on her cheeks like stuck pearls, her cunt a split fig below the great globes of her buttocks on which the knotted tails of the cat were about to descend, while a man in a black mask fingered with his free hand his prick, that curved upwards like a scimitar he held. The picture had a caption 'Reproof of curiosity.' My mother, with all the precision of her eccentricity, had told me what it was that lovers did; I was innocent but not naïve. *The Adventures of Eulalie at the Harem of the Grand Turk* had been printed, according to the flyleaf, in Amsterdam in 1748, a rare collector's piece. Had some ancestor brought it back himself from that northern city? Or had my husband bought it for himself, from one of those dusty little bookshops on the Left Bank where an old man peers at you through spectacles an inch thick, daring you to inspect his wares . . . I turned the pages in the anticipation of fear; the print was rusty. Here was another steel engraving: 'Immolation of the wives of the Sultan'. I knew enough for what I saw in that book to make me gasp.

There was a pungent intensification of the odour of leather that suffused his library; his shadow fell across the massacre.

'My little nun has found the prayerbooks, has she?' he demanded, with a curious mixture of mockery and relish; then, seeing my painful, furious bewilderment, he laughed at me aloud, snatched the book from my hands and put it down on the sofa.

'Have the nasty pictures scared Baby? Baby mustn't play with grownups' toys until she's learned how to handle them, must she?'

Then he kissed me. And with, this time, no reticence. He kissed me and laid his hand imperatively upon my breast, beneath the sheath of ancient lace. I stumbled on the winding stair that led to the bedroom, to the carved, gilded bed on which he had been conceived, I stammered foolishly: We've not taken luncheon yet; and, besides, it is broad daylight . . .

All the better to see you.

He made me put on my choker, the family heirloom of one woman who had escaped the blade. With trembling fingers, I fastened the thing about my neck. It was cold as ice and chilled me. He twined my hair into a rope and lifted it off my shoulders so that he could the better kiss the downy furrows below my ears; that made me shudder. And he kissed those blazing rubies, too. He kissed them before he kissed my mouth. Rapt, he intoned: 'Of her apparel she retains/Only her sonorous jewellery.'

A dozen husbands impaled a dozen brides while the mewing gulls swung on invisible trapezes in the empty air outside.

I was brought to my senses by the intent shrilling of the telephone. He lay beside me, felled like an oak, breathing stertorously, as if he had been fighting with me. In the course of that one-sided struggle, I had seen his deathly composure shatter like a porcelain vase flung against a wall; I had heard him shriek and blaspheme at the orgasm; I had bled. And perhaps I had seen his face without its mask; and perhaps I had not. Yet I had been infinitely dishevelled by the loss of my virginity.

I gathered myself together, reached into the cloisonné cupboard beside the bed that concealed the telephone and addressed the mouthpiece. His agent in New York. Urgent.

I shook him awake and rolled over on my side, cradling my spent body in my arms. His voice buzzed like a hive of distant bees. My husband. My husband, who, with so much love, filled my bedroom with lilies until it looked like an embalming parlour. Those somnolent lilies, that wave their heavy heads, distributing their lush, insolent incense reminiscent of pampered flesh.

When he'd finished with the agent, he turned to me and stroked the ruby necklace that bit into my neck, but with such tenderness now, that I ceased flinching and he caressed my breasts. My dear one, my little love, my child, did it hurt her? He's so sorry for it, such impetuousness, he could not help himself; you see, he loves her so . . . and this lover's recitative of his brought my tears in a flood. I clung to him as though only the one who had inflicted the pain could comfort me for suffering it. For a while, he murmured to me in a voice I'd never heard before, a voice like the soft consolations of the sea. But then he unwound the tendrils of my hair from the buttons of his smoking jacket, kissed my cheek briskly and told me the agent from New York had called with such urgent business that he must leave as soon as the tide was low enough. Leave the castle? Leave France! And would be away for at least six weeks.

'But it is our honeymoon!'

A deal, an enterprise of hazard and chance involving several millions, lay in the balance, he said. He drew away from me into that waxworks stillness of his; I was only a little girl, I did not understand. And, he said unspoken to my wounded vanity, I have had too many honeymoons to find them in the least pressing commitments. I know quite well that this child I've bought with a handful of coloured stones and the pelts of dead beasts won't run away. But, after he'd called his Paris agent to book a passage for the States next day – just one tiny call, my little one – we should have time for dinner together.

And I had to be content with that.

A Mexican dish of pheasant with hazelnuts and chocolate; salad; white, voluptuous cheese; a sorbet of muscat grapes and Asti spumante. A celebration of Krug exploded festively. And then acrid black coffee in precious little cups so fine it shadowed the birds with which they were painted. I had cointreau, he had cognac in the library, with the purple velvet curtains drawn against the night, where he took me to perch on his knee in a leather armchair beside the flickering log fire. He had made me change into the chaste little Poiret shift of white muslin; he seemed especially fond of it, my breasts showed through the flimsy stuff, he said, like little soft white doves that sleep, each one, with a pink eye open. But he would not let me take off my ruby choker, although it was growing very uncomfortable, nor fasten up my descending hair, the sign of a virginity so recently ruptured that still remained a wounded presence between us. He twined his fingers in my hair until I winced; I said, I remember, very little.

'The maid will have changed our sheets already,' he said. 'We do not hang the bloody sheets out of the window to prove to the whole of Brittany you are a virgin, not in these civilised times. But I should tell you it would have been the first time in all my married lives I could have shown my interested tenants such a flag.'

Then I realised, with a shock of surprise, how it must have been my innocence that captivated him – the silent music, he said, of my unknowingness, like *La Terrasse des audiences au clair de lune* played upon a piano with keys of ether. You must remember how ill at ease I was in that luxurious place, how unease had been my constant companion during the whole length of my courtship by this grave satyr who now gently martyrised my hair. To know that my naïvety gave him some pleasure made me take heart. Courage! I shall act the fine lady to the manner born one day, if only by virtue of default.

Then, slowly yet teasingly, as if he were giving a child a great mysterious treat, he took out a bunch of keys from some interior hidey-hole in his jacket – key after key, a key, he said, for every lock in the house. Keys of all kinds – huge, ancient things of black iron; others slender, delicate, almost baroque; wafer-thin Yale keys for safes and boxes. And, during his absence, it was I who must take care of them all.

I eyed the heavy bunch with circumspection. Until that moment, I had not given a single thought to the practical aspects of marriage with a great house, great wealth, a great man, whose key ring was as crowded as that of a prison warder. Here were the clumsy and archaic keys for the dungeons, for dungeons we had in plenty although they had been converted into cellars for his wines; the dusty bottles inhabited in racks all those deep holes of pain in the rock on which the castle was built. There are the keys to the kitchens, this is the key to the picture gallery, a treasure house filled by five centuries of avid collectors – ah! he foresaw I would spend hours there.

He had amply indulged his taste for the Symbolists, he told me with a glint of greed. There was Moreau's great portrait of his first wife, the famous *Sacrificial Victim* with the imprint of the lacelike chains on her pellucid skin. Did I know the story of the painting of that picture? How, when she took off her clothes for him for the first time, she fresh from her bar in Montmartre, she had robed herself involuntarily in a blush that reddened her breasts, her shoulders, her arms, her whole body? He had thought of that story, of that dear girl, when first he had undressed me . . . Ensor, the great Ensor, his monolithic canvas: *The Foolish Virgins*. two or three late Gauguins, his special favourite the one of the tranced brown girl in the deserted house which was called: *Out of the Night We Come, Into the Night We Go*. And, besides the additions he had made himself, his marvellous inheritance of Watteaus, Poussins and a pair of very special Fragonards, commissioned for a licentious ancestor who, it was said, had posed for the master's brush himself with his own two daughters . . . He broke off his catalogue of treasures abruptly.

Your thin white face, chérie; he said, as if he saw it for the first time. Your thin white face, with its promise of debauchery only a connoisseur could detect.

A log fell in the fire, instigating a shower of sparks; the opal on my finger spurted green flame. I felt so giddy as if I were on the edge of a precipice; I was afraid, not so much of him, of his monstrous presence, heavy as if he had been gifted at birth with more specific *gravity* than the rest of us, the presence that, even when I thought myself most in love with him, always subtly oppressed me . . . No. I was not afraid of him; but of myself. I seemed reborn in his unreflective eyes, reborn in unfamiliar shapes. I hardly recognised myself from his description of me and yet, and yet – might there not be a grain of beastly truth in them? And, in the red firelight, I blushed again, unnoticed, to think he might have chosen me because, in my innocence, he sensed a rare talent for corruption.

Here is the key to the china cabinet – don't laugh, my darling; there's a king's ransom in Sèvres in that closet, and a queen's ransom in Limoges. And a key to the locked, barred room where five generations of plate are kept.

Keys, keys, keys. He would trust me with the keys to his office, although I was only a baby; and the keys to his safes, where he kept the jewels I should wear, he promised me, when we returned to Paris. Such jewels! Why, I would be able to change my earrings and necklaces three times a day, just as the Empress Josephine used to change her underwear. He doubted, he said, with that hollow, knocking sound that served him for a chuckle, I would be quite so interested in his share certificates although they, of course, were worth infinitely more.

Outside our firelit privacy, I could hear the sound of the tide drawing back from the pebbles of the foreshore; it was nearly time for him to leave me. One single key remained unaccounted for on the ring and he hesitated over it; for a moment, I thought he was going to unfasten it from its brothers, slip it back into his pocket and take it away with him.

'What is *that* key?' I demanded, for his chaffing had made me bold. 'The key to your heart? Give it me!'

He dangled the key tantalisingly above my head, out of reach of my straining fingers; those bare red lips of his cracked sidelong in a smile.

'Ah, no,' he said. 'Not the key to my heart. Rather, the key to my enfer.'

He left it on the ring, fastened the ring together, shook it musically, like a carillon. Then threw the keys in a jingling heap in my lap. I could feel the cold metal chilling my thighs through my thin muslin frock. He bent over me to drop a beard-masked kiss on my forehead.

'Every man must have one secret, even if only one, from his wife,' he said. 'Promise me this, my whey-faced piano-player; promise me you'll use all the keys on the ring except that last little one I showed you. Play with anything you find, jewels, silver plate; make toy boats of my share certificates, if it pleases you, and send them sailing off to America after me. All is yours, everywhere is open to you – except the lock that this single key fits. Yet all it is is the key to a little room at the foot of the west tower, behind the still-room, at the end of a dark little corridor full of horrid cobwebs that would get into your hair and frighten you if you ventured there. Oh, and you'd find it such a dull little room! But you must promise me, if you love me, to leave it well alone. It is only a private study, a hideaway, a "den", as the English say, where I can go sometimes, on those infrequent yet inevitable occasions when the yoke of marriage seems to weigh too heavily on my shoulders. There I can go, you understand, to savour the rare pleasure of imagining myself wifeless.'

There was a little thin starlight in the courtyard as, wrapped in my furs, I saw him to his car. His last words were, that he had telephoned the mainland and taken a piano-tuner on to the staff; this man would arrive to take up his duties the next day. He pressed me to his vicuña breast, once, and then drove away.

I had drowsed away that afternoon and now I could not sleep. I lay tossing and turning in his ancestral bed until another day-break discoloured the dozen mirrors that were iridescent with the reflections of the sea. The perfume of the lilies weighed on my senses; when I thought that, henceforth, I would always share these sheets with a man whose skin, as theirs did, contained that toad-like, clammy hint of moisture, I felt a vague desolation that within me, now my female wound had healed, there had awoken a certain queasy craving like the cravings of pregnant women for the taste of coal or chalk or tainted food, for the renewal of his caresses. Had he not hinted to me, in his flesh as in his speech and looks, of the thousand, thousand baroque intersections of flesh upon flesh? I lay in our wide bed accompanied by, a sleepless companion, my dark newborn curiosity.

I lay in bed alone. And I longed for him. And he disgusted me.

Were there jewels enough in all his safes to recompense me for this predicament? Did all that castle hold enough riches to recompense me for the company of the libertine with whom I must share it? And what, precisely, was the nature of my desirous dread for this mysterious being who, to show his mastery over me, had abandoned me on my wedding night?

Then I sat straight up in bed, under the sardonic masks of the gargoyles carved above me, riven by a wild surmise. Might he have left me, not for Wall Street but for an importunate mistress tucked away God knows where who knew how to pleasure him far better than a girl whose fingers had been exercised, hitherto, only by the practice of scales and arpeggios? And, slowly, soothed, I sank back on to the heaping pillows; I acknowledged that the jealous scare I'd just given myself was not unmixed with a little tincture of relief.

At last I drifted into slumber, as daylight filled the room and chased bad dreams away. But the last thing I remembered, before I slept, was the tall jar of lilies beside the bed, how the thick glass distorted their fat stems so they looked like arms, dismembered arms, drifting drowned into greenish water.

Coffee and croissants to console this bridal, solitary waking. Delicious. Honey, too, in a section of comb on a glass saucer. The maid squeezed the aromatic juice from an orange into a chilled goblet while I watched her as I lay on the lazy midday bed of the rich. Yet nothing, this morning, gave me more than a fleeting pleasure except to hear that the piano-tuner had been at work already. When the maid told me that, I sprang out of bed and pulled on my old serge skirt and flannel blouse, costume of a student, in which I felt far more at ease with myself than in any of my fine new clothes.

After my three hours of practice, I called the piano-tuner in, to thank him. He was blind, of course; but young, with a gentle mouth and grey eyes that fixed upon me although they could not see me. He was a blacksmith's son from the village across the causeway; a chorister in the church whom the good priest had taught a trade so that he could make a living. All most satisfactory. Yes. He thought he would be happy here. And if, he added shyly, he might sometimes be allowed to hear me play . . . for, you see, he loved music. Yes. Of course, I said. Certainly. He seemed to know that I had smiled.

After I dismissed him, even though I'd woken so late, it was still barely time for my 'five o'clock'. The housekeeper, who, thoughtfully fore-warned by my husband, had restrained herself from interrupting my music, now made me a solemn visitation with a lengthy menu for a late luncheon. When I told her I did not need it, she looked at me obliquely, along her nose. I understood at once that one of my principal functions as châtelaine was to provide work for the staff. But, all the same, I asserted myself and said I would wait until dinner-time, although I looked forward nervously to the solitary meal. Then I found I had to tell her what I would like to have prepared for me; my imagination, still that of a schoolgirl, ran riot. A fowl in cream – or should I anticipate Christmas with a varnished turkey? No; I have decided. Avocado and shrimp, lots of it, followed by no entrée at all. But surprise me for dessert with every ice-cream in the ice box. She noted all down but sniffed; I'd shocked her. Such tastes! Child that I was, I giggled when she left me.

But, now . . . what shall I do, now?

I could have spent a happy hour unpacking the trunks that contained my trousseau but the maid had done that already, the dresses, the tailor-mades hung in the wardrobe in my dressing room, the hats on wooden heads to keep their shape, the shoes on wooden feet as if all these inanimate objects were imitating the appearance of life, to mock me. I did not like to linger in my overcrowded dressing room, nor in my lugubriously lily-scented bedroom. How shall I pass the time?

I shall take a bath in my own bathroom! And found the taps were little dolphins made of gold, with chips of turquoise for eyes. And there was a tank of goldfish, who swam in and out of moving fronds of weeds, as bored, I thought, as I was. How I wished he had not left me. How I wished it were possible to chat with, say, a maid; or the piano-tuner . . . but I knew already my new rank forbade overtures of friendship to the staff.

I had been hoping to defer the call as long as I could, so that I should have something to look forward to in the dead waste of time I foresaw before me, after my dinner was done with, but, at a quarter before seven, when darkness already surrounded the castle, I could contain myself no longer. I telephoned my mother. And astonished myself by bursting into tears when I heard her voice.

No, nothing was the matter. Mother. I have gold bath taps.

I said, gold bath taps!

No; I suppose that's nothing to cry about, Mother.

The line was bad, I could hardly make out her congratulations, her questions, her concern, but I was a little comforted when I put the receiver down.

Yet there still remained one whole hour to dinner and the whole, unimaginable desert of the rest of the evening.

The bunch of keys lay, where he had left them, on the rug before the library fire which had warmed their metal so that they no longer felt cold to the touch but warm, almost, as my own skin. How careless I was; a maid, tending the logs, eyed me reproachfully as if I'd set a trap for her as I picked up the clinking bundle of keys, the keys to the interior doors of this lovely prison of which I was both the inmate and the mistress and had scarcely seen. When I remembered that, I felt the exhilaration of the explorer.

Lights! More lights!

At the touch of a switch, the dreaming library was brilliantly illuminated. I ran crazily about the castle, switching on every light I could find – I ordered the servants to light up all their quarters, too, so the castle would shine like a seaborne birthday cake lit with a thousand candles, one for every year of its life, and everybody on shore would wonder at it. When everything was lit as brightly as the café in the Gare du Nord, the significance of the possessions implied by the bunch of keys no longer intimidated me, for I was determined, now, to search through them all for evidence of my husband's true nature.

His office first, evidently.

A mahogany desk half a mile wide, with an impeccable blotter and a bank of telephones. I allowed myself the luxury of opening the safe that contained the jewellery and delved sufficiently among the leather boxes to find out how my marriage had given me access to a jinn's treasure – parures, bracelets, rings . . . While I was thus surrounded by diamonds, a maid knocked on the door and entered before I spoke; a subtle discourtesy. I would speak to my husband about it. She eyed my serge skirt superciliously; did madame plan to dress for dinner?

She made a moue of disdain when I laughed to hear that, she was far more the lady than I. But imagine – to dress up in one of my Poiret extravaganzas, with the jewelled turban and aigrette on my head, roped with pearl to the navel, to sit down all alone in the baronial dining hall at the head of that massive board at which King Mark was reputed to have fed his knights . . . I grew calmer under the cold eye of her disapproval. I adopted the crisp inflections of an officer's daughter. No. I would not dress for dinner. Furthermore, I was not hungry enough for dinner itself. She must tell the housekeeper to cancel the dormitory feast I'd ordered. Could they leave me sandwiches and a flask of coffee in my music room? And would they all dismiss for the night?

Mais oui, madame.

I knew by her bereft intonation I had let them down again but I did not care; I was armed against them by the brilliance of his hoard. But I would not find his heart amongst the glittering stones; as soon as she had gone, I began a systematic search of the drawers of his desk.

All was in order, so I found nothing. Not a random doodle on an old envelope, nor the faded photograph of a woman. Only the files of business correspondence, the bills from the home farms, the invoices from tailors, the billet-doux from international financiers. Nothing. And this absence of the evidence of his real life began to impress me strangely; there must, I thought, be a great deal to conceal if he takes such pains to hide it.

His office was a singularly impersonal room, facing inwards, on to the courtyard, as though he wanted to turn his back on the siren sea in order to keep a clear head while he bankrupted a small businessman in Amsterdam or – I noticed with a thrill of distaste – engage in some business in Laos that must, from certain cryptic references to his amateur botanist's enthusiasm for rare poppies, be to do with opium. Was he not rich enough to do without crime? Or was the crime itself his profit? And yet I saw enough to appreciate his zeal for secrecy.

Now I had ransacked his desk, I must spend a cool-headed quarter of an hour putting every last letter back where I had found it, and, as I covered the traces of my visit, by some chance, as I reached inside a little drawer that had stuck fast, I must have touched a hidden spring, for a secret drawer flew open within that drawer itself; and the secret drawer contained – at last! – a file marked: *Personal*.

I was alone, but for my reflection in the uncurtained window.

I had the brief notion that his heart, pressed flat as a flower, crimson and thin as tisue paper, lay in this file. It was a very thin one.

I could have wished, perhaps, I had not found that touching, ill-spelt note, on a paper napkin marked *La Coupole*, that began: 'My darling, I cannot wait for the moment when you may make me yours completely.' The diva had sent him a page of the score of *Tristan*, the *Liebestod*, with the single, cryptic word: 'Until . . .' scrawled across it. But the strangest of all these love letters was a postcard with a view of a village graveyard, among mountains, where some black-coated ghoul enthusiastically dug at a grave; this little scene, executed with the lurid exuberance of Grand Guignol, was captioned: 'Typical Transylvanian Scene – Midnight, All Hallows.' And, on the other side, the message: 'On the occasion of this marriage to the descendant of Dracula – always remember, "the supreme and unique pleasure of love is the certainty that one is doing evil." Toutes amitiés, C.'

A joke. A joke in the worst possible taste; for had he not been married to a Romanian countess? And then I remembered her pretty, witty face, and her name – Carmilla. My most recent predecessor in this castle had been, it would seem, the most sophisticated.

I put away the file, sobered. Nothing in my life of family love and music had prepared me for these grown-up games and yet these were clues to his self that showed me, at least, how much he had been loved, even if they did not reveal any good reason for it. But I wanted to know still more; and as I closed the office door and locked it, the means to discover more fell in my way.

Fell, indeed; and with the clatter of a dropped canteen of cutlery, for, as I turned the slick Yale lock, I contrived, somehow, to open up the key ring itself, so that all the keys tumbled loose on the floor, and the very first key I picked out of that pile was, as luck or ill fortune had it, the key to the room he had forbidden me, the room he would keep for his own so that he could go there when he wished to feel himself once more a bachelor.

I made my decision to explore it before I felt a faint resurgence of my ill-defined fear of his waxen stillness. Perhaps I half-imagined, then, that I might find his real self in his den, waiting there to see if indeed I had obeyed him; that he had sent a moving figure of himself to New York, the enigmatic, self-sustaining carapace of his public person, while the real man, whose face I had glimpsed in the storm of orgasm, occupied himself with pressing private business in the study at the foot of the west tower, behind the still-room. Yet, if that were so, it was imperative that I should find him, should know him; and I was too deluded by his apparent taste for me to think my disobedience might truly offend him.

I took the forbidden key from the heap and left the others lying there.

It was now very late and the castle was adrift, as far as it could go from the land, in the middle of the silent ocean where, at my orders, it floated, like a garland of light. And all silent, all still, but for the murmuring of the waves.

I felt no fear, no intimation of dread. Now I walked as firmly as I had done in my mother's house.

Not a narrow, dusty little passage at all; why had he lied to me? but an ill-lit one, certainly; the electricity, for some reason did not extend here, so I retreated to the still-room and found a bundle of waxed tapers in a cupboard, stored there with matches, to light the oak board at grand dinners. I put a match to my little taper and advanced with it in my hand, like a penitent along the corridor hung with heavy, I think Venetian, tapestries. The flame picked out here, the head of a man, there, the rich breast of a woman spilling through a rent in her dress – the Rape of the Sabines, perhaps? The naked swords and immolated horses suggested some grisly mythological subject. The corridor wound downwards; there was an almost imperceptible ramp to the thickly carpeted floor. The heavy hangings on the wall muffled my footsteps, even my breathing. For some reason, it grew very warm, the sweat sprang out in beads on my brow. I could no longer hear the sound of the sea.

A long, a winding corridor, as if I were in the viscera of the castle; and this corridor led to a door of worm-eaten oak, low, round-topped, barred with black iron.

And still I felt no fear, no raising of the hairs on the back of the neck, no pricking of the thumbs.

The key slid into the new lock as easily as a hot knife into butter.

No fear; but hesitation, a holding of the spiritual breath.

If I found some traces of his heart in a file marked: *Personal*, perhaps, here, in his subterranean privacy, I might find a little of his soul. It was the consciousness of the possibility of such a discovery, of its possible strangeness, that kept me for a moment motionless, before in the foolhardiness of my already subtly tainted innocence I turned the key and the door creaked slowly back.

'There is a striking resemblance between the act of love and the ministrations of a torturer,' opined my husband's favourite poet; I had learned something of the nature of that similarity on my marriage bed. And now my taper showed me the outlines of a rack. There was also a great wheel, like the ones I had seen in woodcuts of the martyrdoms of the saints, in my old nurse's little store of holy books. And – just one glimpse of it before my little flame caved in and I was left in absolute darkness – a metal figure, hinged at the side, which I knew to be spiked at the inside and to have the name: the Iron Maiden.

Absolute darkness. And, about me, the instruments of mutilation.

Until that moment, this spoiled child did not know she had inherited nerves and a will from the mother who had defied the yellow outlaws of Indo-China. My mother's spirit drove me on, into the dreadful place, in a cold ecstasy to know the very worst. I fumbled for the matches in my pocket; what a dim lugubrious light they gave! And yet, enough, oh, more than enough, to see a room designed for desecration and some dark night of unimaginable lovers whose embraces were annihilation.

The walls of this stark torture chamber were the naked rock; they gleamed as if they were sweating with fright. At the four corners of the room were funerary urns, of great antiquity, Etruscan, perhaps, and, on three-legged ebony stands, the bowls of incense he had left burning which filled the room with a sacerdotal reek. Wheel, rack and Iron Maiden were, I saw, displayed as grandly as if they were items of statuary and I was almost consoled, then, and almost persuaded myself that I might have stumbled only upon a little museum of his perversity, that he had installed these monstrous items here only for contemplation.

Yet at the centre of the room lay a catafalque, a doomed, ominous bier of Renaissance workmanship, surrounded by long, white candles and, at its foot, an armful of the same lilies with which he had filled my bedroom, stowed in a four-foot-high jar, glazed with a sombre Chinese red. I scarcely dared examine this catafalque and its occupant more closely; yet I knew I must.

Each time I struck a match to light those candles around her bed, it seemed a garment of that innocence of mine for which he had lusted fell away from me.

The opera singer lay, quite naked, under a thin sheet of very rare and precious linen, such as the princes of Italy used to shroud those whom they had poisoned. I touched her, very gently, on the white breast; she was cool, he had embalmed her. On her throat I could see the blue imprint of his strangler's fingers. The cool, sad flame of the candles flickered on her white, closed eyelids. The worst thing was, the dead lips smiled.

Beyond the catafalque, in the middle of the shadows, a white nacreous glimmer; as my eyes accustomed themselves to the gathering darkness, I at last – oh horrors! – made out a skull; yes, a skull, so utterly denuded, now, of flesh, that it scarcely seemed possible the stark bone had once been richly upholstered with life. And this skull was strung up by a system of unseen cords, so that it appeared to hang, disembodied, in the still, heavy air, and it had been crowned with a wreath of white roses, and a veil of lace, the final image of his bride.

Yet the skull was still so beautiful, had shaped with its sheer planes so imperiously the face that had once existed above it, that I recognised her the moment I saw her; face of the evening star walking on the rim of night. One false step, oh, my poor, dear girl, next in the fated sisterhood of his wives; one false step and into the abyss of the dark you stumbled.

And where was she, the latest dead, the Romanian countess who might have thought her blood would survive his depredations? I knew she must be here, in the place that had wound me through the castle towards it on a spool of inexorability. But, at first, I could see no sign of her. Then, for some reason – perhaps some change of atmosphere wrought by my presence – the metal shell of the Iron Maiden emitted a ghostly twang; my feverish imagination might have guessed its occupant was trying to clamber out, though, even in the midst of my rising hysteria, I knew she must be dead to find a home there.

With trembling fingers, I prised open the front of the upright coffin, with its sculpted face caught in a rictus of pain. Then, overcome, I dropped the key I still held in my hand. It dropped into the forming pool of her blood.

She was pierced, not by one but by a hundred spikes, this child of the land of the vampires who seemed so newly dead, so full of blood . . . oh God! how recently had he become a widower? How long had he kept her in this obscene cell? Had it been all the time he had courted me, in the clear light of Paris?

I closed the lid of her coffin very gently and burst into a tumult of sobbing that contained both pity for his other victims and also a dreadful anguish to know I, too, was one of them.

The candles flared, as if in a draught from a door to elsewhere. The light caught the fire opal on my hand so that it flashed, once, with a baleful light, as if to tell me the eye of God – his eye – was upon me. My first thought, when I saw the ring for which I had sold myself to this fate, was, how to escape it.

I retained sufficient presence of mind to snuff out the candles round the bier with my fingers, to gather up my taper, to look around, although shuddering, to ensure I had left behind me no traces of my visit.

I retrieved the key from the pool of blood, wrapped it in my handkerchief to keep my hands clean, and fled the room, slamming the door behind me.

It crashed to with a juddering reverberation, like the door of hell.

I could not take refuge in my bedroom, for that retained the memory of his presence trapped in the fathomless silvering of his mirrors. My music room seemed the safest place, although I looked at the picture of Saint Cecilia with a faint dread; what had been the nature of her martyrdom? My mind was in a tumult; schemes for flight jostled with one another . . . as soon as the tide receded from the causeway, I would make for the mainland – on foot, running, stumbling; I did not trust the leather-clad chauffeur, nor the well-behaved housekeeper, and I dared not take any of the pale, ghostly maids into my confidence, either, since they were his creatures, all. Once at the village, I would fling myself directly on the mercy of the gendarmerie.

But – could I trust them, either? His forefathers had ruled this coast for eight centuries, from this castle whose moat was the Atlantic. Might not the police, the advocates, even the judge, all be in his service, turning a common blind eye to his vices since he was milord whose word must be obeyed? Who, on this distant coast, would believe the white-faced girl from Paris who came running to them with a shuddering tale of blood, of fear, of the ogre murmuring in the shadows? Or, rather, they would immediately know it to be true. But were all honour-bound to let me carry it no further.

Assistance. My mother. I ran to the telephone; and the line, of course, was dead.

Dead as his wives.

A thick darkness unlit by any star, still glazed the windows. Every lamp in my room burned, to keep the dark outside, yet it seemed still to encroach on me, to be present beside me but as if masked by my lights, the night like a permeable substance that could seep into my skin. I looked at the precious little clock made from hypocritically innocent flowers long ago, in Dresden; the hands had scarcely moved one single hour forward from when I first descended to the private slaughterhouse of his. Time was his servant, too; it would trap me, here, in a night that would last until he came back to me, like a black sun on a hopeless morning.

And yet the time might still be my friend; at that hour, that very hour, he set sail for New York.

To know that, in a few moments, my husband would have left France calmed my agitation a little. My reason told me I had nothing to fear; the tide that would take him away to the New World would let me out of the imprisonment of the castle. Surely I could easily evade the servants. Anybody can buy a ticket at the railway station. Yet I was still filled with unease. I opened the lid of the piano; perhaps I thought my own particular magic might help me, now, that I could create a pentacle out of music that would keep me from harm for, if my music had first ensnared him, then might it not also give me the power to free myself from him?

Mechanically, I began to play but my fingers were stiff and shaking. At first, I could manage nothing better than the exercises of Czerny but simply the act of playing soothed me and, for solace, for the sake of the harmonious rationality of its sublime mathematics, I searched among his scores until I found *The Well-Tempered Clavier*. I set myself the therapeutic task of playing all Bach's equations, every one, and, I told myself, if I played them all through without a single mistake – then the morning would find me once more a virgin.

Crash of a dropped stick.

His silver-headed cane! What else! Sly, cunning, he had returned; he was waiting for me outside the door!

I rose to my feet; fear gave me strength. I flung back my head defiantly. 'Come in!' My voice astonished me by its firmness, its clarity.

The door slowly, nervously opened and I saw, not the massive irredeemable bulk of my husband but the slight, stooping figure of the piano-tuner, and he looked far more terrified of me than my mother's daughter would have been of the Devil himself. In the torture chamber, it seemed to me that I would never laugh again; now, helplessly, laugh I did, with relief, and, after a moment's hesitation, the boy's face softened and he smiled a little almost in shame. Though they were blind, his eyes were singularly sweet.

'Forgive me,' said Jean-Yves. 'I know I've given you grounds for dismissing me, that I should be crouching outside your door at midnight . . . but I heard you walking about, up and down – I sleep in a room at the foot of the west tower – and some intuition told me you could not sleep and might, perhaps, pass the insomniac hours at your piano. And I could not resist that. Besides, I stumbled over these – ' '

And he displayed the ring of keys I'd dropped outside my husband's office door, the ring from which one key was missing. I took them from him, looked round for a place to stow them, fixed on the piano stool as if to hide them would protect me. Still he stood smiling at me. How hard it was to make everyday conversation.

'It's perfect,' I said. 'The piano. Perfectly in tune.'

But he was full of the loquacity of embarrassment, as though I would only forgive him for his impudence if he explained the cause of it thoroughly.

'When I heard you play this afternoon, I thought I'd never heard such a touch. Such technique. A treat for me, to hear a virtuoso! So I crept up to your door now, humbly as a little dog might, madame, and put my ear to the keyhole and listened, and listened – until my stick fell to the floor through a momentary clumsiness of mine, and I was discovered.'

He had the most touching ingenuous smile.

'Perfectly in tune,' I repeated. To my surprise, now I had said it, I found I could not say anything else. I could only repeat: 'In tune . . . perfect . . . in tune,' over and over again. I saw a dawning surprise in his face. My head throbbed. To see him, in his lovely, blind humanity, seemed to hurt me very piercingly, somewhere inside my breast; his figure blurred, the room swayed about me. After the dreadful revelation of that bloody chamber, it was his tender look that made me faint.

When I recovered consciousness, I found I was lying in the piano-tuner's arms and he was tucking the satin cushion from the piano-stool under my head.

'You are in some great distress,' he said. 'No bride should suffer so much, so early in her marriage.'

His speech had the rhythms of the countryside, the rhythms of the tides.

'Any bride brought to this castle should come ready dressed in mourning, should bring a priest and a coffin with her,' I said.

'What's this?'

It was too late to keep silent; and if he, too, were one of my husband's creatures, then at least he had been kind to me. So I told him everything, the keys, the interdiction, my disobedience, the room, the rack, the skull, the corpses, the blood.

'I can scarcely believe it,' he said, wondering. 'That man . . . so rich; so well-born.'

'Here's proof,' I said and tumbled the fatal key out of my handkerchief on to the silken rug.

'Oh God,' he said. 'I can smell the blood.'

He took my hand; he pressed his arms about me. Although he was scarcely more than a boy, I felt a great strength flow into me from his touch.

'We whisper all manner of strange tales up and down the coast,' he said. 'There was a Marquis, once, who used to hunt young girls on the mainland; he hunted them with dogs, as though they were foxes. My grandfather had it from his grandfather, how the Marquis pulled a head out of his saddle bag and showed it to the blacksmith while the man was shoeing his horse. "A fine specimen of the genus, brunette, eh, Guillaume?" And it was the head of the blacksmith's wife.'

But, in these more democratic times, my husband must travel as far as Paris to do his hunting in the salons. Jean-Yves knew the moment I shuddered.

'Oh, madame! I thought all these were old wives' tales, chattering of fools, spooks to scare bad children into good behaviour! Yet how could you know, a stranger, that the old name for this place is the Castle of Murder?'

How could I know, indeed? Except that, in my heart, I'd always known its lord would be the death of me.

'Hark!' said my friend suddenly. 'The sea has changed key; it must be near morning. The tide is going down.'

He helped me up. I looked from the window, towards the mainland, along the causeway where the stones gleamed wetly in the thin light of the end of the night and, with an almost unimaginable horror, a horror the intensity of which I cannot transmit to you, I saw, in the distance, still far away yet drawing moment by moment inexorably nearer, the twin headlamps of his great black car, gouging tunnels through the shifting mist.

My husband had indeed returned; this time, it was no fancy.

'The key!' said Jean-Yves. 'It must go back on the ring, with the others. As though nothing had happened.'

But the key was still caked with wet blood and I ran to my bathroom and held it under the hot tap. Crimson water swirled down the basin but, as if the key itself were hurt, the bloody token stuck. The turquoise eyes of the dolphin taps winked at me derisively; they knew my husband had been too clever for me! I scrubbed the stain with my nail brush but still it would not budge. I thought how the car would be rolling silently towards the closed courtyard gate; the more I scrubbed the key, the more vivid grew the stain.

The bell in the gatehouse would jangle. The porter's drowsy son would push back the patchwork quilt, yawning, pull the shirt over his head, thrust his feet into his sabots . . . slowly, slowly; open the door for your master as slowly as you can . . .

And still the bloodstain mocked the fresh water that spilled from the mouth of the leering dolphin.

'You have no more time,' said Jean-Yves. 'He is here. I know it. I must stay with you.'

'You shall not!' I said. 'Go back to your room, now. Please.'

He hesitated. I put the edge of steel in my voice, for I knew I must meet my lord alone.

'Leave me!'

As soon as he was gone, I dealt with the keys and went to my bedroom. The causeway was empty; Jean-Yves was correct, my husband had already entered the castle. I pulled the curtains close, stripped off my clothes and pulled the bedcurtains around me as a pungent aroma of Russian leather assured me my husband was once again beside me.

'Dearest!'

With the most treacherous, lascivious tenderness, he kissed my eyes, and, mimicking the new bride newly awakened, I flung my arms around him, for on my seeming acquiescence depended my salvation.

'Da Silva of Rio outwitted me,' he said wryly. 'My New York agent telegraphed Le Havre and saved me a wasted journey. So we may resume our interrupted pleasures, my love.'

I did not believe one word of it. I knew I had behaved exactly according to his desires; had he not bought me so that I should do so? I had been tricked into my own betrayal to that illimitable darkness whose source I had been compelled to seek in his absence and, now that I had met that shadowed reality of his that came to life only in the presence of its own atrocities, I must pay the price of my new knowledge. The secret of Pandora's box; but he had given me the box, himself, knowing I must learn the secret. I had played a game in which every move was governed by a destiny as oppressive and omnipotent as himself, since that destiny was himself; and I had lost. Lost at the charade of innocence and vice in which he had engaged me. Lost as the victim loses to the executioner.

His hand brushed my breast, beneath the sheet. I strained my nerves yet could not help but flinch at the intimate touch, for it made me think of the piercing embrace of the Iron Maiden and of his lost lovers in the vault. When he saw my reluctance his eyes veiled over and yet his appetite did not diminish. His tongue ran over red lips already wet. Silent, mysterious, he moved away from me to draw off his jacket. He took the gold watch from his waistcoat and laid it on the dressing table, like a good bourgeois; scooped out his rattling loose change and now – oh God! – makes a great play of patting his pockets officiously, puzzled lips pursed, searching for something that he had mislaid. Then turns to me with a ghastly, a triumphant smile.

'But of course! I gave the keys to you!'

'Your keys? Why, of course. Here, they're under the pillow; wait a moment – what – Ah! No . . . now, where can I have left them? I was whiling away the evening without you at the piano, I remember. Of course! The music room!'

Brusquely he flung my negligee of antique lace on the bed.

'Go and get them.'

'Now? This moment? Can't it wait until morning, my darling?'

I forced myself to be seductive, I saw myself, pale, pliant as a plant that begs to be trampled underfoot, a dozen vulnerable appealing girls reflected in as many mirrors, and I saw how he almost failed to resist me. If he had come to me in bed, I would have strangled him, then.

But he half-snarled: 'No. It won't wait. Now.'

The unearthly light of dawn filled the room; had only one previous dawn broken upon me in that vile place? And there was nothing for it but to go and fetch the keys from the music stool and pray he would not examine them too closely, pray to God his eyes would fail him, that he might be struck blind.

When I came back into the bedroom carrying the bunch of keys that jangled at every step like a curious musical instrument, he was sitting on the bed in his immaculate shirtsleeves, his head sunk in his hands.

And it seemed to me he was in despair.

Strange. In spite of my fear of him, that made me whiter than my wrap, I felt there emanate from him, at that moment, a stench of absolute despair, rank and ghastly, as if the lilies that surrounded him had all at once begun to fester, or the Russian leather of his scent were reverting to the elements of flayed hide and excrement of which it was composed. The chthonic gravity of his presence exerted a tremendous pressure on the room, so that the blood pounded in my ears as if we had been precipitated to the bottom of the sea, beneath the waves that pounded against the shore.

I held my life in my hands amongst those keys and, in a moment, would place it between his well-manicured fingers. The evidence of that bloody chamber had showed me I could expect no mercy. Yet, when he raised his head and stared at me with his blind, shuttered eyes as though he did not recognise me, I felt a terrified pity for him, for this man who lived in such strange, secret places that, if I loved him enough to follow him, I should have to die.

The atrocious loneliness of that monster!

The monocle had fallen from his face. His curling mane was disordered, as if he had run his hands through it in his distraction. I saw how he had lost his impassivity and was now filled with suppressed excitement. The hand he stretched out for those counters in his game of love and death shook a little; the face that turned towards me contained a sombre delirium that seemed to me compounded of a ghastly, yes, shame but also of a terrible, guilty joy as he slowly ascertained how I had sinned.

That tell-tale stain had resolved itself into a mark the shape and brilliance of the heart on a playing card. He disengaged the key from the ring and looked at it for a while, solitary, brooding.

'It is the key that leads to the kingdom of the unimaginable,' he said. His voice was low and had in it the timbre of certain great cathedral organs that seem, when they are played, to be conversing with God.

I could not restrain a sob.

'Oh, my love, my little love who brought me a white gift of music,' he said, almost as if grieving. 'My little love, you'll never know how much I hate daylight!'

Then he sharply ordered: 'Kneel!'

I knelt before him and he pressed the key lightly to my forehead, held it there for a moment. I felt a faint tingling of the skin and, when I involuntarily glanced at myself in the mirror, I saw the heart-shaped stain had transferred itself to my forehead, to the space between the eyebrows, like the caste mark of a Brahmin woman. Or the mark of Cain. And now the key gleamed as freshly as if it had just been cut. He clipped it back on the ring, emitting that same, heavy sigh as he had done when I said I would marry him.

'My virgin of the arpeggios, prepare yourself for martyrdom.'

'What form shall it take?' I said.

'Decapitation,' he whispered, almost voluptuously. 'Go and bathe yourself; put on that white dress you wore to hear *Tristan* and the necklace that prefigures your end. And I shall take myself off to the armoury, my dear, to sharpen my great-grandfather's ceremonial sword.'

'The servants?'

'We shall have absolute privacy for our last rites; I have already dismissed them. If you look out of the window you can see them going to the mainland.'

It was now the full, pale light of morning; the weather was grey, indeterminate, the sea had an oily, sinister look, a gloomy day on which to die. Along the causeway I could see trouping every maid and scullion, every potboy and pan-scourer, valet, laundress and vassal who worked in the great house, most on foot, a few on bicycles. The faceless housekeeper trudged along with a great basket in which, I guessed, she'd stowed as much as she could ransack from the larder. The Marquis must have given the chauffeur leave to borrow the motor for the day, for it went last of all, at a stately pace, as though the procession were a cortège and the car already bore my coffin to the mainland for burial.

But I knew no good Breton earth would cover me, like a last, faithful lover; I had another fate.

'I have given them all a day's holiday, to celebrate our wedding,' he said. And smiled.

However hard I stared at the receding company, I could see no sign of Jean-Yves, our latest servant hired but the preceding morning.

'Go, now. Bathe yourself; dress yourself. The lustratory ritual and the ceremonial robing; after that, the sacrifice. Wait in the music room until I telephone for you. No, my dear!' And he smiled, as I started, recalling the line was dead. 'One may call inside the castle just as much as one pleases; but outside – never.'

I scrubbed my forehead with the nail brush as I had scrubbed the key but this red mark would not go away, either, no matter what I did, and I knew I would wear it until I died, though that would not be long. Then I went to my dressing room and put on the white muslin shift, costume of a victim of an auto-da-fé, he had bought me to listen to the *Liebestod* in. Twelve young women combed out twelve listless sheaves of brown hair in the mirrors; soon, there would be none. The mass of lilies that surrounded me exhaled, now, the odour of their withering. They looked like the trumpets of the angels of death.

On the dressing table, coiled like a snake about to strike, lay the ruby choker.

Already almost lifeless, cold at heart, I descended the spiral staircase to the music room but there I found I had not been abandoned.

'I can be of some comfort to you,' the boy said. 'Though not of much use.'

We pushed the piano stool in front of the open window so that, for as long as I could, I would be able to smell the ancient, reconciling smell of the sea that, in time, will cleanse everything, scour the old bones white, wash away all the stains. The last little chambermaid had trotted along the causeway long ago and now the tide, fated as I, came tumbling in, the crisp wavelets splashing on the old stones.

'You do not deserve this,' he said.

'Who can say what I deserve or no?' I said. 'I've done nothing; but that may be sufficient reason for condemning me.'

'You disobeyed him,' he said. 'That is sufficient reason for him to punish you.'

'I only did what he knew I would.'

'Like Eve,' he said.

The telephone rang a shrill imperative. Let it ring. But my lover lifted me up and set me on my feet; I must answer it. The receiver felt heavy as earth.

'The courtyard. Immediately.'

My lover kissed me, he took my hand. He would come with me if I would lead him. Courage. When I thought of courage, I thought of my mother. Then I saw a muscle in my lover's face quiver.

'Hoofbeats!' he said.

I cast one last, desperate glance from the window and, like a miracle, I saw a horse and rider galloping at a vertiginous speed along the causeway, though the waves crashed, now, high as the horse's fetlocks. A rider, her black skirts tucked up around her waist so she could ride hard and fast, a crazy, magnificent horsewoman in widow's weeds.

As the telephone rang again.

'Am I to wait all morning?'

Every moment, my mother drew nearer,

'She will be too late,' Jean-Yves said and yet he could not restrain a note of hope that, though it must be so, yet it might not be so.

The third, intransigent call.

'Shall I come up to heaven to fetch you down, Saint Cecilia? You wicked woman, do you wish me to compound my crimes by desecrating the marriage bed?'

So I must go to the courtyard where my husband waited in his London-tailored trousers and the shirt from Turnbull and Asser, beside the mounting block, with, in his hand, the sword which his great-grandfather had presented to the little corporal, in token of surrender to the Republic, before he shot himself. The heavy sword, unsheathed, grey as that November morning, sharp as childbirth, mortal.

When my husband saw my companion, he observed: 'Let the blind lead the blind, eh? But does even a youth as besotted as you think she was truly blind to her own desires when she took my ring? Give it me back, whore.'

The fires in the opal had all died down. I gladly slipped it from my finger and, even in that dolorous place, my heart was lighter for the lack of it. My husband took it lovingly and lodged it on the tip of his finger; it would go no further.

'It will serve me for a dozen more fiancées,' he said. 'To the block, woman. No – leave the boy; I shall deal with him later, utilising a less exalted instrument than the one with which I do my wife the honour of her immolation, for do not fear that in death you will be divided.'

Slowly, slowly, one foot before the other, I crossed the cobbles. The longer I dawdled over my execution, the more time it gave the avenging angel to descend . . .

'Don't loiter, girl! Do you think I shall lose appetite for the meal if you are so long about serving it? No; I shall grow hungrier, more ravenous with each moment, more cruel . . . Run to me, run! I have a place prepared for your exquisite corpse in my display of flesh!'

He raised the sword and cut bright segments from the air with it, but still I lingered although my hopes, so recently raised, now began to flag. If she is not here by now, her horse must have stumbled on the causeway, have plunged into the sea . . . One thing only made me glad; that my lover would not see me die.

My husband laid my branded forehead on the stone and, as he had done once before, twisted my hair into a rope and drew it away from my neck.

'Such a pretty neck,' he said with what seemd to be a genuine, retrospective tenderness. 'A neck like the stem of a young plant.'

I felt the silken bristle of his beard and the wet touch of his lips as he kissed my nape. And, once again, of my apparel I must retain only my gems; the sharp blade ripped my dress in two and it fell from me. A little green moss, growing in the crevices of the mounting block, would be the last thing I should see in all the world.

The whizz of that heavy sword.

And – a great battering and pounding at the gate, the jangling of the bell, the frenzied neighing of a horse! The unholy silence of the place shattered in an instant. The blade did *not* descend, the necklace did *not* sever, my head did *not* roll. For, for an instant, the beast wavered in his stroke, a sufficient split second of astonished indecision to let me spring upright and dart to the assistance of my lover as he struggled sightlessly with the great bolts that kept her out.

The Marquis stood transfixed, utterly dazed, at a loss. It must have been as if he had been watching his beloved *Tristan* for the twelfth, the thirteenth time and Tristan stirred, then leapt from his bier in the last act, announced in a jaunty aria interposed from Verdi that bygones were bygones, crying over spilt milk did nobody any good and, as for himself, he proposed to live happily ever after. The puppet master, open-mouthed, wide-eyed, impotent at the last, saw his dolls break free of their strings, abandon the rituals he had ordained for them since time began and start to live for themselves; the king, aghast, witnesses the revolt of his pawns.

You never saw such a wild thing as my mother, her hat seized by the winds and blown out to sea so that her hair was her white mane, her black lisle legs exposed to the thigh, her skirts tucked round her waist, one hand on the reins of the rearing horse while the other clasped my father's service revolver and, behind her, the breakers of the savage, indifferent sea, like the witnesses of a furious justice. And my husband stood stock-still, as if she had been Medusa, the sword still raised over his head as in those clockwork tableaux of Bluebeard that you see in glass cases at fairs.

And then it was as though a curious child pushed his centime into the slot and set all in motion. The heavy, bearded figure roared out aloud, braying with fury, and wielding the honourable sword as if it were a matter of death or glory, charged us, all three.

On her eighteenth birthday, my mother had disposed of a man-eating tiger that had ravaged the villages in the hills north of Hanoi. Now, without a moment's hesitation, she raised my father's gun, took aim and put a single, irreproachable bullet through my husband's head.

We lead a quiet life, the three of us. I inherited, of course, enormous wealth but we have given most of it away to various charities. The castle is now a school for the blind, though I pray that the children who live there are not haunted by any sad ghosts looking for, crying for, the husband who will never return to the bloody chamber, the contents of which are buried or burned, the door sealed.

I felt I had the right to retain sufficient funds to start a little music school here, on the outskirts of Paris, and we do well enough. Sometimes we can even afford to go to the Opéra, though never to sit in a box, of course. We know we are the source of many whisperings and much gossip but the three of us know the truth of it and mere chatter can never harm us. I can only bless the – what shall I call it? – the *maternal telepathy* that sent my mother running headlong from the telephone to the station after I had called her, that night. I never heard you cry before, she said, by way of explanation. Not when you were happy. And who ever cried because of gold bath taps?

The night train, the one I had taken; she lay in her berth, sleepless as I had been. When she could not find a taxi at the lonely halt, she borrowed old Dobbin from a bemused farmer, for some internal urgency told her that she must reach me before the incoming tide sealed me away from her for ever. My poor old nurse, left scandalised at home – what? interrupt milord on his honeymoon? – she died soon after. She had taken so much secret pleasure in the fact that her little girl had become a marquise; and now here I was, scarcely a penny the richer, widowed at seventeen in the most dubious circumstances and busily engaged in setting up house with a piano-tuner. Poor thing, she passed away in a sorry state of disillusion! But I do believe my mother loves him as much as I do.

No paint nor powder, no matter how thick or white, can mask that red mark on my forehead; I am glad he cannot see it – not for fear of his revulsion, since I know he sees me clearly with his heart – but, because it spares my shame.

The Courtship of Mr Lyon

Outside her kitchen window, the hedgerow glistened as if the snow possessed a light of its own; when the sky darkened towards evening, an unearthly, reflected pallor remained behind upon the winter's landscape, while still the soft flakes floated down. This lovely girl, whose skin possesses that same, inner light so you would have thought she, too, was made all of snow, pauses in her chores in the mean kitchen to look out at the country road. Nothing has passed that way all day; the road is white and unmarked as a spilled bolt of bridal satin.

Father said he would be home before nightfall.

The snow brought down all the telephone wires; he couldn't have called, even with the best of news.

The roads are bad. I hope he'll be safe.

But the old car stuck fast in a rut, wouldn't budge an inch; the engine whirred, coughed and died and he was far from home. Ruined, once; then ruined again, as he had learnt from his lawyers that very morning; at the conclusion of the lengthy, slow attempt to restore his fortunes, he had turned out his pockets to find the cash for petrol to take him home. And not even enough money left over to buy his Beauty, his girl-child, his pet, the one white rose she said she wanted; the only gift she wanted, no matter how the case went, how rich he might once again be. She had asked for so little and he had not been able to give it to her. He cursed the useless car, the last straw that broke his spirit; then, nothing for it but to fasten his old sheepskin coat around him, abandon the heap of metal and set off down the snow-filled lane to look for help.

Behind wrought-iron gates, a short, snowy drive performed a reticent flourish before a miniature, perfect Palladian house that seemed to hide itself shyly behind snow-laden skirts of an antique cypress. It was almost night; that house, with its sweet, retiring, melancholy grace, would have seemed deserted but for a light that flickered in an upstairs window, so vague it might have been the reflection of a star, if any stars could have penetrated the snow that whirled yet more thickly. Chilled through, he pressed the latch of the gate and saw, with a pang, how, on the withered ghost of a tangle of thorns, there clung, still, the faded rag of a white rose.

The gate clanged loudly shut behind him; too loudly. For an instant, that reverberating clang seemed final, emphatic, ominous as if the gate, now closed, barred all within it from the world outside the walled, wintry garden. And, from a distance, though from what distance he could not tell, he heard the most singular sound in the world: a great roaring, as of a beast of prey.

In too much need to allow himself to be intimidated, he squared up to the mahogany door. This door was equipped with a knocker in the shape of a lion's head, with a ring through the nose; as he raised his hand towards it, it came to him this lion's head was not, as he had thought at first, made of brass, but, instead, of gold. Before, however, he could announce his presence, the door swung silently inward on well-oiled hinges and he saw a white hall where the candles of a great chandelier cast their benign light upon so many, many flowers in great, free-standing jars of crystal that it seemed the whole of spring drew him into its warmth with a profound intake of perfumed breath. Yet there was no living person in the hall.

The door behind him closed as silently as it had opened, yet, this time, he felt no fear although he knew by the pervasive atmosphere of a suspension of reality that he had entered a place of privilege where all the laws of the world he knew need not necessarily apply, for the very rich are often very eccentric and the house was plainly that of an exceedingly wealthy man. As it was, when nobody came to help him with his coat, he took it off himself. At that, the crystals of the chandelier tinkled a little, as if emitting a pleased chuckle, and the door of a cloakroom opened of its own accord. There were, however, no clothes at all in this cloakroom, not even the statutory country-garden mackintosh to greet his own squirearchal sheepskin, but, when he emerged again into the hall, he found a greeting waiting for him at last – there was, of all things, a liver and white King Charles spaniel crouched with head intelligently cocked, on the kelim runner. It gave him further, comforting proof of his unseen host's wealth and eccentricity to see the dog wore, in place of a collar, a diamond necklace.

The dog sprang to its feet in welcome and busily shepherded him (how amusing!) to a snug little leather-panelled study on the first floor, where a low table was drawn up to a roaring log fire. On the table, a silver tray; round the neck of the whisky decanter, a silver tag with the legend: *Drink me*, while the cover of the silver dish was engraved with the exhortation: *Eat me*, in a flowing hand. This dish contained sandwiches of thick-cut roast beef, still bloody. He drank the one with soda and ate the other with some excellent mustard thoughtfully provided in a stoneware pot, and, when the spaniel saw to it he had served himself, she trotted off about her own business.

All that remained to make Beauty's father entirely comfortable was to find, in a curtained recess, not only a telephone but the card of a garage that advertised a twenty-four-hour rescue service; a couple of calls later and he had confirmed, thank God that there was no serious trouble, only the car's age and the cold weather . . . could he pick it up from the village in an hour? And directions to the village, but half a mile away, were supplied, in a new tone of deference, as soon as he described the house from where he was calling.

And he was disconcerted but, in his impecunious circumstances, relieved to hear the bill would go on his hospitable if absent host's account; no question, assured the mechanic. It was the master's custom.

Time for another whisky as he tried, unsuccessfully, to call Beauty and tell her he would be late; but the lines were still down, although, miraculously, the storm had cleared as the moon rose and now a glance between the velvet curtains revealed a landscape as of ivory with an inlay of silver. Then the spaniel appeared again, with his hat in her careful mouth, prettily wagging her tail, as if to tell him it was time to be gone, that this magical hospitality was over.

As the door swung to behind him, he saw the lion's eyes were made of agate.

Great wreaths of snow now precariously curded the rose trees and, when he brushed against a stem on his way to the gate, a chill armful softly thudded to the ground to reveal, as if miraculously preserved beneath it, one last, single, perfect rose that might have been the last rose left living in all the white winter, and of so intense and delicate a fragrance it seemed to ring like a dulcimer on the frozen air.

How could his host, so mysterious, so kind, deny Beauty her present?

Not now distant but close to hand, close as the mahogany front door, rose a mighty, furious roaring; the garden seemed to hold its breath in apprehension. But still, because he loved his daughter, Beauty's father stole the rose.

At that, every window of the house blazed with furious light and a fugal baying, as if a pride of lions, introduced his host.

There is always a dignity about great bulk, an assertiveness, a quality of being more *there* than most of us are. The being who now confronted Beauty's father seemed to him, in his confusion, vaster than the house he owned, ponderous yet swift, and the moonlight glittered on his great, mazy head of hair, on the eyes green as agate, on the golden hairs of the great paws that grasped his shoulders so that their claws pierced the sheepskin as he shook him like an angry child shakes a doll.

This leonine apparition shook Beauty's father until his teeth rattled and then dropped him sprawling on his knees while the spaniel, darting from the open door, danced round them, yapping distractedly, like a lady at whose dinner party blows have been exchanged.

'My good fellow – ' stammered Beauty's father; but the only response was a renewed roar.

'Good fellow? I am no good fellow! I am the Beast, and you must call me Beast, while I call you, Thief!'

'Forgive me for robbing your garden, Beast!'

Head of a lion; mane and mighty paws of a lion; he reared on his hind legs like an angry lion yet wore a smoking jacket of dull red brocade and was the owner of that lovely house and the low hills that cupped it.

'It was for my daughter,' said Beauty's father. 'All she wanted, in the whole world, was one white, perfect rose.'

The Beast rudely snatched the photograph her father drew from his wallet and inspected it, first brusquely, then with a strange kind of wonder, almost the dawning of surmise. The camera had captured a certain look she had, sometimes, of absolute sweetness and absolute gravity, as if her eyes might pierce appearances and see your soul. When he handed the picture back, the Beast took good care not to scratch the surface with his claws.

'Take her her rose, then, but bring her to dinner,' he growled; and what else was there to be done?

Although her father had told her of the nature of the one who waited for her, she could not control an instinctual shudder of fear when she saw him, for a lion is a lion and a man is a man and, though lions are more beautiful by far than we are, yet they belong to a different order of beauty and, besides, they have no respect for us: why should they? Yet wild things have a far more rational fear of us than is ours of them, and some kind of sadness in his agate eyes, that looked almost blind, as if sick of sight, moved her heart.

He sat, impassive as a figurehead, at the top of the table; the dining room was Queen Anne, tapestried, a gem. Apart from an aromatic soup kept hot over a spirit lamp, the food, though exquisite, was cold – a cold bird, a cold soufflé, cheese. He asked her father to serve them from a buffet and, himself, ate nothing. He grudgingly admitted what she had already guessed, that he disliked the presence of servants because, she thought, a constant human presence would remind him too bitterly of his otherness, but the spaniel sat at his feet throughout the meal, jumping up from time to time to see that everything was in order.

How strange he was. She found his bewildering difference from herself almost intolerable; its presence choked her. There seemed a heavy, soundless pressure upon her in his house, as if it lay under water, and when she saw the great paws lying on the arm of his chair, she thought: they are the death of any tender herbivore. And such a one she felt herself to be, Miss Lamb, spotless, sacrificial.

Yet she stayed, and smiled, because her father wanted her to do so; and when the Beast told her how he would aid her father's appeal against the judgement, she smiled with both her mouth and her eyes. But when, as they sipped their brandy, the Beast, in the diffuse, rumbling purr with which he conversed, suggested, with a hint of shyness, of fear of refusal, that she should stay here, with him, in comfort, while her father returned to London to take up the legal cudgels again, she forced a smile. For she knew with a pang of dread, as soon as he spoke, that it would be so and her visit to the Beast must be, on some magically reciprocal scale, the price of her father's good fortune.

Do not think she had no will of her own; only, she was possessed by a sense of obligation to an unusual degree and, besides, she would gladly have gone to the ends of the earth for her father, whom she loved dearly.

Her bedroom contained a marvellous glass bed; she had a bathroom, with towels thick as fleece and vials of suave unguents; and a little parlour of her own, the walls of which were covered with an antique paper of birds of paradise and Chinamen, where there were precious books and pictures and the flowers grown by invisible gardeners in the Beast's hothouses. Next morning, her father kissed her and drove away with a renewed hope about him that made her glad, but, all the same, she longed for the shabby home of their poverty. The unaccustomed luxury about her she found poignant, because it gave no pleasure to its possessor and himself she did not see all day as if, curious reversal, she frightened him, although the spaniel came and sat with her, to keep her company. Today, the spaniel wore a neat choker of turquoises.

Who prepared her meals? Loneliness of the Beast; all the time she stayed there, she saw no evidence of another human presence but the trays of food had arrived on a dumb waiter inside the mahogany cupboard in her parlour. Dinner was eggs Benedict and grilled veal; she ate it as she browsed in a book she had found in the rosewood revolving bookcase, a collection of courtly and elegant French fairy tales about white cats who were transformed princesses and fairies who were birds. Then she pulled a sprig of muscat grapes from a fat bunch for her dessert and found herself yawning; she discovered she was bored. At that, the spaniel took hold of her skirt with its velvet mouth and gave a firm but gentle tug. She allowed the dog to trot before her to the study in which her father had been entertained and there, to her well-disguised dismay, she found her host, seated beside the fire with a tray of coffee at his elbow from which she must pour.

The voice that seemed to issue from a cave full of echoes, his dark, soft rumbling growl; after her day of pastel-coloured idleness, how could she converse with the possessor of a voice that seemed an instrument created to inspire the terror that the chords of great organs bring? Fascinated, almost awed, she watched the firelight play on the gold fringes of his mane; he was irradiated, as if with a kind of halo, and she thought of the first great beast of the Apocalypse, the winged lion with his paw upon the Gospel, Saint Mark. Small talk turned to dust in her mouth; small talk had never, at the best of times, been Beauty's forte, and she had little practice at it.

But he, hesitantly, as if he himself were in awe of a young girl who looked as if she had been carved out of a single pearl, asked after her father's law case; and her dead mother; and how they, who had been so rich, had come to be so poor. He forced himself to master his shyness, which was that of a wild creature, and so, she contrived to master her own – to such effect that soon she was chattering away to him as if she had known him all her life. When the little cupid in the gilt clock on the mantelpiece struck its miniature tambourine, she was astonished to discover it did so twelve times.

'So late! You will want to sleep,' he said.

At that, they both fell silent, as if these strange companions were suddenly overcome with embarrassment to find themselves together, alone, in that room in the depths of winter's night. As she was about to rise, he flung himself at her feet and buried his head in her lap. She stayed stock-still, transfixed; she felt his hot breath on her fingers, the stiff bristles of his muzzle grazing her skin, the rough lapping of his tongue and then, with a flood of compassion, understood: all he is doing is kissing my hands.

He drew back his head and gazed at her with his green, inscrutable eyes, in which she saw her face repeated twice, as small as if it were in bud. Then, without another word, he sprang from the room and she saw, with an indescribable shock, he went on all fours.

Next day, all day, the hills on which the snow still settled echoed with the Beast's rumbling roar: has master gone a-hunting? Beauty asked the spaniel. But the spaniel growled, almost bad-temperedly, as if to say, that she would not have answered, even if she could have.

Beauty would pass the day in her suite reading or, perhaps, doing a little embroidery; a box of coloured silks and a frame had been provided for her. Or, well wrapped up, she wandered in the walled garden, among the leafless roses, with the spaniel at her heels, and did a little raking and rearranging. An idle, restful time; a holiday. The enchantment of that bright, sad pretty place enveloped her and she found that, against all her expectations, she was happy there. She no longer felt the slightest apprehension at her nightly interviews with the Beast. All the natural laws of the world were held in suspension, here, where an army of invisibles tenderly waited on her, and she would talk with the lion, under the patient chaperonage of the brown-eyed dog, on the nature of the moon and its borrowed light, about the stars and the substances of which they were made, about the variable transformations of the weather. Yet still his strangeness made her shiver; and when he helplessly fell before her to kiss her hand, as he did every night when they parted, she would retreat nervously into her skin, flinching at his touch.

The telephoned shrilled; for her. Her father. Such news!

The Beast sunk his great head on to his paws. You will come back to me? It will be lonely here, without you.

She was moved almost to tears that he should care for her so. It was in her heart to drop a kiss upon his shaggy mane but, though she stretched out her hand towards him, she could not bring herself to touch him of her own free will, he was so different from herself. But, yes, she said; I will come back. Soon, before the winter is over. Then the taxi came and took her away.

You are never at the mercy of the elements in London, where the huddled warmth of humanity melts the snow before it has time to settle; and her father was as good as rich again, since his hirsute friend's lawyers had the business so well in hand that his credit brought them nothing but the best. A resplendent hotel; the opera, theatres; a whole new wardrobe for his darling, so she could step out on his arm to parties, to receptions, to restaurants, and life was as she had never known it, for her father had ruined himself before her birth killed her mother.

Although the Beast was the source of this new-found prosperity and they talked of him often, now that they were so far away from the timeless spell of his house it seemed to possess the radiant and finite quality of dream and the Beast himself, so monstrous, so benign, some kind of spirit of good fortune who had smiled on them and let them go. She sent him flowers, white roses in return for the ones he had given her; and when she left the florist, she experienced a sudden sense of perfect freedom, as if she had just escaped from an unknown danger, had been grazed by the possibility of some change but, finally, left intact. Yet, with this exhilaration, a desolating emptiness. But her father was waiting for her at the hotel; they had planned a delicious expedition to buy her furs and she was as eager for the treat as any girl might be.

Since the flowers in the shop were the same all the year round, nothing in the window could tell her that winter had almost gone.

Returning late from supper after the theatre, she took off her earrings in front of the mirror; Beauty. She smiled at herself with satisfaction. She was learning, at the end of her adolescence, how to be a spoiled child and that pearly skin of hers was plumping out, a little, with high living and compliments. A certain inwardness was beginning to transform the lines around her mouth, those signatures of the personality, and her sweetness and her gravity could sometimes turn a mite petulant when things went not quite as she wanted them to go. You could not have said that her freshness was fading but she smiled at herself in mirrors a little too often, these days, and the face that smiled back was not quite the one she had seen contained in the Beast's agate eyes. Her face was acquiring, instead of beauty, a lacquer of the invincible prettiness that characterises certain pampered, exquisite, expensive cats.

The soft wind of spring breathed in from the nearby park through the open window; she did not know why it made her want to cry.

There was a sudden urgent, scrabbling sound, as of claws, at her door.

Her trance before the mirror broke; all at once, she remembered everything perfectly. Spring was here and she had broken her promise. Now the Beast himself had come in pursuit of her! First, she was frightened of his anger; then, mysteriously joyful, she ran to open the door. But it was his liver and white spotted spaniel who hurled herself into the girl's arms in a flurry of little barks and gruff murmurings, of whimpering and relief.

Yet where was the well-brushed, jewelled dog who had sat beside her embroidery frame in the parlour with birds of paradise nodding on the walls? This one's fringed ears were matted with mud, her coat was dusty and snarled, she was thin as a dog that has walked a long way and, if she had not been a dog, she would have been in tears.

After that first, rapturous greeting, she did not wait for Beauty to order her food and water; she seized the chiffon hem of her evening dress, whimpered and tugged. Threw back her head, howled, then tugged and whimpered again.

There was a slow, late train that would take her to the station where she had left for London three months ago. Beauty scribbled a note for her father, threw a coat round her shoulders. Quickly, quickly, urged the spaniel soundlessly; and Beauty knew the Beast was dying.

In the thick dark before dawn, the station master roused a sleepy driver for her. Fast as you can.

It seemed December still possessed his garden. The ground was hard as iron, the skirts of the dark cypress moved on the chill wind with a mournful rustle and there were no green shoots on the roses as if, this year, they would not bloom. And not one light in any of the windows, only, in the topmost attic, the faintest smear of radiance on a pane. The thin ghost of a light on the verge of extinction.

The spaniel had slept a little, in her arms, for the poor thing was exhausted. But now her grieving agitation fed Beauty's urgency and, as the girl pushed open the front door, she saw, with a thrust of conscience, how the golden door knocker was thickly muffled in black crêpe.

The door did not open silently, as before, but with a doleful groaning of the hinges and, this time, on to perfect darkness. Beauty clicked her gold cigarette lighter; the tapers in the chandelier had drowned in their own wax and the prisms were wreathed with dreadful arabesques of cobwebs. The flowers in the glass jars were dead, as if nobody had had the heart to replace them after she was gone. Dust, everywhere; and it was cold. There was an air of exhaustion, of despair in the house and, worse, a kind of physical disillusion, as if its glamour had been sustained by a cheap conjuring trick and now the conjurer, having failed to pull the crowds, had departed to try his luck elsewhere.

Beauty found a candle to light her way and followed the faithful spaniel up the staircase, past the study, past her suite, through a house echoing with desertion up a little back staircase dedicated to mice and spiders, stumbling, ripping the hem of her dress in her haste.

What a modest bedroom! An attic, with a sloping roof, they might have given the chambermaid if the Beast had employed staff. A night light on the mantelpiece, no curtains at the windows, no carpet on the floor and a narrow, iron bedstead on which he lay, sadly diminished, his bulk scarcely disturbing the faded patchwork quilt, his mane a greyish rat's nest and his eyes closed. On the stick-backed chair where his clothes had been thrown, the roses she had sent him were thrust into the jug from the washstand but they were all dead.

The spaniel jumped up on the bed and burrowed her way under the scanty covers, softly keening.

'Oh, Beast,' said Beauty. 'I have come home.'

His eyelids flickered. How was it she had never noticed before that his agate eyes were equipped with lids, like those of a man? Was it because she had only looked at her own face, reflected there?

'I'm dying, Beauty,' he said in a cracked whisper of his former purr.

'Since you left me, I have been sick. I could not go hunting, I found I had not the stomach to kill the gentle beasts, I could not eat. I am sick and I must die; but I shall die happy because you have come to say goodbye to me.'

She flung herself upon him, so that the iron bedstead groaned, and covered his poor paws with her kisses.

'Don't die, Beast! If you'll have me, I'll never leave you.'

When her lips touched the meat-hook claws, they drew back into their pads and she saw how he had always kept his fists clenched, but now, painfully, tentatively, at last began to stretch his fingers. Her tears fell on his face like snow and, under their soft transformation, the bones showed through the pelt, the flesh through the wide, tawny brow. And then it was no longer a lion in her arms but a man, a man with an unkempt mane of hair and, how strange, a broken nose, such as the noses of retired boxers, that gave him a distant, heroic resemblance to the handsomest of all the beasts.

'Do you know,' said Mr Lyon, 'I think I might be able to manage a little breakfast today, Beauty, if you would eat something with me.'

Mr and Mrs Lyon walk in the garden; the old spaniel drowses on the grass, in a drift of fallen petals.

The Tiger's Bride

My father lost me to The Beast at cards.

There's a special madness strikes travellers from the North when they reach the lovely land where the lemon trees grow. We come from countries of cold weather; at home, we are at war with nature but here, ah! you think you've come to the blessed plot where the lion lies down with the lamb. Everything flowers; no harsh wind stirs the voluptuous air. The sun spills fruit for you. And the deathly, sensual lethargy of the sweet South infects the starved brain; it gasps: 'Luxury! more luxury!' But then the snow comes, you cannot escape it, it followed us from Russia as if it ran behind our carriage, and in this dark, bitter city has caught up with us at last, flocking against the windowpanes to mock my father's expectations of perpetual pleasure as the veins in his forehead stand out and throb, his hands shake as he deals the Devil's picture books.

The candles dropped hot, acrid gouts of wax on my bare shoulders. I watched with the furious cynicism peculiar to women whom circumstances force mutely to witness folly, while my father, fired in his desperation by more and yet more draughts of the firewater they call 'grappa', rids himself of the last scraps of my inheritance. When we left Russia, we owned black earth, blue forest with bear and wild boar, serfs, cornfields, farmyards, my beloved horses, white nights of cool summer, the fireworks of the northern lights. What a burden all those possessions must have been to him, because he laughs as if with glee as he beggars himself; he is in such a passion to donate all to The Beast.

Everyone who comes to this city must play a hand with the *grande seigneur*; few come. They did not warn us at Milan, or, if they did, we did not understand them – my limping Italian, the bewildering dialect of the region. Indeed, I myself spoke up in favour of this remote, provincial place, out of fashion two hundred years, because, oh irony, it boasted no casino. I did not know that the price of a stay in its Decembral solitude was a game with Milord.

The hour was late. The chill damp of this place creeps into the stones, into your bones, into the spongy pith of the lungs; it insinuated itself with a shiver into our parlour, where Milord came to play in the privacy essential to him. Who could refuse the invitation his valet brought to our lodging? Not my profligate father, certainly; the mirror above the table gave me back his frenzy, my impassivity, the withering candles, the emptying bottles, the coloured tide of the cards as they rose and fell, the still mask that concealed all the features of The Beast but for the yellow eyes that strayed, now and then, from his unfurled hand towards myself.

'*La Bestia!*' said our landlady, gingerly fingering an envelope with his huge crest of a tiger rampant on it, something of fear, something of wonder in her face. And I could not ask her why they called the master of the place, *La Bestia* – was it to do with the heraldic signature – because her tongue was so thickened by the phlegmy, bronchitic speech of the region I scarcely managed to make out a thing she said except, when she saw me: '*Che bella!*'

Since I could toddle, always the pretty one, with my glossy, nut-brown curls, my rosy cheeks. And born on Christmas Day – her 'Christmas rose,' my English nurse called me. The peasants said: 'The living image of her mother,' crossing themselves out of respect for the dead. My mother did not blossom long; bartered for her dowry to such a feckless sprig of the Russian nobility that she soon died of his gaming, his whoring, his agonising repentances. And The Beast gave me the rose from his own impeccable if outmoded buttonhole when he arrived, the valet brushing the snow off his black cloak. This white rose, unnatural, out of season, that now my nervous fingers ripped, petal by petal, apart as my father magnificently concluded the career he had made of catastrophe.

This is a melancholy, introspective region; a sunless, featureless landscape, the sullen river sweating fog, the shorn, hunkering willows. And a cruel city; the sombre piazza, a place uniquely suited to public executions, under the beetling shadow of that malign barn of a church. They used to hang condemned men in cages from the city walls; unkindness comes naturally to them, their eyes are set so close together, they have thin lips. Poor food, pasta soaked in oil, boiled beef with sauce of bitter herbs. A funereal hush about the place, the inhabitants huddled up against the cold so you can hardly see their faces. And they lie to you and cheat you, innkeepers, coachmen, everybody. God, how they fleeced us.

The treacherous South, where you think there is no winter but forget you take it with you.

My senses were increasingly troubled by the fuddling perfume of Milord, far too potent a reek of purplish civet at such close quarters in so small a room. He must bathe himself in scent, soak his shirts and underlinen in it; what can he smell of, that needs so much camouflage?

I never saw a man so big look so two-dimensional, in spite of the quaint elegance of The Beast, in the old-fashioned tailcoat that might, from its looks, have been bought in those distant years before he imposed seclusion on himself; he does not feel he need keep up with the times. There is a crude clumsiness about his outlines, that are on the ungainly, giant side; and he has an odd air of self-imposed restraint, as if fighting a battle with himself to remain upright when he would far rather drop down on all fours. He throws our human aspirations to the godlike sadly awry, poor fellow; only from a distance would you think The Beast not much different from any other man, although he wears a mask with a man's face painted most beautifully on it. Oh, yes, a beautiful face; but one with too much formal symmetry of feature to be entirely human: one profile of his mask is the mirror image of the other, too perfect, uncanny. He wears a wig, too, false hair tied at the nape with a bow, a wig of the kind you see in old-fashioned portraits. A chaste silk stock stuck with a pearl hides his throat. And gloves of blond kid that are yet so huge and clumsy they do not seem to cover hands.

He is a carnival figure made of papier-mâché and crêpe hair; and yet he has the Devil's knack at cards.

His masked voice echoes as from a great distance as he stoops over his hand and he has such a growling impediment in his speech that only his valet, who understands him, can interpret for him, as if his master were the clumsy doll and he the ventriloquist.

The wick slumped in the eroded wax, the candles guttered. By the time my rose had lost all its petals, my father, too, was left with nothing.

'Except the girl.'

Gambling is a sickness. My father said he loved me yet he staked his daughter on a hand of cards. He fanned them out; in the mirror, I saw wild hope light up his eyes. His collar was unfastened, his rumpled hair stood up on end, he had the anguish of a man in the last stages of debauchery. The draughts came out of the old walls and bit me, I was colder than I'd ever been in Russia, when nights are coldest there.

A queen, a king, an ace. I saw them in the mirror. Oh, I know he thought he could not lose me; besides, back with me would come all he had lost, the unravelled fortunes of our family at one blow restored. And would he not win, as well, The Beast's hereditary palazzo outside the city; his immense revenues; his lands around the river; his rents, his treasure chest, his Mantegnas, his Giulio Romanos, his Cellini salt-cellars, his titles . . . the very city itself.

You must not think my father valued me at less than a king's ransom; but at no more than a king's ransom.

It was cold as hell in the parlour. And it seemed to me, child of the severe North, that it was not my flesh but, truly, my father's soul that was in peril.

My father, of course, believed in miracles; what gambler does not? In pursuit of just such a miracle as this, had we not travelled from the land of bears and shooting stars?

So we teetered on the brink.

The Beast bayed; laid down all three remaining aces.

The indifferent servants now glided smoothly forward as on wheels to douse the candles one by one. To look at them you would think that nothing of any moment had occurred. They yawned a little resentfully; it was almost morning. We had kept them out of bed. The Beast's man brought his cloak. My father sat amongst these preparations for departure, staring on at the betrayal of his cards upon the table.

The Beast's man informed me crisply that he, the valet, would call for me and my bags tomorrow, at ten, and conduct me forthwith to The Beast's palazzo. *Capisco?* So shocked was I that I scarcely did *capisco*; he repeated my orders patiently, he was a strange, thin, quick little man who walked with an irregular jolting rhythm upon splayed feet in curious, wedge-shaped shoes.

Where my father had been red as fire, now he was white as the snow that caked the windowpane. His eyes swam; soon he would cry.

' "Like the base Indian," ' he said; he loved rhetoric. ' "One whose hand,/Like the base Indian, threw a pearl away/Richer than all his tribe . . ." I have lost my pearl, my pearl beyond price.'

At that, The Beast made a sudden, dreadful noise, halfway between a growl and a roar; the candles flared. The quick valet, the prim hypocrite, interpreted unblinkingly: 'My master says: If you are so careless of your treasures, you should expect them to be taken from you.'

He gave us the bow and smile his master could not offer us and they departed.

I watched the snow until, just before dawn, it stopped falling; a hard frost settled, next morning there was a light like iron.

The Beast's carriage, of an elegant if antique design, was black as a hearse and it was drawn by a dashing black gelding who blew smoke from his nostrils and stamped upon the packed snow with enough sprightly appearance of life to give me some hope that not all the world was locked in ice, as I was. I had always held a little towards Gulliver's opinion, that horses are better than we are, and, that day, I would have been glad to depart with him to the kingdom of horses, if I'd been given the chance.

The valet sat up on the box in a natty black and gold livery, clasping, of all things, a bunch of his master's damned white roses as if a gift of flowers would reconcile a woman to any humiliation. He sprang down with preternatural agility to place them ceremoniously in my reluctant hand.

My tear-beslobbered father wants a rose to show that I forgive him. When I break off a stem, I prick my finger and so he gets his rose all smeared with blood.

The valet crouched at my feet to tuck the rugs about me with a strange kind of unflattering obsequiousness yet he forgot his station sufficiently to scratch busily beneath his white periwig with an over-supple index finger as he offered me what my old nurse would have called an 'old-fashioned look', ironic, sly, a smidgen of disdain in it. And pity? No pity. His eyes were moist and brown, his face seamed with the innocent cunning of an ancient baby. He had an irritating habit of chattering to himself under his breath all the time as he packed up his master's winnings. I drew the curtains to conceal the sight of my father's farewell; my spite was sharp as broken glass.

Lost to The Beast! And what, I wondered, might be the exact nature of his 'beastliness'? My English nurse once told me about a tiger-man she saw in London, when she was a little girl, to scare me into good behaviour, for I was a wild wee thing and she could not tame me into submission with a frown or the bribe of a spoonful of jam. If you don't stop plaguing the nursemaids, my beauty, the tiger-man will come and take you away. They'd brought him from Sumatra, in the Indies, she said; his hinder parts were all hairy and only from the head downwards did he resemble a man.

And yet The Beast goes always masked; it cannot be his face that looks like mine.

But the tiger-man, in spite of his hairiness, could take a glass of ale in his hand like a good Christian and drink it down. Had she not seen him do so, at the sign of The George, by the steps of Upper Moor Fields when she was just as high as me and lisped and toddled, too. Then she would sigh for London, across the North Sea of the lapse of years. But, if this young lady was not a good little girl and did not eat her boiled beetroot, then the tiger-man would put on his big black travelling cloak lined with fur, just like your daddy's, and hire the Erl-King's galloper of wind and ride through the night straight to the nursery and –

Yes, my beauty! GOBBLE YOU UP!

How I'd squeal in delighted terror, half believing her, half knowing that she teased me. And there were things I knew that I must not tell her. In our lost farmyard, where the giggling nursemaids initiated me into the mysteries of what the bull did to the cows, I heard about the waggoner's daughter. Hush, hush, don't let on to your nursie we said so; the waggoner's lass, hare-lipped, squint-eyed, ugly as sin, who would have taken her? Yet, to her shame, her belly swelled amid the cruel mockery of the ostlers and her son was born of a bear, they whispered. Born with a full pelt and teeth; that proved it. But, when he grew up, he was a good shepherd, although he never married, lived in a hut outside the village and could make the wind blow any way he wanted to besides being able to tell which eggs would become cocks, which hens.

The wondering peasants once brought my father a skull with horns four inches long on either side of it and would not go back to the field where their poor plough disturbed it until the priest went with them; for this skull had the jaw-bone of a *man*, had it not?

Old wives' tales, nursery fears! I knew well enough the reason for the trepidation I cosily titillated with superstitious marvels of my childhood on the day my childhood ended. For now my own skin was my sole capital in the world and today I'd make my first investment.

We had left the city far behind us and were now traversing a wide, flat dish of snow where the mutilated stumps of the willows flourished their ciliate heads athwart frozen ditches; mist diminished the horizon, brought down the sky until it seemed no more than a few inches above us. As far as eye could see, not one thing living. How starveling, how bereft the dead season of this spurious Eden in which all the fruit was blighted by cold! And my frail roses, already faded. I opened the carriage door and tossed the defunct bouquet into the rucked, frost-stiff mud of the road. Suddenly a sharp, freezing wind arose and pelted my face with a dry rice of powdered snow. The mist lifted sufficiently to reveal before me an acreage of half-derelict façades of sheer red brick, the vast man-trap, the megalomaniac citadel of his palazzo.

It was a world in itself but a dead one, a burned-out planet. I saw The Beast bought solitude, not luxury, with his money.

The little black horse trotted smartly through the figured bronze doors that stood open to the weather like those of a barn and the valet handed me out of the carriage on to the scarred tiles of the great hall itself, into the odorous warmth of a stable, sweet with hay, acrid with horse dung. An equine chorus of neighings and soft drummings of hooves broke out beneath the tall roof, where the beams were scabbed with last summer's swallows' nests; a dozen gracile muzzles lifted from their mangers and turned towards us, ears erect. The Beast had given his horses the use of the dining room. The walls were painted, aptly enough, with a fresco of horses, dogs and men in a wood where fruit and blossom grew on the bough together.

The valet tweaked politely at my sleeve. Milord is waiting.

Gaping doors and broken windows let the wind in everywhere. We mounted one staircase after another, our feet clopping on the marble. Through archways and open doors, I glimpsed suites of vaulted chambers opening one out of another like systems of Chinese boxes into the infinite complexity of the innards of the place. He and I and the wind were the only things stirring; and all the furniture was under dust sheets, the chandeliers bundled up in cloth, pictures taken from their hooks and propped with their faces to the walls as if their master could not bear to look at them. The palace was dismantled, as if its owner were about to move house or had never properly moved in; The Beast had chosen to live in an uninhabited place.

The valet darted me a reassuring glance from his brown, eloquent eyes, yet a glance with so much queer superciliousness in it that it did not comfort me, and went bounding ahead of me on his bandy legs, softly chattering to himself. I held my head high and followed him; but for all my pride, my heart was heavy.

Milord has his eyrie high above the house, a small, stifling, darkened room; he keeps his shutters locked at noon. I was out of breath by the time we reached it and returned to him the silence with which he greeted me. I will not smile. He cannot smile.

In his rarely disturbed privacy, The Beast wears a garment of Ottoman design, a loose, dull purple gown with gold embroidery round the neck that falls from his shoulders to conceal his feet. The feet of the chair he sits in are handsomely clawed. He hides his hands in his ample sleeves. The artificial masterpiece of his face appals me. A small fire in a small grate. A rushing wind rattles the shutters.

The valet coughed. To him fell the delicate task of transmitting to me his master's wishes.

'My master –'

A stick fell in the grate. It made a mighty clatter in that dreadful silence, the valet started, lost his place in his speech, began again.

'My master has but one desire.'

The thick, rich, wild scent with which Milord had soaked himself the previous evening hangs all about us, ascends in cursive blue from the smoke hole of a precious Chinese pot.

'He wishes only –'

Now, in the face of my impassivity, the valet twittered, his ironic composure gone, for the desire of a master, however trivial, may yet sound unbearably insolent in the mouth of a servant and his role of go-between clearly caused him a good deal of embarrassment. He gulped; he swallowed, at last contrived to unleash an unpunctuated flood.

'My master's sole desire is to see the pretty young lady unclothed nude without her dress and that only for the one time after which she will be returned to her father undamaged with bankers' orders for the sum which he lost to my master at cards and also a number of fine presents such as furs, jewels and horses –'

I remained standing. During this interview, my eyes were level with those inside the mask that now evaded mine as if, to his credit, he was ashamed of his own request even as his mouthpiece made it for him. *Agitato, molto agitato*, the valet wrung his white-gloved hands.

'Desnuda – '

I could scarcely believe my ears. I let out a raucous guffaw; no young lady laughs like that! my old nurse used to remonstrate. But I did. And do. At the clamour of my heartless mirth, the valet danced backwards with peturbation, palpitating his fingers as if attempting to wrench them off, expostulating, wordlessly pleading. I felt that I owed it to him to make my reply in as exquisite a Tuscan as I could master.

'You may put me in a windowless room, sir, and I promise you I will pull my skirt up to my waist, ready for you. But there must be a sheet over my face, to hide it; though the sheet must be laid over me so lightly that it will not choke me. So I shall be covered completely from the waist upwards, and no lights. There you can visit me once, sir, and only the once. After that I must be driven directly to the city and deposited in the public square, in front of the church. If you wish to give me money, then I should be pleased to receive it. But I must stress that you should give me only the same amount of money that you would give to any other woman in such circumstances. However, if you choose not to give me a present, then that is your right.'

How pleased I was to see I struck The Beast to the heart! For, after a baker's dozen heart-beats, one single tear swelled, glittering, at the corner of the masked eye. A tear! A tear, I hoped, of shame. The tear trembled for a moment on an edge of painted bone, then tumbled down the painted cheek to fall, with an abrupt tinkle, on the tiled floor.

The valet, ticking and clucking to himself, hastily ushered me out of the room. A mauve cloud of his master's perfume billowed out into the chill corridor with us and dissipated itself on the spinning winds.

A cell had been prepared for me, a veritable cell, windowless, airless, lightless, in the viscera of the palace. The valet lit a lamp for me; a narrow bed, a dark cupboard with fruit and flowers carved on it bulked out of the gloom.

'I shall twist a noose out of my bed linen and hang myself with it,' I said.

'Oh, no,' said the valet, fixing upon me wide and suddenly melancholy eyes. 'Oh, no, you will not. You are a woman of honour.'

And what was *he* doing in my bedroom, this jigging caricature of a man? Was he to be my warder until I submitted to The Beast's whim or he to mine? Am I in such reduced circumstances that I may not have a lady's maid? As if in reply to my unspoken demand, the valet clapped his hands.

'To assuage your loneliness, madame . . .'

A knocking and clattering behind the door of the cupboard; the door swings open and out glides a soubrette from an operetta, with glossy, nut-brown curls, rosy cheeks, blue, rolling eyes; it takes me a moment to recognise her, in her little cap, her white stockings, her frilled petticoats. She carries a looking glass in one hand and a powder puff in the other and there is a musical box where her heart should be; she tinkles as she rolls towards me on her tiny wheels.

'Nothing human lives here,' said the valet.

My maid halted, bowed; from a split seam at the side of her bodice protrudes the handle of a key. She is a marvellous machine, the most delicately balanced system of cords and pulleys in the world.

'We have dispensed with servants,' the valet said. 'We surround ourselves instead, for utility and pleasure, with simulacra and find it no less convenient than do most gentlemen.'

This clockwork twin of mine halted before me, her bowels churning out a settecento minuet, and offered me the bold carnation of her smile. Click, click – she raises her arm and busily dusts my cheeks with pink, powdered chalk that makes me cough, then thrusts towards me her little mirror.

I saw within it not my own face but that of my father, as if I had put on his face when I arrived at The Beast's palace as the discharge of his debt. What, you self-deluding fool, are you crying still? And drunk, too. He tossed back his grappa and hurled the tumbler away.

Seeing my astonished fright, the valet took the mirror away from me, breathed on it, polished it with the ham of his gloved fist, handed it back to me. Now all I saw was myself, haggard from a sleepless night, pale enough to need my maid's supply of rouge.

I heard the key turn in the heavy door and the valet's footsteps patter down the stone passage. Meanwhile, my double continued to powder the air, emitting her jangling tune but, as it turned out, she was not inexhaustible; soon she was powdering more and yet more languorously, her metal heart slowed in imitation of fatigue, her musical box ran down until the notes separated themselves out of the tune and plopped like single raindrops and, as if sleep had overtaken her, at last she moved no longer. As she succumbed to sleep, I had no option but to do so too. I dropped on the narrow bed as if felled.

Time passed but I do not know how much; then the valet woke me with rolls and honey. I gestured the tray away but he set it down firmly beside the lamp and took from it a little shagreen box, which he offered to me.

I turned away my head.

'Oh, my lady!' Such hurt cracked his high-pitched voice! He dextrously unfastened the gold clasp; on a bed of crimson velvet lay a single diamond earring, perfect as a tear.

I snapped the box shut and tossed it into a corner. This sudden, sharp movement must have disturbed the mechanism of the doll; she jerked her arm almost as if to reprimand me, letting out a rippling fart of gavotte. Then she was still again.

'Very well,' said the valet, put out. And indicated it was time for me to visit my host again. He did not let me wash or comb my hair. There was so little natural light in the interior of the palace that I could not tell whether it was day or night.

You would not think the Beast had budged an inch since I last saw him; he sat in his huge chair, with his hands in his sleeves, and the heavy air never moved. I might have slept an hour, a night, or a month, but his sculptured calm, the stifling air remained just as it had been. The incense rose from the pot, still traced the same signature on the air. The same fire burned.

Take off my clothes for you, like a ballet girl? Is that all you want of me?

'The sight of a young lady's skin that no man has seen before – ' stammered the valet.

I wished I'd rolled in the hay with every lad on my father's farm, to disqualify myself from this humiliating bargain. That he should want so little was the reason why I could not give it; I did not need to speak for The Beast to understand me.

A tear came from his other eye. And then he moved; he buried his cardboard carnival head with its ribboned weight of false hair in, I would say, his arms; he withdrew his, I might say, hands from his sleeves and I saw his furred pads, his excoriating claws.

The dropped tear caught upon his fur and shone. And in my room for hours I heard those paws pad back and forth outside my door.

When the valet arrived again with his silver salver, I had a pair of diamond earrings of the finest water in the world; I threw the other into the corner where the first one lay. The valet twittered with aggrieved regret but did not offer to lead me to The Beast again. Instead, he smiled ingratiatingly and confided: 'My master, he say: invite the young lady to go riding.'

'What's this?'

He briskly mimicked the action of a gallop and, to my amazement, tunelessly croaked: 'Tantivy! tantivy! a-hunting we will go!'

'I'll run away, I'll ride to the city.'

'Oh, no,' he said. 'Are you not a woman of honour?'

He clapped his hands and my maidservant clicked and jangled into the imitation of life. She rolled towards the cupboard where she had come from and reached inside it to fetch out over her synthetic arm my riding habit. Of all things. My very own riding habit, that I'd left behind me in a trunk in a loft in the country house outside Petersburg that we'd lost long ago, before, even, we set out on this wild pilgrimage to the cruel South. Either the very riding habit my old nurse had sewn for me or else a copy of it perfect to the lost button on the right sleeve, the ripped hem held up with a pin. I turned the worn cloth about in my hands, looking for a clue. The wind that sprinted through the palace made the door tremble in its frame; had the north wind blown my garments across Europe to me? At home, the bear's son directed the winds at his pleasure; what democracy of magic held this palace and the fir forest in common? Or, should I be prepared to accept it as proof of the axiom my father had drummed into me: that, if you have enough money, anything is possible?

'Tantivy,' suggested the now twinkling valet, evidently charmed at the pleasure mixed with my bewilderment. The clockwork maid held my jacket out to me and I allowed myself to shrug into it as if reluctantly, although I was half mad to get out into the open air, away from this deathly palace, even in such company.

The doors of the hall let the bright day in; I saw that it was morning. Our horses, saddled and bridled, beasts in bondage, were waiting for us, striking sparks from the tiles with their impatient hooves while their stablemates lolled at ease among the straw, conversing with one another in the mute speech of horses. A pigeon or two, feathers puffed to keep out the cold, strutted about, pecking at ears of corn. The little black gelding who had brought me here greeted me with a ringing neigh that resonated inside the mist roof as in a sounding box and I knew he was meant for me to ride.

I always adored horses, noblest of creatures, such wounded sensitivity in their wise eyes, such rational restraint of energy at their high-strung hindquarters. I lirruped and hurrumphed to my shining black companion and he acknowledged my greeting with a kiss on the forehead from his soft lips. There was a little shaggy pony nuzzling away at the *trompe l'oeil* foliage beneath the hooves of the painted horses on the wall, into whose saddle the valet sprang with a flourish as of the circus. Then The Beast wrapped in a black fur-lined cloak, came to heave himself aloft a grave grey mare. No natural horseman he; he clung to her mane like a shipwrecked sailor to a spar.

Cold, that morning, yet dazzling with the sharp winter sunlight that wounds the retina. There was a scurrying wind about that seemed to go with us, as if the masked, immense one who did not speak carried it inside his cloak and let it out at his pleasure, for it stirred the horses' manes but did not lift the lowland mists.

A bereft landscape in the sad browns and sepias of winter lay all about us, the marshland drearily protracting itself towards the wide river. Those decapitated willows. Now and then, the swoop of a bird, its irreconcilable cry.

A profound sense of strangeness slowly began to possess me. I knew my two companions were not, in any way, as other men, the simian retainer and the master for whom he spoke, the one with clawed forepaws who was in a plot with the witches who let the winds out of their knotted handkerchiefs up towards the Finnish border. I knew they lived according to a different logic than I had done until my father abandoned me to the wild beasts by his human carelessness. This knowledge gave me a certain fearfulness still; but, I would say, not much . . . I was a young girl, a virgin, and therefore men denied me rationality just as they denied it to all those who were not exactly like themselves, in all their unreason. If I could see not one single soul in that wilderness of desolation all around me, then the six of us – mounts and riders, both – could boast amongst us not one soul, either, since all the best religions in the world state categorically that not beasts nor women were equipped with the flimsy, insubstantial things when the good Lord opened the gates of Eden and let Eve and her familiars tumble out. Understand, then, that though I would not say I privately engaged in metaphysical speculation as we rode through the reedy approaches to the river, I certainly meditated on the nature of my own state, how I had been bought and sold, passed from hand to hand. That clockwork girl who powdered my cheeks for me; had I not been allotted only the same kind of imitative life amongst men that the doll-maker had given her?

Yet, as to the true nature of the being of this clawed magus who rode his pale horse in a style that made me recall how Kublai Khan's leopards went out hunting on horseback, of that I had no notion.

We came to the bank of the river that was so wide we could not see across it, so still with winter that it scarcely seemed to flow. The horses lowered their heads to drink. The valet cleared his throat, about to speak; we were in a place of perfect privacy, beyond a brake of winter-bare rushes, a hedge of reeds.

'If you will not let him see you without your clothes – '

I involuntarily shook my head –

' – you must, then, prepare yourself for the sight of my master, naked.'

The river broke on the pebbles with a diminishing sigh. My composure deserted me; all at once I was on the brink of panic. I did not think that I could bear the sight of him, whatever he was. The mare raised her dripping muzzle and looked at me keenly, as if urging me. The river broke again at my feet. I was far from home.

'You,' said the valet, 'must.'

When I saw how scared he was I might refuse, I nodded.

The reed bowed down in a sudden snarl of wind that brought with it a gust of the heavy odour of his disguise. The valet held out his master's cloak to screen him from me as he removed the mask. The horses stirred.

The tiger will never lie down with the lamb; he acknowledges no pact that is not reciprocal. The lamb must learn to run with the tigers.

A great, feline, tawny shape whose pelt was barred with a savage geometry of bars the colour of burned wood. His domed, heavy head, so terrible he must hide it. How subtle the muscles, how profound the tread. The annihilating vehemence of his eyes, like twin suns.

I felt my breast ripped apart as if I suffered a marvellous wound.

The valet moved forward as if to cover up his master now the girl had acknowledged him, but I said: 'No.' The tiger sat still as a heraldic beast, in the pact he had made with his own ferocity to do me no harm. He was far larger than I could have imagined. From the poor, shabby things I'd seen once, in the Czar's menagerie at Petersburg, the golden fruit of their eyes dimming, withering in the far North of captivity. Nothing about him reminded me of humanity.

I therefore, shivering, now unfastened my jacket, to show him I would do him no harm. Yet I was clumsy and blushed a little, for no man had seen me naked and I was a proud girl. Pride it was, not shame, that thwarted my fingers so; and a certain trepidation lest this frail little article of human upholstery before him might not be, in itself, grand enough to satisfy his expectations of us, since those, for all I knew, might have grown infinite during the endless time he had been waiting. The wind clattered in the rushes, purled and eddied in the river.

I showed his grave silence my white skin, my red nipples, and the horses turned their heads to watch me, also, as if they, too, were courteously curious as to the fleshly nature of women. Then the Beast lowered his massive head; Enough! said the valet with a gesture. The wind died down. All was still again.

Then they went off together, the valet on his pony, the tiger running before him like a hound, and I walked along the river bank for a while. I felt I was at liberty for the first time in my life. Then the winter sun began to tarnish, a few flakes of snow drifted from the darkening sky and, when I returned to the horses, I found The Beast mounted again on his grey mare, cloaked and masked and once more, to all appearances, a man, while the valet had a fine catch of waterfowl dangling from his hand and the corpse of a young roebuck slung behind his saddle. I climbed up on the black gelding in silence and so we returned to the palace as the snow fell more and more heavily, obscuring the tracks that we had left behind us.

The valet did not return me to my cell but, instead, to an elegant, if old-fashioned boudoir with sofas of faded pink brocade, a jinn's treasury of Oriental carpets, tintinnabulation of cut-glass chandeliers. Candles in antlered holders struck rainbows from the prismatic hearts of my diamond earrings, that lay on my new dressing table at which my attentive maid stood ready with her powder puff and mirror. Intending to fix the ornaments in my ears, I took the looking glass from her hand, but it was in the midst of one of its magic fits again and I did not see my own face in it but that of my father; at first I thought he smiled at me. Then I saw he was smiling with pure gratification.

He sat, I saw, in the parlour of our lodgings, at the very table where he had lost me, but now he was busily engaged in counting out a tremendous pile of banknotes. My father's circumstances had changed already; well-shaven, neatly barbered, smart new clothes. A frosted glass of sparkling wine sat convenient to his hand beside an ice bucket. The Beast had clearly paid cash on the nail for his glimpse of my bosom and paid up promptly, as if it had not been a sight I might have died of showing. Then I saw my father's trunks were packed, ready for departure. Could he so easily leave me here?

There was a note on the table with the money, in a fine hand. I could read it quite clearly. 'The young lady will arrive immediately.' Some harlot with whom he'd briskly negotiated a liaison on the strength of his spoils? Not at all. For, at that moment, the valet knocked at my door to announce that I might leave the palace at any time hereafter, and he bore over his arm a handsome sable cloak, my very own little gratuity, The Beast's morning gift, in which he proposed to pack me up and send me off.

When I looked at the mirror again, my father had disappeared and all I saw was a pale, hollow-eyed girl whom I scarcely recognised. The valet asked politely when he should prepare the carriage, as if he did not doubt that I would leave with my booty at the first opportunity while my maid, whose face was no longer the spit of my own, continued bonnily to beam. I will dress her in my own clothes, wind her up, send her back to perform the part of my father's daughter.

'Leave me alone,' I said to the valet.

He did not need to lock the door, now. I fixed the earrings in my ears. They were very heavy. Then I took off my riding habit, left it where it lay on the floor. But, when I got down to my shift, my arms dropped to my sides. I was unaccustomed to nakedness. I was so unused to my own skin that to take off all my clothes involved a kind of flaying. I thought The Beast had wanted a little thing compared with what I was prepared to give him; but it is not natural for humankind to go naked, not since first we hid our loins with fig leaves. He had demanded the abominable. I felt as much atrocious pain as if I was stripping off my own underpelt and the smiling girl stood poised in the oblivion of her balked simulation of life, watching me peel down to the cold, white meat of contract and, if she did not see me, then so much more like the market place, where the eyes that watch you take no account of your existence.

And it seemed my entire life, since I had left the North, had passed under the indifferent gaze of eyes like hers.

Then I was flinching stark, except for his irreproachable tears.

I huddled in the furs I must return to him, to keep me from the lacerating winds that raced along the corridors. I knew the way to his den without the valet to guide me.

No response to my tentative rap on his door.

Then the wind blew the valet whirling along the passage. He must have decided that, if one should go naked, then all should go naked; without his livery, he revealed himself, as I had suspected, a delicate creature, covered with silken moth-grey fur, brown fingers supple as leather, chocolate muzzle, the gentlest creature in the world. He gibbered a little to see my fine furs and jewels as if I were dressed up for the opera and, with a great deal of tender ceremony, removed the sables from my shoulders. The sables thereupon resolved themselves into a pack of black squeaking rats that rattled immediately down the stairs on their hard little feet and were lost to sight.

The valet bowed me inside The Beast's room.

The purple dressing gown, the mask, the wig, were laid out on his chair; a glove was planted on each arm. The empty house of his appearance was ready for him but he had abandoned it. There was a reek of fur and piss; the incense pot lay broken in pieces on the floor. Half-burned sticks were scattered from the extinguished fire. A candle stuck by its own grease to the mantelpiece lit two narrow flames in the pupils of the tiger's eyes.

He was pacing backwards and forwards, backwards and forwards, the tip of his heavy tail twitching as he paced out the length and breadth of his imprisonment between the gnawed and bloody bones.

He will gobble you up.

Nursery fears made flesh and sinew; earliest and most archaic of fears, fear of devourment. The beast and his carnivorous bed of bone and I, white, shaking, raw, approaching him as if offering, in myself, the key to a peaceable kingdom in which his appetite need not be my extinction.

He went still as stone. He was far more frightened of me than I was of him.

I squatted on the wet straw and stretched out my hand. I was now within the field of force of his golden eyes. He growled at the back of his throat, lowered his head, sank on to his forepaws, snarled, showed me his red gullet, his yellow teeth. I never moved. He snuffled the air, as if to smell my fear; he could not.

Slowly, slowly he began to drag his heavy, gleaming weight across the floor towards me.

A tremendous throbbing, as of the engine that makes the earth turn, filled the little room; he had begun to purr.

The sweet thunder of this purr shook the old walls, made the shutters batter the windows until they burst apart and let in the white light of the snowy moon. Tiles came crashing down from the roof; I heard them fall into the courtyard far below. The reverberations of his purring rocked the foundations of the house, the walls began to dance. I thought: 'It will all fall, everything will disintegrate.'

He dragged himself closer and closer to me, until I felt the harsh velvet of his head against my hand, then a tongue, abrasive as sandpaper. 'He will lick the skin off me!'

And each stroke of his tongue ripped off skin after successive skin, all the skins of a life in the world, and left behind a nascent patina of shiny hairs. My earrings turned back to water and trickled down my shoulders; I shrugged the drops off my beautiful fur.

Puss-in-Boots

Figaro here; Figaro, there, I tell you! Figaro upstairs, Figaro downstairs and – oh, my goodness me, this little Figaro can slip into my lady's chamber smart as you like at any time whatsoever that he takes the fancy for, don't you know, he's a cat of the world, cosmopolitan, sophisticated; he can tell when a furry friend is the Missus' best company. For what lady in all the world could say 'no' to the passionate yet *toujours discret* advances of a fine marmalade cat? (Unless it be her eyes incontinently overflow at the slightest whiff of furr, which happened once, as you shall hear.)

A tom, sirs, a ginger tom and proud of it. Proud of his fine, white shirtfront that dazzles harmoniously against his orange and tangerine tessellations (oh! what a fiery suit of lights have I); proud of his bird-entrancing eye and more than military whiskers; proud, to a fault, some say, of his fine, musical voice. All the windows in the square fly open when I break into impromptu song at the spectacle of the moon above Bergamo. If the poor players in the square, the sullen rout of ragged trash that haunts the provinces, are rewarded with a hail of pennies when they set up their makeshift stage and start their raucous choruses; then how much more liberally do the citizens deluge me with pails of the freshest water, vegetables hardly spoiled and, occasionally, slippers, shoes and boots.

Do you see these fine, high, shining leather boots of mine? A young cavalry officer made me the tribute of, first one; then, after I celebrate his generosity with a fresh obbligato, the moon no fuller than my heart – whoops! I nimbly spring aside – down comes the other. Their high heels will click like castanets when Puss takes his promenade upon the tiles, for my song recalls flamenco, all cats have a Spanish tinge although Puss himself elegantly lubricates his virile, muscular, native Bergamasque with French, since that is the only language in which you can purr.

'*Merrrrrrrrrrci!*'

Instanter I draw my new boots on over the natty white stockings that terminate my hinder legs. That young man, observing with curiosity by moonlight the use to which I put his footwear, calls out: 'Hey, Puss! Puss, there!'

'At your service, sir!'

'Up to my balcony, young Puss!'

He leans out, in his nightshirt, offering encouragement as I swing succinctly up the façade, forepaws on a curly cherub's pate, hindpaws on a stucco wreath, bring them up to meet your forepaws while, first paw forward, hup! on to the stone nymph's tit; left paw down a bit, the satyr's bum should do the trick. Nothing to it, once you know how, rococo's no problem. Acrobatics? Born to them; Puss can perform a back somersault whilst holding aloft a glass of vino in his right paw and *never spill a drop*.

But, to my shame, the famous death-defying triple somersault *en plein air*, that is, in middle air, that is, unsupported and without a safety net, I, Puss, have never yet attempted though often I have dashingly brought off the double tour, to the applause of all.

'You strike me as a cat of parts,' says this young man when I'm arrived at his windowsill. I made him a handsome genuflection, rump out, tail up, head down, to facilitate his friendly chuck under my chin; and, as involuntary free gift, my natural, my habitual smile.

For all cats have this particularity, each and every one, from the meanest alley sneaker to the proudest, whitest she that ever graced a pontiff's pillow – we have our smiles, as it were, painted on. Those small, cool, quiet Mona Lisa smiles that smile we must, no matter whether it's been fun or it's been not. So all cats have a politician's air; we smile and smile and so they think we're villains. But, I note, this young man is something of a smiler hisself.

'A sandwich,' he offers. 'And, perhaps, a snifter of brandy.'

His lodgings are poor, though he's handsome enough and even *en déshabillé*, nightcap and all, there's a neat, smart, dandified air about him. Here is one who knows what's what, thinks I; a man who keeps up appearances in the bedchamber can never embarrass you out of it. And excellent beef sandwiches; I relish a lean slice of roast beef and early learned a taste for spirits, since I started life as a wine-shop cat, hunting cellar rats for my keep, before the world sharpened my wits enough to let me live by them.

And the upshot of this midnight interview? I'm engaged, on the spot, as Sir's valet: *valet de chambre* and, from time to time, his body servant, for, when funds are running low, as they must do for every gallant officer when the pickings fall off, he pawns the quilt, doesn't he. Then faithful Puss curls up on his chest to keep him warm at night. And if he don't like me to knead his nipples, which, out of the purist affection and the desire – ouch! he says – to test the retractability of my claws, I do in moments of absence of mind, then what other valet could slip into a young girl's sacred privacy and deliver her a billet-doux at the very moment when she's reading her prayerbook with her sainted mother? A task I once or twice peform for him, to his infinite gratitude.

And, as you will hear, brought him at last to the best of fortunes for us all.

So Puss got his post at the same time as his boots and I dare say the Master and I have much in common for he's proud as the devil, touchy as tin-tacks, lecherous as liquorice and, though I say it as loves him, as quick-witted a rascal as ever put on clean linen.

When times were hard, I'd pilfer the market for breakfast – a herring, an orange, a loaf; we never went hungry. Puss served him well in the gaming salons, too, for a cat may move from lap to lap with impunity and cast his eye over any hand of cards. A cat can jump on the dice – he can't resist to see it roll! poor thing, mistook it for a bird; and, after I've been, limp-spined, stiff-legged, playing the silly buggers, scooped up to be chastised, who can remember how the dice fell in the first place?

And we had, besides, less . . . gentlemanly means of maintenance when they closed the tables to us, as, churlishly, they sometimes did. I'd perform my little Spanish dance while he went around with his hat: olé! But he only put my loyalty and affection to the test of this humiliation when the cupboard was as bare as his backside; after, in fact, he'd sunk so low as to pawn his drawers.

So all went right as ninepence and you never saw such boon companions as Puss and his master; until the man must needs go fall in love.

'Head over heels, Puss.'

I went about my ablutions, tonguing my arsehole with the impeccable hygienic integrity of cats, one leg stuck in the air like a ham bone; I choose to remain silent. Love? What has my rakish master, for whom I've jumped through the window of every brothel in the city, besides haunting the virginal back garden of the convent and god knows what other goatish errands, to do with tender passion?

'And she. A princess in a tower. Remote and shining as Aldebaran. Chained to a dolt and dragon-guarded.'

I withdrew my head from my privates and fixed him with my most satiric smile; I dared him warble on in that strain.

'All cats are cynics,' he opines, quailing beneath my yellow glare.

It is the hazard of it draws him, see.

There is a lady sits in a window for one hour and one hour only, at the tenderest time of dusk. You can scarcely see her features, the curtains almost hide her; shrouded like a holy image, she looks out on the piazza as the shops shut up, the stalls go down, the night comes on. And this is all the world she ever sees. Never a girl in all Bergamo so secluded except, on Sundays, they let her go to Mass, bundled up in black, with a veil on. And then she is in the company of an aged hag, her keeper, who grumps along grim as a prison dinner.

How did he see that secret face? Who else but Puss revealed it?

Back we come from the tables so late, so very late at night we found, to our emergent surprise that all at once it was early in the morning. His pockets were heavy with silver and both our guts sweetly a-gurgle with champagne; Lady Luck had sat with us, what fine spirits were we in! Winter and cold weather. The pious trot to church already with little lanterns through the chill fog as we go ungodly rolling home.

See, a black barque, like a state funeral; and Puss takes it into his bubbly-addled brain to board her. Tacking obliquely to her side, I rub my marmalade pate against her shin; how could any duenna, be she never so stern, take offence at such attentions to her chargeling from a little cat? (As it turns out, this one: *attishooo!* does.) A white hand fragrant as Arabia descends from the black cloak and reciprocally rubs behind his ears at just the ecstatic spot. Puss lets rip a roaring purr, rears briefly on his high-heeled boots; jig with joy and pirouette with glee – she laughs to see and draws her veil aside. Puss glimpses high above, as it were, an alabaster lamp lit behind by dawn's first flush: her face.

And she smiling.

For a moment, just that moment, you would have thought it was May morning.

'Come along! Come! Don't dawdle over the nasty beast!' snaps the old hag, with the one tooth in her mouth, and warts; she sneezes.

The veil comes down; so cold it is, and dark, again.

It was not I alone who saw her; with that smile he swears she stole his heart.

Love.

I've sat inscrutably by and washed my face and sparkling dicky with my clever paw while he made the beast with two backs with every harlot in the city, besides a number of good wives, dutiful daughters, rosy country girls come to sell celery and endive on the corner, and the chambermaid who strips the bed, what's more. The Mayor's wife, even, shed her diamond earrings for him and the wife of the notary unshuffled her petticoats and if I could, I would blush to remember how her daughter shook out her flaxen plaits and jumped in bed between them and she not sixteen years old. But never the word, 'love', has fallen from his lips, nor in nor out of any of these transports, until my master saw the wife of Signor Panteleone as she went walking out to Mass, and she lifted up her veil though not for him.

And now he is half sick with it and will go to the tables no more for lack of heart and never even pats the bustling rump of the chambermaid in his new-found maudlin celibacy, so we get our slops left festering for days and the sheets filthy and the wench goes banging about bad-temperedly with her broom enough to fetch the plaster off the walls.

I'll swear he lives for Sunday morning, though never before was he a religious man. Saturday nights, he bathes himself punctiliously, even, I'm glad to see, washes behind his ears, perfumes himself, presses his uniform so you'd think he had a right to wear it. So much in love he very rarely panders to the pleasures, even of Onan, as he lies tossing on his couch, for he cannot sleep for fear he miss the summoning bell. Then out into the cold morning, harking after that black, vague shape, hapless fisherman for his sealed oyster with such a pearl in it. He creeps behind her across the square; how can one so amorous bear to be so inconspicuous? And yet, he must; though, sometimes, the old hag sneezes and says she swears there is a cat about.

He will insinuate himself into the pew behind milady and sometimes contrive to touch the hem of her garment, when they all kneel, and never a thought to his orisons; she is the divinity he's come to worship. Then sits silent, in a dream, till bed-time; what pleasure is his company for me?

He won't eat, either. I brought him a fine pigeon from the inn kitchen, fresh off the spit, *parfumé avec* tarragon, but he wouldn't touch it so I crunched it up, bones and all, performing, as ever after meals, my meditative toilette, I pondered, thus: one, he is in a fair way to ruining us both by neglecting his business; two, love is desire sustained by unfulfilment. If I lead him to her bedchamber and there he takes his fill of her lily-white, he'll be right as rain in two shakes and next day tricks as usual.

Then Master and his Puss will soon be solvent once again.

Which, at the moment, very much not, sir.

This Signor Panteleone employs, his only servant but the hag, a kitchen cat, a sleek, spry tabby whom I accost. Grasping the slack of her neck firmly between my teeth, I gave her the customary tribute of a few firm thrusts of my striped loins and, when she got her breath back, she assured me in the friendliest fashion the old man was a fool and a miser who kept herself on short commons for the sake of the mousing and the young lady a soft-hearted creature who smuggled breast of chicken and sometimes, when the hag-dragon-governess napped at midday, snatched this pretty kitty out of the hearth and into her bedroom to play with reels of silk and run after trailed handkerchiefs, when she and she had as much fun together as two Cinderellas at an all-girls' ball.

Poor, lonely lady, married so young to an old dodderer with his bald pate and his goggle eyes and his limp, his avarice, his gore belly, his rheumaticks, and his flag hangs all the time at half-mast indeed; and jealous as he is impotent, tabby declares – he'd put a stop to all the rutting in the world, if he had his way, just to certify his young wife don't get from another what she can't get from him.

'Then shall we hatch a plot to antler him, my precious?'

Nothing loath, she tells me the best time for this accomplishment should be the one day in all the week he forsakes his wife and his counting-house to ride off into the country to extort more grasping rents from starveling tenant farmers. And she's left all alone, then, behind so many bolts and bars you wouldn't believe; all alone – but for the hag!

Aha! This hag turns out to be the biggest snag; an iron-plated, copper-bottomed, sworn man-hater of some sixty bitter winters who – as ill luck would have it – shatters, clatters, erupts into paroxysms of the *sneeze* at the very glimpse of a cat's whisker. No chance of Puss worming his winsome way into *that* one's affections, nor for my tabby neither! But, oh my dear, I say; see how my ingenuity rises to the challenge . . . So we resume the sweetest part of our conversation in the dusty convenience of the coalhole and she promises me, least she can do, to see the fair, hitherto-inaccessible one gets a letter safe if I slip it to her and slip it to her forthwith I do, though somewhat discommoded by my boots.

He spent three hours over his letter, did my master, as long as it takes me to lick the coaldust off my dicky. He tears up half a quire of paper, splays five pen-nibs with the force of his adoration: 'Look not for any peace, my heart; having become a slave to this beauty's tyranny, dazzled am I by this sun's rays and my torments cannot be assuaged.' *That's* not the high road to the rumpling of the bedcovers; she's got *one* ninny between them already!

'Speak from the heart,' I finally exhort. 'And all good women have the missionary streak, sir; convince her her orifice will be your salvation and she's yours.'

'When I want your advice, Puss, I'll ask for it,' he says; all at once hoity-toity. But at last he manages to pen ten pages; a rake, a profligate, a card-sharper, a cashiered officer well on the way to rack and ruin when first he saw, as if it were a glimpse of grace, her face . . . his angel, his good angel, who will lead him from perdition.

Oh, what a masterpiece he penned!

'Such tears she wept at his addresses!' says my tabby friend.

'Oh, Tabs, she sobs – for she calls me "Tabs" – I never meant to wreak such havoc with a pure heart when I smiled to see a booted cat! And put his paper next to her heart and swore, it was a good soul that sent her his vows and she was too much in love with virtue to withstand him. If, she adds, for she's a sensible girl, he's neither old as the hills nor ugly as sin, that is.'

An admirable little note the lady's sent him in return, per Figaro here and there; she adopts a responsive yet uncompromising tone. For, says she, how can she usefully discuss his passion further without a glimpse of his person?

He kisses her letter once, twice, a thousand times; she must and will see me! I shall serenade her this very evening!

So, when dusk falls, off we trot to the piazza, he with an old guitar he pawned his sword to buy and most, if I may say so, outlandishly rigged out in some kind of vagabond mountebank's outfit he bartered his gold-braided waistcoat with poor Pierrot braying in the square for, moon-struck zany, lovelorn loon he was himself and even plastered his face with flour to make it white, poor fool, and so ram home his heartsick state.

There she is, the evening star with the clouds around her; but such a creaking of carts in the square, such a clatter and crash as they dismantle the stalls, such an ululation of ballad-singers and oration of nostrum-peddlers and pertubation of errand boys that though he wails out his heart to her: 'Oh, my beloved!' why she, all in a dream, sits with her gaze in the middle distance where there's a crescent moon stuck on the sky behind the cathedral pretty as a painted stage, and so is she.

Does she hear him?

Not a grace-note.

Does she see him?

Never a glance.

'Up you go, Puss; tell her to look my way!'

If rococo's a piece of cake, that chaste, tasteful, early Palladian stumped many a better cat than I in its time. Agility's not in it, when it comes to Palladian, daring alone will carry the day and, though the first storey's graced with a hefty caryatid whose bulbous loincloth and tremendous pects facilitate the first ascent, the Doric column on her head proves a horse of a different colour, I can tell you. Had I not seen my precious Tabby crouched in the gutter above me keening encouragement, I, even I, might never have braved that flying, upward leap that brought me, as if Harlequin himself on wires, in one bound to her windowsill.

'Dear god!' the lady says, and jumps. I see she, too, ah, sentimental thing! clutches a well-thumbed letter. 'Puss-in-boots!'

I bow her with a courtly flourish. What luck to hear no sniff or sneeze; where's hag? A sudden flux sped her to the privy – not a moment to lose.

'Cast your eye below,' I hiss. 'Him you know of lurks below, in white with the big hat, ready to sing you an evening ditty.'

The bedroom door creaks open, then, and: whee! through the air Puss goes, discretion is the better part. And, for both their sweet sakes I did it, the sight of both their bright eyes inspired me to the never-before-attempted, by me or any other cat, in boots or out of them – the death-defying triple somersault!

And a three-storey drop to ground, what's more; a grand descent.

Only the merest trifle winded. I'm proud to say, I neatly land on all my fours and Tabs goes wild, huzzah! But has my master witnessed my triumph? Has he, my arse. He's tuning up that old mandolin and breaks, as down I come, again into his song.

I would never have said, in the normal course of things, his voice would charm the birds out of the trees, like mine; and yet the bustle died for him, the homeward-turning costers paused in their tracks to hearken, the preening street girls forgot their hard-edged smiles as they turned to him and some of the old ones wept, they did.

Tabs, up on the roof there, prick up your ears! For by its power I know my heart is in his voice.

And now the lady lowers her eyes to him and smiles, as once she smiled at me.

Then, bang! a stern hand pulls the shutters to. And it was as if all the violets in all the baskets of all the flower-sellers drooped and faded at once; and spring stopped dead in its tracks and might, this time, not come at all; and the bustle and the business of the square, that had so magically quieted for his song, now rose up again with the harsh clamour of the loss of love.

And we trudge drearily off to dirty sheets and a mean supper of bread and cheese, all I can steal him, but at least the poor soul manifests a hearty appetite now she knows he's in the world and not the ugliest of mortals; for the first time since that fateful morning, sleeps sound. But sleep comes hard to Puss tonight. He takes a midnight stroll across the square, soon comfortably discusses a choice morsel of salt cod his tabby friend found among the ashes on the hearth before our converse turns to other matters.

'Rats!' she says. 'And take your boots off, you uncouth bugger; those three-inch heels wreak havoc with the soft flesh of my underbelly!'

When we'd recovered ourselves a little, I ask her what she means by those 'rats' of hers and she proposes her scheme to me. How my master must pose as a *rat-catcher* and I, his ambulant marmalade rat-trap. How we will then go kill the rats that ravage milady's bedchamber, the day the old fool goes to fetch his rent, and she can have her will of the lad at leisure for, if there is one thing the hag fears more than a cat, it is a rat and she'll cower in a cupboard till the last rat is off the premises before she comes out. Oh, this tabby one, sharp as a tack is she; I congratulate her ingenuity with a few affectionate cuffs round the head and home again, for breakfast, ubiquitous Puss, here, there and everywhere, who's your Figaro?

Master applauds the rat ploy; but, as to the rats themselves; how are they to arrive in the house in the first place? he queries.

'Nothing easier, sir; my accomplice, a witty soubrette who lives among the cinders, dedicated as she is to the young lady's happiness, will personally strew a large number of dead and dying rats she has herself collected about the bedroom of the said ingénue's duenna, and, most particularly, that of the said ingénue herself. This to be done tomorrow morning, as soon as Sir Pantaloon rides out to fetch his rents. By good fortune, down in the square, plying for hire, a rat-catcher! Since our hag cannot abide either a rat or a cat, it falls to milady to escort the rat-catcher, none other than yourself, sir, and his intrepid hunter, myself, to the site of the infestation.

'Once you're in her bedroom, sir, if *you* don't know what to do, then I can't help you.'

'Keep your foul thoughts to yourself, Puss.'

Some things, I see, are sacrosanct from humour.

Sure enough, prompt at five in the bleak next morning, I observe with my own eyes the lovely lady's lubberly husband hump off on his horse like a sack of potatoes to rake in his dues. We're ready with our sign: SIGNOR FURIOSO, THE LIVING DEATH OF RATS; and in the leathers he's borrowed from the porter, I hardly recognise him myself, not with the false moustache. He coaxes the chambermaid with a few kisses – poor, deceived girl! love knows no shame – and so we install ourselves under a certain shuttered window with the great pile of traps she's lent us, the sign of our profession, Puss perched atop them bearing the humble yet determined look of a sworn enemy of vermin.

We've not waited more than fifteen minutes – and just as well, as many rat-plagued Bergamots approach us already and are not easily dissuaded from employing us – when the front door flies open on a lusty scream. The hag, aghast, flings her arms round flinching Furioso; how fortuitous to find him! But, at the whiff of me, she's sneezing so valiantly, her eyes awash, the vertical gutters of her nostrils aswill with snot, she barely can depict the scenes inside, rattus domesticus dead in her bed and all; and worse! in the Missus' room.

So Signor Furioso and his questing Puss are ushered into the very sanctuary of the goddess, our presence announced by a fanfare from her keeper on the nose harp. *Attishhoooo!!!*

Sweet and pleasant in a morning gown of loose linen, our ingénue jumps at the tattoo of my boot heels but recovers instantly and the wheezing, hawking hag is in no state to sniffle more than: 'Ain't I seen that cat before?'

'Not a chance,' says my master. 'Why, he's come but yesterday with me from Milano.'

So she has to make do with that.

My Tabs has lined the very stairs with rats; she's made a morgue of the hag's room but something more lively of the lady's. For some of her prey she's very cleverly not killed but crippled; a big black beastie weaves its way towards us over the turkey carpet, Puss, pounce! Between scream-ing and sneezing, the hag's in a fine state, I can tell you, though milady exhibits a most praiseworthy and collected presence of mind, being, I guess, a young woman of no small grasp so, perhaps, she has a sniff of the plot already.

My master goes down on hands and knees under the bed.

'My god!' he cries. 'There's the biggest hole, here in the wainscoting, I ever saw in all my professional career! And there's an army of black rats gathering behind it, ready to storm through! To arms!'

But, for all her terror, the hag's loath to leave the Master and me alone to deal with the rats; she casts her eye on a silver-backed hairbrush, a coral rosary, twitters, hovers, screeches, mutters until milady assures her, amidst scenes of rising pandemonium:

'I shall stay here myself and see that Signor Furioso doesn't make off with my trinkets. You go and recover yourself with an infusion of friar's balsam and don't come back until I call.'

The hag departs; quick as a flash, la belle turns the key in the door on her and softly laughs; the naughty one.

Dusting the slut-fluff from his knees, Signor Furioso now stands slowly upright; swiftly, he removes his false moustache, for no element of the farcical must mar this first, delirious encounter of these lovers, must it. (Poor soul, how his hands tremble!)

Accustomed as I am to the splendid, feline nakedness of my kind, that offers no concealment of that soul made manifest in the flesh of lovers, I am always a little moved by the poignant reticence with which humanity shyly hesitates to divest itself of its clutter of concealing rags in the presence of desire. So, first, these two smile, a little, as if to say 'How strange to meet you here!' uncertain of a loving welcome, still. And do I deceive myself, or do I see a tear a-twinkle in the corner of his eye? But who is it steps towards the other first? Why, she; women, I think, are, of the two sexes, the more keenly tuned to the sweet music of their bodies. (A penny for my foul thoughts, indeed! Does she, that wise, grave personage in the negligee, think you've staged this grand charade merely in order to kiss her hand?) But, then – oh, what a pretty blush! steps back; now it's his turn to take two steps forward in the saraband of Eros.

I could wish, though, they'd dance a little faster; the hag will soon recover from her spasms and shall she find them in flagrante?

His hand, then, trembling, upon her bosom; hers, initially more

hesitant, sequentially more purposeful, upon his breeches. Then their
strange trance breaks; that sentimental havering done, I never saw two
fall to it with such appetite. As if the whirlwind got into their fingers,
they strip each other bare in a twinkling and she falls back on the bed,
shows him the target, he displays the dart, scores an instant bullseye.
Bravo! Never can that old bed have shook with such a storm before. And
their sweet choked mutterings, poor things: 'I never . . .' 'My darling
. . .' 'More . . .' And etc. etc. Enough to melt the thorniest heart.

He rises up on his elbows once and gasps at me: 'Mimic the murder of
the rats, Puss! Mask the music of Venus with that clamour of Diana!'

A-hunting we shall go! Loyal to the last, I play catch as catch can with
Tab's dead rats, giving the dying the *coup de grâce* and baying with
resonant vigour to drown the extravagant screeches that break forth from
that (who would have suspected?) more passionate young woman as she
comes off in fine style. (Full marks, Master.)

At that, the old hag comes battering at the door. What's going on?
Whyfor the racket? And the door rattles on its hinges.

'Peace!' cries Signor Furioso. 'Haven't I just now blocked the great
hole?'

But milady's in no hurry to don her smock again, she takes her lovely
time about it; so full of pleasure gratified her languorous limbs you'd
think her very navel smiled. She pecks my master prettily thank-you on
the cheek, wets the gum on his false moustache with the tip of her
strawberry tongue and sticks it back on his upper lip for him, then lets her
wardress into the scene of the faux carnage with the most modest and
irreproachable air in the world.

'See! Puss has slaughtered all the rats.'

I rush, purring proud, to greet the hag; instantly, her eyes o'erflow.

'Why the bedclothes so disordered?' she squeaks, not quite blinded yet, by
phlegm and chose for her post from all the other applications on account of
her suspicious mind, even (oh, dutiful) when in *grande peur des rats*.

'Puss had a mighty battle with the biggest beast you ever saw upon this
very bed; can't you see the bloodstains on the sheets? And now, what do
we owe you, Signor Furioso, for this singular service?'

'A hundred ducats,' says I, quick as a flash, for I know my master, left
to himself, would like an honourable fool, take nothing.

'That's the entire household expenses for a month!' wails avarice's
well-chosen accomplice.

'And worth every penny! For those rats would have eaten us out of
house and home.' I see the glimmerings of sturdy backbone in this little
lady. 'Go, pay them from your private savings that I know of, that you've
skimmed off the housekeeping.'

Muttering and moaning but nothing for it except to do as she is bid; and the furious Sir and I take off a laundry basket full of dead rats as souvenir – we drop it, plop! in the nearest sewer. And sit down to one dinner honestly paid for, for a wonder.

But the young fool is off his feed again. Pushes his plate aside, laughs, weeps, buries his head in his hands and, time and time and time again, goes to the window to stare at the shutters behind which his sweetheart scrubs the blood away and my dear Tabs rests from her supreme exertions. He sits, for a while, and scribbles; rips the page in four, hurls it aside. I spear a falling fragment with a claw. Dear God, he's took to writing poetry.

'I must and will have her for ever,' he exclaims.

I see my plan has come to nothing. Satisfaction has not satisfied him; that soul they both saw in one another's bodies has such insatiable hunger no single meal could ever appease it. I fall to the toilette of my hinder parts, my favourite stance when contemplating the ways of the world.

'How can I live without her?'

You did so for twenty-seven years, sir, and never missed her for a moment.

'I'm burning with the fever of love!'

Then we're spared the expense of fires.

'I shall steal her away from her husband to live with me.'

'What do you propse to live on, sir?'

'Kisses,' he said distractedly. 'Embraces.'

'Well, you won't grow fat on that, sir; though *she* will. And then, more mouths to feed.'

'I'm sick and tired of your foul-mouthed barbs, Puss,' he snaps. And yet my heart is moved, for now he speaks the plain, clear, foolish rhetoric of love and who is there cunning enough to help him to happiness but I? Scheme, loyal Puss, scheme!

My wash completed, I step out across the square to visit that charming she who's wormed her way directly into my own hitherto-untrammelled heart with her sharp wits and her pretty ways. She exhibits warm emotion to see me; and, oh! what news she has to tell me! News of a rapt and personal nature, that turns my mind to thoughts of the future, and, yes, domestic plans of most familial nature. She's saved me a pig's trotter, a whole entire pig's trotter the Missus smuggled to her with a wink. A feast! Masticating, I muse.

'Recapitulate,' I suggest, 'the daily motions of Sir Pantaloon when he's at home.'

They set the cathedral clock by him, so rigid and so regular his habits. Up at the crack, he meagrely breakfasts off yesterday's crusts and a cup of cold water, to spare the expense of heating it up. Down to his counting-house, counting out his money, until a bowl of well-watered gruel at midday. The afternoon he devotes to usury, bankrupting, here, a small tradesman, there, a weeping widow, for fun and profit. Dinner's luxurious, at four; soup, with a bit of rancid beef or a tough bird in it – he's an arrangement with the butcher, takes unsold stock off his hands in return for a shut mouth about a pie that had a finger in it. From four-thirty until five-thirty, he unlocks the shutters and lets his wife look out, oh, don't I know! while hag sits beside her to make sure she doesn't smile. (Oh, that blessed flux, those precious loose minutes that set the game in motion!)

And while she breathes the air of evening, why, he checks up on his chest of gems, his bales of silk, all those treasures he loves too much to share with daylight and if he wastes a candle when he so indulges himself, why, any man is entitled to one little extravagance. Another draught of Adam's ale healthfully concludes the day; up he tucks besides Missus and, since she is his prize possession, consents to finger her a little. He palpitates her hide and slaps her flanks: 'What a good bargain!' Alack, can do no more, not wishing to profligate his natural essence. And so drifts off to sinless slumber amid the prospects of tomorrow's gold.

'How rich is he?'

'Croesus.'

'Enough to keep two loving couples?'

'Sumptuous.'

Early in the uncandled morning, groping to the privy bleared with sleep, were the old man to place his foot upon the subfusc yet volatile fur of a shadow-camouflaged young tabby cat –

'You read my thoughts, my love.'

I say to my master: 'Now, you get yourself a doctor's gown, impedimenta all complete or I'm done with you.'

'What's this, Puss?'

'Do as I say and never mind the reason! The less you know of why, the better.'

So he expends a few of the hag's ducats on a black gown with a white collar and his skull cap and his black bag and, under my direction, makes himself another sign that announces, with all due pomposity, how he is Il Famed Dottore: *Aches cured, pains prevented, bones set, graduate of Bologna, physician extraordinary*. He demands to know, is she to play the invalid to give him further access to her bedroom?

'I'll clasp her in my arms and jump out of the window; we too shall both perform the triple somersault of love.'

'You just mind your own business, sir, and let me mind it for you after my own fashion.'

Another raw and misty morning! Here in the hills, will the weather ever change? So bleak it is, and dreary; but there he stands, grave as a sermon in his black gown and half the market people come with coughs and boils and broken heads and I dispense the plasters and the vials of coloured water I'd forethoughtfully stowed in his bag, he too *agitato* to sell for himself. (And, who knows, might we not have stumbled on a profitable profession for future pursuit, if my present plans miscarry?)

Until dawn shoots his little yet how flaming arrow past the cathedral on which the clock strikes six. At the last stroke, that famous door flies open once again and – *eeeeeeeeeeeeech!* the hag lets rip.

'Oh, Doctor, oh, Doctor, come quick as you can; our good man's taken a sorry tumble!'

And weeping fit to float a smack, she is, so doesn't see the doctor's apprentice is most colourfully and completely furred and whiskered.

The old booby's flat out at the foot of the stair, his head at an acute angle that might turn chronic and a big bunch of keys, still, grinned in his right hand as if they were the keys to heaven marked: *Wanted on voyage*. And Missus, in her wrap, bends over him with a pretty air of concern.

'A fall – ' she begins when she sees the doctor but stops short when she sees your servant, Puss, looking as suitably down-in-the-mouth as his chronic smile will let him, humping his master's stock-in-trade and hawing like a sawbones. 'You, again,' she says, and can't forbear to giggle. But the dragon's too blubbered to hear.

My master puts his ear to the old man's chest and shakes his head dolefully; then takes the mirror from his pocket and puts it to the old man's mouth. Not a breath clouds it. Oh, sad! Oh, sorrowful!

'Dead, is he?' sobs the hag. 'Broke his neck, has he?'

And she slyly makes a little grab for the keys, in spite of her well-orchestrated distress; but Missus slaps her hand and she gives over.

'Let's get him to a softer bed,' says Master.

He ups the corpse, carries it aloft to the room we know full well, bumps Pantaloon down, twitches an eyelid, taps a kneecap, feels a pulse.

'Dead as a doornail,' he pronounces. 'It's not a doctor you want, it's an undertaker.'

Missus has a handkerchief very dutifully and correctly to her eyes.

'You just run along and get one,' she says to hag. 'And then I'll read the will. Because don't think he's forgotten you, thou faithful servant. Oh, my goodness, no.'

So off goes hag; you never saw a woman of her accumulated Christmases spring so fast. As soon as they are left alone, no trifling, this time; they're at it, hammer and tongs, down on the carpet since the bed is *occupé*. Up and down, up and down his arse; in and out, in and out her legs. Then she heaves him up and throws him on the back, her turn at the grind, now, and you'd think she'll never stop.

Toujours discret, Puss occupies himself in unfastening the shutters and throwing the windows open to the beautiful beginning of morning in whose lively yet fragrant air his sensitive nostrils catch the first and vernal hint of spring. In a few moments, my dear friend joins me. I notice already – or is it only my fond imagination? – a charming new *portliness* in her gait, hitherto so elastic, so spring-heeled. And there we sit upon the windowsill like the two genii and protectors of the house; ah, Puss, your rambling days are over. I shall become a hearthrug cat, a fat and cosy cushion cat, sing to the moon no more, settle at last amid the sedentary joys of a domesticity we two, she and I, have so richly earned.

Their cries of rapture rouse me from this pleasant revery.

The hag chooses, *naturellement*, this tender if outrageous moment to return with the undertaker in his chiffoned topper, plus a brace of mutes black as beetles, glum as bailiffs, bearing the elm box between them to take the corpse away in. But they cheer up something wonderful at the unexpected spectacle before them and he and she conclude their amorous interlude amidst roars of approbation and torrents of applause.

But what a racket the hag makes! Police, murder, thieves! Until the Master chucks her purseful of gold back again, for a gratuity. (Meanwhile, I note that sensible young woman, mother-naked as she is has yet the presence of mind to catch hold of her husband's key ring and sharply tug it from his sere, cold grip. Once she's got the keys secure, she's in charge of all.)

'Now, no more of your nonsense!' she snaps to hag. 'If I hereby give you the sack, you'll get a handsome gift to go along with you for now' – flourishing the keys – 'I am a rich widow and here' – indicating to all my bare yet blissful master – 'is the young man who'll be my second husband.'

When the governess found Signor Panteleone had indeed remembered her in his will, left her a keepsake of the cup he drank his morning water from, she made not a squeak more, pocketed a fat sum with thanks and, sneezing, took herself off with no more cries of 'murder' neither. The old buffoon briskly bundled in his coffin and buried; Master comes into a great fortune and Missus rounding out already and they as happy as pigs in plunk.

But my Tabs beat her to it, since cats don't take much time about engendering; three fine, new-minted ginger kittens, all complete with snowy socks and shirtfronts, tumble in the cream and tangle Missus's knitting and put a smile on every face, not just their mother's and proud

father's for Tabs and I smile all day long and, these days, we put our
hearts in it.

So may all your wives, if you need them, be rich and pretty; and all
your husbands, if you want them, be young and virile; and all your cats as
wily, perspicacious and resourceful as:

PUSS-IN-BOOTS.

The Erl-King

The lucidity, the clarity of the light that afternoon was sufficient to itself;
perfect transparency must be impenetrable, these vertical bars of a brass-
coloured distillation of light coming down from sulphur-yellow
interstices in a sky hunkered with grey clouds that bulge with more rain.
It struck the wood with nicotine-stained fingers, the leaves glittered. A
cold day of late October, when the withered blackberries dangled like
their own dour spooks on the discoloured brambles. There were crisp
husks of beechmast and cast acorn cups underfoot in the russet slime of
dead bracken where the rains of the equinox had so soaked the earth that
the cold oozed up through the soles of the shoes, lancinating cold of the
approaching of winter that grips hold of your belly and squeezed it tight.
Now the stark elders have an anorexic look; there is not much in the
autumn wood to make you smile but it is not yet, not quite yet, the
saddest time of the year. Only, there is a haunting sense of the imminent
cessation of being; the year, in turning, turns in on itself. Introspective
weather, a sickroom hush.

The woods enclose. You step between the fir trees and then you are no
longer in the open air; the wood swallows you up. There is no way
through the wood any more, this wood has reverted to its original
privacy. Once you are inside it, you must stay there until it lets you out
again for there is no clue to guide you through in perfect safety; grass
grew over the track years ago and now the rabbits and the foxes make
their own runs in the subtle labyrinth and nobody comes. The trees stir
with a noise like taffeta skirts of women who have lost themselves in
woods and hunt round hopelessly for the way out. Tumbling crows play
tig in the branches of the elms they clotted with their nests, now and then
raucously cawing. A little stream with soft margins of marsh runs
through the wood but it has grown sullen with the time of the year; the
silent, blackish water thickens, now, to ice. All will fall still, all lapse.

A young girl would go into the wood as trustingly as Red Riding Hood
to her granny's house but this light admits no ambiguities and, here, she
will be trapped in her own illusion because everything in the wood is
exactly as it seems.

The woods enclose and then enclose again, like a system of Chinese
boxes opening one into another; the intimate perspectives of the wood

changed endlessly around the interloper, the imaginary traveller walking towards an invented distance that perpetually receded before me. It is easy to lose yourself in these woods.

The two notes of the song of a bird rose on the still air, as if my girlish and delicious loneliness had been made into a sound. There was a little tangled mist in the thickets, mimicking the tufts of old man's beard that flossed the lower branches of the trees and bushes; heavy bunches of red berries as ripe and delicious as goblin or enchanted fruit hung on the hawthorns but the old grass withers, retreats. One by one, the ferns have curled up their hundred eyes and curled back into the earth. The trees threaded a cat's cradle of half-stripped branches over me so that I felt I was in a house of nets and though the cold wind that always heralds your presence, had I but known it then, blew gentle around me, I thought that nobody was in the wood but me.

Erl-King will do you grievous harm.

Piercingly, now, there came again the call of the bird, as desolate as if it came from the throat of the last bird left alive. That call, with all the melancholy of the failing year in it, went directly to my heart.

I walked through the wood until its perspectives converged upon a darkening clearing; as soon as I saw them, I knew at once that all its occupants had been waiting for me from the moment I first stepped into the wood, with the endless patience of wild things, who have all the time in the world.

It was a garden where all the flowers were birds and beasts; ash-soft doves, diminutive wrens, freckled thrushes, robins in their tawny bibs, huge, helmeted crows that shone like patent leather, a blackbird with a yellow bill, voles, shrews, fieldfares, little brown bunnies with their ears laid together along their backs like spoons, crouching at his feet. A lean, tall, reddish hare, up on its great hind legs, nose a-twitch. The rusty fox, its muzzle sharpened to a point, laid its head upon his knee. On the trunk of a scarlet rowan a squirrel clung, to watch him; a cock pheasant delicately stretched his shimmering neck from a brake of thorn to peer at him. There was a goat of uncanny whiteness, gleaming like a goat of snow, who turned her mild eyes towards me and bleated softly, so that he knew I had arrived.

He smiles. He lays down his pipe, his elder bird-call. He lays upon me his irrevocable hand.

His eyes are quite green, as if from too much looking at the wood.

There are some eyes can eat you.

The Erl-King lives by himself all alone in the heart of the wood in a house which has only the one room. His house is made of sticks and stones and has grown a pelt of yellow lichen. Grass and weeds grow in the mossy roof. He chops fallen branches for his fire and draws his water from the stream in a tin pail.

What does he eat? Why, the bounty of the woodland! Stewed nettles; savoury messes of chickweed sprinkled with nutmeg; he cooks the foliage of shepherd's purse as if it were cabbage. He knows which of the frilled, blotched, rotted fungi are fit to eat; he understands their eldritch ways, how they spring up overnight in lightless places and thrive on dead things. Even the homely wood blewits, that you cook like tripe, with milk and onions, and the egg-yolk yellow chanterelle with its fan-vaulting and faint scent of apricots, all spring up overnight like bubbles of earth, sustained by nature, existing in a void. And I could believe that it has been the same with him; he came alive from the desire of the woods.

He goes out in the morning to gather his unnatural treasures, he handles them as delicately as he does pigeon's eggs, he lays them in one of the baskets he weaves from osiers. He makes salads of dandelion that he calls rude names, 'bum-pipes' or 'piss-the-beds,' and flavours them with a few leaves of wild strawberry but he will not touch the brambles, he says the Devil spits on them at Michaelmas.

His nanny goat, the colour of whey, gives him her abundant milk and he can make soft cheese that has a unique, rank, amniotic taste. Sometimes he traps a rabbit in a snare of string and makes a soup or stew, seasoned with wild garlic. He knows all about the wood and the creatures in it. He told me about the grass snakes, how the old ones open their mouths wide when they smell danger and the thin little ones disappear down the old ones' throats until the fright is over and out they come again, to run around as usual. He told me how the wise toad who squats among the kingcups by the stream in summer has a very precious jewel in his head. He said the owl was a baker's daughter; then he smiled at me. He showed me how to thread mats from reeds and weave osier twigs into baskets and into the little cages in which he keeps his singing birds.

His kitchen shakes and shivers with birdsong from cage upon cage of singing birds, larks and linnets, which he piles up one on another against the wall, a wall of trapped birds. How cruel it is, to keep wild birds in cages! But he laughs at me when I say that; laughs, and shows his white, pointed teeth with the spittle gleaming on them.

He is an excellent housewife. His rustic home is spick and span. He puts his well-scoured saucepan and skillet neatly on the hearth side by side, like a pair of polished shoes. Over the hearth hang bunches of drying mushrooms, the thin, curling kind they call jew's-ears, which have grown on the elder trees since Judas hanged himself on one; this is the kind of lore he tells me, tempting my half-belief. He hangs up herbs in bunches to dry, too – thyme, marjoram, sage, vervain, southern wood, yarrow. The room is musical and aromatic and there is always a wood fire crackling in the grate, a sweet, acrid smoke, a bright, glancing flame. But you cannot get a tune out of the old fiddle hanging on the wall beside the birds because all its strings are broken.

Now, when I go for walks, sometimes in the mornings when the frost has put its shiny thumbprint on the undergrowth or sometimes, though less frequently, yet more enticingly, in the evening when the cold darkness settles down, I always go to the Erl-King and he lays me down on his bed of rustling straw where I lie at the mercy of his huge hands.

He is the tender butcher who showed me how the price of flesh is love; skin the rabbit, he says! Off come all my clothes.

When he combs his hair that is the colour of dead leaves, dead leaves fall out of it; they rustle and drift to the ground as though he were a tree and he can stand as still as a tree, when he wants the doves to flutter softly, crooning as they come, down upon his shoulders, those silly, fat, trusting woodies with the pretty wedding rings round their necks. He makes his whistles out of an elder twig and that is what he uses to call the birds out of the air – all the birds come; and the sweetest singers he will keep in cages.

The wind stirs the dark wood; it blows through the bushes. A little of the cold air that blows over graveyards always goes with him, it crisps the hairs on the back of my neck but I am not afraid of him; only afraid of vertigo, of the vertigo with which he seizes me. Afraid of falling down.

Falling as a bird would fall through the air if the Erl-King tied up the winds in his handkerchief and knotted the ends together so they could not get out. Then the moving currents of the air would no longer sustain them and all the birds would fall at the imperative of gravity, as I fall down for him, and I know it is only because he is kind to me that I do not fall still further. The earth with its fragile fleece of last summer's dying leaves and grasses supports me only out of complicity with him, because his flesh is of the same substance as those leaves that are slowly turning into earth.

He could thrust me into the seed-bed of next year's generation and I would have to wait until he whistled me up from my darkness before I could come back again.

Yet, when he shakes out those two clear notes from his bird call, I come, like any other trusting thing that perches on the crook of his wrist.

I found the Erl-King sitting on an ivy-covered stump winding all the birds in the wood to him on a diatonic spool of sound, one rising note, one falling note; such a sweet piercing call that down there came a soft, chirruping jostle of birds. The clearing was cluttered with dead leaves, some the colour of honey, some the colour of cinders, some the colour of earth. He seemed so much the spirit of the place I saw without surprise how the fox laid its muzzle fearlessly upon his knee. The brown light of the end of the day drained into the moist, heavy earth; all silent, all still and the cool smell of night coming. The first drops of rain fell. In the wood, no shelter but his cottage.

That was the way I walked into the bird-haunted solitude of the Erl-King, who keeps his feathered things in little cages he has woven out of osier twigs and there they sit and sing for him.

Goat's milk to drink, from a chipped tin mug; we shall eat the oatcakes he has baked on the hearthstone. Rattle of the rain on the roof. The latch clanks on the door; we are shut up inside with one another, in the brown room crisp with the scent of burning logs that shiver with tiny flame, and I lie down on the Erl-King's creaking palliasse of straw. His skin is the tint and texture of sour cream, he has stiff, russet nipples ripe as berries. Like a tree that bears blossom and fruit on the same bough together, how pleasing, how lovely.

And now – ach! I feel your sharp teeth in the subaqueous depths of your kisses. The equinotical gales seize the bare elms and make them whizz and whirl like dervishes; you sink your teeth into my throat and make me scream.

The white moon above the clearing coldly illuminate the still tableaux of our embracements. How sweet I roamed, or, rather, used to roam; once I was the perfect child of the meadows of summer, but then the year turned, the light clarified and I saw the gaunt Erl-King, tall as a tree with birds in its branches, and he drew me towards him on his magic lasso of inhuman music. If I strung that old fiddle with your hair, we could waltz together to the music as the exhausted daylight founders among the trees; we should have better music than the shrill prothalamions of the larks stacked in their pretty cages as the roof creaks with the freight of birds you've lured to it while we engage in your profane mysteries under the leaves.

He strips me to my last nakedness, that underskin of mauve, pearlised satin, like a skinned rabbit; then dresses me again in an embrace so lucid and encompassing it might be made of water. And shakes over me dead leaves as if into the stream I have become.

Sometimes the birds, at random, all singing, strike a chord.

His skin covers me entirely; we are like two halves of a seed, enclosed in the same integument. I should like to grow enormously small, so that you could swallow me, like those queens in fairy tales who conceive when they swallow a grain of corn or a sesame seed. Then I could lodge inside your body and you could bear me.

The candle flutters and goes out. His touch both consoles and devastates me; I feel my heart pulse, then wither, naked as a stone on the roaring mattress while the lovely, moony night slides through the window to dapple the flanks of this innocent who makes cages to keep the sweet birds in. Eat me, drink me; thirsty, cankered, goblin-ridden, I go back and back to him to have his fingers strip the tattered skin away and clothe me in his dress of water, this garment that drenches me, its slithering odour, its capacity for drowning.

Now the crows drop winter from their wings, invoke the harshest season with their cry.

It is growing colder. Scarcely a leaf left on the trees and the birds come to him in greater numbers because, in this hard weather, it is lean pickings. The blackbirds and thrushes must hunt the snails from hedge bottoms and crack the shells on stones. But the Erl-King gives them corn and when he whistles to them a moment later you cannot see him for the birds that have covered him like a soft fall of feathered snow. He spreads out a goblin feast of fruit for me, such appalling succulence; I lie above him and see the light from the fire sucked into the black vortex of his eye, the omission of light at the centre, there, that exerts on me such a tremendous pressure, it draws me inwards.

Eyes green as apples. Green as dead sea fruit.

A wind rises; it makes a singular, wild, low, rushing sound.

What big eyes you have. Eyes of an incomparable luminósity, the numinous phosphorescence of the eyes of lycanthropes. The gelid green of your eyes fixes my reflective face. It is a preservative, like a green liquid amber; it catches me. I am afraid I will be trapped in it for ever like the poor little ants and flies that stuck their feet in resin before the sea covered the Baltic. He winds me into the circle of his eye on a reel of birdsong. There is a black hole in the middle of both your eyes; it is their still centre, looking there makes me giddy, as if I might fall into it.

Your green eye is a reducing chamber. If I look into it long enough, I will become as small as my own reflection, I will diminish to a point and vanish. I will be drawn down into that black whirlpool and be consumed by you. I shall become so small you can keep me in one of your osier cages and mock my loss of liberty. I have seen the cage you are weaving for me; it is a very pretty one and I shall sit, hereafter, in my cage among the other singing birds but I – I shall be dumb, from spite.

When I realised what the Erl-King meant to do with me, I was shaken with a terrible fear and I did not know what to do for I loved him with all my heart and yet I had no wish to join the whistling congregation he kept in his cages although he looked after them very affectionately, gave them fresh water every day and fed them well. His embraces were his enticements and yet, oh yet! they were the branches of which the trap itself was woven. But in his innocence he never knew he might be the death of me, although I knew from the first moment I saw him how Erl-King would do me grievous harm.

Although the bow hangs beside the old fiddle on the wall, all the strings are broken so you cannot play it. I don't know what kind of tunes you might play on it, if it were strung again; lullabies for foolish virgins, perhaps, and now I know the birds don't sing, they only cry because they can't find their way out of the wood, have lost their flesh when they are dipped in the corrosive pools of his regard and now must live in cages.

Sometimes he lays his head on my lap and lets me comb his lovely hair for him; his combings are leaves of every tree in the wood and dryly susurrate around my feet. His hair falls down over my knees. Silence like a dream in front of the spitting fire while he lies at my feet and I comb the dead leaves out of his languorous hair. The robin has built his nest in the thatch again, this year; he perches on an unburnt log, cleans his beak, ruffles his plumage. There is a plaintive sweetness in his song and a certain melancholy, because the year is over – the robin, the friend of man, in spite of the wound in his breast from which Erl-King tore out his heart.

Lay your head on my knee so that I can't see the greenish inward-turning suns of your eyes any more.

My hands shake.

I shall take two huge handfuls of his rustling hair as he lies half dreaming, half waking, and wind them into ropes, very softly, so he will not wake up, and softly, with hands as gentle as rain, I will strangle him with them.

Then she will open all the cages and let the birds free; they will change back into young girls, every one, each with the crimson imprint of his love-bite on their throats. She will carve off his great mane with the knife he uses to skin the rabbits; she will string the old fiddle with five single strings of ash-brown hair.

Then it will play discordant music without a hand touching it. The bow will dance over the new strings of its own accord and will cry out: 'Mother, mother, you have murdered me!'

The Snow Child

Midwinter – invincible, immaculate. The Count and his wife go riding, he on a grey mare and she on a black one, she wrapped in the glittering pelts of black foxes; and she wore high, black, shining boots with scarlet heels, and spurs. Fresh snow fell on snow already fallen; when it ceased, the whole world was white. 'I wish I had a girl as white as snow,' says the Count. They ride on. They come to a hole in the snow; this hole is filled with blood. He says: 'I wish I had a girl as red as blood.' So they ride on again; here is a raven, perched on a bare bough. 'I wish I had a girl as black as that bird's feathers.'

As soon as he completed her description, there she stood, beside the road, white skin, red mouth, black hair and stark naked; she was the child of his desire and the Countess hated her. The Count lifted her up and sat her in front of him on his saddle but the Countess had only one thought: how shall I be rid of her?

The Countess dropped her glove in the snow and told the girl to get down to look for it; she meant to gallop off and leave her there but the Count said: 'I'll buy you new gloves.' At that, the furs sprang off the Countess's shoulders and twined round the naked girl. Then the Countess threw her diamond brooch through the ice of a frozen pond: 'Dive in and fetch it for me,' she said; she thought the girl would drown. But the Count said: 'Is she a fish to swim in such cold weather?' Then her boots leapt off the Countess's feet and on to the girl's legs. Now the Countess was bare as a bone and the girl furred and booted; the Count felt sorry for his wife. They came to a bush of roses, all in flower. 'Pick me one,' said the Countess to the girl. 'I can't deny you that,' said the Count.

So the girl picks a rose; pricks her finger on the thorn; bleeds; screams; falls.

Weeping, the Count got off his horse, unfastened his breeches and thrust his virile member into the dead girl. The Countess reined in her stamping mare and watched him narrowly; he was soon finished.

Then the girl began to melt. Soon there was nothing left of her but a feather a bird might have dropped; a blood stain, like the trace of a fox's kill on the snow; and the rose she had pulled off the bush. Now the Countess had all her clothes on again. With her long hand, she stroked

her furs. The Count picked up the rose, bowed and handed it to his wife;
when she touched it, she dropped it.

'It bites!' she said.

The Lady of the House of Love

At last the revenants became so troublesome the peasants abandoned the village and it fell solely into the possession of subtle and vindictive inhabitants who manifest their presences by shadows that fall almost inperceptibly awry, too many shadows, even at midday, their shadows that have no source in anything visible; by the sound, sometimes, of sobbing in a derelict bedroom where a cracked mirror suspended from a wall does not reflect a presence; by a sense of unease that will afflict the traveller unwise enough to pause to drink from the fountain in the square that still gushes spring water from a faucet stuck in a stone lion's mouth. A cat prowls in a weedy garden; he grins and spits, arches his back, bounces away from an intangible on four fear-stiffened legs. Now all shun the village below the château in which the beautiful somnambulist helplessly perpetuates her ancestral crimes.

Wearing an antique bridal gown, the beautiful queen of the vampires sits all alone in her dark, high house under the eyes of the portraits of her demented and atrocious ancestors, each one of whom, through her, projects a baleful posthumous existence; she counts out the Tarot cards, ceaselessly construing a constellation of possibilities as if the random fall of the cards on the red plush tablecloth before her could precipitate her from her chill, shuttered room into the country of perpetual summer and obliterate the perennial sadness of a girl who is both death and the maiden.

Her voice is filled with distant sonorities, like reverberations in a cave: now you are at the place of annihilation, now you are at the place of annihilation. And she is herself a cave full of echoes, she is a system of repetitions, she is a closed circuit. 'Can a bird sing only the song it knows or can it learn a new song?' She draws her long, sharp fingernail across the bars of the cage in which her pet lark sings, striking a plangent twang like that of the plucked heartstrings of a woman of metal. Her hair falls down like tears.

The castle is mostly given over to ghostly occupants but she herself has her own suite of drawing room and bedroom. Closely barred shutters and heavy velvet curtains keep out every leak of natural light. There is a round table on a single leg covered with a red plush cloth on which she lays out her inevitable Tarot; this room is never more than faintly illuminated by a heavily shaded lamp on the mantelpiece and the dark red figured wallpaper is obscurely, distressingly patterned by the rain that drives in through the neglected roof and leaves behind it random areas of staining, ominous marks like those left on the sheets by dead lovers. Depredations of rot and fungus everywhere. The unlit chandelier is so heavy with dust the individual prisms no longer show any shapes, industrious spiders have woven canopies in the corners of this ornate and rotting place, have trapped the porcelain vases on the mantelpiece in soft grey nets. But the mistress of all this disintegration notices nothing.

She sits in a chair covered in moth-ravaged burgundy velvet at the low, round table and distributes the cards; sometimes the lark sings, but more often remains a sullen mound of drab feathers. Sometimes the Countess will wake it for a brief cadenza by strumming the bars of its cage; she likes to hear it announce how it cannot escape.

She rises when the sun sets and goes immediately to her table where she plays her game of patience until she grows hungry, until she becomes ravenous. She is so beautiful she is unnatural; her beauty is an abnormality, a deformity, for none of her features exhibit any of those touching imperfections that reconcile us to the imperfections of the human condition. Her beauty is a symptom of her disorder, of her soullessness.

The white hands of the tenebrous belle deal the hand of destiny. Her fingernails are longer than those of the mandarins of ancient China and each is pared to a fine point. These and teeth as fine and white as spikes of spun sugar are the visible signs of the destiny she wistfully attempts to evade via the arcana; her claws and teeth have been sharpened on centuries of corpses, she is the last bud of the poison tree that sprang from the loins of Vlad the Impaler who picnicked on corpses in the forests of Transylvania.

The walls of her bedroom are hung with black satin, embroidered with tears of pearl. At the room's four corners are funerary urns and bowls which emit slumbrous, pungent fumes of incense. In the centre is an elaborate catafalque, in ebony, surrounded by long candles in enormous silver candlesticks. In a white lace negligee stained a little with blood, the Countess climbs up on her catafalque at dawn each morning and lies down in an open coffin.

A chignoned priest of the Orthodox faith staked out her wicked father at a Carpathian crossroad before her milk teeth grew. Just as they staked him out, the fatal Count cried: 'Nosferatu is dead; long live Nosferatu!' Now she possesses all the haunted forests and mysterious habitations of his vast domain; she is the hereditary commandant of the army of shadows who camp in the village below her château, who penetrate the woods in the form of owls, bats and foxes, who make the milk curdle and butter refuse to come, who ride the horses all night in a wild hunt so they are sacks of skin and bone in the morning, who milk the cows dry and, especially, torment pubescent girls with fainting fits, disorders of the blood, diseases of the imagination.

But the Countess herself is indifferent to her own weird authority, as if she were dreaming it. In her dream, she would like to be human; but she does not know if that is possible. The Tarot always shows the same configuration: always she turns up La Papesse, La Mort, La Tour Abolie, wisdom, death, dissolution.

On moonless nights, her keeper lets her out into the garden. This garden, an exceedingly sombre place, bears a strong resemblance to a burial ground and all the roses her dead mother planted have grown up into a huge, spiked wall that incarcerates her in the castle of her inheritance. When the back door opens, the Countess will sniff the air and howl. She drops, now, on all fours. Crouching, quivering, she catches the scent of her prey. Delicious crunch of the fragile bones of rabbits and small, furry things she pursues with fleet, four-footed speed; she will creep home, whimpering, with blood smeared on her cheeks. She pours water from the ewer in her bedroom into the bowl, she washes her face with the wincing, fastidious gestures of a cat.

The voracious margin of huntress's nights in the gloomy garden, crouch and pounce, surrounds her habitual tormented somnambulism, her life or imitation of life. The eyes of this nocturnal creature enlarge and glow. All claws and teeth, she strikes, she gorges, but nothing can console her for the ghastliness of her condition, nothing. She resorts to the magic comfort of the Tarot pack and shuffles the cards, lays them out, reads them, gathers them up with a sigh, shuffles them again, constantly constructing hypotheses about a future which is irreversible.

An old mute looks after her, to make sure she never sees the sun, that all day she stays in her coffin, to keep mirrors and all reflective surfaces away from her – in short, to perform all the functions of the servants of vampires. Everything about this beautiful and ghastly lady is as it should be, queen of night, queen of terror – except her horrible reluctance for the role.

Nevertheless, if an unwise adventurer pauses in the square of the deserted village to refresh himself at the fountain, a crone in a black dress and white apron presently emerges from a house. She will invite you with smiles and gestures; you will follow her. The Countess wants fresh meat. When she was a little girl, she was like a fox and contented herself entirely with baby rabbits that squeaked piteously as she bit into their necks with a nauseated voluptuousness, with voles and fieldmice that palpitated for a bare moment between her embroidress's fingers. But now she is a woman, she must have men. If you stop too long beside the giggling fountain, you will be led by the hand to the Countess's larder.

All day, she lies in her coffin in her negligee of bloodstained lace. When the sun drops behind the mountain, she yawns and stirs and puts on the only dress she has, her mother's wedding dress, to sit and read her cards until she grows hungry. She loathes the food she eats; she would have liked to take the rabbits home with her, feed them on lettuce, pet them and make them a nest in her red-and-black chinoiserie escritoire, but hunger always overcomes her. She sinks her teeth into the neck where an artery throbs with fear; she will drop the deflated skin from which she has extracted all the nourishment with a small cry of both pain and disgust. And it is the same with the shepherd boys and gypsy lads who, ignorant or foolhardy, come to wash the dust from their feet in the water of the fountain; the Countess's governess brings them into the drawing room where the cards on the table always show the Grim Reaper. The Countess herself will serve them coffee in tiny cracked, precious cups, and little sugar cakes. The hobbledehoys sit with a spilling cup in one hand and a biscuit in the other, gaping at the Countess in her satin finery as she pours from a silver pot and chatters distractedly to put them at their fatal ease. A certain desolate stillness of her eyes indicates she is inconsolable. She would like to caress their lean brown cheeks and stroke their ragged hair. When she takes them by the hand and leads them to her bedroom, they can scarcely believe their luck.

Afterwards, her governess will tidy the remains into a neat pile and wrap it in its own discarded clothes. This mortal parcel she then discreetly buries in the garden. The blood on the Countess's cheeks will be mixed with tears; her keeper probes her fingernails for her with a silver toothpick, to get rid of the fragments of skin and bone that have lodged there.

>   Fee fie fo fum
>   I smell the blood of an Englishman.

One hot, ripe summer in the pubescent years of the present century, a young officer in the British army, blond, blue-eyed, heavy-muscled, visiting friends in Vienna, decided to spend the remainder of his furlough exploring the little-known uplands of Romania. When he quixotically decided to travel the rutted cart-tracks by bicycle, he saw all the humour of it: 'on two wheels in the land of the vampires'. So, laughing, he sets out on his adventure.

He has the special quality of virginity, most and least ambiguous of states: ignorance, yet at the same time, power in potentia, and, furthermore, unknowingness, which is not the same as ignorance. He is more than he knows – and has about him, besides, the special glamour of that generation for whom history has already prepared a special, exemplary fate in the trenches of France. This being, rooted in change and time, is about to collide with the timeless Gothic eternity of the vampires, for whom all is as it has always been and will be, whose cards always fall in the same pattern.

Although so young, he is also rational. He has chosen the most rational mode of transport in the world for his trip round the Carpathians. To ride a bicycle is in itself some protection against superstitious fear, since the bicycle is the product of pure reason applied to motion. Geometry at the service of man! Give me two spheres and a straight line and I will show you how far I can take them. Voltaire himself might have invented the bicycle, since it contributes much to man's welfare and nothing at all to his bane. Beneficial to the health, it emits no harmful fumes and permits only the most decorous speeds. How can a bicycle ever be an implement of harm?

A single kiss woke up the Sleeping Beauty in the Wood.

The waxen fingers of the Countess, fingers of a holy image, turn up the card called Les Amoureux. Never, never before . . . never before has the Countess cast herself a fate involving love. She shakes, she trembles, her great eyes close beneath her finely veined, nervously fluttering eyelids; the lovely cartomancer has, this time, the first time, dealt herself a hand of love and death.

> Be he alive or be he dead
> I'll grind his bones to make my bread.

At the mauvish beginnings of evening, the English m'sieu toils up the hill to the village he glimpsed from a great way off; he must dismount and push his bicycle before him, the path too steep to ride. He hopes to find a friendly inn to rest the night; he's hot, hungry, thirsty, weary, dusty . . . At first, such disappointment, to discover the roofs of all the cottages caved in and tall weeds thrusting through the piles of fallen tiles, shutters hanging disconsolately from their hinges, an entirely uninhabited place. And the rank vegetation whispers, as if foul secrets, here, where, if one were sufficiently imaginative, one could almost imagine twisted faces appearing momentarily beneath the crumbling eaves . . . but the adventure of it all, and the consolation of the poignant brightness of the hollyhocks still bravely blooming in the shaggy gardens, and the beauty of the flaming sunset, all these considerations soon overcame his disappointment, even assuaged the faint unease he'd felt. And the fountain where the village women used to wash their clothes still gushed out bright, clear water; he gratefully washed his feet and hands, applied his mouth to the faucet, then let the icy stream run over his face.

When he raised his dripping, gratified head from the lion's mouth, he saw, silently arrived beside him in the square, an old woman who smiled eagerly, almost conciliatorily at him. She wore a black dress and a white apron, with a housekeeper's key ring at her waist; her grey hair was neatly coiled in a chignon beneath the white linen headdress worn by elderly women of that region. She bobbed a curtsy at the young man and beckoned him to follow her. When he hesitated, she pointed towards the great bulk of the mansion above them, whose façade loured over the village, rubbed her stomach, pointed to her mouth, rubbed her stomach again, clearly miming an invitation to supper. Then she beckoned him again, this time turning determinedly upon her heel as though she would brook no opposition.

A great, intoxicated surge of the heavy scent of red roses blew into his face as soon as they left the village, inducing a sensuous vertigo; a blast of rich, faintly corrupt sweetness strong enough, almost, to fell him. Too many roses. Too many roses bloomed on enormous thickets that lined the path, thickets bristling with thorns, and the flowers themselves were almost too luxuriant, their huge congregations of plush petals somehow obscene in their excess, their whorled, tightly budded cores outrageous in their implications. The mansion emerged grudgingly out of this jungle.

In the subtle and haunting light of the setting sun, that golden light rich with nostalgia for the day that was just past, the sombre visage of the place, part manor house, part fortified farmhouse, immense, rambling, a dilapidated eagle's nest atop the crag down which its attendant village meandered, reminded him of childhood tales on winter evenings, when he and his brothers and sisters scared themselves half out of their wits with ghost stories set in just such places and then had to have candles to light them up newly terrifying stairs to bed. He could almost have regretted accepting the crone's unspoken invitation; but now, standing before the door of time-eroded oak while she selected a huge iron key from the clanking ringful at her waist, he knew it was too late to turn back and brusquely reminded himself he was no child, now, to be frightened of his own fancies.

The old lady unlocked the door, which swung back on melo-dramatically creaking hinges, and fussily took charge of his bicycle, in spite of his protests. He felt a certain involuntary sinking of the heart to see his beautiful two-wheeled symbol of rationality vanish into the dark entrails of the mansion, to, no doubt, some damp outhouse where they would not oil or check its tyres. But, in for a penny, in for a pound – in his

youth and strength and blond beauty, in the invisble, even unacknowledged pentacle of his virginity, the young man stepped over the
threshold of Nosferatu's castle and did not shiver in the blast of cold air, as
from the mouth of a grave, that emanated from the lightless, cavernous
interior.

The crone took him to a little chamber where there was a black oak
table spread with a clean white cloth and this cloth was carefully laid with
heavy silverware, a little tarnished, as if someone with foul breath had
breathed on it, but laid with one place only. Curiouser and curiouser;
invited to the castle for dinner, now he must dine alone. All the same, he
sat down as she had bid him. Although it was not yet dark outside, the
curtains were closely drawn and only the sparing light trickling from a
single oil lamp showed him how dismal his surroundings were. The
crone bustled about to get him a bottle of wine and a glass from an ancient
cabinet of wormy oak; while he bemusedly drank his wine, she
disappeared but soon returned bearing a steaming platter of the local
spiced meat stew with dumplings, and a shank of black bread. He was
hungry after his long day's ride, he ate heartily and polished his plate with
the crust, but this coarse food was hardly the entertainment he'd expected
from the gentry and he was puzzled by the assessing glint in the dumb
woman's eyes as she watched him eating.

But she darted off to get him a second helping as soon as he'd finished
the first one and seemed so friendly and helpful, besides, that he knew he
could count on a bed for the night in the castle, as well as his supper, so he
sharply reprimanded himself for his own childish lack of enthusiasm for
the eerie silence, the clammy chill of the place.

When he'd put away the second plateful, the old woman came and
gestured he should leave the table and follow her once again. She made a
pantomine of drinking; he deduced he was now invited to take after-
dinner coffee in another room with some more elevated member of the
household who had not wished to dine with him but, all the same,
wanted to make his acquaintance. An honour, no doubt; in deference to
his host's opinion of himself, he straightened his tie, brushed the crumbs
from his tweed jacket.

He was surprised to find how ruinous the interior of the house was –
cobwebs, worm-eaten beams, crumbling plaster; but the mute crone
resolutely wound him on the reel of her lantern down endless corridors,
up winding staircases, through the galleries where the painted eyes of
family portraits briefly flickered as they passed, eyes that belonged, he
noticed to faces, one and all, of a quite memorable beastliness. At last she
paused and, behind the door where they'd halted, he heard a faint,
metallic twang as of, perhaps, a chord struck on a harpsichord. And then,

wonderfully, the liquid cascade of the song of a lark, bringing to him, in the heart – had he but known it – of Juliet's tomb, all the freshness of morning.

The crone rapped with her knuckles on the panels; the most seductively caressing voice he had ever heard in his life softly called out, in heavily accented French, the adopted language of the Romanian aristocracy: '*Entrez.*'

First of all, he saw only a shape, a shape imbued with a faint luminosity since it caught and reflected in its yellowed surfaces what little light there was in the ill-lit room; this shape resolved itself into that of, of all things, a hooped-skirted dress of white satin draped here and there with lace, a dress fifty or sixty years out of fashion but once, obviously, intended for a wedding. And then he saw the girl who wore the dress, a girl with the fragility of the skeleton of a moth, so thin, so frail that her dress seemed to him to hang suspended, as if untenanted in the dank air, a fabulous lending, a self-articulated garment in which she lived like a ghost in a machine. All the light in the room came from a low-burning lamp with a thick greenish shade on a distant mantelpiece; the crone who accompanied him shielded her lantern with her hand, as if to protect her mistress from too suddenly seeing, or their guest from too suddenly seeing her.

So that it was little by little, as his eyes grew accustomed to the half-dark, that he saw how beautiful and how very young the bedizened scarecrow was, and he thought of a child dressing up in her mother's clothes, perhaps a child putting on the clothes of a dead mother in order to bring her, however briefly, to life again.

The Countess stood behind a low table, beside a pretty, silly, gilt-and-wire birdcage, hands outstretched in a distracted attitude that was almost one of flight, she looked startled by their entry as if she had not requested it. With her stark white face, her lovely death's head surrounded by long dark hair that fell down as straight as if it were soaking wet, she looked like a shipwrecked bride. Her huge dark eyes almost broke his heart with their waiflike, lost look; yet he was disturbed, almost repelled, by her extraordinarily fleshy mouth, a mouth with wide, full, prominent lips of a vibrant purplish-crimson, a morbid mouth. Even – but he put the thought away from him immediately – a whore's mouth. She shivered all the time, a starveling chill, a malarial agitation of the bones. He thought she must be only sixteen or seventeen years old, no more, with the hectic, unhealthy beauty of a consumptive. She was the châtelaine of all this decay.

With many tender precautions, the crone now raised the light she held to show his hostess her guest's face. At that, the Countess let out a faint mewing cry and made a blind, appalled gesture with her hands, as if pushing him away, so that she knocked against the table and a butterfly dazzle of painted cards fell to the floor. Her mouth formed a round 'o' of woe, she swayed a little and then sank into her chair, where she lay as if now scarcely capable of moving. A bewildering reception. Tsk'ing under her breath, the crone busily poked about on the table until she found an enormous pair of dark green glasses, such as blind beggars wear, and perched them on the Countess's nose.

He went forward to pick up her cards for her from a carpet that, he saw to his surprise, was part rotted away, partly encroached upon by all kinds of virulent-looking fungi. He retrieved the cards and shuffled them carelessly together, for they meant nothing to him, though they seemed strange playthings for a young girl. What a grisly picture of a capering skeleton! He covered it up with a happier one – of two young lovers, smiling at one another, and put her toys back into a hand so slender you could almost see the frail net of bones beneath the translucent skin, a hand with fingernails as long, as finely pointed, as banjo picks.

At his touch, she seemed to revive a little and almost smiled, raising herself upright.

'Coffee,' she said. 'You must have coffee.' And scooped up her cards into a pile so that the crone could set before her a silver spirit kettle, a silver coffee pot, cream jug, sugar basin, cups ready on a silver tray, a strange touch of elegance, even if discoloured, in this devastated interior whose mistress ethereally shone as if with her own blighted, submarine radiance.

The crone found him a chair and tittering noiselessly, departed, leaving the room a little darker.

While the young lady attended to the coffee-making, he had time to contemplate with some distaste a further series of family portraits which decorated the stained and peeling walls of the room; these livid faces all seemed contorted with a febrile madness and the blubber lips, the huge, demented eyes that all had in common bore a disquieting resemblance to those of the hapless victim of inbreeding now patiently filtering her fragrant brew, even if some rare grace has so finely transformed those features when it came to her case. The lark, its chorus done, had long ago fallen silent; no sound but the chink of silver on china. Soon, she held out to him a tiny cup of rose-painted china.

'Welcome,' she said in her voice with the rushing sonorities of the ocean in it, a voice that seemed to come elsewhere than from her white, still throat. 'Welcome to my château. I rarely receive visitors and that's a misfortune since nothing animates me half as much as the presence of a stranger . . . This place is so lonely, now the village is deserted, and my one companion, alas, she cannot speak. Often I am so silent that I think I,

too, will soon forget how to do so and nobody here will ever talk any
more.'

She offered him a sugar biscuit from a Limoges plate; her fingernails
struck carillons from the antique china. Her voice, issuing from those red
lips like the obese roses in her garden, lips that do not move – her voice is
curiously disembodied; she is like a doll, he thought, a ventriloquist's
doll, or, more, like a great ingenious piece of clockwork. For she seemed
inadequately powered by some slow energy of which she was not in
control; as if she had been wound up years ago, when she was born, and
now the mechanism was inexorably running down and would leave her
lifeless. This idea that she might be an automaton, made of white velvet
and black fur, that could not move of its own accord, never quite deserted
him; indeed, it deeply moved his heart. The carnival air of her white dress
emphasised her unreality, like a sad Columbine who lost her way in the
wood a long time ago and never reached the fair.

'And the light. I must apologise for the lack of light . . . a hereditary
affliction of the eyes . . .'

Her blind spectacles gave him his handsome face back to himself twice
over; if he presented himself to her naked face, he would dazzle her like
the sun she is forbidden to look at because it would shrivel her up at once,
poor night bird, poor butcher bird.

Vouse serez ma proie.

You have such a fine throat, m'sieu, like a column of marble. When
you came through the door retaining about you all the golden light of the
summer's day of which I know nothing, nothing, the card called 'Les
Amoureux' had just emerged from the tumbling chaos of imagery before
me; it seemed to me you had stepped off the card into my darkness and,
for a moment, I thought, perhaps, you might irradiate it.

I do not mean to hurt you. I shall wait for you in my bride's dress in the
dark.

The bridegroom is come, he will go into the chamber which has been
prepared for him.

I am condemned to solitude and dark; I do not mean to hurt you.

I will be very gentle.

(And could love free me from the shadows? Can a bird sing only the
song it knows, or can it learn a new song?)

See, how I'm ready for you. I've always been ready for you; I've been
waiting for you in my wedding dress, why have you delayed for so long
. . . it will all be over very quickly.

You will feel no pain, my darling.

She herself is a haunted house. She does not possess herself; her ancestors sometimes come and peer out of the windows of her eyes and that is very frightening. She has the mysterious solitude of ambiguous states; she hovers in a no-man's land between life and death, sleeping and waking, behind the hedge of spiked flowers, Nosferatu's sanguinary rosebud. The beastly forebears on the walls condemn her to a perpetual repetition of their passions.

(One kiss, however, and only one, woke up the Sleeping Beauty in the Wood.)

Nervously, to conceal her inner voices, she keeps up a front of inconsequential chatter in French while her ancestors leer and grimace on the walls; however hard she tries to think of any other, she only knows of one kind of consummation.

He was struck, once again, by the birdlike, predatory claws which tipped her marvellous hands; the sense of strangeness that had been growing in him since he buried his head under the streaming water in the village, since he entered the dark portals of the fatal castle, now fully overcame him. Had he been a cat, he would have bounced backwards from her hands on four fear-stiffened legs, but he is not a cat: he is a hero.

A fundamental disbelief in what he sees before him sustains him, even in the boudoir of Countess Nosferatu herself; he would have said, perhaps, that there are some things which, even if they *are* true, we should not believe possible. He might have said: it is folly to believe one's eyes. Not so much that he does not believe in her; he can see her, she is real. If she takes off her dark glasses, from her eyes will stream all the images that populate this vampire-haunted land, but, since he himself is immune to shadow, due to his virginity – he does not yet know what there is to be afraid of – and due to his heroism, which makes him like the sun, he sees before him, first and foremost, an inbred, highly strung girl child, fatherless, motherless, kept in the dark too long and pale as a plant that never sees the light, half-blinded by some hereditary condition of her eyes. And though he feels unease, he cannot feel terror; so he is like the boy in the fairy tale, who does not know how to shudder, and not spooks, ghouls, beasties, the Devil himself and all his retinue could do the trick.

This lack of imagination gives his heroism to the hero.

He will learn to shudder in the trenches. But this girl cannot make him shudder.

Now it is dark. Bats swoop and squeak outside the tightly shuttered windows. The coffee is all drunk, the sugar biscuits eaten. Her chatter comes trickling and diminishing to a stop; she twists her fingers together, picks at the lace of her dress, shifts nervously in her chair. Owls shriek; the impedimenta of her condition squeak and gibber all around us. Now you are at the place of annihilation, now you are at the place of annihilation. She turns her head away from the blue beams of his eyes; she knows no other consummation than the only one she can offer him. She has not eaten for three days. It is dinner-time. It is bed-time.

> *Suivez-moi.*
> *Je vous attendais.*
> *Vouse serez ma proie.*

The raven caws on the accursed roof. 'Dinner-time, dinner-time,' clang the portraits on the walls. A ghastly hunger gnaws her entrails; she has waited for him all her life without knowing it.

The handsome bicyclist, scarcely believing his luck, will follow her into her bedroom; the candles around her sacrificial altar burn with a low, clear flame, light catches on the silver tears stitched to the wall. She will assure him, in the very voice of temptation: 'My clothes have but to fall and you will see before you a succession of mysteries.'

She has no mouth with which to kiss, no hands with which to caress, only the fangs and talons of a beast of prey. To touch the mineral sheen of the flesh revealed in the cool candle gleam is to invite her fatal embrace; hear her low, sweet voice, she will croon the lullaby of the House of Nosferatu.

Embraces, kisses; your golden head, of a lion, although I have never seen a lion, only imagined one, of the sun, even if I've only seen the picture of the sun on the Tarot card, your golden head of the lover whom I dreamed would one day free me, this head will fall back, its eyes roll upwards in a spasm you will mistake for that of love and not of death. The bridegroom bleeds on my inverted marriage bed. Stark and dead, poor bicyclist; he has paid the price of a night with the Countess and some think it too high a fee while some do not.

Tomorrow, her keeper will bury his bones under her roses. The food her roses feed on gives them their rich colour, their swooning odour, that breathes lasciviously of forbidden pleasures.

> *Suivez-moi*

'*Suivez-moi!*'

The handsome bicyclist, fearful for his hostess's health, her sanity, gingerly follows her hysterical imperiousness into the other room; he would like to take her in his arms and protect her from the ancestors who leer down from the walls.

What a macabre bedroom!

His colonel, an old goat with jaded appetites, had given him the visiting card of a brothel in Paris where, the satyr assured him, ten louis would buy just such a lugubrious bedroom, with a naked girl upon a coffin; offstage, the brothel pianist played the *Dies Irae* on a harmonium and, amidst all the perfumes of the embalming parlour, the customer took his necrophiliac pleasure of a pretend corpse. He had good-naturedly refused the old man's offer of such an initiation; how can he now take criminal advantage of the disordered girl with fever-hot, bone-dry, taloned hands and eyes that deny all the erotic promise of her body with their terror, their sadness, their dreadful, balked tenderness?

So delicate and damned, poor thing. Quite damned.

Yet I do believe she scarcely knows what she is doing.

She is shaking as if her limbs are not efficiently joined together, as if she might shake into pieces. She raises her hands to unfasten the neck of her dress and her eyes well with tears, they trickle down beneath the rim of her dark glasses. She can't take off her mother's wedding dress unless she takes off her dark glasses; she fumbled the ritual, it is no longer inexorable. The mechanism within her fails her, now, when she needs it most. When she takes off the dark glasses, they slip from her fingers and smash to pieces on the tiled floor. There is no room in her drama for improvisation; and this unexpected, mundane noise of breaking glass breaks the wicked spell in the room, entirely. She gapes blindly down at the splinters and ineffectively smears the tears across her face with her fist. What is she to do now?

When she kneels to try to gather the fragments of glass together, a sharp sliver pierces deeply into the pad of her thumb; she cries out, sharp, real. She kneels among the broken glass and watches the bright bead of blood form a drop. She has never seen her own blood before, not her *own* blood. It exercises upon her an awed fascination.

Into this vile and murderous room, the handsome bicyclist brings the innocent remedies of the nursery; in himself, by his presence, he is an exorcism. He gently takes her hand away from her and dabs the blood with his own handkerchief, but still it spurts out. And so he puts his mouth to the wound. He will kiss it better for her, as her mother, had she lived, would have done.

All the silver tears fall from the wall with a flimsy tinkle. Her painted ancestors turn away their eyes and grind their fangs.

How can she bear the pain of becoming human?

The end of exile is the end of being.

He was awakened by larksong. The shutters, the curtains, even the long-sealed windows of the horrid bedroom were all opened up and light and air streamed in; now you could see how tawdry it all was, how thin and cheap the satin, the catafalque not ebony at all but black-painted paper stretched on struts of wood, as in the theatre. The wind had blown droves of petals from the roses outside in to the room and their crimson residue swirled fragrantly about the floor. The candles had burnt out and she must have set her pet lark free because it perched on the edge of the silly coffin to sing him its ecstatic morning song. His bones were stiff and aching, he'd slept on the floor with his bundled-up jacket for a pillow, after he'd put her to bed.

But now there was no trace of her to be seen, except, lightly tossed across the crumbled black satin bedcover, a lace negligee lightly soiled with blood, as it might be from a woman's menses, and a rose that must have come from the fierce bushes nodding through the window. The air was heavy with incense and roses and made him cough. The Countess must have got up early to enjoy the sunshine, slipped outside to gather him a rose. He got to his feet, coaxed the lark on to his wrist and took it to the window. At first, it exhibited the reluctance for the sky of a long-caged thing, but, when he tossed it up on to the currents of the air, it spread its wings and was up and away into the clear blue bowl of the heavens; he watched its trajectory with a lift of joy in his heart.

Then he padded into the boudoir, his mind busy with plans. We shall take her to Zurich, to a clinic; she will be treated for nervous hysteria. Then to an eye specialist, for her photophobia, and to a dentist, to put her teeth into better shape. Any competent manicurist will deal with her claws. We shall turn her into the lovely girl she is; I shall cure her of all these nightmares.

The heavy curtains are pulled back, to let in brilliant fusillades of early morning light; in the desolation of the boudoir, she sits at her round table in her white dress, with the cards laid out before her. She has dropped off to sleep over the cards of destiny that are so fingered, so soiled, so worn by constant shuffling that you can no longer make the image out on any single one of them.

She is not sleeping.

In death, she looked far older, less beautiful and so, for the first time, fully human.

I will vanish in the morning light; I was only an invention of darkness.

And I leave you as a souvenir the dark, fanged rose I plucked from between my thighs, like a flower laid on a grave. On a grave.

My keeper will attend to everything.

Nosferatu always attends his own obsequies; she will not go to the graveyard unattended. And now the crone materialised, weeping, and roughly gestured him to be gone. After a search in some foul-smelling outhouses, he discovered his bicycle and, abandoning his holiday, rode directly to Bucharest where, at the poste restante, he found a telegram summoning him to rejoin his regiment at once. Much later, when he changed back into uniform in his quarters, he discovered he still had the Countess's rose, he must have tucked it into the breast pocket of his cycling jacket after he had found her body. Curiously enough, although he had brought it so far away from Romania, the flower did not seem to be quite dead and, on impulse, because the girl had been so lovely and her death so unexpected and pathetic, he decided to try and resurrect her rose. He filled his tooth glass with water from the carafe on his locker and popped the rose into it, so that its withered head floated on the surface.

When he returned from the mess that evening, the heavy fragrance of Count Nosferatu's rose drifted down the stone corridor of the barracks to greet him, and his spartan quarters brimmed with the reeling odour of a glowing, velvet, monstrous flower whose petals had regained all their former bloom and elasticity, their corrupt, brilliant, baleful splendour.

Next day, his regiment embarked for France.

The Werewolf

It is a northern country; they have cold weather, they have cold hearts.

Cold; tempest; wild beasts in the forest. It is a hard life. Their houses are built of logs, dark and smoky within. There will be a crude icon of the virgin behind a guttering candle, the leg of a pig hung up to cure, a string of drying mushrooms. A bed, a stool, a table. Harsh, brief, poor lives.

To these upland woodsmen, the Devil is as real as you or I. More so; they have not seen us nor even know that we exist, but the Devil they glimpse often in the graveyards, those bleak and touching townships of the dead where the graves are marked with portraits of the deceased in the naïf style and there are no flowers to put in front of them, no flowers grow there, so they put out small, votive offerings, little loaves, sometimes a cake that the bears come lumbering from the margins of the forest to snatch away. At midnight especially on Walpurgisnacht, the Devil holds picnics in the graveyards and invites the witches; then they dig up fresh corpses, and eat them. Anyone will tell you that.

Wreaths of garlic on the doors keep out the vampires. A blue-eyed child born feet first on the night of St John's Eve will have second sight. When they discover a witch – some old woman whose cheeses ripen when her neighbour's do not, another old woman whose black cat, oh, sinister! *follows her about all the time,* they strip the crone, search her for marks, for the supernumary nipple her familiar sucks. They soon find it. Then they stone her to death.

Winter and cold weather.

Go and visit grandmother, who has been sick. Take her the oatcakes I've baked for her on the hearthstone and a little pot of butter.

The good child does as her mother bids – five miles' trudge through the forest; do not leave the path because of the bears, the wild boar, the starving wolves. Here, take your father's hunting knife; you know how to use it.

The child had a scabby coat of sheepskin to keep out the cold, she knew the forest too well to fear it but she must always be on her guard. When she heard that freezing howl of a wolf, she dropped her gifts, seized her knife and turned on the beast.

It was a huge one, with red eyes and running, grizzled chops; any but a mountaineer's child would have died of fright at the sight of it. It went for her throat, as wolves do, but she made a great swipe at it with her father's knife and slashed off its right forepaw.

The wolf let out a gulp, almost a sob, when she saw what had happened to it; wolves are less brave than they seem. It went lolloping off disconsolately between the trees as well as it could on three legs, leaving a trail of blood behind it. The child wiped the blade of her knife clean on her apron, wrapped up the wolf's paw in the cloth in which her mother had packed the oatcakes and went on towards her grandmother's house. Soon it came on to snow so thickly that the path and any footsteps, track or spoor that might have been upon it were obscured.

She found her grandmother was so sick she had taken to her bed and fallen into a fretful sleep, moaning and shaking so that the child guessed she had a fever. She felt the forehead, it burned. She shook out the cloth from her basket, to use it to make the old woman a cold compress, and the wolf's paw fell to the floor.

But it was no longer a wolf's paw. It was a hand, chopped off at the wrist, a hand toughened with work and freckled with age. There was a wedding ring on the third finger and a wart on the index finger. By the wart, she knew it for her grandmother's hand.

She pulled back the sheet but the old woman woke up, at that, and began to struggle, squawking, and shrieking like a thing possessed. But the child was strong, and armed with her father's hunting knife; she managed to hold her grandmother down long enough to see the cause of her fever. There was a bloody stump where her right hand should have been, festering already.

The child crossed herself and cried out so loud the neighbours heard her and came rushing in. They knew the wart on the hand at once for a witch's nipple; they drove the old woman, in her shift as she was, out into the snow with sticks, beating her old carcass as far as the edge of the forest, and pelted her with stones until she fell down dead.

Now the child lived in her grandmother's house; she prospered.

The Company of Wolves

One beast and only one howls in the woods by night.

The wolf is carnivore incarnate and he's as cunning as he is ferocious; once he's had a taste of flesh then nothing else will do.

At night, the eyes of wolves shine like candle flames, yellowish, reddish, but that is because the pupils of their eyes fatten on darkness and catch the light from your lantern to flash it back to you – red for danger; if a wolf's eyes reflect only moonlight, then they gleam a cold and unnatural green, a mineral, a piercing colour. If the benighted traveller spies those luminous, terrible sequins stitched suddenly on the black thickets, then he knows he must run, if fear has not struck him stock-still.

But those eyes are all you will be able to glimpse of the forest assassins as they cluster invisibly round your smell of meat as you go through the wood unwisely late. They will be like shadows, they will be like wraiths, grey members of a congregation of nightmare; hark! his long, wavering howl . . . an aria of fear made audible.

The wolfsong is the sound of the rending you will suffer, in itself a murdering.

It is winter and cold weather. In this region of mountain and forest, there is now nothing for the wolves to eat. Goats and sheep are locked up in the byre, the deer departed for the remaining pasturage on the southern slopes – wolves grow lean and famished. There is so little flesh on them that you could count the starveling ribs through their pelts, if they gave you time before they pounced. Those slavering jaws; the lolling tongue; the rime of saliva on the grizzled chops – of all the teeming perils of the night and the forest, ghosts, hobgoblins, ogres that grill babies upon gridirons, witches that fatten their captives in cages for cannibal tables, the wolf is worst for he cannot listen to reason.

You are always in danger in the forest, where no people are. Step between the portals of the great pines where the shaggy branches tangle about you, trapping the unwary traveller in nets as if the vegetation itself were in a plot with the wolves who live there, as though the wicked trees go fishing on behalf of their friends – step between the gateposts of the forest with the greatest trepidation and infinite precautions, for if you stray from the path for one instant, the wolves will eat you. They are grey as famine, they are as unkind as plague.

The grave-eyed children of the sparse villages always carry knives with them when they go to tend the little flocks of goats that provide the homesteads with acrid milk and rank, maggoty cheese. Their knives are half as big as they are, the blades are sharpened daily.

But the wolves have ways of arriving at your own hearthside. We try and try but sometimes we cannot keep them out. There is no winter's night the cottager does not fear to see a lean, grey, famished snout questing under the door, and there was a woman once bitten in her own kitchen as she was straining the macaroni.

Fear and flee the wolf; for, worst of all, the wolf may be more than he seems.

There was a hunter once, near here, that trapped a wolf in a pit. This wolf had massacred the sheep and goats; eaten up a mad old man who used to live by himself in a hut halfway up the mountain and sing to Jesus all day; pounced on a girl looking after the sheep, but she made such a commotion that men came with rifles and scared him away and tried to track him to the forest but he was cunning and easily gave them the slip. So this hunter dug a pit and put a duck in it, for bait, all alive-oh; and he covered the pit with straw smeared with wolf dung. Quack, quack! went the duck and a wolf came slinking out of the forest, a big one, a heavy one, he weighed as much as a grown man and the straw gave way beneath him – into the pit he tumbled. The hunter jumped down after him, slit his throat, cut off all his paws for a trophy.

And then no wolf at all lay in front of the hunter but the bloody trunk of a man, headless, footless, dying, dead.

A witch from up the valley once turned an entire wedding party into wolves because the groom had settled on another girl. She use to order them to visit her, at night, from spite, and they would sit and howl around her cottage for her, serenading her with their misery.

Not so very long ago, a young woman in our village married a man who vanished clean away on her wedding night. The bed was made with new sheets and the bride lay down in it; the groom said, he was going out to relieve himself, insisted on it, for the sake of decency, and she drew the coverlet up to her chin and lay there. And she waited and she waited and then she waited again – surely he's been gone a long time? Until she jumps up in bed and shrieks to hear a howling, coming on the wind from the forest.

That long-drawn, wavering howl has, for all its fearful resonance, some inherent sadness in it, as if the beasts would love to be less beastly if only they knew how and never cease to mourn their own condition. There is a vast melancholy in the canticles of the wolves, melancholy infinite as the forest, endless as these long nights of winter and yet that ghastly sadness, that mourning for their own, irremediable appetites, can never move the heart for not one phrase in it hints at the possibility of redemption; grace could not come to the wolf from its own despair, only through some external mediator, so that, sometimes, the beast will look as if he half welcomes the knife that dispatches him.

The young woman's brothers searched the outhouses and the hay-stacks but never found any remains so the sensible girl dried her eyes and found herself another husband not too shy to piss into a pot who spent the nights indoors. She gave him a pair of bonny babies and all went right as a trivet until, one freezing night, the night of the solstice, the hinge of the year when things do not fit together as well as they should, the longest night, her first good man came home again.

A great thump on the door announced him as she was stirring the soup for the father of her children and she knew him the moment she lifted the latch to him although it was years since she'd worn black for him and now he was in rags and his hair hung down his back and never saw a comb, alive with lice.

'Here I am again, missus,' he said. 'Get me my bowl of cabbage and be quick about it.'

Then her second husband came in with wood for the fire and when the first one saw she'd slept with another man and, worse, clapped his red eyes on her little children who'd crept into the kitchen to see what all the din was about, he shouted: 'I wish I were a wolf again, to teach this whore a lesson!' So a wolf he instantly became and tore off the eldest boy's left foot before he was chopped by the hatchet they used for chopping logs. But when the wolf lay bleeding and gasping its last, the pelt peeled off again and he was just as he had been, years ago, when he ran away from his marriage bed, so that she wept and her second husband beat her.

They say there's an ointment the Devil gives you that turns you into a wolf the minute you rub it on. Or, that he was born feet first and had a wolf for his father and his torso is a man's but his legs and genitals are a wolf's. And he has a wolf's heart.

Seven years is a werewolf's natural span but if you burn his human clothes you condemn him to wolfishness for the rest of his life, so old wives hereabouts think it some protection to throw a hat or an apron at the werewolf, as if clothes made the man. Yet by the eyes, those phosphorescent eyes, you know him in all his shapes; the eyes alone unchanged by metamorphosis.

Before he can become a wolf, the lycanthrope strips stark naked. If you spy a naked man among the pines, you must run as if the Devil were after you.

★

It is midwinter and the robin, the friend of man, sits on the handle of the gardener's spade and sings. It is the worst time in all the year for wolves but this strong-minded child insists she will go off through the wood. She is quite sure the wild beasts cannot harm her although, well-warned, she lays a carving knife in the basket her mother has packed with cheeses. There is a bottle of harsh liquor distilled from brambles; a batch of flat oatcakes baked on the heathstone; a pot or two of jam. The girl will take these delicious gifts to a reclusive grandmother so old the burden of her years is crushing her to death. Granny lives two hours' trudge through the winter woods; the child wraps herself up in her thick shawl, draws it over her head. She steps into her stout wooden shoes; she is dressed and ready and it is Christmas Eve. The malign door of the solstice still swings upon its hinges but she has been too much loved ever to feel scared.

Children do not stay young for long in this savage country. There are no toys for them to play with so they work hard and grow wise but this one, so pretty and the youngest of her family, a little late-comer, had been indulged by her mother and the grandmother who'd knitted her the red shawl that, today, has the ominous if brilliant look of blood on snow. Her breasts have just begun to swell; her hair is like lint, so fair it hardly makes a shadow on her pale forehead; her cheeks are an emblematic scarlet and white and she has just started her woman's bleeding, the clock inside her that will strike, henceforward, once a month.

She stands and moves within the invisible pentacle of her own virginity. She is an unbroken egg; she is a sealed vessel; she has inside her a magic space the entrance to which is shut tight with a plug of membrane; she is a closed system; she does not know how to shiver. She has her knife and she is afraid of nothing.

Her father might forbid her, if he were home, but he is away in the forest, gathering wood, and her mother cannot deny her.

The forest closed upon her like a pair of jaws.

There is always something to look at in the forest, even in the middle of winter – the huddled mounds of birds, succumbed to the lethargy of the season, heaped on the creaking boughs and too forlorn to sing; the bright frills of the winter fungi on the blotched trunks of the trees; the cuneiform slots of rabbits and deer, the herringbone tracks of the birds, a hare as lean as a rasher of bacon streaking across the path where the thin sunlight dapples the russet brakes of last year's bracken.

When she heard the freezing howl of a distant wolf, her practised hand sprang to the handle of her knife, but she saw no sign of a wolf at all, nor of a naked man, neither, but then she heard a clattering among the brushwood and there sprang on to the path a fully clothed one, a very handsome young one, in the green coat and wideawake hat of a hunter, laden with carcasses of game birds. She had her hand on her knife at the first rustle of twigs but he laughed with a flash of white teeth when he saw her and made her a comic yet flattering little bow; she'd never seen such a fine fellow before, not among the rustic clowns of her native village. So on they went, through the thickening light of the afternoon.

Soon they were laughing and joking like old friends. When he offered to carry her basket, she gave it to him although her knife was in it because he told her his rifle would protect them. As the day darkened, it began to snow again; she felt the first flakes settle on her eyelashes but now there was only half a mile to go and there would be a fire, and hot tea, and a welcome, a warm one surely, for the dashing huntsman as well as for herself.

This young man had a remarkable object in his pocket. It was a compass. She looked at the little round glassface in the palm of his hand and watched the wavering needle with a vague wonder. He assured her this compass had taken him safely through the wood on his hunting trip because the needle always told him with perfect accuracy where the north was. She did not believe it; she knew she should never leave the path on the way through the wood or else she would be lost instantly. He laughed at her again; gleaming trails of spittle clung to his teeth. He said, if he plunged off the path into the forest that surrounded them, he would guarantee to arrive at her grandmother's house a good quarter of an hour before she did, plotting his way through the undergrowth with his compass, while she trudged the long way, along the winding path.

I don't believe you. Besides, aren't you afraid of the wolves?

He only tapped the gleaming butt of his rifle and grinned.

Is it a bet? he asked her. Shall we make a game of it? What will you give me if I get to your grandmother's house before you?

What would you like? she asked disingenuously.

A kiss.

Commonplaces of a rustic seduction; she lowered her eyes and blushed.

He went through the undergrowth and took her basket with him but she forgot to be afraid of the beasts, although now the moon was rising, for she wanted to dawdle on her way to make sure the handsome gentleman would win his wager.

Grandmother's house stood by itself a little way out of the village. The freshly falling snow blew in eddies about the kitchen garden and the young man stepped delicately up the snowy path to the door as if he were reluctant to get his feet wet, swinging his bundle of game and the girl's basket and humming a little tune to himself.

There is a faint trace of blood on his chin; he has been snacking on his catch.

He rapped upon the panels with his knuckles.

Aged and frail, granny is three-quarters succumbed to the mortality the ache in her bones promises her and almost ready to give in entirely. A boy came out from the village to build up her hearth for the night an hour ago and the kitchen crackles with busy firelight. She has her Bible for company, she is a pious old woman. She is propped up on several pillows in the bed set into the wall peasant-fashion, wrapped up in the patchwork quilt she made before she was married, more years ago than she cares to remember. Two china spaniels with liver-coloured blotches on their coats and black noses sit on either side of the fireplace. There is a bright rug of woven rags on the pantiles. The grandfather clock ticks away her eroding time.

We keep the wolves outside by living well.

He rapped upon the panels with his hairy knuckles.

It is your granddaughter, he mimicked in a high soprano.

Lift up the latch and walk in, my darling.

You can tell them by their eyes, eyes of a beast of prey, nocturnal, devastating eyes as red as a wound; you can hurl your Bible at him and your apron after, granny, you thought that was a sure prophylactic against these infernal vermin . . . now call on Christ and his mother and all the angels in heaven to protect you but it won't do you any good.

His feral muzzle is sharp as a knife; he drops his golden burden of gnawed pheasant on the table and puts down your dear girl's basket, too. Oh, my God, what have you done with her?

Off with his disguise, that coat of forest-coloured cloth, the hat with the feather tucked into the ribbon; his matted hair streams down his white shirt and she can see the lice moving in it. The sticks in the hearth shift and hiss; night and the forest has come into the kitchen with darkness tangled in its hair.

He strips off his shirt. His skin is the colour and texture of vellum. A crisp stripe of hair runs down his belly, his nipples are ripe and dark as poison fruit but he's so thin you could count the ribs under his skin if only he gave you the time. He strips off his trousers and she can see how hairy his legs are. His genitals, huge. Ah! huge.

The last thing the old lady saw in all this world was a young man, eyes like cinders, naked as a stone, approaching her bed.

The wolf is carnivore incarnate.

When he had finished with her, he licked his chops and quickly dressed himself again, until he was just as he had been when he came through her door. He burned the inedible hair in the fireplace and wrapped the bones up in a napkin that he hid away under the bed in the wooden chest in which he found a clean pair of sheets. These he carefully put on the bed instead of the tell-tale stained ones he stowed away in the laundry basket. He plumped up the pillows and shook out the patchwork quilt, he picked up the Bible from the floor, closed it and laid it on the table. All was as it had been before except that grandmother was gone. The sticks twitched in the grate, the clock ticked and the young man sat patiently, deceitfully beside the bed in granny's nightcap.

Rat-a-tap-tap.

Who's there, he quavers in granny's antique falsetto.

Only your granddaughter.

So she came in, bringing with her a flurry of snow that melted in tears on the tiles, and perhaps she was a little disappointed to see only her grandmother sitting beside the fire. But then he flung off the blanket and sprang to the door, pressing his back against it so that she could not get out again.

The girl looked round the room and saw there was not even the indentation of a head on the smooth cheek of the pillow and how, for the first time she'd seen it so, the Bible lay closed on the table. The tick of the clock cracked like a whip. She wanted her knife from her basket but she did not dare to reach for it because his eyes were fixed upon her – huge eyes that now seemed to shine with a unique, interior light, eyes the size of saucers, saucers full of Greek fire, diabolic phosphorescence.

What big eyes you have.

All the better to see you with.

No trace at all of the old woman except for a tuft of white hair that had caught in the bark of an unburned log. When the girl saw that, she knew she was in danger of death.

Where is my grandmother?

There's nobody here but we two, my darling.

Now a great howling rose up all around them, near, very near as close as the kitchen garden, the howling of a multitude of wolves; she knew the worst wolves are hairy on the inside and she shivered, in spite of the scarlet shawl she pulled more closely round herself as if it could protect her although it was as red as the blood she must spill.

Who has come to sing us carols, she said.

Those are the voices of my brothers, darling; I love the company of wolves. Look out of the window and you'll see them.

Snow half-caked the lattice and she opened it to look into the garden. It was a white night of moon and snow; the blizzard whirled round the gaunt, grey beasts who squatted on their haunches among the rows of winter cabbage, pointing their sharp snouts to the moon and howling as if their hearts would break. Ten wolves; twenty wolves – so many wolves she could not count them, howling in concert as if demented or deranged.

Their eyes reflected the light from the kitchen and shone like a hundred candles.

It is very cold, poor things, she said; no wonder they howl so.

She closed the window on the wolves' threnody and took off her scarlet shawl, the colour of poppies, the colour of sacrifices, the colour of her menses, and, since her fear did her no good, she ceased to be afraid.

What shall I do with my shawl?

Throw it on the fire, dear one. You won't need it again.

She bundled up her shawl and threw it on the blaze, which instantly consumed it. Then she drew her blouse over her head; her small breasts gleamed as if the snow had invaded the room.

What shall I do with my blouse?

Into the fire with it, too, my pet.

The thin muslin went flaring up the chimney like a magic bird and now off came her skirt, her woollen stockings, her shoes, and on to the fire they went, too, and were gone for good. The firelight shone through the edges of her skin; now she was clothed only in her untouched integument of flesh. This dazzling, naked she combed out her hair with her fingers; her hair looked white as the snow outside. Then went directly to the man with red eyes in whose unkempt mane the lice moved; she stood up on tiptoe and unbuttoned the collar of his shirt.

What big arms you have.

All the better to hug you with.

Every wolf in the world now howled a prothalamion outside the window as she freely gave him the kiss she owed him.

What big teeth you have!

She saw how his jaw began to slaver and the room was full of the clamour of the forest's *Liebestod* but the wise child never flinched, even as he answered: All the better to eat you with.

The girl burst out laughing; she knew she was nobody's meat. She laughed at him full in the face, she ripped off his shirt for him and flung it into the fire, in the fiery wake of her own discarded clothing. The flames danced like dead souls on Walpursignacht and the old bones under the bed set up a terrible clattering but she did not pay them any heed.

Carnivore incarnate, only immaculate flesh appeases him.

She will lay his fearful head on her lap and she will pick out the lice from his pelt and perhaps she will put the lice into her mouth and eat them, as he will bid her, as she would do in a savage marriage ceremony.

The blizzard will die down.

The blizzard died down, leaving the mountains as randomly covered with snow as if a blind woman had thrown a sheet over them, the upper branches of the forest pines limed, creaking, swollen with the fall.

Snowlight, moonlight, a confusion of paw-prints.

All silent, all silent.

Midnight; and the clock strikes. It is Christmas day, the werewolves' birthday, the door of the solstice stands wide open; let them all sink through.

See! sweet and sound she sleeps in granny's bed, between the paws of the tender wolf.

Wolf-Alice

Could this ragged girl with brindled lugs have spoken like we do she would have called herself a wolf, but she cannot speak, although she howls because she is lonely – yet 'howl' is not the right word for it, since she is young enough to make the noise the pups do, bubbling, delicious, like that of a panful of fat on the fire. Sometimes the sharp ears of her foster kindred hear her across the irreparable gulf of absence; they answer her from faraway pine forest and the bald mountain rim. Their counterpoint crosses and criss-crosses the night sky; they are trying to talk to her but they cannot do so because she does not understand their language even if she knows how to use it for she is not a wolf herself, although suckled by wolves.

Her panting tongue hangs out; her red lips are thick and fresh. Her legs are long, lean and muscular. Her elbows, hands and knees are thickly callused because she always runs on all fours. She never walks; she trots or gallops. Her pace is not our pace.

Two-legs looks, four-legs sniffs. Her long nose is always a-quivering, sifting every scent it meets. With this useful tool, she lengthily investigates everything she glimpses. She can net so much more of the world than we can through the fine, hairy sensitive filters of her nostrils that her poor eyesight does not trouble her. Her nose is sharper by night than our eyes are by day so it is the night she prefers, when the cool reflected light of the moon does not make her eyes smart and draws out the various fragrances from the woodland where she wanders when she can. But the wolves keep well away from the peasants' shotguns, now, and she will no longer find them there.

Wide shoulders, long arms and she sleeps succinctly curled into a ball as if she were cradling her spine in her tail. Nothing about her is human except that she is *not* a wolf; it is as if the fur she thought she wore had melted into her skin and become part of it, although it does not exist. Like the wild beasts, she lives without a future. She inhabits only the present tense, a fugue of the continuous, a world of sensual immediacy as without hope as it is without despair.

When they found her in the wolf's den beside the bullet-riddled corpse of her foster mother, she was no more than a little brown scrap so snarled in her own brown hair they did not at first think she was a child but a cub;

she snapped at her would-be saviours with her spiky canines until they
tied her up by force. She spent the first days amongst us crouched stock-
still, staring at the whitewashed wall of her cell in the convent to which
they took her. The nuns poured water over her, poked her with sticks to
rouse her. Then she might snatch bread from their hands and race with it
into a corner to mumble it with her back towards them; it was a great day
among the novices when she learned to sit up on her hind legs and beg for
a crust.

They found, if she were treated with a little kindness, she was not
intractable. She learned to recognise her own dish; then, to drink from a
cup. They found that she could quite easily be taught a few, simple tricks
but she did not feel the cold and it took a long time to wheedle a shift over
her head to cover up her bold nakedness. Yet she always seemed wild,
impatient of restraint, capricious in temper; when the Mother Superior
tried to teach her to give thanks for her recovery from the wolves, she
arched her back, pawed the floor, retreated to a far corner of the chapel,
crouched, trembled, urinated, defecated – reverted entirely, it would
seem, to her natural state. Therefore, without a qualm, this nine days'
wonder and continuing embarrassment of a child was delivered over to
the bereft and unsanctified household of the Duke.

Deposited at the castle, she huffed and snuffled and smelled only a reek
of meat, not the least whiff of sulphur, nor of familiarity. She settled
down on her hunkers with that dog's sigh that is only the expulsion of
breath and does not mean either relief or resignation.

The Duke is sere as old paper; his dry skin rustles against the bedsheets
as he throws them back to thrust out his thin legs scabbed with old scars
where thorns score his pelt. He lives in a gloomy mansion, all alone but
for this child who has as little in common with the rest of us as he does.
His bedroom is painted terracotta, rusted with a wash of pain, like the
interior of an Iberian butcher's shop, but for himself, nothing can hurt
him since he ceased to cast an image in the mirror.

He sleeps in an antlered bed of dull black wrought iron until the moon,
the governess of transformations and overseer of somnambulists, pokes
an imperative finger through the narrow window and strikes his face:
then his eyes start open.

At night, those huge, inconsolable, rapacious eyes of his are eaten up
by swollen, gleaming pupil. His eyes see only appetite. These eyes open
to devour the world in which he sees, nowhere, a reflection of himself; he
passed through the mirror and now, henceforward, lives as if upon the
other side of things.

Spilt, glistering milk of moonlight on the frost-crisped grass; on such a
night, in moony, metamorphic weather, they say you might easily find

him, if you had been foolish enough to venture out late, scuttling along by the churchyard wall with half a juicy torso slung across his back. The white light scours the fields and scours them again until everything gleams and he will leave paw-prints in the hoar-frost when he runs howling round the graves at night in his lupine fiestas.

By the red early hour of midwinter sunset, all the doors are barred for miles. The cows low fretfully in the byre when he goes by, the whimpering dogs sink their noses in their paws. He carries on his frail shoulders a weird burden of fear; he is cast in the role of the corpse-eater, the body-snatcher who invades the last privacies of the dead. He is white as leprosy, with scrabbling fingernails, and nothing deters him. If you stuff a corpse with garlic, why, he only slavers at the treat: cadavre provençal. He will use the holy cross as a scratching post and crouch above the font to thirstily lap up holy water.

She sleeps in the soft, warm ashes of the hearth; beds are traps, she will not stay in one. She can perform a few, small tasks to which the nuns trained her, she sweeps up the hairs, vertebrae and phalanges that litter his room into a dustpan, she makes up his bed at sunset, when he leaves it and the grey beasts outside howl, as if they know his transformation is their parody. Unkind to their prey, to their own they are tender; had the Duke been a wolf, they would have angrily expelled him from the pack, he would have had to lollop along miles behind them, creeping in submission on his belly up to the kill only after they had eaten and were sleeping, to gnaw the well-chewed bones and chew the hide. Yet, suckled as she was by wolves on the high uplands where her mother bore and left her, only his kitchen maid, who is not wolf or woman, knows no better than to do his chores for him.

She grew up with wild beasts. If you could transport her, in her filth, rags and feral disorder, to the Eden of our first beginnings where Eve and grunting Adam squat on a daisy bank, picking the lice from one another's pelts, then she might prove to be the wise child who leads them all and her silence and her howling a language as authentic as any language of nature. In a world of talking beasts and flowers, she would be the bud of flesh in the kind lion's mouth: but how can the bitten apple flesh out its scar again?

Mutism is her lot; though, now and then, she will emit an involuntary rustle of sound, as if the unused chords in her throat were a wind-harp that moved with the random impulses of the air, her whisper, more obscure than the voices of the dumb.

Familiar desecrations in the village graveyard. The coffin had been ripped open with the abandon with which a child unwraps a gift on Christmas morning and, of its contents, not a trace could be found but for a rag of the bridal veil in which the corpse had been wrapped that was caught, fluttering, in the brambles at the churchyard gate so they knew which way he had taken it, towards his gloomy castle.

In the lapse of time, the trance of being of that exiled place, this girl grew amongst things she could neither name nor perceive. How did she think, how did she feel, this perennial stranger with her furred thoughts and her primal sentience that existed in a flux of shifting impressions; there are no words to describe the way she negotiated the abyss between her dreams, those wakings strange as her sleepings. The wolves had tended her because they knew she was an imperfect wolf; we secluded her in animal privacy out of fear of her imperfection because it showed us what we might have been, and so time passed, although she scarcely knew it. Then she began to bleed.

Her first blood bewildered her. She did not know what it meant and the first stirrings of surmise that ever she felt were directed towards its possible cause. The moon had been shining into the kitchen when she woke to feel the trickle between her thighs and it seemed to her that a wolf who, perhaps, was fond of her, as wolves were, and who lived, perhaps, in the moon? must have nibbled her cunt while she was sleeping, had subjected her to a series of affectionate nips too gentle to wake her yet sharp enough to break the skin. The shape of this theory was blurred yet, out of it, there took root a kind of wild reasoning, as it might have from a seed dropped in her brain off the foot of a flying bird.

The flow continued for a few days, which seemed to her an endless time. She had, as yet, no direct notion of past, or of future, or of duration, only of a dimensionless, immediate moment. At night, she prowled the empty house looking for rags to sop the blood up; she had learned a little elementary hygiene in the convent, enough to know how to bury her excrement and cleanse herself of her natural juices, although the nuns had not the means to inform her how it should be, it was not fastidiousness but shame that made her do so.

She found towels, sheets and pillowcases in closets that had not been opened since the Duke came shrieking into the world with all his teeth, to bite his mother's nipple off and weep. She found once-worn ball dresses in cobwebbed wardrobes, and, heaped in the corner of his bloody chamber, shrouds, nightdresses and burial clothes that had wrapped items on the Duke's menus. She tore strips of the most absorbent fabrics to clumsily diaper herself. In the course of these prowlings, she bumped against that mirror over whose surface the Duke passed like a wind on ice.

First, she tried to nuzzle her reflection; then, nosing it industriously, she soon realised it gave out no smell. She bruised her muzzle on the cold glass and broke her claws trying to tussle with this stranger. She saw, with irritation, then amusement, how it mimicked every gesture of hers when she raised her forepaw to scratch herself or dragged her bum along the dusty carpet to rid herself of a slight discomfort in her hindquarters. She rubbed her head against her reflected face, to show that she felt friendly towards it, and felt a cold, solid, immovable surface between herself and she – some kind, possibly, of invisible cage? In spite of this barrier, she was lonely enough to ask this creature to try to play with her, baring her teeth and grinning: at once she received a reciprocal invitation. She rejoiced; she began to whirl round on herself, yapping exultantly, but, when she retreated from the mirror, she halted in the midst of her ecstasy, puzzled, to see how her new friend grew less in size.

The moonlight spilled into the Duke's motionless bedroom from behind a cloud and she saw how pale this wolf, not-wolf who played with her was. The moon and mirrors have this much in common: you cannot see behind them. Moonlit and white, Wolf-Alice looked at herself in the mirror and wondered whether there she saw the beast who came to bite her in the night. Then her sensitive ears pricked at the sound of a step in the hall; trotting at once back to her kitchen, she encountered the Duke with the leg of a man over his shoulder. Her toenails clicked against the stairs as she padded incuriously past, she, the serene, inviolable one in her absolute and verminous innocence.

Soon the flow ceased. She forgot it. The moon vanished; but, little by little, reappeared. When it again visited her kitchen at full strength, Wolf-Alice was surprised into bleeding again and so it went on, with a punctuality that transformed her vague grip on time. She learned to expect these bleedings, to prepare her rags against them, and afterwards, neatly bury the dirtied things. Sequence asserted itself with custom and then she understood the circumambulatory principle of the clock perfectly, even if all clocks were banished from the den where she and the Duke inhabited their separate solitudes, so that you might say she discovered the very action of time by means of this returning cycle.

When she curled up among the cinders, the colour, texture and warmth of them brought her foster mother's belly out of the past and printed it on her flesh; her first conscious memory, painful as the first time the nuns combed her hair. She howled a little, in a firmer, deepening trajectory, to obtain the inscrutable consolation of the wolves' response, for now the world around her was assuming form. She perceived an essential difference between herself and her surroundings that you might say she could not put her *finger* on – only, the trees and grass of the meadows outside no longer seemed the emanation of her questing nose and erect ears, and yet sufficient to itself, but a kind of backdrop for her, that waited for her arrivals to give it meaning. She saw herself upon it and her eyes, with their sombre clarity, took on a veiled, introspective look.

She would spend hours examining the new skin that had been born, it seemed to her, of her bleeding, she would lick her soft upholstery with her long tongue and groom her hair with her fingernails. She examined her new breasts with curiosity; the white growths reminded her of nothing so much as the night-sprung puffballs she found, sometimes, on evening rambles in the woods, a natural if disconcerting apparition, but then, to her astonishment, she found a little diadem of fresh hairs tufting between her thighs. She showed it to her mirror littermate, who reassured her by showing her she shared it.

The damned Duke haunts the graveyard; he believes himself to be both less and more than a man, as if his obscene difference were a sign of grace. During the day, he sleeps. His mirror faithfully reflects his bed but never the meagre shape within the disordered covers.

Sometimes, on those white nights when she was left alone in the house, she dragged out his grandmother's ball dress and rolled on suave velvet and abrasive lace because to do so delighted her adolescent skin. Her intimate in the mirror wound the old clothes around herself, wrinkling its nose in delight at the ancient yet still potent scents of musk and civet that woke up in the sleeves and bodices. This habitual, at last boring, fidelity to her very movement finally woke her up to the regretful possibility that her companion was, in fact, no more than a particularly ingenious variety of the shadow she cast on sunlit grass. Had not she and the rest of the litter tussled and romped with their shadows long ago? She poked her agile nose around the back of the mirror; she found only dust, a spider stuck in his web, a heap of rags. A little moisture leaked from the corners of her eyes, yet her relation with the mirror was now far more intimate since she knew she saw herself within it.

She pawed and tumbled the dress the Duke had tucked away behind the mirror for a while. The dust was soon shaken out of it; she experimentally inserted her front legs in the sleeves. Although the dress was torn and crumpled, it was so white and of such a sinuous texture that she thought, before she put it on, she must thoroughly wash off her coat of ashes in the water from the pump in the yard, which she knew how to manipulate with her cunning forepaw. In the mirror, she saw how this white dress made her shine.

Although she could not run so fast on two legs in petticoats, she trotted out in her new dress to investigate the odorous October hedgerows, like a débutante from the castle, delighted with herself but still, now and then, singing to the wolves with a kind of wistful triumph, because now she knew how to wear clothes and had put on the visible sign of her difference from them.

Her footprints on damp earth are beautiful and menacing as those Man Friday left.

The young husband of the dead bride spent a long time planning his revenge. He filled the church with an arsenal of bells, books and candles; a battery of silver bullets; they brought a ten gallon tub of holy water in a wagon from the city, where it had been blessed by the Archbishop himself, to drown the Duke, if the bullets bounced off him. They gathered in the church to chant a litany and wait for the one who would visit the first deaths of winter.

She goes out at night more often now; the landscape assembles itself about her, she informs it with her presence. She is its significance.

It seemed to her the congregation in the church was ineffectually attempting to imitate the wolves' chorus. She lent them the assistance of her own, educated voice for a while, rocking contemplatively on her haunches by the graveyard gate; then her nostrils twitched to catch the rank stench of the dead that told her her co-habitor was at hand; raising her head, who did her new, keen eyes spy but the lord of cobweb castle intent on performing his cannibal rituals?

And if her nostrils flare suspiciously at the choking reek of incense and his do not, that is because she is far more sentient than he. She will, therefore, run, run! when she hears the crack of bullets, because they killed her foster mother; so, with the self-same lilting lope, drenched with holy water, will he run, too, until the young widower fires the silver bullet that bites his shoulder and drags off half his fictive pelt, so that he must rise up like any common forked biped and limp distressfully on as best he may.

When they saw the white bride leap out of the tombstones and scamper off towards the castle with the werewolf stumbling after, the peasants thought the Duke's dearest victim had come back to take matters into her own hands. They ran screaming from the presence of a ghostly vengeance on him.

Poor, wounded thing . . . locked half and half between such strange states, an aborted transformation; an incomplete mystery now he lies writhing on his black bed in the room like a Mycenaean tomb, howls like a wolf with his foot in a trap or a woman in labour, and bleeds.

First, she was fearful when she heard the sound of pain, in case it hurt her, as it had done before. She prowled round the bed, growling, snuffing at his wound that does not smell like her wound. Then, she was pitiful as her gaunt grey mother; she leapt upon his bed to lick, without hesitation, without disgust, with a quick, tender gravity, the blood and dirt from his cheek and forehead.

The lucidity of the moonlight lit the mirror propped against the red wall; the rational glass, the master of the visible, impartially recorded the crooning girl.

As she continued her ministrations, this glass, with infinite slowness, yielded to the reflexive strength of its own material construction. Little by little, there appeared within it, like the image on photographic paper that emerges, first, a formless web of tracery, the prey caught in its own fishing net, then a firmer yet still shadowed outline until at last as vivid as real life itself, as if brought into being by her soft, moist, gentle tongue, finally, the face of the Duke.

BLACK VENUS

Black Venus

Sad; so sad, those smoky-rose, smoky-mauve evenings of late autumn, sad enough to pierce the heart. The sun departs the sky in winding sheets of gaudy cloud; anguish enters the city, a sense of the bitterest regret, a nostalgia for things we never knew, anguish of the turn of the year, the time of impotent yearning, the inconsolable season. In America, they call it 'the Fall', bringing to mind the Fall of Man, as if the fatal drama of the primal fruit-theft must recur again and again, with cyclic regularity, at the same time of every year that schoolboys set out to rob orchards, invoking, in the most everyday image, any child, every child, who, offered the choice between virtue and knowledge, will always choose knowledge, always the hard way. Although she does not know the meaning of the word, 'regret', the woman sighs, without any precise reason.

Soft twists of mist invade the alleys, rise up from the slow river like exhalations of an exhausted spirit, seep in through the cracks in the window frames so that the contours of their high, lonely apartment waver and melt. On these evenings, you see everything as though your eyes are going to lapse to tears.

She sighs.

The custard-apple of her stinking Eden she, this forlorn Eve, bit – and was all at once transported here, as in a dream; and yet she is a *tabula rasa*, still. She never experienced her experience *as* experience, life never added to the sum of her knowledge; rather, subtracted from it. If you start out with nothing, they'll take even that away from you, the Good Book says so.

Indeed, I think she never bothered to bite any apple at all. She wouldn't have known what knowledge was *for*, would she? She was in neither a state of innocence nor a state of grace. I will tell you what Jeanne was like.

She was like a piano in a country were everybody has had their hands cut off.

On these sad days, at those melancholy times, as the room sinks into dusk, he, instead of lighting the lamp, fixing drinks, making all cosy, will ramble on: 'Baby, baby, let me take you back where you belong, back to your lovely, lazy island where the jewelled parrot rocks on the enamel tree and you can crunch sugar-cane between your strong, white teeth, like you did when you were little, baby. When we get there, among the lilting palm-trees, under the purple flowers, I'll love you to death. We'll go back and live together in a thatched house with a veranda overgrown with flowering vine and a little girl in a short white frock with a yellow satin bow in her kinky pigtail will wave a huge feather fan over us, stirring the languishing air as we sway in our hammock, this way and that way . . . the ship, the ship is waiting in the harbour, baby. My monkey, my pussy-cat, my pet . . . think how lovely it would be to live there . . .'

But, on these days, nipped by frost and sulking, no pet nor pussy she; she looked more like an old crow with rusty feathers in a miserable huddle by the smoky fire which she pokes with spiteful sticks. She coughs and grumbles, she is always chilly, there is always a draught gnawing the back of her neck or pinching her ankles.

Go, where? Not *there*! The glaring yellow shore and harsh blue sky daubed in crude, unblended colours squeezed directly from the tube, where the perspectives are abrupt as a child's drawings, your eyes hurt to look. Fly-blown towns. All there is to eat is green bananas and yams and a brochette of rubber goat to chew. She puts on a theatrical shudder, enough to shake the affronted cat off her lap. She hates the cat, anyway. She can't look at the cat without wanting to strangle it. She would like a drink. Rum will do. She twists a flute of discarded manuscript from the wastepaper basket into a spill for her small, foul, black cheroot.

Night comes in on feet of fur and marvellous clouds drift past the windows, those spectral clouds of the night sky that are uncannily visible when no light is there. The whim of the master of the house has not let the windows alone; he had all the panes except the topmost ones replaced with frosted glass so that the inmates could pursue an uninterrupted view of the sky as if they were living in the gondola of a balloon such as the one in which his friend Nadar made triumphant ascents.

At the inspiration of a gust of wind such as now rattles the tiles above us, this handsome apartment with its Persian rugs, its walnut table off which the Borgias served poisons, its carved armchairs from whose bulbous legs grin and grimace the cinquecento faces, the crust of fake Tintorettos on the walls (he's an indefatigable connoisseur, if, as yet, too young to have the sixth sense that tells you when you're being conned) – at the invitation of the mysterious currents of the heavens, this well-appointed cabin will loose its moorings in the street below and take off, depart, whisk across the dark vault of the night, tangling a stillborn, crescent moon in its ropes, nudging a star at lift-off, and will deposit us –

'*No!*' she said. 'Not the bloody parrot forest! Don't take me on the slavers' route back to the West Indies, for godsake! And let the bloody cat out, before it craps on your precious Bokhara!'

They have this in common, neither has a native land, although he likes to pretend she has a fabulous home in the bosom of the blue ocean, he will force a home on her whether she's got one or not, he cannot believe she is as dispossessed as he . . . Yet they are only at home together when contemplating flight; they are both waiting for the wind to blow that will take them to a miraculous elsewhere, a happy land, far, far away, the land of delighted ease and pleasure.

After she's got a drink or two inside her, however, she stops coughing, grows a bit more friendly, will consent to unpin her hair and let him play with it, the way he likes to. And, if her native indolence does not prove too much for her – she is capable of sprawling, as in a vegetable trance, for hours, for days, in the dim room by the smoky fire – nevertheless, she will sometimes lob the butt of her cheroot in the fire and be persuaded to take off her clothes and dance for Daddy who, she will grudgingly admit when pressed, is a good Daddy, buys her pretties, allocates her the occasional lump of hashish, keeps her off the streets.

Nights of October, of frail, sickle moons, when the earth conceals the shining accomplice of assassins in its shadow, to make everything all the more mysterious – on such a night, you could say the moon was black.

This dance, which he wanted her to perform so much and had especially devised for her, consisted of a series of voluptuous poses one following another; private-room-in-a-bordello stuff but tasteful, he preferred her to undulate rhythmically rather than jump about and shake a leg. He liked her to put on all her bangles and beads when she did her dance, she dressed up in the set of clanking jewellery he'd given her, paste, nothing she could sell or she'd have sold it. Meanwhile, she hummed a Creole melody, she liked the ones with ribald words about what the shoemaker's wife did at Mardi Gras or the size of some fisherman's legendary tool but Daddy paid no attention to what song his siren sang, he fixed his quick, bright, dark eyes upon her decorated skin as if, sucker, authentically entranced.

'Sucker!' she said, almost tenderly, but he did not hear her.

She cast a long shadow in the firelight. She was a woman of immense height, the type of those beautiful giantesses who, a hundred years later, would grace the stages of the Crazy Horse or the Casino de Paris in sequin cache-sexe and tinsel pasties, divinely tall, the colour and texture of suede. Josephine Baker! But vivacity, exuberance were never Jeanne's qualities. A slumbrous resentment of anything you could not eat, drink or smoke, i.e. burn, was her salient characteristic. Consumption, combustion, these were her vocations.

She sulked sardonically through Daddy's sexy dance, watching, in a bored, fascinated way, the elaborate reflections of the many strings of glass beads he had given her tracking about above her on the ceiling. She looked like the source of light but this was an illusion; she only shone because the dying fire lit his presents to her. Although his regard made her luminous, his shadow made her blacker than she was, his shadow could eclipse her entirely. Whether she had a good heart or not underneath, is anybody's guess; she had been raised in the School of Hard Knocks and enough hard knocks can beat the heart out of anybody.

Though Jeanne was not prone to introspection, sometimes, as she wriggled around the dark, buoyant room that tugged at its moorings, longing to take off on an aerial quest for the Cythera beloved of poets, she wondered what the distinction was between dancing naked in front of *one* man who paid and dancing naked in front of a group of men who paid. She had the impression that, somewhere in the difference, lay morality. Tutors in the School of Hard Knocks, that is, other chorus girls in the cabaret, where in her sixteenth summer, she had tunelessly croaked these same Creole ditties she now hummed, had told her there was all the difference in the world and, at sixteen, she could conceive of no higher ambition than to be kept; that is, kept off the streets. Prostitution was a question of number; of being paid by more than one person at a time. That was bad. She was not a bad girl. When she slept with anyone else but Daddy, she never let them pay. It was a matter of honour. It was a question of fidelity. (In these ethical surmises slumbered the birth of irony although her lover assumed she was promiscuous because she *was* promiscuous.)

Now, however, after a few crazy seasons in the clouds with him, she sometimes asked herself if she'd played her cards right. If she was going to have to dance naked to earn her keep, anyway, why shouldn't she dance naked for hard cash in hand and earn enough to keep herself? Eh? Eh?

But then, the very thought of organising a new career made her yawn. Dragging herself around madames and music halls and so on; what an effort. And how much to ask? She had only the haziest notion of her own use value.

She danced naked. Her necklaces and earrings clinked. As always, when she finally got herself up off her ass and started dancing she quite enjoyed it. She felt almost warm towards him; her good luck he was young and handsome. Her bad luck his finances were rocky, the opium, the scribbling; that he . . . but, at 'that', she snapped her mind off.

Thinking resolutely of her good luck, she held out her hands to her lover, flashed her teeth at him – the molars might be black stumps, already, but the pointed canines still white as vampires – and invited him to join in the dance with her. But he never would, never. Scared of muzzing his shirt or busting his collar or something, even if, when stoned, he would clap his hands to the rhythm. She liked it when he did that. She felt he was appreciating her. After a few drinks, she forgot the other things altogether, although she guessed, of course. The girls told over the ghoulish litany of the symptoms together in the dressing room in hushed scared voices, peeking at the fortune-telling mirror and seeing, not their rosy faces, but their own rouged skulls.

When she was on her own, having a few drinks in front of the fire, thinking about it, it made her break out in horrible hag's laughter, as if she were already the hag she would become enjoying a grim joke at the expense of the pretty, secretly festering thing she still was. At Walpurgisnacht, the young witch boasted to the old witch: 'Naked on a goat, I display my fine young body.' How the old witch laughed! 'You'll rot!' I'll rot, thought Jeanne, and laughed. This cackle of geriatric cynicism ill became such a creature made for pleasure as Jeanne, but was pox not the emblematic fate of a creature made for pleasure and the price you paid for the atrocious mixture of corruption and innocence this child of the sun brought with her from the Antilles?

For herself, she came clean, arrived in Paris with nothing worse than scabies, malnutrition and ringworm about her person. It was a bad joke, therefore, that, some centuries before Jeanne's birth, the Aztec goddess, Nanahuatzin, had poured a cornucopia of wheelchairs, dark glasses, crutches and mercury pills on the ships of the conquistadores as they took their spoiled booty from the New World to the Old; the raped continent's revenge, perpetrating itself in the beds of Europe. Jeanne innocently followed Nanahuatzin's trail across the Atlantic but she brought no erotic vengeance – she'd picked up the germ from the very first protector. The man she'd trusted to take her away from all that, enough to make a horse laugh, except that she was a fatalist, she was indifferent.

She bent over backwards until the huge fleece of a black sheep, her unfastened hair, spilled on to the Bokhara. She was a supple acrobat; she could make her back into a mahogany rainbow. (Notice her big feet and huge, strong hands, capable enough to have been a nurse's hands.) If he was a connoisseur of the beautiful, she was a connoisseur of the most exquisite humiliations but she had always been too poor to be able to afford the luxury of acknowledging a humiliation as such. You took what came. She arched her back so much a small boy could have run under her. Her reversed blood sang in her ears.

Upside down as she was, she could see, in the topmost right-hand windowpane he had left unfrosted, the sickle moon, precise as if pasted on the sky. This moon was the size of a broad nail-paring; you could see the vague outline of the rest of its surface, obscured by the shadow of the earth as if the earth were clenched between the moon's shining claw-tips, so you could say the moon held the world in its arms. An exceptionally brilliant star suspended from the nether prong on a taut, invisible leash.

The basalt cat, the pride of the home, its excretory stroll along the quai concluded, now whined for readmittance outside the door. The poet let Puss in. Puss leapt into his waiting arms and filled the apartment with a happy purr. The girl plotted to strangle the cat with her long, agile toes but, indulgent from the exercise of her sensuality, she soon laughed to see him loving up the cat with the same gestures, the same endearments, he used on her. She forgave the cat for its existence; they had a lot in common. She released the bow of her back with a twang and plumped on the rug, rubbing her stretched tendons.

He said she danced like a snake and she said, snakes can't dance: they've got no legs, and he said, but kindly, you're an idiot, Jeanne; but she knew he'd never so much as *seen* a snake, nobody who'd seen a snake move – that quick system of transverse strikes, lashing itself like a whip, leaving a rippling snake in the sand behind it, terribly fast – if he'd seen a snake move, he'd never have said a thing like that. She huffed off and contemplated her sweating breasts; she would have liked a bath, anyway, she was a little worried about a persistent vaginal discharge that smelled of mice, something new, something ominous, something horrid. But: no hot water, not at this hour.

'They'll bring up hot water if you pay.'

His turn to sulk. He took to cleaning his nails again.

'You think I don't need a wash because I don't show the dirt.'

But, even as she launched the first darts of a shrew's assault that she could have protracted for a tense, scratchy hour or more, had she been in the mood, she lost the taste for it. She was seized with sudden indifference. What does it matter? we're all going to die; we're as good as dead already. She drew her knees up to her chin and crouched in front of the fire, staring vacantly at the embers. Her face fixed in sullen resentment. The cat drew silently alongside, as if on purpose, adding a touch of satanic glamour, so you could imagine both were having silent conversations with the demons in the flames. As long as the cat left her alone, she let it alone. They were alone together. The quality of the separate self-absorptions of the cat and the woman was so private that the poet felt outmanoeuvred and withdrew to browse in his bookshelves, those rare, precious volumes, the jewelled missals, the incunabula, those books acquired from special shops that incurred damnation if you so much as opened the covers. He cherished his arduously aroused sexuality until she was prepared to acknowledge it again.

He thinks she is a vase of darkness; if he tips her up, black light will spill out. She is not Eve but, herself, the forbidden fruit, and he has eaten her!

> Weird goddess, dusky as night,
> reeking of musk smeared on tobacco,
> a shaman conjured you, a Faust of the savannah,
> black-thighed witch, midnight's child . . .

Indeed, the Faust who summoned her from the abyss of which her eyes retain the devastating memory must have exchanged her presence for his soul; black Helen's lips suck the marrow from the poet's spirit, although she wishes to do no such thing. Apart from her meals and a few drinks, she is without many conscious desires. If she were a Buddhist, she would be halfway on the road to sainthood because she wants so little, but, alas, she is still pricked by needs.

The cat yawned and stretched. Jeanne woke from her trance. Folding another spill out of a dismantled sonnet to ignite a fresh cheroot, her bib of cut glass a-jingle and a-jangle, she turned to the poet to ask, in her inimitable half-raucous, half-caressing voice, voice of a crow reared on honey, with its dawdling accent of the Antilles, for a little money.

Nobody seems to know in what year Jeanne Duval was born, although the year in which she met Charles Baudelaire (1842) is precisely logged and biographies of his other mistresses, Aglaé-Josephine Sabatier and Marie Daubrun, are well documented. Besides Duval, she also used the names Prosper and Lemer, as if her name was of no consequence. Where she came from is a problem; books suggest Mauritius, in the Indian ocean, or Santo Domingo, in the Caribbean, take your pick of two different sides of the world. (Her *pays d'origine* of less importance than it would have been had she been a wine.) Mauritius looks like a shot in the dark based on the fact the Baudelaire spent some time on that island during his abortive trip to India in 1841. Santo Domingo, Columbus' Hispaniola, now the Dominican Republic, a troubled history, borders upon Haiti. Here Toussaint L'Ouverture led a successful slave revolt against French plantation owners at the time of the French Revolution.

Although slavery had been abolished without debate throughout the French possessions by the National Assembly in 1794, it was reimposed in Martinique and Guadeloupe – though not in Haiti – by Napoleon. These slaves were not finally emancipated until 1848. However, African mistresses of French residents were often manumitted, together with their children, and intermarriage was by no means a rare occurrence. A middle-class Creole population grew up; to this class belong the Josephine who became Empress of the French on her marriage to the same Napoleon.

It is unlikely that Jeanne Duval belonged to this class if, in fact, she came from Martinique, which, since she seems to have been Franco-phone, remains a possibility.

He made a note in *Mon Coeur Mis à Nu*: 'Of the People's Hatred of Beauty. Examples: Jeanne and Mme Muller.' (Who was Mme Muller?)

Kids in the streets chucked stones at her, she so tall and witchy and when she was pissed, teetering along with the vulnerable, self-conscious dignity of the drunk which always invites mockery, and, always she held her bewildered head with its enormous, unravelling cape of hair as proudly as if she were carrying upon it an enormous pot full of all the waters of Lethe. Maybe he found her crying because the kids in the street were chucking stones at her, calling her a 'black bitch' or worse and spattering the beautiful white flounces of her crinoline with handfuls of tossed mud they scooped from the gutters where they thought she belonged because she was a whore who had the nerve to sashay to the corner shop for cheroots or *ordinaire* or rum with her nose stuck up in the air as if she were the Empress of all the Africas.

But she was the deposed Empress, royalty in exile, for, of the entire and heterogeneous wealth of all those countries, had she not been dispossessed?

Robbed of the bronze gateway of Benin; of the iron beasts of the Amazons of the court of the King of Dahomey; of the esoteric wisdom of the great university of Timbuktu; of the urbanity of glamorous desert cities before whose walls the horsemen wheel, welcoming the night on trumpets twice the length of their own bodies. The Abyssinia of black saints and holy lions was not even so much as a legend to her. Of those savannahs where men wrestle with leopards she knew not one jot. The splendid continent to which her skin allied her had been excised from her memory. She had been deprived of history, she was the pure child of the colony. The colony – white, imperious – had fathered her. Her mother went off with the sailors and her granny looked after her in one room with a rag-covered bed.

Her granny said to Jeanne: 'I was born in the ship where my mother died and was thrown into the sea. Sharks ate her. Another woman of some other nation who had just still-born suckled me. I don't know anything about my father nor where I was conceived nor on what coast nor in what circumstances. My foster-mother soon died of fever in the plantation. I was weaned, I grew up.'

Nevertheless, Jeanne retained a negative inheritance; if you tried to get her to do anything she didn't want to, if you tried to erode that little steely nugget of her free will, which expressed itself as lethargy, you could see how she had worn away the patience of the missionaries and so come to inherit, not even self-pity, only the twenty-nine legally permitted strokes of the whip.

Her granny spoke Creole, patois, knew no other language, spoke it badly and taught it badly to Jeanne, who did her best to convert it into good French when she came to Paris and started mixing with swells but made a hash of it, her heart wasn't in it, no wonder. It was as though her tongue had been cut out and another one sewn in that did not fit well. Therefore you could say, not so much that Jeanne did not understand the lapidary, troubled serenity of her lover's poetry but, that it was a perpetual affront to her. He recited it to her by the hour and she ached, raged and chafed under it because his eloquence denied her language. It made her dumb, a dumbness all the more profound because it manifested itself in a harsh clatter of ungrammatical recriminations and demands which were not directed at her lover so much – she was quite fond of him – as at her own condition, great gawk of an ignorant black girl, good for nothing: correction, good for only one thing, even if the spirochetes were already burrowing away diligently at her spinal marrow while she bore up the superb weight of oblivion on her Amazonian head.

The greatest poet of alienation stumbled upon the perfect stranger; theirs was a match made in heaven. In his heart, he must have known this.

The goddess of his heart, the ideal of the poet, lay resplendently on the bed in a room morosely papered red and black; he liked to have her make a spectacle of herself, to provide a sumptuous feast for his bright eyes that were always bigger than his belly.

Venus lies on the bed, waiting for a wind to rise: the sooty albatross hankers for the storm. Whirlwind!

She was acquainted with the albatross. A scallop-shell carried her stark naked across the Atlantic; she clutched an enormous handful of dreadlocks to her pubic mound. Albatrosses hitched glides on the gales the wee black cherubs blew for her.

The Albatross can fly around the world in eight days, if only it sticks to the stormy places. The sailors call the huge bird ugly names, goonies, mollyhawks, because of their foolish clumsiness on the ground but wind, wind is their element; they have absolute mastery of it.

Down there, far below, where the buttocks of the world slim down again, if you go far south enough you reach again the realm of perpetual cold that begins and ends our experience of this earth, those ranges of ice mountains where the bull-roaring winds bay and bellow and no people are, only the stately penguin in his frock coat not unlike yours, Daddy, the estimable but, unlike you, uxorious penguin who balances the precious egg on his feet while his dear wife goes out and has as good a time as the Antarctic may afford.

If Daddy were like a penguin, how much more happy we should be; there isn't room for two albatrosses in *this* house.

Wind is the element of the albatross just as domesticity is that of the penguin. In the 'Roaring Forties' and 'Furious Fifties', where the high winds blow ceaselessly from west to east between the remotest tips of the inhabited continents and the blue nightmare of the uninhabitable ice, these great birds glide in delighted glee, south, far south, so far south it inverts the notional south of the poet's parrot-forest and glittering beach; down here, down south, only the phlegmatic monochrome, flightless birds form the audience for the wonderful *aerielistes* who live in the heart of the storm – like the bourgeoisie, Daddy, sitting good and quiet with their eggs on their feet watching artists such as we dare death upon the high trapeze.

The woman and her lover wait for the rising of the wind upon which they will leave the gloomy apartment. They believe they can ascend and soar upon it. This wind will be like that from a new planet.

The young man inhales the aroma of the coconut oil which she rubs into her hair to make it shine. His agonised romanticism transforms this homely odour of the Caribbean kitchen into the perfume of the air of those tropical islands he can sometimes persuade himself are the happy lands for which he longs. His lively imagination performs an alchemical alteration on the healthy tang of her sweat, freshly awakened by dancing. He thinks her sweat smells of cinnamon because she has spices in her pores. He thinks she is made of a different kind of flesh than his.

It is essential to their connection that, if she should put on the private garments of nudity, its non-sartorial regalia of jewellery and rouge, then he himself must retain the public nineteenth-century masculine impedimenta of frock coat (exquisitely cut); white shirt (pure silk, London tailored); oxblood cravat; and impeccable trousers. There's more to *Le Déjeuner sur l'Herbe* than meets the eye. (Manet, another friend of his.) Man does and is dressed to do so; his skin is his own business. He is artful, the creation of culture. Woman is; and is therefore, fully dressed in no clothes at all, her skin is common property, she is a being at one with nature in a fleshly simplicity that, he insists, is the most abominable of artifices.

Once, before she became a kept woman, he and a group of Bohemians contrived to kidnap her from her customers at the cabaret, spirited her, at first protesting, then laughing, off with them, and they wandered along the streets in the small hours, looking for a place to take their prize for another drink and she urinated in the street, right there, didn't announce it; or go off into an alley to do it on her own, she did not even leave go of his arm but straddled the gutter, legs apart and pissed as if it was the most natural thing in the world. Oh, the unexpected Chinese bells of that liquid cascade!

(At which point, his Lazarus arose and knocked unbidden on the coffin-lid of the poet's trousers.)

Jeanne hitched up her skirts with her free hand as she stepped across the pool she'd made, so that he saw where she had splashed her white stockings at the ankle. It seemed to his terrified, exacerbated sensibilities that the liquid was a kind of bodily acid that burned away the knitted cotton, dissolved her petticoat, her stays, her chemise, the dress she wore, her jacket, so that now she walked beside him like an ambulant fetish, savage, obscene, terrifying.

He himself always wore gloves of pale pink kid that fitted as tenderly close as the rubber gloves that gynaecologists will wear. Watching him play with her hair, she tranquilly recollected a red-haired friend in the cabaret who had served a brief apprenticeship in a brothel but retired from the profession after she discovered a significant proportion of her customers wanted nothing more of her than permission to ejaculate into her magnificent Titian mane. (How the girls giggled over that.) The red-haired girl thought that, on the whole, this messy business was less distasteful and more hygienic than regular intercourse but it meant she had to wash her hair so often that her crowning, indeed – she was a squint-eyed little thing – unique glory was stripped of its essential, natural oils. Seller and commodity in one, a whore is her own investment in the world and so she must take care of herself; the squinting red-head decided she dare not risk squandering her capital so recklessly but Jeanne never had this temperament of the tradesperson, she did not feel she was her own property and so she gave herself away to everybody except the poet, for whom she had too much respect to offer such an ambivalent gift for nothing.

'Get it up for me,' said the poet.

'Albatrosses are famous for the courtship antics they carry on throughout the breeding season. These involve grotesque, awkward dancing, accompanied by bowing, scraping, snapping of bills, and prolonged nasal groans.'
Birds of the World, Oliver L. Austin Jnr

They are not great nest builders. A slight depression in the ground will do. Or, they might hollow out a little mound of mud. They will make only the most squalid concessions to the earth. He envisaged their bed, the albatross's nest, as just such a fleeting kind of residence in which Destiny, the greatest madame of all, had closeted these two strange birds together. In this transitory exile, anything is possible.

'Jeanne, get it up for me.'

Nothing is simple for this fellow! He makes a performance worthy of the Comédie Française out of a fuck, bringing him off is a five-act drama with farcical interludes and other passages that could make you cry and, afterwards, cry he does, he is ashamed, he talks about his mother, but Jeanne can't remember her mother and her granny swapped her with a ship's mate for a couple of bottles, a bargain with which her granny said she was well satisfied because Jeanne was already getting into trouble and growing out of her clothes and ate so much.

While they had been untangling together the history of transgression, the fire went out; also, the small, white, shining, winter moon in the top left-hand corner of the top left-hand pane of the few sheets of clear glass in the window had, accompanied by its satellite star, completed the final section of its slow arc over the black sky. While Jeanne stoically laboured over her lover's pleasure, as if he were her vineyard, she laying up treasure in heaven from her thankless toil, moon and star arrived together at the lower right-hand windowpane.

If you could see her, if it were not so dark, she would look like the victim of a robbery; her bereft eyes are like abysses but she will hold him to her bosom and comfort him for betraying to her in his self-disgust those trace elements of common humanity he has left inside her body, for which he blames her bitterly, for which he will glorify her, awarding her the eternity promised by the poet.

The moon and star vanish.

Nadar says he saw her a year or so after, deaf, dumb and paralysed, Baudelaire died. The poet, finally, so far estranged from himself that, in the last months before the disease triumphed over him, when he was shown his reflection in a mirror, he bowed politely, as to a stranger. He told his mother to make sure that Jeanne was looked after but his mother didn't give her anything. Nadar says he saw Jeanne hobbling on crutches along the pavement to the dram-shop; her teeth were gone, she had a mammy-rag tied around her head but you could still see that her wonderful hair had fallen out. Her face would terrify the little children. He did not stop to speak to her.

★

The ship embarked for Martinique.

You can buy teeth, you know; you can buy hair. They make the best wigs from the shorn locks of novices in convents.

The man who called himself her brother, perhaps they *did* have the same mother, why not? She hadn't the faintest idea what had happened to her mother and this hypothetical, high-yellow, demi-sibling popped up in the nick of time to take over her disordered finances with the skill of a born entrepreneur – he might have been Mephistopheles, for all she cared. Her brother. They'd salted away what the poet managed to smuggle to her, all the time he was dying, when his mother wasn't looking. Fifty francs for Jeanne, here; thirty francs for Jeanne, there. It all added up.

She was surprised to find out how much she was worth.

Add to this the sale of a manuscript or two, the ones she hadn't used to light her cheroots with. Some books, especially the ones with the flowery dedications. Sale of cuff-links and drawerful upon drawerful of pink kid gloves, hardly used. Her brother knew where to get rid of them. Later, any memorabilia of the poet, even his clumsy drawings, would fetch a surprising sum. They left a portfolio with an enterprising agent.

In a new dress of black tussore, her somewhat ravaged but carefully repaired face partially concealed by a flattering veil, she chugged away from Europe on a steamer bound for the Caribbean like a respectable widow and she was not yet fifty, after all. She might have been the Creole wife of a minor civil servant setting off home after his death. Her brother went first, to look out the property they were going to buy.

Her voyage was interrupted by no albatrosses. She never thought of the slavers' route, unless it was to compare her grandmother's crossing with her own, comfortable one. You could say that Jeanne had found herself; she had come down to earth, and, with the aid of her ivory cane, she walked perfectly well upon it. The sea air did her good. She decided to give up rum, except for a single tot last thing at night, after the accounts were completed.

Seeing her, now, in her declining years, every morning in decent black, leaning a little on her stick but stately as only one who has snatched herself from the lion's mouth can be. She leaves the charming house, with its vine-covered veranda; 'Good morning, Mme Duval!' sings out the obsequious gardener. How sweet it sounds. She is taking last night's takings to the bank. 'Thank you so much, Mme Duval.' As soon as she had got her first taste of it, she became a glutton for deference.

Until at last, in extreme old age, she succumbs to the ache in her bones and a cortège of grieving girls takes her to the churchyard, she will continue to dispense, to the most privileged of the colonial administration, at a not excessive price, the veritable, the authentic, the true Baudelairean syphilis.

The lines on page 237 are translated from:

SED NON SATIATA

Bizarre déité, brune comme les nuits,
Au parfum mélangé de musc et de havane,
Oeuvre de quelque obi, le Faust de la savane,
Sorcière au flanc d'ébène, enfant des noirs minuits,

Je préfère au constance, à l'opium, au nuits,
L'élixir de ta bouche où l'amour se pavane;
Quand vers toi mes désirs partent en caravane,
Tes yeux sont la citerne où boivent mes ennuis.

Par ces deux grands yeux noirs, soupiraux de ton âme,
Ô démon sans pitié! verse-moi moins de flamme;
Je ne suis pas le Styx pour t'embrasser neuf fois,

Hélas! et je ne puis, Mégère libertine,
Pour briser ton courage et te mettre aux abois,
Dans l'enfer de ton lit devenir Proserpine!

Les Fleurs du Mal, Charles Baudelaire

The other poems in *Les Fleurs du Mal* believed to have been written about Jeanne Duval, are often called the *Black Venus Cycle*, and include 'Les Bijoux', 'La Chevelure', 'Le Serpent qui danse', 'Parfum Exotique', 'Le Chat', 'Je t'adore à l'egal de la voûte nocturne', etc.

The Kiss

The winters in Central Asia are piercing and bleak, while the sweating, foetid summers bring cholera, dysentery and mosquitoes, but, in April, the air caresses like the touch of the inner skin of the thigh and the scent of all the flowering trees douses the city's throat-catching whiff of cesspits.

Every city has its own internal logic. Imagine a city drawn in straightforward, geometric shapes with crayons from a child's colouring box, in ochre, in white, in pale terracotta. Low, blonde terraces of houses seem to rise out of the whitish, pinkish earth as if born from it, not built out of it. There is a faint, gritty dust over everything, like the dust those pastel crayons leave on your fingers.

Against these bleached pallors, the iridescent crusts of ceramic tiles that cover the ancient mausoleums ensorcellate the eye. The throbbing blue of Islam transforms itself to green while you look at it. Beneath a bulbous dome alternately lapis lazuli and veridian, the bones of Tamburlaine, the scourge of Asia, lie in a jade tomb. We are visiting an authentically fabulous city. We are in Samarkand.

The Revolution promised the Uzbek peasant women clothes of silk and on this promise, at least, did not welch. They wear tunics of flimsy satin, pink and yellow, red and white, black and white, red, green and white, in blotched stripes of brilliant colours that dazzle like an optical illusion, and they bedeck themselves with much jewellery made of red glass.

They always seem to be frowning because they paint a thick, black line straight across their foreheads that takes their eyebrows from one side of the face to the other without a break. They rim their eyes with kohl. They look startling. They fasten their long hair in two or three dozen whirling plaits. Young girls wear little velvet caps embroidered with metallic thread and beadwork. Older women cover their heads with a couple of scarves of flower-printed wool, one bound tight over the forehead, the other hanging loosely on the shoulders. Nobody has worn a veil for sixty years.

They walk as purposefully as if they did not live in an imaginary city. They do not know that they themselves and their turbanned, sheepskin-jacketed, booted menfolk are creatures as extraordinary to the foreign eye as a unicorn. They exist, in all their glittering and innocent exoticism, in direct contradiction to history. They do not know what I know about them. They do not know that this city is not the entire world. All they know of the world is this city, beautiful as an illusion, where irises grow in the gutters. In the teahouse a green parrot nudges the bars of its wicker cage.

The market has a sharp, green smell. A girl with black-barred brows sprinkles water from a glass over radishes. In this early part of the year you can buy only last summer's dried fruit – apricots, peaches, raisins – except for a few, precious, wrinkled pomegranates, stored in sawdust through the winter and now split open on the stall to show how a wet nest of garnets remains within. A local speciality of Samarkand is salted apricot kernels, more delicious, even, than pistachios.

An old woman sells arum lilies. This morning, she came from the mountains, where wild tulips have put out flowers like blown bubbles of blood, and the wheedling turtle-doves are nesting among the rocks. This old woman dips bread into a cup of buttermilk for her lunch and eats slowly. When she has sold her lilies, she will go back to the place where they are growing.

She scarcely seems to inhabit time. Or, it is as if she were waiting for Scheherazade to perceive a final dawn had come and, the last tale of all concluded, fall silent. Then, the lily-seller might vanish.

A goat is nibbling wild jasmine among the ruins of the mosque that was built by the beautiful wife of Tamburlaine.

Tamburlaine's wife started to build this mosque for him as a surprise, while he was away at the wars, but when she got word of his imminent return, one arch still remained unfinished. She went directly to the architect and begged him to hurry but the architect told her that he would complete the work on time only if she gave him a kiss. One kiss, one single kiss.

Tamburlaine's wife was not only very beautiful and very virtuous but also very clever. She went to the market, bought a basket of eggs, boiled them hard and stained them a dozen different colours. She called the architect to the palace, showed him the basket and told him to choose any egg he liked and eat it. He took a red egg. What does it taste like? Like an egg. Eat another.

He took a green egg.

What does that taste like? Like the red egg. Try again.

He ate a purple egg.

One eggs tastes just the same as any other egg, if they are fresh, he said.

There you are! she said. Each of these eggs looks different to the rest but they all taste the same. So you may kiss any one of my serving women that you like but you must leave me alone.

Very well, said the architect. But soon he came back to her and this time he was carrying a tray with three bowls on it, and you would have thought the bowls were all full of water.

Drink from each of these bowls, he said.

She took a drink from the first bowl, then from the second; but how she coughed and spluttered when she took a mouthful from the third bowl, because it contained, not water, but vodka.

This vodka and that water both look alike but each tastes quite different, he said. And it is the same with love.

Then Tamburlaine's wife kissed the architect on the mouth. He went back to the mosque and finished the arch the same day that victorious Tamburlaine rode into Samarkand with his army and banners and his cages full of captive kings. But when Tamburlaine went to visit his wife, she turned away from him because no woman will return to the harem after she has tasted vodka. Tamburlaine beat her with a knout until she told him she had kissed the architect and then he sent his executioners hotfoot to the mosque.

The executioners saw the architect standing on top of the arch and ran up the stairs with their knives drawn but when he heard them coming he grew wings and flew away to Persia.

This is a story in simple, geometric shapes and the bold colours of a child's box of crayons. This Tamburlaine's wife of the story would have painted a black stripe laterally across her forehead and done up her hair in a dozen, dozen tiny plaits, like any other Uzbek woman. She would have bought red and white radishes from the market for her husband's dinner. After she ran away from him perhaps she made her living in the market. Perhaps she sold lilies there.

Our Lady of the Massacre

My name is neither here nor there since I used several in the Old World that I may not speak of now; then there is my, as it were, *wilderness* name, that now I never speak of; and, now, what I call myself in *this* place, therefore my name is no clue as to my person nor my life as to my nature. But I first saw light in the county of *Lancashire* in *Old England*, in the Year of Our Lord 16—, my father a poor farm servant, and me mam and he both died of plague when I was a little thing so me and me brothers and sisters left living were put on the parish and what became of them I do not know, but, as for me, I could do a bit of sewing and keep a place clean so when I were nine or ten years of age they set me up as a maid of all work to an old woman that lived in our parish.

This old woman, or *lady* rather, never married and was, as I found out, of the Roman faith, though she kept *that* to herself, and once a good deal richer than she had become. Besides, her father, wanting a son and getting nowt but she, taught her Latin, Greek and a bit of Hebrew and left her a great telescope with which she used to view the heavens from her roof though her sight was too bad to make out much but what she did not see, she made up, for she said she had poor sight for the things of *this* world but clear sight into the one to come. She often let me have a squint at the stars, too, for I was her only companion and she learned me my letters, as you can see, and would have taught me all she knew herself, had she not, as soon as I come to her, cast my *horoscope* for me, her father having left the charts and zodiacal instruments. And, having done so, told me I would not need the language of *Homer* at no time in all my life, but a little conversational Hebrew she *did* teach me, for reasons as follows:

That the stars, whom she had consulted on behalf of her dear child, as she pleased to call me, assured her that I would take a long voyage over the Ocean to the *New World* and there bear a blessed babe whose fathers' fathers never sailed in Noah's Ark. And, from her reading, which had worn her eyes out, she had concluded that those 'red children of the wilderness' could be none other than the Lost Tribe of Israel, so *shalom*, she taught me, besides the words for 'love' and 'hunger', and much else that I have forgotten, so that I could talk to my husband when I met him. And if I had not been a steady girl, she would have turned my head with all her nonsense for she would have it that the stars foretold I should grow up to be nowt less than Our Lady of the Red Men.

For, she says, that country far beyond the sea is named *Virginia*, after the virgin mother of God Almighty, and its rivers flow directly from Eden so, when the natives are converted to the true religion – 'which task I charge you with, child,' and she gives me a mouthful of Ave Marias – when that shall be accomplished, why, the whole world will end and the dead rise up out of their coffins and all go to heaven that deserve it and my little babby sit smiling over everything with a gold crown on his head. Then she'd babble away in Latin and cross herself. But I never told nobody about her *Roman* ways nor about her star-gazing, either, for if they hadn't hanged her for a heretic, they'd have hanged her for a witch, poor creature.

One day the old lass lies down and never gets up again and her cousins come and shift all the goods with a penn'orth of value to 'em but they could find no place for me in their house so I must shift for meself.

I take it into my head to go to *London*, where I persuade myself I can make my fortune, and I walk the highway, sleeping in barns and hedges, for I was hardy, and makes good time – five days. When I gets to London, I stole my first penny loaf, to keep me from starving, which led directly to my undoing, a gentleman that spies me slip the loaf into my pocket, instead of raising a hue and cry, follows me into the streets, takes my arm, inquires: whether it be want or inclination that makes me take it. I flares up at that: Want, sir! says I and he says, such a pretty young 'Lancashire milkmaid' as I was should not want for nothing while he had breath in his body and so flattered and coaxed me that I went with him to a room with a bed in it in a public house where he was well known. When he finds I've never done the thing before, he weeps; beats his breast for shame for debauching me; gives me five gold sovereigns, the most money that ever I saw until then; and departs for, so he says, the church, to pray forgiveness, which is the last that I saw of him. So I went on the common with my first fall, which was a fortunate one, and the 'Lancashire milkmaid' was soon in a fair way of trade as the 'Lancashire whore'.

Now, had I been content with honest whoring, no doubt I would be dressed in silk riding my coach in Cheapside still and never eat the bitter bread of exile. But you could say that, when I clapped my eye on his coin, I was as if struck with love and though want made a thief of me, first, it was avarice perfected me in the art and whoring was my 'cover' for it since my customers, blinded as they were with lust and often fuddled with liquor, were easier to pluck, living, than geese, dead.

It was a gold watch out of the bosom of a city alderman that took me to Newgate for I quarrelled with my landlady over my rent and she took his complaint of me to the magistrate out of spite. So, just as my old Lancashire mistress said, I sailed the Ocean to *Virginia* but I went in a convict transport. They burned my hand, to brand me, as they used convicts, and sold me to work my sentence in the plantation for seven years, after which they said I should be a free woman again.

My master took a liking to me, for I was not yet aged above seventeen, and he had me out of the tobacco fields into his kitchen. But the overseer did not like it, that I should get the taste of his whip no more, and pestered me unmercifully that, since I had been a whore in Cheapside, I should not play the honest maid with him in *Virginia*. Coming at me alone in the house, my master having gone to church, it being Sunday morning, this overseer thrust one hand in my bosom and the other up my skirt, says I shall have it whether I wants it or no. I picked up the big carving knife and whacks off both his ears, first one, then t'other. What a sight! blood enough for pig-sticking; he roars, he curses, I runs out into the garden with the knife in my hand, it dripping.

Seeing me in such a fluster, the gardener coming up with a basket of vegetables cries: 'What's this, Sal?'

'Well,' says I, 'the overseer just now tried to board me and I've had the ears off him and would it had been his pillocks too.'

The gardener, being a good-natured kind of *Negro* man and a slave, hisself, and hisself tickled once too often by the overseer's whip, cannot forbear to laugh but says to me: 'Then you must be off into the wilderness, Sal, and cast your fate to the tender mercies of the savage Indian. For this is a hanging matter.'

He gives me his handkerchief with his bit of dinner in it and a tinder-box he had about him, which I stow away in my apron pocket, and I show the plantation a clean pair of heels, I can tell you, adding to my list of crimes that most heinous: escape from bondage.

I am a good walker as you may judge from my trudge from Lancashire to London and by the time night comes on and I sit down to eat the gardener's bit of bread and bacon there are fifteen odd miles between myself and the plantation and rough going, too, for my master had cleared land from the forest to grow his tobacco. My plan is, to walk until I gets to where the English have no dominion, for I have heard the Spaniards and the French are on this coast, as well, and there, I thought, I'd ply my trade amongst strangers, for a whore needs nowt but her skin to set up business.

You must know I had no knowledge of *geography* and thought, from *Virginia* to *Florida* but ten or twelve days' march, at the most, for I knew it was very far and could think of no distance further than that, for the great vastness of the *Americas* was then unknown to me. As for the Indians, I thought, well! if I can keep off the overseer with my knife, I'd be more than a match for them, if I should meet them, so slept sound under the sky, took a bearing by the sun in the morning and went on.

I had clean water out of the streams and it was the season of berries so I made my breakfast off a bit of fruit but my guts began to rumble by dinner-time and I cast my eye about for more solid fodder. Seeing the brakes full of small beasts and birds unknown to me, I thought: 'How can I go hungry if I use my wits!' So I tied my shoestrings together to make a little snare and trapped a small, brown, furry thing of the rabbit kind, but earless, and slit its throat, skinned it, toasted it on the end of my carving-knife over a fire I made with the blessed tinder-box the gardener give me. So all I wanted was salt and a bit of bread.

After I eat my dinner, I saw how the oak trees were full of acorns at this season and thought that I might grind up those acorns between two flat stones, with a bit of effort, and so get a kind of flour, as had been done at home in times of want. I reasoned how I could mix this flour to dough with water. Then I could bake the dough in cakes in the ashes of my fire and have bread with my meat. And, if I wanted fish on a Friday, as was my Lancashire lady's custom, I could tickle the trout with which the stream abounded, which is a trick every country girl knows and not unlike picking a pocket. Also, it seemed to me, if I dried the mulberries in the sun, they would eat sweet for a month. When I got so far in planning my diet, I thought: why, I can get along here very well in the woods on my own for a while even if I must eat meat without salt!

For, I thought, I have steel and fire and the climate is temperate, the land fruitful; this earthly paradise surely will provide for me! I can build a shelter out of branches and bide my time until the fuss over the lop-eared overseer dies down, then make my way South in my own good time. Besides, to tell the truth, my nostrils were too full of the stink of humanity to relish a quick return to the world in some bordello in *Florida*. But I thought that I should travel on a little more, for safety's sake, into the deep wilderness, so that no hunting party might find me and return me to the noose. Of which I had a very powerful fear and, I may tell you, more dread of the *white man*, which I knew, than of the *red man*, who was at that time unknown to me.

So I walked on another day, taking my living from the country easily enough; then one day more and never heard a voice but the birds' whistle; but the day after that I heard a woman singing and saw one of the savage tribe in a clearing and thought to kill her, before she killed me, but then I saw she had no weapon but was picking herbs and putting them in a fine basket. So I steps back to hide myself from her lest she be some Indian servant of a planter, although I do think that I walk, now, where no person of my country ever trod before. But she hears the leaves move and sees me and jumps as if she'd seen a ghost so that she knocks over her basket and her herbs spill out.

I never think twice about it but step across to pick up the spilled herbs for her as if I was back in Cheapside and run to help some fruit-seller that overturns her basket of apples.

This woman sees the brand on my hand and grunts to herself, as though she knows the meaning of it and will not fear me for it, or, rather, does not fear me because of it, but, all the same, does not like the look of me. She holds back from me though she takes her basket from me again as if to leave me in the forest. But I am struck by her looks, she is a handsome woman, not red but wondrous brown, and it came into my mind to open my bodice, show her my breasts, that, though I had whiter skin, I could give suck as well as she and she reached out and touched my bosom.

She was a woman of about middle age dressed in nowt but a buckskin skirt and she grunted when she saw my stays – for I still wore my *English apparel*, though it was ragged – and motioned me, as I thought, that whalebone was not the fashion among the Indian nation. So off go my stays and I throws them into a bush and breathes easier for it. Then she asks me, by signs, to give her the big knife I'd stuck in my apron.

'Now I'm for it!' I thinks but hands it over and she smiles, though not much, for these savages are not half so free with their feelings as we are, and says in a word I take to mean 'Knife'. I say it after her, pointing to it, but she shakes her head and runs her finger down the blade, so I say, after her: 'Sharp'. Or, a word you might put into English as: acute. And that was the first word of the *Algonkian* language that ever I spoke, though not the last, by any means. Then, seeing this old woman with a shape, not, as I can see, marked by child-bearing, and remembering the Virgin Queen my missus taught me of, I try her out with: '*Shalom*'. Which she politely repeats after me but I can tell it means nowt to her.

She motions me: shall I go with her? I think the overseer will never come to look for me among the *red men*! So I goes with her to the Indian town and in this way, no other, was I 'taken' by 'em although the Minister would have it otherwise, that they took me with violence, against my will, haling me by the hair, and if he wishes to believe it, then let 'im.

Their clean, pretty town was built within a low wood fence or stockade, the houses built of birchbark set in gardens with vines with pumpkins on 'em and the cooking of their meat savouring the air, as it was about dinner-time. They were cooking what they call *succotash*, a great pot on an open fire and a naked savage squatting before it, calm as you please, fanning the flames with a birchbark fan. The town was surrounded by tidy fields of tobacco and corn and a river near. But no kind of beast did I see, nor cows nor horses nor chickens, for they keep none. She takes me to her own lodge, where she lives by herself on account of her business, and gives me water to wash in and a bunch of feathers to dry myself, so that I was much refreshed.

I had heard these Indians were mortal dragons, accustomed to eat the flesh of dead men, but the pretty little naked children playing with their dollies in the dust, oh! never could such little ducks be reared on cannibal meat! And my Indian 'mother', as I soon called her, assured me that though their cousins to the North roasted the thighs of their captives and ceremoniously partook thereof, it was, as you might say, a *sacramental meal*, to honour the departed by devouring him; and I have often disputed with the Minister on this point, that the Iroquois dinner is but the *Mass* in a state of nature. And the Minister will say, either: that I lived so long with Satan that I grew accustomed to his ways, or, that the Romish *Mass* is but the Iroquois feast in britches.

As for me, all I ever eat among the Indians was fish, game or fowl, boiled or broiled, besides corn cooked in various ways, beans, squash in season and etc. and this such a healthy diet that it is very rare to see a sick body amongst them and never did I see there any either shaking with palsy or suffering toothache or with sore eyes or crooked with age.

The weather being warm, at first I blushed to see the nakedness of the savages, for the men were accustomed to go clad in nowt but breech-clouts at that season and the women with only a rag about 'em. But soon I thought nothing of it and exchanged my petticoat for the bucksin one my mother give me and she gave me a necklace, too, of the beads they carve from shells, for she said she had no daughter of her own to pet until the woods sent her this one, whom she was thankful to the English for giving away.

There was no end of the kindness of this woman to me and I lived in her cabin with her, for she had no husband, since she was, as it were the *midwife* of the tribe and all her time taken up with seeing to women in their labour. And it was to make potions to ease the labour pains and the pains of the women in their courses that she was picking herbs in the woods when I first saw her.

How do they live, these so-called demi-devils? The men among them have an easy life, spend all their time in leisure and idleness, except when they are hunting or fighting their enemies, since all their tribes are constantly at war with one another, and with the English, too; and the *werowance*, as they call him, he is not the chief, or ruler of the village, although the English do say that he is so, but, rather, he is the man who goes the first in battle, so he is commonly more courageous a man than the English generals who direct their soldiers from the back.

As for me, I stayed with my Indian mother in her hut and learned from her Indian manners, such as sitting on my knees on the ground to my meat that was spread on a mat before me because they have no furniture. I learned how to cure and dress robes out of buckskin, beaver and other skins, and to embroider them with shell and feather. I had a housewife with me in my apron pocket and my mother was very pleased with the steel needles, likewise with the tinder-box, which she was glad to get, while my carving-knife she thought a wonderfully convenient thing, they having no notion of working metal although the women make good pots out of the river clay and bake them in an open fire very cleverly while you never see a beard on any man, since they contrive to shave themselves all over quite close with razors of stone.

And I should say that one or two *guns* they *did* have, for a little while before I arrived among 'em, there came a Scotsman, swapping guns and liquor in return for dressed robes and, as for the effects of the liquor, I shall say nowt about it except it sends 'em mad, but, as for the guns, they soon learned to use them.

The harvest coming on, they gathered up their corn, a very poor, small sort of corn, to my way of thinking, the heads just *that* much bigger than my thumb, and we dug holes in the ground six or seven feet deep and what of the corn we did not eat we dried and stored away under the earth. But the digging was a great labour for they have no shovels or spades except what they steal from the English so we made shift with sticks or the shoulder-bones of deer. And if I have one quarrel with my tribe, it is that the men will have nothing to do with this *agriculture*, although it is heavy work, but go fishing in the creek or chase deer or engage in dances and such silly performances as they say will make the corn grow.

But my mother said: 'There is no harm in it and it keeps the men *out of the way.*'

By the time the weather turned, I was rattling away in the Indian language as if I'd been born to it, though not a word of Hebrew did it contain so I think my old Lancashire lady was mistaken that they are the Lost Tribe of Israel and, as to converting them to the true religion, I was so busy with one thing and another that it never entered my head. As for my *pale face*, by the end of the harvest it was brown as any of theirs and my mother stained my light hair for me with some darkish dye so they grew accustomed to my presence among them and at six months end you would have thought she whom I called my 'mother' was my own natural mother and I was Indian born and bred, except my blue eyes remained a marvel.

But for all the bonds of affection between us, I might still have thought of journeying on to *Florida* as the weather grew colder, such is the power of custom and habit, had I not cast my eye on a *brave* of that tribe who had no woman for himself and he cast his eye on me but never a word he says, it seems all along he intends to do the *right thing* by me, so it was my mother said to me at last: 'That *Tall Hickory* you know of would like you for his wife.' *Tall Hickory* being what his name signified in English, and as common a kind of name amongst 'em as James or Matthew might be in Lancashire.

And now it comes to it, I wept, for he was a fine man.

'How can I be that good man's wife, mother, for I was a bad woman in my own country.'

'A bad woman?' she says. 'What's this?'

So I told her what I did to earn my living on Cheapside; and how I was a thief by natural vocation. As for my whoring, she was very much surprised to hear that English men would trouble to pay for such a thing as I had to sell, for the Indians exchange it free or not at all, and, as for my virginity being gone, she laughs and says: 'If you were not good, nobody would have had you.' But she grieves over my thievery until at last she says to me: 'Well, child, would you steal away a bowl or *wampun belt* or robe from out of my hut and keep it yourself and deny it to me?'

'How could I do that, mother,' says I. 'If I should need anything, I may use it and give it to you again as you do with our needles and the tinder-box and the knife. And so it is with such-a-one and such-a-one –' naming our neighbours. 'And to tell the truth, there is nowt in all the village excites my old passion of avarice, while as for my dinner, if I need it, I may have a share in any cooking pot in the Indian country, for that is the custom. So neither *desire* nor *want* can make a thief of me, here.'

'Then you are a good woman in spite of yourself among the Indians and so I think you will remain,' she says. 'Why not marry the young fellow?'

Now, certain men of the village, such as the *general*, and the *priest*, as I might call him, seeing he dealt with religion, had not one wife but three or four to till their fields for them and I did not like that. I would be the only one in my husband's lodge, a fancy of the old life that I could not lose. And she puzzles over that, although she herself was never any man's wife, having, so she tells me with a wink, not much liking for the sex and much fondness for her own.

'As for ourselves, we are too seemly and decent a folk for the matter of matrimony to come between a woman and her friends!' she says. 'The more wives a man has, the better company for them, the more knees to dandle the children on and the more corn they can plant so the better they all live together.'

But still I said, I would be his *only wife* or never marry him.

'Listen, my dear,' she said. 'Do you not love me?'

'Indeed I do,' I says, 'with all my heart.'

'Then if your sweetheart should offer to marry us both, would you love me the less for it?'

But I ducked my head and forbore to answer that, for fear she should ask my beau to take her, too, along with me, since I was so struck with him I could not think that any woman, however set in her ways, would not have him if she got half the chance. Then she gives me a clout on the buttocks and cries out: 'Now, child, see what a wretched thing this *jealousy* is, that it can set a daughter against her own mother!'

But she relents to see me cry for shame and says, she is too old and stubborn to think of marriage and, besides, my young man is so taken with me that he will marry me on my own terms in the English fashion. For they are taught to love their wives and let them have their way no matter how many of them they marry and, if I wanted the toil of tilling a patch of corn with nowt but my own two hands, then he would not interfere with that.

We were married about the time they were planting the corn, which they celebrate with a good deal of singing and dancing although it is we squaws who break our backs setting the seed. The season of the anniversary of my arrival in the town passed, winter comes again and by the spring I was well on the way to bringing him a little *brave*. It was marvellous to see the tenderness of my husband's bearing towards me when the sun grew hot and made me sweat, weary, heavy, peevish, so that I often swore I wished meself in England again; but he bore with all.

Now, at this time, the *general* of our village held counsel how all the tribes of this part of the territory should settle their differences and join together in a great army to drive the English off back to where they come from while some of the others said, they should, instead, make treaties with the English against those other tribes who were their *natural enemies* and so get more guns from the English.

But I sent word by my husband – the women did not go to the counsels but were accustomed to let their husbands give their messages – I sent word by him that it would take all the tribes of all the continent to drive away the English, and then the English would only go away to come again in double numbers, so eager were they to 'plant the colony' with me and such poor devils as I had been. So I told them straight they must make a grand, warlike, well-armed confederacy amongst all the Indian nations and never trust a word the English said, for the English would all be thieves if they could, and I was living proof of it, who only left off thieving when there was nothing to steal.

But they took no notice of me, and could not agree about the manner in which, if they should wage it, the war should be waged, whether an attack on Annestown by night, creeping on all fours like bears with bows in their mouths; or picking off the Englishmen one by one when they went hunting or out in lonely places; or meeting 'em head on, like an army. Which they fancied best, because it was most honourable, but, to my way of thinking, putting the head in the beast's mouth. While some still held that the English were their friends because they were their *enemies' enemy*. So they fell to squabbling amongst themselves and nothing came of all the talk which was a great sadness to me, for I was with child and so I wanted a quiet life.

I was scratching away with my pointed stick along the garden bean-row until the very minute the waters broke and I goes running into my mother and, an hour later, as I judge it, for they have no means of keeping exact time, she was washing the blood off my young son.

My young son we named what would be, in English, *Little Shooting Star*, and you may laugh at it, but it is a name fine men have carried. And he is strapped into his little board that he might ride on my back in his birchbark carriage and I was as pleased with him as any woman might be. Which is how the fate my old Lancashire lady foresaw for me came to pass, because my boy's father never sprang from the tribe of Shem, Ham nor Japhet, although his mother resembled more the Mary Magdalene, or repentant harlot, than Mary the Virgin, though the Minister does not hold with that stuff, being a dissenting man, and will not let me speak of it.

But it would come about that the little lad's crown must be of tears, not gold.

Now, the confederacy among the *Algonkians* breaking up, the depredations of the English upon the villages towards the South grew week by week more severe but our fierce braves held them off a while. The generals of this region held a parley, as to whether all stay and defend our villages or else beat a retreat, that is, stir our stumps and pick up our traps and leave our fields and shift westwards a piece, to new pastures, after the harvest, which was in hand. But this latter they were loath to do, since to the West lay the *Rechacrians*, a very warlike tribe not easily crossed. And they sent out a *war party* to give the English a taste of their own medicine, to start off with, but I was full of fear lest my husband not come back.

He paints his face up black and red so the babby cried to see and they do go out and all come back, with blood on their axes, and several scalps of yellow hair that he hangs on the ridgepole of the roof, besides plunder of copper kettles, bullets and gunpowder. Also, alas, rum.

Yet I must say, when I first saw those English topknots, I felt nowt but pleasure though their hair was of my colour; yet the Minister says I am a good girl and God will forgive me for the sins I committed among the Indians.

As for gunpowder, *Tall Hickory*, my husband, told me, when the English first give it to the general, years back, the English told him, with much secret merriment amongst themselves, how he should bury it, like seed corn, and watch the bullets come up. And the Indians held it as a grudge ever after, to have been teased like silly children, when the English would have starved dead if the Red Man had not taught 'em how to plant corn.

Their captive they brought back lashed to the powder barrel and taunted him, how they would set their torches to a slow fuse, left him there in the middle of the village and abused him in their drunkenness for they were devils when they'd got a bit of drink inside 'em, I must admit it.

'Now, my dear,' says my husband, who was stone-cold sober because he'd a mortal terror of the edge of my tongue. 'I must ask you to talk to this fellow in your own language, that we might know if his fellow-countrymen will at last remember certain pledges and treaties formerly made between us or do indeed mean to drive us into the arms of the *Rechacrians,* with whom we are on no friendly terms, so it will be the worse for us, trapped between the two.'

At first I would not do it because I felt some pity for this Englishman, they were very stern with their captives and made a cruel festival out of this one, what with the drink and all. Then I recall how I saw this fellow riding his high horse along the dock at Annestown when the convicts were unloaded in chains from the holds of the ship and all pity left me.

When he hears my English, 'Praise the Lord!' he cries, and tells me straightaway how I must give over my tribes to the whites in the name of God, the King of England, and a free pardon thrown in when he sees my brand. But I shows him the babby and he calls me all kind of foul names, to whore among the heathen, so I shoves a sharp stick in his belly to teach him manners. He squawks at that but will say nothing of the soldiers or where they might be but only: that the damned seed shall be driven from the land. They took him off the barrel, for they did not want to waste good gunpowder on him, and hoist him up over the fire. Soon he was dead.

When I went through his pockets, they were stuffed full of coin and all the children come to play ducks and drakes with gold pieces on the river. But his gold watch I wound up and give my husband in remembrance of the one I robbed the alderman of.

'What's this?' he says in his innocence. Just then it rang the hours of twelve, it being noon, and he screetches out, drops it, it breaks apart, the wheels and springs scatter on the ground, and my husband, poor, superstitious savage that he was for all he was the best man in the world, my husband fell a-shaking and a-trembling and said the watch was 'bad medicine' and boded ill.

So he went off and got drunk with the rest. I go through the papers in the gentleman's pockets and find out we've put an end to the governor of all Virginia and I tells 'em so, full of misgiving at it, but they was all so far gone in liquor no sense to be had out of any of 'em until they slept it off but just before sun-up next day the soldiers came on horseback.

They burned the ripe cornfields and set light to the stockade so it burned and our lodge burned when the powder went up so I saw the massacre bright as day. They put a bullet through my husband's head, he on his feet and all bewildered, I got him out of the lodge when I first heard the fire crackle but he was a big man, couldn't miss him. And the poor drunk, sleepy savages all mown down. I got the baby in my arms and went and hid in the bird-scare in the cornfield, which was a platform on legs with hide over it, and so escaped.

But the soldiers caught hold of my mother as she was running to the river with her hair on fire and she shouts to me, seeing me fleeing: 'You unkind daughter!' For she thought I was hastening to cast my lot in with the English, which was not so, by any means. Then they violated her, then they slit her throat. So all over quickly, by daybreak nowt left but ashes, corpses, the widow mourning her dead children, soldiers leaning on their guns well pleased with their night's work and the courageous manner in which they had revenged the govenor.

The babby bust out crying. One of these brutes, hearing him, came beating among the scorched corn and pushes at the bird-scare, knocks it down so I fell out, flat on my back, the baby tumbles out of my arms and cracks his head open on a stone, sets up a terrible shrieking, even the hardest heart would have run directly to him. But this soldier puts his knee on my belly, unfastens his britches intending to rape me, he'd need the strength of ten to hold me down but all at once leaves off his horrid fumbling, amazed.

'Captain!' he says. 'Look here! Here's a squaw with blue eyes, such as I've never seen before!'

He takes a good handful of my hair and hales me to where the captain of these good soldiers is washing his bloody hands in a basin of water cool as you please while his men pick over the *wampun* and the robes for trophies of war. He asks me, what is my name and whether I speak English; then Dutch; then French; and tries me in Spanish but I will say nothing except, in the Algonkian language: 'I am the widow of *Tall Hickory*.' But he cannot understand that.

They found out I was not indeed a woman of the Indian blood at last by a trick for one of 'em fetched my baby from where they'd left him bawling in the cornfield and showed him his knife, making as if he would stick the sharp blade into my little one.

'Thou shalt not!' I cried out while the others held me back from him or I should have torn out his eyes with my bare hands. How they laughed, when the squaw with feathers in her hair shouted out in broad Lancashire. Then the captain sees my burned hand and calls me a 'runaway' and says there will be a price on my head over and above the bounty on the Indians. And teases me, how they will brand my cheek with 'R' for 'runaway' when we gets to Annestown so I cannot whore among the Indians no more, nor amongst nobody else. But all I want is the loan of his handkerchief, dipped in water, to wipe the cut on the babby's forehead and this he's kind enough to give me, at last.

When I got my babby back and put him to nurse, for he was hungry, then I went along with the soldiers, since I had no choice, my mother and my husband dead and, truth to tell, my spirit broken. And what squaws were left living, that I used to call 'sister', trailed along behind us, for the soldiers wanted women and the women wanted bread and not one brave left living in that part of the New World that now you might call a 'fair garden blasted of folk'. And the river watering this earthly paradise running blood.

The squaws blamed me, how I had brought bad luck on them and cruelly repaid their kindness to me. But, as for me, my grief is mixed with fear over the memory of the overseer I had the ears off of, that all this will end in a *downward drop*, once I am back where the justice is.

We gets to a place with a few houses and they had just finished building a church and: 'Here is a morsel plucked from Satan,' says the one that widowed me to the Minister, who tells me to thank God that I have been rescued from the savage and beg the Good Lord's forgiveness for straying from His ways. Taking my cue from his, I fall to my knees, for I see that repentance is the fashion in these parts and the more of it I show, the better it will be for me. And when they ask my name, I give 'em the name of my old Lancashire lady, which is Mary, and stick by it, so I live on as if I were her ghost, and all her prophecies come true, except it turns out I was Our Lady of the Massacre and I do think my *half-breed* child will bear the mark of *Cain*, for the scar above his left eye never fades.

The Minister's wife come out of the kitchen with an old gown of hers and tells me to cover up my breasts, for shame, but the child cries and will not be pacified. Yet she is decent, and the Minister, also, as their acts now prove for they would not let the soldiers take me to Annestown with them but offered the captain a good sum of money to leave me with them, for the sake of my innocent baby. The captain hums and haws, the Minister adds another guinea, the *fine soldier* pockets the gold and all ride off and the Minister would give my child some Bible name, Isaac or Ishmael or some such name. 'Hasn't he got a good enough name already?' says I. But the Minister says: '*Little Shooting Star* is no name for a Christian,' and a baptised Christian my boy must be if his soul may be admitted to the congregation of the blessed though the poor thing will never find his daddy there. And when shall these dead rise up and be avenged? But, as for me, I will not call him by the name the Minister gave him; nor do I talk to him in any but the Indian language when nobody else is there.

After a while, the tale comes how, two years or more before, the Indians came by stealth to a plantation to the north, murdered an overseer and stole away a bonded servant girl. The gardener saw them drag her off by her yellow hair. I think to meself, how the gardener must have settled a score on his own account, good luck to him, and if they choose to think I was forced into captivity, then they have my leave to do so, if it makes them happy, as long as they leave me be. Which, because the Minister has a powerful desire to save my soul, and his wife fond of the little one, having none of her own, they do, for they've paid out good money to keep us from the law. And don't I earn my keep, do all the rough work, carry water, hew wood.

So I scrubbed the Minister's floor, cooked the dinner, washed the clothes and for all the Minister swears they've come to build the *City of God* in the *New World*, I was the same skivvy as I'd been in Lancashire and no openings for a whore in the *Community of the Saints*, either, if I could have found in my heart the least desire to take up my old trade again. But that I could not; the Indians had damned me for a *good woman* once and for all.

By and by the missus comes to me and says: 'You are still a young woman, Mary, and Jabez Mather says he will have you for a wife since his own died of the flux but he will not take the child so I shall keep him.' But *she* will never have my little lad for her son, nor will I have Jabez Mather for my husband, nor any man living, but sit and weep by the waters of Babylon.

The Cabinet of Edgar Allan Poe

Imagine Poe in the Republic! when he possesses none of its virtues; no Spartan, he. Each time he tilts the jug to greet the austere morning, his sober friends reluctantly concur: 'No man is safe who drinks before breakfast.' Where is the black star of melancholy? Elsewhere; not here. Here it is always morning; stern, democratic light scrubs apparitions off the streets down which his dangerous feet must go.

Perhaps . . . perhaps the black star of melancholy was hiding in the dark at the bottom of the jug all the time . . . it might be the whole thing is a little secret between the jug and himself . . .

He turns back to go and look; and the pitiless light of common day hits him full in the face like a blow from the eye of God. Struck, he reels. Where can he hide, where there are no shadows? They split the Republic in two, they halved the apple of knowledge, white light strikes the top half and leaves the rest in shadow; up here, up north, in the levelling latitudes, a man must make his own penumbra if he wants concealment because the massive, heroic light of the Republic admits of no ambiguities. Either you are a saint; or a stranger. He is a stranger, here, a gentleman up from Virginia somewhat down on his luck, and, alas, he may not invoke the Prince of Darkness (always a perfect gentleman) in his cause since, of the absolute night which is the antithesis to these days of rectitude, there is no aristocracy.

Poe staggers under the weight of the Declaration of Independence. People think he is drunk.

He *is* drunk.

The prince in exile lurches through the new-found land.

So you say he overacts? Very well; he overacts. There is a past history of histrionics in his family. His mother was, as they say, born in a trunk, grease-paint in her bloodstream, and made her first appearance on any stage in her ninth summer in a hiss-the-villain melodrama entitled *Mysteries of the Castle*. On she skipped to sing a ballad clad in the pretty rags of a ballet gypsy.

It was the evening of the eighteenth century.

At this hour, this very hour, far away in Paris, France, in the appalling dungeons of the Bastille, old Sade is jerking off. Grunt, groan, grunt, on to the prison floor . . . aaaagh! He seeds dragons' teeth. Out of each ejaculation spring up a swarm of fully-armed, mad-eyed homunculi. Everything is about to succumb to delirium.

Heedless of all this, Poe's future mother skipped on to a stage in the fresh-hatched American republic to sing an old-world ballad clad in the pretty rags of a ballet gypsy. Her dancer's grace, piping treble, dark curls, rosy cheeks – cute kid! And eyes with something innocent, something appealing in them that struck directly to the heart so that the smoky auditorium broke out in raucous sentimental cheers for her and clapped its leather palms together with a will. A star was born that night in the rude firmament of fit-ups and candle-footlights, but she was to be a shooting star; she flickered briefly in the void, she continued the inevitable trajectory of the meteor, downward. She hit the boards and trod them.

But, well after puberty, she was still able, thanks to her low stature and slim build, to continue to personate children, clever little ducks and prattlers of both sexes. Yet she was versatility personified; she could do you Ophelia, too.

She had a low, melodious voice of singular sweetness, an excellent thing in a woman. When crazed Ophelia handed round the rosemary and rue and sang: 'He is dead and gone, lady,' not a dry eye in the house, I assure you. She also tried her hand at Juliet and Cordelia and, if necessary, could personate the merriest soubrette; even when racked by the nauseas of her pregnancies, still she would smile, would smile and oh! the dazzling candour of her teeth!

Out popped her firstborn, Henry; her second, Edgar, came jostling after to share her knee with her scripts and suckle at her bosom while she learned her lines, yet she was always word-perfect even when she played two parts in the one night, Ophelia or Juliet and then, say, Little Pickle, the cute kid in the afterpiece, for the audiences of those days refused to leave the theatre after a tragedy unless the players changed costumes and came back to give them a little something extra to cheer them up again.

Little Pickle was a trousers' role. She ran back to the green-room and undid the top buttons of her waistcoat to let out a sore, milky breast to pacify little Edgar who, wakened by the hoots and catcalls that had greeted her too voluptuous imitation of a boy, likewise howled and screamed.

A mug of porter or a bottle of whisky stood on the dressing-table all the time. She dipped a plug of cotton in whisky and gave it to Edgar to suck when he would not stop crying.

*

The father of her children was a bad actor and only ever carried a spear in the many companies in which she worked. He often stayed behind in the green-room to look after the little ones. David Poe tipped a tumbler of neat gin to Edgar's lips to keep him quiet. The red-eyed Angel of Intemperance hopped out of the bottle of ardent spirits and snuggled down in little Edgar's longclothes. Meanwhile, on stage, her final child, in utero, stitched its flesh and bones together as best it could under the corset that preserved the theatrical illusion of Mrs Elizabeth Poe's eighteen-inch waist until the eleventh hour, the tenth month.

Applause rocked round the wooden O. Loving mother that she was – for we have no reason to believe that she was not – Mrs Poe exited the painted scene to cram her jewels on her knee while tired tears ran rivers through her rouge and splashed upon their peaky faces. The monotonous clamour of their parents' argument sent them at last to sleep but the unborn one in the womb pressed its transparent hands over its vestigial ears in terror.

(To be born at all might be the worst thing.)

However, born at last this last child was, one July afternoon in a cheap theatrical boarding-house in New York City after many hours on a rented bed while flies buzzed at the windowpanes. Edgar and Henry, on a pallet on the floor, held hands. The midwife had to use a pair of blunt iron tongs to scoop out the reluctant wee thing; the sheet was tented up over Mrs Poe's lower half for modesty so the toddlers saw nothing except the midwife brandishing her dreadful instrument and then they heard the shrill cry of the new-born in the exhausted silence, like the sound of the blade of a skate on ice, and something bloody as a fresh-pulled tooth twitched between the midwife's pincers.

It was a girl.

David Poe spent his wife's confinement in a nearby tavern, wetting the baby's head. When he came back and saw the mess he vomited.

Then, before his sons' bewildered eyes, their father began to grow insubstantial. He unbecame. All at once he lost his outlines and began to waver on the air. It was twilit evening. Mama slept on the bed with a fresh mauve bud of flesh in a basket on the chair beside her. The air shuddered with the beginning of absence.

He said not one word to his boys but went on evaporating until he melted clean away, leaving behind him in the room as proof he had been there only a puddle of puke on the splintered floorboards.

As soon as the deserted wife got out of bed, she posted down to Virginia with her howling brats because she was booked for a tour of the South and she had no money put away so all the babies got to eat was her sweat.

She dragged them with her in a trunk to Charleston; to Norfolk; then back to Richmond.

Down there, it is the foetid height of summer.

Stripped to her chemise in the airless dressing-room, she milks her sore breast into a glass; this latest baby must be weaned before its mother dies.

She coughed. She slapped more, yet more rouge on her now haggard cheekbones. 'My children! what will become of my children?' Her eyes glittered and soon acquired a febrile brilliance that was not of *this* world. Soon she needed no rouge at all; red spots brighter than rouge appeared of their own accord on her cheeks while veins as blue as those in Stilton cheese but muscular, palpitating, prominent, lithe, stood out of her forehead. In Little Pickle's vest and breeches it was not now possible for her to create the least suspension of disbelief and something desperate, something fatal in her distracted playing both fascinated and appalled the witnesses, who could have thought they saw the living features of death itself upon her face. Her mirror, the actress's friend, the magic mirror in which she sees whom she has become, no longer acknowledged any but a death's head.

The moist, sullen, Southern winter signed her quietus. She put on Ophelia's madwoman's nightgown for her farewell.

When she summoned him, the spectral horseman came. Edgar looked out of the window and saw him. The soundless hooves of black-plumed horses struck sparks from the stones in the road outside. 'Father!' said Edgar; he thought their father must have reconstituted himself at this last extremity in order to transport them all to a better place but, when he looked more closely, by the light of a gibbous moon, he saw the sockets of the coachman's eyes were full of worms.

They told her children that now she could come back to take no curtain-calls no matter how fiercely all applauded the manner of her going. Lovers of the theatre plied her hearse with bouquets: 'And from her pure and uncorrupted flesh May violets spring.' (Not a dry eye in the house.) The three orphaned infants were dispersed into the bosoms of charitable protectors. Each gave the clay-cold cheek a final kiss; then they too kissed and parted, Edgar from Henry, Henry from the tiny one who did not move or cry but lay still and kept her eyes tight shut. When shall these three meet again? The church bell tolled: never never never never never.

Kind Mr Allan of Virginia, Edgar's own particular benefactor, who would buy his bread, henceforward, took his charge's little hand and led him from the funeral. Edgar parted his name in the middle to make room for Mr Allan inside it. Edgar was then three years old. Mr Allan ushered him into Southern affluence, down there; but do not think his mother left Edgar empty handed, although the dead actress was able to leave him only what could not be taken away from him, to wit, a few tattered memories.

TESTAMENT OF MRS ELIZABETH POE

Item: nourishment. A tit sucked in a green-room, the dug snatched away from the toothless lips as soon as her cue came, so that, of nourishment, he would retain only the memory of hunger and thirst endlessly unsatisified.

Item: transformation. This is a more ambivalent relic. Something like this . . . Edgar would lie in prop-baskets on heaps of artificial finery and watch her while she painted her face. The candles made a profane altar of the mirror in which her vague face swam like a magic fish. If you caught hold of it, it would make your dreams come true but Mama slithered through all the nets which desire set out to catch her.

She stuck glass jewels in her ears, pinned back her nut-brown hair and tied a muslin bandage round her head, looking like a corpse for a minute. Then on went the yellow wig. Now you see her, now you don't; brunette turns blonde in the wink of an eye.

Mama turns round to show how she has changed into the lovely lady he glimpsed in the mirror.

'Don't touch me, you'll mess me.'

And vanishes in a susurration of taffeta.

Item: that women possess within them a cry, a thing that needs to be extracted . . . but this is only the dimmest of memories and will reassert itself in vague shapes of unmentionable dread only at the prospect of carnal connection.

Item: the awareness of mortality. For, as soon as her last child was born, if not before, she started to rehearse in private the long part of dying; once she began to cough she had no option.

Item: a face, the perfect face of a tragic actor, his face, white skin stretched tight over fine, white bones in a final state of wonderfully lucid emaciation.

Ignited by the tossed butt of a still-smouldering cigar that lodged in the cracks of the uneven floorboards, the theatre at Richmond where Mrs Poe had made her last appearance burned to the ground three weeks after her death. Ashes. Although Mr Allan told Edgar how all of his mother that was mortal had been buried in her coffin, Edgar knew the somebody elses she so frequently became lived in her dressing-table mirror and were not constrained by the physical laws that made her body rot. But now the mirror, too, was gone; and all the lovely and untouchable, volatile, unreal mothers went up together in a puff of smoke on a pyre of props and painted scenery.

The sparks from this conflagration rose high in the air, where they lodged in the sky to become a constellation of stars which only Edgar saw and then only on certain still nights of summer, those hot, rich, blue, mellow nights the slaves brought with them from Africa, weather that ferments the music of exile, weather of heartbreak and fever. (Oh, those voluptuous nights, like something forbidden!) High in the sky these invisible stars marked the points of a face folded in sorrow.

NATURE OF THE THEATRICAL ILLUSION; everything you see is false.

Consider the theatrical illusion with special reference to this impressionable child, who was exposed to it at an age when there is no reason for anything to be real.

He must often have toddled on to the stage when the theatre was empty and the curtains down so all was like a parlour prepared for a séance, waiting for the moment when the eyes of the observers make the mystery.

Here he will find a painted backdrop of, say, an antique castle – a castle! such as they don't build here; a Gothic castle all complete with owls and ivy. The flies are painted with segments of trees, massy oaks or something like that, all in two dimensions. Artificial shadows fall in all the wrong places. Nothing is what it seems. You knock against a gilded throne or horrid rack that looks perfectly solid, thick, immovable, and you kick it sideways, it turns out to be made of papier mâché, it is as light as air – a child, you yourself, could pick it up and carry it off with you and sit in it and be a king or lie in it and be in pain.

A creaking, an ominous rattling scares the little wits out of you; when you jump round to see what is going on behind your back, why, the very castle is in mid-air! Heave-ho and up she rises, amid the inarticulate cries and muttered oaths of the stagehands, and down comes Juliet's tomb or Ophelia's sepulchre, and a super scuttles in, clutching Yorrick's skull.

The foul-mouthed whores who dandle you on their pillowy laps and tip mugs of sour porter against your lips now congregate in the wings, where they have turned into nuns or something. On the invisible side of the plush curtain that cuts you off from the beery, importunate, tobacco-stained multitude that has paid its pennies on the nail to watch these transcendent rituals now come the thumps, bangs and clatter that make the presence of their expectations felt. A stagehand swoops down to scoop you up and carry you off, protesting, to where Henry, like a good boy, is already deep in his picture book and there is a poke of candy for you and the corner of a handkerchief dipped in moonshine and Mama in crown and train presses her rouged lips softly on your forehead before she goes down before the mob.

On his brow her rouged lips left the mark of Cain.

Having, at an impressionable age, seen with his own eyes the nature of the mystery of the castle – that all its horrors are so much painted cardboard and yet they terrify you – he saw another mystery and made less sense of it.

Now and then, as a great treat, if he kept quiet as a mouse, because he begged and pleaded so, he was allowed to stay in the wings and watch; the round-eyed baby saw that Ophelia could, if necessary, die twice nightly. All her burials were premature.

A couple of brawny supers carried Mama on stage in Act Four, wrapped in a shroud, tipped her into the cellarage amidst displays of grief from all concerned but up she would pop at curtain-call having shaken the dust off her graveclothes and touched up her eye make-up, to curtsy with the rest of the resurrected immortals, all of whom, even Prince Hamlet himself, turned out, in the end, to be just as un-dead as she.

How could he, then, truly believe she would not come again, although, in the black suit that Mr Allan provided for him out of charity, he toddled behind her coffin to the cemetery? Surely, one fine day, the spectral coachman would return again, climb down from his box, throw open the carriage door and out she would step wearing the white nightdress in which he had last seen her, although he hoped this garment had been laundered in the interim since he last saw it all bloody from a haemorrhage.

Then a transparent constellation in the night sky would blink out; the scattered atoms would reassemble themselves to the entire and perfect Mama and he would run directly to her arms.

It is the mid-morning of the nineteenth century. He grows up under the black stars of the slave states. He flinches from that part of women the sheet hid. He becomes a man.

As soon as he becomes a man, affluence departs from Edgar. The heart and pocketbook that Mr Allan opened to the child now pull themselves together to expel. Edgar shakes the dust of the sweet South off his heels. He hies north, up here, to seek his fortune in the places where the light does not permit that chiaroscuro he loves; now Edgar Poe must live by his disordered wits.

The dug was snatched from the milky mouth and tucked away inside the bodice; the mirror no longer reflected Mama but, instead, a perfect stranger. He offered her his hand; smiling a tranced smile, she stepped out of the frame.

'My darling, my sister, my life and my bride!'

He was not put out by the tender years of this young girl whom he soon married; was she not just Juliet's age, just thirteen summers?

The magnificent tresses forming great shadowed eaves above her high forehead were the raven tint of nevermore, black as his suits the seams of which his devoted mother-in-law painted with ink so that they would not advertise to the world the signs of wear and, nowadays, he always wore a suit of sables, dressed in readiness for the next funeral in a black coat buttoned up to the stock and he never betrayed his absolute mourning by so much as one flash of white shirtfront. Sometimes, when his wife's mother was not there to wash and starch his linen, he economised on laundry bills and wore no shirt at all.

His long hair brushes the collar of this coat, from which poverty has worn off the nap. How sad his eyes are; there is too much of sorrow in his infrequent smile to make you happy when he smiles at you and so much of bitter gall, also, that you might mistake his smile for a grimace or a *grue* except when he smiles at his young wife with her forehead like a tombstone. Then he will smile and smile with as much posthumous tenderness as if he saw already: *Dearly beloved wife of . . .* carved above her eyebrows.

For her skin was white as marble and she was called – would you believe! – 'Virginia', a name that suited his expatriate's nostalgia and also her condition, for the childbride would remain a virgin until the day she died.

Imagine the sinless children lying in bed together! The pity of it!

For did she not come to him stiffly armoured in taboos – taboos against the violation of children; taboos against the violation of the dead – for, not to put too fine a point on it, didn't she always look like a walking corpse? But such a pretty, pretty corpse!

And, besides, isn't an undemanding, economic, decorative corpse the perfect wife for a gentleman in reduced circumstances, upon whom the four walls of paranoia are always about to converge?

Virginia Clemm. In the dialect of northern England, to be 'clemmed' is to be very cold. 'I'm fair clemmed.' Virginia Clemm.

She brought with her a hardy, durable, industrious mother of her own, to clean and cook and keep accounts for them and to outlive them, and to outlive them both.

Virginia was not very clever; she was by no means a sad case of arrested development, like his real, lost sister, whose life passed in a dream of non-being in her adopted home, the vegetable life of one who always declined to participate, a bud that never opened. (A doom lay upon them; the brother, Henry, soon died.) But the slow years passed and Virginia stayed as she had been at thirteen, a simple little thing whose sweet disposition was his only comfort and who never ceased to lisp, even when she started to rehearse the long part of dying.

She was light on her feet as a revenant. You would have thought she never bent a stem of grass as she passed across their little garden. When she spoke, when she sang, how sweet her voice was; she kept her harp in their cottage parlour, which her mother swept and polished until all was like a new pin. A few guests gathered there to partake of the Poes' modest hospitality. There was his brilliant conversation though his women saw to it that only tea was served, since all knew his dreadful weakness for liquor, but Virginia poured out with so much simple grace that everyone was charmed.

They begged her to take her seat at her harp and accompany herself in an Old World ballad or two. Eddy nodded gladly: 'yes', and she lightly struck the strings with white hands of which the long, thin fingers were so fine and waxen that you would have thought you could have set light to the tips to make of her hand the flaming Hand of Glory that casts all the inhabitants of the house, except the magician himself, into a profound and death-like sleep.

She sings: *Cold blows the wind, tonight, my love,*
        And a few drops of rain.

With a taper made from a manuscript folded into a flute, he slyly takes a light from the fire.

    I never had but one true love
    In cold earth she was lain.

He sets light to her fingers, one after the other.

    A twelve month and a day being gone
    The dead began to speak.

Eyes close. Her pupils contain in each a flame.

    Who is that sitting on my grave
    Who will not let me sleep?

All sleep. Her eyes go out. She sleeps.

He rearranges the macabre candelabra so that the light from her glorious hand will fall between her legs and then he busily turns back her petticoats; the mortal candles shine. Do not think it is not love that moves him; only love moves him.

He feels no fear.

An expression of low cunning crosses his face. Taking from his back pocket a pair of enormous pliers, he now, one by one, one by one by one, extracts the sharp teeth just as the midwife did.

All silent, all still.

Yet, even as he held aloft the last fierce canine in triumph above her prostrate and insensible form in the conviction he had at last exorcised the demons from desire, his face turned ashen and sear and he was overcome with the most desolating anguish to hear the rumbling of the wheels outside. Unbidden, the coachman came; the grisly emissary of her high-born kinsman shouted imperiously: 'Overture and beginners, please!' She popped the plug of spiritous linen between his lips; she swept off with a hiss of silk.

The sleepers woke and told him he was drunk; but his Virginia breathed no more!

After a breakfast of red-eye, as he was making his toilet before the mirror, he suddenly thought he would shave off his moustache in order to become a different man so that the ghosts who had persistently plagued him since his wife's death would no longer recognise him and would leave him alone. But, when he was clean-shaven, a black star rose in the mirror and he saw that his long hair and face folded in sorrow had taken on such a marked resemblance to that of his loved and lost one that he was struck like a stock or stone, with the cut-throat razor in his hand.

And, as he continued, fascinated, appalled, to stare in the reflective glass at those features that were his own and yet not his own, the bony casket of his skull began to agitate itself as if he had succumbed to a tremendous attack of the shakes.

Goodnight, sweet prince.

He was shaking like a backcloth about to be whisked off into oblivion.

Lights! he called out.

Now he wavered; horrors! *He was starting to dissolve!*

Lights! more lights! he cried, like the hero of a Jacobean tragedy when the murdering begins, for the black star was engulfing him.

On cue, the laser light on the Republic blasts him.

His dust blows away on the wind.

Overture and Incidental Music for
A Midsummer Night's Dream

Call me the Golden Herm.

My mother bore me in the Southern wild but, 'she, being mortal, of that boy did die,' as my Aunt Titania says, though 'boy' in the circumstances is pushing it, a bit, she's censoring me, there, she's rendering me unambiguous in order to get the casting director out of a tight spot. For 'boy' is correct, as far as it goes, but insufficient. Nor is the sweet South in the least wild, oh, dear, no! It is the lovely land where the lemon trees grow, multiplied far beyond the utmost reaches of your stultified Europocentric imaginations. Child of the sun am I, and of the breezes, juicy as mangoes, that mythopoeically caress the Coast of Coramandel far away on the porphyry and lapis lazuli Indian shore where everything is bright and precise as lacquer.

My Aunt Titania. Not, I should assure you, my *natural* aunt, no blood bond, no knot of the umbilical in the connection, but my mother's best friend, to whom, before she departed, she entrusted me, and, therefore, always called by me 'auntie'.

Titania, she, the great fat, showy, pink and blonde thing, the Memsahib, I call her, Auntie Tit-tit-tit-ania (for her tits are the things you notice first, size of barrage balloons), Tit-tit-tit-omania boxed me up in a trunk she bought from the Army and Navy Stores, labelled it 'Wanted on Voyage' (oh, yes, indeed!) and shipped me here.

Here! to – *Atishoo!* – catch my death of cold in this dripping bastard wood. Rain, rain, rain, rain, rain!

'Flaming June', the sarcastic fairies mutter, looking glum, as well they might, poor dears, their little wings all sodden and plastered to their backs, so water-logged they can hardly take off and no sooner airborne than they founder in the pelting downpour, crash-land among the plashy bracken furls amid much piteous squeaking. 'Never such weather,' complain the fairies, amid the brakes of roses putting on – I must admit – a brave if pastel-coloured floral show amidst the inclemency of the weather, and the flat dishes of the pale wild roses spill over with the raindrops that have collected upon them as the bushes shudder in the reverberations of dozens and dozens of teeny tiny sneezes, for no place on their weeny anatomies to store a handkerchief and all the fairies have got shocking colds as well as I.

Nothing in my princely, exquisite, peacock-jewelled heredity prepared me for the dank, grey, English midsummer. A midsummer nightmare, I call it. The whirling winds have wrenched the limbs off even the hugest oaks and brought down altogether the more tottery elms so that they sprawl like collapsed drunks athwart dishevelled fairy rings. Thunder, lightning, and, at night, the blazing stars whizz down and bomb the wood . . . nothing temperate about your temperate climate, dear, I snap at Aunt Titania, but she blames it all on Uncle Oberon, whose huff expresses itself in thunder and he makes it rain when he abuses himself, which it would seem he must do almost all the time, thinking of me, the while, no doubt. Of ME!

> For Oberon is passing fell and wrath
> Because that she, as her attendant hath
> A lovely boy, stolen from an Indian king;
> She never had so sweet a changeling;
> And jealous Oberon would have the child!

'Boy' again, see; which isn't the half of it. Misinformation. The patriarchal version. No king had nothing to do with it; it was all between my mother and my auntie, wasn't it.

Besides, is a child to be stolen? Or given? Or taken? Or sold in bondage, dammit? Are these blonde English fairies the agents of proto-colonialism?

To all this, in order to preserve my complicated integrity, I present a façade of passive opposition. I am here. I am.

I am Herm, short for *hermaphrodite verus*, one testis, one ovary, half of each but all complete and more, much more, than the sum of my parts. This elegantly retractable appendage, here . . . is *not* the tribade's well-developed clit, but the veritable reproductive erectile tissue, while the velvet-lipped and deliciously closable aperture below it is, I assure you, a viable avenue of the other gender. So there.

Take a look. I'm not shy. Impressive, huh?

And I am called the Golden Herm, for I am gold all over; when I was born, wee, tiny, playful cherubs filled their cheeks and lungs and blew, blew the papery sheets of beaten gold all over my infant limbs, to which they stuck and clung. See me shine!

And here I stand, under the dripping trees, in the long, rank, soaking grass among draggletail dog-daisies and the branched candelabras of the buttercups from whom the gusty rain has knocked off all the petals, leaving their warty green heads bald. And the bloody crane's bill. And the stinging nettles, those Portuguese men-o'-war of the woodland, who gave me so many nasty shocks when I first met them. And pease-blossom and mustard-seed and innumerable unknown-to-me weeds, the dreary, washed-out, pinks, yellows and Cambridge blues of them. Boring. In the underpinnings of the trees, all soggy and floral as William Morris wallpaper in an abandoned house, I, in order to retain my equilibrium and psychic balance, meditate in the yogic posture known as The Tree, that is, on one leg.

Bearer of both arrow and target, wound and bow, spoon and porringer, in my left hand I hold a lotus, looking a bit the worse for wear by now. My snake coils round my other arm.

I am golden, stark naked and bi-partite.

On my golden face, a fixed, archaic grin. Except when –

Atishoo!

Damn' occidental common cold virus.

Atishoo.

The Golden Herm stood in the green wood.

This wood is, of course, nowhere near Athens; the script is a positive maze of false leads. The wood is really located somewhere in the English midlands, possibly near Bletchley, where the great decoding machine was sited. Correction: this wood *was* located in the English midlands until oak, ash and thorn were chopped down to make room for a motorway a few years ago. However, since the wood existed only as a structure of the imagination, in the first place, it will remain, in the second place, as a green, decorative margin to the eternity the poet promised for himself. The English poet; his is, essentially, an English wood. It is *the* English wood.

The English wood is nothing like the dark, necromantic forest in which the Northern European imagination begins and ends, where its dead and the witches live, and Baba-yaga stalks about in her house with chicken's feet looking for children in order to eat them. No. There is a qualitative, not a quantitative, difference between this wood and that forest. The difference does not exist just because a wood contains fewer trees than a forest and covers less ground. That is just one of the causes of the difference and does not explain the effects of the difference.

For example, an English wood, however marvellous, however metamorphic, cannot, by definition, be trackless, although it might well be formidably labyrinthine. Yet there is always a way out of a maze, and, even if you cannot find it for a while, you know that it is there. A maze is a construct of the human mind, and not unlike it; lost in the wood, this analogy will always console. But to be lost in the forest is to be lost to *this* world, to be abandoned by the light, to lose yourself utterly with no guarantee you will either find yourself or else be found, to be committed against your will – or, worse, of your own desire – to a perpetual absence from humanity, an existential catastrophe, for the forest is as infinitely boundless as the human heart.

But the wood is finite, a closure; you purposely mislay your way in the wood, for the sake of the pleasure of roving, the temporary confusion of direction is in the nature of a holiday from which you will come home refreshed, with your pockets full of nuts, your hands full of wildflowers and the cast feather of a bird in your cap. That forest is haunted; this wood is enchanted.

The very perils of the wood, so many audio-visual aids to a pleasurable titillation of mild fear; the swift rattle of an ascending pheasant, velvet thud of an owl, red glide of the fox – these may all 'give you a fright', but, here, neither hobgoblin nor foul fiend can daunt your spirit because the English lobs and hobs reflect nothing more than a secular faith in the absence of harm in nature, part of the credit sheet of a temperate climate. (Here that, Herm? No tigers burn bright, here; no scaly pythons, no armoured scorpions.) Since the last English wolf was killed, there is nothing savage among the trees to terrify you. All is mellow in the filtered light, where Robin Wood, the fertility spirit, lurks in the green shade; this wood is kind to lovers.

Indeed, you might call the wood the common garden of the village, a garden almost as intentionally wild as one of Bacon's 'natural wildernesses', where every toad carries a jewel in its head and all the flowers have names, nothing is unknown – this kind of wilderness is not an otherness.

And always something to eat! Mother Nature's greengrocery store; sorrel for soup, mushrooms, dandelion and chickweed – there's your salad, mint and thyme for seasoning, wild strawberries and blackberries and, in the autumn, a plenitude of nuts. Nebuchadnezzar, in an English wood, need not have confined his appetite to grass.

The English wood offers us a glimpse of a green, unfallen world a little closer to Paradise than we are.

Such is the English wood in which we see the familiar fairies, the blundering fiancés, the rude mechanicals. This is the true Shakespearian wood – but it is not the wood of Shakespeare's time, which did not know itself to be Shakespearian, and therefore felt no need to keep up appearances. No. The wood we have just described is that of nineteenth-century nostalgia, which disinfected the wood, cleansing it of the grave, hideous and elemental beings with which the superstition of an earlier age had filled it. Or, rather, denaturing, castrating these beings until they came to look just as they do in those photographs of fairy folk that so enraptured Conan Doyle. It is Mendelssohn's wood.

'Enter these enchanted woods . . .' who could resist such a magical invitation?

However, as it turns out, the Victorians did not leave the woods in quite the state they might have wished to find them.

The Puck was obsessively fascinated by the exotic visitor. In some respects, it was the attraction of opposites, for, whereas the Golden Herm was sm-o-o-o-th, the Puck was hairy. On these chill nights of June, Puck inside his hairy pelt was the only one kept warm at all. Hairy. Shaggy. Especially about the thighs. (And, h'm, on the palms of his hands.)

Shaggy as a Shetland pony when naked and sometimes goes on all fours. When he goes on all fours, he whinnies; or else he barks.

He is the lub, the lubber fiend, and sometimes he plays at being the nut-brown house-sprite for whom a bowl of milk is left outside the door, although, if you want to be rid of him, you must leave him a pair of trousers; he thinks a gift of trousers is an insult to his sex, of which he is most proud. Nesting in his luxuriant pubic curls, that gleam with the deep-fried gloss of the woodcarvings of Grinling Gibbons, see his testicles, wrinkled ripe as medlars.

Puck loves hokey-pokey and peek-a-boo. He has relations all over the place – in Iceland, the *puki*; the Devonshire *pixy*; the *spook* of the Low Countries are all his next of kin and not one of them is up to any good. That Puck!

The tender little exiguities that cluster round the Queen of the Fairies do not like to play with the Puck because he is so rough and rips their painted wings in games of tag and pulls the phantasmal legs off the grey gnats that draw Titania's wee coach through the air, kisses the girls and makes them cry, creeps up and swings between the puce, ithyphallic foxglove spires above Titania's bed so the raindrops fall and scatter in a drenching shower and up she wakes. Spiteful!

Puck is no more polymorphously perverse than all the rest of these sub-microscopic particles, his peers, yet there is something particularly rancid and offensive about his buggery and his undinism and his frotteurism and his scopophilia and his – indeed, my very paper would *blush*, go pink as an invoice, should I write down upon it some of the things Puck gets up to down in the reeds by the river, as he is distantly related to the great bad god Pan and, when in the mood, behaves in a manner uncommon in an English wood, although familiar in the English public school.

By the Puck's phallic orientation, you know him for a creature of King Oberon's.

Hairy Puck fell in love with Golden Herm and often came to frolic round the lovely living statue in the moonlit glade, although he could not, happily for the Herm, get near enough to touch because Titania forethoughtfully had thrown a magical *cordon sanitaire* around her lovely adoptive, so that s/he was, as it were, in an invisible glass case, such as s/he might find herself in, some centuries later, in the Victoria and Albert Museum. Against this transparent, intangible barrier, the Puck often flattened still further his already snub nose.

The Herm removed his/her left foot from its snug nest in her/his crotch and placed it on the ground. With one single, fluent, gracile movement of transition, s/he shifted on to the *other* leg. The lotus and the snake, on either arm, stayed where they were.

The Puck, pressed tight against Titania's magic, sighed heavily, stepped back a few paces and began energetically to play with himself.

Have *you* seen fairy sperm? We mortals call it, cuckoo spit.

And no passing, clayey mortal, tramping through the wood on great, heavy feet, scattering the fairies who twitter like bats in their fright, just as such a mortal could never hear them, so he would never spot the unafraid Herm, sticking stock-still as a trance.

And if you *did* chance to spy him/her, you would think the little yellow idol was a talisman dropped from a gypsy pocket, perhaps, or a charm fallen off a girl's bracelet, or else the gift from inside a very expensive cracker.

Yet, if you picked up the beautiful object and held it on the palm of your hand, you would feel how warm it was, as if somebody had been holding it tight before you came and only just put it down.

And, if you watched long enough, you would see the golden sequins of the eyelids move.

At which a wind of strangeness would rise and blow away the wood and all within it.

Just as your shadow can grow big and then shrink to almost nothing, and then swell up, again, so can *these* shadows, these insubstantial bubbles of the earth, these 'beings' to whom the verb, 'to be', may not be properly applied, since, in our sense, they are not. They *cannot* be; they cannot cast their own shadows, for who has seen the shadow of a shadow? Their existences are necessarily moot – do *you* believe in fairies? Their lives lead always just teasingly almost out of the corners of the eyes of their observers, so it is possible they were only, all the time, a trick of the light

. . . such half-being, with such a lack of public acknowledgement, is not conducive to any kind of visual consistency among them. So they may take what shapes they please.

The Puck can turn himself into anything he likes: a three-legged stool, in order to perpetrate the celebrated trick ('Then slip I from her bum, down topples she') so beloved in the lower forms of grammar schools when the play is read aloud round the class because it is suitable for children because it is about fairies; a baby Fiat; a grand piano; anything!

Except the lover of the Golden Herm.

In his spare moments, when he was not off about his Master's various businesses, the Puck, wistfully lingering outside the Herm's magic circle like an urchin outside a candy shop, concluded that, in order to take full advantage of the sexual facilities offered him by the Herm, should the barrier between them ever be removed – and, unlikely as this eventuality might be, the Puck's motto was 'Be Prepared'! – if there was to be intercourse between himself and the Golden Herm, then the Herm's partner would require a similar set of equipment to the Herm in order to effect maximally satisfactory congress.

Then the Puck further concluded that the equipment of the Herm's hypothetical partner would need, however, to be attached in *reversed order* to that of the Herm, in order to procure a perfect fit and no fumbling; the Puck, a constant inquisitive spy on mortal couples come to make the beast with two backs in what they mistakenly believed to be privacy, had noticed there is a vexed question of handedness about caresses, so that all right-handed lovers truly require left-handed lovers during the pre-liminaries to the act, and Mother Nature, when she cast the human mould, took no account of foreplay, which alone distinguishes us from the beasts when we are being beastly.

Try, try as he might, try and try again, the Puck could not get it quite right, although, after strenuous effort, he at last succeeded in turning himself into a perfect simulacrum of the Herm and would, at odd moments, adopt the Herm's form and posture and stand facing him in the wood, a living mirror of the living statue, except for the fierce erection the satyromaniac Puck could not subdue when in the presence of his love.

The Herm continued to smile inscrutably, except when he sneezed.

But all of them can grow BIG! then shrink down to . . . the size of dots, of less than dots, again. Every last one of them is of such elastic – since incorporeal – substance. Consider the Queen of the Fairies.

Her very name, Titania, bears witness to her descent from the giant race of the Titans; and 'descend' might seem apt enough, at first, to describe the declension when she manifests herself under her alias, Mab, or, in Wales, Mabh, and rules over the other diminutives, herself the size of the solitaire in an engagement ring, as infinitely little as her forebears were infinitely large.

'Now, I do call my horned master, the Horn of Plenty, but as for my missus –' said the Puck, in his inimitable Worcestershire drawl.

Like a Japanese water-flower dropped in a glass of water, Titania grows . . .

In the dewy wood tinselled with bewildering moonlight, the bumbling, tumbling babies of the fairy crèche trip over the hem of her dress, which is no more nor less than the margin of the wood itself; they stumble in the tangled grass as they play with the coneys, the quick brown fox-cubs, the russet fieldmice and the wee scraps of grey voles, blind velvet Mole and striped Brock with his questing snout – all the denizens of the woodland are her embroiderings, and the birds flutter round her head, settle on her shoulders and make their nests in her great abundance of disordered hair, in which are plaited poppies and the ears of wheat.

The arrival of the Queen is announced by no fanfare of trumpets but the ash-soft lullaby of wood doves and the liquid coloratura blackbird. Moonlight falls like milk upon her naked breasts.

She is like a double bed; or, a table laid for a wedding breakfast; or, a fertility clinic.

In her eyes are babies. When she looks at you, you helplessly reduplicate. Her eyes provoke engendering.

Correction: used to provoke.

But not *this* year. Frosts have blasted the fruit blossom, rain has rotted all the corn so her garland is not gold but greenish and phosphorescent with blight. The acres of the rye have been invaded with ergot and, this year, eating bread will make you mad. The floods broke down the Bridge of Ware. The beasts refuse to couple; the cow rejects the bull and the bull keeps himself to himself. Even the goats, hitherto synonymous with lechery, prefer to curl up with a good book. The very worms no longer agitate the humus with their undulating and complex embraces. In the wood, a chaste, conventual calm reigns over everything, as if the foul weather had put everybody off.

The wonderful giantess manifested herself with an owl on her shoulder and an apron-full of roses and of babies so rosy the children could scarcely be distinguished from the flowers. She picked up her defunct friend's child, the Herm. The Herm stood on one leg on the palm of Titania's hand and smiled the inscrutable, if manic, smile of the figures in Hindu erotic sculpture.

'My husband shall not have you!' cried Titania. 'He shan't! *I* shall keep you!'

At that, thunder crashed, the heavens, which, for a brief moment, had sealed themselves up, now reopened again with redoubled fury, and all the drenched babies in Titania's pinafore coughed and sneezed. The worms in the rosebuds woke up at the clamour and began to gnaw.

But the Queen stowed the tiny Herm safe away between her breasts as if s/he were a locket and herself diminished until she was a suitable size to enjoy her niece or nephew or nephew/niece *à choix* in the obscurity of an acorn-cup.

'But she cannot put horns on her husband, for he is antlered, already,' opined the Puck, changing back into himself and skipping across the glade to the heels of his master. For no roe-buck now raises his head behind that gorse bush to watch these goings on; Oberon is antlered like a ten-point stag.

Among the props of the Globe Theatre, along with the thunder-making machine and the bearskins, is listed a 'robe for to go invisible'. By his coat, you understand that Oberon is to remain unseen as he broods magisterial but impotent above the scarcely discernible quiverings among last year's oak leaves that conceal his wife and the golden bone of contention that has come between the elemental lovers.

High in the thick of a dripping hedge of honeysuckle, a wee creature was extracting a tritonic, numinous, luxuriantly perfumed melody from the pan-pipes of the wild woodbine. The tune broke off as the player convulsed with ugly coughing. He gobbed phlegm, that flew through the air until its trajectory was interrupted by a cowslip, to whose freckled ear the translucent pustule clung. The infinitesimal then took up his tootling again.

The Herm's golden skin is made of beaten gold but the flesh beneath it has been marinated in: black pepper, red chilli, yellow turmeric, cloves, coriander, cumin, fenugreek, ginger, mace, nutmeg, allspice, khuskhus, garlic, tamarind, coconut, candlenut, lemon grass, galangal and now and then you get – phew! – a whiff of asafoetida. Hot stuff! Were the Herm to be served piled up on a lordly platter and garnished with shreds of its own outer casing, s/he would then resemble that royal dish, *moglai biriani*, which is decorated with edible gold shavings in order, so they say, to aid digestion. Nothing so deliciously aromatic as the Herm has ever been scented before in England's green and pleasant land, still labouring as it is at this point in time under its unrelieved late medieval diet of boiled cabbage. The Herm is hot and sweet as if drenched in sun and honey, but Oberon is the colour of ashes.

The Puck, tormented for lack of the Herm, pulled up a mandrake and sunk his prodigious tool in the cleft of the reluctant root, which shrieked mournfully but to no avail as old shaggylugs had his way with it.

Distemperate weather! It's raining, it's pouring; the earth is in estrangement from itself, the withering buds tumble out of the Queen's apron and rot on the mulch, for Oberon has put a stop to reproduction. But still Titania hugs the Herm to her shrivelling bosoms and will not let her husband have the wee thing, not even for one minute. Did she not give a sacred promise to a friend?

What does the Herm want?

The Herm wants to know what 'want' means.

'I am unfamiliar with the concept of desire. I am the unique and perfect, paradigmatic Hermaphrodite, provoking on all sides desire yet myself transcendent, the unmoved mover, the still eye of the tempest, exemplary and self-sufficient, the beginning and the end.'

Titania, despairing of the Herm's male aspect, inserted a tentative forefinger in the female orifice. The Herm felt bored.

Oberon watched the oak leaves shiver and said nothing, for he was choked with balked longing for the golden, half and halfy thing with its salivatory perfume. He took off his invisible disguise and made himself gigantic and bulked up in the night sky over the wood, arms akimbo, blotting out the moon, naked but for his buskins and his great codpiece. The mossy antlers on his forehead aren't the half of it, he wears a crown made out of yellowish vertebrae of unmentionable mammals, down from beneath which his black hair drops straight as light. Since he is in his malign aspect, he has put on, furthermore, a necklace of suggestively little skulls, which might be those of the babies he has plucked from human cradles – do not forget, in German, they call him Erl-King.

His face, breast and thighs he has daubed with charcoal; Oberon, lord of night and silence, of the grave silence of endless night, Lord of Plutonic dark. His hair, long, it never saw scissors; but he has this peculiarity – no hair at all on either chop or chin, nor his shins, neither, but all his face bald as an egg except for the eyebrows, that meet in the middle.

Indeed, who in their right minds would trust a child to this man?

When Oberon cheers up a bit, he lets the sun come out and then he'll hang little silver bells along his codpiece and they go jingle jangle jingle when he walks up and down and round about, the pretty chinking sounds suspended wriggling in the air like homunculi wherever he has passed.

And if he is not a creature of the dream, then surely you have forgotten your dreams.

The Puck, too, yearning and thwarted as he was, found himself helplessly turning himself into the thing he longed for, and, under the faintly twitching oak leaves, became yellow, metallic, double-sexed and extravagantly precious-looking. There the Puck stood on one leg, the living image of the Herm, and glittered.

Oberon saw him.

Oberon stooped down and picked up the Puck and stood him, a simulated Yogic tree, on his palm. A misty look came into Oberon's eyes. The Puck knew he had no option but to go through with it.

Atishoo!

Titania tenderly wiped the Herm's nose with the edge of her petticoat, on which the flowers are all drooping, shedding embroidery stitches, the fruits are cankering and spotting and coming undone for, if Oberon is the Horn of Plenty, then Titania is the Cauldron of Generation and, unless he gives her a stir, now and then, with his great pot stick, the cauldron will go off the boil.

Lie close and sleep, said Titania to the Herm. My fays shall lullaby you as we cuddle up on my mattress of dandelion down.

The draggled fairies obediently started in on a chorus of: 'Ye spotted snakes with double tongue,' but were all so afflicted by coughing and sneezing and rawness of the throat and rheumy eyes and gasping for breath and all the other symptoms of rampant influenza that their hoarse voices petered out before they reached the bit about the newts and after that the only sound in the entire wood was the pit-pattering of the rain on the leaves.

The orchestra has laid down its instruments. The curtain rises. The play begins.

Peter and the Wolf

At length the grandeur of the mountains becomes monotonous; with familiarity, the landscape ceases to provoke awe and wonder and the traveller sees the alps with the indifferent eye of those who always live there. Above a certain line, no trees grow. Shadows of clouds move across the bare alps as freely as the clouds themselves move across the sky.

A girl from a village on the lower slopes left her widowed mother to marry a man who lived up in the empty places. Soon she was pregnant. In October, there was a severe storm. The old woman knew her daughter was near her time and waited for a message but none arrived. After the storm passed, the old woman went up to see for herself, taking her grown son with her because she was afraid.

From a long way off, they saw no smoke rising from the chimney. Solitude yawned round them. The open door banged backwards and forwards on its hinges. Solitude engulfed them. There were traces of wolf-dung on the floor so they knew wolves had been in the house but left the corpse of the young mother alone although of her baby nothing was left except some mess that showed it had been born. Nor was there a trace of the son-in-law but a gnawed foot in a boot.

They wrapped the dead in a quilt and took it home with them. Now it was late. The howling of the wolves mutilated the approaching silence of the night.

Winter came with icy blasts, when everyone stays indoors and stokes the fire. The old woman's son married the blacksmith's daughter and she moved in with them. The snow melted and it was spring. By the next Christmas, there was a bouncing grandson. Time passed. More children came.

When the eldest grandson, Peter, reached his seventh summer, he was old enough to go up the mountain with his father, as the men did every year, to let the goats feed on the young grass. There Peter sat in the new sunlight, plaiting the straw for baskets, until he saw the thing he had been taught most to fear advancing silently along the lea of an outcrop of rock. Then another wolf, following the first one.

If they had not been the first wolves he had ever seen, the boy would not have inspected them so closely, their plush, grey pelts, of which the hairs are tipped with white, giving them a ghostly look, as if they were on the point of dissolving at the edges; their sprightly, plumey tails; their acute, inquisitive masks.

Then Peter saw that the third wolf was a prodigy, a marvel, a naked one, going on all fours, as they did, but hairless as regards the body although hair grew around its head.

The sight of this bald wolf so fascinated him that he would have lost his flock, perhaps himself been eaten and certainly been beaten to the bone for negligence had not the goats themselves raised their heads, snuffed danger and run off, bleating and whinnying, so that the men came, firing guns, making hullabaloo, scaring the wolves away.

His father was too angry to listen to what Peter said. He cuffed Peter round the head and sent him home. His mother was feeding this year's baby. His grandmother sat at the table, shelling peas into a pot.

'There was a little girl with the wolves, granny,' said Peter. Why was he so sure it had been a little girl? Perhaps because her hair was so long, so long and lively. 'A little girl about my age, from her size,' he said.

His grandmother threw a flat pod out of the door so the chickens could peck it up.

'I saw a little girl with the wolves,' he said.

His grandmother tipped water into the pot, got up from the table and hung the pot of peas on the hook over the fire. There wasn't time, that night, but next morning, very early, she herself took the boy back up the mountain.

'Tell your father what you told me.'

They went to look at the wolves' tracks. On a bit of dampish ground they found a print, not like that of a dog's pad, much less like that of a child's footprint, yet Peter worried and puzzled over it until he made sense of it.

'She was running on all fours with her arse stuck up in the air . . . therefore . . . she'd put all her weight on the ball of her foot, wouldn't she? And splay out her toes, see . . . like that.'

He went barefoot in summer, like all the village children; he inserted the ball of his own foot in the print, to show his father what kind of mark he would have made if he, too, always ran on all fours.

'No use for a heel, if you run that way. So she doesn't have a heelprint. Stands to reason.'

At last his father made a slow acknowledgement of Peter's powers of deduction, giving the child a veiled glance of disquiet. It was a clever child.

They soon found her. She was asleep. Her spine had grown so supple she could curl into a perfect C. She woke up when she heard them and ran, but somebody caught her with a sliding noose at the end of a rope;

the noose over her head jerked tight and she fell to the ground with her eyes popping and rolling. A big, grey, angry bitch appeared out of nowhere but Peter's father blasted it to bits with his shotgun. The girl would have choked if the old woman hadn't taken her head on her lap and pulled the knot loose. The girl bit the grandmother's hand.

The girl scratched and fought until the men tied her wrists and ankles together with twine and slung her from a pole to carry her back to the village. Then she went limp. She didn't scream or shout, she didn't seem to be able to, she made only a few dull, guttural sounds in the back of her throat, and, though she did not seem to know how to cry, water trickled out of the corners of her eyes.

How burned she was by the weather! Bright brown all over; and how filthy she was! Caked with mud and dirt. And every inch of her chestnut hide was scored and scabbed with dozens of scars of sharp abrasions of rock and thorn. Her hair dragged on the ground as they carried her along; it was stuck with burrs and it was so dirty you could not see what colour it might be. She was dreadfully verminous. She stank. She was so thin that all her ribs stuck out. The fine, plump, potato-fed boy was far bigger than she, although she was a year or so older.

Solemn with curiosity, he trotted behind her. Granny stumped alongside with her bitten hand wrapped up in her apron. Once the girl was dumped on the earth floor of her grandmother's house, the boy secretly poked at her left buttock with his forefinger, out of curiosity, to see what she felt like. She felt warm but hard. She did not so much as twitch when he touched her. She had given up the struggle; she lay trussed on the floor and pretended to be dead.

Granny's house had the one large room which, in winter, they shared with the goats. As soon as it caught a whiff of her, the big tabby mouser hissed like a pricked balloon and bounded up the ladder that went to the hayloft above. Soup smoked on the fire and the table was laid. It was now about supper-time but still quite light; night comes late on the summer mountain.

'Untie her,' said the grandmother.

Her son wasn't willing at first but the old woman would not be denied, so he got the breadknife and cut the rope round the girl's ankles. All she did was kick, but when he cut the rope round her wrists, it was if he had let a fiend loose. The onlookers ran out of the door, the rest of the family ran for the ladder to the hayloft but Granny and Peter both ran to the door, to shoot the bolt, so she could not get out.

The trapped one knocked round the room. Bang – over went the table. Crash, tinkle – the supper dishes smashed. Bang, crash tinkle – the dresser fell forward upon the hard white shale of crockery it shed in falling. Over went the meal barrel and she coughed, she sneezed like a child sneezes, no different, and then she bounced around on fear-stiffened legs in a white cloud until the flour settled on everything like a magic powder that made everything strange. Her first frenzy over, she squatted a moment, questing with her long nose and then began to make little rushing sorties, now here, now there, snapping and yelping and tossing her bewildered head.

She never rose up on two legs; she crouched, all the time, on her hands and tiptoes, yet it was not quite like crouching, for you could see how all fours came naturally to her as though she had made a different pact with gravity than we have, and you could see, too, how strong the muscles in her thighs had grown on the mountain, how taut the twanging arches of her feet, and that indeed, she only used her heels when she sat back on her haunches. She growled; now and then she coughed out those intolerable, thick grunts of distress. All you could see of her rolling eyes were the whites, which were the bluish, glaring white of snow.

Several times, her bowels opened, apparently involuntarily. The kitchen smelled like a privy yet even her excrement was different to ours, the refuse of raw, strange, unguessable, wicked feeding, shit of a wolf. Oh, horror!

She bumped into the hearth, knocked over the pan hanging from the hook and the spilled contents put out the fire. Hot soup scalded her forelegs. Shock of pain. Squatting on her hindquarters, holding the hurt paw dangling piteously from its wrist before her, she howled, in high, sobbing arcs.

Even the old woman, who had contracted with herself to love the child of her dead daughter, was frightened when she heard the girl howl.

Peter's heart gave a hop, a skip, so that he had a sensation of falling; he was not conscious of his own fear because he could not take his eyes off the sight of the crevice of her girl-child's sex, that was perfectly visible to him as she sat there square on the base of her spine. The night was now as dark as, at this season, it would go – which is to say, not very dark; a white thread of moon hung in the blond sky at the top of the chimney so that it was neither dark nor light indoors yet the boy could see her intimacy clearly, as if by its own phosphorescence. It exercised an absolute fascination upon him.

Her lips opened up as she howled so that she offered him, without her own intention or volition, a view of a set of Chinese boxes of whorled flesh that seemed to open one upon another into herself, drawing him into an inner, secret place in which destination perpetually receded before him, his first, devastating, vertiginous intimation of infinity.

She howled.

And went on howling until, from the mountain, first singly, then in a complex polyphony, answered at last voices in the same language.

She continued to howl, though now with a less tragic resonance.

Soon it was impossible for the occupants of the house to deny to themselves that the wolves were descended on the village in a pack.

Then she was consoled, sank down, laid her head on her forepaws so that her hair trailed in the cooling soup, and so closed up her forbidden book without the least notion she had ever opened it or that it was banned. Her heavy eyelids closed on her brown, bloodshot eyes. The household gun hung on a nail over the fireplace where Peter's father had put it when he came in but when the man set his foot on the top rung of the ladder in order to come down for his weapon, the girl jumped up, snarling and showing her long yellow canines.

The howling outside was now mixed with the agitated dismay of the domestic beasts. All the other villagers were well locked up at home.

The wolves were at the door.

The boy took hold of his grandmother's uninjured hand. First the old woman would not budge but he gave her a good tug and she came to herself. The girl raised her head suspiciously but let them by. The boy pushed his grandmother up the ladder in front of him and drew it up behind them. He was full of nervous dread. He would have given anything to turn time back, so that he might have run, shouting a warning, when he first caught sight of the wolves, and never seen her.

The door shook as the wolves outside jumped up at it and the screws that held the socket of the bolt to the frame cracked, squeaked and started to give. The girl jumped up, at that, and began to make excited little sallies back and forth in front of the door. The screws tore out of the frame quite soon. The pack tumbled over one another to get inside.

Dissonance. Terror. The clamour within the house was that of all the winds of winter trapped in a box. That which they feared most, outside, was now indoors with them. The baby in the hayloft whimpered and its mother crushed it to her breast as if the wolves might snatch this one away, too; but the rescue party had arrived only in order to collect their fosterling.

They left behind a riotous stench in the house, and white tracks of flour everywhere. The broken door creaked backwards and forwards on its hinges. Black sticks of dead wood from the extinguished fire were scattered on the floor.

Peter thought the old woman would cry, now, but she seemed unmoved. When all was safe, they came down the ladder one by one and, as if released from a spell of silence, burst into excited speech except for the mute old woman and the distraught boy. Although it was well past midnight, the daughter-in-law went to the well for water to scrub the wild smell out of the house. The broken things were cleared up and thrown away. Peter's father nailed the table and the dresser back together. The neighbours came out of their houses, full of amazement; the wolves had not taken so much as a chicken from the hen-coops, not snatched even a single egg.

People brought beer into the starlight, and schnapps made from potatoes, and snacks, because the excitement had made them hungry. That terrible night ended up in one big party but the grandmother would eat or drink nothing and went to bed as soon as her house was clean.

Next day, she went to the graveyard and sat for a while beside her daughter's grave but she did not pray. Then she came home and started chopping cabbage for the evening meal but had to leave off because her bitten hand was festering.

That winter, during the leisure imposed by the snow, after his grandmother's death, Peter asked the village priest to teach him to read the Bible. The priest gladly complied; Peter was the first of his flock who had ever expressed any interest in learning to read.

The boy became very pious, so much so that his family were startled and impressed. The younger children teased him and called him 'Saint Peter' but that did not stop him sneaking off to church to pray whenever he had a spare moment. In Lent, he fasted to the bone. On Good Friday, he lashed himself. It was as if he blamed himself for the death of the old lady, as if he believed he had brought into the house the fatal infection that had taken her out of it. He was consumed by an imperious passion for atonement. Each night, he pored over his book by the flimsy candlelight, looking for a clue to grace, until his mother shooed him off to sleep.

But, as if to spite the four evangelists he nightly invoked to protect his bed, the nightmare regularly disordered his sleeps. He tossed and turned on the rustling straw pallet he shared with two little ones.

Delighted with Peter's precocious intelligence, the priest started to teach him Latin. Peter visited the priest as his duties with the herd permitted. When he was fourteen, the priest told his parents that Peter should now go to the seminary in the town in the valley where the boy would learn to become a priest himself. Rich in sons, they spared one to God, since his books and his praying made him a stranger to them. After the goats came down from the high pasture for the winter, Peter set off. It was October.

At the end of his first day's travel, he reached a river that ran from the mountain into the valley. The nights were already chilly; he lit himself a fire, prayed, ate bread and cheese his mother had packed for him and slept as well as he could. In spite of his eagerness to plunge into the white world of penance and devotion that awaited him, he was anxious and troubled for reasons he could not explain to himself.

In the first light, the light that no more than clarifies darkness like egg shells dropped in cloudy liquid, he went down to the river to drink and to wash his face. It was so still he could have been the one thing living.

Her forearms, her loins and her legs were thick with hair and the hair on her head hung round her face in such a way that you could hardly make out her features. She crouched on the other side of the river. She was lapping up water so full of mauve light that it looked as if she were drinking up the dawn as fast as it appeared yet all the same the air grew pale while he was looking at her.

Solitude and silence; all still.

She could never have acknowledged that the reflection beneath her in the river was that of herself. She did not know she had a face; she had never known she had a face and so her face itself was the mirror of a different kind of consciousness than ours is, just as her nakedness, without innocence or display, was that of our first parents, before the Fall. She was hairy as Magdalen in the wilderness and yet repentance was not within her comprehension.

Language crumbled into dust under the weight of her speechlessness.

A pair of cubs rolled out of the bushes, cuffing one another. She did not pay them any heed.

The boy began to tremble and shake. His skin prickled. He felt he had been made of snow and now might melt. He mumbled something, or sobbed.

She cocked her head at the vague, river-washed sound and the cubs heard it, too, left off tumbling and ran to burrow their scared heads in her side. But she decided, after a moment, there was no danger and lowered her muzzle, again, to the surface of the water that took hold of her hair and spread it out around her head.

When she finished her drink, she backed a few paces, shaking her wet pelt. The little cubs fastened their mouths on her dangling breasts.

Peter could not help it, he burst out crying. He had not cried since his grandmother's funeral. Tears rolled down his face and splashed on the grass. He blundered forward a few steps into the river with his arms held open, intending to cross over to the other side to join her in her marvellous and private grace, impelled by the access of an almost visionary ecstasy. But his cousin took fright at the sudden movement, wrenched her teats away from the cubs and ran off. The squeaking cubs scampered behind. She ran on hands and feet as if that were the only way to run towards the high ground, into the bright maze of the uncompleted dawn.

When the boy recovered himself, he dried his tears on his sleeve, took off his soaked boots and dried his feet and legs on the tail of his shirt. Then he ate something from his pack, he scarcely knew what, and continued on the way to the town; but what would he do at the seminary, now? For now he knew there was nothing to be afraid of.

He experienced the vertigo of freedom.

He carried his boots slung over his shoulder by the laces. They were a great burden. He debated with himself whether or not to throw them away but, when he came to a paved road, he had to put them on, although they were still damp.

The birds woke up and sang. The cool, rational sun surprised him; morning had broken on his exhilaration and the mountain now lay behind him. He looked over his shoulder and saw, how, with distance, the mountain began to acquire a flat, two-dimensional look. It was already turning into a picture of itself, into the postcard hastily bought as a souvenir of childhood at a railway station or a border post, the newspaper cutting, the snapshot he would show in strange towns, strange cities, other countries he could not, at this moment, imagine, whose names he did not yet know, places where he would say, in strange languages, 'That was where I spent my childhood. Imagine!'

He turned and stared at the mountain for a long time. He had lived in it for fourteen years but he had never seen it before as it might look to someone who had not known it as almost a part of the self, so, for the first time, he saw the primitive, vast, magnificent, barren, unkind, simplicity of the mountain. As he said goodbye to it, he saw it turn into so much scenery, into the wonderful backcloth for an old country tale, tale of a child suckled by wolves, perhaps, or of wolves nursed by a woman.

Then he determinedly set his face towards the town and tramped onwards, into a different story.

'If I look back again,' he thought with a last gasp of superstitious terror, 'I shall turn into a pillar of salt.'

The Kitchen Child

'Born in a trunk', they say when a theatrical sups grease-paint with
mother's milk, and if there be a culinary equivalent of the phrase then
surely I merit it, for was I not conceived the while a soufflé rose? A lobster
soufflé, very choice, twenty-five minutes in a medium oven.

And the very first soufflé that ever in her life as cook me mam was
called upon to make, ordered up by some French duc, house guest of Sir
and Madam, me mam pleased as punch to fix it for him since few if any
fins becs pecked their way to our house, not even during the two weeks of
the Great Grouse Shoot when nobs rolled up in droves to score the
feathered booty of the skies. Especially not then. Palates like shoe leather.
'Pearls before swine,' my mother would have said as she reluctantly sent
the four and twenty courses of her Art up to the dining room, except that
pigs would have exhibited more gourmandise. I tell you, the English
country house, yes! that's the place for grub; but, only when Sir and
Madam are *pas chez lui*. It is the staff who keep up the standards.

For Madam would touch nothing but oysters and grapes on ice three
times a day, due to the refinement of her sensibility, while Sir fasted until
a devilled bone at sundown, his tongue having been burned out by curry
when he was governing a bit of Poonah. (I reckon those Indians hotted up
his fodder out of spite. Oh, the cook's vengeance, when it strikes –
terrible!) And as for the Shooters of Grouse, all they wanted was
sandwiches for hors d'oeuvres, sandwiches for entrées, followed by
sandwiches, sandwiches, sandwiches, and their hip flasks kept re-
plenished, oh, yes, wash it down with the amber fluid and who can tell
how it tastes?

So me mam took great pains with the construction of this, her very first
lobster soufflé, sending the boy who ground knives off on his bike to the
sea, miles, for the beast itself and then the boiling of it alive, how it come
squeaking piteously crawling out of the pot etc. etc. etc. so me mam all
a-flutter before she so much as separated the eggs.

Then, just as she bent over the range to stir the flour into the butter, a
pair of hands clasped tight around her waist. Thinking, at first, it was but
kitchen horseplay, she twitched her ample hips to put him off as she slid
the egg yolks into the roux. But as she mixed in the lobster meat, diced
up, all nice, she felt those hands stray higher.

That was when too much cayenne went in. She always regretted that. And as she was folding in the toppling contents of the bowl of beaten egg-white, God knows what it was he got up to but so much so she flings all into the white dish with abandon and:

'To hell with it!'

Into the oven goes the soufflé; the oven door slams shut. I draw a veil.

'But, mam!' I often begged her. '*Who was that man?*'

'Lawks a mercy, child,' says she. 'I never thought to ask. I were that worried the wallop I give the oven door would bring the soufflé down.'

But, no. The soufflé went up like a montgolfier and, as soon as its golden head knocked imperiously against the oven door, she bust through the veil I have discreetly drawn over this scene of passion and emerged, smoothing her apron, in order to extract the exemplary dish amidst oohs and aahs and of the assembled kitchen staff, some forty-five in number.

But not quite exemplary. The cook met her match in the eater. The housekeeper brings his plate herself, slaps it down. 'He said: "*Trop de cayenne,*" and scraped it off his plate into the fire,' she announces with a gratified smirk. She is a model of refinement and always very particular about her aspirates. She hiccups. She even says the 'h' in 'hic'.

My mother weeps for shame.

'What we need here is a congtinental – hic – chef to improve *le ton*,' menaces the housekeeper, tossing me mam a killing look as she sweeps out the door for me mam is a simple Yorkshire lass for all she has magic in her fingers but no room for two queens in this hive, the housekeeper hates her. And the housekeeper is pricked perpetually by the fancy for the importation of a Carême or a Soyer with moustaches like hatracks to *croquembouche* her and *milly filly* her as is all the rage.

'For isn't it Alberlin, chef to the dear Devonshires; and Crépin, at the Duchess of Sutherland's. Then there's Labalme, with the Duke of Beaufort's household, doncherno . . . and the Queen, bless her, has her Ménager . . . while we're stuck with that fat cow who can't speak nothing but broad Yorkshire, never out of her carpet slippers . . .'

Conceived upon a kitchen table, born upon a kitchen floor; no bells rang to welcome me but, far more aptly, my arrival heralded by a bang! bang! bang! on every skillet in the place, a veritable fusillade of copper-bottom kitchen tympani; and the merry clatter of ladle against dish-cover; and the very turnspit dogs all went: 'Bow wow!'

It being, as you might yourself compute, a good three months off October, Sir and Madam being in London the housekeeper maintains a fine style all by herself, sitting in her parlour partaking of the best Bohea

from a Meissen cup, to which she adds a judicious touch of rum from the
locked bottles to which she's forged a key in her ample leisure. The
housekeeper's little skivvy, that she keeps to fetch, carry and lick boot,
just topping the tea-cup up with old Jamaica, all hell breaks loose below
stairs as if a Chinese orchestra started up its woodblocks and xylophones,
crash, wallop.

'What on earth are the – hick – lower ordures up to?' elocutes the
housekeeper in ladylike and dulcet tones, giving the ear of the skivvy a
quick but vicious tug to jerk the gossip out of her.

'Oh, madamissima!' quavers the poor little skivvyette. ''Tis nobbut
the cook's babby!'

'The cook's baby?!?'

Due to my mother's corpulence, which is immense, she's round as the
'o' in 'obese', and the great loyalty and affection towards her of all the
kitchen staff, the housekeeper knew nothing of my imminence but, amid
her waxing wroth, also glad to hear it, since she thought she spied a way
to relieve my mother of her post due to this unsolicited arrival and then
nag Sir and Madam to get in some mincing and pomaded gent to
chaudfroid and gêlée and butter up. Below stairs she descends forthwith, a
stately yet none too stable progress due to the rum with a dash of tea she
sips all day, the skivvy running in front of her to throw wide the door.

What a spectacle greets her! Raphael might have sketched it, had he
been in Yorkshire at the time. My mother, wreathed in smiles, enthroned
on a sack of spuds with, at her breast, her babe, all neatly swaddled in a
new-boiled pudding cloth and the entire kitchen brigade arranged around
her in attitudes of adoration, each brandishing a utensil and giving out
therewith that merry rattle of the ladles, yours truly's first lullaby.

Alas, my cradle song soon peters out in the odd thwack and tinkle as
the housekeeper cast her coldest eye.

'What's – hic – this?'

'A bonny boy!' croons me mam, planting a smacking kiss on the tender
forehead pressed against her pillowing bosom.

'Out of the house for this!' cries the housekeeper. 'Hic,' she adds.

But what a clang and clamour she unleashes with that demand; as if
she'd let off a bomb in a hardware store, for all present (except my mother
and myself) attack their improvised instruments with renewed vigour,
chanting in unison:

'The kitchen child! The kitchen child! You can't turn out the kitchen
child!'

And that was the truth of the matter; who else could I claim as my
progenitor if not the greedy place itself, that, if it did not make me, all the
same, it caused me to be made? Not one scullery maid nor the littlest

vegetable boy could remember who or what it was which visited my mother that soufflé morning, every hand in the kitchen called to cut sandwiches, but some fat shape seemed to have haunted the place, drawn to the kitchen as a ghost to the dark; had not that gourmet duc kept a gourmet valet? Yet his outlines melt like aspic in the heat from the range.

'The kitchen child!'

The kitchen brigade made such a din that the housekeeper retreated to revive herself with another tot of rum in her private parlour, for, faced with a mutiny amongst the pans, she discovered little valour in her spirit and went to sulk in her tent.

The first toys I played with were colanders, egg whisks and saucepan lids. I took my baths in the big tureen in which the turtle soup was served. They gave up salmon until I could toddle because, as for my crib, what else but the copper salmon kettle? And this kettle was stowed way up high on the mantelshelf so I could snooze there snug and warm out of harm's way, soothed by the delicious odours and appetising sounds of the preparation of nourishment, and there I cooed my way through babyhood above that kitchen as if I were its household deity high in my tiny shrine.

And, indeed, is there not something holy about a great kitchen? Those vaults of soot-darkened stone far above me, where the hams and strings of onions and bunches of dried herbs dangle, looking somewhat like the regimental banners that unfurl above the aisles of old churches. The cool, echoing flags scrubbed spotless twice a day by votive persons on their knees. The scoured gleam of row upon row of metal vessels dangling from hooks or reposing on their shelves till needed with the air of so many chalices waiting for the celebration of the sacrament of food. And the range like an altar, yes, an altar, before which my mother bowed in perpetual homage, a fringe of sweat upon her upper lip and fire glowing in her cheeks.

At three years old she gave me flour and lard and straightaway I invented shortcrust. I being too little to manage the pin, she hoists me on her shoulders to watch her as she rolls out the dough upon the marble slab, then sets me to stamp out the tartlets for myself, tears of joy at my precocity trickling down her cheeks, lets me dollop on the damson jam and lick the spoon for my reward. By three and a half, I've progressed to rough puff and, after that, no holding me. She perches me on a tall stool so I can reach to stir the sauce, wraps me in her pinny that goes round and round and round me thrice, tucks it in at the waist else I trip over it head first into my own Hollandaise. So I become her acolyte.

Reading and writing come to me easy. I learn my letters as follows: A for asparagus, *asperges au beurre fondue* (though never, for my mother's sake, with a *sauce bâtarde*); B for *boeuf*, baron of, roasted mostly, with a *pouding Yorkshire* patriotically sputtering away beneath it in the dripping pan; C for carrots, *carrottes*, *choufleur*, *camembert* and so on, right down to *Zabaglione*, although I often wonder what use the X might be, since it figures in no cook's alphabet.

And I stick as close to that kitchen as the *croûte* to a *pâté* or the mayonnaise to an *oeuf*. First, I stand on that stool to my saucepans; then on an upturned bucket; then on my own two feet. Time passes.

Life in this remote mansion flows by a tranquil stream, only convulsing into turbulence once a year and then for two weeks only, but that fuss enough, the Grouse Shoot, when they all come from town to set us by the ears.

Although Sir and Madam believe their visit to be the very and unique reason for the existences of each and every one of us, the yearly climacteric of our beings, when their staff, who, as far as *they* are concerned, sleep out a hibernation the rest of the year, now spring to life like Sleeping Beauty when her prince turns up, in truth, we get on so well without them during the other eleven and a half months that the arrival of Themselves is a chronic interruption of our routine. We sweat out the fortnight of their presence with as ill a grace as gentlefolk forced by reduced circumstances to take paying guests into their home, and as for *haute cuisine*, forget it; sandwiches, sandwiches, sandwiches, all they want is sandwiches.

And never again, ever again, a special request for a soufflé, lobster or otherwise. Me mam always a touch broody come the Grouse Shoot, moody, distracted, and, even though no order came, nevertheless, every year, she would prepare her lobster soufflé all the same, send the grinding boy off for the lobster, boil it alive, beat the eggs, make the panada etc. etc. etc., as if the doing of the thing were a magic ritual that would raise up out of the past the great question mark from whose loins her son had sprung so that, perhaps, she could get a good look at his face, this time. Or, perhaps, there was some other reason. But she never said either way. In due course, she could construct the airiest, most savoury soufflé that ever lobster graced; but nobody arrived to eat it and none of the kitchen had the heart. So, fifteen times in all, the chickens got that soufflé.

Until, one fine October day, the mist rising over the moors like the steam off a *consommé*, the grouse taking last hearty meals like condemned men, my mother's vigil was at last rewarded. The house party arrives and as it does we hear the faint, nostalgic wail of an accordion as a closed barouche comes bounding up the drive all festooned with the *lys de France*.

Hearing the news, my mother shakes, comes over queer, has to have a sit down on the marble pastry slab whilst I, oh, I prepare to meet my maker, having arrived at the age when a boy most broods about his father.

But what's this? Who trots into the kitchen to pick up the chest of ice the duc ordered for the bottles he brought with him but a beardless boy of his own age or less! And though my mother tries to quizz him on the whereabouts of some other hypothetical valet who, once upon a time, might possibly have made her hand tremble so she lost control of the cayenne, he claims he cannot understand her Yorkshire brogue, he shakes his head, he mimes incomprehension. Then, for the third time in all her life, my mother wept.

First, she wept for shame because she'd spoiled a dish. Next, she wept for joy, to see her son mould the dough. And now she weeps for absence.

But still she sends the grinding boy off for a lobster, for she must and will prepare her autumn ritual, if only as a wake for hope or as the funeral baked meats. And, taking matters into my own hands, I use the quickest method, the dumb waiter, above stairs to make a personal inquiry of this duc as to where his staff might be.

The duc, relaxing before dinner, popping a cork or two, is wrapped up in a velvet quilted smoking jacket much like the coats they put on very well-bred dogs, warming his slippered (Morocco) feet before the blazing fire and singing songs to himself in his native language. And I never saw a fatter man; he'd have given my mother a stone or two and not felt the loss. Round as the 'o' in 'rotund'. If he's taken aback by the apparition of this young chef out of the panelling, he's too much of a gent to show it by a jump or start, asks, what can he do for me? nice as you like and, in my best culinary French, my *petit poi de française*, I stammer out:

'The valet de chambre who accompanied you (garni de) those many years past of your last visit – '

'Ah! Jean-Jacques!' he readily concurs. '*Le pauvre*,' he adds.

He squints lugubriously down his museau.

'*Une crise de foie. Hélas, il est mort.*'

I blanche like an endive. He, being a perfect gentleman, offers me a restorative snifter of his bubbly, brought as it has been all the way from his own cellars, he don't trust Sir's incinerated tastes, and I can feel it put hairs on my chest as it goes eructating down. Primed by another bottle, in which the duc joins me with that easy democratic affability which is the mark of all true aristocrats, I give him an account of what I take to be the circumstances of my conception, how his defunct valet wooed and won my mother in the course of the cooking of a lobster soufflé.

'I well remember that soufflé,' says the duc. 'Best I ever eat. Sent my compliments to the chef by way of the concierge, only added the advice of a truly exigeant gourmet to go easy on the cayenne, next time.'

So that was the truth of it! The spiteful housekeeper relaying only half the message!

I then relate the touching story, how, every Grouse Shoot after, my mother puts up a lobster soufflé in (I believe) remembrance of Jean-Jacques, and we share another bottle of bubbly in memory of the departed until the duc, exhibiting all the emotion of a tender sensibility, says through a manly tear:

'Tell you what, me lad, while your maman is once again fixing me up this famous lobster soufflé, I shall myself, as a tribute to my ex-valet, slip down – '

'Oh, sir!' I stammer. 'You are too good!'

Forthwith I speed to the kitchen to find my mother just beginning the béchamel. Presently, as the butter melts like the heart of the duc melted when I told him her tale, the kitchen door steals open and in tippytoes Himself. Never a couple better matched for size, I must say. The kitchen battalion all turn their heads away, out of respect for this romantic moment, but I myself, the architect of it, cannot forbear to peep.

He creeps up behind her, his index finger pressed to his lips to signify caution and silence, and extends his arm, and, slowly, slowly, slowly, with infinite delicacy and tact, he lets his hand adventure athwart her flank. It might have been a fly alighting on her bum. She flicks a haunch, like a mare in the field, unmoved, shakes in the flour. The duc himself quivers a bit. An expression as of a baby in a sweetie shop traverses his somewhat Bourbonesque features. He is attempting to peer over her shoulder to see what she is up to with her *batterie de cuisine* but his *embonpoint* gets in the way.

Perhaps it is to shift her over a bit, or else a genuine tribute to her large charms, but now, with immense if gigantic grace, he *gooses* her.

My mother fetches out a sigh, big enough to blow away the beaten egg-whites but, great artist that she is, her hand never trembles, not once, as she folds in the yolks. And when the ducal hands stray higher – not a mite of agitation stirs the spoon.

For it is, you understand, the time for seasoning. And in goes just sufficient cayenne, this time. Not a grain more. Huzzah! This soufflé will be – I flourish the circle I have made with my thumb and forefinger, I simulate a kiss.

The egg-whites topple into the panada; the movements of her spoon are quick and light as those of a bird caught in a trap. She upturns all into the soufflé dish.

He tweaks.

And *then* she cries: 'To hell with it!' Departing from the script, my mother wields her wooden spoon like a club, brings it, smack! down on to the duc's head with considerable force. He drops on to the flags with a low moan.

'Take that,' she bids his prone form. Then she smartly shuts the soufflé in the oven.

'How could you!' I cry.

'Would you have him spoil my soufflé? Wasn't it touch and go, last time?'

The grinding boy and I get the duc up on the marble slab, slap his face, dab his temples with the oven cloth dipped in chilled chablis, at long last his eyelids flicker, he comes to.

'*Quelle femme,*' he murmurs.

My mother, crouching over the range stopwatch in hand, pays him no heed.

'She feared you'd spoil the soufflé,' I explain, overcome with embarrassment.

'What dedication!'

The man seems awestruck. He stares at my mother as if he will never get enough of gazing at her. Bounding off the marble slab as sprightly as a man his size may, he hurls himself across the kitchen, falls on his knees at her feet.

'I beg you, I implore you –'

But my mother has eyes only for the oven.

'*Here* you are!' Throwing open the door, she brings forth the veritable queen of all the soufflés, that spreads its archangelic wings over the entire kitchen as it leaps upwards from the dish in which the force of gravity alone confines it. All present (some forty-seven in number – the kitchen brigade with the addition of me, plus the duc) applaud and cheer.

The housekeeper is mad as fire when my mother goes off in the closed barouche to the duc's very own regal and French kitchen but she comforts herself with the notion that now she can persuade Sir and Madam to find her a spanking new chef such as Soyer or Carême to twirl their moustaches in her direction and *gateau Saint-Honoré* her on her birthday and indulge her in not infrequent *babas au rhum*. But – I am the only child of my mother's kitchen and now I enter into my inheritance; besides, how can the housekeeper complain? Am I not the youngest (Yorkshire born) French chef in all the land?

For am I not the duc's stepson?

The Fall River Axe Murders

Lizzie Borden with an axe
Gave her father forty whacks
When she saw what she had done
She gave her mother forty-one.

Children's rhyme

Early in the morning of the fourth of August, 1892, in Fall River, Massachusetts.

Hot, hot, hot . . . very early in the morning, before the factory whistle, but, even at this hour, everything shimmers and quivers under the attack of white, furious sun already high in the still air.

Its inhabitants have never come to terms with these hot, humid summers – for it is the humidity more than the heat that makes them intolerable; the weather clings like a low fever you cannot shake off. The Indians who lived here first had the sense to take off their buckskins when hot weather came and sit up to their necks in ponds; not so the descendants of the industrious, self-mortifying saints who imported the Protestant ethic wholesale into a country intended for the siesta and are proud, proud! of flying in the face of nature. In most latitudes with summers like these, everything slows down, then. You stay all day in penumbra behind drawn blinds and closed shutters; you wear clothes loose enough to make your own breeze to cool yourself when you infrequently move. But the ultimate decade of the last century finds us at the high point of hard work, here; all will soon be bustle, men will go out into the furnace of the morning well wrapped up in flannel underclothes, linen shirts, vests and coats and trousers of sturdy woollen cloth, and they garrotte themselves with neckties, too, they think it is so virtuous to be uncomfortable.

And today it is the middle of a heat wave; so early in the morning and the mercury has touched the middle eighties, already, and shows no sign of slowing down its headlong ascent.

As far as clothes were concerned, women only appeared to get off more lightly. On this morning, when, after breakfast and the performance of a few household duties, Lizzie Borden will murder her parents, she will, on rising, don a simple cotton frock – but, under that, went a long, starched cotton petticoat; another short, starched cotton petticoat; long drawers; woollen stockings; a chemise; and a whalebone corset that took her viscera in a stern hand and squeezed them very tightly. She also strapped a heavy linen napkin between her legs because she was menstruating.

In all these clothes, out of sorts and nauseous as she was, in this dementing heat, her belly in a vice, she will heat up a flat-iron on a stove and press handkerchiefs with the heated iron until it is time for her to go down to the cellar woodpile to collect the hatchet with which our imagination – 'Lizzie Borden with an axe' – always equips her, just as we always visualise St Catherine rolling along her wheel, the emblem of her passion.

Soon, in just as many clothes at Miss Lizzie wears, if less fine, Bridget, the servant girl, will slop kerosene on a sheet of last night's newspaper crumpled with a stick or two of kindling. When the fire settles down, she will cook breakfast; the fire will keep her suffocating company as she washes up afterwards.

In a serge suit, one look at which would be enough to bring you out in prickly heat, Old Borden will perambulate the perspiring town, truffling for money like a pig until he will return home mid-morning to keep a pressing appointment with destiny.

But nobody here is up and about, yet; it is still early morning, before the factory whistle, the perfect stillness of hot weather, a sky already white, the shadowless light of New England like blows from the eye of God, and the sea, white, and the river, white.

If we have largely forgotten the physical discomforts of the itching, oppressive garments of the past and the corrosive effects of perpetual physical discomfort on the nerves, then we have mercifully forgotten, too, the smells of the past, the domestic odours – ill-washed flesh; infrequently changed underwear; chamber-pots; slop-pails; inadequately plumbed privies; rotting food; unattended teeth; and the streets are no fresher than indoors, the omnipresent acridity of horse piss and dung, drains, sudden stench of old death from butchers' shops, the amniotic horror of the fishmonger.

You would drench your handkerchief with cologne and press it to your nose. You would splash yourself with parma violet so that the reek of fleshly decay you always carried with you was overlaid by that of the embalming parlour. You would abhor the air you breathed.

Five living creatures are asleep in a house on Second Street, Fall River. They comprise two old men and three women. The first old man owns all the women by either marriage, birth or contract. His house is narrow as a coffin and that was how he made his fortune – he used to be an undertaker but he has recently branched out in several directions and all his branches bear fruit of the most fiscally gratifying kind.

But you would never think, to look at his house, that he is a successful and a prosperous man. His house is cramped, comfortless, small and mean – 'unpretentious', you might say, if you were his sycophant – while Second Street itself saw better days some time ago. The Borden house – see 'Andrew J. Borden' in flowing script on the brass plate next to the door – stands by itself with a few scant feet of yard on either side. On the left is a stable, out of use since he sold the horse. In the back lot grow a few pear trees, laden at this season.

On this particular morning, as luck would have it, only one of the two Borden girls sleeps in their father's house. Emma Lenora, his oldest daughter, has taken herself off to nearby New Bedford for a few days, to catch the ocean breeze, and so she will escape the slaughter.

Few of their social class stay in Fall River in the sweating months of June, July and August but, then, few of their social class live on Second Street, in the low part of town where heat gathers like fog. Lizzie was invited away, too, to a summer house by the sea to join a merry band of girls but, as if on purpose to mortify her flesh, as if important business kept her in the exhausted town, as if a wicked fairy spelled her in Second Street, she did not go.

The other old man is some kind of kin of Borden's. He doesn't belong here; he is visiting, passing through, he is a chance bystander, he is irrelevant.

Write him out of the script.

Even though his presence in the doomed house is historically unimpeachable, the colouring of this domestic apocalypse must be crude and the design profoundly simplified for the maximum emblematic effect.

Write John Vinnicum Morse out of the script.

One old man and two of his women sleep in the house on Second Street.

The City Hall clock whirrs and sputters the prolegomena to the first stroke of six and Bridget's alarm clock gives a sympathetic skip and click as the minute-hand stutters on the hour; back the little hammer jerks, about to hit the bell on top of her clock, but Bridget's damp eyelids do not shudder with premonition as she lies in her sticking flannel nightgown under one thin sheet on an iron bedstead, lies on her back, as the good nuns taught her in her Irish girlhood, in case she dies during the night, to make less trouble for the undertaker.

She is a good girl, on the whole, although her temper is sometimes uncertain and then she will talk back to the missus, sometimes, and will be forced to confess the sin of impatience to the priest. Overcome by heat and nausea – for everyone in the house is going to wake up sick today – she will return to this little bed later in the morning. While she snatches a few moments rest, upstairs, all hell will be let loose, downstairs.

A rosary of brown glass beads, a cardboard-backed colour print of the Virgin bought from a Portuguese shop, a flyblown photograph of her solemn mother in Donegal – these lie or are propped on the mantelpiece that, however sharp the Massachusetts winter, has never seen a lit stick. A banged tin trunk at the foot of the bed holds all Bridget's worldly goods.

There is a stiff chair beside the bed with, upon it, a candlestick, matches, the alarm clock that resounds the room with a dyadic, metallic clang, for it is a joke between Bridget and her mistress that the girl could sleep through anything, *anything*, and so she needs the alarm as well as all the factory whistles that are just about to blast off, just this very second about to blast off . . .

A splintered deal washstand holds the jug and bowl she never uses; she isn't going to lug water up to the third floor just to wipe herself down, is she? Not when there's water enough in the kitchen sink.

Old Borden sees no necessity for baths. He does not believe in total immersion. To lose his natural oils would be to rob his body.

A frameless square of mirror reflects in corrugated waves a cracked, dusty soap dish containing a quantity of black metal hairpins.

On bright rectangles of paper blinds move the beautiful shadows of the pear trees.

Although Bridget left the door open a crack in forlorn hopes of coaxing a draught into the room, all the spent heat of the previous day has packed itself tightly into her attic. A dandruff of spent whitewash flakes from the ceiling where a fly drearily whines.

The house is thickly redolent of sleep, that sweetish, clinging smell. Still, all still; in all the house nothing moving except the droning fly. Stillness on the staircase. Stillness pressing against the blinds. Stillness, mortal stillness in the room below, where Master and Mistress share the matrimonial bed.

Were the drapes open or the lamp lit, one could better observe the differences between this room and the austerity of the maid's room. Here is a carpet splashed with vigorous flowers, even if the carpet is of the cheap and cheerful variety; there are mauve, ochre and harsh cerise flowers on the wallpaper, even though the wallpaper was old when the Bordens arrived in the house. A dresser with another distorting mirror; no mirror in this house does not take your face and twist it. On the dresser, a runner embroidered with forget-me-nots; on the runner, a bone comb missing three teeth and lightly threaded with grey hairs, a hairbrush backed with ebonised wood, and a number of lace mats underneath small china boxes holding safety-pins, hairnets etc. The little hairpiece that Mrs Borden attaches to her balding scalp for daytime wear is curled up like a dead squirrel. But of Borden's male occupation of this room there is no trace because he has a dressing room of his own, through *that* door, on the left . . .

What about the other door, the one next to it?

It leads to the back stairs.

And that yet other door, partially concealed behind the head of the heavy, mahogany bed?

If it were not kept securely locked, it would take you into Miss Lizzie's room.

One peculiarity of this house is the number of doors the rooms contain and, a further peculiarity, how all these doors are always locked. A house full of locked doors that open only into other rooms with other locked doors, for, upstairs and downstairs, all the rooms lead in and out of one another like a maze in a bad dream. It is a house without passages. There is no part of the house that has not been marked as some inmate's personal territory; it is a house with no shared, no common spaces between one room and the next. It is a house of privacies sealed as close as if they had been sealed with wax on a legal document.

The only way to Emma's room is through Lizzie's. There is no way out of Emma's room. It is a dead end.

The Bordens' custom of locking all the doors, inside and outside, dates from a time, a few years ago, shortly before Bridget came to work for them, when the house was burgled. A person unknown came through the side door while Borden and his wife had taken one of their rare trips out together; he had loaded her into a trap and set out for the farm they owned at Swansea to ensure his tenant was not bilking him. The girls stayed at home in their rooms, napping on their beds or repairing ripped hems or sewing loose buttons more securely or writing letters or contemplating acts of charity among the deserving poor or staring vacantly into space.

I can't imagine what else they might do.

What the girls do when they are on their own is unimaginable to me.

Emma is more mysterious by far than Lizzie, for we know much less about her. She is a blank space. She has no life. The door from her room leads only into the room of her sister.

'Girls' is, of course, a courtesy term. Emma is well into her forties, Lizzie in her thirties, but they did not marry and so live in their father's house, where they remain in a fictive, protracted childhood.

While the master and the mistress were away and the girls asleep or otherwise occupied, some person or persons unknown tiptoed up the back stairs to the matrimonial bedroom and pocketed Mrs Borden's gold watch and chain, the coral necklace and silver bangle of her remote childhood, and a roll of dollar bills Old Borden kept under clean union suits in the third drawer of the bureau on the left. The intruder attempted to force the lock of the safe, that featureless block of black iron like a slaughtering block or an altar sitting squarely next to the bed on Old Borden's side, but it would have taken a crowbar to penetrate adequately the safe and the intruder tackled it with a pair of nail scissors that were lying handy on the dresser so *that* didn't come off.

Then the intruder pissed and shat on the cover of the Bordens' bed, knocked the clutter of this and that on the dresser to the floor, smashing everything, swept into Old Borden's dressing room there to maliciously assault the funeral coat as it hung in the moth-balled dark of his closet with the self-same nail scissors that had been used on the safe (the nail scissors now split in two and were abandoned on the closet floor), retired to the kitchen, smashed the flour crock and the treacle crock, and then scrawled an obscenity or two on the parlour window with the cake of soap that lived beside the scullery sink.

What a mess! Lizzie stared with vague surprise at the parlour window; she heard the soft bang of the open screen door, swinging idly, although there was no breeze. What was she doing, standing clad only in her corset in the middle of the sitting room? How had she got there? Had she crept down when she heard the screen door rattle? She did not know. She could not remember.

All that happened was: all at once here she is, in the parlour, with a cake of soap in her hand.

She experienced a clearing of the senses and only then began to scream and shout.

'Help! We have been burgled! Help!'

Emma came down and comforted her, as the big sister had comforted the little one since babyhood. Emma it was who cleared from the sitting-room carpet the flour and treacle Lizzie had heedlessly tracked in from the kitchen on her bare feet in her somnambulist trance. But of the missing jewellery and dollar bills no trace could be found.

I cannot tell you what effect the burglary had on Borden. It utterly disconcerted him; he was a man stunned. It violated him, even. He was a man raped. It took away his hitherto unshakeable confidence in the integrity inherent in things.

The burglary so moved them that the family broke its habitual silence with one another in order to discuss it. They blamed it on the Portuguese, obviously, but sometimes on the Canucks. If their outrage remained constant and did not diminish with time, the focus of it varied according to their moods, although they always pointed the finger of suspicion at the strangers and newcomers who lived in the gruesome ramparts of the company housing a few squalid blocks away. They did not always suspect the dark strangers exclusively; sometimes they thought the culprit might very well have been one of the mill-hands fresh from saucy Lancashire across the ocean who committed the crime, for a slum landlord has few friends among the criminal classes.

However, the possibility of a poltergeist occurs to Mrs Borden, although she does not know the word; she knows, however, that her younger stepdaughter is a strange one and could make the plates jump out of sheer spite, if she wanted to. But the old man adores his daughter. Perhaps it is then, after the shock of the burglary, that he decides she needs a change of scene, a dose of sea air, a long voyage, for it was after the burglary he sent her on the grand tour.

After the burglary, the front door and the side door were always locked three times if one of the inhabitants of the house left it for just so much as to go into the yard and pick up a basket of fallen pears when pears were in season or if the maid went out to hang a bit of washing or Old Borden, after supper, took a piss under a tree.

From this time dated the custom of locking all the bedroom doors on the inside when one was on the inside oneself or on the outside when one was on the outside. Old Borden locked his bedroom door in the morning, when he left it, and put the key in sight of all on the kitchen shelf.

The burglary awakened Old Borden to the evanescent nature of private property. He thereafter undertook an orgy of investment. He would forthwith invest his surplus in good brick and mortar, for who can make away with an office block?

A number of leases fell in simultaneously at just this time on a certain street in the downtown area of the city and Borden snapped them up. He owned the block. He pulled it down. He planned the Borden building, an edifice of shops and offices, dark red brick, deep tan stone, with cast-iron detail, from whence, in perpetuity, he might reap a fine harvest of unsaleable rents, and this monument, like that of Ozymandias, would long survive him – and, indeed, stands still, foursquare and handsome, the Andrew Borden Building, on South Main Street.

Not bad for a fish peddler's son, eh?

For, although 'Borden' is an ancient name in New England and the Borden clan between them owned the better part of Fall River, our Borden, Old Borden, these Bordens, did not spring from a wealthy branch of the family. There were Bordens and Bordens and he was the son of a man who sold fresh fish in a wicker basket from house to house to house. Old Borden's parsimony was bred of poverty but learned to thrive best on property, for thrift has a different meaning for the poor; they get no joy of it, it is stark necessity to them. Whoever heard of a penniless miser?

Morose and gaunt, this self-made man is one of few pleasures. His vocation is capital accumulation.

What is his hobby?

Why, grinding the faces of the poor.

First, Andrew Borden was an undertaker, and death, recognising an accomplice, did well by him. In the city of spindles, few made old bones; the little children who laboured in the mills died with especial frequency. When he was an undertaker, no! – it was not true he cut the feet off corpses to fit into a job lot of coffins bought cheap as Civil War surplus! That was a rumour put about by his enemies!

With the profits from his coffins, he bought up a tenement or two and made fresh profit off the living. He bought shares in the mills. Then he invested in a bank or two, so that now he makes a profit on money itself, which is the purest form of profit of all.

Foreclosures and evictions are meat and drink to him. He loves nothing better than a little usury. He is halfway on the road to his first million.

At night, to save the kerosene, he sits in lampless dark. He waters the pear trees with his urine; waste not, want not. As soon as the daily newspapers are done with, he rips them up in geometric squares and stores them in the cellar privy so that they all can wipe their arses with them. He mourns the loss of the good organic waste that flushes down the WC. He would like to charge the very cockroaches in the kitchen rent. And yet he has not grown fat on all this; the pure flame of his passion has melted off his flesh, his skin sticks to his bones out of sheer parsimony. Perhaps it is from his first profession that he has acquired his bearing, for he walks with the stately dignity of a hearse.

To watch Old Borden bearing down the street towards you was to be filled with an instinctual respect for mortality, whose gaunt ambassador he seemed to be. And it made you think, too, what a triumph over nature it was when we rose up to walk on two legs instead of four, in the first place! For he held himself upright with such ponderous assertion it was a perpetual reminder to all who witnessed his progress how it is not *natural* to be upright, that it is a triumph of will over gravity, in itself a transcendence of the spirit over matter.

His spine is like an iron rod, forged, not born, impossible to imagine that spine of Old Borden's curled up in the womb in the big C of the foetus; he walks as if his legs had joints at neither knee nor ankle so that his feet hit the trembling earth like a bailiff pounding a door.

He has a white, chin-strap beard, old-fashioned already in those days. He looks as if he'd gnawed his lips off. He is at peace with his god for he has used his talents as the Good Book says he should.

Yet do not think he has no soft spot. Like Old Lear, his heart – and, more than that, his cheque-book – is putty in his youngest daughter's hands. On his pinky – you cannot see it, it lies under the covers – he wears a gold ring, not a wedding ring but a high-school ring, a singular trinket for a fabulously misanthropic miser. His youngest daughter gave it to him when she left school and asked him to wear it, always, and so he always does, and will wear it to the grave to which she is going to send him later in the morning of this combustible day.

He sleeps fully dressed in a flannel nightshirt over his long-sleeved underwear, and a flannel nightcap, and his back is turned towards his wife of thirty years, as is hers to his.

They are Mr and Mrs Jack Spratt in person, he tall and gaunt as a hanging judge and she, such a spreading, round little doughball. He is a miser, while she is a glutton, a solitary eater, most innocent of vices and yet the shadow or parodic vice of his, for he would like to eat up all the world, or, failing that, since fate has not spread him a sufficiently large table for his ambitions, he is a mute, inglorious Napoleon, he does not know what he might have done because he never had the opportunity – since he has not access to the entire world, he would like to gobble up the city of Fall River. But she, well, she just gently, continuously stuffs herself, doesn't she; she's always nibbling away at something, at the cud, perhaps.

Not that she gets much pleasure from it, either; no gourmet, she, forever meditating the exquisite difference between a mayonnaise sharpened with a few drops of Orleans vinegar or one pointed up with a squeeze of fresh lemon juice. No. Abby never aspired so high, nor would she ever think to do so even if she had the option; she is satisfied to stick to simple gluttony and she eschews all overtones of the sensuality of indulgence. Since she relishes not one single mouthful of the food she eats, she knows her ceaseless gluttony is no transgression.

Here they lie in bed together, living embodiments of two of the Seven Deadly Sins, but he knows his avarice is no offence because he never spends any money and she knows she is not greedy because the grub she shovels down gives her dyspepsia.

She employs an Irish cook and Bridget's rough-and-ready hand in the kitchen fulfils Abby's every criterion. Bread, meat, cabbage, potatoes – Abby was made for the heavy food that made her. Bridget merrily slaps on the table boiled dinners, boiled fish, cornmeal mush, Indian pudding, johnnycakes, cookies.

But those cookies . . . ah! there you touch on Abby's little weakness. Molasses cookies, oatmeal cookies, raisin cookies. But when she tackles a sticky brownie, oozing chocolate, then she feels a queasy sense of having gone almost too far, that sin might be just around the corner if her stomach did not immediately palpitate like a guilty conscience.

Her flannel nightdress is cut on the same lines as his nightshirt except for the limp flannel frill round the neck. She weighs two hundred pounds. She is five feet nothing tall. The bed sags on her side. It is the bed in which his first wife died.

Last night, they dosed themselves with castor oil, due to the indisposition that kept them both awake and vomiting the whole night before that; the copious results of their purges brim the chamber-pots beneath the bed. It is fit to make a sewer faint.

Back to back they lie. You could rest a sword in the space between the old man and his wife, between the old man's backbone, the only rigid thing he ever offered her, and her soft, warm, enormous bum. Their purges flailed them. Their faces show up decomposing green in the gloom of the curtained room, in which the air is too thick for flies to move.

The youngest daughter dreams behind the locked door.

Look at the sleeping beauty!

She threw back the top sheet and her window is wide open but there is no breeze, outside, this morning, to shiver deliciously the screen. Bright sun floods the blinds so that the linen-coloured light shows us how Lizzie has gone to bed as for a levée in a pretty, ruffled nightdress of snatched white muslin with ribbons of pastel pink satin threaded through the eyelets of the lace, for is it not the 'naughty Nineties' everywhere but dour Fall River? Don't the gilded steamships of the Fall River Line signify all the squandered luxury of the Gilded Age within their mahogany and chandeliered interiors? But don't they sail *away* from Fall River, to where, elsewhere, it is the Belle Epoque? In New York, Paris, London, champagne corks pop, in Monte Carlo the bank is broken, women fall backwards in a crisp meringue of petticoats for fun and profit, but not in Fall River. Oh, no. So, in the immutable privacy of her bedroom, for her own delight, Lizzie puts on a rich girl's pretty nightdress, although she lives in a mean house, because she is a rich girl, too.

But she is plain.

The hem of her nightdress is rucked up above her knees because she is a restless sleeper. Her light, dry, reddish hair, crackling with static, slipping loose from the night-time plait, crisps and stutters over the square pillow at which she clutches as she sprawls on her stomach, having rested her cheek on the starched pillowcase for coolness' sake at some earlier hour.

Lizzie was not an affectionate diminutive but the name with which she had been christened. Since she would always be known as 'Lizzie', so her father reasoned, why burden her with the effete and fancy prolongation of 'Elizabeth'? A miser in everything, he even cropped off half her name before he gave it to her. So 'Lizzie' it was, stark and unadorned, and she is a motherless child, orphaned at two years old, poor thing.

Now she is two-and-thirty and yet the memory of that mother she cannot remember remains an abiding source of grief: 'If mother had lived, everything would have been different.'

How? Why? Different in what way? She wouldn't have been able to answer that, lost in a nostalgia for unknown love. Yet how could she have been loved better than by her sister, Emma, who lavished the pent-up treasures of a New England spinster's heart upon the little thing? Different, perhaps, because her natural mother, the first Mrs Borden, subject as she was to fits of sudden, wild, inexplicable rage, might have taken the hatchet to Old Borden on her own account? But Lizzie *loves* her father. All are agreed on that. Lizzie adores the adoring father who, after her mother died, took to himself another wife.

Her bare feet twitch a little, like those of a dog dreaming of rabbits. Her sleep is thin and unsatisfying, full of vague terrors and indeterminate menaces to which she cannot put a name or form once she is awake. Sleep opens within her a disorderly house. But all she knows is, she sleeps badly, and this last, stifling night has been troubled, too, by vague nausea and the gripes of her female pain; her room is harsh with the metallic smell of menstrual blood.

Yesterday evening she slipped out of the house to visit a woman friend. Lizzie was agitated; she kept picking nervously at the shirring on the front of her dress.

'I am afraid . . . that somebody . . . will *do* something,' said Lizzie.

'Mrs Borden . . .' and here Lizzie lowered her voice and her eyes looked everywhere in the room except at Miss Russell . . . 'Mrs Borden – oh! will you ever believe? Mrs Borden thinks somebody is trying to *poison* us!'

She used to call her stepmother 'mother', as duty bade, but, after a quarrel about money after her father deeded half a slum property to her stepmother five years before, Lizzie always, with cool scrupulosity, spoke of 'Mrs Borden' when she was forced to speak of her, and called her 'Mrs Borden' to her face, too.

'Last night, Mrs Borden and poor father were so sick! I heard them, through the wall. And, as for me, I haven't felt myself all day, I have felt so strange. So very . . . strange.'

For there were those somnambulist fits. Since a child, she endured occasional 'peculiar spells', as the idiom of the place and time called odd lapses of behaviour, unexpected, involuntary trances, moments of disconnection. Those times when the mind misses a beat. Miss Russell hastened to discover an explanation within reason; she was embarrassed to mention the 'peculiar spells'. Everyone knew there was nothing odd about the Borden girls.

'Something you ate? It must have been something you have eaten. What was yesterday's supper?' solicitously queried kind Miss Russell.

'Warmed-over swordfish. We had it hot for dinner though I could not take much. Then Bridget heated up the leftovers for supper but, again, for myself, I could only get down a forkful. Mrs Borden ate up the remains and scoured her plate with her bread. She smacked her lips but then was sick all night.' (Note of smugness, here.)

'Oh, Lizzie! In all this heat, this dreadful heat! Twice-cooked fish! You know how quickly fish goes off in this heat! Bridget should have known better than to give you twice-cooked fish!'

It was Lizzie's difficult time of the month, too; her friend could tell by a certain haggard, glazed look on Lizzie's face. Yet her gentility forbade her to mention that. But how could Lizzie have got it into her head that the entire household was under siege from malign forces without?

'There have been threats,' Lizzie pursued remorselessly, keeping her eyes on her nervous fingertips. 'So many people, you understand, dislike father.'

This cannot be denied. Miss Russell politely remained mute.

'Mrs Borden was so very sick she called the doctor in and Father was abusive towards the doctor and shouted at him and told him he would not pay a doctor's bills whilst we had our own good castor oil in the house. He shouted at the doctor and all the neighbours heard and I was so ashamed. There is a man, you see . . .' and here she ducked her head, while her short, pale eyelashes beat on her cheek bones . . . 'such a man, a *dark* man, with the aspect, yes of death upon his face, Miss Russell, a dark man I've seen outside the house at odd, at unexpected hours, early in the morning, late at night, whenever I cannot sleep in this dreadful shade if I raise the blind and peep out, there I see him in the shadows of the pear trees, in the yard, a dark man . . . perhaps he puts poison in the milk, in the mornings, after the milkman fills his can. Perhaps he poisons the ice, when the iceman comes.'

'How long has he been haunting you?' asked Miss Russell, properly dismayed.

'Since . . . the burglary,' said Lizzie and suddenly looked Miss Russell full in the face with a kind of triumph. How large her eyes were; prominent, yet veiled. And her well-manicured fingers went on pecking away at the front of her dress as if she were trying to unpick the shirring.

Miss Russell knew, she just *knew*, this dark man was a figment of Lizzie's imagination. All in a rush, she lost patience with the girl; dark men standing outside her bedroom window, indeed! Yet she was kind and cast about for ways to reassure.

'But Bridget is up and about when the milkman, the iceman call and the whole street is busy and bustling, too; who would dare to put poison in either milk or ice-bucket while half of Second Street looks on? Oh, Lizzie, it is the dreadful summer, the heat, the intolerable heat that's put us all out of sorts, makes us fractious and nervous, makes us sick. So easy to imagine things in this terrible weather, that taints the food and sows worms in the mind . . . I thought you'd planned to go away, Lizzie, to the ocean. Didn't you plan to take a little holiday, by the sea? Oh, do go! Sea air would blow away these silly fancies!'

Lizzie neither nods nor shakes her head but continues to worry at her shirring. For does she not have important business in Fall River? Only that morning, had she not been down to the drug-store to try to buy some prussic acid herself? But how can she tell kind Miss Russell she is gripped by an imperious need to stay in Fall River and murder her parents?

She went to the drug-store on the corner of Main Street in order to buy prussic acid but nobody would sell it to her, so she came home empty-handed. Had all that talk of poison in the vomiting house put her in mind of poison? The autopsy will reveal no trace of poison in the stomachs of either parent. She did not try to poison them; she only had it in mind to poison them. But she had been unable to buy poison. The use of poison had been denied her; so what can she be planning, now?

'And this dark man,' she pursued to the unwilling Miss Russell, 'oh! I have seen the moon glint upon an *axe*!'

When she wakes up, she can never remember her dreams; she only remembers she slept badly.

Hers is a pleasant room of not ungenerous dimensions, seeing the house is so very small. Besides the bed and the dresser, there is a sofa and a desk; it is her bedroom and also her sitting room and her office, too, for the desk is stacked with account books of the various charitable organisations with which she occupies her ample spare time. The Fruit and Flower Mission, under whose auspices she visits the indigent old in hospital with gifts; the Women's Christian Temperance Union, for whom she extracts signatures for petitions against the Demon Drink; Christian Endeavour, whatever that is – this is the golden age of good works and she flings herself into committees with a vengeance. What would the daughters of the rich do with themselves if the poor ceased to exist?

There is the Newsboys Thanksgiving Dinner Fund; and the Horse-trough Association; and the Chinese Conversion Association – no class nor kind is safe from her merciless charity.

Bureau; dressing-table; closet; bed; sofa. She spends her days in this room, moving between each of these dull items of furniture in a circumscribed, undeviating, planetary round. She loves her privacy, she loves her room, she locks herself up in it all day. A shelf contains a book or two: *Heroes of the Mission Field*, *The Romance of Trade*, *What Katy Did*. On the walls, framed photographs of high-school friends, sentimentally inscribed, with, tucked inside one frame, a picture postcard showing a black kitten peeking through a horseshoe. A watercolour of a Cape Cod seascape executed with poignant amateur incompetence. A monochrome photograph or two of works of art, a Della Robbia madonna and the Mona Lisa; these she bought in the Uffizi and the Louvre respectively when she went to Europe.

Europe!

For don't you remember what Katy did next? The story-book heroine took the steamship to smoky old London, to elegant, fascinating Paris, to sunny, antique Rome and Florence, the story-book heroine sees Europe reveal itself before her like an interesting series of magic-lantern slides on a gigantic screen. All is present and all unreal. The Tower of London; click. Notre Dame; click. The Sistine Chapel; click. Then the lights go out and she is in the dark again.

Of this journey she retained only the most circumspect of souvenirs, that madonna, that Mona Lisa, reproductions of objects of art conse-crated by a universal approval of taste. If she came back with a bag full of memories stamped 'Never to be Forgotten', she put the bag away under the bed on which she had dreamed of the world before she set out to see it and on which, at home again, she continued to dream, the dream having been transformed not into lived experience but into memory, which is only another kind of dreaming.

Wistfully: 'When I was in Florence . . .'

But then, with pleasure, she corrects herself: 'When *we* were in Florence . . .'

Because a good deal, in fact most, of the gratification the trip gave her came from having set out from Fall River with a select group of the daughters of respectable and affluent mill-owners. Once away from Second Street, she was able to move comfortably in the segment of Fall River society to which she belonged by right of old name and new money but from which, when she was at home, her father's plentiful personal eccentricities excluded her. Sharing bedrooms, sharing state-rooms, sharing berths, the girls travelled together in a genteel gaggle that bore its doom already upon it, for they were the girls who would not marry, now, and any pleasure they might have obtained from the variety and excitement of the trip was spoiled in advance by the knowledge they were eating up what might have been their own wedding-cake, using up what should have been, if they'd had any luck, their marriage settlements.

All girls pushing thirty, privileged to go out and look at the world before they resigned themselves to the thin condition of New England spinsterhood; but it was a case of look, don't touch. They knew they must not get their hands dirtied or their dresses crushed by the world, while their affectionate companionship en route had a certain steadfast, determined quality about it as they bravely made the best of the second-best.

It was a sour trip, in some ways, sour; and it was a round trip, it ended at the sour place from where it had set out. Home, again; the narrow house, the rooms all locked like those in Bluebeard's castle, and the fat, white stepmother whom nobody loves sitting in the middle of the spider web, she has not budged a single inch while Lizzie was away but she has grown fatter.

This stepmother oppressed her like a spell.

The days open their cramped spaces into other cramped spaces and old furniture and never anything to look forward to, nothing.

When Old Borden dug in his pocket to shell out for Lizzie's trip to Europe, the eye of God on the pyramid blinked to see daylight, but no extravagance is too excessive for the miser's younger daughter who is the wild card in his house and, it seems, can have anything she wants, play ducks and drakes with her father's silver dollars if it so pleases her. He pays all her dressmakers' bills on the dot and how she loves to dress up fine! She is addicted to dandyism. He gives her each week in pin-money the same as the cook gets for wages and Lizzie gives that which she does not spend on personal adornment to the deserving poor.

He would give his Lizzie anything, anything in the world that lives under the green sign of the dollar.

She would like a pet, a kitten or a puppy, she loves small animals and birds, too, poor, helpless things. She piles high the bird-table all winter. She used to keep some white pouter pigeons in the disused stable, the kind that look like shuttlecocks and go 'vroo croo', soft as a cloud.

Surviving photographs of Lizzie Borden show a face it is difficult to look at as if you knew nothing about her; coming events cast their shadow across her face, or else you see the shadows these events have cast – something terrible, something ominous in this face with its jutting, rectangular jaw and those mad eyes of the New England saints, eyes that belong to a person who does not listen to you . . . fanatic's eyes, you might say, if you knew nothing about her. If you were sorting through a box of old photographs in a junk shop and came across this particular, sepia, faded face above the choked collars of the 1890s, you might murmur when you saw her: 'Oh, what big eyes you have!' as Red Riding Hood said to the wolf, but then you might not even pause to pick her out and look at her more closely, for hers is not, in itself, a striking face.

But as soon as the face has a name, once you recognise her, when you know who she is and what it was she did, the face becomes as if of one possessed, and now it haunts you, you look at it again and again, it secretes mystery.

This woman, with her jaw of a concentration-camp attendant, and such eyes . . .

In her old age, she wore pince-nez, and truly with the years the mad light has departed from those eyes or else is deflected by her glasses – if, indeed, it *was* a mad light, in the first place, for don't we all conceal somewhere photographs of ourselves that make us look like crazed assassins? And, in those early photographs of her young womanhood, she herself does not look so much like a crazed assassin as somebody in extreme solitude, oblivious of that camera in whose direction she obscurely smiles, so that it would not surprise you to learn that she is blind.

There is a mirror on the dresser in which she sometimes looks at those times when time snaps in two and then she sees herself with blind, clairvoyant eyes, as though she were another person.

'Lizzie is not herself, today.'

At those times, those irremediable times, she could have raised her muzzle to some aching moon and howled.

At other times, she watches herself doing her hair and trying her clothes on. The distorting mirror reflects her with the queasy fidelity of water. She puts on dresses and then she takes them off. She looks at herself in her corset. She pats her hair. She measures herself with the tape-measure. She pulls the measure tight. She pats her hair. She tries on a hat, a little hat, a chic little straw toque. She punctures it with a hatpin. She pulls the veil down. She pulls it up. She takes the hat off. She drives the hatpin into it with a strength she did not know she possessed.

Time goes by and nothing happens.

She traces the outlines of her face with an uncertain hand as if she were thinking of unfastening the bandages on her soul but it isn't time to do that, yet: she isn't ready to be seen, yet.

She is a girl of Sargasso calm.

She used to keep her pigeons in the loft above the disused stable and feed them grain out of the palms of her cupped hands. She liked to feel the soft scratch of their beaks. They murmured 'vroo croo' with infinite tenderness. She changed their water every day and cleaned up their leprous messes but Old Borden took a dislike to their cooing, it got on his nerves, who'd have thought he *had* any nerves but he invented some, they got on them, one afternoon he took out the hatchet from the woodpile in the cellar and chopped those pigeons' heads right off, he did.

Abby fancied the slaughtered pigeons for a pie but Bridget the servant girl put her foot down, at that: what?!? make a pie out of Miss Lizzie's beloved turtledoves? JesusMaryandJoseph!!! she exclaimed with characteristic impetuousness, what can they be thinking of! Miss Lizzie so nervy with her funny turns and all! (The maid is the only one in the house with any sense and that's the truth of it.) Lizzie came home from the Fruit and Flower Mission for whom she had been reading a tract to an old woman in a poorhouse: 'God bless you, Miss Lizzie.' At home all was blood and feathers.

She doesn't weep, this one, it isn't her nature, she is still waters, but, when moved, she changes colour, her face flushes, it goes dark, angry, mottled red. The old man loves his daughter this side of idolatry and pays for everything she wants, but all the same he killed her pigeons when his wife wanted to gobble them up.

That is how she sees it. That is how she understands it. She cannot bear to watch her stepmother eat, now. Each bite the woman takes seems to go: 'Vroo croo.'

Old Borden cleaned off the hatchet and put it back in the cellar, next to the woodpile. The red receding from her face, Lizzie went down to inspect the instrument of destruction. She picked it up and weighed it in her hand.

That was a few weeks before, at the beginning of the spring.

Her hands and feet twitch in her sleep; the nerves and muscles of this complicated mechanism won't relax, just won't relax, she is all twang, all tension, she is taut as the strings of a wind-harp from which random currents of the air pluck out tunes that are not our tunes.

At the first stroke of the City Hall clock, the first factory hooter blares, and then, on another note, another, and another, the Metacomet Mill, the American Mill, the Mechanics Mill . . . until every mill in the entire town sings out aloud in a common anthem of summoning and hot alleys where the factory folk live blacken with the hurrying throng: hurry! scurry! to loom, to bobbin, to spindle, to dye-shop as to places of worship, men, and women, too, and children, the streets blacken, the sky darkens as the chimneys now belch forth, the clang, bang, clatter of the mills commences.

Bridget's clock leaps and shudders on its chair, about to sound its own alarm. Their day, the Bordens' fatal day, trembles on the brink of beginning.

Outside, above, in the already burning air, see! the angel of death roosts on the roof-tree.

AMERICAN GHOSTS AND OLD WORLD WONDERS

Lizzie's Tiger

John Ford's 'Tis Pity She's a Whore

Gun for the Devil

The Merchant of Shadows

The Ghost Ships

In Pantoland

Ashputtle or *The Mother's Ghost*

Alice in Prague or *The Curious Room*

Impressions: The Wrightsman Magdalene

Lizzie's Tiger

When the circus came to town and Lizzie saw the tiger, they were living on Ferry Street, in a very poor way. It was the time of the greatest parsimony in their father's house; everyone knows the first hundred thousand is the most difficult and the dollar bills were breeding slowly, slowly, even if he practised a little touch of usury on the side to prick his cash in the direction of greater productivity. In another ten years' time, the War between the States would provide rich pickings for the coffin-makers, but, back then, back in the Fifties, well – if he had been a praying man, he would have gone down on his knees for a little outbreak of summer cholera or a touch, just a touch, of typhoid. To his chagrin, there had been nobody to bill when he had buried his wife.

For, at that time, the girls were just freshly orphaned. Emma was thirteen, Lizzie four – stern and square, a squat rectangle of a child. Emma parted Lizzie's hair in the middle, stretched it back over each side of her bulging forehead and braided it tight. Emma dressed her, undressed her, scrubbed her night and morning with a damp flannel, and humped the great lump of little girl around in her arms whenever Lizzie would let her, although Lizzie was not a demonstrative child and did not show affection easily, except to the head of the house, and then only when she wanted something. She knew where the power was and, intuitively feminine in spite of her gruff appearance, she knew how to court it.

That cottage on Ferry – very well, it was a slum; but the undertaker lived on unconcerned among the stiff furnishings of his defunct marriage. His bits and pieces would be admired today if they turned up freshly beeswaxed in an antique store, but in those days they were plain old-fashioned, and time would only make them more so in that dreary interior, the tiny house he never mended, eroding clapboard and diseased paint, mildew on the dark wallpaper with a brown pattern like brains, the ominous crimson border round the top of the walls, the sisters sleeping in one room in one thrifty bed.

On Ferry, in the worst part of town, among the dark-skinned Portuguese fresh off the boat with their earrings, flashing teeth and incomprehensible speech, come over the ocean to work the mills whose newly erected chimneys closed in every perspective; every year more chimneys, more smoke, more newcomers, and the peremptory shriek of the whistle that summoned to labour as bells had once summoned to prayer.

The hovel on Ferry stood, or, rather, leaned at a bibulous angle on a narrow street cut across at an oblique angle by another narrow street, all the old wooden homes like an upset cookie jar of broken gingerbread houses lurching this way and that way, and the shutters hanging off their hinges and windows stuffed with old newspapers, and the snagged picket fence and raised voices in unknown tongues and howling of dogs who, since puppyhood, had known of the world only the circumference of their chain. Outside the parlour window were nothing but rows of counterfeit houses that sometimes used to scream.

Such was the anxious architecture of the two girls' early childhood.

A hand came in the night and stuck a poster, showing the head of a tiger, on to a picket fence. As soon as Lizzie saw the poster, she wanted to go to the circus, but Emma had no money, not a cent. The thirteen-year-old was keeping house at that time, the last skivvy just quit with bad words on both sides. Every morning, Father would compute the day's expenses, hand Emma just so much, no more. He was angry when he saw the poster on the fence; he thought the circus should have paid him rental for the use. He came home in the evening, sweet with embalming fluid, saw the poster, purpled with fury, ripped it off, tore it up.

Then it was supper-time. Emma was no great shakes at cookery and Father, dismissing the possibility of another costly skivvy until such time as plague struck, already pondered the cost-efficiency of remarriage; when Emma served up her hunks of cod, translucently uncooked within, her warmed-over coffee and a dank loaf of baker's bread, it almost put him in a courting mood, but that is not to say his meal improved his temper. So that, when his youngest climbed kitten-like upon his knee and, lisping, twining her tiny fingers in his gunmetal watch-chain, begged small change for the circus, he answered her with words of unusual harshness, for he truly loved this last daughter, whose obduracy recalled his own.

Emma unhandily darned a sock.

'Get that child to bed before I lose my temper!'

Emma dropped the sock and scooped up Lizzie, whose mouth set in dour lines of affront as she was borne off. The square-jawed scrap, deposited on the rustling straw mattress – oat straw, softest and cheapest – sat where she had been dropped and stared at the dust in a sunbeam. She seethed with resentment. It was moist midsummer, only six o'clock and still bright day outside.

She had a whim of iron, this one. She swung her feet on to the stool upon which the girls climbed down out of bed, thence to the floor. The kitchen door stood open for air behind the screen door. From the parlour came the low murmur of Emma's voice as she read *The Providence Journal* aloud to Father.

Next-door's lean and famished hound launched itself at the fence in a frenzy of yapping that concealed the creak of Lizzie's boots on the back porch. Unobserved, she was off – off and away! – trotting down Ferry Street, her cheeks pink with self-reliance and intent. She would not be denied. The circus! The word tinkled in her head with a red sound, as if it might signify a profane church.

'That's a tiger,' Emma had told her as, hand in hand, they inspected the poster on their fence.

'A tiger is a big cat,' Emma added instructively.

How big a cat?

A *very* big cat.

A dumpy, red-striped, regular cat of the small, domestic variety greeted Lizzie with a raucous mew from atop a gatepost as she stumped determinedly along Ferry Street; our cat, Ginger, whom Emma, in a small ecstasy of sentimental whimsy presaging that of her latter protracted spinsterhood, would sometimes call Miss Ginger, or even Miss Ginger Cuddles. Lizzie, however, sternly ignored Miss Ginger Cuddles. Miss Ginger Cuddles sneaked. The cat put out a paw as Lizzie brushed past, as if seeking to detain her, as if to suggest she took second thoughts as to her escapade, but, for all the apparent decision with which Lizzie put one firm foot before the other, she had not the least idea where the circus might be and would not have got there at all without the help of a gaggle of ragged Irish children from Corkey Row, who happened by in the company of a lean, black and tan, barking dog of unforeseen breed that had *this* much in common with Miss Ginger Cuddles, it could go wither it pleased.

This free-ranging dog with its easy-going grin took a fancy to Lizzie and, yapping with glee, danced around the little figure in the white pinafore as it marched along. Lizzie reached out to pat its head. She was a fearless girl.

The child-gang saw her pet their dog and took a fancy to her for the same reason as crows settle on one particular tree. Their wild smiles circled round her. 'Going to the circus, are ye? See the clown and the ladies dancing?' Lizzie knew nothing about clowns and dancers, but she nodded, and one boy took hold of one hand, another of the other, so they raced her off between them. They soon saw her little legs could not keep up their pace, so the ten-year-old put her up on his shoulders where she rode like a lord. Soon they came to a field on the edge of town.

'See the big top?' There was a red and white striped tent of scarcely imaginable proportions, into which you could have popped the entire house on Ferry, and the yard too, with enough room to spare inside for another house, and another – a vast red and white striped tent, with ripping naphtha flares outside and, besides this, all manner of other tents, booths and stalls, dotted about the field, but most of all she was impressed by the great number of people, for it seemed to her that the whole town must be out tonight, yet, when they looked closely at the throng, nowhere at all was anyone who looked like she did, or her father did, or Emma; nowhere that old New England lantern jaw, those ice-blue eyes.

She was a stranger among these strangers, for all here were those the mills had brought to town, the ones with different faces. The plump, pink-cheeked Lancashire mill-hands, with brave red neckerchiefs; the sombre features of the Canucks imbibing fun with characteristic gloom; and the white smiles of the Portuguese, who knew how to enjoy themselves, laughter tripping off their tipsy-sounding tongues.

'Here y'are!' announced her random companions as they dumped her down and, feeling they had amply done their duty by their self-imposed charge, they capered off among the throng, planning, perhaps, to slither under the canvas and so enjoy the shows for free, or even to pick a pocket or two to complete the treat, who knows?

Above the field, the sky now acquired the melting tones of the end of the day, the plush, smoky sunsets unique to these unprecedented industrial cities, sunsets never seen in this world before the Age of Steam that set the mills in motion that made us all modern.

At sunset, the incomparably grave and massive light of New England acquires a monumental, a Roman sensuality; under this sternly voluptuous sky, Lizzie abandoned herself to the unpremeditated smells and never-before-heard noises – hot fat in a vat of frying doughnuts; horse-dung; boiling sugar; frying onions; popping corn; freshly churned earth; vomit; sweat; cries of vendors; crack of rifles from the range; singsong of the white-faced clown, who clattered a banjo, while a woman in pink fleshings danced upon a little stage. Too much for Lizzie to take in at once, too much for Lizzie to take in at all – too rich a feast for her senses, so that she was taken a little beyond herself and felt her head spinning, a vertigo, a sense of profound strangeness overcoming her.

All unnoticeably small as she was, she was taken up by the crowd and tossed about among insensitive shoes and petticoats, too close to the ground to see much else for long; she imbibed the frenetic bustle of the midway through her nose, her ears, her skin that twitched, prickled, heated up with excitement so that she began to colour up in the way she had, her cheeks marked with red, like the marbling on the insides of the family Bible. She found herself swept by the tide of the crowd to a long table where hard cider was sold from a barrel.

The white tablecloth was wet and sticky with spillage and gave forth a dizzy, sweet, metallic odour. An old woman filled tin mugs at the barrel spigot, mug after mug, and threw coins on to other coins into a tin box – splash, chink, clang. Lizzie clung on to the edge of the table to prevent herself being carried away again. Splash, chink, clang. Trade was brisk, so the old woman never turned the spigot off and cider cascaded on to the ground on the other side of the table.

The devil got into Lizzie, then. She ducked down and sneaked in under the edge of the tablecloth, to hide in the resonant darkness and crouch on the crushed grass in fresh mud, as she held out her unobserved hands under the discontinuous stream from the spigot until she collected two hollowed palmfuls, which she licked up, and smacked her lips. Filled, licked, smacked again. She was so preoccupied with her delicious thievery that she jumped half out of her skin when she felt a living, quivering thing thrust into her neck in that very sensitive spot where her braids divided. Something moist and intimate shoved inquisitively at the nape of her neck.

She craned round and came face to face with a melancholy piglet, decently dressed in a slightly soiled ruff. She courteously filled her palms with cider and offered it to her new acquaintance, who sucked it up eagerly. She squirmed to feel the wet quiver of the pig's curious lips against her hands. It drank, tossed its pink snout, and trotted off out the back way from the table.

Lizzie did not hesitate. She followed the piglet past the dried-cod smell of the cider-seller's skirts. The piglet's tail disappeared beneath a cart piled with fresh barrels that was pulled up behind the stall. Lizzie pursued the engaging piglet to find herself suddenly out in the open again, but this time in an abrupt margin of pitch black and silence. She had slipped out of the circus grounds through a hole in their periphery, and the dark had formed into a huge clot, the night, whilst Lizzie was underneath the table; behind her were the lights, but here only shadowy undergrowth, stirring, and then the call of a night bird.

The pig paused to rootle the earth, but when Lizzie reached out to stroke it, it shook its ears out of its eyes and took off at a great pace into the countryside. However, her attention was immediately diverted from this disappointment by the sight of a man who stood with his back to the lights, leaning slightly forward. The cider-barrel-spigot sound repeated itself. Fumbling with the front of his trousers, he turned round and tripped over Lizzie, because he was a little unsteady on his feet and she was scarcely to be seen among the shadows. He bent down and took hold of her shoulders.

'Small child,' he said, and belched a puff of acridity into her face. Lurching a little, he squatted right down in front of her, so they were on the same level. It was so dark that she could see of his face only the hint of moustache above the pale half-moon of his smile.

'Small girl,' he corrected himself, after a closer look. He did not speak like ordinary folks. He was not from around these parts. He belched again, and again tugged at his trousers. He took firm hold of her right hand and brought it tenderly up between his squatting thighs.

'Small girl, do you know what *this* is for?'

She felt buttons; serge; something hairy; something moist and moving. She didn't mind it. He kept his hand on hers and made her rub him for a minute or two. He hissed between his teeth: 'Kissy, kissy from Missy?'

She *did* mind that and shook an obdurate head; she did not like her father's hard, dry, imperative kisses, and endured them only for the sake of power. Sometimes Emma touched her cheek lightly with unparted lips. Lizzie would allow no more. The man sighed when she shook her head, took her hand away from the crotch, softly folded it up on its fingers and gave her hand ceremoniously back to her.

'Gratuity,' he said, felt in his pocket and flipped her a nickel. Then he straightened up and walked away. Lizzie put the coin in her pinafore pocket and, after a moment's thought, stumped off after the funny man along the still, secret edges of the field, curious as to what he might do next.

But now surprises were going on all round her in the bushes, mewings, squeaks, rustlings, although the funny man paid no attention to them, not even when a stately fat woman rose up under his feet, huge as a moon and stark but for her stays, but for black cotton stockings held up by garters with silk rosettes on them, but for a majestic hat of black leghorn with feathers. The woman addressed the drunken man angrily, in a language with a good many ks in it, but he ploughed on indifferently and Lizzie scuttled unseen after, casting an inquisitive backward glance. She had never seen a woman's naked breasts since she could remember, and this pair of melons jiggled entrancingly as the fat woman shook her fist in the wake of the funny man before she parted her thighs with a wet smack and sank down on her knees again in the grass in which something unseen moaned.

Then a person scarcely as tall as Lizzie herself, dressed up like a little drummer-boy, somersaulted – head over heels – directly across their paths, muttering to himself as he did so. Lizzie had just the time to see that, although he was small, he was not shaped quite right, for his head seemed to have been pressed into his shoulders with some violence, but then he was gone.

Don't think any of this frightened her. She was not the kind of child that frightens easily.

Then they were at the back of a tent, not the big, striped tent, but another, smaller tent, where the funny man fumbled with the flap much as he had fumbled with his trousers. A bright mauve, ammoniac reek pulsed out from this tent; it was lit up inside like a Chinese lantern and glowed. At last he managed to unfasten and went inside. He did not so much as attempt to close up after him; he seemed to be in as great a hurry as the tumbling dwarf, so she slipped through too, but as soon as she was inside, she lost him, because there were so many other people there.

Feet of customers had worn all the grass from the ground and it had been replaced by sawdust, which soon stuck all over the mudpie Lizzie had become. The tent was lined with cages on wheels, but she could not see high enough to see what was inside them, yet, mixed with the everyday chatter around her, she heard strange cries that did not come from human throats, so she knew she was on the right track.

She saw what could be seen: a young couple, arm in arm, he whispering in her ear, she giggling; a group of three grinning, gaping youths, poking sticks within the bars; a family that went down in steps of size, a man, a woman, a boy, a girl, a boy, a girl, a boy, a girl, down to a baby of indeterminate sex in the woman's arms. There were many more present, but these were the people she took account of.

The gagging stench was worse than a summer privy and a savage hullabaloo went on all the time, a roaring as if the sea had teeth.

She eeled her way past skirts and trousers and scratched, bare legs of summer boys until she was standing beside the biggest brother of the staircase family at the front of the crowd, but still she could not see the tiger, even if she stood on tiptoe, she saw only wheels and the red and gold base of the cage, whereon was depicted a woman without any clothes, much like the one in the grass outside only without the hat and stockings, and some foliage, with a gilded moon and stars. The brother of the staircase family was much older than she, perhaps twelve, and clearly of the lower class, but clean and respectable-looking, although the entire family possessed that pale, peculiar look characteristic of the mill operatives. The brother looked down and saw a small child in a filthy pinafore peering and straining upwards.

'*Veux-tu voir le grand chat, ma petite?*'

Lizzie did not understand what he said, but she knew what he was saying and nodded assent. Mother looked over the head of the good baby in the lace bonnet as her son heaved Lizzie up in his arms for a good look.

'*Les poux . . .*' she warned, but her son paid her no heed.

'*Voilà, ma petite!*'

The tiger walked up and down, up and down; it walked up and down like Satan walking about the world and it burned. It burned so brightly, she was scorched. Its tail, thick as her father's forearm, twitched back and forth at the tip. The quick, loping stride of the caged tiger; its eyes like yellow coins of a foreign currency; its round, innocent, toy-like ears; the stiff whiskers sticking out with an artificial look; the red mouth from which the bright noise came. It walked up and down on straw strewn with bloody bones.

The tiger kept its head down; questing hither and thither though in quest of what might not be told. All its motion was slung from the marvellous haunches it held so high you could have rolled a marble down its back, if it would have let you, and the marble would have run down an oblique angle until it rolled over the domed forehead on to the floor. In its hind legs the tense muscles keened and sang. It was a miracle of dynamic suspension. It reached one end of the cage in a few paces and whirled around upon itself in one liquid motion; nothing could be quicker or more beautiful than its walk. It was all raw, vivid, exasperated nerves. Upon its pelt it bore the imprint of the bars behind which it lived.

The young lad who kept hold of her clung tight as she lunged forward towards the beast, but he could not stop her clutching the bars of the cage with her little fingers and he tried but he could not dislodge them. The tiger stopped in its track halfway through its mysterious patrol and looked at her. Her pale-blue Calvinist eyes of New England encountered with a shock the flat, mineral eyes of the tiger.

It seemed to Lizzie that they exchanged this cool regard for an endless time, the tiger and herself.

Then something strange happened. The svelte beast fell to its knees. It was as if it had been subdued by the presence of this child, as if this little child of all the children in the world, might lead it towards a peaceable kingdom where it need not eat meat. But only 'as if'. All we could see was, it knelt. A crackle of shock ran through the tent; the tiger was acting out of character.

Its mind remained, however, a law unto itself. We did not know what it was thinking. How could we?

It stopped roaring. Instead it started to emit a rattling purr. Time somersaulted. Space diminished to the field of attractive force between the child and the tiger. All that existed in the whole world now were Lizzie and the tiger.

Then, oh! then . . . it came towards her, as if she were winding it to her on an invisible string by the exercise of pure will. I cannot tell you how much she loved the tiger, nor how wonderful she thought it was. It was the power of her love that forced it to come to her, on its knees, like a penitent. It dragged its pale belly across the dirty straw towards the bars where the little soft creature hung by its hooked fingers. Behind it followed the serpentine length of its ceaselessly twitching tail.

There was a wrinkle in its nose and it buzzed and rumbled and they never took their eyes off one another, though neither had the least idea what the other meant.

The boy holding Lizzie got scared and pummelled her little fists, but she would not let go a grip as tight and senseless as that of the newborn. Crack! The spell broke.

The world bounded into the ring.

A lash cracked round the tiger's carnivorous head, and a glorious hero sprang into the cage brandishing in the hand that did not hold the whip a three-legged stool. He wore fawn breeches, black boots, a bright red jacket frogged with gold, a tall hat. A dervish, he; he beckoned, crouched, pointed with the whip, menaced with the stool, leaped and twirled in a brilliant ballet of mimic ferocity, the dance of the Taming of the Tiger, to whom the tamer gave no chance to fight at all.

The great cat unpeeled its eyes off Lizzie's in a trice, rose up on its hind legs and feinted at the whip like our puss Ginger feints at a piece of paper dangled from a string. It batted at the tamer with its enormous paws, but the whip continued to confuse, irritate and torment it and, what with the shouting, the sudden, excited baying of the crowd, the dreadful confusion of the signs surrounding it, habitual custom, a lifetime's training, the tiger whimpered, laid back its ears and scampered away from the whirling man to an obscure corner of the stage, there to cower, while its flanks heaved, the picture of humiliation.

Lizzie let go of the bars and clung, mudstains and all, to her young protector for comfort. She was shaken to the roots by the attack of the trainer upon the tiger and her four-year-old roots were very near the surface.

The tamer gave his whip a final, contemptuous ripple around his adversary's whispers that made it sink its huge head on the floor. Then he placed one booted foot on the tiger's skull and cleared his throat for speech. He was a hero. He was a tiger himself, but even more so, because he was a man.

'Ladies and gentlemen, boys and girls, this incomparable TIGER known as the Scourge of Bengal, and brought alive-oh to Boston from its native jungle but three short months before this present time, now, at my imperious command, offers you a perfect imitation of docility and obedience. But do not let the brute deceive you. Brute it was, and brute it remains. Not for nothing did it receive the soubriquet of Scourge for, in its native habitat, it thought nothing of consuming a dozen brown-skinned heathen for its breakfast and following up with a couple of dozen more for dinner!'

A pleasing shudder tingled through the crowd.

'This tiger,' and the beast whickered ingratiatingly when he named it, 'is the veritable incarnation of blood lust and fury; in a single instant, it can turn from furry quiescence into three hundred pounds, yes, three hundred POUNDS of death-dealing fury.

'The tiger is the cat's revenge.'

Oh, Miss Ginger, Miss Ginger Cuddles, who sat mewing censoriously on the gatepost as Lizzie passed by; who would have thought you seethed with such resentment!

The man's voice dropped to a confidential whisper and Lizzie, although she was in such a state, such nerves, recognised this was the same man as the one she had met behind the cider stall, although now he exhibited such erect mastery, not a single person in the tent would have thought he had been drinking.

'What is the nature of the bond between us, between the Beast and Man? Let me tell you. It is fear. Fear! Nothing but fear. Do you know how insomnia is the plague of the tamer of cats? How all night long, every night, we pace our quarters, impossible to close our eyes for brooding on what day, what hour, what moment the fatal beast will choose to strike?

'Don't think I cannot bleed, or that they have not wounded me. Under my clothes, my body is a palimpsest of scars, scar upon scar. I heal only to be once more broken open. No skin of mine that is not scar tissue. And I am always afraid, always; all the time in the ring, in the cage, now, this moment – this very moment, boys and girls, ladies and gentlemen, you see before you a man in the grip of mortal fear.

'Here and now I am in terror of my life.

'At this moment I am in this cage within a perfect death trap.'

Theatrical pause.

'But,' and here he knocked the tiger's nose with his whipstock, so that it howled with pain and affront, 'but . . .' and Lizzie saw the secret frog he kept within his trousers shift a little, '. . . BUT I'm not half so scared of the big brute as it is of me!'

He showed his red maw in a laugh.

'For I bring to bear upon its killer instinct a rational man's knowledge of the power of fear. The whip, the stool, are instruments of bluff with which I create his fear in my arena. In my cage, among my cats, I have established a hierarchy of FEAR and among my cats you might well say I am TOP DOG, because I know that all the time they want to kill me, that is their project, that is their intention . . . but as for them, they just don't know what I might do next. No, sir!'

As if enchanted by the notion, he laughed out loud again, but by now the tiger, perhaps incensed by the unexpected blow on the nose, rumbled out a clear and incontrovertible message of disaffection and, with a quick jerk of its sculptured head, flung the man's foot away so that, caught off-balance, he half toppled over. And then the tiger was no longer a thing of stillness, of hard edges and clear outlines, but a whizz of black and red, maw and canines, in the air. On him.

The crowd immediately bayed.

But the tamer, with enormous presence of mind, seeing as how he was drunk, and, in the circumstances, with almost uncanny physical agility, bounced backwards on his boot-heels and thrust the tool he carried in his left hand into the fierce tiger's jaws, leaving the tiger worrying, gnawing, destroying the harmless thing, as a ragged black boy quickly unlatched the cage door and out the tamer leaped, unscathed, amidst hurrahs.

Lizzie's stunned little face was now mottled all over with a curious reddish-purple, with the heat of the tent, with passion, with the sudden access of enlightenment.

To see the rest of the stupendous cat act, the audience would have had to buy another ticket for the Big Top, besides the ticket for the menagerie, for which it had already paid, so, reluctant on the whole to do that, in spite of the promise of clowns and dancing ladies, it soon got bored with watching the tiger splintering the wooden stool, and drifted off.

'Eh bien, ma petite,' said her boy-nurse to her in a sweet, singsong, crooning voice. 'Tu as vu la bête! La bête du cauchemar!'

The baby in the lace bonnet had slept peacefully through all this, but now began to stir and mumble. Its mother nudged her husband with her elbow.

'On va, Papa?'

The crooning, smiling boy brought his bright pink lips down on Lizzie's forehead for a farewell kiss. She could not bear that; she struggled furiously and shouted to be put down. With that, her cover broke and she burst out of her disguise of dirt and silence; half the remaining gawpers in the tent had kin been bleakly buried by her father, the rest owed him money. She was the most famous daughter in all Fall River.

'Well, if it ain't Andrew Borden's little girl! What are they Canucks doing with little Lizzie Borden?'

John Ford's
'Tis Pity She's a Whore

There was a rancher had two children, a son and then a daughter. A while after that, his wife died and was buried under two sticks nailed together to make a cross because there was no time, yet, to carve a stone.

Did she die of the loneliness of the prairies? Or was it anguish that killed her, anguish, and nostalgia for the close, warm, neighbourly life she had left behind her when she came to this emptiness? Neither. She died of the pressure of that vast sky, that weighed down upon her and crushed her lungs until she could not breathe any more, as if the prairies were the bedrock of an ocean in which she drowned.

She told her boy: 'Look after your sister.' He, blond, solemn, little; he and Death sat with her in the room of logs her husband split to build. Death, with high cheek-bones, wore his hair in braids. His invisible presence in the cabin mocked the existence of the cabin. The round-eyed boy clutched his mother's dry hand. The girl was younger.

Then the mother lay with the prairies and all that careless sky upon her breast, and the children lived in their father's house. So they grew up. In his spare time the rancher chiselled at a rock: 'Beloved wife of . . . mother of . . .' beneath the space at the top he had left for his own name.

America begins and ends in the cold and solitude. Up here, she pillows her head upon the Arctic snow. Down there, she dips her feet in the chilly waters of the South Atlantic, home of the perpetually restless albatross. America, with her torso of a woman at the time of this story, a woman with an hour-glass waist, a waist laced so tightly it snapped in two, and we put a belt of water there. America, with your child-bearing hips and

NOTE:
  John Ford (1586–c. 1639). English dramatist of the Jacobean period. His tragedy, '*Tis Pity She's a Whore*, was published in 1633. 'Deep in a dump John Ford alone was got/With folded arms and melancholy hat.' (*Choice Drollery*, 1656.)
  John Ford (1895–1973). American film-maker. Filmography includes: *Stagecoach* (1938); *My Darling Clementine* (1946); *She Wore a Yellow Ribbon* (1949). 'My name is John Ford. I make Westerns.' (*John Ford*, Andrew Sinclair, New York 1979.)

your crotch of jungle, your swelling bosom of a nursing mother and your cold head, your cold head.

Its central paradox resides in this: that the top half doesn't know what the bottom half is doing. When I say the two children of the prairie, suckled on those green breasts, were the pure children of the continent, you know at once that they were *norteamericanos*, or I would not speak of them in the English language, which was their language, the language that silences the babble of this continent's multitude of tongues.

Blond children with broad, freckled faces, the boy in dungarees and the little girl in gingham and sunbonnet. In the old play, one John Ford called them Giovanni and Annabella; the other John Ford, in the movie, might call them Johnny and Annie-Belle.

Annie-Belle will bake bread, tramp the linen clean and cook the beans and bacon; this lily of the West had not spare time enough to pause and consider the lilies of the field, who never do a hand's turn. No, sir. A woman's work is never done and she became a woman early.

The gaunt paterfamilias would drive them into town to church on Sundays with the black Bible on his knee wherein their names and dates of birth were inscribed. In the buggy, his shy, big-boned, tow-headed son in best, dark, Sunday clothes, and Annie-Belle, at thirteen, fourteen, increasingly astonished at and rendered shy by her own lonely flowering. Fifteen. How pretty she was growing! They came to pray in God's house that, like their own, was built of split logs. Annie-Belle kept her eyes down; she was a good girl. They were good children. The widower drank, sometimes, but not much. They grew up in silence, in the enormous silence of the empty land, the silence that swallowed up the Saturday-night fiddler's tune, mocked the rare laughter at weddings and christenings, echoed, a vast margin, around the sermons of the preacher.

Silence and space and an unimaginable freedom which they dare not imagine.

Since his wife died, the rancher spoke rarely. They lived far out of town. He had no time for barn-raisings and church suppers. If she had lived, everything would have been different, but he occupied his spare moments in chiselling her gravestone. They did not celebrate Thanksgiving for he had nothing for which to give thanks. It was a hard life.

The Minister's wife made sure Annie-Belle knew a thing or two when she judged it about the time the girl's bleeding started. The Minister's wife, in a vague, pastoral way, thought about a husband for Annie-Belle, a wife for Johnny. 'Out there, in that little house on the prairie, so lonesome . . . Nobody for those young folks to talk to 'cept cows, cows, cows.'

*

What did the girl think? In summer, of the heat, and how to keep flies out of the butter; in winter, of the cold. I do not know what else she thought. Perhaps, as young girls do, she thought that a stranger would come to town and take her away to the city and so on, but, since her imagination began and ended with her experience, the farm, work, the seasons, I think she did not think so far, as if she knew already she was the object of the object of her own desire for, in the bright light of the New World, nothing is obscure. But when they were children, all they knew was they loved each other just as, surely, a brother or a sister should.

She washed her hair in a tub. She washed her long, yellow hair. She was fifteen. It was spring. She washed her hair. It was the first time that year. She sat on the porch to dry her hair, she sat in the rocking-chair which her mother selected from the Sears' Roebuck catalogue, where her father would never sit, now. She propped a bit of mirror on the porch railing. It caught the sun and flashed. She combed out her wet hair in the mirror. There seemed to be an awful lot of it, tangling up the comb. She wore only her petticoat, the men were off with the cattle, nobody to see her pale shoulders except that Johnny came back. The horse threw him, he knocked his head against the stone. Giddy, he came back to the house, leading his pony, and she was busy untangling her hair and did not see him, nor have a chance to cover herself.

'Why, Johnny, I declare – '

Imagine an orchestra behind them: the frame house, the porch, the rocking-chair endlessly rocking, like a cradle, the white petticoat with eyelet lace, her water-darkened hair hanging on her shoulders and little trickles running down between her shallow breasts, the young man leading the limping pony, and, inexhaustible as light, around them the tender land.

The 'Love Theme' swells and rises. She jumps up to tend him. The jogged mirror falls.

'Seven years' bad luck – '

In the fragments of the mirror, they kneel to see their round, blond, innocent faces that, superimposed upon one another, would fit at every feature, their faces, all at once the same face, the face that never existed until now, the pure face of America.

EXTERIOR. PRAIRIE. DAY
(Long shot) Farmhouse.
(Close up) Petticoat falling on to porch of
farmhouse.

Wisconsin, Ohio, Iowa, Missouri, Kansas, Minnesota, Nebraska, the

Dakotas, Wyoming, Montana . . . Oh, those enormous territories! That green vastness, in which anything is possible.

> EXTERIOR. PRAIRIE. DAY
> (Close up) Johnny and Annie–Belle kiss.
> 'Love Theme' up.
> Dissolve.

No. It wasn't like that! Not in the least like that.
He put out his hand and touched her wet hair. He was giddy.

Annabella: Methinks you are not well.
Giovanni: Here's none but you and I. I think you love me, sister.
Annabella: Yes, you know I do.

And they thought, then, that they should kill themselves, together now, before they did it; they remembered tumbling together in infancy, how their mother laughed to see their kisses, their embraces, when they were too young to know they should not do it, yet even in their loneliness on the enormous plain they knew they must not do it . . . do what? How did they know what to do? From watching the cows with the bull, the bitch with the dog, the hen with the cock. They were country children. Turning from the mirror, each saw the other's face as if it were their own.

[*Music plays.*]
Giovanni: Let not this music be a dream, ye gods.
   For pity's sake, I beg you!
[*She kneels.*]
Annabella: On my knees,
   Brother, even by our mother's dust, I charge you
   Do not betray me to your mirth or hate.
   Love me, or kill me, brother.
[*He kneels.*]
Giovanni: On my knees,
   Sister, even by our mother's dust, I charge you
   Do not betray me to your mirth or hate.
   Love me, or kill me, sister.

> EXTERIOR. FARMHOUSE PORCH. DAY
> Upset water-tub, spilling over discarded
>   petticoat.
> Empty rocking-chair, rocking, rocking.

*

It is the boy – or young man, rather – who is the most mysterious to me. The eagerness with which he embraces his fate. I imagine him mute or well-nigh mute; he is the silent type, his voice creaks with disuse. He turns the soil, he breaks the wills of the beautiful horses, he milks the cows, he works the land, he toils and sweats. His work consists of the vague, undistinguished 'work' of such folks in the movies. No cowboy, he, roaming the plains. Where the father took root, so has the son, in the soil that was never before broken until now.

And I imagine him with an intelligence nourished only by the black book of the father, and hence cruelly circumscribed, yet dense with allusion, seeing himself as a kind of Adam and she his unavoidable and irreplaceable Eve, the unique companion of the wilderness, although by their toil he knows they do not live in Eden and of the precise nature of the forbidden thing he remains in doubt.

For surely it cannot be this? This bliss? Who could forbid such bliss!

Was it bliss for her, too? Or was there more of love than pleasure in it? 'Look after your sister.' But it was she who looked after him as soon as she knew how and pleasured him in the same spirit as she fed him.

Giovanni: I am lost forever.

Lost in the green wastes, where the pioneers were lost. Death with his high cheek-bones and his braided hair helped Annie-Belle take off her clothes. She closed her eyes so that she could not see her own nakedness. Death showed her how to touch him and him her. There is more to it than farmyard ways.

> INTERIOR. MINISTER'S HOUSE. DAY
> Dinner-table. Minister's wife dishing portions
>   from a pot for her husband and her son.
>
> MINISTER'S WIFE: 'Tain't right, just
>   ain't right, those two out there, growing up like
>   savages, never seeing nobody.
>
> MINISTER'S SON: She's terribly pretty, Mama.
>
> The Minister's wife and the Minister turn to
> look at the young man. He blushes slowly
>   but comprehensively.

The rancher knew nothing. He worked. He kept the iron core of grief within him rustless. He looked forward to his solitary, once-monthly drink, alone on the porch, and on those nights they took a chance and slept together in the log cabin under the patchwork quilt made in the 'log cabin' pattern by their mother. Each time they lay down there together, as if she obeyed a voice that came out of the quilt telling her to put the light out, she would extinguish the candle flame between her finger-tips. All around them, the tactility of the dark.

She pondered the irreversibility of defloration. According to what the Minister's wife said, she had lost everything and was a lost girl. And yet this change did not seem to have changed her. She turned to the only one she loved, and the desolating space around them diminished to that of the soft grave their bodies dented in the long grass by the creek. When winter came, they made quick, dangerous love among the lowing beasts in the barn. The snow melted and all was green enough to blind you and there was a vinegarish smell from the rising of the sharp juices of spring. The birds came back.

A dusk bird went chink-chink-chink like a single blow on the stone xylophone of the Chinese classical orchestra.

> EXTERIOR. FARMHOUSE PORCH. DAY
> Annie-Belle, in apron, comes out on
>   homestead porch; strikes metal triangle.
>
> ANNIE-BELLE: Dinner's ready!
>
> INTERIOR. FARMHOUSE. NIGHT
> Supper-table. Annie-Belle serves beans. None
>   for herself.
>
> JOHNNY: Annie-Belle, you're not eating
>   anything tonight.
>
> ANNIE-BELLE: Can't rightly fancy anything
>   tonight.

The dusk bird went chink-chink-chink with the sound of a chisel on a gravestone.

He wanted to run away with her, west, further west, to Utah, to California where they could live as man and wife, but she said: 'What about Father? He's lost enough already.' When she said that, she put on, not his face, but that of their mother, and he knew in his bones the child inside her would part them.

The Minister's son, in his Sunday coat, came courting Annie-Belle. He is the second lead, you know in advance, from his tentative manner and mild eyes; he cannot long survive in this prairie scenario. He came courting Annie-Belle although his mother wanted him to go to college. 'What will you do at college with a young wife?' said his mother. But he put away his books; he took the buggy to go out and visit her. She was hanging washing out on the line.

Sound of the wind buffeting the sheets, the very sound of loneliness.

Soranzo: Have you not the will to love?
Annabella: Not you.
Soranzo: Who, then?
Annabella: That's as the fates infer.

She lowered her head and drew her foot back and forth in the dust. Her breasts hurt, she felt queasy.

> EXTERIOR. PRAIRIE. DAY
> Johnny and Annie-Belle walking on the
> prairie.
>
> ANNIE-BELLE: I think he likes me, Johnny.
>
> Pan blue sky, with clouds. Johnny and Annie-
> Belle, dwarfed by the landscape, hand in
> hand, heads bowed. Their hands slowly
> part.
>
> Now they walk with gradually increasing
> distance between them.

The light, the unexhausted light of North America that, filtered through celluloid, will become the light by which we see America looking at itself.

Correction: will become the light by which we see *North* America looking at itself.

> EXTERIOR. FARMHOUSE PORCH. DAY
> Row of bottles on a fence.
> Bang, bang, bang. Johnny shoots the bottles
> one by one.
> Annie-Belle on porch, washing dishes in a tub.
> Tears run down her face.
>
> EXTERIOR. FARMHOUSE PORCH. DAY
> Father on porch, feet up on railing, glass and
> bottle to hand.

Sun going down over prairies.
Bang, bang, bang.

(Father's point of view) Johnny shooting
   bottles off the fence.

Clink of father's bottle against glass.

EXTERIOR. FARMHOUSE. DAY
Minister's son rides along track in long shot.
Bang, bang, bang.

Annie–Belle, clean dress, tidy hair, red eyes,
   comes out of house on to porch. Clink of
   father's bottle against glass.

EXTERIOR. FARMHOUSE. DAY
Minister's son tethers horse. He has brushed
   his Sunday coat. In his hand, a posy of
   flowers – cottage roses, sweetbrier, daisies.
   Annie–Belle smiles, takes posy.

ANNIE–BELLE: Oh!

Holds up pricked forefinger; blood drops on
   to a daisy.

MINISTER'S SON: Let me . . .

Takes her hand. Kisses the little wound.

. . . make it better.

Bang. Bang. Bang.
Clink of bottle on glass.

(Close up) Annie–Belle, smiling, breathing in
   the scent from her posy.

And, perhaps, had it been possible, she would have learned to love the
Minister's gentle son before she married him, but, not only was it
impossible, she also carried within her the child that meant she must be
married quickly.

INTERIOR. CHURCH. DAY
Harmonium. Father and Johnny by the altar.
Johnny white, strained; father stoical.
Minister's wife thin-lipped, furious.

Minister's son and Annie-Belle, in simple
white cotton wedding-dress, join hands.

MINISTER: Do you take this woman . . .

(Close up) Minister's son's hand slipping
wedding ring on to Annie-Belle's finger.

INTERIOR. BARN. NIGHT
Fiddle and banjo old-time music.
Vigorous square dance going on; bride and
groom lead.
Father at table, glass in hand.
Johnny, beside him, reaching for bottle.

Bride and groom come together at end of
dance; groom kisses bride's cheek. She
laughs.

(Close up) Annie-Belle looking shyly up at the
Minister's son.

The dance parts them again; as Annie-Belle is
handed down the row of men, she staggers
and faints.

Consternation.

Minister's son and Johnny both run towards
her.

Johnny lifts her up in his arms, her head on
his shoulder. Eyes opening. Minister's son
reaches out for her. Johnny lets him take
hold of her.

She gazes after Johnny beseechingly as he
disappears among the crowd.

Silence swallowed up the music of the fiddle and the banjo; Death with
his hair in braids spread out the sheets on the marriage bed.

INTERIOR. MINISTER'S HOUSE. BEDROOM.
NIGHT
Annie-Belle in bed, in a white nightgown,
clutching the pillow, weeping. Minister's
son, bare back, sitting on side of bed with

his back to camera, head in hands.

In the morning, her new mother-in-law heard her vomiting into the chamber-pot and, in spite of her son's protests, stripped Annie-Belle and subjected her to a midwife's inspection. She judged her three months gone, or more. She dragged the girl round the room by the hair, slapped her, punched her, kicked her, but Annie-Belle would not tell the father's name, only promised, swore on the grave of her dead mother, that she would be a good girl in future. The young bridegroom was too bewildered by this turn of events to have an opinion about it; only, to his vague surprise, he knew he still loved the girl although she carried another man's child.

'Bitch! Whore!' said the Minister's wife and struck Annie-Belle a blow across the mouth that started her nose bleeding.

'Now, stop that, Mother,' said the gentle son. 'Can't you see she ain't well?'

The terrible day drew to its end. The mother-in-law would have thrown Annie-Bell out on the street, but the boy pleaded for her, and the Minister, praying for guidance, found himself opening the Bible at the parable of the woman taken in adultery and meditated well upon it.

'Only tell me the name of the father,' her young husband said to Annie-Belle.

'Better you don't know it,' she said. Then she lied: 'He's gone, now; gone out west.'

'Was it – ?' naming one or two.

'You never knew him. He came by the ranch on his way out west.'

Then she burst out crying again, and he took her in his arms.

'It will be all over town,' said the mother-in-law. 'That girl made a fool of you!'

She slammed the dishes on the table and would have made the girl eat out the back door, but the young husband laid her a place at table with his own hand and led her in and sat her down in spite of his mother's black looks. They bowed their heads for grace. Surely, the Minister thought, seeing his boy cut bread for Annie-Belle and lay it on her plate, my son is a saint. He began to fear for him.

'I won't do anything unless you want,' her husband said in the dark after the candle went out.

The straw with which the mattress was stuffed rustled beneath her as she turned away from him.

INTERIOR. FARMHOUSE KITCHEN. NIGHT
Johnny comes in from outside, looks at father

asleep in rocking-chair.

Picks up some discarded garment of Annie-
     Belle's from the back of a chair, buries
     face in it.

Shoulders shake.

Opens cupboard, takes out bottle.

Uncorks with teeth. Drinks.

Bottle in hand, goes out on porch.

EXTERIOR. PRAIRIE. NIGHT

(Johnny's point of view) Moon rising over
     prairie: the vast, the elegiac plain.

'Landscape Theme' rises.

INTERIOR. MINISTER'S SON'S ROOM. NIGHT

Annie-Belle and Minister's son in bed.
     Moonlight through the curtains. Both lie
     there, open-eyed. Rustle of mattress.

ANNIE-BELLE: You awake?

Minister's son moves away from her.

ANNIE-BELLE: Reckon I never properly
     knowed no young man before . . .

MINISTER'S SON: What about—

ANNIE-BELLE (shrugging the question off):
     Oh . . .

Minister's son moves towards her.

For she did not consider her brother in this new category of 'young
men'; he was herself. So she and her husband slept in one another's arms,
that night, although they did nothing else for she was scared it might
harm the baby and he was so full of pain and glory it was scarcely to be
borne, it was already enough, or too much, holding her tight, in his
terrible innocence.

It was not so much that she was pliant. Only, fearing the worst, it
turned out that the worst had already happened; her sin found her out, or,
rather, she found out she had sinned only when he offered his
forgiveness, and, from her repentance, a new Annie-Belle sprang up, for
whom the past did not exist.

She would have said to him: 'It did not signify, my darling; I only did it
with my brother, we were alone together under the vast sky that made us

scared and so we clung together and what happened, happened.' But she knew she must not say that, that the most natural love of all was just precisely the one she must not acknowledge. To lie down on the prairie with a passing stranger was one thing. To lie down with her father's son was another. So she kept silent. And when she looked at her husband, she saw, not herself, but someone who might, in time, grow even more precious.

The next night, in spite of the baby, they did it, and his mother wanted to murder her and refused to get the breakfast for this prostitute, but Annie-Belle served them, put on an apron, cut the ham and cooked it, then scrubbed the floor with such humility, such evidence of gratitude that the older woman kept her mouth shut, her narrow lips tight as a trap, but she kept them shut for if there was one thing she feared, it was the atrocious gentleness of her menfolk. And. So.

Johnny came to the town, hungering after her; the gates of Paradise slammed shut in his face. He haunted the backyard of the Minister's house, hid in the sweetbrier, watched the candle in their room go out and still he could not imagine it, that she might do it with another man. But. She did.

At the store, all gossip ceased when she came in; all eyes turned towards her. The old men chewing tobacco spat brown streams when she walked past. The women's faces veiled with disapproval. She was so young, so unaccustomed to people. They talked, her husband and she; they would go, just go, out west, still further, west as far as the place where the ocean starts again, perhaps. With his schooling, he could get some clerking job or other. She would bear her child and he would love it. Then she would bear *their* children.

'Yes,' she said. 'We shall do that,' she said.

EXTERIOR. FARMHOUSE. DAY
Annie-Belle drives up in trap.
Johnny comes out on porch, in shirt-sleeves,
    bottle in hand.
Takes her reins. But she doesn't get down
    from the trap.

ANNIE-BELLE: Where's Daddy?

Johnny gestures towards the prairie.

ANNIE-BELLE (not looking at Johnny): Got
    something to tell him.

(Close up) Johnny.

JOHNNY: Ain't you got nothing to tell me?

(Close up) Annie-Belle.

ANNIE-BELLE: Reckon I ain't.

(Close up) Johnny.

JOHNNY: Get down and visit a while, at least.

(Close up) Annie-Belle.

ANNIE-BELLE: Can't hardly spare the time.

(Close up) Johnny and Annie-Belle.

JOHNNY: Got to scurry back, get your
   husband's dinner, is that it?

ANNIE-BELLE: Johnny . . . why haven't you
   come to church since I got married,
   Johnny?

Johnny shrugs, turns away.

EXTERIOR. FARMHOUSE. DAY
Annie-Belle gets down from trap, follows
   Johnny towards farmhouse.

ANNIE-BELLE: Oh, Johnny, you *knowed* we
   did wrong.

Johnny walks towards farmhouse.

ANNIE-BELLE: I count myself fortunate
   to have found forgiveness.

JOHNNY: What are you going to tell Daddy?

ANNIE-BELLE: I'm going out west.

Giovanni: What, chang'd so soon! hath your new sprightly lord
   Found out a trick in night-games more than we
   Could know in our simplicity? – Ha! is't so?
   Or does the fit come on you, to prove treacherous
   To your past vows and oaths?
Annabella: Why should you jest
   At my calamity.

EXTERIOR. FARMHOUSE. DAY

JOHNNY: Out west?

Annie-Belle nods.

JOHNNY: By yourself?

Annie-Belle shakes her head.

JOHNNY: With him?

Annie-Belle nods.
Johnny puts hand on porch rail, bends
  forward, hiding his face.

ANNIE-BELLE: It is for the best.

She puts her hand on his shoulder. He reaches
  out for her. She extricates herself. His
  hand, holding bottle; contents of bottle run
  out on grass.

ANNIE-BELLE: It was wrong, what we did.

JOHNNY: What about . . .

ANNIE-BELLE: It shouldn't ever have been
  made, poor little thing. You won't never
  see it. Forget everything. You'll find
  yourself a woman, you'll marry.

Johnny reaches out and clasps her roughly to
  him.

'No,' she said; 'never. No.' And fought and bit and scratched: 'Never!
It's wrong. It's a sin.' But, worse than that, she said: 'I don't want to,' and
she meant it, she knew she must not or else her new life, that lay before
her, now, with the radiant simplicity of a child's drawing of a house,
would be utterly destroyed. So she got free of him and ran to the buggy
and drove back lickety-split to town, beating the pony round the head
with the whip.

Accompanied by a black trunk like a coffin, the Minister and his wife
drove with them to a railhead such as you have often seen on the movies –
the same telegraph office, the same water-tower, the same old man with
the green eyeshade selling tickets. Autumn was coming on. Annie-Belle
could no longer conceal her pregnancy, out it stuck; her mother-in-law

could not speak to her directly but addressed remarks through the
Minister, who compensated for his wife's contempt by showing Annie-
Belle all the honour due to a repentant sinner.

She wore a yellow ribbon. Her hair was long and yellow. The
repentant harlot has the surprised look of a pregnant virgin.

She is pale. The pregnancy does not go well. She vomits all morning.
She bleeds a little. Her husband holds her hand tight. Her father came last
night to say goodbye to her; he looks older. He does not take care of
himself. That Johnny did not come set the tongues wagging; the gossip
is, he refuses to set eyes on his sister in her disgrace. That seems the only
thing to explain his attitude. All know he takes no interest in girls himself.

'Bless you, children,' says the Minister. With that troubling air of
incipient sainthood, the young husband settles his wife down on the
trunk and tucks a rug round her legs for a snappy wind drives dust down
the railroad track and the hills are October mauve and brown. In the
distance, the train whistle blows, that haunting sound, blowing across
endless distance, the sound that underlines the distance.

> EXTERIOR. FARMHOUSE. DAY
> Johnny mounts horse. Slings rifle over
>   shoulder.
> Kicks horse's sides.
>
> EXTERIOR. RAILROAD. DAY
> Train whistle. Burst of smoke.
> Engine pulling train across prairie.
>
> EXTERIOR. PRAIRIE. DAY
> Johnny galloping down track.
>
> EXTERIOR. RAILROAD. DAY
> Train wheels turning.
>
> EXTERIOR. PRAIRIE. DAY
> Hooves churning dust.
>
> EXTERIOR. STATION. DAY
>
> MINISTER'S WIFE: Now, you take care of
>   yourself, you hear? And – (but she can't
>   bring herself to say it).
>
> MINISTER: Be sure to tell us about the baby
>   as soon as it comes.

> (Close up) Annie-Belle smiling gratefully.
> Train whistle.

And see them, now, as if posing for the photographer, the young man and the pregnant woman, sitting on a trunk, waiting to be transported onwards, away, elsewhere, she with the future in her belly.

> EXTERIOR. STATION. DAY
> Station master comes out of ticket-office.
>
> STATION MASTER: Here she comes!
>
> (Long shot) Engine appearing round bend.
>
> EXTERIOR. STATION. DAY
> Johnny tethers his horse.
>
> ANNIE-BELLE: Why, Johnny, you've come to
> say goodbye after all!
>
> (Close up) Johnny, racked with emotion.
>
> JOHNNY: He shan't have you. He'll never
> have you. Here's where you belong, with
> me. Out here.

Giovanni: Thus die, and die by me, and by my hand!
   Revenge is mine; honour doth love command!
Annabella: Oh, brother, by your hand!

> EXTERIOR. STATION. DAY
>
> ANNIE-BELLE: Don't shoot – think of the
> baby! Don't –
>
> MINISTER'S SON: Oh, my God –
>
> Bang, bang, bang.

Thinking to protect his wife, the young husband threw his arms around her and so he died, by a split second, before the second bullet pierced her and both fell to the ground as the engine wheezed to a halt and passengers came tumbling off to see what Wild West antics were being played out while the parents stood and stared and did not believe, did not believe.

Seeing some life left in his sister, Johnny sank to his knees beside her and her eyes opened up and, perhaps, she saw him, for she said:

Annabella: Brother, unkind, unkind . . .

So that Death would be well satisfied, Johnny then put the barrel of the rifle into his mouth and pulled the trigger.

> EXTERIOR. STATION. DAY
> (Crane shot) The three bodies, the Minister
> comforting his wife, the passengers
> crowding off the train in order to look at
> the catastrophe.

> The 'Love Theme' rises over a pan of the
> prairie under the vast sky, the green breast
> of the continent, the earth, beloved, cruel,
> unkind.

NOTE:
The Old World John Ford made Giovanni cut out Annabella's heart and carry it on stage; the stage direction reads: *Enter Giovanni, with a heart upon his dagger.* The New World John Ford would have no means of representing this scene on celluloid, although it is irresistibly reminiscent of the ritual tortures practised by the Indians who lived here before.

Gun for the Devil

A hot, dusty, flyblown Mexican border town – a town without hope, without grace, the end of the road for all those who've the misfortune to find themselves washing up here. The time is about the turn of the century, long after the heroic period of the West is past; and there was never anything heroic about these border raiders, this poverty-stricken half-life they lead. The Mendozas, a barbarous hierarchy of bandits, run the town, its corrupt sheriff, its bank, the telegraph – everything. Even the priest is an appointment of theirs.

The only establishment in the town with a superficial veneer of elegance is the bar-cum-whorehouse. This is presided over by a curious, apparently ill-matched couple – an ageing, drunken, consumptive European aristocrat and his mistress, the madame, who keeps him. She's called Roxana, a straightforward, ageing, rather raddled, unimaginative, affectionate woman.

She is the sister of Maria Mendoza, the bandit's wife – that's how she obtained the brothel concession. Roxana and her man, the dying, despairing man they call the Count, arrived, the pair of them, out of nowhere, a few years back, penniless, in rags; they'd begged a ride in a farm cart . . . 'I've come home, Maria, after all this time . . . there's nowhere else to go.' Roxana'd had a lot of experience in the trade; with her brother-in-law's blessing, with his finance, she opened up a bar-cum-brothel and staffed it with girls who'd got good reason to lie low for a while – not, perhaps, the best class of whore. Five of them. But they suit the customers very well; they keep Mendoza's desperadoes out of trouble, they service his visitors – and sometimes there's a casual visitor, a stray passerby, a travelling salesman, say, or a smuggler. The brothel prospers.

And the Count, in his soiled, ruffled shirt and threadbare suits of dandified black, lends a little class to the joint; so his life has come to this, he serves to ornament his mistress's bar. A certain bitterness, a dour dignity, characterises the Count.

The Count lets visitors buy drinks for him; he is a soak, but a distinguished one, nevertheless. He keeps a margin of distance about himself – he has his pride, still, even if he's dying. He's rumoured to have been, in his day, in the Old Country, a legendary marksman. The girls chatter among themselves. Julie, the Yankee, says she's heard that he and Roxana used to do an act in a circus. He used to shoot all her clothes off her until she was as naked as the day she was born. As the day she was born!

But hadn't he killed Roxana's lover, no, not her lover but some man she'd been sold to, some seamy story . . . wasn't it in San Francisco, on the waterfront? No, no, no – everything happened in Austria, or Germany, or wherever it is he comes from, long before he met Roxana. He's not touched a gun since he met Roxana. He never shoots, now, even if his old-fashioned, long-barrelled rifle hangs on the wall . . . look! He was *too good* a shot; they said that only the devil himself – it's best not to pay attention to such stories, even if Maddalena once worked in a house in San Francisco where Roxana used to work and somebody told her – but the Count's shadow falls across the wall; they hush, even if Maddalena furtively crosses herself.

In this town, nobody asks any questions. Who would live here if they had the option to live anywhere else? Poor Teresa Mendoza, pretty as a picture, sweet sixteen, sullen, dissatisfied, she got a few ideas above her station when they sent her off to a convent to learn how to read and write. What does she need to read and write for? Not when she's condemned to live like a pig. But she's going to get married, isn't she? To a rich man? Yes, but he's a rich bandit!

In the afternoon, the slack time, Roxana and her sister sit in Roxana's boudoir with the shades down against the glaring sun, rocking on cane rocking-chairs, smoking cigars together and gently tippling tequila. Maria Mendoza is a roaring, mannish, booted and spurred bandit herself; savage, illiterate, mother of one daughter only, the beautiful Teresa. 'We finally fixed it, Roxana; signed, sealed and almost delivered . . . See, here's the picture of Teresa's fiancé . . . isn't he a handsome man? Eh? Eh?'

Roxana looks at the cherished photograph dubiously. Another bandit, even if a more powerful one than Mendoza himself! At least she, Roxana, has managed to get herself a man who doesn't wear spurs to bed. And Teresa hasn't even met her intended . . . 'No, no!' cries Maria. 'That's not necessary. Love will come, as soon as they're married, once he gets his leg over her . . . and the babies, my Teresa's babies, my grand-children, growing up in his enormous house, surrounded by servants bowing and scraping.' But Roxana is less certain and shakes her head doubtfully. 'Anyway, there's nothing Teresa can do about it,' says her mother firmly; 'it's all been fixed up by Mendoza, she'll be the bandit queen of the entire border. That's a lot better than living like a pig in this hole.'

The Mendozas do indeed live like pigs, behind a stockade, in a filthy, gypsy-like encampment of followers and hangers-on in the grounds of what was once, before the Mendozas took it over, a rather magnificent Spanish colonial hacienda. Now Mendoza himself, Teresa's hulking brute of a father, gallops his horse down the corridors, shoots out the windowpanes in his drunkenness. Teresa, the spoiled only daughter, screams at him in fury: 'We live like pigs! Like pigs!'

Problems in the brothel! The pianist has run off with the prettiest of all the girls; they're heading south to start up their own place, she reckons her husband won't chase her down as far as Acapulco. They wait for the stagecoach to take them away, sitting on barrels in the general store with their bags piled around them; the coach drops one passenger, the driver goes off to water the horses. Any work here for a piano-player? Why, what a coincidence!

He's from the north, a gringo. And a city boy, too, in a velvet coat, with such long, white fingers! He winces when he hears gunfire – a Mendoza employee boisterously shooting at chickens in the gutter. How pale he is . . . a handsome boy, nice, refined, educated voice. Is there even the trace of a foreign accent?

Like the Count, he is startlingly alien in this primitive, semi-desert environment.

Roxana melts maternally at the sight of him; he delights the Count by playing a little Brahms on the out-of-tune, honky-tonk piano. The Count's eyes mist over; he remembers . . . The conservatoire at Vienna? Can it be possible? How extraordinary . . . so you were studying at the conservatoire at Vienna? Although Roxana's delighted with her new employee, her lip curls, she is a natural sceptic. But he's the best piano-player she's ever heard.

And, anyway, nobody really asks questions in this town, or believes any answers, for that matter. He must have his reasons for holing up in this godforsaken place. The job's yours, Johnny; you get a little room over the porch to sleep in, with a lock on it to keep the girls out. They get bored . . . don't let them bother you.

But Johnny is in the grip of a singular passion; he is a grim and dedicated being. He ignores the girls completely.

In his bedroom, Johnny places photographs of a man and a woman – his parents – on the splintered pine dressing-table; pins up a poster for the San Francisco Opera House on the wall, *Der Freischütz*. He addresses the photographs. 'I've found out where they live, I've tracked them to their lair. It won't be long now, Mother and Father. Not long.'

Hoofbeats outside. Maria Mendoza is coming to visit her sister, riding astride, like a man, while her daughter rides side-saddle like a lady, even if her hair is an uncombed haystack. She looks the wild bandit-child she is. But – now she's an engaged woman, her father forbids her to visit the brothel, even to pay a formal call on her good aunt! Ride back home, Teresa!

Sullen, she turns her horse round. Looking back at the brothel as she trots away, she sees Johnny gazing at her from his window; their eyes meet, Johnny's briefly veil.

Teresa is momentarily confused; then spurs her horse cruelly, gallops off, like a wild thing.

In the small hours, when the brothel has finally closed down for the night, Johnny plays Chopin for the Count. Tears of sentimental nostalgia roll down the old man's cheeks. And Vienna . . . is it still the same? Try not to remember . . . he pours himself another whisky. Then Johnny asks him softly, is it true what he's heard . . . stories circulating in the faraway Austro-Hungarian Empire; the Count starts.

The old legend, about the man who makes a pact with the devil to obtain a bullet that cannot miss its target . . .

An old legend, says the Count. In the superstitious villages, they believe such things still.

All kinds of shadows drift in through the open window.

The old legend, given a new lease of life by the exploits of a certain aristocrat, who vanished suddenly, left everything. And the Mendozas, here, the bandits – aren't they all damned? Vicious, cruel . . . wouldn't a man who's sold his soul to the devil feel safest amongst the damned? Amongst whores and murderers?

The Count, shuddering, pours yet another whisky.

Is it true what they used to whisper, that the Count – this Count, you! old man – had a reputation as a marksman so extraordinary that everyone thought he had supernatural powers?

The Count, recovering himself, says: 'They said that of Paganini, that he must have learned how to play the fiddle from the devil. Since no human being could have played so well.'

'And perhaps he did,' says Johnny.

'You're a musician, not a murderer, Johnny.'

'Stranglers and piano-players both need long fingers. But a bullet is more merciful,' suggests Johnny obliquely.

Out of some kind of dream into which he's abruptly sunk, the Count says: 'The seventh bullet belongs to the devil. That is how you pay – '

But tonight, he won't, can't say any more. He lurches off to bed, to Roxana, who's waiting for him, as she always does. But why, oh why, is the old man crying? The whisky makes you into a baby . . . but Roxana takes care of you, she's always taken care of you, ever since she found you.

Roxana mothers the newcomer, Johnny, too, but she also watches him, with troubled eyes. All he does is play the piano and brood obsessively over the Mendoza gunmen as they sport and play in the bar. Sometimes he inspects the Count's old rifle, hung up on the wall, strokes the barrel, caresses the stock; but he knows nothing about the arts of death at all. Nothing! And he takes no interest in the girls, that's unhealthy.

It seems to Roxana that there's a likeness between her old man and the young one. That crazy, black-clad dignity. They always seem to be chatting to one another and sometimes they talk in German. Roxana hates that, it makes her feel shut out, excluded.

Can he be, can young Johnny be . . . some son the Count begot and then abandoned, a child he'd never known, come all this way to find him?

Could it be?

Old man and young one, with eyes the same shape, hands the same shape . . . could it be?

And if it is, why don't they tell her, Roxana?

Secrets make her feel shut out, excluded. She sits in her room on the rocking-chair in the dusk, sipping tequila.

Voices below – in German. She goes to her window, watches the Count and the piano-player wander off together in the direction of the little scummy pond in front of the brothel, which is set back off the main street.

She crosses herself, goes on rocking.

'Speak English, we must leave the Old World and its mysteries behind us,' says the Count. 'The old, weary, exhausted world. Leave it behind! This is a new country, full of hope . . .'

He is heavily ironic. The ancient rocks of the desert lour down in the sunset.

'But the landscape of this country is more ancient by far than we are, strange gods brood over it. I shall never be friends with it, never.'

Aliens, strangers, the Count and Johnny watch the Mendozas ride out on the rampage, led by Teresa's father; a band of grizzled hooligans, firing off their guns, shouting.

Johnny, calm, quiet, tells the Count how the Mendozas killed his parents when they raided a train for the gold the train carried. His parents, both opera singers, on their way back across the continent from California, from a booking in San Francisco . . . and he far away, in Europe.

Mendoza himself tore the earrings from his mother's ears. And raped her. And somebody shot his father when his father tried to stop the rape. And then they shot his mother because she was screaming so loudly.

Calm, quiet, Johnny recounts all.

'We all have our tragedies.'

'Some tragedies we can turn back on the perpetrators. I've planned my revenge. A suitably operatic revenge. I shall seduce the beautiful señorita and give her a baby. And if I can't shoot her father and mother, I shall find some way of strangling them with my beautiful pianist's hands.'

Quiet, assured, deadly – but incompetent. He doesn't know one end of a gun from the other; never raised his hand in anger in his life.

But he's been brooding on this revenge ever since the black-edged letter arrived at his lodgings in Vienna; in Vienna, where he heard how a nobleman made a pact with the devil, once, to ensure no bullet he ever fired would miss the mark . . .

'If you've planned it all so well, if you're dedicated to your vengeance . . .'

Johnny nods. Quiet, assured, deadly.

'If you're quite determined, then . . . you belong to the devil already. And a bullet is indeed more merciful than anger, if accurately fired.'

And the Count has always hated Mendoza's contempt for himself and Roxana, who live on Mendoza's charity.

But Johnny has never used a gun in his life. Old man, old man, what have you to lose? You've nothing, you've come to a dead end, kept by a whore in a flyblown town at the end of all the roads you ever took . . . give me a gun that will never miss a shot; that will fire by itself. I know you know how to get one. I know –

'I have nothing to lose,' says the Count inscrutably. 'Except my sins, Johnny. Except my sins.'

Teresa, sixteen, sullen, pretty, dissatisfied, retreats into her bedroom, into the depths of an enormous, gilded, four-poster bed looted from a train especially for her, surrounded by a jackdaw's nest of tawdry, looted glitter, gorges herself on chocolates, leafs through very very old fashion magazines. She hugs a scrawny kitten, her pet. Chickens roost on the canopy of her bed. Maa! maa! a goat pokes its head in through the open window. Teresa twitches with annoyance. You call this living?

Her door bursts open. An excited dog follows a flock of squawking chickens into the room; all the chickens roosting on the bed rise up, squawking. Chaos! The dog jumps on to the bed, begins to gnaw at the bloody something he carries in his mouth. Kitten rises on its hind legs to bat at the dog. Teresa hurls chocolates, magazines, screaming – insupportable! She storms out of the room.

In the courtyard, her mother is slaughtering a screaming pig. That's the sort of thing the Mendoza womenfolk enjoy! Ugh. Teresa's made for better things, she knows it.

She wanders disconsolately out into the dusty street. Empty. Like my life, like my life.

Willows bend over the scummy pool in front of Roxana's brothel; it has a secluded air.

Teresa skulks beside the pool, sullenly throwing stones at her own reflection. Morning, slack time; in voluptuous déshabillé, the whores lean over the veranda: 'Little Teresa! Little Teresa! Come in and see your auntie!' They laugh at her in her black stockings, her convent-girl dress, her rumpled hair.

Roxana's doing the books, behind the bar, with a pair of wire-rimmed glasses propped on her nose. The Count pours himself elevenses – she looks up, is about to remonstrate with him, thinks better of it, returns to her sums. Morning sunshine; outside on the veranda, the whores giggle and wave at Teresa.

Johnny idly begins to play a Strauss waltz. Roxana's foot taps a little.

The Count puts down his whisky. Smiles. He approaches Roxana, presents his arm. She's startled – then blushes, beams like a young girl. Takes off her glasses, pats her hair, glances at herself in the mirror behind the bar, pleasantly flustered. Seeing her pleasure, the Count becomes more courtly still. Still quite a fine figure of a man! And she, when she smiles, you see what a pretty girl she must have been.

Johnny flourishes the keys; he's touched. He begins to play a Strauss waltz in earnest.

Roxana takes the Count's proffered arm; they dance.

'Look! Look! Roxana's dancing!'

The whores flock back into the room, laughing, admiring. And begin to dance with one another, girl with girl, in their spoiled negligees, their unlaced corsets, petticoats, torn stockings.

Maddalena, partnerless, lingers on the veranda, teasing Teresa. Music spills out of the brothel.

'Teresa! Teresa! Come and dance with me!'

Slowly, slowly, Teresa arrives at the veranda, climbs the stairs, peers through a window as, flushed and breathless, the dancers collapse in a laughing heap.

She and Johnny exchange a flashing glance. But her aunt catches sight of her. 'Teresa, Teresa, scram! This is no place for you!'

At the Mendozas' dinner-table, her father sits picking his teeth with his knife.

'I want to learn the piano, papa.'

He continues to pick his teeth with his knife. She didn't want to learn the piano at the damn convent; why does she want to learn it now? To be a lady, Papa; isn't she going to have a grand wedding, marry a fine man? 'Papa, I want to learn the piano.'

Teresa is spoiled, indulged in everything. But her father likes to tease her; he'll drag out her pleading as long as he can. He doesn't often have his daughter pleading with him. He cuts himself a chunk more meat, munches.

'And who will teach you piano in his hole, hm?'

'Johnny. Johnny at Aunt Roxana's.'

He's suddenly really angry. You see what an animal he can become.

'What? My daughter learn piano in a brothel? Under the eye of that fat whore, Roxana?'

Maria leaps to her sister's defence, surging down on her husband with the carving knife held high. 'Don't you insult my sister!'

Mendoza twists her wrist; she drops the knife. 'I'm not having my daughter mixing with whores!'

'I want to learn piano,' the spoiled child insists.

'Over my dead body will you go to Roxana's to learn the piano, not now you are an engaged girl.'

'Then, papa, buy me a piano, let Johnny come here to teach me.'

A creaking wagon delivers a shiny, new, baby grand in the courtyard of the rotting hacienda, among the grunting pigs and flapping chickens.

Effortlessly, it's installed in Teresa's room; entranced, she picks at the notes. 'Kitty, kitty, the young man in the black jacket is coming to teach me piano . . .'

Her mother chaperones her, sitting, lolling in a rocking-chair, sipping tequila. Johnny, neat, elegant, a stranger, damned, with a portfolio of music under his arm, has come to give Teresa lessons. First, scales . . . soon, Czerny exercises. Johnny waits, watchful, biding his time.

Bored, her mother sips tequila and nods off to sleep . . . A Czerny exercise; Teresa hasn't quite mastered it. Making a mess of it, in fact. On purpose? Johnny's presence makes her flutter.

Johnny stands behind her, showing her where to put her hands. His long, white hands cover her little, brown paws with the bitten fingernails.

She turns to him. They kiss. She's eager, willing; he's surprised by her enthusiasm, almost taken aback. Despises her. It's going to be almost too easy!

But where is the seduction to be accomplished? Not in Teresa's bedroom, with her mother dozing in the rocking-chair. Not in Johnny's room at the brothel, either, under Aunt Roxana's watchful eye.

'In church, Johnny; nobody will look for lovers there.'

A huge, cavernous, almost cathedral, built in expectation of mass conversions among the Indians, now almost in ruins, on a kind of bluff, brooding over the half-ruined village. Empty. And they make love on the floor of the church, the savage child, the vengeance-seeker. Afterwards, triumphant, she buries her face in his breast, shrieking for glee; he is detached, rejoicing in his own coldness, his own wickedness.

Naked, Teresa wanders down the aisle of the church towards the altar, stands looking up vaguely at the rococo Christ. She pokes out her tongue at her saviour.

'I'll be here again, soon. I'm going to be married.'

'Married?'

'To a fine bandit gentleman.' Makes a face. 'Because I have no brothers, I am the heiress. My son will inherit everything, but first I must be married.'

'Oh, no,' says Johnny, lost, gone into his vengeance. 'You won't be married. I won't let you be married.'

Suspicious, at first. Then . . . 'Do you love me?' Exultant, shouting. 'So you love me! You must love me! You'll take me away!'

The Count rummages through a trunk in his and Roxana's bedroom, he gets out old books and curious instruments. The room is full of mysterious shadows. Roxana tries the door, finds that it is locked; she rattles the handle agitatedly. 'What are you up to? What secrets do you have from me? Is it the old secret? Is it — '

The Count lets her in, takes her into his arms. 'He'll take the burden from me, Roxana. He wants to, he's willing, he knows . . .'

'Your . . . son has come to set you free?'

'Not my son, Roxana.'

She is so relieved that she almost forgets the dark import of what he's saying. Yet she must ask him: 'And what's the price?'

'High, Roxana. Do you love a poor old man, do you love him more than you love your kin?'

Wide-eyed, she stares at him.

'Yes, old man, I do believe I do, It's been so long, now, since we've been together . . .'

'We'll be together for ever, Roxana.'

So he goes on assembling his occult materials and now she helps him. She has only one reservation. 'The little Teresa, nothing must happen to her . . .'

'No. Not Teresa. What harm has she ever done to anyone? Not Teresa.'

An eclipse of the moon. In the church, in darkness, at the altar, the

Count and Johnny summon the appropriate demon – the Archer of the Dark Abyss. Such a storm! Out of nowhere, a great wind, whirling the dust into a sandstorm. Roxana, alone in her bedroom full of curious shadows, draws the shutters close and mutters prayers, incantations.

The great wind blows open the doors of the church, sets them creaking on their hinges. Out of the sandstorms, hallucinatory figures emerge and merge, figures of demons or gods not necessarily those of Europe. The unknown continent, the new world, issues forth its banned daemonology.

The Count has summoned up more than he bargained for. He and Johnny crouch in the pentacle; Aztec and Toltec gods appear in giant forms. The church seems to have disappeared.

When the ritual is done, all clears; the interior of the church is a shambles, however, the Christ over the altar cast down on its face. Johnny and the Count pick themselves up from the floor, where the wind has left them. The Count is coughing horribly, his face is livid; the rite has nearly killed him.

Outside, all is calm now, a clear, bright night. The moon is back in the heavens again. Johnny, a man in the grip of a mania, stern, firm, helps the shaking Count to his feet.

'Where is the weapon?'

'He has come. He's waiting. He'll give it to us.'

Outside, against the wall, so still he's almost part of the landscape, an Indian sits in the dark, poncho, slouch hat, waiting, impassive.

The Count, leaning heavily on Johnny, greets the Indian with some courtly ceremony. But Johnny barks: 'Got the gun?'

'I got it.'

The gun changes hands. Johnny grabs it.

'How much?'

'On account,' says the Indian and grins. 'On account.'

He tips his hat. His pony, in the graveyard, grazes on a grave. The two Europeans watch him walk towards his pony, mount, ride. In the immense stillness of the night, his hoofbeats diminish.

Johnny inspects the Winchester repeater in his hands; it looks perfectly normal. Not used to guns, he handles it clumsily. His disappointment is obvious.

'What's so special about it? Could have bought one in the store.'

'It will fire seven bullets,' says the Count, impassive as any Indian. 'And the seventh bullet is the one that *he* put in it, it belongs to him.'

'But – '

'The seventh bullet is the devil's own. He will fire the seventh shot for you, even though you pull the trigger. But the other six can't miss their targets. Though you've never used a gun before.'

Incredulous, Johnny takes aim, fires at a movement in the darkness. He rushes towards the scream. His target, Teresa's kitten, dead.

'Five left now, for your own use,' says the Count. 'Use them sparingly. They come at a high price.'

Teresa wants her kitten. 'Kitty! Kitty!' But the kitten doesn't come. 'The dogs have eaten it,' says Teresa's mother. 'And hold still, Teresa, you're wriggling like an eel; how can I fit your wedding-dress . . . ?'

It's a store-bought wedding-dress, come on the stagecoach from Mexico City. All white lace. And a veil! In front of the clouded mirror in Teresa's bedroom, Maria pops the veil on her daughter's head; what a picture. But Teresa sulks.

'I don't want to get married.'

Too bad, Teresa! Tomorrow you must and will get married.

I won't. I won't!

You won't wheedle your father out of this one, not this time.

Teresa, in her wedding finery, picks out a few notes of the 'Wedding March' on her piano; furious, she slams the lid shut.

Johnny, at the piano in the whorehouse, plays a few bars of the 'Wedding March'; a wedding guest, drunk, flings his glass at the mirror behind the bar, smashing it. The whores superstitiously huddle and mutter. The place is packed out with wedding guests, all notable villains. But there is too much tension to be any joy. Roxana, unsmiling, rings up the price of a replacement mirror on her cash register. The Count, morose, stoops over his drink at the bar. The wedding guests treat him with genial contempt.

Teresa creeps out of her bedroom window, steals along the street, conceals herself hastily in the shadows when an Indian on a pony comes riding down the street.

Her lover waits for her by the scummy pond. Take me away. Save me! He strokes her hair with the first sign of tenderness. Perhaps he *will* take her away, if she can bear to look at him after the holocaust. Perhaps . . .

It's very late, now. Only the Count stays up. He's gazing at the recumbent form of a wedding guest passed out on the floor, snoring. The whores have stuck a feather hat on the visitor's head, taken off his trousers, daubed his face with rouge.

When Johnny comes in, the Count silently pours him a drink. He looks at the boy with, almost, love – certainly with some emotion.

'I could almost ask you . . .'

Johnny smiles, shakes his head, whistles a few bars of Chopin's 'Funeral March'.

'But then . . . be good to the little Teresa. "The prince of darkness is a gentleman . . ."'

Maybe. Maybe not. But, maybe . . .

How Teresa's hair tangles in the comb! A great bustle in the Mendoza encampment; they've got a carriage for her, decked it with exuberant paper flowers. But she herself is nervous, anxious; she chews at her underlip, she lets the women dress her as if she were a doll. Her mother, oddly respectable in black, weeps copiously. Teresa, in her wedding-dress and veil, suddenly turns to her mother and hugs her convulsively. The woman returns the embrace fiercely.

Johnny kisses the photographs of his father and mother. It's time. Unhandily carrying the rifle, in his music student's black velvet jacket, elegant, deadly, mad, he goes towards the church.

They've put back the rococo, suffering Christ; Johnny crouches beneath him, hiding under the skirts of the altar cloth. He tests the weight of the gun in his hand, peers through the sights.

The Count won't go to the wedding. No, he won't! He won't get out of bed. Please, Roxana, don't you go to the wedding, either! What? Not see my little niece Teresa get married? And you should come, too, you irreligious old man. Aren't you fond of Teresa?

But the Count is sick this morning. He can't crawl out of bed. He coughs, stares at the ominous bloodstains on his handkerchief.

'I'm dying, Roxana. Don't leave me.'

Though the bridegroom has arrived already, a huge brute, the image of Teresa's father. He takes his place before the altar. The congregation rustles. The organ plays softly.

Roxana, late, troubled, untidily dressed, slips in at the back of the church.

Teresa steps out of the flower-decorated carriage in front of the church. She's really worried, now, looking desperately around for Johnny. Her mother kisses her, again; this time, the girl doesn't respond, she's got too much on her mind. Her mother and the Mendoza womenfolk enter the church. Her father, a little dressed up, boots polished, offers her his arm.

Traditional gasps as she walks down the aisle – isn't she lovely! Even if her eyes search round and round the church for her rescuer. Where can he be? What will he do to save me?

The organ rings out.

Teresa arrives beside her bridegroom. From beneath her veil, she gives him a swift glance of furious dislike. The priest says the first words of the wedding service.

Johnny flings back the altar cloth, leaps on the altar, shoots point-blank the wide-eyed, open-mouthed Mendoza.

Mendoza tumbles backwards down the altar steps.

Silence. Then, shouting. Then, gunfire. Havoc!

But no bullet can touch Johnny; he shoots the bridegroom as the bridegroom leaps forward to attack him; shoots three – four – into the crowd of Mendoza desperadoes, two men fall.

Teresa, in her wedding finery, stands speechless, shocked.

Her mother, wailing, rushes from the crowd towards her dead husband.

Johnny aims, shoots Maria. She drops dead on to the body of her husband.

Teresa at last wakes up. She rushes through the havoc in the church; she is appalled, the world has come to an end.

Roxana fights free of the crowd and goes running after her. The church is a mêlée of shots, noise, gunsmoke.

Outside the church, the girl and woman meet. Teresa can't speak. Roxana hugs her, grabs her hand, pulls her down the path, towards the whorehouse.

Johnny erupts from the church door. Now he's like a mad dog. Blazing, furious, deadly – carrying a gun.

By the scummy pool, Roxana hears Johnny coming after them. She drags Teresa faster, faster – the girl stumbles over her white lace hem, now filthy with dust and blood. Faster, faster – he's coming, the murderer's coming, the devil himself is coming!

The Count's mistress and the beloved little Teresa run towards the whorehouse, where the Count gazes out of the window; run towards him, with the madman hot on their heels.

The Count opens the whorehouse door.

He's carrying the rifle that hangs on the wall of the bar.

Slowly, shakily, he raises it.

He's aiming at Johnny.

Teresa sees him, breaks free of Roxana's hand, dashes back towards her lover – to try to protect him? Some reason, sufficient to her hysteria.

Johnny, startled, halts; so the old man's turned against him, has he? The old man's turned his own magic rifle on the young one, the acolyte!

He takes aim at the Count, fires the seventh bullet.

He's forgotten it's the seventh bullet, forgotten everything except the sudden ease with which he can kill.

He fires the seventh bullet and Teresa drops dead by the side of the scummy pool. Her lace train slides down into the water.

The Count bursts into a great fit of tears. Roxana kneels by the dead girl, uselessly speaks to her, closes her eyes gently. Crosses herself. Gives the weeping Count, slumped on the whorehouse veranda, a long, dark look.

The crowd spills out of the church.
Johnny drops his gun, turns, runs.

Coda

Almost the desert. White, fantastic rocks, sand, burning sun. Johnny
stole one of the Mendozas' horses; now it founders beneath him. He
shades his eyes; there's a village in the distance . . .

But this village seems deserted. A weird, shabby figure in his music-
student's black jacket, he draws water from the well, drinks. At last, a
thin, ragged, filthy child emerges from the derelict house.

'The smallpox came. All dead, all dead.'

Flies buzz on an unburied corpse in a murky interior. Johnny retches.
He's white-faced, fevered – you would have said, a man with the devil
pursuing him.

At the end of the village, gazing across the acres of desert before him, a
figure is propped against the wall, a figure so still, so silent as at first to
seem part of the landscape. He smiles to see Johnny stumbling towards
him.

'I was waiting for you,' says the Indian who sold Johnny the gun. 'We
have some business to conclude.'

The Merchant of Shadows

I killed the car. And at once provoked such sudden, resonant quiet as if, when I switched off the ignition, I myself brought into being the shimmering late afternoon hush, the ripening sun, the very Pacific that, way below, at the foot of the cliff, shattered its foamy peripheries with the sound of a thousand distant cinema organs.

I'd never get used to California. After three years, still the enchanted visitor. However frequently I had been disappointed, I still couldn't help it, I still tingled with expectation, still always thought that something wonderful might happen.

Call me the Innocent Abroad.

All the same, you can take the boy out of London but you can't take London out of the boy. You will find my grasp of the local lingo enthusiastic but shaky. I call gas 'petrol', and so on. I don't intend to go native, I'm not here for good, I'm here upon a pilgrimage. I have hied me, like a holy palmer, from the dishevelled capital of a foggy, three-cornered island on the other side of the world where the light is only good for water-colourists to this place where, to wax metaphysical about it, Light was made Flesh.

I am a student of Light and Illusion. That is, of cinema. When first I clapped my eyes on that HOLLYWOODLAND sign back in the city now five hours' hard drive distant, I thought I'd glimpsed the Holy Grail.

And now, as if it were the most everyday thing in the world, I was on my way to meet a legend. A living legend, who roosted on this lonely cliff-top like a forlorn seabird.

I was parked in a gravelled lot where the rough track I'd painfully negotiated since I left the minor road that brought me from the freeway terminated. I shared the parking lot with a small, red, crap-caked Toyota truck that, some time ago, had seen better days. There was straw in the back. Funny kind of transportation for a legend. But I knew she was in there, behind the gated wall in front of me, and I needed a little time along with the ocean before the tryst began. I climbed out of the car and crept close to the edge of the precipice.

The ocean shushed and tittered like an audience when the lights dim before the main feature.

The first time I saw the Pacific, I'd had a vision of sea gods, but not the ones *I* knew, oh, no. Not even Botticelli's prime 36B cup blonde ever came in on *this* surf. My entire European mythology capsized under the crash of waves Britannia never ruled and then I knew that the denizens of these deeps are *sui generis* and belong to no mythology but their weird own. They have the strangest eyes, lenses on stalks that go flicker, flicker, and give you the truth twenty-four times a second. Their torsos luminesce in every shade of technicolor but have no depth, no substance, no dimensionality. Beings from a wholy strange pantheon. Beautiful – but alien.

Aliens were somewhat on my mind, however, perhaps because I was somewhat alienated myself in LA, but also due to the obsession of my room-mate. While I researched my thesis, I was rooming back there in the city in an apartment over a New Age bookshop-cum-healthfood restaurant with a science fiction freak I'd met at a much earlier stage of studenthood during the chance intimacy of the mutual runs in Barcelona. Now he and I subsisted on brown rice courtesy of the Japanese waitress from downstairs, with whom we were both on, ahem, intimate terms, and he was always talking about aliens. He thought most of the people you met on the streets were aliens cunningly simulating human beings. He thought the Venusians were behind it.

He said he had tested Hiroko's reality quotient sufficiently and *she* was clear, but I guessed from his look he wasn't too sure about me. That shared diarrhoea in the Plaza Real was providing a shaky bond. I stayed out of the place as much as possible. I kept my head down at school all day and tried to manifest humanity as well as I knew how whenever I came home for a snack, a shower and, if I got the chance, one of Hiroko's courteous if curiously impersonal embraces. Now my host showed signs of getting into leather. Would it soon be time to move?

It must be the light that sends them crazy, that white light now refracting from the sibilant Pacific, the precious light that, when it is distilled, becomes the movies. *Ars Magna Lucis et Umbrae*, the Great Art of Light and Shade as Athanias Kircher put it, he who tinkered with magic lanterns four centuries ago in the Gothic north.

And from that Gothic north had come the object of the quest that brought me to this luminous hill-top – a long-dead Teutonic illusionist who'd played with light and shade as well as any. You know him as Hank Mann, that 'dark genius of the screen', the director with 'the occult touch', that neglected giant etc. etc. etc.

But stay, you may ask, how can a dead man, no matter how occult his touch, be the object of a quest?

Aha! In that cliff-top house he'd left the woman, part of whose legend was she was his widow.

He had been her ultimate husband. First (silent movies) she'd hitched up with an acrobatic cowboy and, when a pinto threw him, she'd joined a *soi-disant* Viennese tenor for a season of kitschissimo musicals during early sound. Hank Mann turned her into an icon after he rescued her off a cardboard crag where he'd come upon her, yodelling. When Mann passed on, she shut up marital shop entirely, and her screen presence acquired the frozen majesty of one appreciating, if somewhat belatedly, the joys of abstinence. She never did another on-screen love scene, either.

If you are a true buff, you know that he was born Heinrich von Mannheim. One or two titles in two or three catalogues survive from his early days at UFA, plus a handful of scratched, faded stills.

My correspondence with his relict, conducted through somebody who pp'd for her in an illegible scrawl, finally produced this invitation. I'd been half-stunned with joy. I was, you understand, writing my thesis about Mannheim. He had become my pet, my hobby, my obsession.

But you must understand that I was prevaricating out of pure nerves. For she was far, far more than a Hollywood widow; she was the Star of Stars, no less, the greatest of them all . . . dubbed by *Time* magazine the 'Spirit of the Cinema' when, on her eightieth birthday, she graced its cover for the seventh time, with a smile like open day in a porcelain factory and a white lace mantilla on the curls that time had bleached with its inexorable peroxide. And had she not invited me, me! to call for a chat, a drink, at this ambiguous hour, martini-time, the blue hour, when you fold up the day and put it away and shake out the exciting night?

Only surely she was well past the expectation of exciting times. She had become what Hiroko's people call a 'living national treasure'. Decade after ageless decade, movie after movie, 'the greatest star in heaven'. That was the promo. She'd no especial magic, either. She was no Gish, nor Brooks, nor Dietrich, nor Garbo, who all share the same gift, the ability to reveal otherness. She *did* have a certain touch-me-not thing, that made her a natural for *film noir* in the Forties. Otherwise, she possessed only the extraordinary durability of her presence, as if continually incarnated afresh with the passage of time due to some occult operation of the Great Art of Light and Shade.

One odd thing. As Svengali, Hank Mann had achieved a posthumous success. Although it was he who had brushed her with stardust (she'd been a mere 'leading player' up till then), her career only acquired that touch of the fabulous after he adjourned to the great cutting room in the sky.

There was a scent of jasmine blowing over the wall from an invisible garden. I deeply ingested breath. I checked out my briefcase: notebook, recorder, tapes. I checked that the recorder contained tape. I was nervous as hell. And then there was nothing for it but, briefcase in hand, to summon the guts to stride up to her gate.

It was an iron gate with a sheet of zinc behind the wrought squiggles so you couldn't see through and, when I reached up to ring the bell, this gate creaked open of its own accord to let me in and then swung to behind me with a disconcerting, definitive clang. So there I was.

A plane broke the darkening dish of sky, that sealed up again behind it. Inside the garden, it was very quiet. Nobody came to meet me.

A flight of rough-cut stone steps led up to a pool surrounded by clumps of sweet-smelling weeds; I recognised lavender. A tree or two dropped late summer leaves on scummy water and, when I saw that pool, I couldn't help it, I started to shiver; I'll tell you why in a minute. That untended pool, in which a pair of dark glasses with one cracked lens rested on an emerald carpet of algae, along with an empty gin bottle.

On the terrace, a couple of rusty, white-enamelled chairs, a lop-sided table. Then, fringed by a clump of cryptomeria, the house von Mannheim caused to be erected for his bride.

That house made the Bauhaus look baroque. An austere cube of pure glass, it exhibited the geometry of transparency at its most severe. Yet, just at that moment, it took all the red light of the setting sun into itself and flashed like a ruby slipper. I knew the wall of the vast glittering lounge gaped open to admit me, and only me, but I thought, well, if nobody has an objections, I'll just stick around on the terrace for a while, keep well away from that glass box that looks like nothing so much as the coffin for a classical modernist Snow White; let the lady come out to me.

No sound but the deep, distant bass of the sea; a gull or two; pines, hushing one another.

So I waited. And waited. And I found myself wondering just what it was the scent of jasmine reminded me of, in order to take my mind off what I knew damn well the swimming pool reminded me of – *Sunset Boulevard*, of course. And I knew damn well, of course I knew, that this was indeed the very pool in which my man Hank Mann succumbed back in 1940, so very long ago, when not even I nor my blessed mother, yet, was around to so much as piss upon the floor.

I waited until I found myself growing impatient. How does one invoke the Spirit of Cinema? Burn a little offering of popcorn and old fan magazines? Offer a libation of Jeyes' Fluid mixed with Kia Ora orange?

I found myself vengefully asserting that I knew one or two things about her old man that perhaps she never knew herself. For example, his grandmother's maiden name (Ernst). I knew he entered UFA and swept the cutting-room floor. I talked to the son he left behind in Germany shortly after conceiving him. Nice old buffer, early sixties, retired bank

THE MERCHANT OF SHADOWS

clerk, prisoner of war in Norfolk, England, 1942–6, perfect English, never so much as met his father, no bitterness. Brought up exclusively by the first Frau Mannheim, actress. He showed me a still. Kohled eyes, expressionist cheek-bones, star of Mannheim's UFA one-reeler of *The Fall of the House of Usher*, now lost. Frau von Mannheim, victim of the Dresden fire raid. Hm. Her son expressed no bitterness at that, either, and I felt ashamed until he told me she'd ended up the official mistress of a fairly nasty Nazi. Then I felt better.

I'd actually got to meet the second Mrs Mann, now a retired office cleaner and full-time lush in downtown LA. Once a starlet; lack of exposure terminated her career. Once a call girl. Age terminated her career. The years had dealt hardly with her. Vaguely, she recalled him, a man she once married. She'd had a hangover, he moved into her apartment. She'd still had a hangover. Then he moved out. *God*, she'd had a hangover. They divorced and she married somebody else, whose name escaped her. She accepted ten bucks off me with the negligent grace of habitual custom. I couldn't think why he'd married her and she couldn't remember.

Anyway, after I'd donated ten bucks and packed up my tape recorder, she, as if now I'd paid she felt she owed, started to rummage around amongst the cardboard boxes – shoe boxes, wine crates – with which her one-room competency was mostly furnished. Things tipped and slithered everywhere, satin dancing slippers, old hats, artificial flowers; spilled face powder rose up in clouds and out of the clouds, she, wheezing with triumph, emerged with a photograph.

Nothing so quaint as out-of-date porn. It was an artfully posed spanking pic. I knew him at once, with his odd, soft, pale, malleable face, the blond, slicked-down hair, the moustache, in spite of the gym slip, suspenders and black silk stockings; he sprawled athwart the knee of the second Mrs Mann, who sported a long-line leather bra and splendid boots. Hand raised ready to smack his exposed botty, she turned upon the camera a toothy smile. She'd been quite pretty, in a spit-curled way. She said I could have the snap for a couple of hundred dollars but I was on a tight budget and thought it wouldn't add much to the history of film.

Foresightfully, von Mannheim had left Germany in good time, but he started over in Hollywood at the bottom (forgive the double entendre). His ascent, however, was brisk. Assistant art director, assistant director, director.

The masterpiece of Mann's Hollywood period is, of course, *Paracelsus* (1937), with Charles Laughton. Laughton's great bulk swims into pools of scalding light out of greater or lesser shoals of darkness like a vast monster of the deep, a great, black whale. The movie haunts you like a bad dream. Mann did not try to give you a sense of the past; instead, *Paracelsus* looks as if it had been made in the middle ages – the gargoyle faces, bodies warped with ague, gaunt with famine, a claustrophobic sense of a limited world, of chronic, cramped unfreedom.

The Spirit of Cinema cameos in *Paracelsus* as the Gnostic goddess of wisdom, Sophia, in a kind of Rosicrucian sabbat scene. They were married, by then. Mann wanted his new bride nude for this sabbat, which caused a stir at the time and eventually he was forced to shoot only her disembodied face floating above suggestive shadow. Suggestive, indeed; from his piece of sleight of hand sprang two myths, one, easily discredited by aficionados of the rest of her oeuvre, that she had the biggest knockers in the business, the other, less easily dismissed, that she was thickly covered with body hair from the sternum to the knee. Even Mann's ex-assistant director believed the latter. 'Furry as a spider,' he characterised her. 'And just as damn lethal.' I'd smuggled a half-pint of Jack Daniels into his geriatric ward; he waxed virulent, he warned me to take a snake-bite kit to the interview.

Paracelsus was, needless to say, one of the greatest box-office disasters in the history of the movies. Plans were shelved for his long-dreamed-of *Faust*, with the Spirit either as Gretchen or as Mephistopheles, or as Gretchen doubling *with* Mephistopheles, depending on what he said in different interviews. Mann was forced to perpetrate a hack job, a wallowing melo with the Spirit as twins, a good girl in a blonde wig and a bad girl in a black one, from which his career never recovered and her own survival truly miraculous.

Shortly after this notorious stinker was released to universal jeers, he did the *A Star is Born* bit, although he walked, not into the sea, but into the very swimming pool, that one over there, in which his relict now disposes of her glassware.

As for the Spirit, she found a new director, was rumoured to have undergone a little, a very little plastic surgery, and, the next year, won her first Oscar. From that time on, she was unstoppable, though always she carried her tragedy with her, like a permanent widow's veil, giving her the spooky allure of a born-again *princesse lointaine*.

Who liked to keep her guests waiting.

In my nervous ennui, I cast my eyes round and round the terrace until I came upon something passing strange in the moist earth of a flowerbed.

Moist, therefore freshly watered, though not by whatever it was had left such amazing spoor behind it. No big-game hunter I, but I could have sworn that, impressed on the soil, as if in fresh concrete outside Graumann's Chinese Theatre, was the print, unless the tiger lilies left it, of a large, clawed paw.

Did you know a lion's mane grows grey with age? I didn't. But the geriatric feline that now emerged from a clump of something odorous beneath the cryptomeria had snow all over his hairy eaves. He appeared as taken aback to see me as I was to bump into him. Our eyes locked. Face like a boxer with a broken nose. Then he tilted his enormous head to one side, opened his mouth – God, his breath was foul – and roared like the last movement of Beethoven's Ninth. With a modest blow of a single paw, he could have batted me arse over tip off the cliff half-way to Hawaii. I wouldn't say it was much comfort to see he'd had his teeth pulled out.

'Aw, come on, Pussy, he don't want to be gummed to death,' said a cracked, harsh, aged, only residually female voice. 'Go fetch Mama, now, there's a good boy.'

The lion grumbled a little in his throat but trotted off into the house with the most touching obedience and I took breath, again – I noticed I'd somehow managed not to for some little time – and sank into one of the white metal terrace chairs. My poor heart was going pit-a-pat, I can tell you, but the *personage* who had at last appeared from somewhere in the darkening compound neither apologised for nor expressed concern about my nasty shock. She stood there, arms akimbo, surveying me with a satirical, piercing, blue eye.

Except for the jarring circumstances that in one hand she held a stainless steel, many-branched candlestick of awesomely chaste design, she looked like a superannuated lumberjack, plaid shirt, blue jeans, workboots, butch leather belt with a giant silver skull and crossbones for a buckle, coarse, cropped, grey hair escaping from a red bandana tied Indian-style around her head. Her skin was wrinkled in pinpricks like the surface of Parmesan cheese and a putty grey in colour.

'You the one that's come about the thesis?' she queried. Her diction was pure hillbilly.

I burbled in the affirmative.

'He's come about the thesis,' she repeated to herself sardonically and discomforted me still further by again cackling to herself.

But now an ear-splitting roar announced action was about to commence. This Ma, or Pa, Kettle person set down her candlestick on the terrace table, briskly struck a match on the seat of her pants and applied the flame to the wicks, dissipating the gathering twilight as She rolled out the door. Rolled. She sat in a chrome and ivory leather wheel-chair as if upon a portable throne. Her right hand rested negligently on the lion's mane. She was a sight to see.

How long had she spent dressing up for the interview? Hours. Days. Weeks. She had on a white satin bias-cut lace-trimmed negligee circa

1935, her skin had that sugar almond, one hundred per cent Max Factor look and she wore what I assumed was a wig due to the unnatural precision of the snowy curls. Only she'd gone too far with the wig; it gave her a Medusa look. Her mouth looked funny because her lips had disappeared with age so all that was left was a painted-in red trapezoid.

But she didn't look her age, at all, at all – oh, no; she looked a good ten or fifteen years younger, though I doubt the vision of a sexy septua-genarian was the one for which she'd striven as she decked herself out. Impressive, though. Impressive as hell.

And you knew at once this was the face that launched a thousand ships. Not because anything lovely was still smouldering away in those old bones; she'd, as it were, transcended beauty. But something in the way she held her head, some imperious arrogance, demanded that you look at her and keep on looking.

At once I went into automatic, I assumed the stance of gigolo. I picked up her hand, kissed it, said: '*Enchanté*', bowed. Had I not been wearing sneakers, I'd have clicked my heels. The Spirit appeared pleased but not surprised by this, but she couldn't smile for fear of cracking her make-up. She whispered me a throaty greeting, eyeing me in a very peculiar way, a way that made the look in the lion's eye seem positively vegetarian.

It freaked me. She freaked me. It was her *star quality*. So *that*'s what they mean! I thought. I'd never before, nor am I likely to again, encountered such psychic force as streamed out of that frail little old lady in her antique lingerie and her wheel-chair. And, yes, there was something undeniably erotic about it, although she was old as the hills; it was as though she got the most extraordinary sexual charge from being looked at and this charge bounced back on the looker, as though some mechanism inside herself converted your regard into sexual energy. I wondered, not quite terrified, if I was for it, know what I mean.

And all the time I kept thinking, it kept running through my head: 'The phantom is up from the cellars again!'

Night certainly brought out the scent of jasmine.

She whispered me a throaty greeting. Her faded voice meant you had to crouch to hear her, so her cachou-flavoured breath stung your cheek, and you could tell she loved to make you crouch.

'My sister,' she husked, gesturing towards the lumberjack lady who was watching this performance of domination and submission with her thumbs stuck in her belt and an expression of unrelieved cynicism on her face. Her sister. God.

The lion rubbed its head against my leg, making me jump, and she pummelled its greying mane.

'And this – oh! you'll have seen him a thousand times; more exposure than any of us. Allow me to introduce Leo, formerly of MGM.'

The old beast cocked its head from side to side and roared again, in unmistakable fashion, as if to identify itself. Mickey Mouse does her chauffeuring. Every morning, she takes a ride on Trigger.

'*Ars gratia artis*,' she reminded me, as if guessing my thoughts. 'Where could he go, poor creature, when they retired him? Nobody would touch a fallen star. So he came right here, to live with Mama, didn't you, darling.'

'Drinkies!' announced Sister, magnificently clattering a welcome, bottle-laden trolley.

After the third poolside martini, which was gin at which a lemon briefly sneered, I judged it high time to broach the subject of Hank Mann. It was pitch dark by then, a few stars burning, night sounds, sea sounds, the creak of those metal chairs that seemed to have been designed, probably on purpose, by the butch sister, to break your balls. But it was difficult to get a word in. The Spirit was briskly checking out my knowledge of screen history.

'No, the art director certainly was *not* Ben Carré, how absurd to think that! . . . My goodness me, young man, Wallace Reid was dead and buried by then, and good riddance to bad rubbish . . . Edith Head? Edith Head design Nancy Carroll's patent leather evening dress? Who put that into your noddle?'

Now and then the lion sandpapered the back of my hand with its tongue, as if to show sympathy. The butch sister put away gin by the tumblerful, two to my one, and creaked resonantly from time to time, like an old door.

'No, no, no, young man! Laughton certainly was *not* addicted to self-abuse!'

And out of the dark it came to me that that dreamy perfume of jasmine issued from no flowering shrub but, instead, right out of the opening sequence of *Double Indemnity*, do you remember? And I suffered a ghastly sense of incipient humiliation, of impending erotic doom, so that I shivered, and Sister, alert and either comforting or complicitous, sloshed another half pint of gin into my glass.

Then Sister belched and announced: 'Gonna take a leak.'

Evidently equipped with night vision, she rolled off into the gloaming from whence, after a pause, came the tinkle of running water. She'd gone back to Nature as far as toilet training was concerned, cut out the frills. The raunchy sound of Sister making pee-pee brought me down to earth again. I clutched my tumbler, for the sake of holding something solid.

'About thish time,' I said, 'you met Hank Mann.'

Night and candlelight turned the red mouth black, but her satin dress
shone like water with plankton in it.

'Heinrich,' she corrected with a click of orthodontics; and then, or so it
seemed, fell directly into the trance for, all at once, she fixed her gaze on
the middle distance and said no more.

I thankfully took advantage of her lapse of attention to pour my gin
down the side of my chair, trusting that by the morrow it would be
indistinguishable from lion piss. Sister, clanking her death's head belt-
buckle as she readjusted her clothing, came back to us and juggled ice and
lemon slices as if nothing untoward was taking place. Then, in a perfectly
normal, even conversational tone, the Spirit said: 'White kisses, red
kisses. And coke in a golden casket on top of the baby grand. Those were
the days.'

Sister t'sked, possibly with irritation.

'Reckon you've had a skinful,' said Sister. 'Reckon you deserve a stiff
whupping.'

That roused the Spirit somewhat, who chuckled and lunged at the gin
which, fortunately, stood within her reach. She poured a fresh drink
down the hatch in a matter of seconds, then made a vague gesture with
her left hand, inadvertently biffing the lion in the ear. The lion had dozed
off and grumbled like an empty stomach to have his peace disturbed.

'They wore away her face by looking at it too much. So we made her a
new one.'

'Hee haw, hee haw,' said Sister. She was not braying but laughing.

The Spirit propped herself on the arm of her wheel-chair and pierced
me with a look. Something told me we had gone over some kind of edge.
Nancy Carroll's evening dress, indeed. Enough of that nonsense. Now
we were on a different plane.

'I used to think of prayer wheels,' she informed me. 'Night after night,
prayer wheels ceaselessly turning in the darkened cathedrals, those
domed and gilded palaces of the Faith, the Majestics, the Rialtos, the
Alhambras, those grottoes of the miraculous in which the creatures of the
dream came out to walk within the sight of men. And the wheels spun out
those subtle threads of light that wove the liturgies of that reverential age,
the last great age of religion. While the wonderful people out there in the
dark, the congregation of the faithful, the company of the blessed, they
leant forward, they aspired upwards, they imbibed the transmission of
divine light.

'Now, the priest is he who prints the anagrams of desire upon the
stock; but whom does he project upon the universe? Another? Or,
himself?'

All this was somewhat more than I'd bargained for. I fought with the gin fumes reeling in my head, I needed all my wits about me. Moment by moment, she became more gnomic. Surreptitiously, I fumbled with my briefcase. I wanted to get that tape recorder spooling away, didn't I; why, it might have been Mannheim talking.

'Is he the one who interprets the spirit or does the spirit speak through him? Or is he only, all the time, nothing but the merchant of shadows? 'Hic,' she interrupted herself.

Then Sister, whose vision was not one whit impaired by time or liquor, extended her trousered leg in one succinct and noiseless movement and kicked my briefcase clear into the pool, where it dropped with a liquid plop.

In spite of the element of poetic justice in it, that my file on Mannheim should suffer the same fate as he, I must admit that now I fell into a great fear. I even thought they might have lured me here to murder me, this siren of the cinema and her weird acolyte. Remember, they had made me quite drunk; it was a moonless night and I was far from home; and I was trapped helpless among these beings who could only exist in California, where the light made movies and madness. And one of them had just arbitrarily drowned the poor little tools of my parasitic trade, leaving me naked and at their mercy. The kindly lion shook himself awake and licked my hand again, perhaps to reassure me, but I wasn't expecting it and jumped half out of my skin.

The Spirit broke into speech again.

'She is only in semi-retirement, you know. She still spends three hours every morning looking through the scripts that almost break the mailman's back as he staggers beneath them up to her cliff-top retreat.

'Age does not wither her; we've made quite sure of that, young man. She still irradiates the dark, for did we not discover the true secret of immortality together? How to exist almost and only in the eye of the beholder, like a genuine miracle?'

I cannot say it comforted me to theorise this lady was, to some degree, possessed, and so was perfectly within her rights to refer to herself in the third person in that ventriloquial, insubstantial voice that scratched the ear as smoke scratches the back of the throat. But by whom or what possessed? I felt very close to the perturbed spirit of Heinrich von Mannheim and the metaphysics of the Great Art of Light and Shade, I can tell you. And speaking of the latter – Athanias Kircher, author, besides, of *Spectacula Paradoxa Rerum* (1624), *The Universal Theatre of Paradoxes*.

Her eyelids were drooping now, and as they closed her mouth fell open, but she spoke no more.

The Sister broke the silence as if it were wind.

'That's about the long and short of it, young man,' she said. 'Got enough for your thesis?'

She heaved herself up with a sigh so huge that, horrors! it blew out all the candles and then, worse and worse! she left me alone with the Spirit. But nothing more transpired because the Spirit seemed to have passed, if not on, then out, flat out in her wheel-chair, and the inner light that brought out the shine on her satin dress was extinguished too. I saw nothing, until a set of floods concealed in the pines around us came on and everything was visible as common daylight, the old lady, the drowsing lion, the depleted drinks trolley, the slices of lemon ground into the terrace by my nervous feet, the little plants pushing up between the cracks in the paving, the black water of the swimming pool in which my over-excited, suddenly light-wounded senses hallucinated a corpse.

Which last resolved itself, as I peered, headachy and blinking, into my own briefcase, opened, spilling out a floating debris of papers and tape boxes. I poured myself another gin, to steady my nerves. Sister appeared again, right behind my shoulder, making me jog my elbow so gin soaked my jeans. Her Indian headband had knocked rakishly askew, giving her a piratical air. In close-up, her bones, clearly visible under her ruined skin, reminded me of somebody else's, but I was too chilled, drunk and miserable to care whose they might be. She was cackling to herself, again.

'We hates y'all with the tape recorders,' she said. 'Reckon us folks thinks you is dancin' on our graves.'

She aimed a foot at the brake on the Spirit's wheel-chair and briskly pushed it and its unconscious contents into the house. The lion woke up, yawned like the opening of the San Andreas fault and padded after. The sliding door slid to. After a moment, a set of concealing crimson curtains swished along the entire length of the glass wall and that was that. I half-expected to see the words, THE END, come up on the curtains, but then the lights went off and I was in the dark.

Unwilling to negotiate the crazy steps down to the gate, I reached sightlessly for the gin and sucked it until I fell into a troubled slumber.

And I awoke me on the cold hill-side.

Well, not exactly. I woke up to find myself tucked into the back seat of my own VW, parked on the cliff beside the Toyota truck in the grey hour before dawn, my frontal lobes and all my joints a-twang with pain. I didn't even try the gate of the house. I got out of the car, shook myself, got back in again and headed straight home. After a while, on the perilous road to the freeway, I saw in the driving mirror a vehicle approaching me from behind. It was the red Toyota truck. Sister, of course, at the wheel.

She overtook me at illicit speed, blasting the horn joyously, waving with one hand, her face split in a toothless grin. When I saw that smile, even though the teeth were missing, I knew who she reminded me of – of a girl in a dirndl on a cardboard alp, smiling because at last she saw approaching her the man who would release her . . . If I hadn't, in the interests of scholarship, sat yawning through that dire operetta in the viewing booth, I would never have so much as guessed.

She must have hated the movies. Hated them. She had the lion in back. They looked as if they were enjoying the ride. Probably Leo had smiled for the cameras once too often, too. They parked at the place where the cliff road ended and waited there, quite courteously, until I was safely embarked among the heavy traffic, out of their lives.

How had they found a corpse to substitute for von Mannheim? A corpse was never the most difficult thing to come by in Southern California, I suppose. I wondered if, after all those years, they finally decided to let me in on the masquerade. And, if so, why.

Perhaps, having constructed this masterpiece of subterfuge, von Mannheim couldn't bear to die without leaving some little hint, somewhere, of how, having made her, he then *became* her, became a better she than she herself had ever been, and wanted to share with his last little acolyte, myself, the secret of his greatest hit. But, more likely, he simply couldn't resist turning himself into the Spirit one last time, couldn't let down his public . . . for they weren't to know I'd seen a picture of him in a frock, already, were they, although in those days, he still wore a moustache. And that clinched it, in my own mind, when I remembered the second Mrs Mann's spanking picture, although this conviction did not make me any the less ill at ease.

In the healthfood restaurant, Hiroko slapped the carrot-juicer with a filthy cloth and fed me brown rice and chilled bean-curd with chopped onion and ginger on top, pursing her lips with distaste; she herself only ate Kentucky fried chicken. Business was slack in the mid-afternoon and I wanted her to come upstairs with me for a while, to remind me there was more to flesh than light and illusion, but she shook her head.

'Boring,' she said, offensively. After a while she added, though in no conciliatory tone, 'Not just you. Everything. California. I've seen this movie. I'm going home.'

'I thought you said you felt like an enemy alien at home, Hiroko.'

She shrugged, staring through her midnight bangs at the white sunlight outside.

'Better the devil you know,' she said.

I realised I was just a wild oat to her, a footnote to her trip, and, although she had been just the same to me, all the same I grew glum to realise how peripheral I was, and suddenly wanted to go home, too, and longed for rain again, and television, that secular medium.

The Ghost Ships

A CHRISTMAS STORY

> Therefore that whosoever shall be found observing any such day as
> Christmas or the like, either by forebearing of labor, feasting, or any other
> way upon any such account aforesaid, every person so offending shall pay
> for every offense five shillings as a fine to the county.

Statute enacted by the General Court of
Massachusetts, May 1659, repealed 1681

'Twas the night before Christmas. Silent night, holy night. The snow lay
deep and crisp and even. Etc. etc. etc.; let these familiar words conjure up
the traditional anticipatory magic of Christmas Eve, and then – forget it.

Forget it. Even if the white moon above Boston Bay ensures that all is
calm, all is bright, there will be no Christmas *as such* in the village on the
shore that now lies locked in a precarious winter dream.

(Dream, that uncensorable state. They would forbid it if they could.)

At that time, for we are talking about a long time ago, about three and a
quarter hundred years ago, the newcomers had no more than scribbled
their signatures on the blank page of the continent that was, as it lay under
the snow, no whiter nor more pure than their intentions.

They plan to write more largely; they plan to inscribe thereon the name
of God.

And that was why, because of their awesome piety, tomorrow, on
Christmas Day, they will wake, pray and go about their business as if it
were any other day.

For them, all days are holy but none are holidays.

New England is the new leaf they have just turned over; Old England is
the dirty linen their brethren at home have just – did they not recently win
the English Civil War? – washed in public. Back home, for the sake of
spiritual integrity, their brothers and sisters have broken the graven images
in the churches, banned the playhouses where men dress up as women,
chopped down the village Maypoles because they welcome in the spring
in altogether too orgiastic a fashion.

Nothing particularly radical about that, given the Puritans' basic
premises. Anyone can see at a glance that a Maypole, proudly erect upon

the village green as the sap is rising, is a godless instrument. The very thought of Cotton Mather, with blossom in his hair, dancing round the Maypole makes the imagination reel. No. The greatest genius of the Puritans lay in their ability to sniff out a pagan survival in, say, the custom of decorating a house with holly for the festive season; they were the stuff of which social anthropologists would be made!

And their distaste for the icon of the lovely lady with her bonny babe – Mariolatry, graven images! – is less subtle than their disgust at the very idea of the festive season itself. It was the *festivity* of it that irked them.

Nevertheless, it assuredly *is* a gross and heathenish practice, to welcome the birth of Our Saviour with feasting, drunkenness, and lewd displays of mumming and masquerading.

We want none of that filth in this new place.

No, thank you.

As midnight approached, the cattle in the byres lumbered down upon their knees in homage, according to the well-established custom of over sixteen hundred English winters when they had mimicked the kneeling cattle in the Bethlehem stable; then, remembering where they were in the nick of time, they hastily refrained from idolatry and hauled themselves upright.

Boston Bay, calm as milk, black as ink, smooth as silk. And suddenly, at just the hour when the night spins on its spindle and starts to unravel its own darkness, at what one could call, elsewhere, the witching hour –

> I saw three ships come sailing in,
> Christmas Day, Christmas Day,
> I saw three ships come sailing in
> On Christmas Day in the morning.

Three ships, silent as ghost ships; ghost ships of Christmas past.

And what was in those ships all three?

Not, as in the old song, 'the Virgin Mary and her baby'; that would have done such grievous damage to the history of the New World that you might not be reading this in the English language even. No; the imagination must obey the rules of actuality. (Some of them, anyway.)

Therefore I imagine that the first ship was green and leafy all over, built of mossy Yule logs bound together with ivy. It was loaded to the gunwales with roses and pomegranates, the flower of Mary and the fruit that represents her womb, and the mast was a towering cherry tree which, now and then, leaned down to scatter ripe fruit on the water in memory of the carol that nobody in New England now sang. The Cherry Tree Carol, that tells how, when Mary asked Joseph to pick her some cherries, he was jealous and spiteful and told her to ask the father of her unborn child to help her pick them – and, at that, the cherry tree bowed down so low the cherries dangled in her lap, almost.

Clinging to the mast of this magic cherry tree was an abundance of equally inadmissible mistletoe, sacred since the dawn of time, when the Druids used to harvest it with silver sickles before going on to perform solstitial rites of memorable beastliness at megalithic sites all over Europe.

Yet more mistletoe dangled from the genial bundle of evergreens, the kissing bough, that invitation to the free exchange of precious bodily fluids.

And what is that bunch of holly, hung with red apples and knots of red ribbon? Why, it is a wassail bob.

This is what you did with your wassail bob. You carried it to the orchard with you when you took out a jar of hard cider to give the apple trees their Christmas drink. All over Somerset, all over Dorset, everywhere in the apple-scented cider country of Old England, time out of mind, they souse the apple trees at Christmas, get them good and drunk, soak them.

You pour the cider over the tree trunks, let it run down to the roots. You fire off guns, you cheer, you shout. You serenade the future apple crop and next year's burgeoning, you 'wassail' them, you toast their fecundity in last year's juices.

But not in *this* village. If a sharp smell of fruit and greenery wafted from the leafy ship to the shore, refreshing their dreams, all the same, the immigration officials at the front of the brain, the port of entry for memory, sensed contraband in the incoming cargo and snapped: 'Permission to land refused!'

There was a furious silent explosion of green leaves, red berries, white berries, of wet, red seeds from bursting pomegranates, of spattering cherries and scattering flowers; and cast to the winds and scattered was the sappy, juicy, voluptuous flesh of all the wood demons, tree spirits and fertility goddesses who had ever, once upon a time, contrived to hitch a ride on Christmas.

Then the ship and all it had contained were gone.

But the second ship now began to belch forth such a savoury aroma from a vent amidships that the most abstemious dreamer wrinkled his nose with pleasure. This ship rode low in the water, for it was built in the unmistakable shape of a pie dish and, as it neared shore, it could be seen that the deck itself was made of piecrust just out of the oven, glistening with butter, gilded with egg yolk.

Not a ship at all, in fact, but a Christmas pie!

But now the piecrust heaved itself up to let tumbling out into the water a smoking cargo of barons of beef gleaming with gravy, swans upon spits and roast geese dripping hot fat. And the figurehead of this jolly vessel was a boar's head, wreathed in bay, garlanded in rosemary, a roasted apple in its mouth and sprigs of rosemary tucked behind its ears. Above, hovering a pot of mustard, with wings.

Those were hungry days in the new-found land. The floating pie came wallowing far closer in than the green ship had done, close enough for the inhabitants of the houses on the foreshore to salivate in their sleep.

But then, with one accord, they recalled that burnt offerings and pagan sacrifice of pig, bird and cattle could never be condoned. In unison, they rolled over on to their other sides and turned their stern backs.

The ship span round once, then twice. Then, the mustard pot swooping after, it dove down to the bottom of the sea, leaving behind a bobbing mass of sweetmeats that dissipated itself gradually, like sea wrack, leaving behind only a single cannonball of the plum-packed Christmas pudding of Old England that the sea's omnivorous belly found too much, too indigestible, and rejected it, so that the pudding refused to sink.

The sleepers, freed from the ghost not only of gluttony but also of dyspepsia, sighed with relief.

Now there was only one ship left.

The silence of the dream lent this apparition an especial eeriness.

This last ship was packed to the gunwales with pagan survivals of the most concrete kind, the ones in – roughly – human shape. The masts and spars were hung with streamers, paperchains and balloons, but the gaudy decorations were almost hidden by the motley crew of queer types aboard, who would have been perfectly visible from the shore in every detail of their many-coloured fancy dress had anyone been awake to see them.

Reeling to and fro on the deck, tumbling and dancing, were all the mummers and masquers and Christmas dancers that Cotton Mather hated so, every one of them large as life and twice as unnatural. The rouged men dressed as women, with pillowing bosoms; the clog dancers, making a soundless rat-a-tat-tat on the boards with their wooden shoes;

the sword dancers whacking their wooden blades and silently jingling the little bells on their ankles. All these riotous revellers used to welcome in the festive season back home; it was they who put the 'merry' into Merry England!

And now, horrors! they sailed nearer and nearer the sanctified shore, as if intent on forcing the saints to celebrate Christmas whether they wanted to or no.

The saint the Church disowned, Saint George, was there, in paper armour painted silver, with his old foe, the Turkish knight, a chequered tablecloth tied round his head for a turban, fencing with clubs as they used to every Christmas in the Old Country, going from house to house with the mumming play that was rooted far more deeply in antiquity than the birth it claimed to celebrate.

This is the plot of the mumming play: Saint George and the Turkish knight fight until Saint George knocks the Turkish knight down. In comes the Doctor, with his black bag, and brings him back to life again – a shocking mockery of death and resurrection. (Or else a ritual of revivification, depending on one's degree of faith, and also, of course, depending on one's degree of faith in what.)

The master of these floating revels was the Lord of Misrule himself, the clown prince of Old Christmas, to which he came from fathoms deep in time. His face was blackened with charcoal. A calf's tail was stitched on to the rump of his baggy pants, which constantly fell down, to be hitched up again after a glimpse of his hairy buttocks. His top hat sported paper roses. He carried an inflated bladder with which he merrily battered the dancing heads around him. He was a true antique, as old as the festival that existed at midwinter before Christmas was ever thought of. Older.

His descendants live, all year round, in the circus. He is mirth, anarchy and terror. Father Christmas is his bastard son, whom he has disowned for not being obscene enough.

The Lord of Misrule was there when the Romans celebrated the Winter Solstice, the hinge on which the year turns. The Romans called it Saturnalia and let the slaves rule the roost for the duration, when all was topsy-turvy and almost everything that occurred would have been illegal in the Commonwealth of Massachusetts at the time of the ghost ships, if not today.

Yet from the phantom festival on the bedizened deck came the old, old message: during the twelve days of Christmas, nothing is forbidden, everything is forgiven.

A merry Christmas is Cotton Mather's worst nightmare.

★

If a little merriment imparts itself to the dreams of the villagers, they do not experience it as pleasure. They have exorcised the vegetables, and the slaughtered beasts; they will not tolerate, here, the riot of unreason that used to mark, over there, the inverted season of the year when nights are longer than days and the rivers do not run and you think that when the sun sinks over the rim of the sea it might never come back again.

The village raised a silent cry: Avaunt thee! Get thee hence!

The riotous ship span round once, twice – a third time. And then sank, taking its Dionysiac crew with it.

But, just as he was about to be engulfed, the Lord of Misrule caught hold of the Christmas pudding that still floated on the water. This Christmas pudding, sprigged with holly, stuffed with currants, raisins, almonds, figs, compressed all the Christmas contraband into one fearful sphere.

The Lord of Misrule drew back his arm and bowled the pudding towards the shore.

Then he, too, went down. The Atlantic gulped him. The moon set, the snow came down again and it was a night like any other winter night.

Except, next morning, before dawn, when all rose to pray in the shivering dark, the little children, thrusting their feet reluctantly into their cold shoes, found a juicy resistance to the progress of their great toes and, investigating further, discovered to their amazed and secret glee, each child a raisin the size of your thumb, wrinkled with its own sweetness, plump as if it had been soaked in brandy, that came from who knows where but might easily have dropped out of the sky during the flight overhead of a disintegrating Christmas pudding.

In Pantoland

'I'm bored with television,' announced Widow Twankey from her easy chair in the Empyrean, switching off *The Late Show* and adjusting his/her falsies inside her outrageous red bustier. 'I will descend again to Pantoland!'

> In Pantoland,
> Everything is grand.

Well, let's not exaggerate – grandish. Not like what it used to be but, then, what is. Even so, all still brightly coloured – garish, in fact, all your primaries, red, yellow, blue. And all excessive, so that your castle has more turrets than a regular castle, your forest is considerably more impenetrable than the average forest and, not infrequently, your cow has more than its natural share of teats and udders. We're talking multiple projections, here, spikes, sprouts, boobs, bums. It's a bristling world, in Pantoland, either phallic or else demonically, aggressively female and there's something archaic behind it all, archaic in the worst sense. Something positively filthy.

But all also two-dimensional, so that Maid Marian's house, in Pantoland's fictive Nottingham, is flat as a pancake. The front door may well open when she goes in, but it makes a hollow sound behind her when she slams it shut and the entire façade gets the shivers. Robin serenades her from below; she opens her window to riposte and what you see behind her of her bedroom is only a painted bedhead on a painted wall.

Of course, the real problem here is that it is Baron Hardup of Hardup Hall, father of Cinderella, stepfather of the Ugly Sisters, who, these barren days, all too often occupies the post of Minister of Finance in Pantoland. Occasionally, even now, the free-spenders such as Princess Badroulbador take things into their own hands and then you get some wonderful effects, such as a three-masted galleon in full sail breasting through tumultuous storms with thunder booming and lightning breaking about the spars as the gallant ship takes Dick Whittington and his cat either away from or else back to London amidst a nostalgic series of *tableaux vivants* of British naval heroes such as Raleigh, Drake, Captain Cook and Nelson, discovering things or keeping the Channel safe for

English shipping, while Dick gives out a full-throated contralto rendition of 'If I had a hammer' with a chorus of rats in masks and tights, courtesy of the Italia Conti school.

Illusion and transformation, kitchen into palace with the aid of gauze etc. etc. etc. You know the kind of thing. It all costs money. And, sometimes, as if it were the greatest illusion of all, there might be an incursion of the real. Real horses, perhaps, trotting, neighing and whinnying, large as life. Yet 'large as life' isn't the right phrase, at all, at all. 'Large as life' they might be, in the context of the auditorium, but when the proscenium arch gapes as wide as the mouth of the ogre in *Jack and the Beanstalk*, those forty white horses pulling the glass coach of the princess look as little and inconsequential as white mice. They are real, all right, but insignificant, and only raise a laugh or round of applause if one of them inadvertently drops dung.

And sometimes there'll be a dog, often one of those sandy-coloured, short-haired terriers. On the programmes, it will say: 'Chuckles, played by himself,' just above where it says: 'Cigarettes by Abdullah.' (Whatever happened to Abdullah?) Chuckles does everything they taught him at dog-school – fetches, carries, jumps through a flaming hoop – but now and then he forgets his script, forgets he lives in Pantoland, remembers he is a real dog precipitated into a wondrous world of draughts and pungency and rustlings. He will run down to the footlights, he will look out over the daisy field of upturned, expectant faces and, after a moment's puzzlement, give a little questioning bark.

It was not like this when Toto dropped down into Oz; it is more like it was when Toto landed back, alas, in Kansas. Chuckles does not like it. Chuckles feels let down.

Then Robin Hood or Prince Charming or whoever it is has the titular – and 'tits' is the operative word with this one – ownership of Chuckles in Pantoland, scoops him up against her bosom and he has been saved. He has returned to Pantoland. In Pantoland, he can live for ever.

In Pantoland, which is the carnival of the unacknowledged and the fiesta of the repressed, everything is excessive and gender is variable.

A Brief Look at the Citizens of Pantoland

THE DAME

Double-sexed and self-sufficient, the Dame, the sacred transvestite of Pantoland, manifests him/herself in a number of guises. For example he/she might introduce him/herself thus:

'My name is Widow Twankey.' Then sternly adjure the audience:
'Smile when you say that!'

Because Twankey rhymes with – pardon me, vicar; and,

> Once upon a distant time,
> They talked in Pantoland in rhyme . . .

but now they talk in double entendre, which is a language all of its own
and is accented, not with the acute or grave, but with the eyebrows.
Double entendre. That is, everyday discourse which has been dipped in
the infinite riches of a dirty mind.

She/he stars as Mother Goose. In *Cinderella*, you get two for the price
of one with the Ugly Sisters. If they throw in Cinders' stepmother, that's
a bonanza, that's three. Then there is Jack's Mum in *Jack and the Beanstalk*
where the presence of cow and stem in close proximity rams home the
'phallic mother' aspect of the Dame. The Queen of Hearts (who stole
some tarts). Granny in *Red Riding Hood*, where the wolf – 'Ooooer!' –
gobbles her up. He/she pops up everywhere in Pantoland, tittering and
squealing: 'Look out, girls! There's a man!!!' wherever the Principal Boy
(q.v.) appears.

Big wigs and round spots of rouge on either cheek and eyelashes longer
than those of Daisy the Cow; crinolines that dip and sway and support a
mass of crispy petticoats out of which comes running Chuckles the Dog
dragging behind him a string of sausages plucked, evidently, from the
Dame's fundament.

'Better out than in.'

He/she bestrides the stage. His/her enormous footsteps resonate with
the antique past. She brings with him the sacred terror inherent in those of
his/her avatars such as Lisa Maron, the androgynous god-goddess of the
Abomey pantheon; the great god Shango, thunder deity of the Yorubas,
who can be either male or female; the sacrificial priest who, in the Congo,
dressed like a woman and was called 'Grandma'.

The Dame bends over, whips up her crinolines; she has three pairs of
knee-length bloomers, which she wears according to mood.

One pair of bloomers is made out of the Union Jack, for the sake of
patriotism.

The second pair of bloomers is quartered red and black, in memory of
Utopia.

The third and vastest pair of bloomers is scarlet, with a target on the
seat, centred on the arsehole, and *this* pair is wholly dedicated to
obscenity.

Roars. Screams. Hoots.

She turns and curtsies. And what do you know, she/he has shoved a truncheon down her trousers, hasn't she?

In Burgundy, in the Middle Ages, they held a Feast of Fools that lasted all through the dead days, that vacant lapse of time during which, according to the hairy-legged mythology of the Norsemen, the sky wolf ate up the sun. By the time the sky wolf puked it up again, a person or persons unknown had fucked the New Year back into being during the days when all the boys wore sprigs of mistletoe in their hats. Filthy work, but *somebody* had to do it. By the fourteenth century, the far-from-hairy-legged Burgundians had forgotten all about the sky wolf, of course; but had they also forgotten the orgiastic non-time of the Solstice, which, once upon a time, was also the time of the Saturnalia, the topsy-turvy time, 'the Liberties of December', when master swapped places with slave and anything could happen?

The mid-winter carnival in Old Burgundy, known as the Feast of Fools, was reigned over in style by a man dressed as a woman whom they used to call Mère Folle, Crazy Mother.

Crazy Mother turns round and curtsies. She pulls the truncheon out of her bloomers. All shriek in terrified delight and turn away their eyes. But when the punters dare to look again, they encounter only his/her seraphic smile and, lo and behold! the truncheon has turned into a magic wand.

When Widow Twankey/the Queen of Hearts/Mother Goose taps Daisy the Cow with her wand, Daisy the Cow gives out with a chorus of 'Down by the Old Bull and Bush'.

THE BEASTS

1 *The Goose* in *Mother Goose* is, or so they say, the Hamlet of animal roles, introspective and moody as only a costive bird straining over its egg might be. There is a full gamut of emotion in the Goose role – loyalty and devotion to her mother; joy and delight at her own maternity; heartbreak at loss of egg; fear and trembling at the wide variety of gruesome possibilities which might occur if, in the infinite intercouplings of possible texts which occur all the time in the promiscuity of Pantoland, one story effortlessly segues into another story, so that *Mother Goose* twins up with *Jack and the Beanstalk*, involving an egg-hungry ogre, or with *Robin Hood*, incorporating a goose-hungry Sheriff of Nottingham.

Note that the Goose, like the Dame, is a female role usually, though not always, played by a man. But the Goose does not represent the exaggerated and parodic femininity of Widow Twankey. The Goose's femininity is real. She is all woman. Witness the centrality of the egg in her life. So the Goose deserves an interpreter with the sophisticated

technique and empathy for gender of the *onnagata*, the female imper-
sonators of the Japanese Kabuki theatre, who can make you weep at the
sadness inherent in the sleeves of a kimono as they quiver with suppressed
emotion at a woman's lot.

Because of this, and because she is the prime focus of all attention, the
Goose in *Mother Goose* is the premier animal role, even more so than . . .

2 *Dick Whittington's Cat*: Dick Whittington's cat is the Scaramouche of
Pantoland, limber, agile, and going on two legs more often than on four
to stress his status as intermediary between the world of the animals and
our world. If he possesses some of the chthonic ambiguity of all dark
messengers between different modes of being, nevertheless he is never
less than a perfect valet to his master and hops and skips at Dick's bidding.
His is therefore less of a starring role than the Goose, even if his rat-
catching activities are central to the action and it is a difficult to imagine
Dick without his cat as Morecambe without Wise.

Note that this cat is male almost to a fault, unquestionably a tom-cat,
and personated by a man; some things are sacrosanct, even in Pantoland.
A tom-cat is maleness personified, whereas . . .

3 *Daisy the Cow* is so female it takes two whole men to represent her, one
on his own couldn't hack it. The back legs of the pantomime quadruped
are traditionally a thankless task, but the front end gets the chance to
indulge in all manner of antics, flirting, flattering, fluttering those endless
eyelashes and, sometimes, if the coordination between the two ends is
good enough, Daisy does a tap-dance, which makes her massive udder
with its many dangling teats dip and sway in the most salacious manner,
bringing back home the notion of a basic crudely reproductive female
sexuality of which those of us who don't lactate often do not like to be
reminded. (They have lactation, generation all the time in mind in
Pantoland.)

This rude femaleness requires two men to mimic it, as I've said;
therefore you could call Daisy a Dame, squared.

These three are the principal animal leads in Pantoland, although Mother
Hubbard, a free-floating Dame who might turn up in any text, always
comes accompanied by her dog but, more often than not, Chuckles gets
in on the act here, and *real* animals don't count. Pantomime horses can
crop up anywhere and mimic rats are not confined to *Dick Whittington* but
inhabit Cinderella's kitchen, even drive her coach; there are mice and
lizards too. Birds. You need robins to cover up the Babes in the Wood.
Emus, you get sometimes. Ducks. You name it.

When Pantoland was young, and I mean *really* young, before it got stage-struck, in the time of the sky wolf, when fertility festivals filled up those vacant, dark, solstitial days, we used to see no difference between ourselves and the animals. Bruno the Bear and Felix the Cat walked and talked amongst us. We lived with, we loved, we married the animals (*Beauty and the Beast*). The Goose, the Cat and Daisy the Cow have come to us out of the paradise that little children remember, when we thought we could talk to the animals, to remind us how once we knew that the animals were just as human as we were, and that made us more human too.

THE PRINCIPAL BOY

What an armful! She is the grandest thing in Pantoland.

Look at those arms! Look at those thighs! Like tree trunks, but like sexy tree trunks. Her hats are huge and plumed with feathers; her gleaming, exiguous little knicks are made of satin and trimmed with sequins. As Prince Charming, she is a veritable spectacle of pure glamour although, as Jack, her costume might start off a touch more pleasant and, as Dick, she needs to look like a London apprentice for a while before she gets to try on that Lord Mayor schmutter. For Robin Hood, she'll wear green; as Aladdin, the East is signified by her turban.

You can tell she is supposed to be a man not by her shape, which is a conventional hour-glass, but by her body language. She marches with as martial a stride as it is possible to achieve in stiletto heels and throws out her arms in wide, generous, all-encompassing, patriarchal gestures, as if she owned the earth. Her maleness has an antique charm, even, nowadays, a touch of wistful Edwardiana about it; no Principal Boy worth her salt would want to personate a New Man, after all. She's gone to the bother of turning herself into a Principal Boy to get away from the washing-up, in the first place.

In spite of her spilling physical luxuriance, which ensures that, unlike the more ambivalent Dame, the Principal Boy is always referred to as a 'she', her voice is a deep, dark brown and, when raised in song, could raise the dead. Who, who ever heard her, could ever forget a Principal Boy of the Old School leading the chorus in a rousing military parade and rendition of, say, 'Where are the boys of the Old Brigade?'

Come to that, where *are* the Principal Boys of the Old Brigade? In these anorexic times, there is less and less thigh to slap. Girls, nowadays, are big-bosomed, all right, due to implants, but not deep-chested any more. Principal Boys used to share a hollow-voiced, bass-baritone bonhomie with department-store Father Christmases but 'Ho! ho! ho!' is heard no more in the land. In these lean times, your average Principal Boy looks more like a Peter Pan, and pre-pubescence isn't what you're aiming for at a fertility festival, although the presence of actual children, in great numbers, laughing at that which they should not know about, is indispensable as having established the success of preceding fertility festivals.

The Principal Boy is a male/female cross, like the Dame, but she is never played for laughs. No. She is played for thrills, for adventure, the romance. So, after innumerable adventures, she ends up with the Principal Girl in a number where their voices soar and swoon together as in the excruciatingly erotic climactic aria of Monteverdi's *L'Incoronazione di Poppaea*, performed as it is in the present day always by two ladies, one playing Nero, one Poppaea, due to male castrati being thin on the ground in spite of the population explosion. And, as Principal Boy and Principal Girl duet, their four breasts in two décolletages jostle one another for pre-eminence in the eyes of all observers. This is a thrill indeed but will not make babies unless they then dash out and borrow the turkey-baster from the Christmas-dinner kitchen. There is a kind of censorship inherent in the pantomime.

But the question of gender remains vague because you have to hang on to the idea that the Principal Boy is all boy and all girl *at the same time*, a door that opens both ways, just as the Dame is Mother Eve and Old Adam in one parcel; they are both doors that open both ways, they are the Janus faces of the season, they look backwards and forwards, they bury the past, they procreate the future, and, by rights, these two should belong together for they are and are not ambivalent and the Principal Girl (q. does *not* v. in this work of reference) is nothing more than a pretty prop, even when eponymous as in *Cinderella* and *Snow White*.

Widow Twankey came out of retirement and, gorged on anthropology, dropped down on stage in Pantoland.

'I have come back to earth and I feel randy!'

She/he didn't have to say a word. The décor picked up on her unutterance and all the pasteboard everywhere shuddered.

The Dame and the Principal Boy come together by chance in the Chinese laundry. Aladdin has brought in his washing. They exchange some banter about smalls and drawers, eyeing one another up. They know that this time, for the first time since censorship began, the script will change.

'I feel randy,' said Widow Twankey.

What is a fertility festival without a ritual copulation?

But it isn't as simple as that. For now, oh! now the hobby-horse is quite forgot. The Phallic Mother and the Big-Breasted Boy must take second place in the contemporary cast-list to some cricketer who does not even know enough to make an obscene gesture with his bat, since, in the late twentieth century, the planet is over-populated and four breasts in harmony is what we need more of, rather than babies, so Widow Twankey ought to go and have it off with Mother Hubbard and stop bothering Aladdin, really she/he ought.

Do people still believe in Pantoland?

If you believe in Pantoland, put your palms together and give a big hand to . . .

If you *really* believe in Pantoland, put your – pardon me, vicar –

A fertility festival without a ritual copulation is . . . nothing but a pantomime.

Widow Twankey has come back to earth to restore the pantomime to its original condition.

But, before scarlet drawers and satin knicks could hit the floor, a hook dropped out of the flies and struck Widow Twankey between the shoulders. The hook lodged securely in her red satin bustier; shouting and screaming, with a great display of scrawny shin, she was hauled back up where she had come from, in spite of her raucous protests, and deposited back amongst the dead stars, leaving the Principal Boy at a loss for what to do except to briskly imitate George Formby and start to sing 'Oh, Mr Wu, I'm telling you . . .'

As Umberto Eco once said, 'An everlasting carnival does not work.' You can't keep it up, you know; nobody ever could. The essence of the carnival, the festival, the Feast of Fools, is transience. It is here today and gone tomorrow, a release of tension not a reconstitution of order, a refreshment . . . after which everything can go on again exactly as if nothing had happened.

Things don't change because a girl puts on trousers or a chap slips on a frock, you know. Masters were masters again the day after Saturnalia ended; after the holiday from gender, it was back to the old grind . . .

Besides, all that was years ago, of course. That was before television.

Ashputtle
or *The Mother's Ghost*

THREE VERSIONS OF ONE STORY

I THE MUTILATED GIRLS

But although you could easily take the story away from Ashputtle and centre it on the mutilated sisters – indeed, it would be easy to think of it as a story about cutting bits off women, so that they will *fit in*, some sort of circumcision-like ritual chop, nevertheless, the story always begins not with Ashputtle or her stepsisters but with Ashputtle's mother, as though it is really always the story of her mother even if, at the beginning of the story, the mother herself is just about to exit the narrative because she is at death's door: 'A rich man's wife fell sick, and, feeling that her end was near, she called her only daughter to her bedside.'

Note the absence of the husband/father. Although the woman is defined by her relation to him ('a rich man's wife') the daughter is unambiguously hers, as if hers alone, and the entire drama concerns only women, takes place almost exclusively among women, is a fight between two groups of women – in the right-hand corner, Ashputtle and her mother; in the left-hand corner, the stepmother and *her* daughters, of whom the father is unacknowledged but all the same is predicated by both textual and biological necessity.

In the drama between two female families in opposition to one another because of their rivalry over men (husband/father, husband/son), the men seem no more than passive victims of their fancy, yet their significance is absolute because it is ('a rich man', 'a king's son') economic.

Ashputtle's father, the old man, is the first object of their desire and their dissension; the stepmother snatches him from the dead mother before her corpse is cold, as soon as her grip loosens. Then there is the young man, the potential bridegroom, the hypothetical son-in-law, for whose possession the mothers fight, using their daughters as instruments of war or as surrogates in the business of mating.

If the men, and the bank balances for which they stand, are the passive victims of the two grown women, then the girls, all three, are animated solely by the wills of their mothers. Even if Ashputtle's mother dies at the beginning of the story, her status as one of the dead only makes her position more authoritative. The mother's ghost dominates the narrative and is, in a real sense, the motive centre, the event that makes all the other events happen.

On her death bed, the mother assures the daughter: 'I shall always look after you and always be with you.' The story tells you how she does it.

At this point, when her mother makes her promise, Ashputtle is nameless. She is her mother's daughter. That is all we know. It is the stepmother who names her Ashputtle, as a joke, and, in doing so, wipes out her real name, whatever that is, banishes her from the family, exiles her from the shared table to the lonely hearth among the cinders, removes her contingent but honourable status as daughter and gives her, instead, the contingent but disreputable status of servant.

Her mother told Ashputtle she would always look after her, but then she died and the father married again and gave Ashputtle an imitation mother with daughters of her own whom she loves with the same fierce passion as Ashputtle's mother did and still, posthumously, does, as we shall find out.

With the second marriage comes the vexed question: who shall be the daughters of the house? Mine! declares the stepmother and sets the freshly named, non-daughter Ashputtle to sweep and scrub and sleep on the hearth while her daughters lie between clean sheets in Ashputtle's bed. Ashputtle, no longer known as the daughter of her mother, nor of her father either, goes by a dry, dirty, cindery nickname for everything has turned to dust and ashes.

Meanwhile, the false mother sleeps on the bed where the real mother died and is, presumably, pleasured by the husband/father in that bed, unless there is no pleasure in it for her. We are not told what the husband/ father does as regards domestic or marital function, but we can surely make the assumption that he and the stepmother share a bed, because that is what married people do.

And what can the real mother/wife do about it? Burn as she might with love, anger and jealousy, she is dead and buried.

The father, in this story, is a mystery to me. Is he so besotted with his new wife that he cannot see how his daughter is soiled with kitchen refuse and filthy from her ashy bed and always hard at work? If he sensed there was a drama in hand, he was content to leave the entire production to the women for, absent as he might be, always remember that it is in *his* house where Ashputtle sleeps on the cinders, and he is the invisible link that binds both sets of mothers and daughters in their violent equation. He is the unmoved mover, the unseen organising principle, like God, and, like God, up he pops in person, one fine day, to introduce the essential plot device.

Besides, without the absent father there would be no story because there would have been no conflict.

If they had been able to put aside their differences and discuss everything amicably, they'd have combined to expel the father. Then all the women could have slept in one bed. If they'd kept the father on, he could have done the housework.

This is the essential plot device introduced by the father: he says, 'I am about to take a business trip. What presents would my three girls like me to bring back for them?'

Note that: his *three* girls.

It occurs to me that perhaps the stepmother's daughters were really, all the time, his own daughters, just as much his own daughters as Ashputtle, his 'natural' daughters, as they say, as though there is something inherently unnatural about legitimacy. *That* would realign the forces in the story. It would make his connivance with the ascendancy of the other girls more plausible. It would make the speedy marriage, the stepmother's hostility, more probable.

But it would also transform the story into something else, because it would provide motivation, and so on; it would mean I'd have to provide a past for all these people, that I would have to equip them with three dimensions, with tastes and memories, and I would have to think of things for them to eat and wear and say. It would transform 'Ashputtle' from the bare necessity of fairy tale, with its characteristic copula formula, 'and then', to the emotional and technical complexity of bourgeois realism. They would have to learn to think. Everything would change.

I will stick with what I know.

What presents do his three girls want?

'Bring me a silk dress,' said his eldest girl. 'Bring me a string of pearls,' said the middle one. What about the third one, the forgotten one, called out of the kitchen on a charitable impulse and drying her hands, raw with housework, on her apron, bringing with her the smell of old fire?

'Bring me the first branch that knocks against your hat on the way home,' said Ashputtle.

Why did she ask for that? Did she make an informed guess at how little he valued her? Or had a dream told her to use this random formula of unacknowledged desire, to allow blind chance to choose her present for her? Unless it was her mother's ghost, awake and restlessly looking for a way home, that came into the girl's mouth and spoke the request for her.

He brought her back a hazel twig. She planted it on her mother's grave and watered it with tears. It grew into a hazel tree. When Ashputtle came out to weep upon her mother's grave, the turtle dove crooned: 'I'll never leave you, I'll always protect you.'

Then Ashputtle knew that the turtle dove was her mother's ghost and she herself was still her mother's daughter, and although she had wept and wailed and longed to have her mother back again, now her heart sank a little to find out that her mother, though dead, was no longer gone and henceforward she must do her mother's bidding.

Came the time for that curious fair they used to hold in that country, when all the resident virgins went to dance in front of the king's son so that he could pick out the girl he wanted to marry.

The turtle dove was mad for that, for her daughter to marry the prince. You might have thought her own experience of marriage might have taught her to be wary, but no, needs must, what else is a girl to do? The turtle dove was mad for her daughter to marry so she flew in and picked up the new silk dress with her beak, dragged it to the open window, threw it down to Ashputtle. She did the same with the string of pearls. Ashputtle had a good wash under the pump in the yard, put on her stolen finery and crept out the back way, secretly, to the dancing grounds, but the stepsisters had to stay home and sulk because they had nothing to wear.

The turtle dove stayed close to Ashputtle, pecking her ears to make her dance vivaciously, so that the prince would see her, so that the prince would love her, so that he would follow her and find the clue of the fallen slipper, for the story is not complete without the ritual humiliation of the other woman and the mutilation of her daughters.

The search for the foot that fits the slipper is essential to the enactment of this ritual humiliation.

The other woman wants that young man desperately. She would do anything to catch him. Not losing a daughter, but gaining a son. She wants a son so badly she is prepared to cripple her daughters. She takes up a carving knife and chops off her elder daughter's big toe, so that her foot will fit the little shoe.

Imagine.

Brandishing the carving knife, the woman bears down on her child, who is as distraught as if she had not been a girl but a boy and the old woman was after a more essential portion than a toe. 'No!' she screams. 'Mother! No! Not the knife! No!' But off it comes, all the same, and she throws it in the fire, among the ashes, where Ashputtle finds it, wonders at it, and feels both awe and fear at the phenomenon of mother love.

Mother love, which winds about these daughters like a shroud.

The prince saw nothing familiar in the face of the tearful young woman, one shoe off, one shoe on, displayed to him in triumph by her mother, but he said: 'I promised I would marry whoever the shoe fitted so I will marry you,' and they rode off together.

The turtle dove came flying round and did not croon or coo to the bridal pair but sang a horrid song: 'Look! Look! There's blood in the shoe!'

The prince returned the ersatz ex-fiancée at once, angry at the trick, but the stepmother hastily lopped off her other daughter's heel and pushed *that* poor foot into the bloody shoe as soon as it was vacant so, nothing for it, a man of his word, the prince helped up the new girl and once again he rode away.

Back came the nagging turtle dove: 'Look!' And, sure enough, the shoe was full of blood again.

'Let Ashputtle try,' said the eager turtle dove.

So now Ashputtle must put her foot into the hideous receptacle, this open wound, still slick and warm as it is, for nothing in any of the many texts of this tale suggests the prince washed the shoe out between the fittings. It was an ordeal in itself to put a naked foot into the bloody shoe, but her mother, the turtle dove, urged her to do so in a soft, cooing croon that could not be denied.

If she does not plunge without revulsion into this open wound, she won't be fit to marry. That is the song of the turtle dove, while the other mad mother stood impotently by.

Ashputtle's foot, the size of the bound foot of a Chinese woman, a stump. Almost an amputee already, she put her tiny foot in it.

'Look! Look!' cried the turtle dove in triumph, even while the bird betrayed its ghostly nature by becoming progressively more and more immaterial as Ashputtle stood up in the shoe and commenced to walk around. Squelch, went the stump of the foot in the shoe. Squelch. 'Look!' sang out the turtle dove. 'Her foot fits the shoe like a corpse fits the coffin!'

'See how well I look after you, my darling!'

2 THE BURNED CHILD

A burned child lived in the ashes. No, not really burned – more charred, a little bit charred, like a stick half-burned and picked off the fire. She looked like charcoal and ashes because she lived in the ashes since her mother died and the hot ashes burned her so she was scabbed and scarred. The burned child lived on the hearth, covered in ashes, as if she were still mourning.

After her mother died and was buried, her father forgot the mother and forgot the child and married the woman who used to rake the ashes, and that was why the child lived in the unraked ashes, and there was nobody to brush her hair, so it stuck out like a mat, nor to wipe the dirt off her scabbed face, and she had no heart to do it for herself, but she raked the ashes and slept beside the little cat and got the burned bits from the bottom of the pot to eat, scraping them out, squatting on the floor, by herself in front of the fire, not as if she were human, because she was still mourning.

Her mother was dead and buried, but felt perfect exquisite pain of love when she looked up through the earth and saw the burned child covered in ashes.

'Milk the cow, burned child, and bring back all the milk,' said the stepmother, who used to rake the ashes and milk the cow, once upon a time, but the burned child did all that, now.

The ghost of the mother went into the cow.

'Drink milk, grow fat,' said the mother's ghost.

The burned child pulled on the udder and drank enough milk before she took the bucket back and nobody saw, and time passed, she drank milk every day, she grew fat, she grew breasts, she grew up.

There was a man the stepmother wanted and she asked him into the kitchen to get his dinner, but she made the burned child cook it, although the stepmother did all the cooking before. After the burned child cooked the dinner the stepmother sent her off to milk the cow.

'I want that man for myself,' said the burned child to the cow.

The cow let down more milk, and more, and more, enough for the girl to have a drink and wash her face and wash her hands. When she washed her face, she washed the scabs off and now she was not burned at all, but the cow was empty.

'Give your own milk, next time,' said the ghost of the mother inside the cow. 'You've milked me dry.'

The little cat came by. The ghost of the mother went into the cat.

'Your hair wants doing,' said the cat. 'Lie down.'

The little cat unpicked her raggy lugs with its clever paws until the burned child's hair hung down nicely, but it had been so snagged and tangled that the cat's claws were all pulled out before it was finished.

'Comb your own hair, next time,' said the cat. 'You've maimed me.'

The burned child was clean and combed, but stark naked.

There was a bird sitting in the apple tree. The ghost of the mother left the cat and went into the bird. The bird struck its own breast with its beak. Blood poured down on to the burned child under the tree. It ran over her shoulders and covered her front and covered her back. When the bird had no more blood, the burned child got a red silk dress.

'Make your own dress, next time,' said the bird. 'I'm through with that bloody business.'

The burned child went into the kitchen to show herself to the man. She was not burned any more, but lovely. The man left off looking at the stepmother and looked at the girl.

'Come home with me and let your stepmother stay and rake the ashes,' he said to her and off they went. He gave her a house and money. She did all right.

'Now I can go to sleep,' said the ghost of the mother. 'Now everything is all right.'

3 TRAVELLING CLOTHES

The stepmother took the red-hot poker and burned the orphan's face with it because she had not raked the ashes. The girl went to her mother's grave. In the earth her mother said: 'It must be raining. Or else it is snowing. Unless there is a heavy dew tonight.'

'It isn't raining, it isn't snowing, it's too early for the dew. My tears are falling on your grave, mother.'

The dead woman waited until night came. Then she climbed out and went to the house. The stepmother slept on a feather bed, but the burned child slept on the hearth among the ashes. When the dead woman kissed her, the scar vanished. The girl woke up. The dead woman gave her a red dress.

'I had it when I was your age.'

The girl put the red dress on. The dead woman took worms from her eyesockets; they turned into jewels. The girl put on a diamond ring.

'I had it when I was your age.'

They went together to the grave.

'Step into my coffin.'

'No,' said the girl. She shuddered.

'I stepped into *my* mother's coffin when I was your age.'

The girl stepped into the coffin although she thought it would be the death of her. It turned into a coach and horses. The horses stamped, eager to be gone.

'Go and seek your fortune, darling.'

Alice in Prague
or *The Curious Room*

This piece was written in praise of Jan Svankmayer,
the animator of Prague, and his film of *Alice*

In the city of Prague, once, it was winter.

Outside the curious room, there is a sign on the door which says
'Forbidden'. Inside, inside, oh, come and see! The celebrated DR DEE.

The celebrated Dr Dee, looking for all the world like Santa Claus on
account of his long, white beard and apple cheeks, is contemplating his
crystal, the fearful sphere that contains everything that is, or was, or ever
shall be.

It is a round ball of solid glass and gives a deceptive impression of
weightlessness, because you can see right through it and we falsely
assume an equation between lightness and transparency, that what the
light shines through cannot be there and so must weigh nothing. In fact,
the Doctor's crystal ball is heavy enough to inflict a substantial injury and
the Doctor's assistant, Ned Kelly, the Man in the Iron Mask, often
weighs the ball in one hand or tosses it back and forth from one to the
other hand as he ponders the fragility of the hollow bone, his master's
skull, as it pores heedless over some tome.

Ned Kelly would blame the murder on the angels. He would say the
angels came out of the sphere. Everybody knows the angels live there.

The crystal resembles: an aqueous humour, frozen:

> a glass eye, although without any iris or
> pupil – just the sort of transparent eye, in
> fact, which the adept might construe as apt
> to see the invisible;

> a tear, round, as it forms within the eye, for
> a tear acquires its characteristic shape of a
> pear, what we think of as a 'tear' shape, only
> in the act of falling;

the shining drop that trembles, sometimes, on the
tip of the Doctor's well-nigh senescent, tending
towards the flaccid, yet nevertheless sustainable
and discernible morning erection, and
always reminds him of

a drop of dew,

a drop of dew endlessly, tremulously about to fall
from the unfolded petals of a rose and, therefore,
like the tear, retaining the perfection of its
circumference only by refusing to sustain free fall,
remaining what it is, because it refuses to become
what it might be, the antithesis of metamorphosis;

and yet, in old England, far away, the sign of the
Do Drop Inn will always, that jovial pun, show an
oblate spheroid, heavily tinselled, because the
sign-painter, in order to demonstrate the idea of
'drop', needs must represent the dew in the act of
falling and therefore, for the purposes of this
comparison, *not* resembling the numinous ball
weighing down the angelic Doctor's outstretched
palm.

For Dr Dee, the invisible is only another unexplored country, a brave
new world.

The hinge of the sixteenth century, where it joins with the seventeenth
century, is as creaky and judders open as reluctantly as the door in a
haunted house. Through that door, in the distance, we may glimpse the
distant light of the Age of Reason, but precious little of that is about to fall
on Prague, the capital of paranoia, where the fortune-tellers live on
Golden Alley in cottages so small, a good-sized doll would find itself
cramped, and there is one certain house on Alchemist's Street that only
becomes visible during a thick fog. (On sunny days, you see a stone.)
But, even in the fog, only those born on the Sabbath can see the house
anyway.

Like a lamp guttering out in a recently vacated room, the Renaissance
flared, faded and extinguished itself. The world had suddenly revealed
itself as bewilderingly infinite, but since the imagination remained, for
after all it is only human, finite, our imaginations took some time to catch

up. If Francis Bacon will die in 1626 a martyr to experimental science, having contracted a chill whilst stuffing a dead hen with snow on Highgate Hill to see if that would keep it fresh, in Prague, where Dr Faustus once lodged in Charles Square, Dr Dee, the English expatriate alchemist, awaits the manifestation of the angel in the Archduke Rudolph's curious room, and we are still fumbling our way towards the end of the previous century.

The Archduke Rudolph keeps his priceless collection of treasures in this curious room; he numbers the Doctor amongst these treasures and is therefore forced to number the Doctor's assistant, the unspeakable and iron-visaged Kelly, too.

The Archduke Rudolph has crazy eyes. These eyes are the mirrors of his soul.

It is very cold this afternoon, the kind of weather that makes a person piss. The moon is up already, a moon the colour of candlewax and, as the sky discolours when the night comes on, the moon grows more white, more cold, white as the source of all the cold in the world, until, when the winter moon reaches its chill meridian, everything will freeze – not only the water in the jug and the ink in the well, but the blood in the vein, the aqueous humour.

Metamorphosis.

In their higgledy-piggledy disorder, the twigs on the bare trees outside the thick window resemble those random scratchings made by common use that you only see when you lift your wineglass up to the light. A hard frost has crisped the surface of the deep snow on the Archduke's tumbled roofs and turrets. In the snow, a raven: caw!

Dr Dee knows the language of birds and sometimes speaks it, but what the birds say is frequently banal; all the raven said, over and over, was: 'Poor Tom's a-cold!'

Above the Doctor's head, slung from the low-beamed ceiling, dangles a flying turtle, stuffed. In the dim room we can make out, amongst much else, the random juxtaposition of an umbrella, a sewing machine and a dissecting table; a raven and a writing desk; an aged mermaid, poor wizened creature, cramped in a foetal position in a jar, her ream of grey hair suspended adrift in the viscous liquid that preserves her, her features rendered greenish and somewhat distorted by the flaws in the glass.

Dr Dee would like, for a mate to this mermaid, to keep in a cage, if alive, or, if dead, in a stoppered bottle, an angel.

It was an age in love with wonders.

*

Dr Dee's assistant, Ned Kelly, the Man in the Iron Mask, is also looking for angels. He is gazing at the sheeny, reflective screen of his scrying disc which is made of polished coal. The angels visit him more frequently than they do the Doctor, but, for some reason, Dr Dee cannot see Kelly's guests, although they crowd the surface of the scrying disc, crying out in their high, piercing voices in the species of bird-creole with which they communicate. It is a great sadness to him.

Kelly, however, is phenomenally gifted in this direction and notes down on a pad the intonations of their speech which, though he doesn't understand it himself, the Doctor excitedly makes sense of.

But, today, no go.

Kelly yawns. He stretches. He feels the pressure of the weather on his bladder.

The privy at the top of the tower is a hole in the floor behind a cupboard door. It is situated above another privy, with another hole, above another privy, another hole, and so on, down seven further privies, seven more holes, until your excreta at last hurtles into the cesspit far below. The cold keeps the smell down, thank God.

Dr Dee, ever the seeker after knowledge, has calculated the velocity of a flying turd.

Although a man could hang himself in the privy with ease and comfort, securing the rope about the beam above and launching himself into the void to let gravity break his neck for him, Kelly, whether at stool or making water, never allows the privy to remind him of the 'long drop' nor even, however briefly, admires his own instrument for fear the phrase 'well-hung' recalls the noose which he narrowly escaped in his native England for fraud, once, in Lancaster; for forgery, once, in Rutlandshire; and for performing a confidence trick in Ashby-de-la-Zouch.

But his ears were cropped for him in the pillory at Walton-le-Dale, after he dug up a corpse from a churchyard for purposes of necromancy, or possibly of grave-robbing, and this is why, in order to conceal this amputation, he always wears the iron mask modelled after that which will be worn by a namesake three hundred years hence in a country that does not yet exist, an iron mask like an upturned bucket with a slit cut for his eyes.

Kelly, unbuttoning, wonders if his piss will freeze in the act of falling; if, today, it is cold enough in Prague to let him piss an arc of ice.

No.

He buttons up again.

Women loathe this privy. Happily, few venture here, into the magician's tower, where the Archduke Rudolph keeps his collection of wonders, his proto-museum, his '*Wunderkammer*', his '*cabinet de curiosités*', that *curious room* of which we speak.

There's a theory, one I find persuasive, that the quest for knowledge is, at bottom, the search for the answer to the question: 'Where was I before I was born?'

In the beginning was . . . what?

Perhaps, in the beginning, there was a curious room, a room like this one, crammed with wonders; and now the room and all it contains are forbidden you, although it was made just for you, had been prepared for you since time began, and you will spend all your life trying to remember it.

Kelly once took the Archduke aside and offered him, at a price, a little piece of the beginning, a slice of the fruit of the Tree of the Knowledge of Good and Evil itself, which Kelly claimed he had obtained from an Armenian, who had found it on Mount Ararat, growing in the shadows of the wreck of the Ark. The slice had dried out with time and looked very much like a dehydrated ear.

The Archduke soon decided it was a fake, that Kelly had been fooled. The Archduke is *not* gullible. Rather, he has a boundless desire to know *everything* and an exceptional generosity of belief. At night, he stands on top of the tower and watches the stars in the company of Tycho Brahe and Johann Kepler, yet by day, he makes no move nor judgement before he consults the astrologers in their zodiacal hats and yet, in those days, either an astrologer or an astronomer would be hard put to it to describe the difference between their disciplines.

He is not gullible. But he has his peculiarities.

The Archduke keeps a lion chained up in his bedroom as a species of watch-dog or, since the lion is a member of the *Felis* family and not a member of the *Cave canem* family, a giant guard-cat. For fear of the lion's yellow teeth, the Archduke had them pulled. Now that the poor beast cannot chew, he must subsist on slop. The lion lies with his head on his paws, dreaming. If you could open up his brain this moment, you would find nothing there but the image of a beefsteak.

Meanwhile, the Archduke, in the curtained privacy of his bed, embraces something, God knows what.

Whatever it is, he does it with such energy that the bell hanging over the bed becomes agitated due to the jolting and rhythmic lurching of the bed, and the clapper jangles against the sides.

Ting-a-ling!

The bell is cast out of *electrum magicum*. Paracelsus said that a bell cast out of *electrum magicum* would summon up the spirits. If a rat gnaws the Archduke's toe during the night, his involuntary start will agitate the bell immediately so the spirits can come and chase the rat away, for the lion, although *sui generis* a cat is not sufficiently a cat in spirit to perform the domestic functions of a common mouser, not like the little calico beastie who keeps the good Doctor company and often, out of pure affection, brings him furry tributes of those she has slain.

Though the bell rings, softly at first, and then with increasing fury as the Archduke nears the end of his journey, no spirits come. But there have been no rats either.

A split fig falls out of the bed on to the marble floor with a soft, exhausted plop, followed by a hand of bananas, that spread out and go limp, as if in submission.

'Why can't he make do with meat, like other people,' whined the hungry lion.

Can the Archduke be effecting intercourse with a fruit salad?

Or with Carmen Miranda's hat?

Worse.

The hand of bananas indicates the Archduke's enthusiasm for the newly discovered Americas. Oh, brave new world! There is a street in Prague called 'New World' (*Novy Svet*). The hand of bananas is freshly arrived from Bermuda via his Spanish kin, who know what he likes. He has a particular enthusiasm for weird plants, and every week comes to converse with his mandrakes, those warty, shaggy roots that originate (the Archduke shudders pleasurably to think about it) in the sperm and water spilled by a hanged man.

The mandrakes live at ease in a special cabinet. It falls to Ned Kelly's reluctant duty to bathe each of these roots once a week in milk and dress them up in fresh linen nightgowns. Kelly, reluctantly, since the roots, warts and all, resemble so many virile members, and he does not like to handle them, imagining they raucously mock his manhood as he tends them, believing they unman him.

The Archduke's collection also boasts some magnificent specimens of the *coco-de-mer*, or double coconut, which grows in the shape, but exactly the shape, of the pelvic area of a woman, a foot long, heft and clefted, I kid you not. The Archduke and his gardeners plan to effect a vegetable marriage and will raise the progeny – *man-de-mer* or *coco-drake* – in his own greenhouses. (The Archduke himself is a confirmed bachelor.)

★

The bell ceases. The lion sighs with relief and lays his head once more upon his heavy paws: 'Now I can sleep!'

Then, from under the bed curtains, on either side of the bed, begins to pour a veritable torrent that quickly forms into dark, viscous, livid puddles on the floor.

But, before you accuse the Archduke of the unspeakable, dip your finger in the puddle and lick it.

Delicious!

For these are sticky puddles of freshly squeezed grape juice, and apple juice, and peach juice, juice of plum, pear, or raspberry, strawberry, cherry ripe, blackberry, black currant, white currant, red . . . The room brims with the delicious ripe scent of summer pudding, even though, outside, on the frozen tower, the raven still creaks out his melancholy call:

'Poor Tom's a-cold!'

And it is midwinter.

Night was. Widow Night, an old woman in mourning, with big, black wings, came beating against the window; they kept her out with lamps and candles.

When he went back into the laboratory, Ned Kelly found that Dr Dee had nodded off to sleep as the old man often did nowadays towards the end of the day, the crystal ball having rolled from palm to lap as he lay back in the black oak chair, and now, as he shifted at the impulse of a dream, it rolled again off his lap, down on to the floor, where it landed with a soft thump on the rushes – no harm done – and the little calico cat disabled it at once with a swift blow of her right paw, then began to play with it, batting it that way and this before she administered the *coup de grâce*.

With a gusty sigh, Kelly once more addressed his scrying disc, although today he felt barren of invention. He reflected ironically that, if just so much as one wee feathery angel ever, even the one time, should escape the scrying disc and flutter into the laboratory, the cat would surely get it.

Not, Kelly knew, that such a thing was possible.

If you could see inside Kelly's brain, you would discover a calculating machine.

Widow Night painted the windows black.

Then, all at once, the cat made a noise like sharply crumpled paper, a noise of inquiry and concern. A rat? Kelly turned to look. The cat, head on one side, was considering, with such scrupulous intensity that its prickled ears met at the tips, something lying on the floor beside the crystal ball, so that at first it looked as if the glass eye had shed a tear.

But look again.

Kelly looked again and began to sob and gibber.

The cat rose up and backed away all in one liquid motion, hissing, its bristling tail stuck straight up, stiff as a broom handle, too scared to permit even the impulse of attack upon the creature, about the size of a little finger, that popped out of the crystal ball as if the ball had been a bubble.

But its passage has not cracked or fissured the ball; it is still whole, has sealed itself up again directly after the departure of the infinitesimal child who, suddenly released from her sudden confinement, now experimentally stretches out her tiny limbs to test the limit of the new invisible circumference around her.

Kelly stammered: 'There must be some rational explanation!'

Although they were too small for him to see them, her teeth still had the transparency and notched edges of the first stage of the second set; her straight, fair hair was cut in a stern fringe; she scowled and sat upright, looking about her with evident disapproval.

The cat, cowering ecstatically, now knocked over an alembic and a quantity of *elixir vitae* ran away through the rushes. At the bang, the Doctor woke and was not astonished to see her.

He bade her a graceful welcome in the language of the tawny pippit.

How did she get there?

She was kneeling on the mantelpiece of the sitting room of the place she lived, looking at herself in the mirror. Bored, she breathed on the glass until it clouded over and then, with her finger, she drew a door. The door opened. She sprang through and, after a brief moment's confusing fish-eye view of a vast, gloomy chamber, scarcely illuminated by five candles in one branched stick and filled with all the clutter in the world, her view was obliterated by the clawed paw of a vast cat extended ready to strike, hideously increasing in size as it approached her, and then, splat! she burst out of 'time will be' into 'time was', for the transparent substance which surrounded her burst like a bubble and there she was, in her pink frock, lying on some rushes under the gaze of a tender ancient with a long, white beard and a man with a coal-scuttle on his head.

Her lips moved but no sound came out; she had left her voice behind in the mirror. She flew into a tantrum and beat her heels upon the floor, weeping furiously. The Doctor, who, in some remote time past, raised children of his own, let her alone until, her passion spent, she heaved and grunted on the rushes, knuckling her eyes; then he peered into the depths of a big china bowl on a dim shelf and produced from out of it a strawberry.

The child accepted the strawberry suspiciously, for it was, although not large, the size of her head. She sniffed it, turned it round and round, and then essayed just one little bite out of it, leaving behind a tiny ring of white within the crimson flesh. Her teeth were perfect.

At the first bite, she grew a little.

Kelly continued to mumble: 'There must be some rational explanation.'

The child took a second, less tentative bite, and grew a little more. The mandrakes in their white nightgowns woke up and began to mutter among themselves.

Reassured at last, she gobbled the strawberry all up, but she had been falsely reassured; now her flaxen crown bumped abruptly against the rafters, out of the range of the candlestick so they could not see her face but a gigantic tear splashed with a metallic clang upon Ned Kelly's helmet, then another, and the Doctor, with some presence of mind, before they needed to hurriedly construct an Ark, pressed a phial of *elixir vitae* into her hand. When she drank it, she shrank down again until soon she was small enough to sit on his knee, her blue eyes staring with wonder at his beard, as white as ice-cream and as long as Sunday.

But she had no wings.

Kelly, the faker, knew there *must* be a rational explanation but he could not think of one.

She found her voice at last.

'Tell me,' she said, 'the answer to this problem: the Governor of Kgoujni wants to give a very small dinner party, and invites his father's brother-in-law, his brother's father-in-law, his father-in-law's brother, and his brother-in-law's father. Find the number of guests.'[1]

At the sound of her voice, which was as clear as a looking-glass, everything in the curious room gave a shake and a shudder and, for a moment, looked as if it were painted on gauze, like a theatrical effect, and might disappear if a bright light were shone on it. Dr Dee stroked his beard reflectively. He could provide answers to many questions, or knew where to look for answers. He had gone and caught a falling starre – didn't a piece of it lie beside the stuffed dodo? To impregnate the aggressively phallic mandrake, with its masculinity to the power of two, as implied by its name, was a task which, he pondered, the omnivorous Archduke, with his enthusiasm for erotic esoterica, might prove capable of. And the answer to the other two imponderables posed by the poet were obtainable, surely, through the intermediary of the angels, if only one scried long enough.

He truly believed that nothing was unknowable. That is what makes him modern.

But, to the child's question, he can imagine no answer.

Kelly, forced against his nature to suspect the presence of another world that would destroy his confidence in tricks, is sunk in introspection, and has not even heard her.

However, such magic as there is in *this* world, as opposed to the worlds that can be made out of dictionaries, can only be real when it is artificial and Dr Dee himself, whilst a member of the Cambridge Footlights at university, before his beard was white or long, directed a famous production of Aristophanes' *Peace* at Trinity College, in which he sent a grocer's boy right up to heaven, laden with his basket as if to make deliveries, on the back of a giant beetle.

Archytas made a flying dove of wood. At Nuremberg, according to Boterus, an adept constructed both an eagle and a fly and set them to flutter and flap across his laboratory, to the astonishment of all. In olden times, the statues that Daedalus built raised their arms and moved their legs due to the action of weights, and of shifting deposits of mercury. Albertus Magnus, the Great Sage, cast a head in brass that spoke.

Are they animate or not, these beings that jerk and shudder into such a semblance of life? Do these creatures believe themselves to be human? And if they do, at what point might they, by virtue of the sheer intensity of their belief, become so?

(In Prague, the city of the Golem, an image can come to life.)

The Doctor thinks about these things a great deal and thinks the child upon his knee, babbling about the inhabitants of another world, must be a little automaton popped up from God knows where.

Meanwhile, the door marked 'Forbidden' opened up again.

It came in.

It rolled on little wheels, a wobbling, halting, toppling progress, a clockwork land galleon, tall as a mast, advancing at a stately if erratic pace, nodding and becking and shedding inessential fragments of its surface as it came, its foliage rustling, now stuck and perilously rocking at a crack in the stone floor with which its wheels cannot cope, now flying helter-skelter, almost out of control, wobbling, clicking, whirring, an electric juggernaut evidently almost on the point of collapse; it has been a heavy afternoon.

But, although it looked as if eccentrically self-propelled, Arcimboldo the Milanese pushed it, picking up bits of the thing as they fell off, tut-tutting at its ruination, pushing it, shoving it, occasionally picking it up bodily and carrying it. He was smeared all over with its secretions and looked forward to a good wash once it had been returned to the curious room from whence it came. There, the Doctor and his assistant will take it apart until the next time.

This thing before us, although it is not, was not and never will be alive, *has* been animate and will be animate again, but, at the moment, not, for now, after one final shove, it stuck stock-still, wheels halted, wound down, uttering one last, gross, mechanical sigh.

A nipple dropped off. The Doctor picked it up and offered it to the child. Another strawberry! She shook her head.

The size and prominence of the secondary sexual characteristics indicate this creature is, like the child, of the feminine gender. She lives in the fruit bowl where the Doctor found the first strawberry. When the Archduke wants her, Arcimboldo, who designed her, puts her together again, arranging the fruit of which she is composed on a wicker frame, always a little different from the last time according to what the greenhouse can provide. Today, her hair is largely composed of green muscat grapes, her nose a pear, eyes filbert nuts, cheeks russet apples somewhat wrinkled – never mind! The Archduke has a penchant for older women. When the painter got her ready, she looked like Carmen Miranda's hat on wheels, but her name was 'Summer'.

But now, what devastation! Hair mashed, nose squashed, bosom puréed, belly juiced. The child observed this apparition with the greatest interest. She spoke again. She queried earnestly:

'If 70 per cent have lost an eye, 75 per cent an ear, 80 per cent an arm, 85 per cent a leg: what percentage, *at least*, must have lost all four?'[2]

Once again, she stumped them. They pondered, all three men, and at last slowly shook their heads. As if the child's question were the last straw, 'Summer' now disintegrated – subsided, slithered, slopped off her frame into her fruit bowl, whilst shed fruit, some almost whole, bounced to the rushes around her. The Milanese, with a pang, watched his design disintegrate.

It is not so much that the Archduke likes to pretend this monstrous being is alive, for nothing inhuman is alien to him; rather, he does not care whether she is alive or no, that what he wants to do is to plunge his member into her artificial strangeness, perhaps as he does so imagining himself an orchard and this embrace, this plunge into the succulent flesh, which is not flesh as we know it, which is, if you like, the living metaphor – '*fica*' – explains Arcimboldo, displaying the orifice – this intercourse with the very flesh of summer will fructify his cold kingdom, the snowy country outside the window, where the creaking raven endlessly laments the inclement weather.

'Reason becomes the enemy which withholds from us so many possibilities of pleasure,' said Freud.

One day, when the fish within the river freeze, the day of the frigid lunar noon, the Archduke will come to Dr Dee, his crazy eyes resembling, the one, a blackberry, the other, a cherry, and say: transform me into a harvest festival!

So he did; but the weather got no better.

Peckish, Kelly absently demolished a fallen peach, so lost in thought he never noticed the purple bruise, and the little cat played croquet with the peach stone while Dr Dee, stirred by memories of his English children long ago and far away, stroked the girl's flaxen hair.

'Whither comest thou?' he asked her.

The question stirred her again into speech.

'A and B began the year with only £1,000 apiece,' she announced, urgently.

The three men turned to look at her as if she were about to pronounce some piece of oracular wisdom. She tossed her blonde head. She went on.

'They borrowed nought; they stole nought. On the next New Year's Day they had £60,000 between them. How did they do it?'[3]

They could not think of a reply. They continued to stare at her, words turning to dust in their mouths.

'How did they do it?' she repeated, now almost with desperation, as if, if they only could stumble on the correct reply, she would be precipitated back, diminutive, stern, rational, within the crystal ball and thence be tossed back through the mirror to 'time will be', or, even better, to the book from which she had sprung.

'Poor Tom's a-cold,' offered the raven. After that, came silence.

NOTE:

The answers to Alice's conundrums:

  1 One.

  2 Ten.

  3 They went that day to the Bank of England. A stood in front of it, while B went round and stood behind it.

Problems and answers from *A Tangled Tale*, Lewis Carroll, London, 1885.

Alice was invented by a logician and therefore she comes from the world of nonsense, that is, from the world of *non-sense* – the opposite of common sense; this world is constricted by logical deduction and is created by language, although language shivers into abstractions within it.

Impressions: The Wrightsman
Magdalene

For a woman to be a virgin and a mother, you need a miracle; when a woman is not a virgin, nor a mother, either, nobody talks about miracles. Mary, the mother of Jesus, together with the other Mary, the mother of St John, and the Mary Magdalene, the repentant harlot, went down to the seashore; a woman named Fatima, a servant, went with them. They stepped into a boat, they threw away the rudder, they permitted the sea to take them where it wanted. It beached them near Marseilles.

Don't run away with the idea the South of France was an easy option compared to the deserts of Syria, or Egypt, or the wastes of Cappadocia, where other early saints, likewise driven by the imperious need for solitude, found arid, inhospitable crevices in which to contemplate the ineffable. There were clean, square, white, Roman cities all along the Mediterranean coast everywhere except the place the three Marys landed with their servant. They landed in the middle of a malarial swamp, the Camargue. It was not pleasant. The desert would have been more healthy.

But there the two stern mothers and Fatima – don't forget Fatima – set up a chapel, at the place we now call Saintes-Maries-de-la-Mer. There they stayed. But the other Mary, the Magdalene, the not-mother, could not stop. Impelled by the demon of loneliness, she went off on her own through the Camargue; then she crossed limestone hill after limestone hill. Flints cut her feet, sun burned her skin. She ate fruit that had fallen from the tree of its own accord, like a perfect Manichean. She ate dropped berries. The black-browed Palestinian woman walked in silence, gaunt as famine, hairy as a dog.

She walked until she came to the forest of the Sainte-Baume. She walked until she came to the remotest part of the forest. There she found a cave. There she stopped. There she prayed. She did not speak to another human being, she did not see another human being, for thirty-three years. By then, she was old.

Mary Magdalene, the Venus in sackcloth. Georges de La Tour's picture does not show a woman in sackcloth, but her chemise is coarse and simple enough to be a penitential garment, or, at least, the kind of garment that shows you were not thinking of personal adornment when you put it on. Even though the chemise is deeply open on the bosom, it does not seem to disclose flesh as such, but a flesh that has more akin to the wax of the burning candle, to the way the wax candle is irradiated by its own flame, and glows. So you could say that, from the waist up, this Mary Magdalene is on the high road to penitence, but, from the waist down, which is always the more problematic part, there is the question of her long, red skirt.

Left-over finery? Was it the only frock she had, the frock she went whoring in, then repented in, then set sail in? Did she walk all the way to the Sainte-Baume in this red skirt? It doesn't look travel-stained or worn or torn. It is a luxurious, even scandalous skirt. A scarlet dress for a scarlet woman.

The Virgin Mary wears blue. Her preference has sanctified the colour. We think of a 'heavenly' blue. But Mary Magdalene wears red, the colour of passion. The two women are twin paradoxes. One is not what the other is. One is a virgin and a mother; the other is a non-virgin, and childless. Note how the English language doesn't contain a specific word to describe a woman who is grown-up, sexually mature and *not* a mother, unless such a woman is using her sexuality as her profession.

Because Mary Magdalene is a woman and childless she goes out into the wilderness. The others, the mothers, stay and make a church, where people come.

But why has she taken her pearl necklace with her? Look at it, lying in front of the mirror. And her long hair has been most beautifully brushed. Is she, yet, fully repentant?

In Georges de La Tour's painting, the Magdalene's hair is well brushed. Sometimes the Magdalene's hair is as shaggy as a Rastafarian's. Sometimes her hair hangs down upon, is inextricably mixed up with, her furs. Mary Magdalene is easier to read when she is hairy, when, in the wilderness, she wears the rough coat of her own desires, as if the desires of her past have turned into the hairy shirt that torments her present, repentant flesh.

Sometimes she wears only her hair; it never saw a comb, long, matted, unkempt, hanging down to her knees. She belts her own hair round her waist with the rope with which, each night, she lashes herself, making a rough tunic of it. On these occasions, the transformation from the young lovely, voluptuous Mary Magdalene, the happy non-virgin, the party girl, the woman taken in adultery – on these occasions, the transformation is complete. She has turned into something wild and strange, into a female version of John the Baptist, a hairy hermit, as good as naked, transcending gender, sex obliterated, nakedness irrelevant.

Now she is one with such pole-sitters as Simeon Stylites, and other solitary cave-dwellers who communed with beasts, like St Jerome. She eats herbs, drinks water from the pool; she comes to resemble an even earlier incarnation of the 'wild man of the woods' than John the Baptist. Now she looks like hairy Enkidu, from the Babylonian *Epic of Gilgamesh*. The woman who once, in her grand, red dress, was vice personified, has now retired to an existential situation in which vice simply is not possible. She has arrived at the radiant, enlightened sinlessness of the animals. In her new, resplendent animality, she is now beyond choice. Now she has no option but virtue.

But there is another way of looking at it. Think of Donatello's Magdalene, in Florence – she's dried up by the suns of the wilderness, battered by wind and rain, anorexic, toothless, a body entirely annihilated by the soul. You can almost smell the odour of the kind of sanctity that reeks from her – it's rank, it's raw, it's horrible. By the ardour with which she has embraced the rigorous asceticism of penitence, you can tell how much she hated her early life of so-called 'pleasure'. The mortification of the flesh comes naturally to her. When you learn that Donatello intended the piece to be not black but gilded, that does not lighten its mood.

Nevertheless, you can see the point that some anonymous Man of the Enlightenment on the Grand Tour made two hundred years ago – how Donatello's Mary Magdalene made him 'disgusted with penitence'.

Penitence becomes sado-masochism. Self-punishment is its own reward.

But it can also become kitsch. Consider the apocryphal story of Mary of Egypt. Who was a beautiful prostitute until she repented and spent the remaining forty-seven years of her life as a penitent in the desert, clothed only in her long hair. She took with her three loaves and ate a mouthful of bread once a day, in the mornings; the loaves lasted her out. Mary of Egypt is clean and fresh. Her face stays miraculously unlined. She is as untouched by time as her bread is untouched by appetite. She sits on a rock in the desert, combing out her long hair, like a lorelei whose water has turned to sand. We can imagine how she smiles. Perhaps she sings a little song.

Georges de La Tour's Mary Magdalene has not yet arrived at an ecstasy of repentance, evidently. Perhaps, indeed, he has pictured her as she is just about to repent – before her sea voyage in fact, although I would prefer to think that this bare, bleak space, furnished only with the mirror, is that of her cave in the woods. But this is a woman who is still taking care of herself. Her long, black hair, sleek as that of a Japanese woman on a painted scroll – she must just have finished brushing it, reminding us that she is the patron saint of hairdressers. Her hair is the product of culture, not left as nature intended. Her hair shows she has just used the mirror as an instrument of worldly vanity. Her hair shows that, even as she meditates upon the candle flame, *this* world still has a claim upon her.

Unless we are actually watching her as her soul is drawn out into the candle flame.

We meet Mary Magdalene in the gospels, doing something extra-ordinary with her hair. After she massaged Jesus's feet with her pot of precious ointment, she wiped them clean with her hair, an image so astonishing and erotically precise it is surprising it is represented so rarely in art, especially that of the seventeenth century, when religious excess and eroticism went so often together. Magdalene, using her hair, that beautiful net with which she used to snare men as – well, as a mop, a washcloth, a towel. And a slight element of the perverse about it, too. All in all, the kind of *gaudy gesture* a repentant prostitute *would* make.

She has brushed her hair, perhaps for the last time, and taken off her pearl necklace, also for the last time. Now she is gazing at the candle flame, which doubles itself in the mirror. Once upon a time, that mirror was the tool of her trade; it was within the mirror that she assembled all the elements of the femininity she put together for sale. But now, instead of reflecting her face, it duplicates the pure flame.

When I was in labour, I thought of a candle flame. I was in labour for nineteen hours. At first the pains came slowly and were relatively light; it was easy to ride them. But when they came more closely together, and grew more and more intense, then I began to concentrate my mind upon an imaginary candle flame.

Look at the candle flame as if it is the only thing in the world. How white and steady it is. At the core of the white flame is a cone of blue, transparent air; that is the thing to look at, that is the thing to concentrate on. When the pains came thick and fast, I fixed all my attention on the blue absence at the heart of the flame, as though it were the secret of the flame and, if I concentrated enough upon it, it would become *my* secret, too.

Soon there was no time to think of anything else. By then, I was entirely subsumed by the blue space. Even when they snipped away at my body, down below, to finally let the baby out the easiest way, all my attention was concentrated on the core of the flame.

Once the candle flame had done its work, it snuffed itself out; they wrapped my baby in a shawl and gave him to me.

Mary Magdalene meditates upon the candle flame. She enters the blue core, the blue absence. She becomes something other than herself.

The silence in the picture, for it is the most silent of pictures, emanates not from the darkness behind the candle in the mirror but from these two candles, the real candle and the mirror candle. Between them, the two candles disseminate light and silence. They have tranced the woman into enlightenment. She can't speak, won't speak. In the desert, she will grunt, maybe, but she will put speech aside, after this, after she has meditated upon the candle flame and the mirror. She will put speech aside just as she has put aside her pearl necklace and will put away her red skirt. The new person, the saint, is being born out of this intercourse with the candle flame.

But something has already been born out of this intercourse with the candle flame. See. She carries it already. She carries where, if she were a Virgin mother and not a sacred whore, she would rest her baby, not a living child but a *memento mori*, a skull.

UNCOLLECTED STORIES

The Scarlet House
The Snow Pavilion
The Quilt Maker

The Scarlet House

I remember, I'd been watching a hawk. There was an immense sky of the most innocent blue, blue of a bowl from which a child might just have drunk its morning milk and left behind a few whitish traces of cloud around the rim, and, imprinted on this sky, a single point of perfect stillness – a hawk over the ruins. A hawk so still he seemed the central node of the sky and the source of the heavy silence which fell down on the ruins like invisible rain; an immobile hawk so high above the turning world that I was sure he would see a half rotating hemisphere below him; and, over this hemisphere, scampered the plump vole or delicious bunny that did not know it had been pinioned already by the eyebeam of its feathered, taloned fate imminent in the air. Morning, silence, a hawk, his prey and ruins. If I try very hard, I can also add to this landscape with my little tent, my half-track and, piece by piece, all my naturalist's equipment . . . I must have gone out to collect samples of the desolate flora of this empty place. Above the green abandonment of the deserted city, where the little foxes played, a rapt hawk gathered to himself all its haunted stillness.

Hawk plummets. He's unpremeditated and precise as Zen swordsmen, his fall subsumed to the aerial whizz of the rope that traps me.

I am sure of it – beat me as much as you like; I remember it perfectly. Don't I?

The Count sits in a hall hung with embroideries depicting all the hierarchy of hell, a place, he claims, not unlike the Scarlet House. Soon, everywhere will be like the Scarlet House. Chaos is coming, says the Count, and giggles; the Count ends all his letters 'yours entropically' and signs them with the peacock's quill dipped in the blood of a human sacrifice. Why did you come to these abandoned regions, my dear, surely you'd heard rumours that I and my fabulous retinue had already installed ourselves in the ruins, preparing chaos with the aid of a Tarot pack?

But I had no notion who the Count was when his bodyguard captured me. They stood around me as I writhed on the ground and they showed their fangs at me; they all file their canines to a point, it is a sign of machismo among them. They wore jackets of black leather brightly studded with cabbalistic patterns; tall boots; snug leggings of black leather; and slick black helmets that fitted closely over the head and over the mouth, too, leaving only their pale eyes visible. Their eyes glittered like pebbles in a brook. They were armed with hand-guns and their belts bristled with knives. Each carried a coil of rope. A silence so perfect that it might never have been broken resumed itself after the hawk fell.

They hauled me off at the end of the rope they tied to the back of one of their motorcycles and made me run, tumble, bounce behind them on my way to the Scarlet House, though I must admit they drove quite slowly, so I was not much injured. The Scarlet House was built of white concrete and looked to me very much like a hospital, a large terminal ward. A few days in bed there, and the gravel rash, the grazes and bruises healed.

I remember everything perfectly. I know the ruins exist; at nights, I can hear the foxes barking in New Bond Street. That sound confirms the existence of the ruins though, of course, I can see nothing from the windows.

Meanwhile, in this blind place, the Count consults maps of the stars with the aid of his adviser, whose general efficiency is hindered by the epileptic fits with which he is afflicted. Though at the best of times his wits are out of order; he drools, too. His star-spangled robes are dabbled with spittle and spilled food and other randomly spattered bodily effluvia, for he's quite shameless in his odd little lusts and pleasures and the Count lets him indulge them all. He's the licensed fool and may even pull out his prick and play with it at mealtimes, and woe betide you if you flinch from one of his random displays of slobbering affection, for that's a sure sign you aren't in tune with chaos. But I'm not sure if he's a fool all the time; sometimes his eyes focus on me with the assessing glint of a used-car dealer. Then I am afraid he may be wondering what I can remember.

When he's been a good fool and made the Count chuckle, the Count tells Madame Schreck to give him access to one of the youngest of the girls. There are girls as young as twelve or thirteen and Fool likes his women just out of the shell. The Fool takes his present down to the dungeons. We won't see *her* again.

But was she not almost as good as dead the moment she set foot inside the Scarlet House? The moment of capture had sealed her fate.

As for myself, I am sure I was captured by the bikers, in the ruins. I am perfectly confident that is how I came to the Scarlet House. Yet the Count assures me, with equal, if not superior confidence, that I am mistaken, so that I am not sure which of us to believe.

The Count is dedicated to the obliteration of memory.

Memory, says the Count, is the main difference between man and the beasts; the beasts were born to live but man was born to remember. Out of his memory, he made abstract patterns of significant forms. Memory is the grid of meaning we impose on the random and bewildering flux of the world. Memory is the line we pay out behind us as we travel through time – it is the clue, like Ariadne's, which means we do not lose our way. Memory is the lasso with which we capture the past and haul it from chaos towards us in nicely ordered sequences, like those of baroque keyboard music. The Count grimaces when he says that because he hates music even more that he hates mathematics but he loves to listen to screaming. 'The entropic rhetoric of the scream', he calls it. Madame Schreck screeches for him sometimes at night, to augment his pleasure if we girls have screamed ourselves hoarse and cannot make any more noise.

Memory, origin of narrative; memory, barrier against oblivion; memory, repository of my being, those delicate filaments of myself I weave, in time into a spider's web to catch as much world in it as I can. In the midst of my self-spun web, there I can sit, in the serenity of my self-possession. Or so I would, if I could.

Because my memory is undergoing a sea-change. Though I am certain I remember, I am no longer sure what it is I remember nor, indeed, the reason why I should remember it.

Everyday, the Count attempts to erase the tapes from my memory. He has perfected a complex system of forgetting. Although I passionately assert how I was seized by the bikers in the ruins of New Bond Street, I know this assertion is no more than my last, paltry line of defence against the obliterations of the Count. He has already implanted in me a set of pseudo-memories, all of which sometimes play in my head together, throwing me into a dreadful confusion so that, though I remember everything, I have no means of ascertaining the actuality of those memories, which all return to me with shimmering vividness and a sense of lived and quantified experience. All of them.

Dear god, all of them.

Remembering is the first stage of absolute forgetfulness, says the occult Count, who goes by contraries. So I have been precipitated into a fugue of all the memories of all the women in the Scarlet House, where I live, now. This is his harem. We are left in the cruel care of Madame Schreck, who eats small birds such as fig-peckers and thrushes; she puts a whole one, spit-grilled, into her huge, red mouth as lusciously as if it were a liqueur chocolate and then she spits the bones out like the skin and pips of a grape. And she's got other, extravagant tastes as well; she likes to gorge upon the unborn young of rabbits. She acquires the foetuses from laboratories; she has them cooked for her in a cream sauce enriched with the addition of the yolk of an egg. She's a messy eater, she spills sauce on her bare belly and one of us must lick it off for her. She throws open her legs and shows us her hole; the way down and out, she says.

The count comes personally to the Scarlet House to give us our lessons. He always brings with him a brace of pigs on silken leashes which we girls must caress. The Count believes the pig is the prime example of perfected evolution, the multivorous beast that lives in shit, most entropic of substances, and consumes its own farrow, if it gets half the chance.

Like time, says the Count; like time.

Time, which is the enemy of memory.

The past is very much like the future.

I descended at dusk from a train on which I had been the only passenger in a dank, chill compartment lit only by one greenish, meagre gas mantle; its pair, on the other side of a mirror so scratched and defaced I could not see my own reflection in it, was broken. A mess of sandwich wrappings and orange peel littered the grimy floor. It had been a gloomy journey, across a fen shrouded in mist of autumn, an unpeopled landscape, flat, water-logged, dotted here and there with pollarded willows with their melancholy look of men whose arms have been lopped off or mutilated women with whips upon their heads. I descended from the train at that lonely halt as night was falling; a man with a seamed, shuttered face came to take my ticket and, without a single word, humped my little tin trunk for me out of the ramshackle, wooden station to a shabby carriage in the lane outside, a shabby carriage with, between its shafts, a starveling pony whose ribs poked out under its drab, glossless coat. On the driving seat sat a thin, dark man in black livery who, to my shocked horror, I perceived possessed no mouth at all. I started back; but the station master grabbed my hand and all but forced me into the carriage, then slammed the door on me.

As the poor beast began painfully to drag the carriage forward, I glimpsed the last of the world in which, until that aghast moment, I'd spent twenty-two years of girlhood; into the darkness before me I took the grinning face of the station master, pressed in farewell at the smeared window, transformed by a sudden rush of malevolent glee to a mask of pure evil.

I knew I must try to escape and tussled weakly with the door but it was locked fast. The inexorable carriage, lurching, ponderous, took me into the deepening shadows of the night, which seemed to be moving across the fen to engulf me. I lay back upon the leather seat and gave way to helpless tears.

At last we entered a dark courtyard virtually enclosed by tall, black trees; the gates shut immediately after we were inside. When the pony halted, the macabre coachman came to let me out. He reached for my hand to help me down with a certain courtesy and I had no choice but to touch him. His flesh felt as dank as the wet, night air of the fens which surrounded us.

Yet when I brought myself to look at his ghastly face in order to thank him, I saw his eyes speak though he had no mouth nor none of the necessary appendages of lips, teeth and tongue with which to do so, his grave eyes, the colour of the inside of the ocean, told me I was a young girl much to be pitied and, in luminous depths, I perceived the most dreadful intimation of my fate. At the door of the rambling, brick-built, red-tiled place, half farmhouse, half country mansion and now, had I but known it, wholly dedicated to the Count's experiments, Madame Schreck waited to greet me in the scarlet splendour of her satin dress that laid open to the view of her breasts and the unimaginable wound of her sex – Madame Schreck, whom I would learn to fear far more than death itself, since death is finite.

Now you are at the place of annihilation, now you are at the place of annihilation.

Yet this version of my capture, in which despair settles slowly like a fall of grey snow upon the landscape through which I travelled towards the moment when hope vanished, sometimes seems to me to have altogether too literary a flavour – too much of a nineteenth-century quality, with its railway trains, its advertisment in the personal column of *The Times* for a governess that drew me, like a Brontë heroine, on a spool of fate over the bleak flat-lands. There's the inky, over-written smell of pseudo-memory about the gas lights and the mute coachman, though my skin still shudders from the remembered touch of his skin and I will never be able to forget his eyes.

But the Count, the Morpholytic Kid who presides over the death of forms, assures me that now the process of forgetting is well under way so that I can remember both the past and the future with equal facility, since both are illusory. I've made up a past out of some novelette once read on a train, perhaps; and I've guessed at a future. For there are no foxes in New Bond Street. Nor will they frolic in New Bond Street until the cards fall in such a way that the foxes will bound out, barking, from beneath them. Time past and time future combine to distort my memory.

But I have one memory I sometimes think must be the most authentic, since it is by far the most ghastly.

My beloved father has a straight back and an erect gait in spite of the seventy summers that have turned his hair to a spume of white foam. We sit at a round tea-table with a red plush cover in our pleasant apartment, the windows open on to a balcony where a little breeze stirs the heavy heads of my fine show of geraniums, white, salmon pink and scarlet, all banked together, exuding a delicious, spicy odour.

How I loved that room . . . the slippery horsehair sofa with the paisley shawl thrown over it and the piles of cushions my mother had embroidered with all manner of brightly coloured butterflies and flowers; the rosewood cabinet filled with china shepherdesses and bird-catchers, all covered with a fine bloom of dust – I'm not the best of housekeepers; there is a stain on the Persian carpet which marks the spot where I spilled a bowl of hot chocolate when I was six years old. There is a china bowl filled with pot pourri on the mantlepiece.

My mother used to make pot pourri every summer; she would bring back the flowers from our house in the country. Now she is dead but she still presides over our tea-table; there on the wall she smiles at us from a bird's-eye maple frame, a tinted photograph taken shortly after she and my father were married. She's still very young, not much older than I am now; she wears a wide straw hat decorated with pink ribbon and a bunch of daisies. Its brim gently shades her eyes, of which the long lashes are so dark they look like the fringed centres of anemones. Her eyes are a mysterious, darkish green.

They say I have her eyes.

Some women can take their eyes out, says the Count; he is always particularly angry if when he is engaged in erasing the tapes of memory, I begin – as I sometimes, quite helplessly, do – to repeat, over and over again, as if one tape were stuck: 'They say I have my mother's eyes, they say I have my mother's eyes.' Then he beats me with a knotted whip until my shoulders bleed; when visiting his women, he never forgets a whip. Then he hands me over to Madame Schreck for a spell in the sensory deprivation unit, I must crawl into the oblivion of her hole for a while.

My father and I sit under my mother's photograph in an old-fashioned room in which everything is loved because it is familiar. Twenty-two years of my life have unfurled in this room like a slow, quiet fan. I pour tea for my father from a silver pot with a spout like the neck of a swan. The cups have narrow stems and are made of fine, white porcelain with scrolls of faded gold around the rims. My own cup cracked under its weight of years long ago; I remember how my father carefully riveted it together again, until it was as good as new. There is a glass saucer containing a sliced lemon on the table, its sharp, clean scent refreshes this sultry July afternoon. The light falls in regular parallelograms through our slatted blinds so we know we are in control of the weather. In the park outside, a few birds cheep the exhausted songs of high summer.

The staccato click of bootheels. The peremptory barrage of gloved fists on the panels of the door. When the old man reaches for the revolver he always wears in the holster under his armpit, they gun him down. His white hair floods with blood as red as the painted house of Madame

Schreck, who is waiting for me in the subterranean torture-chamber deep at the heart of the maze of my brain, the Minotaur with the head of a woman and the orifice of a sow.

My father tumbles across the tea-table. Cups, saucers fly apart in shards as he crashes down. His fingers grasp at the empty air to catch one last, lost handful of world between them before it slips away from him for ever.

Then they seized me, stripped me, raped me on the silk birds of the Persian carpet under my mother's picture, threw a coat over me, thrust a gun in my back and forced me down the echoing staircase to the armoured car waiting outside. I had been a virgin. I was in great pain.

Madame Schreck, in a smart uniform of drab olive, with sheer black stockings and those six-inch heels of hers that stab the linoleum as she walks, took my particulars at the mahogany desk. When I refused to tell her where my brother was, she made me lie down on the camp-bed in the corner of the room, under a propaganda poster of the Count riding upon a winged snake and, with judicious impassivity, she applied the lighted end of her cigarette to the interior membrane of my labia minor. Through the open window, I remember, I saw a hawk immobile at the central node of the blue sky of the midsummer. From his spread wings dropped a silence that stunned me more than the pain she inflicted.

An orderly took me to the Scarlet House, a block-house with red-painted doors. He had almost to carry me because I could scarcely walk. There was no mouth in his face. No mouth. His eyes were feral, wild, scarcely human.

'Aha!' says the Count in a great good humour; 'Your memory is playing tricks on you!'

He himself, such is his magnanimity, received me in a vast, echoing hall hung with extravagant tapestries. I retain only the most confused recollections of its exterior but I know the inside perfectly well, now. It is a maze of cells like the inside of a brain. He took away my old coat that was still bundled around my shoulders and dropped it into an incinerator. Then he showed me the sacrificial knife, which is made of black obsidian, and said to me: 'As of the present moment you inhabit the world no longer since the least impulse of my will can cause you to disappear from it.'

But his methods are more subtle than the knife. Dedicated as he is to the dissolution of forms, he intends to erode my sense of being by equipping me with a multiplicity of beings, so that I confound myself with my own profusion of pasts, presents and futures.

I am eroding, I am wearing away. I am being stroked as smooth as stone is by the hands of the sea; the elements that went to make up my uniqueness fall apart as he erases the tapes of my memory and makes his own substitutions. For, if my first capture incorporates within it ruins that do not yet exist and my second capture resonates with too many echoes of books I might have read, then my third and by far my most moving capture might only recapitulate a Middle-European nightmare, an episode from Prague or Vienna seen in a movie, perhaps, or told me by a complete stranger during the exposed privacy of a long train journey. For sometimes I cannot believe I've suffered so much.

If only I could remember everything perfectly, just as it happened, then loaded with the ambivalent burden of my past, I should be free.

But in this brothel where memory's the prostitute there is no such thing as freedom; all is governed by the fall of the cards. Madame Schreck, of course, is the High Priestess or Female Pope. The Count has given her a blue robe to wear over that terrible red dress that reminds us all, every time we see it, of the irresoluble and animal part of ourselves we all hold in common, since we are women. She is the paradigm of sexuality. At her hairy hole we all pay homage as if it were the mouth of an oracular cave.

When we play the Tarot Game, Madame Schreck sits on a small throne. They bring down the Count's special book, the book in black ink on purple paper that he keeps hanging from a twisted beam in his private apartments; they open it up and spread it out on her open lap, to mimic her sex, which is also a forbidden book.

The Tarot Game is like those games of chess that medieval princes performed on the black and white marble chequered floors of their palaces, using men for pieces. They'd dress one team in black and one team in white; the knights would be mounted on suitably caparisoned chargers who sometimes unloaded a freight of dung as they stepped delicately sideways, to prove the game was real. The bishops would be properly mitred; the pawns, no doubt, dressed as common militia. The Count plays the Game of Tarot with a major arcana of fourteen of his retinue. If Madame Schreck adopts the emblems of the Papess to the manner born, the Fool remains himself, of course. They mask themselves and perform random dances to sounds not unlike screaming that the Count extorts from an electronic synthesiser. He reads the patterns the hallucinated pack make at random and so he invokes chaos. He has methodology. He is a scientist, in his way.

Now, altogether I've been erased and substituted and played back so many times my memory is nothing but a palimpsest of possibilities and probabilities, there are some elements he cannot rid me of and these, interestingly enough, are not those of blood on an old man's hair or his leather-clad minions closing in on me with mineral menace of eyes like stones; no. There is a hawk, drawing towards it in a still sky all the elements of which a complex world was once composed. And some man haunts the labyrinths inside my head and he was born without a mouth. And there are certain kinds of eyes, those eyes that, once seen, can never be forgotten.

When I helplessly repeat, 'I saw a hawk, I saw a hawk, I saw a hawk . . . ' or, 'They say I have my mother's eyes', the Count half flays me alive. His anger is a nervous reflex, like the crazy courage of a coward in arms against his own weakness; that still, in my extremity, I should persist in remembering reminds him of the possibility, which is appalling to him, that there might be a remedy for chaos.

I need hardly tell you that we, the women of the Scarlet House, live in absolute isolation, although the planned interpenetration of all our experience gives us a vague but pervasive sense of closeness to one another. When on a pillow wet with tears, I live over again the fatal moment of capture, it might be your dread I feel, or yours, or yours – a different kind of dread than mine which, nevertheless, I experience as though it were my own and so I draw nearer to you all.

Yet our lives have contracted to the limitations imposed upon us by the grisly machinery of the Count's harem. We are not ourselves; we are his playing cards, a shifting chorus to the Count, to Madame Schreck, to the Fool and to the others I do not know but only see on the nights he plays the Tarot Game, hieratic figures like apparitions from a forgotten theogony who rise and fall at the random dictates of whim. 'God is random,' says the Count who believes in the irresolute triumph of time over its own rectification, memory.

We whisper among ourselves, of course, like toys might in the privacy of the toy cupboard after the little master is tucked up in bed for the night. Our whispers are soft, awed by the predicament in which we find ourselves. In the night-time darkness of our quarters, we cannot make out one another's features. Our disembodied voices rustle like dead leaves and sometimes we stretch out our hands to touch one another, lightly, to lay a finger on one another's mouths to assure ourselves a voice issues from that aperture. Like drifting cobwebs, the insubstantial caresses linger for a moment upon our skins. We manifest ourselves in a ghostly fashion for are we not already shadows? Phantoms of the dead, phantoms of the living, there is little to choose between two states of limbo.

Nevertheless, I have certain precious mnemonics. A hawk; a man without a mouth; and eyes without a face. As long as I retain them in my memory, even if I forget any kind of context for them, then I can keep back something of myself from the Count's dissolving

philosophy. He may beat me as much as he pleases; I'm not afraid of
encountering Death's grisly skeleton in the gavotte of the arcana, and
that's something.

(If you *do* find yourself partnering the skeleton, you vanish, of course.)

The Fool never says a word but only screeches and babbles; he's
growing perfect, he's quite forgotten how to speak. When the Count
beats me and I scream, he says: '*Now* you're talking! Who needs words?'

We are his harem and also his finishing school. The curriculum is
divided into three parts. First, we learn how to forget; second, we forget
how to speak; third, we cease to exist.

There are no mirrors in the Scarlet House because mirrors propagate
souls. A mirror shows you who you are and not one single one of us
poor girls has the slightest notion of what that might have been. Yet, when
the Count beats us, we feel pain and so we know we are still living, not
yet quite annihilated, and the anguish that overcomes me when I
remember I am no longer myself is quite real and persists all the time.

Yet the fugue of our common memory is also a kind of consolation.
Though I am not myself, sometimes, when we are forced to play at the
Tarot Game, I and the rest of the minor arcana, I sense I may be, in some
as yet formless and incoherent way, almost a legion of selves. When we
lie in our sleeping quarters and touch one another to confirm that the
ripped envelopes of our bodies are still there, even if the contents have all
been misdirected, it is almost as though my body had been transformed
into one of those many-limbed and many-headed effigies sculptured in
Indian temples – no point, any longer, in trying to ascertain the original
from my bewilderment. The more the Count scrambles the tapes, the
more the harem becomes one single woman with a multiplicity of hands
and eyes and no name, no past, no future – first, a being in a void; and,
soon, a void itself.

Chaos is like a vat of acid. Everything disintegrates.

Nevertheless, I cling to my mnemonics like a drowning man to a spar.
As time passes and wears me away, I meditate upon them more and
more. I am beginning to reconcile myself completely to the fact that they
may not contain any element at all of real memory. It was hard to bear, at
first, but soon I understood how the hawk, the face without a mouth, the
eyes without a face, are all the residue of the world I still carry with me
that does *not* elude me and, if they are not precisely memories, then they
may be, in some sense, like those odds and ends that all refugees carry with
them, from which they refuse to be parted, although they're quite
insignificant – a spoon with a bent handle, say; or a tram ticket issued by a
city that no longer exists. Small items, meaningless in themselves, and
yet keys to an entire system of meanings, if only I can remember . . .

The hawk, now. If I think about the hawk long enough, I remember that I do not remember it. That's a painful beginning; but one must begin somewhere. There was a sky, certainly; there's plenty of sky outside the Scarlet House, though we see none of it inside. Sky. Now, the hawk – down! he comes, like a butcher's cleaver thwacking through meat. The hawk drops on the plump, careless bunny romping through the clover and young grass; the hawk's eye, like a telescopic lens, zooms in on me as I lie in the sun with the smell of fresh grass in my clothes. Yes. I remember the green scent of a summer's day, not unlike the spicy odour of crushed geranium leaves. (Concentrate of fleshly impressions, any fleshly impression; reef it in from the past, from the time before my time in the Scarlet House. Scent of grass, of geraniums, of slivered lemons. All these scents bring back the world.)

As I lie in the fresh grass I have reconstructed out of memory, I begin to perceive some element of paranoia in the image of the hawk. For I did not know that I was watched. I was ignorant of my clawed, feathered fate. And so I will be seized by force. Capture; and rape, from the Latin, *rapere*, to seize by force . . . *that's* a curious pedantic bunny to hunt out from the back alleys of memory. I must have studied Latin, once, though for what purpose I can't imagine. So the capture and the rape elide. Man is an animal who insists on making *patterns*, says the Count contemptuously; all the world you think so highly of is nothing but pretty floral wallpaper pasted up over chaos.

The Count prepares chaos in his crucible. When he plays his Tarot Game, he makes an institution out of chaos. He signs himself, yours entropically, with the quill of a hawk dipped in the blood of ruptured virginities.

The hawk drops. They throw me down on the silk birds of the antique Persian carpet and rape me. And, to my amazement, a pattern emerges, although it is stylised as those woven birds I may once have walked on. For the hawk is nothing more and nothing less than the memory of my capture, preserved as an image, or an icon.

I cannot tell you with what inexpressible relief I greeted the concretisation, not of a memory, but of an inter-connection that made some sense in my plight to me. It was as if I'd gone to the confused jumble of limbs and hands and eyes scattered promiscuously on the floor of the harem and unerringly been able to pick out my own hand, screw it back on to my wrist and feel the blood flow back into it. Or pull out my mother's eyes from the mess, wipe them carefully on my sleeve and slip them back into my own eye sockets, where they belong.

Now, these are my mother's eyes that jumped out of the old photograph into my head; and there are also the eyes of the mute coachman that were full so full of pity for me that my heart stopped momentarily, out of fear for my own predicament. Those eyes, too, are rimmed with endless black lashes, they've been put in with a sooty finger. They move me as only the mute language of the eye can do and I do not know if, indeed, they are my own eyes, because there are no mirrors here, or if they are the eyes of somebody I loved, once, before they dissolved in my memory. However, I must slip these eyes back into some head or other; any head will do, to make sense of those eyes which will continue to speak even if the mouth is sealed up.

Those eyes hold all the speech which will be denied to me when forgetting forges my lips together and I cannot speak at all, like the mute coachman, like the mute orderly whose eyes had been excised and replaced with those of a beast of prey. Or else with stones, like the bikers, whose mouths were hidden by their leather hoods so you could not tell whether they had mouths or no.

And so I established the declension of my undoing, from capture to annihilation: the hawk, the face without a mouth, the eyes without a face. After that will come nothing. I shall be perfectly silent.

When I perceived I'd organised these disparate elements into a grid, or system of connections, I felt for the first time I entered the obscure portals of the Scarlet House, a flood of joy. I examined the abused flesh of my breasts and belly and felt, not sorrow I'd been so mauled, but anger the Count had mistreated me; and what if it's only that the puppet turns against the puppet-master: Isn't the puppet-master dependent on the submission of his dolls for his authority? Can't I, in the systematic randomness of my connections, control the Game?

The ghost reassembles the events that rendered it into non-being. As it does so, hourly it grows more substantial.

And where there's no hope, there's no fear, either. Not even fear of Madame Schreck, through whose hole we must all crawl to extinction, one day; unless it is the way to freedom.

This morning, the Count busily erased all the tapes of my Viennese apocalypse; I am glad of it, it was a vile memory and I am heartily sorry for whoever it was among my companions to whom it belonged. He tittered with his habitual beastly glee when at last he'd rid me of the compulsion, that nervous, that hiccuping reiteration; 'They say I have my mother's eyes.' But that was because he does not know I no longer need to remember it, whether it were true or no; I know all that I need to know to enable me to endure the time of the torturers and all its second-hand furniture of fear – the magic robes, the book of pretend-spells, the silence of the fool, the extinction of the whore.

This world's a vile oubliette. Yet in its refuse I will find the key to free me.

The Snow Pavilion

The motor stalled in the middle of a snowy landscape, lodged in a rut, wouldn't budge an inch. How I swore! I'd planned to be snug in front of a roaring fire, by now, a single malt on the mahogany wine-table (a connoisseur's piece) beside me, the five courses of Melissa's dinner savourously aromatising the kitchen; to complete the décor, a labrador retriever's head laid on my knee as trustingly as if I were indeed a country gentleman and lolled by rights among the chintz. After dinner, before I read our customary pre-coital poetry aloud to her, my elegant and accomplished mistress, also a connoisseur's piece, might play the piano for her part-time pasha while I sipped black, acrid coffee from her precious little cups.

Melissa was rich, beautiful and rather older than I. The servants slipped me looks of sly complicity; no matter how carefully I rumpled my sheets, they knew when a bed hadn't been slept in. The master of the house had a pied-à-terre in London when the House was sitting and the House was sitting tight. I'd met him only once, at the same dinner party where I'd met her – he'd been off-hand with me, gruff. I was young and handsome and full of promise; my relations with husbands rarely prospered. Wives were quite amother matter. Women, as Mayakovosky justly opined, are very partial to poets.

And now her glamorous motor car had broken down in the snow. I'd borrowed it for a trip to Oxford, ostensibly to buy books, utilising, with my instinctual cunning, the weather as an excuse. Last night, the old woman had been shaking her mattress with a vengeance – such snow! When I woke up the bedroom was full of luminous snow light, catching in the coils of Melissa's honey-coloured hair, and I'd experienced, once again, but, this time, almost uncontrollably, the sense of claustrophobia that sometimes afflicted me when I was with her.

I'd said, let's read some snowy poetry together, after dinner tonight, Melissa, a tribute of white verses to the iconography of the weather. Any excuse, no matter how far fetched, to get her out of the house – too much luxury on an empty stomach, that was the trouble. Always the same eyes too big for his belly, as grandma used to say; grandma spotted the trait when this little fellow lisped and toddled and pissed the bed before he knew what luxury was, even. Cultural indigestion, I tell you, the gripe in the bowels of your spirit. How can I get out of here, away from her subtly flawed antique mirrors, her French perfume decanted into eighteenth-century crystal bottles, her inscrutably smirking ancestresses in their gilt, oval frames? And her dolls, worst of all, her blasted dolls.

Those dolls that had never have been played with, her fine collection of antique women, part of the apparatus of Melissa's charm, her piquant originality that lay well on the safe side of quaint. A dozen or so of the finest lived in her bedroom in a glass-fronted, satinwood cabinet lavishly equipped with such toyland artefacts and miniature sofas and teeny-tiny grand pianos. They had heads made of moulded porcelain, each dimple and bee-stung underlip sculpted with loving care. Their wigs and over-lifelike eyelashes were made of real hair. She told me their eyes had been manufactured by the same craftsman in glass who made those terribly precious paperweights filled with magic snowstorms. Whenever I woke up in Melissa's bed, the first thing I saw were a dozen pairs of shining eyes that seemed to gleam wetly, as if in lacrimonious accusation of my presence there, for the dolls, like Melissa, were perfect ladies and I, in my upwardly social mobile nakedness – a nakedness that was, indeed, the essential battledress for such storm-troopers as I! – patently no gentleman.

After three days of that kind of style, I badly needed to sit in a public bar, drink coarse pints of bitter, swap double entendres with the barmaid; but I could hardly tell milady that. Instead, I must use my vocation to justify my day off. Lend me the car, Melissa, so that I can drive to Oxford and buy a book of snowy verses, since there's no such book in the house. And I'd made my purchase and managed to fit in my bread, cheese and badinage as well. A good day. Then, almost home again and here I was, stuck fast.

The fields were all brim-full of snow and the dark sky of late afternoon already swollen and discoloured with the next fall. Flocks of crows wheeled endlessly upon the invisible carousels of the upper air, occasionally emitting a rusty caw. A glance beneath the bonnet showed me only that I did not know what was wrong and must get out to trudge along a lane where the mauve shadows told me snow and the night would arrive together. My breath smoked. I wound Melissa's husband's muffler round my neck and dug my fists into his sheepskin pockets; his borrowed coat kept me snug and warm although the cold made the nerves in my forehead hum with a thin, high sound like that of the wind in telephone wires.

The leafless trees, the hillside quilted by intersections of dry-stone walling – all had been subdued to monochrome by the severity of last night's blizzard. Snow clogged every sound but that of the ironic punctuation of the crows. No sign of another presence; the pastoral cows were all locked up in the steaming byre, Colin Clout and Hobbinol sucked their pipes by the fireside in pastoral domesticity. Who would be outside, today, when he could be warm and dry, inside.

Too white. It is too white, out. Silence and whiteness at such a pitch of twinned intensity you know what it must be like to live in a country where snow is not a charming, since infrequent, visitor that puts its cold garlands on the trees so prettily we think they are playing at blossoming. (What an aptly fragile simile, with its Botticellian nuance. I congratulated myself.) No. Today is as cold as the killing cold of the perpetually white countries; today's atrocious candour is that of those white freckles that are the stigmata of frostbite.

My sensibility, the exquisite sensibility of a minor poet, tingled and crisped at the sight of so much whiteness.

I was certain that soon I'd come to a village where I could telephone Melissa; then she would send the village taxi for me. But the snow-fields now glimmered spectrally in an ever-thickening light and still there was no sign of life about me in the whole, white world but for the helmeted crows creaking down towards their nests.

Then I came to a pair of wrought-iron gates standing open on a drive. There must be some mansion or other at the end of the drive that would offer me shelter and, if they were half as rich as they ought to be, to live in such style, then they would certainly know Melissa and might even have me driven back to her by their own chauffeur in a warm car that would smell deliciously of new leather. I was sure they must be rich, the country side was lousy with the rich; hadn't I flattened a brace of pheasants on my way to Oxford? Encouraged, I turned in between the gate-posts, on which snarled iron gryphons sporting circumcision caps of snow.

The drive wound through an elm copse where the upper limbs of the bare trees were clogged with beastly lice of old crows' nests. I could tell that nobody had come this way since the snow fell, for only rabbit slots and the cuneiform prints of birds marked surfaces already crisping with frost. The drive took me uphill. My shoes and trouser bottoms were already wet through; it grew darker, colder and the old woman must have given her mattress a tentative shake or two, again, for a few more flakes drifted down and caught on my eyelashes so I first saw that house through a dazzle as of unshed tears, although, I assure you, I was out of the habit of crying.

I had reached the brow of a hill. Before me, in a hollow, magically surrounded by a snowy formal garden, lay a jewel of a mansion in a voluptuous style of English renaissance and every one of its windows blazed with light. I imagined myself describing it to Melissa – 'a vista like visible Debussy'. Enchanting. But, though lights streamed out in every direction, all was silent except for the crackling of the frosty trees. Lights and frost; in the winter sky above me, stars were coming out. Especially for my cultured patroness, I made an elision of the stars in the mansion of the heavens and the lights of the great house. So who was it, this snowy afternoon, who'd bagged a triad of fine images for her? Why, her clever boy! How pleased she'd be. And now I could declare the image factory closed for the day and get on with the real business of living, the experience of which that lovely house seemed to promise me in such abundance.

Yet, since the place was so well lit, the front door at the top of the serpentine staircase left open as for expected guests, why were there still no traces of arrivals or departures in the snow on which my footprints extended backwards to the lane and Melissa's abandoned car? And no figures to be glimpsed through any window, nor sound of life at all?

The vast empty hall serenely dominated by an immense chandelier, the faceted pendants of which chinked faintly in the currents of warm air and stippled with shifting, prismatic shadows walls wreathed in white stucco. This chandelier intimidated me, like too grand a butler but, all the same, I found the bellpull and tugged it. Somewhere inside a full-mouthed bell tolled; its reverberations set the chandelier a-tinkle but even when everything settled down again, nobody came.

I hauled again on the bellpull; still no reply, but a sudden wind blew a flurry of snow or sleet around me into the hall. The chandelier rocked musically in the draught. Behind me, outside, the air was full of the taste of snow – the storm was about to begin again. Nothing for it but to step bravely over the indifferent threshold and stamp my feet on the doormat with enough éclat to announce my arrival to the entire ground floor.

It was by far the most magnificent house I'd ever seen, and warm, so warm my frozen fingers throbbed. Yet all was white inside as the night outside, white walls, white paint, white drapes and a faint perfume everywhere, as though many rich women in beautiful dresses had drifted through the hall on their way to drinks before dinner, leaving behind them their spoor of musk and civet. The very air, here, mimicked the caress of their naked arms, intimate, voluptuous, rare.

My nostrils flared and quivered. I should have liked to have made love to every one of those lovely beings whose presence here was most poignant in her absence; it was a house built and furnished only for pleasure, for the indulgence of the flesh, for elegant concupiscence. I felt like Mignon in the land of the lemon trees; this is the place where I would like to live. I screwed up sufficient wincing courage to shout out: 'Anyone at home?' But only the chandelier tinkled in reply.

Then, a sudden creak behind me; I spun round to see the door swing to on its hinges with a soft, inexorable click. At that, the chandelier above me seemed to titter uncontrollably, as if with glee to see me locked in.

It is the wind, only the wind. Try to believe it is only the wind that blew the door shut behind you, keep a strong hold on that imagination of yours. Stop that shaking, all at once uneasy; walk slowly to the door, don't look nervous. It is the wind. Or else – perhaps – a trick of the owners, a practical joke. I grasped the notion gratefully. I knew the rich loved practical jokes.

But as soon as I realised it must be a practical joke, I knew I was not alone in the house because its apparent emptiness was all part of the joke. Then I exchanged one kind of unease for another. I became terribly self-conscious. Now I must watch my step; whatever happened, I must look as if I knew how to play the game in which I found myself. I tried the door but I was locked firmly in, of course. In spite of myself, I felt a faint panic, stifled it . . . No, you are *not* at their mercy.

The hall remained perfectly empty. Closed doors on either side of me; the staircase swept up to an empty landing. Am I to meet my hosts in embarrassment and humiliation, will they all come bouncing – 'boo!' – out of hidey holes in the panelling, from behind sweeping curtains to make fun of me? A huge mirror behind an extravagant arrangement of arum lilies showed me a poor poet not altogether convincingly rigged out in borrowed country squire's gear. I thought, how pinched and pale my face looks; a face that's eaten too much bread and margarine in its time. Come, now, liven up! You left bread and margarine behind you long ago, at grandma's house. Now you are a house-guest of the Lady Melissa. Your car has just broken down in the lane; you are looking for assistance.

Then, to my relief but also my increased disquiet, I saw a face behind my own, reflected, like mine, in the mirror. She must have known I could spy her, peeking at me behind my back. It was a pale, soft, pretty face, streaming blonde hair, and it sprang out quite suddenly from the reflections of the backs of the lilies. But when I turned, she – young, tricksy, fleet of foot – was gone already, though I could have sworn I heard a carillon of giggles, unless my sharp, startled movement had disturbed the chandelier, again.

This fleeting apparition let me know for sure I was observed. ('How amusing, a game of hide-and-seek. All the same, do you think, perhaps, the chauffeur could . . .') With the sullen knowledge of myself as appointed clown, I opened the first door I came to on the ground floor, expecting to discover my tittering audience awaiting me.

It was perfectly empty.

A white on white reception room, all bleached, all pale, sidetables of glass and chrome, artefacts of white lacquer, upholstery of thick, white

velvet. Company was expected; there were decanters, bowls of ice,
dishes of nuts and olives. I was tempted to swallow a cut-glass tumbler
full of something-or-other, to snatch a handful of salted almonds – I was
parched and starving, only that pub sandwich since breakfast. But it
would never do to be caught in the act by the fair-haired girl I'd glimpsed
in the hall. Look, she's left her doll behind her, forgotten in the deep
cushioning of an armchair.

How the rich indulge their children! Not a doll so much as a little work
of art; the cash register at the back of my mind rang up twenty guineas at
the sight of this floppy Pierrot with his skull-cap, his white satin pyjamas
with the black buttons down the front, all complete, and that authentic
pout of comic sadness on his fine china face. *Mon ami Pierrot*, poor old
fellow, limp limbs a-dangle, all anguished sensibility and no moral fibre.
I know how you feel. But, as I exchanged my glance of pitying
complicity with him, there came a sharp, melodious twang like a note
from an imperious tuning fork, from beyond the half-open double doors.
After a startled moment, I sprang into the dining room, summoned.

I had never seen anything like that dining room, except at the movies –
not even at the dinner where I'd met Melissa. Fifteen covers laid out on a
tongue-shaped spit of glass; but I hardly had time to take in the
splendour of the fine china, the lead crystal, because the door into the
hall still swung on its hinges and I knew I had missed her by seconds. So
the daughter of the house is indeed playing 'catch' with me; and where has
she got to, now?

Soft, softly on the white carpets; I leave deep prints behind me but do
not make a sound. And still no sign of life, only the pale shadows of the
candles; yet, somehow, everywhere a sense of hushed expectancy, as of
the night before Christmas.

Then I heard a patter of running footsteps. But these footsteps came
from a part of the house where no carpets muffled them, somewhere high
above me. As I poised, ears a-twitch, there came from upstairs or
downstairs, or milady's chamber, a spring of thin, high laughter agitating
the chandeliers; then the sound of many, many running feet overhead.
For a moment, the whole house seemed to tremble with unseen
movement; then, just as suddenly, all was silent again.

I resolutely set myself to search the upper rooms.

All these rooms were quite empty. But my always nascent paranoia,
now tingling at the tip of every nerve, assured me they had all been
vacated the very moment I entered them. Every now and then, as I made
my increasingly grim-faced tour of the house, I heard bursts of all kinds
of delicious merriments but never from the room next to the one in which
I stood. These voices started and stopped as if switched on and off and, of

course, were part and parcel of the joke; this joke was, my unease. In what, by its size and luxury, must have been the master bedroom, the polar bearskin rug thrown over the bed was warm and rumpled as if someone had just been lying there and now hid, perhaps, in the ivorine wardrobe, enjoying my perplexity. And I could have wrecked their fun if only – if only! – I had the courage to fling open the pale doors and catch my reluctant hosts crouching, as I thought, among the couture. But I did not dare do that.

The staircarpets gave way to scrubbed boards and still I had not seen anything living except the possibility of a face in the mirror, although the entire house was full of evidence of life. These upper floors were dimly lit, only single lights in holders at intervals along the walls, but one door was standing open and light spilled out onto the passage, like an invitation.

A good fire glowed in a neat little range where nightclothes were warming on the brass fender. I felt a sudden, sharp pang of disappointment to find her trail lead me to the nursery; I had been duped of all the fleshly adventures the house had promised me and that, damn them, must be part of the joke, too. All the same, if I indulged the fancy of the child I'd seen in the mirror, perhaps I might engage the fancy of her mother, who must be still young enough to enjoy the caress of a bearskin bedstead; and not, I'd be bound, inimical to poetry, either.

This mother, who had condemned even the nursery to whiteness, white walls, white painted furniture, white rug, white curtains, all chic as hell. Even the child had been made a slave to fashion. Yet, though the nursery itself had succumbed to the interior designer's snowdrift that had engulfed the entire house, its inhabitants had not. I'd never seen so many dolls before, not even in Melissa's cabinet, and all quite exquisite, as if they'd just come from the shop, although some of them must be older than I was. How Melissa would have loved them!

Dolls sat on shelves with their legs stuck out before them, dolls spilled from toychests. Fine ladies in taffeta bustles and French hats, babies in every gradation of cuteness. A limp-limbed, golden-haired creature in pink satin sprawled as if in sensual abandon on the rug in front of the fire. A wonderfully elaborate lady in a kitsch Victorian pelisse of maroon silk, with brown hair under a feather straw bonnet, lay in an armchair by the fire with as proprietorial an air as if the room belonged to her. A delicious lass in a purple velvet riding habit occupied the saddle of the wonderful albino rocking horse.

Now at last I was surrounded by beautiful women and they were dumb repositories of all the lively colours that had been exiled from the place, vivid as a hot-house, but none of them existed, all were mute, were fictions and that multitude of glass eyes, like tears congealed in time, made me feel very lonely.

Outside, the snow flurried against the windows; the storm had begun in earnest. Inside, there was still one threshold left to cross. I guessed she would be there, waiting for me, whoever she was, although I hesitated, if only momentarily, before the door that lead to the night nursery, as if unseen gryphons might guard it.

Faint glow of a night light on the mantelpiece; a dim tranquillity, here, where the air is full of the warm, pale smells of childhood, of clean hair, of soap, of talcum powder, the incenses of her sanctuary. And the moment I entered the night nursery, I could hear her transparent breathing; she had hardly hidden herself at all, not even pulled the covers of her white-enamelled crib around her. I had taken the game seriously but she, its instigator, had not; she had fallen fast asleep in the middle of it, her eyelids buttoned down, her long, blonde, patrician hair streaming over the pillow.

She wore a white, fragile, lace smock and her long, white stockings were fine as the smoky breath of a winter's morning. She had kicked off her white kid sandals. This little hunter, this little quarry, lay curled up with her thumb wedged, baby-like, in her mouth.

The wind yowled in the chimney and snow pelted the window. The curtains were not yet drawn so I closed them for her and at once the room denied tempest, so I could have thought I had been snug all my life. Weariness came over me; I sank down in the basketwork chair by her bed. I was loath to leave the company of the only living thing I'd found in the mansion and even if Nanny brusquely stormed in to interrogate me, I reassured myself that she must know how fond her little charge was of hide-and-seek indeed, must have been in complicity with the game, to let me wander about the nursery suite in this unconventional fashion. And if Mummy came in, now, for goodnight kisses? Well so much the better; I should be discovered demonstrating the tenderness of a poet at the cradle of a child.

If nobody came? I would endure the anti-climax; I'd just take the weight off my feet for a while, and then slip out. Yet I must admit I felt a touch of disappointment as time passed and I was forced reluctantly to abandon all hope of an invitation to dinner. They'd forgotten all about me! Careless even of their own games, they had left off playing in the middle of the chase, just as the child had done, and retired into the immutable privacy of the rich. I promised myself that at least I'd help myself to half a tumbler of good whisky on my way out, to see me warmly back to the lane and the stark trudge home.

The child stirred in her sleep and muttered indecipherably. Her fists clenched and unclenched. Her cheeks were delicately flushed a pale, luminous pink. Such skin – the fine texture of childhood, the incomparable down of skin that has never gone out in the cold. The more I watched beside her, the frailer she looked, the more transparent. I had never, in my life before, watched beside a sleeping child. The milky smell of innocence and sentiment suffused the night nursery.

I had anticipated, I suppose, some sort of gratified lust from this game of hide-and-seek through the mansion if not the satisfaction of lust of the flesh, then that of lust of the spirit, of vanity; but the more I mimicked tenderness towards the sleeper, the more tender I became. Oh, my shabby-sordid life! I thought. How she, in her untouchable sleep, judges me.

Yet she was not a peaceful sleeper. She twitched like a dog dreaming of rabbits and sometimes she moaned. She snuffled constantly and then, quite loudly, coughed. The cough rumbled in her narrow chest for a long time and it struck me that the child, so pale and sleeping with such racked exhaustion, was a sick child. A sick, spoiled little girl who ruled the household with a whim, and yet, poor little tyrant, went unloved; they must have been glad she had dropped off to sleep, so they could abandon the game she had forced them to play. She had fairy-tale, flaxen hair and eyelids so delicate the eyes beneath them almost showed glowing through; and if, indeed, it had been she who secreted all the grumbling grown-ups in their wardrobes and bathrooms and wound me through the house on an invisible spool towards her, well, I could scarcely begrudge her her fun. And her game had been as much with those grown-ups as it had been with me; hadn't she tidied them all away as if they'd been dolls she'd stowed in the huge toychest of this exquisite house?

When I thought of that, I went so far in forgiveness as to stroke her eggshell cheek with my finger. Her skin was soft as plumage of snow and sensitive as that of the princess in the story of the princess and the pea; when I touched her, she stirred. She shrugged away from my touch, muttering, and rolled over uneasily. As she did so, a gleaming bundle slithered from between her covers on to the floor, banging its china head on the scrubbed linoleum.

She must have tiptoed down to collect her forgotten doll while I went prowling about the bedrooms. Here he was again, her Pierrot in his shining white pyjamas, her little friend. Perhaps her only friend. I bent to pick him up from the floor for her and, as I did so, something caught the light and glittered at the corner of his huge, tragic, glass eye. A sequin? A brilliant? The moon is your country, old chap; perhaps they've put stars in your eyes for you.

I looked more closely.

It was wet.

It was a tear.

Then I felt a succinct blow on the back of my neck, so sudden, so powerful, so unexpected that I felt only a vague astonishment as I pitched forward on my face into a black vanishment.

When I opened my eyes, I saw a troubled absence of light around me; when I tried to move, a dozen little daggers serrated me. It was terribly cold and I was lying on, yes, marble, as if I was already dead, and I was trapped inside a little hill of broken glass inside the wet carapace of Melissa's husband's sheepskin coat that was sodden with melting snow.

After a few, careful, agonising twitches, I thought it best to stay quite still in this dank, lightless hall where the snow drove in through an open door whose outline I could dimly see against the white night outside. Slow as a dream, the door shifted back and forth on rusty hinges with a raucous, mechanical, monotonous caw, like that of crows.

I tried to piece together what had happened to me. I guessed I lay on the floor of the hall of the house I could have sworn I'd just explored, though I could see very little of its interior in the ghostly light – but all must once have been painted white, though now sadly and obscenely scribbled over by rude village boys with paint and chalks. The despoiled pallor reflected itself in a cracked mirror of immense size on the wall.

Perhaps I had been trapped by the fall of a chandelier. Certainly, I had been caught in the half-shattered glass viscera of the chandelier that I thought I'd just seen multiplying its reflections in another hall than the one in which I lay and every bone in my body ached and throbbed. If time had loosened the chandelier from its moorings in the flaking plaster above me, the chandelier might very well have come tumbling down on me as I sheltered from the storm that howled and gibbered around the house but then it might have killed me and I knew by my throbbing bruises that I was still alive. But had I not just walked through this very hall when it was warm and perfumed and suave with money? Or had I not.

Then I was pierced by a beam of light that struck cold green fire from the prisms around me. The invisible behind the flashlight addressed me unceremoniously in a cracked, old woman's voice, a crone's voice. Who be you? What be you up to?

Trapped in the splintered glass, the splintered light, I told her how my car had broken down in the snow and I had come here for assistance. This alibi now seemed to me a very feeble one.

I could not see the old woman at all, could not even make out her vague shape behind the light, but I told her I was staying with the Lady Melissa, to impress her old country crone's snobbery. She exclaimed and muttered when she heard Melissa's name; when she spoke again, her manner was almost excessively conciliatory. She has to be careful, poor old woman, all alone in the house; thieves come for lead from the roof and young couples up to no good come and so on and on. But, if I am the Lady Melissa's guest, then she is sure it is perfectly all right for me to shelter here. No, there is no telephone. I must wait here till the storm dies down. The new snow will have blocked the lane by now – we are quite cut off! she says; and titters.

I must follow her carefully, walk this way; she gives me a hand out of the mess, so much broken glass . . . take care. What a crash, when the chandelier came down! You'd have thought the world had come to an end. Come with her, she has her rooms; she is quite cosy, sir, with a roaring fire. (What weather, eh?)

She lit me solicitously out of the glass trap and took me past our phantoms moving like deep sea fish in the choked depths of the mirror; up the stairs we went, through the ruins of the house I thought I had explored in my waking faint or system of linked hallucinations, snow induced, or, perhaps, induced by a mild concussion. For I am shaky and a little nauseous; I grasp the banisters too tight.

The doors shudder on their hinges. I glimpse rooms with the furniture spookily shrouded in white sheets but the beam of her torch does not linger on anything; her carpet slippers go flipperty-flopperty, flipperty-flopperty, she is an intrepid negotiator of the shadows. And still I cannot see her clearly, although I hear the rustle of her dress and smell her musty, frowsty, second-hand clothes store, typical crone smell, like grandma's smell, smell of my childhood women.

She has, of course, ensconced herself in the nursery. And how I gasped, in my mild fever, to see so many dolls had set up camp in this decay!

Dolls everywhere higgledy-piggledy, dolls thrust down the sides of chairs, dolls spilled out of tea chests, dolls propped up on the mantelpiece with blank, battered faces. Had she gathered all the dolls of all the departed daughters of the house here, around her, for company? The dolls stared at me dumbly from glass eyes that might hold in suspension the magic snow-storm that trapped me here; I felt I was the cynosure of all their blind eyes.

And have I indeed met any of these now moth-gnawed creatures in this room before? When I first fainted in the hall, did I fall back in time to encounter on a white beach of years ago this young lady, whose heavy head drops forward on her bosom since her limp body has lost too much sawdust to continue to support it? The struts of her satin crinoline, stove in like a broken umbrella. Her blousy neighbour's dark red silk dress has faded to a thin pink but she has not lost her parasol because it had been sewn to her hand and her straw bonnet with the draggled feathers still hangs by a few threads from the brunette wig now awry on a china scalp.

And I almost tripped over a poor corpse on the floor in a purplish jacket of balding velvet, her worn, wax face raddled with age, only a few strands left of all that honey-coloured hair . . .

Yet if any of the denizens of that imaginary nursery were visiting this one, slipped out of my dream through a warp of the imagination, then I couldn't recognise them, thank God, among the dolls half loved to death and now scattered about a room whose present owner had consecrated it to a geriatric cosiness. Nevertheless, I felt a certain sense of disquiet, not so much fear as foreboding; but I was too preoccupied with my physical discomfort, my horrid aches, pains and scratches, to pay much attention to a prickling of the nerves.

And in the old woman's room, all was as comforting as a glowing fire, a steaming kettle could make it, even if eldritchly illuminated by a candle stuck in its own grease on to the mantelpiece. The very homeliness of the room went some way towards restoring my battered spirits and the crone made me very welcome, bustled me out of the sheepskin coat with almost as much solicitude as if she knew who it belonged to, set me down in an armchair. In its red plush death-throes, this armchair looked nothing like those bleached, remembered splendours; I told myself the snow had got into my eyes and brain. The old woman crouched down to take off my wet shoes for me; poured me thick, rich tea from her ever-ready pot; cut me a slice of dark gingerbread that she kept in an old biscuit tin with a picture of kittens on the lid. No spook or phantom could have had a hand in the making of that sagging, treacly, indigestible goody! I felt better, already; outside, the blizzard might rage but I was safe and warm, inside, even if in the company of an authentic crone.

For such she undeniably was, bent almost to a hoop with age, salt and pepper hair skewered up on top of her head with tortoiseshell pins, a face so eroded with wrinkles it was hard to tell whether she was smiling or not. She and her quarters had not seen soap and water for a long time and the lingering, sour, rank odour of uncaredforness faintly repelled me but the tea went down like blood. And don't you remember the slops and old clothes smell of grandma's kitchen? Colin Clout's come home again, with a vengeance.

She poured tea for herself and perched on top of the pile of old newspapers and discarded clothing that cushioned her own chair at the other side of the fire, to sip from her cup and chatter about the violence of the weather whilst I went on thawing myself out, eyeing – nervously, I must admit – the dolls propped on every flat surface, the roomful of bedizened raggle-taggles.

When she saw me looking at the dolls, she said: 'I see you're admiring my beauties.' Meanwhile, snow drove against the curtainless windowpanes like furious birds and blasts echoed through the house. The old woman thrust her empty cup away in the grate, all at once moved as if by a sudden sense of purpose; I saw I must pay in kind for my kind reception, I must give her a piece of undivided attention. She scooped up an armful of dolls and began to introduce them to me one by one. Dotty. Quite dotty, poor old thing.

The Hon. Frances Brambell had one eye out and her bell-shaped, satin skirt had collapsed but she must have been a pretty acquisition to the toy cupboard in her day; time, however, has its revenges, the three divorces, the voluntary exile in Morocco, the hashish, the gigolos, the slow erosion of her beauty . . . how it made the old woman chuckle! But how enchanting the girl had looked when she was presented, the ostrich feathers nodding above her curls! I looked from the old woman to the doll and back again; now the crone was animated, a thick track of spittle descended her chin. With an ironic laugh, she tossed the Hon. Frances Brambell to one side; the china head bounced off the wall and her limbs jerked a little before she lay still on the floor.

Seraphine, Duchess of Pyke, wore faded maroon silk and what had once been a feathered hat. She hailed, initially, from Paris and still possessed a certain style, even in her old age, although the Duchess had been by no means a model of propriety and, even if she carried off her acquired rank to the manner born, there is no more perfect a lady than one who is no better than she should be, suggested the old woman. In a paroxysm of wheezing laughter, she cast the Duchess and her pretensions on top of the Hon. Frances Brambell and told me now I must meet Lady Lucy, ah! she would be a marchioness when she inherited but had been infected with moth in her most sensitive parts and grown emaciated, in spite of her pretty velvet riding habit. She always wore purple, the colour of passion. The sins of the fathers, insinuated this gossipy harridan, a congenital affliction . . . the future held in store for the poor girl only clinics, sanatoria, a wheel-chair, dementia, premature death.

Each doll's murky history was unfolded to me; the old woman picked them up and dismissed them with such confident authority I soon realised she knew all the little girls whose names she'd given to the dolls intimately. She must have been the nanny here, I thought; and stayed on after the family all left the sinking ship, after her last charge, that little daughter who might, might she not? have looked just like my imaginary blonde heiress, ran off with a virile but uncouth chauffeur, or, perhaps, the black saxophonist in the dance band of an ocean liner. And the retainer inherited the desuetude. In the old days, she must have wiped their pretty noses for them, cut their bread and butter into piano keys for them . . . all the little girls must once have played in this very nursery, come for tea with the young mistress, gone out riding on ponies, grown up to come to dances in wonderful dresses, stayed over for house parties, golf by day, affairs of the heart by night. Had my Melissa, herself, danced here, perhaps, in her unimaginable adolescence?

I thought of all the beautiful women with round, bare shoulders discreet as pearls going in to dinner in dresses as brilliant as the hot-house flowers that surrounded them, handsomely set off by the dinner-jackets of their partners, though they would have been far more finely accessorised by me – women who had once filled the whole house with that ineffable perfume of sex and luxury that drew me greedily to Melissa's bed. And time, now, frosting those lovely faces, the years falling on their head like snow.

The wind howled, the logs hissed in the grate. The crone began to yawn and so did I. I can easily curl up in this armchair beside the fire; I'm half asleep already – please don't trouble yourself. But, no; I must have the bed, she said.

You shall sleep in the bed.

And, with that, cackled furiously, jolting me from my bitter-sweet reverie. Her rheumy eyes flashed; I was stricken with the ghastly notion she wanted to sacrifice me to some aged lust of hers as the price of my night's lodging but I said: 'Oh, I can't possibly take your bed, please no!' But her only reply was to cackle again.

When she rose to her feet, she looked far taller than she had been, she towered over me. Now, mysteriously, she resumed her old authority; her word was law in the nursery. She grasped my wrist in a hold like lockjaw and dragged me, weakly protesting, to the door that I knew, with a shock of perfect recognition, led to the night nursery.

I was cruelly precipitated back into the heart of my dream.

Beyond the door, on the threshold of which I stumbled, all was as it had been before, as if the night nursery were the changeless, unvaryingly eye of the storm and its whiteness that of a place beyond the spectrum of colours. The same scent of washed hair, the dim tranquillity of the night light. The white-enamelled crib, with its dreaming occupant. The storm crooned a lullaby; the little heiress of the snow pavilion had eyelids like carved alabaster that hold the light in a luminous cup, but she was a flawed jewel, this one, a shattered replica, a drawing that has been scribbled over, and, for the first time in all that night, I felt a pure fear.

The old woman softly approached her charge, and plucked an object, some floppy, cloth thing, from between the covers, where it had lain in the child's pale arms. And this object she, cackling again with obscure glee, handed to me as ceremoniously as if it were a present from a Christmas tree. I jumped when I touched Pierrot, as if there were an electric charge in his satin pyjamas.

He was still crying. Fascinated, fearful, I touched the shining teardrop pendant on his cheek and licked my finger. Salt. Another tear welled up from the glass eye to replace the one I had stolen, then another, and another. Until the eyelids quivered and closed. I had seen his face before, a face that had eaten too much bread and margarine in its time. A magic snow-storm blinded my eyes; I wept, too.

Tell Melissa the image factory is bankrupt, grandma.

Diffuse, ironic benediction of the night light. The sleeping child extended her warm, sticky hand to grasp mine; in a terror of consolation, I took her in my arms, in spite of her impetigo, her lice, her stench of wet sheets.

The Quilt Maker

One theory is, we make our destinies like blind men chucking paint at a wall; we never understand nor even see the marks we leave behind us. But not too much of the grandly accidental abstract expressionist about *my* life, I trust; oh, no. I always try to live on the best possible terms with my unconscious and let my right hand know what my left is doing and, fresh every morning, scrutinise my dreams. Abandon, therefore, or rather, deconstruct the blind-action painter metaphor; take it apart, formalise it, put it back together again, strive for something a touch more hard-edged, intentional, altogether less arty, for I do believe we all have the right to choose.

In patchwork, a neglected household art neglected, obviously, because my sex excelled in it – well, there you are; that's the way it's been, isn't it? Not that I have anything against fine art, mind; nevertheless, it took a hundred years for fine artists to catch up with the kind of brilliant abstraction that any ordinary housewife used to be able to put together in only a year, five years, ten years, without making a song and dance about it.

However, in patchwork, an infinitely flexible yet harmonious overall design is kept in the head and worked out in whatever material happens to turn up in the ragbag: party frocks, sackcloth, pieces of wedding-dress, of shroud, of bandage, dress shirts etc. Things that have been worn out or torn, remnants, bits and pieces left over from making blouses. One may appliqué upon one's patchwork birds, fruit and flowers that have been clipped out of glazed chintz left over from covering armchairs or making curtains, and do all manner of things with this and that.

The final design is indeed modified by the availability of materials; but not, necessarily, much.

For the paper patterns from which she snipped out regular rectangles and hexagons of cloth, the thrifty housewife often used up old love letters.

With all patchwork, you must start in the middle and work outward, even on the kind they call 'crazy patchwork', which is made by feather-stitching together arbitrary shapes scissored out at the maker's whim.

Patience is a great quality in the maker of patchwork.

The more I think about it, the more I like this metaphor. You can really make this image work for its living; it synthesises perfectly both the miscellany of experience and the use we make of it.

Born and bred as I was in the Protestant north working-class tradition, I am also pleased with the metaphor's overtones of thrift and hard work. Patchwork. Good.

Somewhere along my thirtieth year to heaven – a decade ago now I was in the Greyhound Bus Station in Houston, Texas, with a man I was then married to. He gave me an American coin of small denomination (he used to carry about all our money for us because he did not trust me with it). Individual compartments in a large vending machine in this bus station contained various cellophane-wrapped sandwiches, biscuits and candy bars. There was a compartment with two peaches in it, rough-cheeked Dixie Reds that looked like Victorian pincushions. One peach was big. The other peach was small. I conscientiously selected the smaller peach.

'Why did you do that?' asked the man to whom I was married.

'Somebody else might want the big peach,' I said,

'What's that to you?' he said.

I date my moral deterioration from this point.

No; honestly. Don't you see, from this peach story, how I was brought up? It wasn't – truly it wasn't – that I didn't think I deserved the big peach. Far from it. What it was, was that all my basic training, all my internalised values, told me to leave the big peach there for somebody who wanted it more than I did.

Wanted it; desire, more imperious by far than need. I had the greatest respect for the desires of other people, although, at that time, my own desires remained a mystery to me. Age has not clarified them except on matters of the flesh, in which now I know very well what I want; and that's quite enough of that, thank you. If you're looking for true confessions of that type, take your business to another shop. Thank you.

The point of this story is, if the man who was then my husband hadn't told me I was a fool to take the little peach, then I would never have left him because, in truth, he was, in a manner of speaking, always the little peach to me.

Formerly, I had been a lavish peach thief, but I learned to take the small one because I had never been punished, as follows:

Canned fruit was a very big deal in my social class when I was a kid and during the Age of Austerity, food-rationing and so on. Sunday teatime; guests; a glass bowl of canned peach slices on the table. Everybody gossiping and milling about and, by the time my mother put the teapot on the table, I had surreptitiously contrived to put away a good third of those peaches, thieving them out of the glass bowl with my crooked forepaw the way a cat catches goldfish. I would have been shall we say, for the sake of symmetry – ten years old; and chubby.

My mother caught me licking my sticky fingers and laughed and said I'd already had my share and wouldn't get any more, but when she filled the dishes up, I got just as much as anybody else.

I hope you understand, therefore, how, by the time two more decades had rolled away, it was perfectly natural for me to take the little peach; had I not always been loved enough to feel I had some to spare? What a dangerous state of mind I was in, then!

As any fool could have told him, my ex-husband is much happier with his new wife; as for me, there then ensued ten years of grab, grab, grab didn't there, to make up for lost time.

Until it is like crashing a soft barrier, this collision of my internal calendar, on which dates melt like fudge, with the tender inexorability of time of which I am not, quite, yet, the ruins (although my skin fits less well than it did, my gums recede apace, I crumple like chiffon in the thigh). Forty.

The significance, the real significance, of the age of forty is that you are, along the allotted span, nearer to death than to birth. Along the lifeline I am now past the halfway mark. But, indeed, are we not ever, in some sense, past that halfway mark, because we know when we were born but we do not know . . .

So, having knocked about the four corners of the world awhile, the ex-peach thief came back to London, to the familiar seclusion of privet hedges and soiled lace curtains in the windows of tall, narrow terraces. Those streets that always seem to be sleeping, the secrecy of perpetual Sunday afternoons; and in the long, brick-walled back gardens, where the little town foxes who subsist off mice and garbage bark at night, there will be the soft pounce, sometimes, of an owl. The city is a thin layer on top of a wilderness that pokes through the paving stones, here and there, in tufts of grass and ragwort. Wood doves with mucky pink bosoms croon in the old trees at the bottom of the garden; we double-bar the door against burglars, but that's nothing new.

Next-door's cherry is coming out again. It's April's quick-change act: one day, bare; the next dripping its curds of bloom.

One day, once, sometime after the incident with the little peach, when I had put two oceans and a continent between myself and my ex-husband, while I was earning a Sadie Thompsonesque living as a barmaid in the

Orient, I found myself, on a free weekend, riding through a flowering grove on the other side of the world with a young man who said: 'Me Butterfly, you Pinkerton.' And, though I denied it hotly at the time, so it proved, except, when I went away, it was for good. I never returned with an American friend, grant me sufficient good taste.

A small, moist, green wind blew the petals of the scattering cherry blossom through the open windows of the stopping train. They brushed his forehead and caught on his eyelashes and shook off on to the slatted wooden seats; we might have been a wedding party, except that we were pelted, not with confetti, but with the imagery of the beauty, the fragility, the fleetingness of the human condition.

'The blossoms always fall,' he said.

'Next year, they'll come again,' I said comfortably; I was a stranger here, I was not attuned to the sensibility, I believed that life was for living not for regret.

'What's that to me?' he said.

You used to say you would never forget me. That made me feel like the cherry blossom, here today and gone tomorrow; it is not the kind of thing one says to a person with whom one proposes to spend the rest of one's life, after all. And, after all that, for three hundred and fifty-two in each leap year, I never think of you, sometimes. I cast the image into the past, like a fishing line, and up it comes with a gold mask on the hook, a mask with real tears at the ends of its eyes, but tears which are no longer anybody's tears.

Time has drifted over your face.

The cherry tree in next-door's garden is forty feet high, tall as the house, and it has survived many years of neglect. In fact, it has not one but two tricks up its arboreal sleeve; each trick involves three sets of transformations and these it performs regularly as clockwork each year, the first in early, the second in late spring. Thus:

one day, in April, sticks; the day after, flowers; the third day, leaves. Then –

through May and early June, the cherries form and ripen until, one fine day, they are rosy and the birds come, the tree turns into a busy tower of birds admired by a tranced circle of cats below. (We are a neighbourhood rich in cats.) The day after, the tree bears nothing but cherry pits picked perfectly clean by quick, clever beaks, a stone tree.

The cherry is the principal monument of Letty's wild garden. How wonderfully unattended her garden grows all the soft months of the year, from April through September! Dandelions come before the swallow does and languorously blow away in drifts of fuzzy seed. Then up sprouts a long bolster of creeping buttercups. After that, bindweed distributes its white cornets everywhere, it climbs over everything in Letty's garden, it swarms up the concrete post that sustains the clothesline on which the lady who lives in the flat above Letty hangs her underclothes out to dry, by means of a pulley from her upstairs kitchen window. She never goes in to the garden. She and Letty have not been on speaking terms for twenty years.

I don't know why Letty and the lady upstairs fell out twenty years ago when the latter was younger than I, but Letty already an old woman. Now Letty is almost blind and almost deaf but, all the same, enjoys, I think, the changing colours of this disorder, the kaleidoscope of the seasons variegating the garden that neither she nor her late brother have touched since the war, perhaps for some now forgotten reason, perhaps for no reason.

Letty lives in the basement with her cat.

Correction. Used to live.

Oh, the salty realism with which the Middle Ages put skeletons on gravestones, with the motto: 'As I am now, so ye will be!' The birds will come and peck us bare.

I heard a dreadful wailing coming through the wall in the middle of the night. It could have been either of them, Letty or the lady upstairs, pissed out of their minds, perhaps, letting it all hang out, shrieking and howling, alone, driven demented by the heavy anonymous London silence of the fox-haunted night. Put my ear nervously to the wall to seek the source of the sound. 'Help!' said Letty in the basement. The cow that lives upstairs later claimed she never heard a cheep, tucked up under the eaves in dreamland sleep while I leaned on the doorbell for twenty minutes, seeking to rouse her. Letty went on calling 'Help!' Then I telephoned the police, who came flashing lights, wailing sirens, and double-parked dramatically, leaping out of the car, leaving the doors swinging; emergency call.

But they were wonderful. Wonderful. (We're not black, any of us, of course.) First, they tried the basement door, but it was bolted on the inside as a precaution against burglars. Then they tried to force the front door, but it wouldn't budge, so they smashed the glass in the front door and unfastened the catch from the inside. But Letty for fear of burglars, had locked herself securely in her basement bedroom, and her voice floated up the stairs: 'Help!'

So they battered her bedroom door open too, splintering the jamb, making a terrible mess. The cow upstairs, mind, sleeping sweetly throughout, or so she later claimed. Letty had fallen out of bed, bringing the bedclothes with her, knotting herself up in blankets, in a grey sheet, an old patchwork bedcover lightly streaked at one edge with dried shit, and she hadn't been able to pick herself up again, had lain in a helpless tangle on the floor calling for help until the coppers came and scooped her up and tucked her in and made all cosy. She wasn't surprised to see the police; hadn't she been calling: 'Help'? Hadn't help come?

'How old are you, love,' the coppers said. Deaf as she is, she heard the question, the geriatric's customary trigger. 'Eighty,' she said. Her age is the last thing left to be proud of. (See how, with age, one defines oneself by age, as one did in childhood.)

Think of a number. Ten. Double it. Twenty. Add ten again. Thirty. And again. Forty. Double that. Eighty. If you reverse this image, you obtain something like those Russian wooden dolls, in which big babushka contains a middling babushka who contains a small babushka who contains a tiny babushka and so on *ad infinitum.*

But I am further away from the child I was, the child who stole the peaches, than I am from Letty. For one thing, the peach thief was a plump brunette; I am a skinny redhead.

Henna. I have had red hair for twenty years. (When Letty had already passed through middle age.) I first dyed my hair red when I was twenty. I freshly henna'd my hair yesterday.

Henna is a dried herb sold in the form of a scum-green-coloured powder. You pour this powder into a bowl and add boiling water; you mix the powder into a paste using, say, the handle of a wooden spoon. (It is best not to let henna touch metal, or so they say.) This henna paste is no longer greyish, but now a dark vivid green, as if the hot water had revived the real colour of the living leaf, and it smells deliciously of spinach. You also add the juice of a half a lemon; this is supposed to 'fix' the final colour. Then you rub this hot, stiff paste into the roots of your hair.

(However did they first think of it?)

You're supposed to wear rubber gloves for this part of the process, but I can never be bothered to do that, so, for the first few days after I have refreshed my henna, my fingertips are as if heavily nicotine-stained. Once the green mud has been thickly applied to the hair, you wrap it in an impermeable substance – a polythene bag, or kitchen foil and leave it to cook. For one hour: auburn highlights. For three hours: a sort of vague russet halo around the head. Six hours: red as fire.

Mind you, henna from different *pays d'origines* has different effects – Persian henna, Egyptian henna, Pakistani henna, all these produce different tones of red, from that brick red usually associated with the idea of henna to a dark, burning, courtesan plum or cockatoo scarlet. I am a connoisseur of henna, by now, 'an unpretentious henna from the southern slope', that kind of thing. I've been every redhead in the book. But people think I am naturally redheaded and even make certain tempestuous allowances for me, as they did for Rita Hayworth, who purchased red hair at the same mythopoeic counter where Marilyn Monroe acquired her fatal fairness. Perhaps I first started dyeing my hair in order to acquire the privileged irrationality of redheads. Some men say they adore redheads. These men usually have very interesting psychosexual problems and shouldn't be let out without their mothers.

When I combed Letty's hair next morning, to get her ready for the ambulance, I saw telltale scales of henna'd dandruff lying along her scalp, although her hair itself is now a vague salt and pepper colour and, I hazard, has not been washed since about the time I was making the peach decision in the Houston, Texas, bus station. At that time, I had appropriately fruity – tangerine-coloured – hair in, I recall, a crewcut as brutal as that of Joan of Arc at the stake such as we daren't risk now, oh, no. Now we need shadows, my vain face and I; I wear my hair down to my shoulders now. At the moment, henna produces a reddish-gold tinge on me. That is because I am going grey.

Because the effect of henna is also modified by the real colour of the hair beneath. This is what it does to white hair:

In Turkey, in a small country town with a line of poplar trees along the horizon and a dirt-floored square, chickens, motorbikes, apricot sellers, and donkeys, a woman was haggling for those sesame-seed-coated bracelets of bread you can wear on your arm. From the back, she was small and slender; she was wearing loose, dark-blue trousers in a peasant print and a scarf wound round her head, but from beneath this scarf there fell the most wonderful long, thick, Rapunzel-like plait of golden hair. Pure gold; gold as a wedding ring. This single plait fell almost to her feet and was as thick as my two arms held together. I waited impatiently to see the face of this fairy-tale creature.

Stringing her breads on her wrist, she turned; and she was old.

'What a life,' said Letty, as I combed her hair.

Of Letty's life I know nothing. I know one or two things about her: how long she has lived in this basement – since before I was born, how she used to live with an older brother, who looked after her, an *older* brother. That he, last November, fell off a bus, what they call a 'platform accident', fell off the platform of a moving bus when it slowed for the stop at the bottom of the road and, falling, irreparably cracked his head on a kerbstone.

Last November, just before the platform accident, her brother came knocking at our door to see if we could help him with a light that did not work. The light in their flat did not work because the cable had rotted away. The landlord promised to send an electrician but the electrician never came. Letty and her brother used to pay two pounds fifty pence a week rent. From the landlord's point of view, this was not an economic rent; it would not cover his expenses on the house, rates etc. From the point of view of Letty and her late brother, this was not an economic rent, either, because they could not afford it.

Correction: Letty and her brother could not afford it because he was too proud to allow the household to avail itself of the services of the caring professions, social workers and so on. After her brother died, the caring professions visited Letty *en masse* and now her financial position is easier, her rent is paid for her.

Correction: *was* paid for her.

We know her name is Letty because she was banging out blindly in the dark kitchen as we/he looked at the fuse box and her brother said fretfully: 'Letty, give over!'

What Letty once saw and heard before the fallible senses betrayed her into a world of halftones and muted sounds is unknown to me. What she touched, what moved her, are mysteries to me. She is Atlantis to me. How she earned her living, why she and her brother came here first, all the real bricks and mortar of her life have collapsed into a rubble of forgotten past.

I cannot guess what were or are her desires.

She was softly fretful herself, she said: 'They're not going to take me away, are they?' Well, they won't let her stay here on her own, will they, not now she has proved that she can't be trusted to lie still in her own bed without tumbling out arse over tip in a trap of blankets, incapable of righting herself. After I combed her hair, when I brought her some tea, she asked me to fetch her porcelain teeth from a saucer on the dressing table, so that she could eat the biscuit. 'Sorry about that,' she said. She asked me who the person standing beside me was; it was my own reflection in the dressing-table mirror, but, all the same, oh, yes, she was in perfectly sound mind, if you stretch the definition of 'sound' only a very little. One must make allowances. One will do so for oneself.

She needed to sit up to drink tea, I lifted her. She was so frail it was like picking up a wicker basket with nothing inside it; I braced myself for a burden and there was none, she was as light as if her bones were filled with air like the bones of birds. I felt she needed weights, to keep her from floating up to the ceiling following her airy voice. Faint odour of the lion house in the bedroom and it was freezing cold, although, outside, a good deal of April sunshine and the first white flakes of cherry blossom shaking loose from the tight buds.

Letty's cat came and sat on the end of the bed. 'Hello, pussy,' said Letty.

One of those ill-kempt balls of fluff old ladies keep, this cat looks as if he's unravelling, its black fur has rusted and faded at the same time, but some cats are naturals for the caring professions – they will give you mute company long after anyone else has stopped tolerating your babbling, they don't judge, don't give a damn if you wet the bed and, when the eyesight fades, freely offer themselves for the consolation of still sentient fingertips. He kneads the shit-stained quilt with his paws and purrs.

The cow upstairs came down at last and denied all knowledge of last night's rumpus; she claimed she had slept so soundly she didn't hear the doorbell or the forced entry. She must have passed out or something, or else wasn't there at all but out on the town with her man friend. Or, her man friend was here with her *all the time* and she didn't want anybody to know so kept her head down. We see her man friend once or twice a week as he arrives crabwise to her door with the furtiveness of the adulterer. The cow upstairs is fiftyish, as well preserved as if she'd sprayed herself all over with the hair lacquer that keeps her bright brown curls in tight discipline.

No love lost between her and Letty. 'What a health hazard! What a fire hazard!' Letty, downstairs, dreamily hallucinating in the icy basement as the cow upstairs watches me sweep up the broken glass on the hall floor. 'She oughtn't to be left. She ought to be in a home.' The final clincher: 'For her *own good.*'

Letty dreamily apostrophised the cat; they don't let cats into any old people's homes that I know of.

Then the social worker came; and the doctor; and, out of nowhere, a great-niece, probably summoned by the social worker, a great-niece in her late twenties with a great-great-niece clutching a teddy bear. Letty is pleased to see the great-great-niece, and this child is the first crack that appears in the picture that I'd built up of Letty's secluded, lonely old age. We hadn't realised there were kin; indeed, the great-niece puts us in our place good and proper. 'It's up to family now,' she said, so we curtsy and retreat, and this great-niece is sharp as a tack, busy as a bee, proprietorial yet tender with the old lady. 'Letty, what have you got up to now?' Warding us outsiders off; perhaps she is ashamed of the shit- stained quilt, the plastic bucket of piss beside Letty's bed.

As they were packing Letty's things in an airline bag the great-niece brought, the landlord – by a curious stroke of fate – chose this very day to collect Letty's rent and perked up no end, stroking his well-shaven chin, to hear the cow upstairs go on and on about how Letty could no longer cope, how she endangered property and life on the premises by forcing men to come and break down doors.

What a life.

Then the ambulance came.

Letty is going to spend a few days in hospital.

This street is, as estate agents say, rapidly improving; the lace curtains are coming down, the round paper lampshades going up like white balloons in each front room. The landlord had promised the cow upstairs five thousand pounds in her hand to move out after Letty goes, so that he can renovate the house and sell it with vacant possession for a tremendous profit.

We live in hard-nosed times.

The still unravished bride, the cherry tree, takes flowering possession of the wild garden; the ex-peach thief contemplates the prospect of ripe fruit the birds will eat, not I. Curious euphemism 'to go', meaning death, to depart on a journey.

Somewhere along another year to heaven, I elicited the following laborious explanation of male sexual response, which is the other side of the moon, the absolute mystery, the one thing I can never know.

'You put it in, which isn't boring. Then you rock backwards and forwards. That can get quite boring. Then you come. That's not boring.'

For 'you', read 'him'.

'You come; or as we Japanese say, go.'

Just so. '*Ikimasu*,' to go. The Japanese orgasmic departure renders the English orgasmic arrival, as if the event were reflected in the mirror and the significance of it altogether different – whatever significance it may have, that is. Desire disappears in its fulfilment, which is cold comfort for hot blood and the reason why there is no such thing as a happy ending.

Besides all this, Japanese puts all its verbs at the ends of its sentences, which helps to confuse the foreigner all the more, so it seemed to me they themselves never quite knew what they were saying half the time.

'Everything here is arsy-varsy.'

'No. Where you are is arsy-varsy.'

And never the twain shall meet. He loved to be bored; don't think he was contemptuously dismissive of the element of boredom inherent in sexual activity. He adored and venerated boredom. He said that dogs, for example, were never bored, nor birds, so, obviously, the capacity that distinguished man from the other higher mammals, from the scaled and feathered things, was that of boredom. The more bored one was, the more one expressed one's humanity.

He liked redheads. 'Europeans are so colourful,' he said.

He was a tricky bugger, that one, a Big Peach, all right; face of Gérard Philipe, soul of Nechaev. I grabbed, grabbed and grabbed and, since I did not have much experience in grabbing, often bit off more than I could chew. Exemplary fate of the plump peach-thief; someone refuses to be assimilated. Once a year, when I look at Letty's cherry tree in flower, I put the image to work, I see the petals fall on a face that looked as if it had been hammered out of gold, like the mask of Agamemnon which Schliemann found at Troy.

The mask turns into a shining carp and flips off the hook at the end of the fishing line. The one that got away.

Let me not romanticise you too much. Because what would I do if you *did* resurrect yourself? Came knocking at my door in all your foul, cool, chic of designer jeans and leather blouson and your pocket stuffed with G.N.P., arriving somewhat late in the day to make an honest woman of me as you sometimes used to threaten that you might? 'When you're least expecting it . . . .' God, I'm forty, now. Forty! I had you marked down for a Demon Lover; what if indeed you popped up out of the grave of the heart bright as a button with an American car purring outside waiting to whisk me away to where the lilies grow on the bottom of the sea? 'I am now married to a house carpenter,' as the girl in the song exclaimed hurriedly. But all the same, off she went with the lovely cloven-footed one. But I wouldn't. Not I.

And how very inappropriate too, the language of antique ballads in which to address one who knew best the international language of the jukebox. You'd have one of those Wurlitzer Cadillacs you liked, that you envied G.I.s for, all ready to humiliate me with; it would be bellowing out quadraphonic sound. The Everly Brothers. Jerry Lee Lewis. Early Presley. ('When I grow up,' you reveried, 'I'm going to Memphis to marry Presley.') You were altogether too much, you pure child of the late twentieth century, you person from the other side of the moon or mirror, and your hypothetical arrival is a catastrophe too terrifying to contemplate, even in the most plangent state of regret for one's youth.

I lead a quiet life in South London. I grind my coffee beans and drink my early cup to a spot of early baroque on the radio. I am now married to a house carpenter. Like the culture that created me, I am receding into the past at a rate of knots. Soon I'll need a whole row of footnotes if anybody under thirty-five is going to comprehend the least thing I say.

And yet . . .

*

Going out into the back garden to pick rosemary to put inside a chicken, the daffodils in the uncut grass, enough blackbirds out to make a pie.

Letty's cat sits on Letty's windowsill. The blinds are drawn; the social worker drew them five days ago before she drove off in her little Fiat to the hospital, following Letty in the ambulance. I call to Letty's cat but he doesn't turn his head. His fluff has turned to spikes, he looks spiny as a horse-chestnut husk.

Letty is in hospital supping broth from a spouted cup and, for all my kind heart, of which I am so proud, my empathy and so on, I myself had not given Letty's companion another thought until today, going out to pick rosemary with which to stuff a roast for our greedy dinners.

I called him again. At the third call, he turned his head. His eyes looked as if milk had been poured into them. The garden wall too high to climb since now I am less limber than I was, I chucked half the contents of a guilty tin of cat food over. Come and get it.

Letty's cat never moved, only stared at me with its curtained eyes. And then all the fat, sleek cats from every garden up and down came jumping, leaping, creeping to the unexpected feast and gobbled all down, every crumb, quick as a wink. What a lesson for a giver of charity! At the conclusion of this heartless banquet at which I'd been the thoughtless host, the company of well-cared-for beasts stretched their swollen bellies in the sun and licked themselves, and then, at last, Letty's cat heaved up on its shaky legs and launched itself, plop on to the grass.

I thought, perhaps he got a belated whiff of cat food and came for his share, too late, all gone. The other cats ignored him. He staggered when he landed but soon righted himself. He took no interest at all in the stains of cat food, though. He managed a few doddering steps among the dandelions. Then I thought he might be going to chew on a few stems of medicinal grass; but he did not so much lower his head towards it as let his head drop, as if he had no strength left to lift it. His sides were caved-in under stiff, voluminous fur. He had not been taking care of himself. He peered vaguely around, swaying.

You could almost have believed, not that he was waiting for the person who always fed him to come and feed him again as usual, but that he was pining for Letty herself.

Then his hind legs began to shudder involuntarily. He so convulsed himself with shuddering that his hind legs jerked off the ground; he danced. He jerked and shuddered, shuddered and jerked, until at last he vomited up a small amount of white liquid. Then he pulled himself to his feet again and lurched back to the windowsill. With a gigantic effort, he dragged himself up.

Later on, somebody jumped over the wall, more sprightly than I and left a bowl of bread and milk. But the cat ignored that too. Next day, both were still there, untouched.

The day after that, only the bowl of sour sops, and cherry blossom petals drifting across the vacant windowsill.

Small sins of omission remind one of the greater sins of omission; at least sins of commission have the excuse of choice, of intention. However:

May. A blowy, bright-blue, bright-green morning; I go out on the front steps with a shifting plastic sack of garbage and what do I see but the social worker's red Fiat putter to a halt next door.

In the hospital they'd henna'd Letty. An octogenarian redhead, my big babushka who contains my forty, my thirty, my twenty, my ten years within her fragile basket of bones, she has returned, not in a humiliating ambulance, but on her own two feet that she sets down more firmly than she did. She has put on a little weight. She has a better colour, not only in her hair but in her cheeks.

The landlord, foiled.

Escorted by the social worker, the district nurse, the home help, the abrasive yet not ungentle niece, Letty is escorted down the unswept, grass-grown basement stairs into her own scarcely used front door that someone with a key has remembered to unbolt from inside for her return. Her new cockatoo crest – whoever henna'd her really understood henna – points this way and that way as she makes sure that nothing in the street has changed, even if she can see only large blocks of light and shadow, hear, not the shrieking blackbirds, but only the twitch of the voices in her ear that shout: 'Carefully does it, Letty.'

'I can manage,' she said tetchily.

The door the policemen battered in closes upon her and her chattering entourage.

The window of the front room of the cow upstairs slams down, bang.

And what am I to make of that? I'd set it up so carefully, an enigmatic structure about evanescence and ageing and the mists of time, shadows lengthening, cherry blossom, forgetting, neglect, regret . . . the sadness, the sadness of it all . . .

But. Letty. Letty came home.

In the corner shop, the cow upstairs, mad as fire: 'They should have certified her'; the five grand the landlord promised her so that he could sell the house with vacant possession has blown away on the May wind that disintegrated the dandelion clocks. In Letty's garden now is the time for fierce yellow buttercups; the cherry blossom is over, no regrets.

I hope she is too old and too far gone to miss the cat.

Fat chance.

I hope she never wonders if the nice warm couple next door thought of feeding him.

But she has come home to die at her own apparently ample leisure in the comfort and privacy of her basement; she has exercised, has she not, her right to choose, she has turned all this into crazy patchwork.

Somewhere along my thirtieth year, I left a husband in a bus station in Houston, Texas, a town to which I have never returned, over a quarrel about a peach which, at the time, seemed to sum up the whole question of the rights of individuals within relationships, and, indeed, perhaps it did.

As you can tell from the colourful scraps of oriental brocade and Turkish homespun I have sewn into this bedcover, I then (call me Ishmael) wandered about for a while and sowed (or sewed) a wild oat or two into this useful domestic article, this product of thrift and imagination, with which I hope to cover myself in my old age to keep my brittle bones warm. (How cold it is in Letty's basement.)

But, okay, so I always said the blossom would come back again, but Letty's return from the clean white grave of the geriatric ward is *ridiculous!* And, furthermore, when I went out into the garden to pick a few tulips, there he is, on the other side of the brick wall, lolling voluptuously among the creeping buttercups, fat as butter himself – Letty's been feeding him up.

'I'm pleased to see *you*,' I said.

In a Japanese folk tale it would be the ghost of her cat, rusty and tactile as in life, the poor cat pining itself from death to life again to come to the back door at the sound of her voice. But we are in South London on a spring morning. Lorries fart and splutter along the Wandsworth Road. Capital Radio is braying from an upper window. An old cat, palpable as a second-hand fur coat, drowses among the buttercups.

We know when we were born but –

the times of our reprieves are equally random.

Shake it out and look at it again, the flowers, fruit and bright stain of henna, the Russian dolls, the wrinkling chiffon of the flesh, the old songs, the cat, the woman of eighty; the woman of forty, with dyed hair and most of her own teeth, who is *ma semblable, ma soeur.* Who now recedes into the deceptive privacy of a genre picture, a needlewoman, a quilt maker, a middle-aged woman sewing patchwork in a city garden, turning her face vigorously against the rocks and trees of the patient wilderness waiting round us.

Appendix

AFTERWORD TO *FIREWORKS*

I started to write short pieces when I was living in a room too small to write a novel in. So the size of my room modified what I did inside it and it was the same with the pieces themselves. The limited trajectory of the short narrative concentrates its meaning. Sign and sense can fuse to an extent impossible to achieve among the multiplying ambiguities of an extended narrative. I found that, though the play of surfaces never ceased to fascinate me, I was not so much exploring them as making abstractions from them, I was writing, therefore, tales.

Though it took me a long time to realise why I liked them, I'd always been fond of Poe, and Hoffman – Gothic tales, cruel tales, tales of wonder, tales of terror, fabulous narratives that deal directly with the imagery of the unconscious – mirrors; the externalised self; forsaken castles; haunted forests; forbidden sexual objects. Formally the tale differs from the short story in that it makes few pretences at the imitation of life. The tale does not log everyday experience, as the short story does; it interprets everyday experience through a system of imagery derived from subterranean areas behind everyday experience, and therefore the tale cannot betray its readers into a false knowledge of everyday experience.

The Gothic tradition in which Poe writes grandly ignores the value systems of our institutions; it deals entirely with the profane. Its great themes are incest and cannibalism. Character and events are exaggerated beyond reality, to become symbols, ideas, passions. Its style will tend to be ornate, unnatural – and thus operate against the perennial human desire to believe the word as fact. Its only humour is black humour. It retains a singular moral function – that of provoking unease.

The tale has relations with subliterary forms of pornography, ballad and dream, and it has not been dealt with kindly by literati. And is it any wonder? Let us keep the unconscious in a suitcase, as Père Ubu did with his conscience, and flush it down the lavatory when it gets too troublesome.

So I worked on tales. I was living in Japan; I came back to England in 1972. I found myself in a new country. It was like waking up, it was a rude awakening. We live in Gothic times. Now, to understand and to interpret is the main thing; but my method of investigation is changing.

These stories were written between 1970 and 1973 and are arranged in chronological order, as they were written. There is a small tribute to Defoe, father of the bourgeois novel in England, inserted in the story 'Master'.

First Publications

'The Man Who Loved a Double Bass' first appeared in *Storyteller Contest*, July 1962. 'A Very, Very Great Lady and Her Son at Home' was first published in *Nonesuch*, in Autumn 1965 and 'A Victorian Fable (with Glossary)' was also published in *Nonesuch*, in Summer/Autumn 1966.

'A Souvenir of Japan', 'The Executioner's Beautiful Daughter', 'The Loves of Lady Purple', 'The Smile of Winter', 'Penetrating to the Heart of the Forest', 'Flesh and the Mirror', 'Master', 'Reflections' and 'Elegy for a Freelance', written between 1970 and 1973, were all originally published in *Fireworks: Nine Profane Pieces* (Quartet Books, 1974).

'The Bloody Chamber' and 'The Tiger's Bride' first appeared in *The Bloody Chamber and Other Stories* (Victor Gollancz, 1979). 'The Courtship of Mr Lyon' was originally published in British *Vogue*, 'Puss-in-Boots' appeared in the anthology *The Straw and the Gold*, edited by Emma Tennant (Pierrot Books, 1979). 'The Erl-King' appeared in *Bananas* (October, 1977), 'The Snow Child' was broadcast on the BBC Radio Four programme *Not Now, I'm Listening*. 'The Lady of the House of Love' was first published in *The Iowa Review* (Summer/Autumn 1975), 'The Werewolf' in *South-West Arts Review* (No 2, October, 1977), 'The Company of Wolves' in *Bananas* (April, 1977) and 'Wolf-Alice' in *Stand* (Winter, 1978, vol. 2, No 2).

'Black Venus' first appeared in *Next Editions* in 1980, 'The Kiss' was originally published in *Harper's and Queen*, in 1977, 'Our Lady of the Massacre' appeared in *The Saturday Night Reader* as 'Captured by the Red Man' in 1979. 'The Cabinet of Edgar Allan Poe' was published in *Interzone* in 1982, as was 'Overture and Incidental Music for *A Midsummer Night's Dream*'. 'Peter and the Wolf' is from *Firebird 1*, 1982. A version of 'The Kitchen Child' was published in *Vogue*, 1979, and 'The Fall River Axe Murder' originally appeared in *The London Review of Books* in 1981 under the title 'Mis-en-Scene for Parricide'.

A version of 'Lizzie's Tiger' was first published in *Cosmopolitan* in September 1981, and broadcast on Radio Three. 'John Ford's *'Tis Pity She's a Whore*' originally appeared in *Granta 25*, Autumn, 1988. 'Gun for the Devil' was written as a draft for a screenplay and published in *American Ghosts and Old World Wonders* (Chatto & Windus, 1993). 'The Merchant of Shadows' was published in the *London Review of Books* in

October 1989. 'Alice in Prague or The Curious Room' appeared in *Spell*, [Swiss Papers in English Language and Literature], (vol 5, 1990) and 'The Ghost Ships' was first published in *American Ghosts and Old World Wonders* (Chatto & Windus, 1993). 'In Pantoland' was originally published in the *Guardian* in December 1991. 'Ashputtle or The Mother's Ghost' was first published in the *Virago Book of Ghost Stories* (Virago, 1987), and a shorter version was published in *Soho Square*. A version of 'Impressions: The Wrightsman Magdalene' originally appeared in *FMR Magazine* in February 1992.

'The Snow Pavilion' is published here for the first time. 'The Scarlet House' was originally published in *A Book of Contemporary Nightmares* (Michael Joseph, 1977) and 'The Quilt Maker' was published in *Sex and Sensibility: Stories by Contemporary Women Writers from Nine Countries* (Sidgwick & Jackson, 1981).

Fabulist, feminist, social critic, and weaver of tales, Angela Carter has numerous volumes of work available from Penguin, including:

☐ **THE BLOODY CHAMBER**
ISBN 0-14-017821-X

☐ **BURNING YOUR BOATS**
ISBN 0-14-025528-1

☐ **FIREWORKS**
ISBN 0-14-010588-3

☐ **HEROES AND VILLAINS**
ISBN 0-14-023464-0

☐ **THE INFERNAL DESIRE MACHINES OF DOCTOR HOFFMAN**
ISBN 0-14-023519-1

☐ **LOVE**
ISBN 0-14-010851-3

☐ **THE MAGIC TOYSHOP**
ISBN 0-14-025640-7

☐ **NIGHTS AT THE CIRCUS**
ISBN 0-14-007703-0

☐ **SAINTS AND STRANGERS**
ISBN 0-14-008973-X

☐ **SHADOW DANCE**
ISBN 0-14-025524-9

☐ **WISE CHILDREN**
ISBN 0-14-017530-X

FOR THE BEST IN PAPERBACKS, LOOK FOR THE

In every corner of the world, on every subject under the sun, Penguin represents quality and variety—the very best in publishing today.

For complete information about books available from Penguin—including Penguin Classics, Penguin Compass, and Puffins—and how to order them, write to us at the appropriate address below. Please note that for copyright reasons the selection of books varies from country to country.

In the United States: Please write to *Penguin Group (USA), P.O. Box 12289 Dept. B, Newark, New Jersey 07101-5289* or call *1-800-788-6262.*

In the United Kingdom: Please write to *Dept. EP, Penguin Books Ltd, Bath Road, Harmondsworth, West Drayton, Middlesex UB7 0DA.*

In Canada: Please write to *Penguin Books Canada Ltd, 10 Alcorn Avenue, Suite 300, Toronto, Ontario M4V 3B2.*

In Australia: Please write to *Penguin Books Australia Ltd, P.O. Box 257, Ringwood, Victoria 3134.*

In New Zealand: Please write to *Penguin Books (NZ) Ltd, Private Bag 102902, North Shore Mail Centre, Auckland 10.*

In India: Please write to *Penguin Books India Pvt Ltd, 11 Panchsheel Shopping Centre, Panchsheel Park, New Delhi 110 017.*

In the Netherlands: Please write to *Penguin Books Netherlands bv, Postbus 3507, NL-1001 AH Amsterdam.*

In Germany: Please write to *Penguin Books Deutschland GmbH, Metzlerstrasse 26, 60594 Frankfurt am Main.*

In Spain: Please write to *Penguin Books S. A., Bravo Murillo 19, 1° B, 28015 Madrid.*

In Italy: Please write to *Penguin Italia s.r.l., Via Benedetto Croce 2, 20094 Corsico, Milano.*

In France: Please write to *Penguin France, Le Carré Wilson, 62 rue Benjamin Baillaud, 31500 Toulouse.*

In Japan: Please write to *Penguin Books Japan Ltd, Kaneko Building, 2-3-25 Koraku, Bunkyo-Ku, Tokyo 112.*

In South Africa: Please write to *Penguin Books South Africa (Pty) Ltd, Private Bag X14, Parkview, 2122 Johannesburg.*